COCKY SUITS CHICAGO

BOOKS 1-4

ALEX WOLF

SLOANE HOWELL

HE'S A...

COCKY
Playboy

— A COCKY SUITS NOVEL —

SLOANE HOWELL
ALEX WOLF

TATE

NOTHING in my life can ever be easy.

I glance at the clock on the wall of my hotel suite. I knew this would happen. Weston knows I hate getting assignments at the last minute and rushing to prepare. I'm going to be late. I'm *never* late. He's probably already on his first drink at the bar. I could use a drink about now.

I make it a priority to be organized and professional. It's impossible when he throws stuff at me and makes unreasonable demands. My temples throb with the tension headache slowly radiating through my brain. I rub my fingers in soothing circles above my eyes, hoping to escape the pain. In haste, I toss a few Advil in my mouth, take a drink of water, and toss my head back to swallow.

The room is nicer than I imagined for a quick trip: queen-sized bed, high thread-count sheets, walk in shower, hardwood floors. I shouldn't expect any less from Weston. He's a heavy hitter.

I need to get my ass in gear and out of this hotel room. Weston Hunter is not the kind of man you keep waiting. He runs one of the most successful law firms in Dallas—The Hunter Group. He brought me to Chicago to aid in a merger that could be huge for our firm. It's an amazing, though stressful, opportunity. I can't help but feel this is my big test. Trial by fire.

I'm a senior associate and this is my shot at making partner.

I'm the best lawyer at the firm. It's not a brag, Weston's told me before.

However, I'm underprepared and that doesn't sit well with me. Back in the Dallas office I was reading over a deposition when Weston barged in and hollered for me to grab a bag and meet him at the airport. I don't know what he was thinking.

Maybe he's the boss and can do as he pleases?

3

I fuss over my hair one last time in the mirror. There's one strand that refuses to behave. This shit happens when I'm in a hurry. Everything falls apart.

Giving up on my hair, I slip on a pair of black heels and smooth my hand down the front of my skirt. I pick a stray piece of lint from the back as I twist around in the mirror. My blouse appears crisp and wrinkle free. My jacket completes the ensemble.

Finally, all the paperwork is organized into neat piles on the coffee table. Lists of clients, checklists of shit that needs done for due diligence. It's all there. I breathe easy, gather the files, and tuck the hotel key into my wristlet.

Satisfied I have everything, I walk from the room and get on the elevator. It moves at a snail's pace. If I wasn't afraid of working up a sweat, I'd have taken the stairs to get me to the lobby faster. It never fails; the minute I'm in a hurry, Father Time makes things stand still. It'd be just my luck for the thing to stop working.

I watch the numbers slowly change from one floor to the next. To make things better, I'm stuck with an older woman wearing enough perfume to choke a horse. I hope the freesia scent doesn't cling to my clothes.

Arriving in the lobby, I barely give the concierge time to open the door as I rush out to the street in hopes of catching a cab. I wave my hand at one passing by, calling out, "Taxi!" and it rolls to a stop.

Perfect timing for once.

I make it four steps when a shoulder slams into me out of nowhere. My folder flies through the air. The papers explode like a flock of pigeons and float down to the sidewalk. Catching my balance after managing not to snap a heel, I watch in horror as my hard work scatters itself along the sidewalk.

I throw my hands up. "Really?"

What are the chances?

I shake my head. It'll be a miracle if the wind doesn't carry my papers off to the suburbs of Chicago. I let out an annoyed huff and glance to the perpetrator who caused this misfortune. My eyes start at his Berluti shoes and work their way up a Burberry three-piece that's tailored perfectly to his frame. Icy blue eyes meet my gaze paired with a mischievous smirk. A smirk that would no doubt be sexy under different circumstances. Damn, he's hot. His smoldering stare is something out of the movies.

"You could have said excuse me, or sorry at least." I narrow my eyes on him then drop down to gather my papers. His cologne lands in my nose and smells so good it should be banned. Warmth spreads through my veins as I inhale the intoxicating scent.

A low snicker passes between his perfectly sculpted lips. "You bumped into me, *sweetheart.*" His voice is low and comes out like a primal growl that would make me weak in the knees if he wasn't such an arrogant prick.

I suck in a breath and get a grip on myself, shaking off the sexual thoughts rushing to the forefront of my mind. It's just that I have a thing for sexy voices. Sure, I love a good-looking man as much as the next single woman, but give me a deep voice that vibrates down to my core and it does something to me. This jerk has the voice and the looks that go with it. I bet that neatly trimmed beard would work wonders against my thighs.

Regardless of my impure thoughts, he picked the wrong woman to mess with.

"Sweetheart?" I roll my eyes. "No. I recall the moment perfectly. You barreled into me and nearly knocked me to the ground." I glance to the sidewalk. "Look at my papers."

I watch his eyes flit from my cleavage to the strewn papers on the ground and back to my breasts. He makes no attempt to hide the fact he's ogling the twins.

I point two fingers at him then at my face as I speak. "My eyes are right here, buddy."

He stares like I'm on a display, put there solely for his amusement. Those blue eyes cut into me like glaciers. "Buddy." He snorts. "Have to admit, I like the view of you on your knees in front of me."

"In your dreams, pal."

"Highly doubtful." He rubs his jaw, still smirking. Those blue eyes pierce straight through me once more.

He must see I'm thinking about what he said, me on my knees in front of him. I bet he's hung like a damn horse. Jerks usually are, in my experience anyway. I mentally smack myself. I need to snap out of it.

Sneering, I move to gather my papers.

The hottie in the suit bends down to help. He reaches for my folder, and I smack his large hand.

"I've got it." Cute or not, this guy is an ass and gets on my last nerve. Not to mention nobody touches my work. Nobody!

"Have a nice evening." He huffs out a breath and has the nerve to climb into my cab.

"What the hell?" I yell at him and throw my hand up. "That's *my* cab. I'm in a hurry."

He shoots me a sly wink. A grin spreads across his smug face and his pearly whites flash. "I'm in a hurry too, *sweetheart*." He smacks the door of the cab twice. "Spoils of war."

"Asshole!"

The cab speeds off.

I grind my teeth and continue trying to make heads or tails of the mess he's left me in. This is just great. Now, I have to go back into the hotel and fix everything. All my hard work is ruined. The papers are all out of order. Hours of my life wasted.

My phone pings, and I know it's Weston ready to chew my ass out for not being there. It's not like I'm wasting his time on purpose. Rain drops plop on my head and thrum on the ground, and at this moment, I don't know how things could get any worse. I clutch everything under my arm and run as fast as my heels allow back into the hotel lobby before the rain ruins my hair.

Shaking my head, I hop back in the elevator and make it to my room. One glance in the mirror and rage consumes me. I look like a wet rat with smudged makeup. Grabbing a towel, I wrap my hair up and hustle to get organized once more. If I ever see that bastard again, he's a dead man.

———

WALKING into the bar thirty minutes late, I'm surprised to find Weston still there. I square my shoulders and approach. He's perched on a stool nursing a tumbler of whiskey. I lay the files on the stained oak bar top and situate myself on the stool next to him.

He rubs his chin. His eyes are two dark slits and burn a hole into me. I know I messed up, but it wasn't my fault.

"Where the hell have you been?" His voice is low but lethal. "Why didn't you answer the phone?" He grips the glass and taps the side for the bartender to pour him a refill.

"You done?"

Weston doesn't respond. He simply takes a long swig of the dark brown liquid.

"I would've been here half an hour ago if some jerk didn't knock my papers everywhere and steal my cab. Then came the damn rain." I huff out a breath and that stupid curl springs to my forehead. I blow it out of my eyes and wait for Weston to respond. I'm sure he's going to rip my ass and threaten to fire me, but with the mood I'm in, I almost welcome it so I can argue with him. We both know he won't follow through on any threats and I need to let off some steam.

Weston halfway laughs to himself.

"What?" I shoot a glare in his direction.

"Nothing, that's just how I met Brooke. Stole her cab. Granted I didn't knock her on her ass."

I narrow my eyes and try to reclaim some amount of dignity. Through gritted teeth I say, "He *didn't* knock me on my ass."

Weston sighs. "Whatever, Decker left already. Got tired of waiting. You made me look incompetent."

"I'm not a miracle worker. I warned you I didn't have enough time to get everything ready. I'd barely checked in when you demanded this shit." I pat the folder I carried in. "Did you want half-assed work? Because that's *not* what you pay me for, and you know it."

"Whatever. You win." He shakes his head and orders me a drink. "You look like you need one. Just make sure you're prepared for the meeting tomorrow."

I smirk. "I always am, when given an *appropriate* amount of time." I knock back the drink. I deserve it after the day I've had. Weston settles the bill.

"Tate?"

"Yeah?"

He grins and nods at my head. "Do something about that hair."

I scowl back at him. *Asshole.*

He snickers.

I know it looks like a ball of fuzz on my head after the rain and towel drying it. It couldn't be helped.

Weston stands up. "Let's head back to the hotel. You can get room service and fix whatever this shit's supposed to be." He motions to the papers hanging from my file.

I had them all color-coded at least. I suppose they could be worse.

We share a cab back and go our separate ways in the lobby. Arriving in my room, I toss the files on the table and kick off my heels. I trade my business attire for my robe. Falling into the couch, I grab the menu for room service and scan the choices available. With a big day tomorrow, I don't want anything heavy. I settle on a grilled chicken salad and a fruit bowl for dessert. The files can wait until after I eat. What I really want is a nice warm soak in the tub. That stupid jerk and his mesmerizing blue eyes. My cheeks flush and heat spreads down my neck and across my chest at the thought of his face between my legs.

On my knees my ass, buddy. Put your mouth where it belongs.

My mind flashes to his smoldering stare. It's been too long since I've had sex. That's all these thoughts are. But I can't get him out of my head. His stupid smirk. His deep voice. His large hands. That heavenly cologne. It's like I can still smell it. And for God's sake, that cocky wink he threw my way as he took off in my cab.

The saddest part is, it's his arrogance that's doing things to me. I don't want him to be sweet. I want him to be commanding and dominate me, but I want him to work for it. I want to put up a fight and make him earn every inch.

My fingers trail between my breasts as the fantasy plays out in my mind. I pinch one of my nipples and picture those striking blue eyes. He was gorgeous. I want him to make some smartass comment so I can shove my pussy on his mouth to shut him up. I smirk at the thought as my fingers move farther south. I picture that devilish grin as the tip of my finger circles my clit.

A rap at the door echoes through the room, interrupting my fantasy.

I jump. *Shit.*

"Room service."

"Coming!" I shake my head at my choice of word and attempt to stifle the laugh building in my chest. I yank my robe closed and head for the door. I don't have on a bra and don't want the guy thinking his tip is me flashing my breasts. I open the door and a younger man wheels a cart in. I tell him thanks and grab some cash from my wallet to give him a decent gratuity because I feel guilty about what I was doing, even though he has no clue. He gives me a polite thank you and is on his way.

I walk to the bathroom and wet my face with a cool cloth and get ready to eat and forget about those blue eyes and that smart mouth.

I smother my salad in Italian dressing and stab a chunk of chicken with my fork. My stomach growls as I chew. I hadn't realized how hungry I was until now.

Despite the food, I can't stop thinking about that guy. I'm here for a job not to meet Mr. Wrong. That's all that cocky man would be. Another jerk to cross off the list of men who can't handle me.

I know I'm difficult to please. Working in a male dominated field I have to be. I can dish it out with the best of them. Some men appreciate I can hold my own while others find it intimidating. Putting up walls helps keep things professional and focused on work abilities, not how I look in a skirt.

Tomorrow should be interesting. We're meeting with a group of brothers who run a huge law firm here. The Hunter Group is merging with them. I can't help but wonder if they're anything like Weston and the guys back in Dallas.

DECKER

I HOPE today's meeting with Weston and his senior associate goes better than yesterday's attempt. I stopped by the bar, Label Fifty-one, but had to skip out early to meet up with my current fuck buddy. At least I got the letter of intent signed while Weston was there. No backing out of the merger now.

Anyway, the fuck buddy… she works in pediatrics. She's a surgeon and just as busy as me, if not more so. She knows the deal and doesn't expect our relationship to go anywhere outside of the hotel suites we meet up in. She's career driven, and I respect that about her. I admire a woman who knows what she wants and goes for it. Yesterday was our last fling and it was perfect. There were no emotions tied to it at all. We both knew the score, and it was simply about physical release.

The position she's been vying for in LA landed in her lap last week. She leaves today, actually. I sent her some flowers wishing her the best. I know I'll never hear from her again and I don't expect to. I'm good with that. It is what it is.

The sex was good but neither of us recognized it as anything more than a basic need. I'm a busy man with a lot on my plate. Getting emotionally involved with someone is the last thing I need.

Weston and I were supposed to go over some high-level plans for the merger, but his associate never showed up. I desperately need this union with The Hunter Group to be a success. Maybe, after it's complete, I could think about meeting someone long-term. I'd have more time. Right now, it's just not possible.

I've known Weston Hunter since my college days, but that doesn't mean I can afford to not take this seriously. In my private bathroom, I straighten my tie once more. I want Weston to be on board with everything that needs to happen. I have to make sure my people are taken care of in the long-term as well as the short-term. If we can pull it off, there is a lot of mutual benefit to go around the table.

I exit the bathroom and make my way through the office while giving everything a once over. Quinn, my assistant, has assured me everything is in place, but I'm not risking it. There's no room for mistakes. Everything has to be perfect. It's tough to be taken seriously, given my past. Most people see my name and it conjures up images of what they've read in tabloids or seen on gossip sites. None of it has anything to do with what I can do in a courtroom.

I pass my two younger brothers, the twins, Deacon and Dexter. Dexter has a scar over his left brow from a skateboard accident, and tattoos barely peek out from under his suit. It's the only way most people can tell them apart. Dexter scared the shit out of the whole family when he crashed on a makeshift ramp in our driveway. There was so much blood I thought he was dead. I just knew Mom was going to kill me because I was supposed to be watching him and he was trying to show off in front of my friends.

Deacon walks ahead repositioning a few pens, then puts them back where they were. He looks up to verify I'm watching as he grins.

I silently curse him under my breath. They both love fucking with me, have since we were kids.

Dexter laughs.

Deacon glances at me and holds his hands up in mock surrender. "Just making sure they're perfectly aligned with a proper radius to maximize client reach potential. Can't have anyone leaning over too far and have their tie land in a cup of coffee."

Dexter holds in a laugh and looks like he might piss himself.

Deacon maintains a perfect deadpan stare and turns to Quinn. "Might want to check the chairs with a tape measure. Make sure they're all four inches from the edge of the table. Four inches, Quinn. Not five, not three. Four! I saw a few that might be outside a tolerable variance. Don't forget to wipe them down with sanitizer."

Dexter has to turn and stare at the wall to try and compose himself.

I clench my jaw and do my best to ignore them. They love to talk shit and get me riled up. Any other day I would give in and laugh with them. I can be self-deprecating when I need to be. But today is different. I know they don't get how important this is to me. They can afford to goof off. They may be partners, but they don't actively manage the firm, and this deal isn't riding on their asses. The deal I haven't told them about yet, because I don't want to hear their shit. I'll deal with that later.

"Quinn, is the coffee fresh?"

Quinn glares at Deacon, and when I turn around to face her, she schools her features in a hurry. "Yes, Mr. Collins. Everything is ready to go."

Deacon grins at her. "Did you check the temperature? Needs to be a sweltering one hundred…"

I've finally had enough and shoot him a glare that says *shut the fuck up, now*.

He silences immediately.

I turn back to Quinn. "You're sure it's fresh?"

I can tell she's slightly annoyed, given that she pays as much attention to detail as I do, but like a good employee she puts on a smile and reassures me for the thousandth time.

I turn around to get one last look. Everything really does look great. The long table has a file sitting in front of each chair with our company branding on the front. The coffee, water, croissants, donuts, and juice are neatly on display on a table at the back of the room. Quinn will be on hand to serve everyone and to assist me if I need her.

Donavan, my third brother, walks into the conference room and stands stiff as a board like a soldier in front of me. "Sorry I'm late, *Drill Sergeant!*" He hollers the last two words and drags out the syllables like we're on the set of *Full Metal Jacket.*

They all die laughing.

I lower my voice and try not to grin. "You motherfuckers about finished?" I shoot all three of them a dirty look then straighten Donavan's tie. I'm not even going to ask why it's so damn crooked. I already have a good idea what he's been up to this morning, judging by the lipstick stain on the collar of his shirt. I'd hate to see his dry-cleaning bill with the way he goes through women and suits.

Deacon walks up, finally serious. "Lighten up, bro. You're going to stroke out if you don't keep your blood pressure down."

"Needs to stroke something," says Donavan. "Relieve some pressure." He waggles his eyebrows at me.

I grip the Windsor knot on his tie and shove it up toward his neck a little harder than I need to, as if I'm straightening it.

He starts to choke, and finally it's me who gets to laugh.

Children. That's exactly what they are.

If I wasn't afraid of Weston being on his way in right now, I'd throttle all of them. "We're done joking. They'll be here soon." I take a step back and wave a finger in front of all three of their faces. "You assholes fuck up this meeting and you'll be proofreading trusts in the goddamn…"

I hear a throat clear and turn to see Quinn is at the doorway. Weston is behind her, and there's a woman with him, but I can't see her yet, just a pair of tanned calves and heels. "Mr. Hunter and Ms. Reynolds for you, sir."

"Thanks, Quinn."

She nods and turns to them.

I glare at my brothers who scurry like fleas to take their seats. They're lucky I love them. I'm doing this as much for them as I am for me. I'm not the only one who will benefit, though I'd be lying if I didn't say some days I dream of what it would've been like if I were an only child. A hell of a lot less stressful, that's for damn sure. I do love them, though. They're assholes, but I wouldn't trade them for anything.

Weston Hunter, head of The Hunter Group, fills the doorway. He's a bit of a prick, just like me, and he knows it. It's probably why we get along so well. I don't know how Brooke, his wife, puts up with him. He shoots me a smug grin as we shake hands, and Quinn shows him to his seat. As he strolls through the room greeting and shaking hands with my brothers, I look behind him.

No. Fucking. Way.

My breath catches in my throat. It's the damn woman I ran into on the sidewalk yesterday in front of the hotel. The smoking-hot one. If I'm being totally honest, I pictured her while I was banging Jessica for the last time. There was just something about her. She was so damn sassy and defiant—flustered. And now, she's walking right into my conference room.

I watch and wait for her to recognize me. It would be highly entertaining if I didn't have so much at stake with this deal.

She's ridiculously sexy. I'll give her that. Her tan legs are lethal in the form-fitting skirt she's wearing. Her spiked, pointy-toed heels would feel good digging into my ass. I can picture her legs wrapped around me as I thrust into her.

What the fuck are you doing? Compose yourself.

Her dirty-blonde hair is pinned neatly to her head other than the one curl she keeps fidgeting with behind her ear. I want to kiss her there, right in that spot, and watch her blush. Like she did yesterday in the street.

Those lovely honey-brown eyes meet mine.

It takes all of a split-second for the recognition to set in. At first, it's surprise, then she scowls at me like she could tear my head off and shit down my throat.

Without thinking, I smirk at her and shoot her a wink. Fuck, I hope my brothers didn't notice or Weston for that matter. I can't seem to help myself. There's something about her. Something that gets under my skin in the best and worst ways possible.

"Decker Collins." I shoot her my best crowd pleaser smile.

"Tate Reynolds." Her words are short and laced with venom.

My cock twitches at the sound of her voice and scent of her perfume. Cinnamon and vanilla? Smells like a damn cinnamon roll I'd love to sink my teeth into. She looks poised—all business. I bet I could break right through her tough demeanor, though. Grip her by the hair and smack her ass once, and she'd be all mine. Despite my best attempts, my mind races with dirty thoughts of sending everyone out of the damn room and bending her over the table to find out.

I'd lift her skirt and rip her panties. Bite her neck and pull her hair just to hear her moan. She'd pretend to fight it at first, with her sassy attitude, trying to have the upper hand, but before I was done, she'd be begging for more.

I look down and realize I'm still shaking her hand as she tries to pull away.

What the hell is wrong with me?

TATE

I TAKE my seat feeling those blue eyes I dreamed of last night lighting a fire in my chest. It makes me hate him all over again, that he can have this effect on me. I'm Tate Reynolds. I can hold my own with any man in a suit. I shouldn't be letting this prick toy with my emotions. I damn sure shouldn't be attracted to him.

"Missed you yesterday for drinks, Tate." The jerk from yesterday stares at me, clearly amused with himself. His lips are curved upward, his eyes meet mine, and I swear the man is laughing on the inside at this cruel twist of fate the universe has played on us. I remember it all too well. How good he smelled. How attractive he was and still is. The man is perfection in the looks and voice department. Too bad the asshole seems to be in charge of things here. The universe is a real dick sometimes.

"It's Ms. Reynolds." Tate is my name but that's too personal, and this is work.

Weston leans in as Decker Collins—of course he has a hot name—gets on with his PowerPoint presentation outlining the overview of the merger.

As my eyes dart around the table, his associates appear confused.

Weston whisper-growls in my ear, "What the fuck is your problem with Decker?" I know he isn't pleased with my behavior and he can read body-language like a hawk. Couple that with the way I spoke to Decker and Weston looks like he'd pounce on me if we weren't in the middle of a meeting.

The bastard had the nerve to wink at me when no one was paying attention. If he wants my approval, he's going about it the wrong way. I'm not some little tart he can shoot a flirtatious smile at to get his way. I'm Texas born and bred. I'm as tough if not tougher than any man in this room. I can hold my own.

I whisper, "He was the guy who stole my cab and made me late."

Weston snickers and shakes his head. "Of course he was." His eyes narrow.

"It's done now. Whatever happened yesterday doesn't exist. You need to be professional."

I feel like a child who's had her hand smacked for sticking it in the candy drawer in the kitchen. And I'll be damned if Decker Collins isn't a piece of candy I'd like to sample. He's infuriating. He makes a PowerPoint presentation sexy. How is that even possible?

I try not to sulk in my seat as Weston takes over talking about the merger between our two firms and how they'll be absorbed into The Hunter Group and the appropriate steps moving forward.

Decker's brothers look around the room like they want to jump out the window. Something is off.

"What is all this?" I think the guy's name is Donavan, and he's damn near seething as he stares at Decker. They all look like cardboard cutouts of one another, but Donavan has slightly different features than the others. Deacon and Dexter appear to be identical twins except one of them has a scar over his eye. I have no idea how their mother kept track of all of them with their looks and names. It's quite a chore.

"What merger?" says Deacon.

"You're selling the firm?" says Dexter.

I look to Weston during the outburst and interruption, but he's staring at Decker Collins with a *what the fuck* expression on his face. He's not exactly angry, but he isn't happy. Looks like Decker Collins didn't tell his brothers about his plans for the firm.

Decker pushes his chair back, stands up, and puts both his palms on the table, commanding the room as he towers over the rest of us with a look of pure power and dominance. Man can he rock a suit like nobody's business. I hadn't realized how tall the smug jerk was until now. With a stern expression on his face, he glares at his brothers and says, "This merger is in the best interest of everyone in this room. A letter of intent has been signed. It's happening. Get on board."

The men continue arguing as though Weston and I aren't here. I know when to fight my battles and right now isn't the time. It is kind of shitty that he didn't discuss it with anyone. He's the only managing partner, but still. The man is a definite egomaniac.

Weston remains composed and nods toward the table at the back of the room. That's my cue to make an escape. I'm here to back up Weston, not assert my opinion on family matters.

I slip off to the back where Decker's assistant stands by the table with the food spread. The whole meeting is a disaster, but I can tell Weston isn't thrown off by the family drama. He looks amused, like this isn't his first rodeo with the Collins boys. The man is used to family squabbles anyway, so he'll be able to smooth this over far better than I could. He has a firm with his own brothers, so I guess it's relatable for him. Things have gotten heated between them in the past as well. Everyone wants to be the leader of the pack. The room is full of alpha males who all think they're the boss. I feel dizzy with the testosterone cocktail that's filled the air.

I accept the assistant's offer for a cup of coffee and ignore the brooding suits until Weston finally interjects and puts a stop to all the bickering.

"Listen, Decker. I don't know what's going on here, but I trust you'll get your house in order. I have a flight back to Dallas I can't miss." Weston pushes up his sleeve and glances at his watch. I can see annoyance flickering in his eyes. He's always on a tight schedule trying to balance the business and his family life.

I have none of that on my plate. My career comes first always. I can't remember the last time I had a steady boyfriend. Most men are intimidated by me because I can beat them in the courtroom and best them at their own sports.

"Tate will be staying on a day-to-day basis to transition everything smoothly. She'll be doing due diligence, checking for conflicts of interest, making introductions to clients. She's more than capable of handling whatever you need."

I nearly spit out my coffee. Did he just say he was leaving me here until the merger is complete? No way. He must be insane. Did he not listen to a thing I told him earlier about his friend? Not to mention, I'm not prepared.

Decker smirks at me and shoots me another stupid wink. I scowl at him and Weston. What's Weston thinking? I can't work side by side with this asshole. I move toward Weston once the meeting is over and the room has cleared. "What did you mean you're leaving me here to see things through? I can do this from Dallas."

"I meant exactly what I said. I need you here. You'll need to meet with clients and I want you close to this, keeping an eye on shit."

"I just... I don't know if I can work with him."

"I thought I told you yesterday didn't happen."

"Come on. You weren't there. You didn't hear how he spoke to me. The guy is a major jackass."

Weston shakes his head, clearly still pissed off about the way the meeting went, and now he's having to deal with me.

I already know I shouldn't have said anything. I should keep my head down and do my damn job, but Christ, I really don't know if I can work with Decker Collins without murdering the winking son of a bitch. I can already tell his brothers hate my guts.

Weston puts hands on both my shoulders and makes sure the Collins brothers aren't paying attention. "I can't believe I have to say this to you of all people, Tate. But I don't give a flying fuck what happened about a cab. You're an adult. Grow up and do your damn job."

I swallow my pride. I'm being a brat. I know I am. I don't know why Decker gets to me, but he does. That man makes me want to choke him... or kiss him. I put on my best all-business face and nod. "No, you're right. I apologize. Consider it done."

"Good. I don't want to hear anything else about it. Decker is a good guy, you'll see. I've known him for years. I know you can handle him. This is an opportunity to level up, Tate. You've never let me down before. Don't start now."

My chest swells with pride. This is my shot.

I nod and he returns it. I walk him out as we go over the finer details about my living arrangement for the duration of my stay. I'm given a company card for allowances, meals, and professional attire. Not that I'm concerned with money, but it's a nice perk of the job. I bring in a lot of big clients to the firm and Weston rewards me handsomely for it. We part ways and I stop and wait for an elevator.

I watch as Weston walks into Decker's office and hope I can pull off the impossible. When I turn around, the Collins brothers stand in the hallway staring at me. They definitely do not look happy I'll be sticking around. For some reason, I can't stand there and look at their ridiculous stares. I walk off and go in search of the bathroom to get my shit together. I'm a professional. There's no way they'll get to me. I just need to go scream into the toilet or flush myself down it first.

Damn Decker Collins and those blue eyes.

DECKER

"WELL THAT COULD HAVE GONE OVER BETTER. What the fuck did you ambush them for?"

I ignore Weston's question. I have my reasons. "They'll come around," I tell Weston as he helps himself to a drink from the shelf behind my desk. "So will your associate." I grin and take the drink he poured for me. "You know I bumped into her yesterday… on the sidewalk outside of her hotel."

"And?"

"She's easy on the eyes and has… personality." I take another sip of whiskey and think about how sexy she looks when she gets all flustered and angry. I bet she's insane in bed. Bet she'd scratch her nails down my back. I'd love to have her saying my name as I fucked an orgasm out of her.

Weston gives me a look like he can read my thoughts. The dirty ones I'm having about Tate Reynolds and ripping her tight skirt down her legs and spanking her ass over my desk for being a smartass during the meeting.

"She may have mentioned you were the one who ruined her day, but I am warning you now, Tate is a professional and she'll chew your goddamn head off and spit it out. I'm not bullshitting. She is a fucking shark."

"I have enough shit to worry about without fucking someone in my office. You know me better than that. And you of all people understand the ramifications. I know what's at stake." I don't shit where I eat. Nothing will happen with the woman, despite my impure thoughts. I can't say I was never tempted in the past, but I keep work and my personal life completely separate. Tate is very tempting, but I won't let anything get in the way of this deal.

"Indeed." Weston raises his rocks glass.

Quinn buzzes me. "The car is downstairs to take Mr. Hunter to the airport, sir."

"That's my cue to leave you to the wolves." Weston shakes my hand and leaves me to deal with my asshole brothers. The door closes and I fall back on the leather sofa in the corner of my office that overlooks Millennium Park. If I want to see Lake Michigan, I can see it from the roof deck. I go there often to clear my head. It's my favorite spot.

I know I have about two minutes before my asshat brothers barge in demanding answers. It'll be even worse now that Weston's gone. Rubbing my temples, I pop an aspirin and prepare to defend my choice in merging the firm. I've worked my goddamn ass off to build this place up, but The Hunter Group will take us to the next level.

I buzz Quinn.

"Yes, Mr. Collins?"

"Put Tate in the corner office. The one with the gorgeous view of the lake."

That office is at the other end of the floor. I'm putting her there because having some distance between us will make it easier. I'm physically attracted to the woman and need to keep things strictly professional between us no matter how hard my cock grows at her smartass remarks.

"Give her a tour and anything else she needs."

"Yes, sir."

"Thank you."

"You're most welcome."

My office door bursts open, and my brothers quickly fill the room.

"Don't you assholes know how to knock?" I take another sip of whiskey. I'm going to need it to put up with them. The three of them enter the room and take up the three hardback leather chairs facing my desk.

"I thought you were building the firm up for the family? This was supposed to be our legacy and what, you're just gonna sell us out to the Hunter Group?"

"What part of merger don't you get? Every single thing I'm doing is for the good of this firm and all of you. Nothing has changed. It's going to be better for everyone. You'll see. Being under The Hunter umbrella will bring us more clients which means more billable hours. We can hire more attorneys and take a lot of the workload off ourselves. Our current growth rate can't sustain what we're doing. We'll meet our goals faster with less of the work. I don't get why you're so upset." I thought they would be happy. I know I work them hard. I run myself into the ground keeping things at the level we're at. I don't understand what the issue is here.

"I like shit the way it is," Deacon says, and Dexter nods his head.

Fucking twins.

Donavan is quiet, taking it all in. I expected his support most of all.

I put my palm to my forehead. "Well, I don't, and you know exactly why. I don't need you to fight me on this. I need you to shape up and get with the program. This is a game changer that will be better for me and…"

"It's just sudden." Donavan finally opens his mouth.

Dexter and Deacon both remain quiet.

I narrow my eyes at them. "It's happening. End of discussion. Don't the three of you have clients or cases to be working on?" I don't always like being the hardass around here, but someone has to be, and I fit the role easily. I'm the big brother and it's always been up to me to set the example. My brothers have always looked up to me, so it really chaps my ass when they second guess my decision making. They should know I would never enter into a merger that wouldn't benefit both our family and the firm.

This firm is my baby; I would never just give it away.

I look around at them. "Look, you'll all have partner status and easier jobs. It's just a name change, that's all. Extra support. It's going to be fine, you'll see."

They all nod like they trust me—or maybe they've just given up—and file out of my office.

My line buzzes. It's Quinn. "Ms. Reynolds is all settled in her office, sir."

"Thank you. Did she find everything to her liking?"

"I believe so."

"Good. Thanks."

I end the call and lean back in my chair, my thoughts drifting back to Tate Reynolds and those spiked heels she's wearing today.

Finishing off my drink, I think I'll go check in on her and see how she likes that view. I know I shouldn't, but the whiskey is loosening me up a little.

I can't help but hope this merger will give me more of what I need—time.

TATE

"Downstairs on the third floor is the cafeteria and the main supply room, but we also have a small break room and storage closet on this floor. The best part of the whole building is the roof deck. Follow me."

Quinn leads me to the most gorgeous scene I've ever laid eyes on. Clear as day I can see a panoramic view of Lake Michigan. The water is beautiful. I could stand up here forever, watching all the boats and just gazing at the blueish green that stretches to the horizon. A few buildings away I see a rooftop botanical garden.

"Perfect, right?"

I nod at Quinn and continue taking in the breathtaking view, falling in love with the scenery.

"Wait until you get to your office. You can see the lake and part of the park." Her dark brows wiggle.

Quinn is pretty with soft feminine features. Peach-colored cheeks, green eyes, and auburn hair. She's dressed in a dark green skirt and jacket combination that really pops with her pale skin. I hope she's someone I can grab lunch with during my time here. She's friendly, and I like her style.

I've never been to Chicago until this trip, but I can see how people love the place. I've heard the food is amazing and I can't wait to try out a few different restaurants.

We go back down so she can show me to my office. The view is better than I imagined. My office is huge and located in the corner with floor-to-ceiling windows. Decker has outdone himself. I was expecting him to shove me in a closet like Harry Potter just for the hell of it. He strikes me as the type. The kind of man who is an asshole just because he can be. I have a desk that's much larger than I'll ever need. It also has a sitting area that overlooks part of the park and Lake Michigan.

Maybe I could get used to this place after all.

"I'll be doubling as your assistant until one is assigned to you. If you need to reach me, I'm line four. If there is anything I can get you, just give me a buzz. Coffee. Whatever you need, I'm at your disposal."

"Thank you." The door closes behind her, and I get my laptop set up and arrange things the way I want them on the desk. I shoot my assistant in Dallas an email. Quinn is nice but I'm used to Danelle. We already have a system in place and she just gets me.

Danelle,

I need a list of touristy things to do in Chicago. Preferably on the weekend. Throw in some good places to eat too. Also go through my contacts and see if I have any friends living in the city I could set up lunch with. I need my favorite black pants and those snakeskin heels...the ones that give me three inches in height. Overnight them to me, please.

I'm attaching the contact information for an assistant at this firm. Please see that you get her a cheat sheet to make my time here easier.

Thanks so much!

Tate Reynolds, Senior Associate

The Hunter Group

AFTER I HIT SEND, the door to my office swings open. I glance up from my computer screen and Decker Collins strolls in like he's the king of the castle. Just like him to show up and shit on my parade just as I start to like the place. I guess, technically, he is the king, but his arrogance is unsettling. The cocky jerk smirks at me again. He does that a lot and the sad part is deep down I'm starting to enjoy it.

"Didn't get to give you a tour. Thought I'd stop by and make sure Quinn got you settled in okay and that everything is to your liking. I'll set you up with your own assistant as soon as I find someone capable of filling the position." Why does it sound so sexual when he says filling the position? And why am I squirming in my seat as he speaks? This is ridiculous.

I lick my lips and feel parched all of a sudden. I'm sure my dry mouth has nothing to do with the sexy bastard standing in my office. "Thank you. The view is spectacular. Yours must be amazing if you gave me this one."

"Actually..." He strolls casually to the window and gazes at the picture-perfect scene. "This one's my favorite. It used to be mine."

Why would he give up his favorite office?

"I prefer being closer to the elevator." He answers before I can respond as though he can read my thoughts.

Who the hell factors proximity to the elevator to choose an office? Damn. I'm anal and not even that bad. I wonder if he has some sort of complex. I bet he's a time management freak and clocks himself in the damn pisser. He probably counts how many steps it is from his office to the front door of the building and tries to shave off a few seconds every day.

Poking fun at his routine sets my mind at ease.

I wish he'd quit grinning at me.

My brow lifts into an arch. "The elevator? You moved offices to be closer to the elevator?"

"Yup." He pops the P.

I sense there's more he isn't sharing with me. Reading men is one of my talents. It has allowed me to be successful at the ripe old age of twenty-eight. I credit the ability to growing up with brothers who loved to hold shit in and never wanted to share their feelings. Being surrounded by their friends made it easy for me to pick up on men's social cues.

He pulls away from the window and comes toward my desk. The man stalks toward me like a lion ready to pounce on his next meal. I watch with fascination as he pushes the sleeves of his shirt up, revealing his muscular forearms. I've always found men's arms to be sexy.

Decker's are up there close to a ten. Who am I kidding? They're perfect like the rest of him. Nothing but corded muscle and rough sinew, yet tanned and smooth like he actually uses lotion. A few veins run from under his sleeves and snake down to his wrists.

He glances at his Rolex. I expected an Apple watch. I'm impressed to see some men are still old fashioned in that sense. Everyone is so plugged into their devices. It's the first endearing quality I've noticed about the man.

"I thought we could meet up for drinks later. We didn't get off to a great start."

"You stole my cab yesterday, left me in the rain with my papers—talked all this shit, and now you want to have drinks?" Wow, I should shut up, but I guess that'd been building at the back of my mind.

Decker grins—the most facetious grin I've ever seen in my life—like he relishes the conflict and wants to verbally spar. "First, I offered to help pick up your papers and you declined. Second, this is business only. No pleasure involved." He leans across my desk and my heart rate speeds up tenfold. "Pencil me in on your calendar. It's not a request." He taps the empty square in front of me.

My breath catches in my throat at his close proximity. I need to make a note to keep him at arm's length at all times. If he gets much closer, my brain might shut down.

"Um..." My voice comes out in a sultry whisper that's highly inappropriate but I can't stop it.

Decker gets up and starts to the door. "I don't know how you do things down in Texas, but here in Chicago, *sweetheart*, we do business over drinks." He mocks my accent by drawing out his words in an exaggerated southern drawl.

Before I can turn him down, the door shuts behind him.

I roll my eyes and sink back in my chair, nibbling the tip of my fingernail as I look down at my desk.

The blank space on my calendar stares back, mocking me. I should stand him up, but Weston's voice harps in the back of my mind. This man shouldn't get under my skin, but he does. I can get the job done. Weston always tells me I'm the best he's got, so I need to believe it too. Grabbing my favorite pen, I mark drinks with Decker Collins into my schedule a little too roughly and ink bleeds on the paper, ruining my pretty penmanship.

IT'S NOT A DATE.

I skim the racks at Ikram, settling on a Narciso Rodriguez number. It's black with a white abstract pattern and something that can double as work attire. A pair of Dolce & Gabbana heels, and a new necklace and bracelet complete the look. Finally satisfied, I get everything boxed up and head out front to find a cab.

On the way back to my hotel I rack my brain trying to figure out what on earth we need to meet for drinks about. Anything Decker wants to discuss can be done at the office. Hell, he can do it on the phone if he wants.

The only thought running through my mind is he wants me there in person. The thought sends a shiver up my spine for two different reasons. One, maybe he's attracted to me and wants to get me drunk and do naughty things to me. Two, maybe he wants to actually discuss work and be an insufferable prick the entire time. Nothing good can come of this, yet I can't help but notice I just bought an entire new outfit I don't need, but it's perfect and I look hot as shit in it.

I shake my head as the cabbie pulls up to the curb and drops me in front of the hotel.

It's going to be a long night.

LATER, as I get ready in my hotel room, I can't help but feel this is very much a date. I've analyzed this situation from front to back, replaying every word in my mind and every one of Decker's reactions and the inflection in his voice. He said it wasn't a date, and I don't want it to be because we work together. But still... despite all my reservations, I have that giddy feeling all girls get before a first date.

Butterflies flutter around in my stomach. I primp in the mirror touching up my makeup and taking my hair down. I run my fingers through the waves and spritz it with some hairspray. I look over my appearance and know I'm spending more time than I usually would for a business meeting. Apparently, a girl has to look good when going out for the night in a new city even if it is just for drinks with a colleague.

I'm doomed.

DECKER

I HOP out of the shower and wrap a towel around my waist. Water trickles down my torso as I stand at the sink to brush my teeth. I don't know why I'm making a big deal about going out for drinks with Tate. I only asked because I thought maybe it would loosen her up and help with the transition for the merger if I get to know her better. She can learn a little more about me in a more intimate setting while still keeping things neutral outside the office. I probably wouldn't have been such a prick to her the first time I met her if I knew I'd have to work with her.

Yeah, you would. Who are you kidding?

The only problem is from the moment I crashed into her on the sidewalk, I haven't been able to get her out of my head. Her cute accent. The fact she gives me shit right back as good as I dish it out. She's got—something. Gumption, maybe? Attitude? I just like the way she challenges me, both of us competing to be the dominant voice in the conversation. Nothing more.

So why the hell am I so damn nervous? This is not a damn date. I'm Decker Collins. I don't need to stick my dick in the company gene pool to get laid. I can fuck any eligible woman in Chicago I want. I have. I don't do relationships or the dating scene. My life doesn't allow for it. It's why arrangements like I had with Jessica are key. Tate doesn't strike me as the type of woman I could get away with just fucking occasionally mid-day in a hotel room. A woman like her doesn't even need a man, but I bet she still wants the fairytale romance all the same. All women want that shit, even if they act like they don't.

I hear the backdoor shut. Molly, my housekeeper, is here. Over the next several minutes I finish getting dressed in something a little more casual than the usual suit and tie I wear for work. I go with a pair of dark jeans and a grey fitted v-neck. I pocket my wallet and head to the kitchen to greet Molly.

She's been with me for years and does an excellent job keeping my household running efficiently. Her dark hair is swept back in a tight bun that rests neatly on her head. There are streaks of gray around her temples. She's already busying herself with dinner though I won't be around to eat it until later.

"Good evening, Miss Molly. Something smells good."

"I'm making chicken parm, a garden salad, and cheesy garlic bread." The woman can cook anything. Her Italian is to die for. No one can top her in the kitchen.

"Sounds perfect. I have to go out, but I'll be back no later than nine."

"No worries. Take your time. I'll hold down the fort."

Molly is truly a godsend, and I don't know what I'd do without her. She's like family. I grab my keys off the hook and go into the garage and hop in the Audi.

TEN MINUTES LATE, I find Tate waiting for me in the lounge at The Violet Hour. I couldn't be the first one here, looking all desperate. The Violet Hour is known for its speakeasy vibe and their house bourbon. I've only been here a couple of times and forget about their no cell phone in the lounge rule and switch my phone to vibrate. I slip it back into my pocket when I see the sign. I grab a chair and slide it next to Tate's so we can talk privately away from the chatter at the bar.

I let the server know I'll have whatever Tate is having. She's dressed to kill in her black and white dress. Fuck me, she's even hotter than she was the previous two times we met. Her heels have sexy black leather straps that wrap around her ankles in an erotic fashion, and suddenly I feel way underdressed.

"Two Midnight Stingers," she says.

The bartender scurries off and a moment later returns with the drinks. The whole time he was away, I had to will myself not to stare at Tate in her goddamn dress.

Once the bartender is gone, I break the ice. "Enjoying the city?"

She regards me for a few long seconds, like she's plotting, trying to figure out my motivations for this little get together. "Undecided, but I do love the view from my office."

That's something I've noticed about her. She's always watching, observing, her mind always working, taking in information. When she mentions the view, I can't help but think how much I'm enjoying the view in front of me. "Is our office different from Dallas?"

"Not much." She takes a sip from her tumbler, eyeing me over the brim of her glass looking like an angel sent here to torture me. The glow of the candle illuminates her hair. "Remind me. How do you know Weston?"

I smile. "We went to law school together. After I gave up baseball to pursue law that is."

"You played for Illinois. I read about you."

"You did your homework. Only heard good things I hope." I'm impressed she went to the trouble. I can imagine the shit she came across on the gossip sites that call me a playboy.

"Maybe," she says as we both take a drink. "What was that like? The baseball?"

"Loved it. I lived for the game, but it was exhausting and a lot of hard work."

"If you could go back and do things differently... would you have pursued baseball instead of law?"

It's not the question I expect, and it catches me off guard for a second. I right the ship before she can tell something is off. "No. Part of me wonders what if, but things turned out good. I got to play ball for a while and things worked out." I made my peace with the choice I made a long time ago. I wouldn't trade the life I have today for anything in the world.

"You miss the recognition that came with it?" Her tongue darts out as she beams at me, tapping her nails on her glass in need of another drink.

"No. I didn't like the attention." I signal for a refill.

"Trying to get me drunk? Thought this was business." She wraps her red painted nails around her bourbon-filled glass.

Talking to Tate comes naturally. She's great at conversation and a good listener. I need to change the subject, though. She always just dives straight into the uncomfortable. Ignoring her comment, I say, "Enough about me. Tell me about you. You grew up in Texas?"

"I did. I have two older brothers who didn't mind me tagging along on their fishing and hunting trips."

"You fish and hunt?"

"I'm a southern girl. I can drink like a fish and swim like one too." She laughs, a real, genuine laugh this time.

"I see that. Bet you put the men in Dallas to shame."

She brings her rocks glass up toward her lips but lets it rest against her chin. "I do my best."

"Kicking ass and taking names?"

"Something like that. I keep them in line and crack the whip when I need to." There's a naughty sparkle in her eyes, but maybe it's the flame from the candle.

"You really as tough as Weston says? Or is he just talking shit?"

The corners of her lips curl up into a grin. "Oh, I imagine you'll find out soon enough, counselor."

I can't help but smile. Fuck, this woman is perfect.

She glances around the bar. "You bring all your colleagues here?"

I stroke my jaw. We're both playing with fire. "This is only my third time here. So, to answer your question, no."

"Just me, huh? Does that make me special?"

She's special all right. A damn temptress.

Her Cupid's bow lips curve upward forming a delicious smirk.

"You're something... I just haven't figured out what yet." Knocking back my drink, I place the empty tumbler on the table between us.

27

She finishes hers. Her fingers linger on the table, her red nails on display. I imagine them scratching down my back after I've peeled that dress from her.

I shake myself out of these thoughts. I should get going, but I can't seem to pull myself away from her. The low lights, the proximity of our chairs, her cinnamon vanilla scent—it all mingles together, and I inch closer. I think the bourbon has gone straight to my dick and my brain is no longer able to function.

Tate licks her tempting red lips. Lips I want to kiss but know I shouldn't. Those gorgeous honey-brown eyes meet mine full of playfulness. I lean forward, determined to see if her mouth tastes as sweet as I imagine. This is it, the moment of truth. There's no coming back, but I'm determined to feel her lips on mine.

Her eyelashes flutter and she doesn't stop me. I lean in farther, our mouths just inches apart, close enough I can feel her breath play across my chin.

Fuck it.

I go for it. The one thing that could tank this deal, and one of the dumbest decisions I could possibly make.

My phone vibrates in my pocket.

I pull away and glance at my watch; I see it's already after nine. I lost track of the time. It's not hard to do with the gorgeous Tate Reynolds sitting next to me at the bar. Her eyes remain locked on mine the entire time, probably wondering what the fuck I'm doing. She lets out a small flustered sigh, but, other than that, her poker face remains.

When I pull my phone from my pocket and read the message, my heart damn near beats out of my chest. "Fuck. I gotta go."

Tate frowns, but tries to hide it almost immediately.

"Sorry." I slip money to the server for our drinks and head out of the bar.

We accomplished no work whatsoever. We didn't even discuss the merger.

I did learn one thing about myself, though.

I want Tate Reynolds—bad.

TATE

THINGS ARE weird the next day when I walk into the office. Quinn strolls by and says hello, nothing new there. I catch the other three Collins brothers brooding at me from their desks. They're not hard to miss. The whole office is made out of glass walls, so a ton of natural sunlight filters through the building.

I spot Decker at the end of the hall, so I start in his direction. I can't stop thinking about how close he was to my mouth last night, and how badly I wanted him to kiss me. It would've been a mistake, so I'd breathed easy when his phone rang.

The last thing I want is for things to be weird, but I'm drawn to him like a moth to a flame. He has a way about him that pulls me in like a tractor beam and turns me into a mindless buffoon. As soon as he spots me, he takes off in the other direction.

Just like all the men in your life, scared.

I suppose it's not a bad thing. I'm here to do one thing and one thing only—my job. I head to my office and pull out my highlighter. It's not hard to get lost in my work, and that's exactly what I plan to do. I need to go through the client lists of both firms and make sure there are no conflicts of interest, clients suing each other, etc. Anything I find must be resolved and signed off on by Weston. It's a shitload of work, but that's what Weston pays me for. I make it through a few lines of a contract before the words all jumble together and nothing makes sense. My brain can't process anything, and it's all because of the memory of Decker Collins' mouth inches from mine, hanging there, lingering.

I can't help but think about what it'd be like in my ear, whispering all kinds of dirty words about what he wanted to do to me. How he'd order me to get on my knees, with his hand gripping the back of my neck and pushing me down.

Goosebumps pebble all over my body and I shiver a little in the best kind of way at the thought. How am I supposed to get any work done knowing he's in the same proximity as me? He could barge into my office at any moment and I'd be helpless, a slave to him.

I have to get out of here for a bit.

It's almost lunch time so I gather up my paperwork and decide I can get more done in my hotel room for an hour with no distractions. I stop by Quinn's desk on my way and let her know I'm going to lunch.

As I head toward the elevator, Decker walks out of his office and we nearly collide again. This time, he doesn't barrel over me with his shoulder. His eyes widen when he sees me, and the look on his face says he's warring with himself.

He starts to say something, but no words come out, and then he just walks past me.

"You're really gonna ghost me? Just like that?"

He freezes in his tracks, his Salvatore Ferragamo dress shoes squeaking on the tile as he stops. His hands ball into fists at his sides, then he slowly releases the tension from his body and turns around.

"Everything going okay?" He nods to the folder tucked under my arm.

"Yeah. Gonna head to the hotel and work during lunch. I can't get anything done in my office for some reason." I take a few steps toward him.

He looks like he wants to retreat, but quickly remembers his name is on the wall, and stands his ground.

I take another step closer. "We should talk about what happened last night."

"Funny, I was thinking we should do the exact opposite."

"Typical man," I say, before realizing I said it out loud.

Decker smirks at my response. "Now's not the time, *Tate*."

Why does he have to use my first name and keep things unprofessional? I'm trying to do the exact opposite. All I want to tell him is it's a good thing his phone rang before we made a mistake we both regretted. That way we can put last night behind us. "It's Ms. Reynolds." My words come out harsher than intended.

"Well, Ms. Reynolds." He takes a step closer to me. "*Now* is not the time. I'm busy and this is hardly the setting to have such a conversation." Sarcasm oozes from his tone as he mocks me in his most professional voice possible. I want to grab his tie and give it a yank, just to choke him a little bit, nothing serious.

"Well then, Mr. Collins. I guess I'll be on my way. I'll have work for you and Weston to review by tomorrow morning." I turn toward the elevator.

"Ms. Reynolds?"

I whip around. "Yes?"

He glances around to make sure the coast is clear, then lowers his voice. "Try not to think about me too much while you're reading those documents." The asshole winks and walks off.

Ugh! Fuck you, Decker Collins.

BACK AT THE HOTEL, I can't think of anything but Decker in his damn suit. It pisses me off even more because he told me not to think about him and it's all I can do. I have forty-five minutes to get some work done without the possibility of interruption and all I want to do is run my hand between my legs and pretend it's Decker's tongue.

I turn the TV on and crank up the volume, trying anything to create some white noise in the background to pull my thoughts back to work. Finally, I manage to get about ten pages highlighted with notes.

Only forty to go. No problem at all, Tate.

Even the voice in my head gives me shit.

It'll have to do. Usually, I would've had this work moved off my plate in the first hour I was at work. I don't know what I'm going to do about this whole Decker situation, but I need to fix it in a hurry. That's how I live my life, figuring out the problem and solving it.

Riding Decker like a bull is out of the question, so what can I possibly do? I tap my chin, trying to find a solution. Being efficient in my work is vital to my success. Maybe I can run everything through Weston, then he can discuss it with Decker, and cut the gorgeous, blue-eyed man out of the equation. Any face-to-face stuff I can punt to Quinn, have her run interference.

Then, I'll never have to see him, won't have to correspond with him, and I can finally focus. I solidify the plan in my brain. Now, I just need to execute it.

It'll be easier said than done, but all I can do is hope.

DECKER

I SIT AT MY DESK, poring over my emails for the day. I prefer to knock them out as they come in, so nothing lingers that I can forget about. Fucking Tate and her smart mouth. I know I should go easier on her, try and smooth things over. She's just so—Tate. I'm used to confrontation, but she takes it to a whole other level. What the hell? Like I was just going to discuss almost kissing her right there in the hallway of the firm?

Having drinks with her in the bar was a bad idea. God, that fuck-me dress, and those hot-as-hell heels. I couldn't help myself. I'm only human.

Thank God my phone went off, and I had an excuse to get out of there. I sat up all night dealing with that message and now I'm sleep deprived and crankier than usual.

I pull up a Word doc and type out anything that could go wrong by pursuing Tate. Making lists helps me compartmentalize and think things through.

Could ruin merger.

You can't date anyone right now.

Don't shit where you eat.

She has to leave for Dallas when this is over.

Typing it out helps me reason through the situation and get my thoughts organized. I was so close to kissing her I could practically taste the booze on her lips. The funny thing was, she didn't pull back, or lean into it. She just sat there, expecting it to happen. Wanting it to happen?

Fuck Weston for sending her here. She's driving me insane.

I hop up from the desk, feeling better about the situation after making my list. Now, all I have to do is keep my dick in check. About the time I walk through the door, the elevator dings and out steps the temptress from hell. My immediate reaction is to retreat back into my office until the coast is clear, but she catches me hesitating out of the corner of her eye. I can't look like some pussy and run away from her. There's no way in hell that will ever happen.

Shit.

She turns on her heel and heads right at me while glancing around to make sure the coast is clear. "Now seems like a good time to talk." She doesn't slow down as she barrels right past me with her color-coded files.

I appreciate how organized she is and at the same time I want to smack her ass and send her right back out the door. Who the hell does she think she is barging into my office? Like she can't read my fucking name plastered everywhere.

I turn and glance at the door, debating if I should leave it open. I decide on open, that way if she starts in on me, I won't be tempted to grab her by the hair and kiss the breath from her lungs.

She stops in front of my desk and plops down on one of the chairs.

"Make yourself comfortable." Sarcasm oozes from my voice, hopefully some contempt too as I stroll around and sit down behind the desk, steepling my fingers.

"Nothing about our situation is comfortable. We need to remedy that right now."

"What'd you have in mind?" I can't help but smirk. I'm not used to someone else taking charge and steamrolling me in a conversation, but something about Tate doing it amuses me. I give her my best *I don't give a shit* look to let her know she's wasting my time.

She keeps on like she doesn't notice the way I'm speaking to her. "I've been thinking, maybe I just send everything to Weston and relay messages through Quinn. It'll put some distance between us."

I pretend to think it over, but really, I know the wait is killing her. I should agree to it. It's a reasonable plan, but I can't help myself. Torturing Tate Reynolds has apparently become my new favorite thing to do. I find myself wanting to disagree with her one-hundred percent of the time, just to see how she reacts.

"I don't think that's necessary. We're both professionals."

"It's not working, Decker."

"It's Mr. Collins. Let's keep things professional, shall we?"

Her jaw clenches and her face turns slightly pink. Not an embarrassed pink. It's a pissed-off pink, and it's perfect.

"*Mr.* Collins, it's not working."

"Working fine for me." I stand up as though that's the final word and start toward the door. "And that's really all that matters now, isn't it, *Ms.* Reynolds?"

She stands up and steps right in front of me.

I'm a head taller and I make it obvious I'm looking down my nose at her. "Anything else?"

She tosses the folder on my desk and crosses her arms over her chest. It pushes her tits up so her cleavage stares me in the face. Fuck, I can already feel my cock hardening.

She stands there, trying not to look pissed, but her breaths are shallow, and I can practically hear her heartbeat pounding. "We're not done here."

I look past her and fake a laugh. "Funny, I thought this was my office." I turn toward the lobby and point. "Oh look, there's my goddamn name on the wall."

Tate lets out an exasperated sigh. "Don't do this alpha male bullshit. I'm trying to get this deal done and get out of your hair. Why are you being a prick?"

I lean down, close enough I can smell the cinnamon body wash she must use. "Because I'm not the one with the problem. I'm going on about my work fine. Why should I alter my schedule and routine just to accommodate you?"

I expect her to be taken aback, but she's not. She glares at me with a look that belongs in the fucking World Series of Poker. "Don't be an asshole. You might pull it off with other people, but I see right through it." She leans forward and gives me a better view of her breasts.

Fucking hell. Her tits are perfect, and now I'll have to pretend not to stare at her ass when she leaves, if she ever does.

I can't take this much longer. She's one remark away from getting bent over my desk. My palms are on the verge of twitching. I have to tone down this conversation and get her out of my office before I do something I'll definitely regret. I do my best to remove all sarcasm from my voice and give her an honest reply. "Look, I won't ask you to meet me outside work anymore. That was my fault. *This* is me being a professional and taking responsibility. Now, do your job, and we won't have any more problems. *But*, if I need to talk to you, I'm not going through Weston or chasing down Quinn in my own damn office. I'm busy as hell and I don't have the time. You're stuck with me while you're here. Deal with it."

She shakes her head, almost grinning, and picks up her file from the desk. "Men and their big egos," she mumbles as she walks out of the room.

Like a complete jackass, I can't let it go. "Not the only big thing around here, *sweetheart*."

I expect her to stop in her tracks, but she doesn't. No, Tate Reynolds heels clack on the floor as she sashays her ass in her skirt and stomps out of the office.

I'll be damned if it isn't a perfect ass too.

I stare at the door to my bathroom for a split-second. I'm going to have to rub one out or that woman is going to give me an aneurysm.

TATE

"You got that report for me yet? I don't see it in my inbox." Weston sighs into the phone.

"I'm working on it. You'll have it soon. Things are going great here."

"That's what I like to hear. Get me that report." The call goes dead, and I place the phone on the receiver.

It's been a little over two weeks since the confrontation in Decker's office, and despite the fact he didn't seem too enthusiastic about my plan, that's how everything has worked out. I know it's what I said I wanted, but now, something feels off about this whole situation. It's almost like I miss his sarcastic remarks.

I suppose it's been a good thing, though. Let things simmer down and get tempers in check. It's allowed me to get some work done and I'm ahead of schedule. I've met with a few of the larger clients and haven't found any causes for concern. Things have gone incredibly smooth and I hold out hope it'll last.

Conversations with Decker all happen through his assistant, text, or email. Maybe he's just been busy. He does run a giant law firm after all.

Regardless, I can never catch him in his office to go over the reports before I send them off to Weston. Quinn took a personal day today and I can't find Decker anywhere in the building. I went to the cafeteria, and the woman working the coffee bar said I just missed him. The thought of him fetching his own coffee does make me smile. With Quinn gone today, I suppose he has no choice.

I go back upstairs and he's still not in yet. I feel as though I'm the cat and he's the dang mouse. Like our roles are reversed. He should be chasing me. I shake my head and stop outside an office when I notice Dexter and Deacon have some kind of golf simulation set up, complete with a net and a TV screen. Come to think of it, I never see them doing any actual work. It's like they're hitching a ride off Decker and making boatloads of money in the process.

These two have given me the cold shoulder the entire time I've been here, and I think now is as good a time as any to fuck with them. "Is this how you spend time that should be used netting more billable hours? No wonder Decker called Weston." I make a tsk sound and interrupt their little game.

Dexter puffs out his chest. "Getting ready to take some prospective clients out on the course."

"Oh, I'm sure you'll land some absolute whales with that swing." I look at his pitiful stance and smirk at how he's holding the driver completely wrong.

Dexter does some little shimmy and questions his grip on the club by adjusting his hands. "Like you know anything about golf."

Deacon laughs and slaps his brother's chest. "I bet Tate handles balls with the best of them."

"Step aside boys. I'll show you how it's done once. It's five-hundred an hour for future lessons." I grab the club from Dexter's grip and take a practice swing. My skirt tightens on my legs, so I shimmy it up on over my knees.

"Can definitely handle the wood," Dexter says with a snicker.

Deacon shakes his head, but I laugh. I'm used to shit talking with men.

I line up my swing and drill the ball straight into the net. A virtual golf ball on the TV soars through the air straight down the fairway. I twirl the club in my hands then flip it on the ground at their feet.

They both stand there with their mouths wide open.

"Run your mouth some more, boys."

"Maybe I should be sending Tate to play a few holes with the Branson brothers." Decker steps under the door frame.

My stomach coils up like a spring and goosebumps pebble down my arms at the sound of his voice. I look over and he's leaning in the doorway watching me. He's wearing gray slacks with a white button down. His tie is loosened around the collar and his hair is messy like he's been running his fingers through it.

My cheeks tingle as he stares me down. "Wouldn't want clients leaving when I kick their ass." I start toward the door.

Decker moves so I can exit. He follows but can't see the satisfied smile on my face. There's something about him walking after me that sets the world right.

"You'd let them win, *sweetheart.*"

I spin around. The way the term of endearment rolls off his tongue grates on my nerves, and judging by the wicked glint in his eyes, he knows it.

"I never let anyone else win in life or the courtroom."

"You'd let them win if I told you to." He smirks. "I hear you've been looking for me."

"I need you to take a look at something before I send it off to Weston. He's already irritated I haven't sent it yet. I get the feeling you've been avoiding me. Care to tell me why?"

"Ohh, Tate." He mocks me with his tone. "I've just been busy, you know? Running a law firm. Sorry I wasn't here to hold your hand the past few weeks."

"If any hand holding were needed, I think we know it'd be me holding yours."

"If only that were true."

We round a corner where no one can see and he grabs my hand, rubbing his fingers over my knuckles in a lazy pattern. I can't help but imagine his fingers touching me elsewhere. Heat blooms across my chest and funnels down between my legs at the thought of Decker taking me into my office and doing all the dirty things I've thought about.

"Where's this report you're so bent out of shape over?"

"On my desk." I smile at him and sway my hips as I walk over to retrieve it. I start to tease him but think better of it. I grab the accordion folder and hand it off to him.

"I'll get this back to you Monday morning."

"Good."

He pins me with his gaze, and we have a mini staring contest before he finally blinks. I warned him, I never let anyone win.

He lingers at the door and finally says, "What are you up to this weekend?"

"Dinner and a show with a friend."

The way his jaw ticks at the fact it might be a man sends a thrill of pleasure through me. I shouldn't toy with him, but I can't help myself. There's no way I'm telling him I'm meeting up with Alexis, a married mother of two. He can stew on it.

"HOLY SHIT, LOOK AT YOU, GIRL," says Alexis as I walk toward her in the hotel lobby. "What's it been? Five years?"

I squint. "More like seven. I still can't believe you went and got married and started having babies. We had a plan."

Her grin widens. "Plans change. One day you'll meet your Tucker."

"That man is one of a kind. I'll give you that. If I didn't love you so much, I might have tried to steal him away."

Her arm goes around my neck, pulling me in for a tight squeeze.

"Oomph. You're choking me."

She releases me from her death grip. "Sorry. I'm just so happy you're in town. How long are you here for?"

"However long I'm needed."

"Well, I hope it's a long time. Anyway, Tucker is with the girls for the evening. I thought maybe we could get to the club a little early for a few drinks and an appetizer before the show starts."

"Sounds perfect."

We grab a cab to a place called Lazy Bird. It's tucked away in the basement of The Hoxton Hotel. It has a bit of the same speakeasy vibe as The Violet Hour, the place Decker almost kissed me. I wonder to myself what he's doing this weekend besides working on that report.

We're too early for the live music, but we'll get enough of that when we see

West Side Story later at the Civic Opera House. It's not too crowded and the atmosphere is laid back and friendly. Alexis orders us a couple of Blackthorns, a house drink made with Irish whiskey. It's a bit malty but goes down smooth.

Alexis and I grew up together but went our separate ways after high school. I pursued law and she earned her teaching degree. She tucks her strawberry, bobbed hair behind her ear and sips on her drink. "Tell me everything. Work, relationships, spill the tea, bitch."

"There's not much to tell, really."

"Puhlease. I've spent all my free time with the girls for the past five years. I need some adult talk."

"Honestly, I work a lot for one of the most prestigious law firms in the country. It's my dream job. I have a fabulous apartment in Dallas. I'm happy."

"And... you're still single? Tell me the juicy bits. I want to live vicariously through you."

"Yup. Single and not so ready to mingle." I gaze lazily around the room taking note of the décor. There's an old fireman's map of the city hanging on the wall.

"Why not? You're a total catch."

I swallow my drink quickly. "I don't need a man to be happy. I have B.O.B."

"Who's he?"

I can't stop laughing. "Battery operated boyfriend."

Her brows go up. "Oh."

"Don't you..."

"God no. Tucker would have a stroke. He'd get jealous of the competition."

I snort and change the subject. "Tell me about the girls."

"Mags, Maggie is my oldest. She's my tomboy. She reminds me of you in ways. She loves sports and is looking forward to camp this summer. It's for soccer. Then there is my Bella bean. She was a preemie and still small for her age, but she has the loudest personality. Kid is always singing and making a spectacle of herself."

"She's just like you then." I grin.

"Totally." She laughs. "Drives her father crazy."

"I can't imagine living with two of you."

"Hilarious." We chit chat a bit more about her decision to return to work now that her girls are both in school. "What about you, though? Think you'll ever settle down and do the family thing?"

"Maybe for the right guy, if I ever meet him. But I love my work. The job I'm in town for is my big shot at making partner at the firm. Life's good the way it is. I work a lot. Don't have time to get involved with someone."

"You'll meet your Mr. Right. I know it."

"Mr. Right Hand." I wiggle my fingers at her, and she can't stop laughing. I shake my head and order another drink. I don't want to think about dating anyone at the moment.

DECKER

Looking at the time in the right-side corner of my computer screen, I should be long gone by now, but I'm late getting this report back to Tate. Weston wants biweekly reports of our status. I should've had it ready this morning, but my weekend got away from me. I expected Tate to be on my ass over it, but I've been too busy to cross paths with her. My morning was spent with one of my largest clients. Cole Miller owns a billion-dollar franchise of fitness centers and spas geared toward females, and there was an incident over the weekend. An employee snapped a photo of one of the patrons and posted it to their social media. They made derogatory comments, and the victim lawyered up. I've spent the majority of my day combing over the membership terms and agreement while waiting for him to get me a copy of his liability insurance policy.

The whole thing is a real shitstorm. He issued an apology on behalf of the company, but people are out for blood. It's being tried in the court of Twitter and frontier justice is on the horizon. The post has been removed but there are screenshots floating around. I have my team sending cease and desist letters out to people posting about the gym. It's already getting nasty. Cole has a reputation for being a bit of a brawler and a player. He's a former MMA fighter and the media loves dragging his name through the gutter of every rag tag gossip mag and site.

I know how the guy feels; I've experienced their wrath before.

Picking the phone up, I dial my house. Molly picks up on the third ring. "Collins' residence."

I scrub a hand over my face. "I'm just wrapping things up here at the office. I should be home within the hour. Is she upset?" I didn't expect to be here so late and miss dinner tonight.

Molly's tone softens. "She's fine. She knows you're doing the best you can."

I groan internally and stare out at the Chicago skyline. The Willis Tower lights up. I wish things could be different. "Tell her I love her, and I'll be there as soon as I can."

"I will. Oh, there's a plate for you in the oven."

I grip the phone tighter. "Thanks, Molly." I end the call. Guilt eats at me, but some things can't be helped. I can't be two places at once.

Not needing to hurry any longer, I run the report once more and get it ready to leave on Tate's desk so it will be waiting for her first thing in the morning.

I stick the file under my arm, grab my briefcase, and lock up for the night. I nod at Gene, one of our security officers as he does his sweep of the floor. "Night, Mr. Collins." He clicks his flashlight off.

"Has everyone gone home?"

"I believe so." He steps into the elevator and holds the door open. "Going down?"

"Not yet. Have to drop this off first." I motion toward him with the file in my hand.

The elevator door shuts, and I continue to Tate's office. As I near, I notice a soft glow of yellow light on the floor. If I were a coward, I'd leave the file on Quinn's desk with instructions for her to see Tate receives it first thing, but I'm no pussy. I can't go around avoiding her simply because I find her attractive.

Tapping my knuckles lightly on the heavy door, I wait for her to invite me in. The sound of her heels clacking across the floor grows louder as she approaches. My heartbeat kicks up a notch.

The door pulls open, and her eyes widen when she sees me.

"Mind if I come in?" I take a step forward, not bothering to wait for permission.

She steps back, opening the door wider to put more distance between us. "It's your building."

She looks much taller today, and I can't help but look at her feet to see what shoes she's wearing. They're snakeskin, and she looks hot as fuck in them. I drop the file on her desk and my briefcase in one of the chairs.

"Wh-what are you doing?"

"Going over the report. I made a few notes and I'm busy tomorrow. Have a big case developing."

"No need. I took care of it. In the future if you say you'll have a report on my desk in the morning, I expect it to be on time."

"Is that so?"

Tate doesn't respond. She stands there, fuming.

I stroke my beard, amused. "I don't need you riding me, sweetheart."

"Listen up, *sweetheart*." She takes a few steps toward me and her eyes flash with irritation.

I don't know whether to be intimidated or turned on.

Tate puts both hands on her hips. "If I were riding you, you'd damn sure know it."

My teeth clench. The thought of her straddling me plays front and center in my mind. She'd be in nothing but those fuck-me stilettos. Her hair would tumble down her back while she bounced on my thighs, grinding on my cock, my fingers biting the curves of her hips. It would culminate with her bow-shaped lips forming a perfect O while she comes.

"That a promise?" My gaze rakes over her body, taking her in as she stares me down. She's wearing a yellow skirt that's brighter than the sun, her tanned thighs peeking out the bottom. The top two buttons of her blouse are undone providing a glimpse of dark lace underneath. With every breath she takes, her breasts expand and contract and I don't know how much more of this shit I can take.

I cross the room in three long strides. Grabbing her face between my palms, I look into her eyes ready to get lost in them. Those tempting red lips part, and her mocha-scented breath wafts over me. Tate leans in, and my hard cock brushes up against her stomach. The smell of her perfume invades my nose, and all I can think about is claiming her mouth, until Weston's voice sounds in the dark recesses of my mind and tells me not to get involved or I'll blow more than just a load in my pants.

I mentally curse Weston Hunter for sending Tate Reynolds here to torture me.

Dropping my hands, I pull away as my pulse hammers in my ears.

"This can't happen." I storm toward the door not looking back and suck in a deep breath. I'm losing my goddamn mind.

Fuck, this woman is impossible to be near.

TATE

Kicking off my heels, I don't care where they land. I unzip the back of my skirt allowing it to drop to the floor and pool at my feet as I hastily unbutton my top.

Goddamn Decker Collins.

I'm so turned on right now I can't see straight. I told myself I'd never let a man get me flustered, but that's exactly what I am. My heartbeat is still ringing in my ears after that shit he pulled a while ago at the office. Who does he think he is?

"Think you can play these games with me, Decker Collins?" I say to no one in particular as I fight with my blouse before finally yanking it over my head.

Screw him. I need to release this pent-up frustration. I'm wound up tight and I need an orgasm like an alcoholic needs a drink. That smug, freaking jerk. His face flashes to my mind and warmth spreads through my veins. Once my top is off, next goes the bra. I fan out on the bed. My fingers move at their own accord rubbing over one of my nipples, pretending it's Decker's tongue trailing lazy circles around it.

I sigh.

He has me all twisted up inside. Rolling over to the side of the bed, I bend down to my suitcase and my hand goes into a frenzy searching for the one thing that can alleviate this stress, B.O.B. Once he's in my grip, all feels right with the world again.

Nobody can get me off better than me.

I slide my panties down my legs and roll to my back. Visions of Decker filter through my memory, but it's not enough. I prop my phone up on the nightstand and pull his photo up online. It's a few years old and he's volunteering at some baseball thing for a charity group. Shirtless and squirting water in his mouth, his abs are on display, and the dark hair of his happy trail coming up from his pants sends a thrill through me. It's why I chose this picture. I stare at Decker in his gray sweats that hang low on his hips and show off the vee that points like an arrow straight down to his cock.

Sliding my vibrator between my thighs, the hum starts at a gentle pace, but increases with intensity as my hips arch. Back and forth, I slide my favorite toy through my slick folds pretending it's Decker who's touching me. I want to feel that stubble on his jaw scratch between my thighs as his tongue licks right where I need it to. I can practically smell his earthy scent as I stare harder at the picture, enjoying thoughts of his tense body pressing down on mine. My fantasy is nothing but him taking control and pleasuring me. I spread my legs farther apart and tease at my nipples with my free hand. A moan passes through my lips.

I'm getting close.

Grinding my hips up and down, I rub over my clit. It's absolute heaven. My orgasm starts to build and then my stupid screen cuts off to a call from a number I don't recognize.

Ugh!

I snatch my phone from the nightstand after all thoughts of an orgasm dissipate. I slide my thumb across the screen and yell, "What?"

"Tate?"

Shit. This can't be happening.

I clutch the phone to my chest and get all tingly at the sound. Decker fucking Collins. The current bane of my existence. He must be calling from his house phone. I can't even respond because I'm so out of breath and worked up.

"What the hell are you doing?"

I finally manage to compose myself after a few deep breaths. "None of your business," I say a little harsher than intended, but he makes me crazy.

"Why don't you call me back when you have your shit together."

The sound of his commanding voice does something to me. The man sets my blood on fire in the best and worst ways possible. Desire hums through every cell in my body.

Without thinking I say, "Don't you dare hang up." I can't see him, but I know he smirks on the other end.

"Are you under the impression I'm obligated to take orders from you?"

"Yes." Usually, the sound of his smartass professional voice drives me up the wall, but right now my body is all about it. I power my vibrator back on, knowing he can hear, but I don't care. My body has temporarily overridden my brain.

"What the hell is that sound? Is that an electric toothbrush?"

"It's my vibrator. I'm not on company time. You don't get me all worked up then bounce. I have needs."

There's a moment of stunned silence. I picture him sitting there, absolutely flustered and it sends another pulse of electricity down to my clit. Then, I think of him processing this information and his cock growing hard in his pants. Something about it turns me on more than I've ever been turned on in my life.

"Jesus Christ." After a few quick beats, Decker lowers his voice as if someone might hear and says, "Tate... we can't do this."

"Don't be a little bitch. You started this up, *sweetheart*, and now you're going to finish it."

"It's not appropriate." His voice comes out on a groan and my pussy clenches at the sound.

"We're way past appropriate. I'm two seconds away from going to the nearest bar and finding someone who can take care of it if you can't." I let out a gasp as I hit a higher level of intensity on B.O.B.

"The fuck you will." His voice booms from the speaker on my phone.

Please don't stop talking, Decker.

"What the hell are you gonna do about it then?"

"You want to get off, *sweetheart?*" He draws out the last word.

I smirk. "What are you doing right now, Decker?" I close my eyes to picture whatever he's about to say. I want every damn detail he has to offer.

"I'm in my home office sunk down in my chair with my pants unzipped. My fist is wrapped around my cock. I'm thinking about how big it would look with your small hands wrapped around it."

Of course, his fantasy is me pleasuring him. I can't judge him too harshly for it. My thoughts are the exact same with the roles reversed. "Mmm." My teeth dig into my bottom lip. "Tell me what you would've done to me at the office if you hadn't walked out like a pussy."

"I would've shoved you up against the window and yanked your skirt up over your ass."

"Mmm, go on."

"Know what? Fuck your little script. Let me ask you something, Tate." His voice is so goddamn commanding I might come before he even asks the question.

"Okay."

"Can you feel my teeth nibbling at the shell of your ear and down your neck as I pull your panties aside?"

Holy fuck.

I like where this is headed, but he starts up again before I can even answer his question.

"Can you feel it when I slide a finger inside your tight little pussy?"

"Yes." My word comes out on a pant and I wonder if he even heard it.

A slight groan filters through the receiver and answers my question for me.

I close my eyes, focusing on nothing but the sound of his voice and the feel of my vibrator, gliding it back and forth, imagining his touch... his mouth... his thick cock.

"Can you feel my thumb rubbing your clit while my finger finds that spot deep inside you that nobody else has ever pleasured before?"

"God, Decker."

"Yeah, Tate, I know everything you want. You want my tongue on your pussy, the feel of my face brushing up against your thighs while you squeeze your legs around my head and come all over my mouth."

I might die. The orgasm is front and center and I'm doing everything I can to hold it back.

"Once you come all over my face, I'd bend you over my desk, spank your ass and fist your hair and make you beg for my cock inside you."

I don't know how much more of this I can take. I find myself decreasing the intensity on B.O.B. just to make it last longer.

"I'm so fucking hard, Tate. You have no idea what you do to me. For the past few weeks all I've thought about is tasting that smartass mouth of yours and fucking you so hard you feel me inside you weeks later."

"Don't stop. Keep talking."

"I love that sassy little attitude of yours. It makes me want to fuck you even harder, until you finally submit."

His words send a shiver coursing down my spine to my toes. His voice is the sexiest sound in the world right now.

"What else?"

"Those fucking heels you had on tonight... I want you in nothing but those, down on your goddamn knees, begging for my cock in your mouth. I want that red lipstick you love smeared all over it as you take me into your throat. I want you gagging on my dick while I pull on your hair until I come in that pretty little mouth."

"More. Dirtier." I don't know if he can get much dirtier, but I can't help but want to see where he goes from here.

"Know what I'm going to do, Tate? I'm going to slip into your office first thing tomorrow morning and crawl under your desk. You won't know I'm there until I grip your thighs and shove my tongue in your hot cunt. While you're typing at your computer, you'll be fucking my mouth non-stop. You won't get off until I say you can and at the last second, I'll shove inside you so I can feel you come all over my dick."

I whimper, losing complete control at his filthy talk. My orgasm quakes through my body and my eyes roll back in my head, my legs thrashing on the sheets. My hips lift high off the bed and every muscle in my body spasms at the thought of Decker Collins under my desk tomorrow.

I already know he did that shit on purpose and I don't even care. It's all I'll think about tomorrow and I probably won't be able to concentrate on anything else.

"Did you just come?"

"Mhmm."

"Good." He groans out the word. "I'm close too."

I grin, fully sated... well almost. "How close are you?"

"So fucking close. Fuck." His voice is strained, and it might be the hottest thing I've ever heard in my life.

"I bet you look hot as fuck right now fisting your cock. If I was there, I'd run my tongue all the way up your shaft and lick the tip, just to get a sample." I can picture him now, snug in his leather chair, looking like the king of his castle, ready to come. "I'm so wet for you right now, Decker. You have no idea."

"So fucking close. Don't Stop. Keep going."

Then, I hear it. The slapping sound of his hand stroking his cock furiously through the phone. It sends another wave of shivers through my body and goosebumps pebble up and down my arms. I squirm on the bed, thinking about him pumping up and down on his dick while he thinks about me.

I smile at the thought and say, "Thanks for the orgasm, I feel much better now." I end the call and laugh into my pillow.

Decker tries to call me back and I send him to voicemail.

One day, he'll learn—I always win.

Always.

TATE

I HAVEN'T SEEN Decker since I walked in the building this morning. Part of me wants to give him a smug look of satisfaction and part of me is a little mortified at what I did last night. That's beside the point, though. Something else has come up.

One of my biggest clients in Austin, BankIt, emailed me a lawsuit that's been filed against them. They're a tech start up and developed a personal finance app that uses a proprietary algorithm to help people manage their stock portfolios. A disgruntled employee was let go six months ago and has since went to work for another tech outfit in Chicago, broke his non-compete, and handed the algorithm to his new employer.

To top it off, the company in Chicago is suing my client for stealing their intellectual property.

The best part—Donavan Collins signed the fucking thing.

I march toward Donavan's office. He's leaned back in his large office chair with a look of satisfaction plastered across his face and the phone to his ear.

I tap my knuckles twice on his glass door.

He motions for me to come in. "I need to call you back." He hangs up the phone. "How can I help you, Ms. Reynolds?"

I can't help but notice there's a hint of smugness when he says my name. Surely, he doesn't know the people he's suing are Hunter Group clients or he'd never have been stupid enough to bring this suit.

I take two large strides and drop a stapled set of legal documents on his desk. "You know about this lawsuit filed last week?"

He leans over and grins at the papers. "Of course, I do. My name's on them isn't it?"

"It needs to be dropped."

Donavan let's out the fakest laugh I've ever heard. "That's a good one."

"I'm not fucking with you. Squash it."

His eyes narrow. "Not gonna happen. This is one of my biggest clients. And why would I do that, anyway?"

"Because BankIt is a Hunter Group client and this is a clear conflict of interest. We can't merge the firms when we have clients suing each other."

Donavan leans back in his chair. "Well, perhaps you should talk to BankIt, and get them to settle the case so we can move forward."

This fucking guy.

"My client isn't settling this frivolous bullshit. Your guys stole the algorithm from a disgruntled employee and now you have the balls to pull this shit?"

"If you'd cared to read the suit, you'd know we have R&D records…"

I cut him off before he can finish. "I don't give a shit what evidence you've manufactured to build your case. I know these guys personally. I brought them to the firm. They're geniuses, much smarter than you and I. They've been working on this for years. It's their baby."

"Guess we'll have to see it play out in court, then." Donavan stands up like the meeting is over.

I step right in his face. "I want it dropped. I don't have time to deal with this bullshit. I know what you're doing."

"And what am I doing?"

"You're doing this to fuck with Decker and the merger."

"I'm doing this because I believe in the laws of a free market."

I shake my head. It's difficult not to laugh at how ridiculous he sounds. "You take this to court and I'm going to kick your ass so hard you feel my Jimmy Choos in your goddamn throat. And not because I'm better than you, which I am. But because your case has no merit. It's fucking laughable."

Donavan smirks. "Guess we'll see then, won't we?"

I turn on my heel and march out of his office.

Fucking Collins brothers.

DECKER

"WHERE THE HELL'S MY COFFEE?" I bark the question at an empty room when I get to the office and my usual cup isn't on my desk. "And where the fuck is Quinn?"

I pull up my schedule and my new emails. I smooth a palm over my head and cup the back of my neck, trying to rub the knot out of it. I didn't sleep for shit last night after that little stunt Tate pulled. The woman completely threw me off guard. I called to tell her I left my briefcase in her office. I wasn't prepared for the late-night phone sex that followed.

Fuck, I've never been so worked up in my life.

I've never met a soul like her. A woman who takes complete charge. Says what the fuck she means and takes whatever she wants. I was weak last night, and I never should've given in to the temptation. It took everything I had not to leave in the middle of the night, drive to her hotel, and fuck an apology out of her.

I head to the break room to get my own damn coffee still wondering where the hell my assistant is. I know she didn't call off and she's never late. On my way back to my office I pass Tate. She's talking to Brenda, Dexter's legal assistant. She smirks at me and shoots me a wink. It sends my blood boiling, knowing she got the best of me. Her casual attitude raises the hair on the back of my neck.

I try to ignore her and burn my lip on my coffee. Quinn steps off the elevator carrying a bag and steaming cup from a fancy bakery down the street. I start to ask why she's bringing me something she knows I won't eat when she hands it to Tate.

Goddamn it.

Not only is Tate fucking with my head, she's got my assistant running errands for her. Scowling, I retreat to my office. I arrive at my desk and realize I don't have my damn briefcase. It's still in Tate's office. Blowing on my coffee, I take another sip. I'll need the caffeine to make it through this shit show of a morning.

Nothing is going my way, and everything is getting under my skin. I should've finished the job myself last night to alleviate some of this pent-up frustration, but I was too irritated to do a damn thing.

Donavan taps on my door and I motion him in.

He shuts the door behind him. "I gotta say this, so hear me out."

"Okay." I take a seat, and he pulls up a chair. He sounds serious and Donavan isn't one to speak his mind unless he means it.

"This merger is a mistake. This firm was supposed to be about us. And you brought in your college pal and his associate is walking around here like she runs the damn place. She's fucking with my cases and has your assistant getting her breakfast. I just overheard her barking orders at Brenda, moving Dexter's schedule around. What the fuck, bro?"

Blood rushes to my face. It's one thing for me to be pissed at Tate, but I won't tolerate it from him. "Are you seriously wasting my time with this petty bullshit? I expect more from you."

"I've tried to refrain out of respect but this merger is a mistake."

"I don't need this." I push up from the chair and stalk out of my office.

I go to the one spot where I feel like I can breathe and clear my head. The one place I can get away from everyone.

I step out on the roof deck, and there she is. Her hair is down, and her curls blow with the breeze, wild and untamed just like her. Tate Reynolds is a damn force to be reckoned with and she knows it. I stand quietly and watch her as she stares out at the lake.

I start to turn back. I don't have the energy to spar with her right now but change my mind after the first step.

No. This is my spot. This is my goddamn firm, at least until the papers are signed.

Sensing my approach, she spins around and those passionate eyes of hers burn a hole in my chest.

Not this time. I hold her gaze. "This is my spot. How'd you find it?"

"Quinn showed it to me my first day. But you're a big boy. Didn't your parents teach you to share?"

I take a seat in one of the deck chairs. I wave my hand for her to join me.

Tate sits on another and reclines back.

I lean back as well, closing my eyes as sunshine beams down on us. "I have three brothers. I've had to share my entire life."

I feel her eyes on me and glance over in her direction.

"Everything?" She grins to insinuate we're talking about her.

"*Almost* everything." I make the point clear, though I'm certain Dexter and Deacon have pulled the twin switcharoo on women in the past. That's not my style.

"They don't like me much."

"It's not you they don't like. Well, the twins anyway. I hear you pissed off Donavan." I lean up, because the conversation has switched to a serious tone.

"He's acting like an idiot, but I can handle him."

"Yeah, I'm sure you can." I sigh. "They don't like change. They're used to doing whatever they want and maybe that's part of the problem. You intimidate them. And I've seen your work at The Hunter Group."

"Been reading up on me?"

"What kind of attorney would I be if I didn't? You're not the only one who knows how to research." I shoot her a playful grin. The more we talk the better I feel and the tension slips away.

"I'm not sorry about last night. You had it coming."

Pushing my sleeve up, I check the time and know I need to get back downstairs. "I'd love to stay here and tell you all the reasons you're wrong, but I have a meeting. Lunch, Friday?"

"That depends... is it for business or pleasure?"

"Pleasure." The word comes out before I can stop it.

"I'm not good enough to take to dinner?"

She never gives an inch, and I think that's what I enjoy most about her. I lick my lips, considering how to answer. "I have personal obligations in the evenings."

"Fucking hell, Decker. Don't tell me you have a girlfriend." She pushes up from the chair and turns her nose down at me. Her arms wrap around her waist and she looks away.

"I don't have a girlfriend. I just can't do most nights and it's not up for discussion. Just say yes."

"Fine. I'll have lunch with you Friday."

"Good. I'll send you the details after my meeting. I need my briefcase from your office. I left it in one of your chairs."

"I already sent it back with Quinn. I wouldn't be stealing your assistant all the time if you'd find me one."

"I'll see what I can do." With that, I stand up and leave.

I have a date with Tate Reynolds. It's exciting and scares the shit out of me at the same time.

TATE

I CAN'T BELIEVE I agreed to lunch with Decker. I promised myself after the other night I wouldn't pursue my feelings any further, but he seemed so sincere when we were out on the roof deck I couldn't bring myself to say no. I know I'm bordering on inappropriate for the office with the sexy red dress and heels I'm wearing today but it's Friday and most places have casual Friday. I know I'm reaching for an excuse to wear it, but I want to look irresistible for him. I want the man to eat his heart out. I have a matching jacket over the top half, but come lunch that sucker is coming off.

I know I'm playing with fire and there's a possibility I could get burned but I'm going forward with our lunch date. It's just two people sharing a meal together, nothing more. But sweet lord the things his voice does to me.

Last night I thought about him while I touched myself in the shower.

I fiddle with my lipstick and tuck the tube back in my clutch.

Decker knocks on my door. "You ready? I made reservations."

"All set." I log out of my computer and set my email to away, so we won't be disturbed on our date by new messages coming through on my phone.

I can't help but notice Donavan glaring as we make our way out of the office. I flash him a smirk and keep walking. I should tell Decker about the bullshit suit and go straight over Donavan's head, but I don't want to ruin the lunch date. It's going to come up sometime soon, but not today.

I follow Decker into the elevator and the moment the door closes all the air pulls from my lungs. There's an electric current, some kind of magnetism between us. He stares ahead as we come to a stop on another floor. The elevator begins to fill, pushing me so close I can smell his cologne. I press into his side, unable to escape.

The elevator ride can't end soon enough. I need some physical distance from him.

We finally step through the door and I breathe a sigh of relief. After hailing a cab and a quick ride through downtown, we end up at a place called NoMi. The hostess seats us by a window overlooking Michigan Avenue. Decker's wearing a dark blue Tom Ford paired with a baby blue shirt. It makes his eyes pop against his tan skin and dark hair.

He does the honor of ordering for us while I freshen up in the ladies' room. You can tell a lot about a man by how he feeds you. The restaurant is gorgeous and the food smells amazing as I return to the table. He stands and pulls my chair out for me like a true gentleman. It's nice to see a northern city boy with some manners.

I sip my water and our Caesar salads arrive.

"Aren't you going to ask what I ordered you?"

"No. I want to be surprised."

"*That* surprises me."

I pause in the middle of stabbing my lettuce with my fork. "Why's that?"

"You seem to enjoy control."

"Any woman can be made submissive under the right circumstances." I shove my food in my mouth and the white dressing drips down my chin.

Decker stares right at my mouth, his eyes lingering on the sauce. I dab a napkin to my face, knowing what the image does to him after our conversation the other night.

"Oops. I'm a little messy."

He clears his throat and takes a gulp of water. "You're evil. You know that?"

"I've been told."

"You know a little about me. Tell me about you."

"Hmm. Well I grew up in a little rural Texas town. When I'm not kicking ass in the courtroom, I take my nephews fishing."

His eyes roam my dress, all the way down to my shoes. "I still don't believe you fish."

"I won the junior bass tournament two years in a row."

He looks skeptical and shovels a few more bites of salad into his mouth.

"It's true. I even have one of those singing fish plaques to prove it."

"Don't tell me. It sings *Take Me to the River*."

"Liked *The Sopranos*, did you?" I grin.

"Guilty. I used to watch it on the way to away games in my baseball days."

"Figured you'd be too busy trying to pick up adoring fans."

"That too."

The waiter clears our salad plates and replaces them with New York strips.

I cut into the juicy meat. It's red in the middle. My dad always told me a real man knows how a steak should be cooked, and if he doesn't I should run for the hills. "Now I'm impressed."

"I didn't take you for a soup and salad kind of woman."

"Got that right," I say with a mouth full of steak.

"How old are your nephews?"

"Max is seven, Braxton is ten, and Camden's thirteen and girl crazy."

"Most boys are."

"Are you? You don't have a girlfriend... you say you don't date but this is a date."

"Can't give away all my secrets." He grins as he deflects the question about his personal life.

I want to push him further for more details, but he's still closed off. There's something he's hiding. I don't have any idea what it is, but it sets off all kinds of warning bells in my brain. I hope he doesn't have a closet full of crazy girlfriends or former fuck buddies. He could be a dominant and into the BDSM scene, but I don't see it. He's alpha but there's something I can't put my finger on. It bugs me. I'll have to spend more time feeling him out.

Our meal goes quickly, and as we walk back, Decker points out the different buildings to me. The Willis Tower, Trump Tower... to name a few.

I offer him a smile as we come to a stop outside the office building. "I had a good time." I actually mean what I said. It was really nice.

"Maybe we can do this again sometime?"

"I'd like that." I move to return to work when he grabs my hand, stopping me.

He spins me around quickly and I feel dizzy, like I'm on a carnival ride. He gazes at my lips and I part them wondering if he's finally going to kiss me. When his eyes meet mine, I can't read him. I should push him away and get back inside to work, but I can't. Because of one simple fact, despite how wrong it is and how much trouble I could get into—I want Decker Collins to kiss me. Right here in front of the office building, no matter who is watching, I want him to put his lips on mine and kiss me so hard my fingers and toes go numb.

I'm not a girl who sits around and waits for men to make a move, though. "Decker, if you're going to kiss me—just do it."

His smile broadens and he lets out a hoarse, "Fuck it." He grabs my face and plants his mouth firmly on mine. Our lips collide, mouths opening, and I invite him in. His tongue tastes like wine as he thrusts into my mouth, licking and swirling.

Finally, I pull away, breathless, and delirious. Decker Collins kissed me, and it was everything I had hoped it would be and more.

His fingers grip mine and he tugs me away from the building. With his free hand he hails us a cab.

My brows knit together. "What are you doing?"

"Fuck work. It can wait."

My pulse races as my heart pounds against my rib cage.

I get into the cab. Excitement courses through my veins.

Is he taking me home with him?

TATE

THE CAB COMES to a stop outside Wrigley Field.

Not what I expected, but Decker looks giddy like a little boy in a candy store. We slide out of the cab and he slips the driver a few bills. At admission he hands over his season tickets and escorts me to a suite. I settle into my seat and kick my heels off, tucking my legs underneath me.

Bringing my knuckles to his lips, he grazes them with a tender kiss. It's an intimate and sweet action that sparks some kind of hope that he's finally opening up to me. Maybe there really is more to him than just a cocky asshole who looks gorgeous in a suit.

Dropping my hand, he says, "I love my family and the law. This is the only other thing that compares." It seems as though he's choosing his words carefully.

That wall is still up, but I'll tear it down. I feel like I'm already halfway there.

"Baseball?"

Decker nods. "I sneak out here every chance I get." His face lights up as he stares out at the field below. These seats must cost him a fortune. We're only a few spots away from the owner's box. I don't know a lot about baseball, my brothers were more into hunting and football in Texas. I played soccer myself.

"You wanted to play here?"

"That was the dream. I grew up watching the Cubs. Andre Dawson, Ryne Sandberg, Mark Grace." He has this far off look in his eyes, and I wonder why he quit if he loved it so much. Everything I know about him says he should've ended up playing on the field we're staring at.

"What made you give it up?"

He pauses and takes a deep breath, collecting himself. "Life. I had what it took, but I knew I couldn't play forever and had to grow up sometime. The shelf-life of a baseball player isn't very long. You're always one injury away from having nothing."

His answer is a bullshit copout, but I don't call him on it. Nobody gives up on a dream that easily. They all know the risks and don't care. We're getting along and I'm enjoying myself, though. I'm not about to ruin this with an unnecessary argument.

He pulls out his phone and shoots a message to Quinn that we aren't coming back to the office. I don't know what she'll think but I don't really care.

Right now, everything is perfect. This day with Decker is an unexpected but happy surprise. He's nothing like I thought when I first met him on the sidewalk. He's cocky but there's a sweet layer to him I'm slowly discovering. Weston told me he was a great guy. Maybe I was wrong to judge him so soon.

I put my shoes back on and excuse myself for a trip to the bathroom. When I return, he's chatting with some other men in suits.

"Tate." He motions me over and hands me a cup of beer. "This is Mikey Sullivan and Horace Martinez. They're clients at the firm and good friends."

"Nice to meet you." I extend my free hand.

"Tate's a temporary transplant at the firm. She's out of Dallas."

"I hope you keep her. I wouldn't mind meeting someone so beautiful in the courtroom."

Decker locks an arm around my hip in a possessive manner, but manages to keep a cordial, joking tone. "Careful, Mikey, she's lethal."

"I'd die happy." The man is attractive, but the way he looks at me all hungry like a wolf does nothing for me when I'm here with Decker.

On the inside, I'm rolling my eyes but, on the outside, I plaster on my beauty pageant smile and battle the urge to put him in his place. The last thing I want is to piss off one of Decker's clients when we're having a great time. "Excuse me, boys. I'm here to see asses in those tight baseball pants."

Decker releases my hip, and I move to the edge of the box to watch more of the game, away from the boys and their likely misogynistic conversation. I know how men in suits talk and it's usually better for my career to just walk away.

I can hear Decker's conversation transpiring behind me. "Shit, you weren't kidding. I might be in love with your friend."

"Get in line. The whole office is in love with her."

Everyone but your brothers.

"You still owe me a round of drinks after I schooled you on the golf course," one of the men says to Decker.

"You promised me a rematch, but on my terms."

The man laughs. "No way am I getting on a baseball field with you."

Decker finally says, "I'll have my assistant call yours and we'll get those drinks. I need to get back."

They say their goodbyes and a moment later Decker's strong arm slides around my shoulders. His lips are at my ear. "Enjoying the game?"

I take a sip of stale Old Style beer. I think to myself only Cubs fans could enjoy this swill, but there's something alluring about a stale beer and a baseball game. "Mhmm."

His fingers bite into my shoulder with possession. It's sexy. I like seeing him in his element. He's a fierce lawyer but this is where his heart lies. Decker belongs on that field.

"Holy shit is that, Jose Balinger?"

"Didn't know you were a fan." Decker leans back, a surprised look on his face. "Thought you weren't really into baseball."

"I'm not." I take another drink of my beer. "It's my nephew. The girl-crazy one."

"I bet you'd be the best aunt in the world if you brought him an autographed ball."

"Shut up." I smack his chest nearly spilling my beer in the process.

He laughs and holds out a hand. "Come on, it's almost the seventh inning stretch."

"I haven't the slightest clue what that means but okay."

His hand wraps around mine after we discard our empty cups. As we walk down toward the dugout, his thumb strokes the inside of my wrist and every little touch leads me closer to temptation. His hands are magical and even a brush of his finger sends electricity shivering across my skin.

Decker let's go of my hand and cups his hands around his mouth leaning forward over the dugout. "Hey JoJo!"

The player Camden is crazy about turns around and smiles at Decker. He jogs over and I can't get past the fact the man my nephew worships is coming over to us. "Hey, Collins. What's up?"

"This is my friend, Tate. Think you could get her a ball signed for her nephew?"

"No problemo."

"Thanks. Just give me a call and I'll get it from you later."

I'm flabbergasted. I don't know why I'm being so silly and starstruck, but I am.

"It's that easy for you, huh?"

"We played together in college."

I wonder if it's bittersweet for Decker, but he doesn't seem sad about it.

"I'd get him a ball right now, but they aren't allowed to sign during the games. Some MLB rule. I'll get it to you, though, so you can send it to your nephew."

"That's just—thank you." My face has to be pink. Camden is going to go insane.

Decker gets us a couple of hotdogs and we drink another beer while we watch the rest of the game. We're getting ready to leave the stadium when I remember I never turned my phone back on. The minute I power it on it lights up with notifications and a call comes through from Weston.

"I need to take this." I step off to the side and answer the call. "Hello."

"Where the hell are you? I've been trying to call you all afternoon."

"Um… I'm at a game."

"Baseball?" He sounds super pissed off. "I'm not fucking paying you to go to ballgames with Decker."

I clench my fist and suck in a breath as Decker shoots his brows up at me. I pray he doesn't hear the way Weston is talking to me through the phone.

"Listen, Weston. We're a week ahead of schedule."

"I don't give a fuck."

Decker definitely hears that part as it booms through my phone. "Let me talk to him." Decker reaches for my phone, but I step away so he's out of earshot.

"I have something I need to talk to you about on Monday."

"Oh, the BankIt lawsuit? Yeah, I would've expected to hear it from the attorney responsible for reviewing conflicts of interest."

Shit!

"I'm handling it."

"I fucking hope so." He hangs up.

I should take Weston chewing my ass out as a sign to put a stop to this flirtation brewing with Decker, but I don't. It makes me more determined to see where this leads. I always do what's right and I'm never selfish, but today I'm damn sure going to be.

Decker stands in front of me. "You've been working your ass off. Ignore him."

"I've been dealing with Weston for years. I'll be fine. I can fight my own battles." My chest heaves and Decker pulls me in close.

"I know you can." His mouth crashes down on mine, stealing my breath away. We kiss and the rest of the world melts away. In his arms I forget why I'm in Chicago and focus on kissing him back. As our tongues dance, his cock hardens against my stomach.

He pulls away. "Let's get out of here."

Decker whisks me toward a cab, and I feel drunk on this man. As soon as I slide into the seat, he's next to me firing off the address to my hotel to the driver.

"Why my hotel?"

He leans in close and moves my hair away from my ear. "Because, *sweetheart*, I'm going to peel this red dress off and do everything I said on the phone the other night."

My heart pounds in my chest and his hand moves to my upper thigh. His tongue darts out and licks the shell of my ear and his lips move to my throat.

Decker's other hand caresses my jaw, his thumb rubbing over my mouth. I suck his finger between my lips knowing what it does to him… painting the image he's been thinking about of me going down on my knees for him. If we had the privacy here, I'd unzip his pants and give him a preview.

Sliding his fingers further up my thigh, he teases at the apex where my pelvis and leg meets. "I know this pussy is wet for me." His voice is pure gravel.

We both know we're about to cross a line we can't come back from.

Arriving at the hotel, the ride up the elevator is torturous. All I want is to get him alone and hold him to his promise. I can already feel the wetness on my thighs. Decker stands behind me, his erection pressing against the center of my backside.

We get to my door and he shoves me up against it before I can unlock it. "This is coming off." He fingers the strap of my dress and I nod in response. "Where's your key?"

I dig around in my clutch for the plastic card frustrated with every second separating fantasy from reality. A bolt retracts, the door swings open, and I start to kick off my shoes when he shakes his head. "I want those on and this off." He moves to unzip my dress as the door sucks shut behind us.

My dress falls to my feet leaving me in my strapless red lace bra and matching panties.

"Fucking Christ." The way Decker stares at my body heats me up in ways I couldn't have imagined before now.

He starts unbuttoning his shirt.

I move toward him and grab a pillow off the sofa. I drop it down on the floor. "You. Couch. Now." I smirk and go down on my knees to the pillow.

Decker grins at me with those blue eyes hungry with desire. He does what I tell him but still manages to look powerful and in control as if he's amused. He sinks down on the sofa and spreads his legs apart.

I unzip his pants, eager to get my mouth on him and hear him moan. I grip his thick length over his boxer briefs and flutter my lashes, toying with him as I rub my fingers along his shaft. His eyes burn into mine.

The head of his cock pokes through the slit of his boxers and I kiss the tip.

He groans and fists my hair, giving it a gentle tug. "Put it in your mouth, Tate."

I flick my tongue out and swirl it around the crown, teasing him, drawing the process out in leisurely strokes and kisses. His grip tightens in my hair, so hard his knuckles dig against my scalp, and I smile to myself, loving the effect I have on him.

I give in and free him from the constraints of his boxers getting an eyeful of how thick he is.

Right when I'm about to take him in my mouth, his damn cell phone rings.

A sigh escapes his parted lips as his head drops back against the cushions in frustration.

I fall back on my calves while he digs the mood killer out of his pocket.

One glance at the screen and his entire demeanor changes. "I'm sorry. I have to take this."

"Decker Collins." He listens for a moment and his face pales. He flies up off the couch so fast he nearly barrels right over me. "I'll be right there."

His hands are a blur, furiously tucking everything back in his pants, then he zips them up. "I'm so sorry. I hate to do this right now, but I have to go. It's a family emergency."

"I understand." I move to grab my dress. "I can come with you." I clutch the thin material to my chest.

"No!" He snaps at me, harsher than he's ever been.

I flinch at the unexpected tone of his voice.

He rakes his fingers through his hair and takes a ragged breath, then holds a hand out at me. "I'm just—I'm sorry, Tate. I didn't mean it to come out like that. You just can't."

I do my best to keep my composure. I've never heard him speak to me like that. It's one thing when he's being a prick or sarcastic. This was more. It was pure —I don't even know the right word for it. It wasn't anger. It was just a tone that suggested it wasn't up for discussion or debate, at all. Whatever it was, it socked me in my chest and knocked me speechless.

"I'll call you as soon as I can." The door slams shut with his departure and I'm not sure how I feel about what just transpired.

TATE

It's been days and I haven't heard from Decker. I tried to text him to make sure he was okay and never got a response. I did my best not to take it personally, but we had this wonderful date and things were going perfect. I thought maybe it was leading to something, but perhaps I was just caught up in the moment. It's past ten and he hasn't been in the office all morning. I'm not sure if something is really wrong or if he's avoiding me.

There's one thing I do know. I'm not putting any more effort in with a guy who clearly doesn't have his shit together. I'm a little surprised Weston is getting into bed with someone who seems so all over the damn place. I lied to my boss and feel shitty about it. I told Weston we were at the game with potential clients when I finally called him back. It wasn't a complete fib. There were clients there. I put my ass on the line and for what? A little tonsil hockey and phone sex? I nearly snap my pen in half.

My line buzzes. It's Quinn. "I wanted to let you know Mr. Collins is in."

"Thank you."

I take my lunch in my office, trying to give Decker an opportunity to come to me, but so far, he hasn't shown his face. I'm pissed off and hurt. It's a bad combination for him. I guess I had him all wrong. I've had enough waiting and decide to say screw it. I close down my computer and strut down the hall.

I walk in and stare him down with my hands planted on my hips. He looks up from some paperwork and his mouth opens then shuts. I tap my foot as my anger reaches the boiling point. "Well?"

"Tate… this can't happen. And we aren't having this conversation right now."

"The hell we aren't."

"Lower your voice." He stands up and moves past me to shut the door.

The second it closes, I whirl around and start in on him. "What was that the other night? Where have you been? You couldn't even shoot me a courtesy text to say oh hey I'm alive don't worry? You said you'd call." I fold my arms over my chest.

"You were worried about me?" His gaze softens a little at my words.

It's an unexpected reaction, but I pinch my brows together. "I actually do have some business to discuss with you, but that's beside the point. I know you feel the same way, so quit fucking around."

"Don't do this to me right now. Just don't push this, please." He leans against the door.

"You're not getting off easy this time, Collins. Tell me right now. What. Do. You. Want. From. Me?"

"Fine. You know what I want?" He takes a step toward me with wild eyes. It's kind of hot and primal.

My pulse hammers and my breaths become shallow. "No, but I'm kind of digging you being all hot and pissed off. It makes me want to find out."

"Is that so?" He reaches behind him and locks the door after closing the blinds.

I nod, desperate for him to make a move. He's so close and the sexual tension radiating from his body is off the charts intense. Christ, when this man starts brooding my legs turn to Jello and my brain to mush.

He crosses the room and yanks me into his heaving chest. No more words pass between us. His mouth comes down hard on mine and it's game over. Everything fades away—where we are, all my thoughts, the BankIt lawsuit. His mouth is on mine and there's no way I could stop it, even if I wanted to.

Pawing at my skirt, he shoves it up my hips. He backs me over to his desk, and tugs my panties down to my ankles. A tingling sensation radiates from my clit, traverses my body, and threatens to blast out of my limbs.

I kick my panties off and sit on the edge of his desk. Decker drops to his knees and buries his face between my thighs, licking and sucking everywhere but where I need him the most. He teases me, licking all around my legs at the edge of my pussy, but never making contact. Every nerve ending in my body fires at once and I'm already on the cusp of the greatest orgasm of my life.

I grip the edge of the desk as his facial scruff rubs my inner thigh. Threading my fingers through his dark hair, I give it a yank bringing his mouth closer to my pussy.

When he slides two fingers inside me, my head tilts back and I damn near lose it right there. Decker owns my body. I'm completely lost to him. His mouth hums on my clit while his fingers make a *come here* motion inside me, hitting all the right spots in rapid succession. In and out, his fingers glide into my tight center. I'm a ticking time bomb as he hits me in delicious strokes that have me near the edge of orgasmic bliss. I throw my head back once more, panting. Decker works my pussy better than any man ever has. That's for damn sure.

My muscles clench, tightening my legs around his face. I'm two seconds from coming all over his mouth.

Decker pulls back and I try to yank at his hair, drag his mouth back to me. It's no use. My limbs are puddles already, and he's too strong.

Decker smirks. "Oh no, *sweetheart*. The first time you come for me, it'll be on my cock."

I don't hate it quite so much this time when he calls me sweetheart. In fact, it's kind of hot.

"Is that so?"

Decker's brooding stare bores into me. He undoes his belt and unzips his pants. "You're goddamn right."

I'm not one to take orders in life or the bedroom, but fuck if I wouldn't follow Decker Collins off the edge of a cliff right now. He's so intense and commanding. Veins bulge on his neck and I can't help but notice the urgency with which he got his pants undone, like he couldn't live if he wasn't inside me as soon as possible. Even with his disheveled dress shirt on I can tell he has the body of a Greek god. He's nothing but corded muscle and rough sinew. Veins snake down his forearms as his pants and briefs hit the floor.

His cock springs free and wobbles in front of me before he fists it in his hand. Sweet lord, he's even thicker than I remembered from the hotel room.

My legs hook around his waist and I yank him closer to me.

He stares down at my pussy and slides the head of his cock back and forth over my clit.

I squirm and paw at the desk because it's damn near too much to handle all at once.

Decker smirks, knowing he's in total control of the situation, and slaps the head of his cock on top of my clit.

"Shit, Decker." My hands grip the edge of the desk even tighter.

"I love the way you say my name when you want me inside you."

Oh. My. God.

Decker glances around the room and I wonder what the fuck he's waiting for.

"You on the pill?"

I nod, emphatically. I'm tired of waiting.

"Good. I got checked out. I'm clean. I can show you…"

"Shut up and fuck me."

His lips curve up into a devilish grin. He hooks an arm around one of my legs and keeps me spread open as he slides the tip of his cock into my entrance. "Fuck." That's the only word that comes from his beautiful mouth as he fills my pussy. His eyes roll back slightly toward the ceiling, then fall back on me. The intense stare returns, and he leans down and moves his other hand to the back of my neck, angling my eyes up to him.

Pure possession washes over his face as he heats me to a million degrees on the inside with nothing but his stare. "This pussy is mine."

And you're done for, Tate.

There's something about the way his fingers dig into my skin, the way he looks at me, the way he moves—Decker Collins owns me and he damn well knows it.

I try to think of something sarcastic to say, something defiant, that will piss him off and make him take me to places I've never been before, but every thought in my mind vanishes as he pushes himself in and out of me.

His thighs slap against my ass, and I let out a whimper. Decker clamps a hand over my mouth and I bite his finger as he thrusts inside me. It wasn't meant to be sexual. I literally needed some reprieve from the intense feeling of his cock filling me to the brim. He's rock-solid and stretches me from the inside in the best possible way.

"Fuck, this pussy is tight."

God, his filthy mouth has me coming undone all over again. If he so much as brushes a finger over my clit, I'll combust.

I have to do something. Something to take my mind off what's happening, or I might just pass out. What's that trick they say guys do to make them last longer? Think about car engines or their grandma? Instead, my body instinctively tries to piss Decker Collins off, so he'll pound into me even harder. "Shut up and fuck me, Collins. You talk too much."

A sly grin spreads across his arrogant face, and his hands grip the tops of my thighs, holding me in place. He stares down where we're connected, and his hands spread me farther apart, so he can watch his cock going in and out of me.

I don't know why, but it's hot as all hell. My heartbeat redlines, higher than I thought possible, and all the intense nerve firings in my body amplify by a thousand.

The two of us move together in perfect harmony. His hips speed up, until smacking sounds of wet flesh on flesh echo through the room.

His lips meet mine and our tongues intertwine, then he presses his forehead to mine so that our mouths are inches apart. I feel his labored breaths on my mouth, and I hear every little grunt that parts his lips.

Through his rough pants he says, "Can you taste your pussy on my mouth, *Tate*?"

Jesus, this man.

"Fuck, Decker." It's all I can think to say. My brain has passed the point of being able to have a meaningful conversation. And the way he said my name at the end of his question—it sends my pending orgasm front and center in my mind.

I dig my fingernails into his forearms like I'm holding on for dear life. "I'm so close."

"Me too." He grunts out his response as his hips go to warp speed. My head bounces back and forth and everything blurs at the force of his hips crashing into me.

The stems of my heels dig into the top of his ass, cutting into him with every thrust. He picks up the pace and I reach between us to circle my clit. My whole body quakes the second my finger hits my sensitive bundle of nerves, and the orgasm rolls through me in huge, uncontrolled waves. My thighs quiver and I gasp. My hands reach out, grasping for anything I can grab hold of. Fuzzy stars firework in front of my eyes and nothing but pure pleasure rips through my veins. Finally, my pussy clamps down on his cock.

It elicits a loud groan from deep in Decker's throat.

Right when I think the orgasm subsides, and my mind returns to a state of normalcy, Decker grunts—loud. It's primal and raw, like a caveman. He shoves his cock so far into me I think he hits places no man has ever been.

"Fuck... Tate..." His dick jerks inside me, and he lets loose.

I stare up at his face, trying to log every reaction in my long-term memory. Every groan, every wrinkle that forms as every muscle in his body contracts. Hot jets of come shoot into my pussy and it streams out the sides of his cock and runs down my inner thighs.

He convulses a few more times, until he's emptied himself, then slowly a satisfied smile spreads across his face. I can only imagine the ridiculous, cheesy grin I must be wearing as well. I'll never tell Decker Collins this, but it was by far the best sex I've ever had in my life. It wasn't even sex, it was an experience.

I've never even come close to coming that hard, not even at home with B.O.B.

Placing a gentle kiss on my lips, Decker slides his cock out of me, and I immediately miss the connection. Tiny beads of sweat roll down from his forehead when he pulls back.

I can feel his hot come trickling out of me, but I can't even be bothered to worry about it. The way he now looks at me, all soft and sweet, like he feels something for me—like he's a different man for a few brief seconds.

I like it.

We kiss again and then I lean back to gaze into his eyes, seeing him a bit differently than before.

"Was that so hard?" I ask.

"It's still hard."

I giggle at that and he helps me to my feet and leads me into his private bathroom. Decker grabs a washcloth and wipes his orgasm from my inner thighs, then leaves to give me a moment of privacy. I straighten my hair and dab at my skin with a tissue to get the smudged lipstick look off my face. My lips are swollen from kissing him, but other than that, there's no sign I've been freshly and properly fucked.

I exit the bathroom, and he grins while he fixes his desk and rearranges his files. I move toward him and kiss his cheek, wondering where this leaves us now.

Before I can ask, there's a knock at the door.

I'm on my way out so I unlock it and Decker walks up behind me with a hand on the small of my back.

The door swings open and a woman stands in front of it. I give her an uneasy smile and she shoots a daggered glare right at me. I look back at Decker, but he stares at her with utter confusion written on his face. Then it turns to mixed annoyance and surprise. He clearly knows her, but she doesn't look like an attorney. She doesn't even look like she belongs in the building.

She's wearing jeans, a t-shirt, and sneakers with her hair pulled up in a ponytail. Her arms fold over her chest, and she just stands there like it's a showdown in an old western movie.

Shit, it's his girlfriend. Or wife.

"Monica?" He says her name like he hasn't seen her in years and they just ran into each other at the mall.

Did she hear us? Who the hell is this lady?

DECKER

THIS CAN'T BE FUCKING HAPPENING. The world hates me.

My head is about to explode. I stare at the woman who changed the course of my life fourteen years ago. She doesn't look much different now than she did then. Big green eyes and pink lips—just like Jenny's.

I swallow—hard—as a million different emotions swarm through my body. Anger is front and center. I bite back a lot of what I want to say and go with the obvious. "What the fuck are you doing here?"

"Our daughter was in the hospital and you didn't think it was something I should know about? Why didn't you call?"

Tate whips around, hurt and confusion written on her face. "Daughter? Are you married?"

My jaw tightens and I narrow my eyes on Monica. She never fails to leave destruction in her wake. I put a hand on Tate's shoulder, wondering how I'll ever dig myself out of this one. Tate doesn't seem the type of person to wait idly until I can give her all the facts. She probably wants to kick me in the balls, and maybe even a few other things that would inflict maximum pain. I try to tell her with my eyes that I'm sorry, and all of this has a rational explanation. "I'll explain later. I promise." I gesture to Monica. "Right now, I need to talk to her in my office. I'm sorry."

Tate's expression falls and her face pales. I feel like an asshole, but she'll have to understand. Surely, she'll give me the benefit of the doubt. Monica shoots Tate a smug smile and saunters past her and into my office.

Tate stands there with a shocked expression on her face, waiting for an explanation I can't give her in this moment. I shoot her my best *I'm sorry* look once more and brush a finger along her jaw, then I close the door.

I turn to meet Monica's hateful sneer.

"Banging your secretary in your office now?"

I hold up a finger and glare daggers right at her. "Don't. It's none of your fucking business and she's not a secretary. Why are you here?" I stomp to my bar and pour a glass of whiskey. I need something to dull the pain in my chest from the way Tate looked at me while I closed the door. Why does life have to constantly fuck with me like this? Why couldn't I have two minutes to at least enjoy the fact I fucked Tate so hard she came all over my cock? In my office no less.

That's every man's fantasy rolled up into one, and Monica shows up unannounced and ruins everything.

I take a hard pull from the tumbler and close my eyes as the warm liquid glides down my throat. I open my eyes back up, hoping she'll be gone, and this is some sort of twisted dream, but no dice. "It's been fourteen years." I scoff, shaking my head. "Now you're here. Like you're entitled to barge into my office and demand information on a child you don't even know. Fuck that and fuck you."

Monica shuffles her feet and cocks a hip out, like she's entitled to be defiant in my goddamn building. "That's no way to talk to the mother of your child."

I slam the tumbler down on my desk and take two quick steps toward her before I catch myself. I would never lay hands on a woman, but this is the closest I've ever come to being angry enough. "You're not her mother. Don't feed me that bullshit. Dealing with manipulating assholes is what I do. You're out of your league." I pause and take a deep breath, trying my best to calm down and be the mature person in this situation. "Look, I stepped up to the plate. You stuck your hand out for money."

She starts to say something, and I cut her off, figuring the best way to get her out of my office is to just feed her the facts as quickly as possible, even though she doesn't deserve them. I have damage control to do with Tate and, for all I know, she could already be on a plane heading to DFW.

"Look, we thought she had appendicitis, but she didn't. You've never cared enough to show up before, so that's not why you're here. What is it? You need money? How much?" I take two strides behind my desk and open the drawer, looking for my checkbook. I know how the game is played.

"Wow, Decker. Is that how you really feel about me?" She sniffles and wipes at her crocodile tears.

I'm not falling for her shit. Maybe, I was a little harsh in the beginning because of the Tate situation. That isn't Monica's fault. But I still need to draw some boundaries, or she'll think she can show up whenever she wants, and that's not something I can tolerate.

"I came here hoping I could see her. I want to be a part of her life. I know I made mistakes, but you didn't make it easy on me. I didn't ask for any of this. I wasn't ready, but you were."

I scoff. "That's ridiculous, Monica. You think I was ready? I was terrified. I had the world in my hands. My dream was right there. All I had to do was reach out and take it, but you walked away." I pause, because as much as I want to shake the shit out of Monica right now, I'm being way too harsh. Back then, she was honest about everything, and a deal was made. Truth be told, she did me a favor. It still doesn't excuse her showing up unannounced like this.

Monica looks away and lets out a shaky breath.

"Look, just tell me what you really need and stop playing games. You've got me by the balls for another four years until she's eighteen. What will it cost? I know you don't want anything to do with Jenny. She's a good kid and doing great. If you want pictures or updates, I'll send them to you over email, if you're interested. But you can't show up in our lives. Just tell me how much you need." All I can focus on is wishing Monica would get the fuck out so I can go to Tate and explain it all. This isn't how I imagined telling her I'm a single father who's just trying to balance running a law office and a family.

Monica squares her shoulders and lifts her chin. "I— I want to move to San Diego. I met someone."

I reach for a pen. "Done. Is that it? I have shit to do."

"It's really that simple? You'll just give me the money and that's it?"

I put my empty glass on my desk and stalk toward her, getting up in her face. "I love Jenny more than anything in this world, and I'll do whatever it takes to keep her safe and as close to me as possible. You don't need to use it as leverage. We made a deal, and I plan to honor that deal. You agreed to have Jenny. I agreed to raise her on my own and take care of any financial needs of yours for not terminating the pregnancy. But you are not allowed to come into our lives. She's my child. *Mine*!" I jab my index finger into my chest.

Monica has no claim on her. She hasn't been there day in and day out making sure she was happy, healthy, and safe. I've been here. I'm a damn good father and Monica knows that. Maybe if I actually thought she wanted to be part of Jenny's life it could be up for discussion. I'd let Jenny make that decision. She's old enough now. But this surprise bullshit is unacceptable.

Monica buries her face in her hands and looks up at me with a sadness in her eyes. "Am I that bad? You think I'd hurt her?"

I stare back at her. I don't want to feel bad for her but in a way, I do, because she's the one who missed out. If she only knew the experiences she could have shared with Jenny, all the pure joy I've been able to feel. She's the best damn kid. She's just—perfect. Our daughter is good and caring. She's sweet and smart. So damn smart.

Contrary to what Monica probably thinks, I don't hate her as much as I wish I could. I soften my tone and put a hand on her shoulder.

She glances up to me with what looks like genuine tears.

"You're not a bad person. A little selfish, maybe." I grin, trying to lighten the mood. "You weren't ready to have a kid. and I can never fully repay you for doing what you did. I'll always be grateful for that, more than you can know." Without Monica, I wouldn't have Jenny. It's that simple. I owe her.

Monica tilts her head to the side and walks over to my bookcase and picks up a picture of Jenny. "She has your smile, you know? My eyes. You're in for it when she starts high school. I was boy crazy. If she's anything like me..." She trails off seeing my eyes darken.

Jenny is nothing like her.

"Right." She puts the frame back down, sensing she's getting a little too comfortable with things.

I start for the door to hold it open, hoping Monica will take the hint. "If you need money, just call and ask for it. You don't have to pretend. Just be who you are. But you staying away... that was your way of being a good mother because she didn't need you part time in her life, and I appreciate that."

Monica wanders her way toward the door, not fast enough for my liking, but making progress. "I didn't mean for things to be this way. I just..."

"I know." I give her a weak smile. "When are you planning on going?"

"In a week."

I rub my jaw and glance into the hallway, making my intentions even more clear that it's time for her to leave. "You have my number. Just call. I'll get you the money. But don't show up unannounced and make a scene. We'll have big problems if this happens again."

"Okay. Thanks, Decker."

"Don't mention it."

Monica finally leaves for what I hope is the last time ever. I meant what I said though, I'd pay anything to keep her away. Jenny doesn't need that bullshit in her life. I pour myself another drink and something black under the edge of my desk catches my eye. I bend down and grab the black scrap of lace. *Tate's panties.*

Fuck.

I shove them in my pocket. We need to talk. I pick up my phone and buzz her office but there's no answer. Not good.

Maybe she's on the roof deck. That's the first place I decide to check.

When I get there, she's nowhere to be found. The woman isn't in her office or the cafeteria either. I catch Quinn coming out of the supply room. Her face is flushed but I don't bother asking why.

"Have you seen Tate?"

"Oh. Um she took off early. Said she wasn't feeling well. I think she was going back to her hotel, but she didn't really say. Just the impression I got."

"Thanks." I storm into my office and grab my keys and my cell phone.

TATE

I STARE at Decker's office door after it shuts in my face and I'm speechless. I can still feel the caress of his finger on my cheek. The touch of his lips on my neck and the fullness of him inside me.

Now, he possibly has a wife or girlfriend. He *definitely* has a daughter.

How did I not see this coming?

There were warning signs, but I was so caught up in my attraction I couldn't see them clearly. Or maybe I just didn't *want* to see them. I'd noticed a girl's picture in his office, but she looked like a teenager. The fact he was busy on nights and weekends was a dead giveaway.

I was stupid. I didn't want to see anything past his gorgeous blue eyes and the way he made my heart race just by staring at me or walking toward me a certain way. My head spins. I do the walk of shame to my office, feeling totally exposed. People go about their work like usual, but my paranoid mind runs a marathon, judging every glance or gesture as an assault on my conscience.

Finally, I arrive at my office and grab my bag. I can't be here right now. Who knows if that woman will make a scene. She clearly could sense what we were up to when she came through the door. She could probably smell the fresh sex in the air.

Quinn stops me before I get to the elevator. She puts a hand on my forearm in a comforting, motherly sort of way. I imagine that's the easiest way for her to get Decker's ass moving to get things done, so she does it to everyone. Or, maybe she's genuinely concerned about me. "You okay? You don't look so hot."

"I need to leave. Can you…" I can't even finish the sentence. I can't say his name right now.

She cuts me off. "Sure. Feel better."

I'm sure she knows. Assistants always know more than anyone thinks they do.

It's part of their job; to anticipate future needs and make sure tasks are accomplished in a timely manner. Quinn seems more adept than most, so I have to hold back the embarrassment I feel in every molecule of my body as I try to get out of the office as soon as humanly possible.

I nod at her and step into the elevator feeling like everything is moving in slow motion. The back of my neck is clammy with sweat and my stomach tightens. Nausea washes through me and bile creeps up my throat. I feel like I might hurl. Decker Collins fooled me, but that man isn't going to get the best of me. No man has before, and he isn't going to be the first. I just need to get my shit together and focus. Take this afternoon to get a grip on myself, and then it'll be smooth sailing until I'm back in Dallas, kicking grown men's asses in the courtroom like I was born to do.

I walk aimlessly toward my hotel and stop off at a bar for a drink. I don't even know the name of the place, but it appears I'm not the only person having a terrible day. I glance at the man sitting on the barstool next to me. He grips his hair and his head hangs over his empty drink. There's a wedding band on the counter and a stack of divorce papers. Sucks to be him. I can relate, somewhat.

"What can I get you?" The bartender stops in front of me with a towel over his shoulder. He's wearing a black tank muscle shirt and his large biceps are covered in tattoos.

"Something hard, and pour this guy another." I hook my thumb toward the depressed man.

The bartender shoots me a wink. "Coming right up."

The man next to me looks up when his drink magically refills. "I didn't…"

"It's my treat." I hold up the rocks glass the bartender sets in front of me, toasting both of our defeats. Maybe tomorrow will improve both of our lives.

Highly unlikely, but it's important to stay positive.

"Thanks." His eyes are red and rimmed with tears. Poor bastard. Someone did a number on him. I know the feeling intimately. Decker just fucked me in more ways than one.

I knock back the amber colored liquor and toss a hundred on the bar. "Tip yourself and get this guy a few more rounds."

I should go back to my hotel, but if Decker is looking for me, he'll show up there and I don't want to see his smug face. I need to think three steps ahead of him to get my mojo back. I can still feel his cock inside me, and it doesn't make this any easier. It's not going to make this helpless feeling go away. This feeling I told myself I'd never experience again, that I'd guard myself against until my dying breath. It's worse this time.

I honestly don't know if I've ever felt this way about another man, and it's insane. We don't even know each other that well. Clearly, considering he has a daughter, and maybe even a wife or girlfriend.

Stop it, Tate. This isn't helping.

I pull out my phone and call Alexis. "Hey. What are you and the girls up to?" I hear them squealing in the background and I smile.

"Not much, why?"

I swirl my glass around, watching the ice cubes clank against the glass. "Can I come over?"

"Sure. I'll text you the address."

"See you soon."

I give the bartender a nod, then turn to the man with the divorce papers. I glance down then back at him. "Nowhere to go from here but up."

He holds up his glass with a knowing look as I back away and walk through the door.

I hail a cab and give the driver the address.

ALEXIS LIVES in a two-story brick home in a quiet neighborhood. She even has a white picket fence to round out the perfect suburban scenery. Part of me envies her. She has the American dream. A loving husband who only has eyes for her. Two beautiful kids. A nice home.

What do I have?

A hotel room, more work than I should be able to handle, and a prick who pulled the wool over my eyes. They say comparison is a thief of joy and it can be. I walk up the driveway and smile at the chalk hopscotch drawn on the sidewalk that leads to the front porch.

I don't even get to ring the doorbell before Alexis opens the bright red door and tugs me inside. The girls are in the middle of the living room. One is wearing a pink tutu and the other has on athletic shorts.

"Girls," their mother snaps to get their attention as they play tug of war with the video game controller. "Can you two stop for five seconds and say hello to my friend, Tate?"

They both look up at me. Each of them gives me a quick, "Hi," then they go back to what they were doing.

Alexis rolls her eyes. "Have kids, they said. It's fun." She grins at me and I laugh. "Let's go to the kitchen. I have wine."

"Perfect."

I have a seat at the breakfast bar while she gets glasses.

She places them on the counter, slides one over by the stem, and gives me a look.

"What?" I take a sip and play coy.

"Out with it. What happened?"

"Nothing." I shrug. "Can't I just want to see my friend?" I do my best to smile, but it doesn't work. Not even close.

"Bullshit. We may have been apart for a long-ass time but I'm still your friend and can sense when something is wrong."

I lick my lips and take a longer drink. I really should slow down or I'll end up drunk. With my luck, Weston will call, and I'll slur my words all over the place. I can't think of a more perfect ending to this ridiculous day.

"Tate." She grates my name out like she would with her kids.

I smirk and give her the *I don't want to talk about it, but I know you're going to make me* stare. "Fine. I met someone and he wasn't who I thought he was."

"What'd he do? I have two shovels and a plastic tarp in the garage. We can bury him out back and plant flowers over his grave."

I laugh. I can always count on Alexis no matter how much time has passed. We've always just gotten one another. "He wasn't honest with me and it bit us both in the ass. I straight up asked the dude if he was involved with anyone and he told me no. I knew he was hiding something, but I couldn't put my finger on what. I overlooked all the warning signs and red flags and went with my heart. Turns out he has a kid and possibly a wife or girlfriend. She turned up outside his door right after we—" I glance around making sure the girls aren't around to hear me. "Well, use your imagination." I suck down the rest of my wine.

Alexis looks up at the corner of the ceiling, quietly contemplating the most embarrassing day of my life. "Well, that sucks." She takes a few more seconds to collect her thoughts. "Do you know for sure they're still together? Could it have been bad timing? Did he say what was going on?"

"Nope. He practically kicked me out and slammed the door in my face. What's left to say?" I grind my teeth, the rational part of my brain glad the wine glass is empty because I might down another one like I'm drinking at a college frat party.

Alexis stares at me long enough for it to be awkward. I can't tell if she's contemplating or if she's upset with me, though I can't imagine what I could have possibly done. "Do you like this guy?"

I sigh and lean back. "Thought I did."

"Then yes, there's a lot left to say. Did you give him a chance to explain?"

I don't like where this is headed and my face heats up. I say to her through my teeth, "No. I left the office and came here."

"Oh God, you work together?" She shakes her head in that motherly way, like she wants to scold both of us and put us in time out.

I want to get upset at it, but inside I'm looking at myself the same way. How could I fuck up so bad? How could I be so stupid? "Yup. At least until I go back to Dallas. Which I'm thinking should be sooner rather than later. I shouldn't have gotten involved."

"Probably so. The situation sounds complicated." She reaches out and squeezes my hand.

"Your girls are being quiet." I tilt my head toward the living room, trying anything to distract Alexis from the problem at hand. I think it's more to take my mind off what I feel and all the thoughts running through my brain. We both pause to listen.

Alexis crosses the kitchen and looks in on them. "All that fighting must have knocked them out. They're asleep."

I stand up, not wanting to wear out my welcome. "I should go. You should enjoy your quiet."

"Nonsense. Stay for dinner. I'm sure Tucker would love to see you."

I shake my head. "Next time," I promise and give her a hug.

As I head toward the door, Alexis stops me. "I don't want to sound condescending, so don't take what I'm about to say that way."

I step back and look her in the eyes. "Okay."

"Maybe you should give him a chance to explain. At least five minutes. Maybe it's just a misunderstanding, and your feelings and everything that's going on are amplifying it into a bigger issue than it is. I say this as your friend and an outside observer looking in. I know I don't have all the details, but I don't think it could hurt, if you can manage it."

I nod. "I'll think about it."

I mean what I say. I will definitely think about it. There's only one problem. I don't know if I want to give him a chance to explain, because a part of me just wants to see him, touch him again, and I'm afraid I might believe whatever he tells me, even if it's not the truth.

TATE

THE CAB DROPS me back at the hotel. I'm exhausted. The doorman smiles at me but I don't have the energy to offer him one in return. It's been a hell of a day. I start toward the elevators when I see him.

Gotta be fucking kidding me.

Decker Collins is sunk down in one of the high-back cream-colored chairs turning his cell phone over in his hands. He hasn't noticed me, and I want to keep it that way. I fall into step with one of the bellboys pushing a luggage cart, praying I can avoid him.

I stupidly look back in his direction and those icy blues slam into me. My face heats.

"Tate!" He hops up, rushing toward me as I get into the elevator. I shake my head as the doors start to close.

At the last minute he squeezes in. "Just listen."

"I'm not discussing this with you in an elevator." I hiss the words in his general direction and stare at the ceiling. I can't look at him right now. He'll win me over, somehow, I just know he will. I can't allow that to happen.

Yes, he deserves a shot at an explanation, but later, after I've calmed down and can think rationally about the whole situation.

We arrive on my floor, and I step out hoping I can make it inside my room without him barging his way in.

It doesn't happen. The man is on my heels.

Part of me smiles on the inside at how insistent he's being, and that's exactly what scares me. Decker Collins has an ability to grind me down until I don't even recognize myself in the mirror. Until I'm acting like a giddy teenage girl with a crush on the quarterback.

I groan internally and unlock the door. There's no point in fighting him. He's determined to talk to me, and my mind is one big jumble of frayed wires and misfiring neurons.

Decker comes in behind me. His hair is disheveled, and he looks like shit. *Good.*

I kick my shoes off and place my bag on a chair.

"Will you look at me? Fuck, Tate. Let me explain." He reaches for one of my arms from behind.

I can't see him do it, but I can just feel it. There's no explanation for how two people can be in sync to each other's thoughts and actions this quickly, but I feel it with Decker, and I can't give in to it. I just can't.

I spin around and yank my arm back to avoid his touch. The touch that will have me melting in his arms like nothing ever happened. "There's nothing to say. You were right. We shouldn't have gotten involved. Now look at us." I wave an arm between us. "I didn't come to Chicago for this bullshit. I don't want it in my life."

He takes a step back and raises both his hands. "I owe you an explanation."

"No. Really. Please don't. I don't need to hear any lines or lies. You don't owe me anything, Decker. Okay, we had sex, and it was great. That's the end of it. No strings attached."

His face falls, just slightly. Not in a disappointed way. In a way that says he failed me. "I want to tell you everything, Tate."

"Decker." I let out a sigh.

His blue eyes plead with me and I don't know what to do. This is new territory for me. Why can't he just give me a day or two to process? What is it with men not being able to take a hint?

I do my best to avoid the way he looks at me, but it's impossible. It's excruciating, because I want him no matter what. I want his arms around me. I want him to comfort me and tell me whatever I want to hear that will make it all better.

I absolutely hate myself for feeling this way right now. It's like my heart is sitting on the chopping block, and I've just offered to have a knife plunged into it.

He grabs my hand.

I look away and stare off at the wall, knowing I should yank my hand away from him, but I can't and it eats me up inside.

"I didn't lie to you. I'm not with anyone." He sighs, and stares right at me, like he can sense my apprehension. "I don't mean to make you uncomfortable right now." He lets go of my hand and backs away toward the door.

My eyes drift over to his. This wasn't how I expected him to react. I thought he'd say and do whatever he could to try to get in my head again.

"This was a mistake. I should've given you more time. I apologize. I just wanted you to know that nothing back there was what it seemed, and I want you to give me a chance to explain. Nothing more."

I nod to him, as if to say *thank you, and you can go now.*

"My schedule is full this week with that gym bullshit. And I know you need a few days to process things. But Saturday night. Come to dinner at my place. I'll cook and we can talk about it then. Please."

"I don't think…" I take a step back, trying to escape his pleading gaze.

His face tightens and his brows narrow in on me. "Stop thinking so damn much and just say yes. Seven pm. Saturday night. Say you'll come."

"If I say yes, will you leave me alone?"

He nods. "You won't hear from me all week unless it's work related."

"Fine. I'll come. But no bullshit. You'll give me the truth. I deserve it, and my bullshit meter is off the charts. If I detect a hint of a lie, I'll be gone."

"Okay." He nods again.

"Now go. I need to be alone."

"Thank you. You won't regret it." He turns the knob, pushes the door open, and walks out of the room.

As the door closes, I stumble back against the wall. I need to tell him about the BankIt lawsuit, but I just can't bring myself to do it right now. I can't introduce even more tension into the situation. It's like the entire world crashes into my chest all at once. How does this man make me feel so helpless? So, not myself? My lungs constrict when I exhale, like I was holding my breath the entire time he was talking to me. It's so bad I don't know if I'm having a panic attack or hyperventilating. He's just so intense, and gorgeous, and forceful yet respectful and sweet at the same time. After a few moments, my breathing returns to normal.

If there's one thing I know, it's that I've never felt this way in my entire life, and I really hope my brain decides to act normal again before dinner on Saturday. I don't know if I can survive much more of this.

DECKER

"WHAT ARE WE DOING HERE? You never do the shopping these days." Jenny raises her brows at me.

I can't help but smile any time I look at her. She's beautiful, smart, funny, and everything I want her to be and more. She really is the perfect daughter, which makes things easy for me as far as raising her goes. Things could've been a million times worse. We're a team, though. Always have been, and every day I wait for it to happen, for her to have a defiant streak, for us to grow apart. It never comes.

I grab a cart and pull up the ingredient list on my phone. I give Jenny a look that says *sorry*. It's been like this for about six weeks, me working crazy hours. Once this merger goes through, things will be different, and I'll be home every night for dinner.

"I told you. I'm making dinner and I invited a friend."

Jenny grins from ear-to-ear. "Oh, is this friend a girl?" She drags the word out in a singsong voice. She beams at me with the same green eyes her mother has. It takes my mind back to the moment in my office. The worst possible timing in the history of the universe.

I haven't heard from Monica since then, but I'm sure she'll be calling soon with her hand out. I'll happily cut her a damn check and send her on her way to wherever it is she said she's going. I've kept tabs on her over the years. Made sure she kept her distance from Jenny. Monica is, well, Monica. To her credit, she's never pretended to be anything she wasn't, for the most part. Her little act at the office was totally out of character and I wonder what brought it on.

I guess she does always seem to put on an act when she's asking for money. She never just comes out and says it. We have to go through the same song and dance. Maybe it's a defense mechanism and she's just embarrassed or ashamed.

Her showing up like that really did a number on me, though. Thank God Monica didn't come to the house. That's the only silver lining I can take away from the experience.

Jenny makes a show of clearing her throat to get my attention. "Well... Dad? Is it a woman?"

"Maybe." I smile thinking about Tate.

I kept my word and my distance all week. It was damn hard, and she made sure to look hot as fuck every single day too. Every time I sat at my desk, all I could do was think about fucking her on it. The way my thighs clapped against her ass, and the way she clamped down on my cock when she came.

I wouldn't have had time to pursue her this week, even if she'd given me a chance to. The firm representing the victim in the social media body shaming case played hardball, but I think we're going to be able to reach a settlement outside of court.

Jenny hooks an arm in mine as we slowly ease our way up the aisle. "So, what are you making?"

"Grandma's meatloaf."

Jenny's eyes dart up to mine. "Do you even know how to make it? Why don't you just have Molly do it?"

I grab a carton of eggs and put them in the top of the cart, thinking about when Jenny was a baby and small enough to sit in the same spot with her chubby little legs dangling through the holes. Seems like a lifetime ago. I shrug. "Tate's special."

Jenny unhooks her arm from mine and spins around, stopping us in the aisle. Her face lights up. "So it *is* a girl? Is she your girlfriend?"

I don't know if I like how excited she seems to be over this. I don't know what to think. Part of me thinks I was hasty to invite Tate over. I don't know if I should be bringing her to my house, introducing her to my little two-person ecosystem. The other part of me knows this is the best way to explain my life to her. To let her see the real me and not the uptight asshole Decker Collins who struts around the office making impossible demands of people. "No. Maybe. I don't know. What's with all the questions? Feel like I'm on The First 48."

"I'm just curious. You've never mentioned a woman before." She glances down one of the other aisles. "Any woman, for that matter."

I give her a playful punch on the shoulder. "Just help me with the list and stop acting so—girly."

Jenny laughs at that one. "Don't know if you know this, Dad, but I am a girl. And I'm in my formative years where I gush over romances and teen heartthrobs, so while this dinner takes place, I'll be deciding if I can 'ship' you two."

I stare at her like she's an alien from outer space, having no clue what the hell she's talking about. Finally, I shake my head to rid myself of whatever teenage jargon she's speaking. "Go see if you can find a can of breadcrumbs." Kid is too smart for her own good.

She runs off down another aisle to get them. I survive the rest of the trip without another sixty-question interrogation.

I GET busy banging around the kitchen with the pots and pans trying to figure out where Molly puts everything. I think my entire kitchen has been rearranged over the last month and a half, and I have no clue where anything is. It eats at me that I've grown so distant. It's like I don't even know my own house. Part of me, I think, worries about the fact it seems like I'm not needed at home. Like Jenny and Molly can get on without me.

It gnaws at my stomach. One day, I'm aware, Jenny will be out on her own, living by herself. But that day should be far off in the distance. I tell myself it will all go back to normal as soon as the merger is finalized.

Molly has been making all the meals around here and normally on the weekend all I have to do is order takeout or pop something from the freezer in the oven when I'm not working. I used to cook every night. I start chopping the onions and get the meat ready.

Jenny sits at the table with her homework spread out. She's working on an English paper. "How did you meet her?"

I stop dicing the onions, and I glance up at Jenny. "Work."

I spray my hands with cooking oil, so the meat won't stick to my fingers, and begin mixing everything together.

"She a lawyer too?"

I walk over and look at the blank screen on her laptop that's open next to her book. "Don't you have a paper to write?"

"Answer the question, Dad. Stop deflecting."

I'm being cross examined in my own home. I ignore her and set the timer on the oven and put the pan of meatloaf in. Next, I move on to peeling the potatoes.

"If you're not going to write anything, you wanna help with the corn?"

"Sure. I got writer's block anyway." She puts her stuff away then joins me at the sink to shuck the corn.

My eyes dart back and forth between our hands. This is perfect. I miss it so much. Us, together, making dinner. I don't normally turn into a sap, well, ever really. But something in this moment, thinking about all the time I've missed with her lately, it hits me all at once. "I miss this. I know I've been working a lot lately. I want more than just making it home in time to tell you goodnight."

Jenny glances up at me and smiles. "I know you'd be here if you could. And I'm glad you met someone. You deserve to have fun and be happy. I worry about you being lonely."

I nod, trying to keep my emotions in check. "I'm fine, slugger. That's why this merger is so important, though. It'll give me more time with you."

"You need a life too. When I'm at college I don't want you sitting here all alone and pathetic."

I laugh. "Don't worry about your old man. I'll be okay as long as you're happy. That's all that matters to me."

"And impressing this Tate girl." She grins. "Is she pretty?"

"Yeah, sweetie. She's pretty. You'll see." I shake my head and suck in a breath. Tate is a little fireball. The woman is something else. I can't remember ever feeling this way.

"How old is she?"

"Go set the table."

I glance at the clock on the stove. Damn, it's 6:45. She'll be here before everything is ready.

"Fine." Jenny rolls her eyes but smiles.

While she puts the plates out, she looks over. "Maybe you'll have time for me *and* to have a life, once the merger is done."

"That's the plan, but you always come first. You know that, right?" I turn on some water in the sink and scrub what I can of the dirty dishes so I don't have to deal with them later. Something my mother used to do while she was cooking. She said no one wants to go to bed with a dirty kitchen or wake up to one either.

I think she'd like Tate. My parents retired to Florida a few years ago.

I drain the water off the potatoes and Jenny gets out the mixer. She's always loved helping me in the kitchen, ever since she was a little girl.

"This is nice, Dad. I've missed your cooking. Molly is great and all, but nothing compares to yours."

I smile at her, but the guilt eats at me again.

In a few years she'll be off to college and I don't want her high school years to pass me by. I already feel like I blinked, and she went from baby to a young woman overnight. I absolutely cannot fuck up this merger.

I find myself thinking about something else too.

I want Jenny to like Tate. I'm not sure what I'll do if the two of them don't hit it off.

A knock sounds at the front door right as the corn is about to boil over.

"I'll get it." Jenny grins and grabs me by both shoulders like she's giving me a pep talk. "Don't be so nervous, slugger."

I laugh. That's what I always called her when she was a toddler and it stuck. I look around the room and pray this goes well. If it doesn't, I don't know if I can handle it.

TATE

THE WHOLE CAB ride to Decker's, my leg won't stop bouncing up and down. He stayed true to his promise and gave me space to think about things. I still don't know what to expect tonight. I'm a wreck. Will his kid be there? I've never been involved with a single dad before.

It's not a deal breaker for me, him having a kid, I'm just not experienced with this sort of thing. I clutch the wine bottle in my hand as the cab rolls to a stop outside a modern two-story home with sand-colored brick. It has beautiful curb appeal.

I pay the driver and start up the stone-lined walkway. I let out a breath and smooth my hand down the front of my black wrap dress, hoping I didn't overdo it. I have no idea how casual or formal this is supposed to be. I knock softly and think about chickening out for a minute when the door swings open. A tall, teenage girl stands before me wearing a grin that matches her father's. It has to be her.

"Hi. You must be Tate. I'm Jenny. Dad's in the kitchen." She holds her hand out to mine.

"Oh. Hi. Yes. Tate. That's me." I roll my eyes at myself for being a bumbling idiot.

"Here." She reaches for the wine. "I can take that."

"Err. Okay."

Did I just hand booze to his minor daughter?

"Follow me." She motions me inside, and I take in my surroundings. The foyer holds a small table housed under an oval mirror. There's a picture frame with a collage of Jenny's school photos in it. A delicious smell hits my nose. I recognize sautéed onions and garlic. We pass an open floor living and dining room area. There's a double staircase that goes up to the second level with a balcony that overlooks the downstairs. Beyond that is a home office, and I assume a bathroom.

We walk into the kitchen, and I giggle at Decker's apron. He scurries around the kitchen in a frenzy. God, he looks so—different. So domesticated. Cooking dinner, rushing around like everything has to be perfect; he's even more attractive than he already was, if that's possible.

"You came." The surprise is evident in his tone.

"You cook." I walk over to greet him and tug on the strings of his apron. "Do you clean too?"

"Dad cooks all the time," Jenny states eagerly. "He's a great cook." She smiles at me then looks up at Decker.

He gives her a look I could only classify as the *dad stare*.

Jenny takes the hint and starts for one of the bedrooms. "I'm going to go check my, umm, homework." She walks up another staircase off the side of the kitchen. Either she's being sweet and giving us a moment alone, or Decker used some coded message to tell her to get lost.

I take a step toward the island and inspect the meal he's preparing. "Didn't think I'd come?"

Decker leans over with his elbows on the counter. "There were doubts, but I'm glad you did. I just wanted you to get a look at the real me. I'm not always the person you see around the office."

I nod. "So this is the real you?"

"Yeah. My life's not as glamorous as you'd think."

I don't know if I'm ready to have a serious conversation with him yet, so I change the subject. "So, what are you cooking for me?"

He backs away from the counter a tad. "Best meatloaf in the world."

I scrunch up my nose. "I hate meatloaf."

"Seriously?"

"No. Actually I've never had it."

"You've never had meatloaf?" Jenny comes from behind me and appears at my side. She's returned wearing a sundress and her hair is swept back in a low-hanging ponytail. She's tall and lean like her father.

"Nope. What's in it?"

"Meat," they both say at the same time.

Decker stares at me for a few long moments, then cocks up an eyebrow. "You've really never had it?"

"Of course I've had meatloaf. I'm a southern girl. Don't be ridiculous."

We all laugh.

The three of us sit at the table. Decker is at the head; Jenny is to his right and I sit to his left.

They both stare at me, anxiously waiting for me to take a bite of this world's best meatloaf. It smells fantastic, but they've adorned it with a lofty title. I'll hate to crush their spirits if it doesn't live up to the hype. I'm nervous as all hell, the way they're both leaning in before I'm about to take a bite. It's not the greatest situation in the world, having two people stare at your mouth. Shit, what if I hate it? What if it's so bad I spit it out or gag?

Well, here goes nothing.

The meat is juicy and flavored with onions. I finally finish chewing and swallow.

Jenny nods like she's willing me to enjoy it.

"My mother's recipe," says Decker.

I look back and forth at both of them, doing my best to maintain a poker face. For some reason, teasing out my reaction is a lot of fun. They both look like they might come out of their chairs at the same time and shake me, demanding my opinion.

Finally, I smile really big. "My God, that's good."

They both turn and grin big cheesy smiles at each other. "Told you," says Decker.

"You mean I told *you*," says Jenny.

I can't help but grin. This really is—nice. Jenny is a total sweetheart and Decker looks happier than I've ever seen him. We eat in a comfortable silence for a few minutes.

Before it turns awkward, I look up at Jenny. "So, what grade are you in?"

"Eighth."

"Favorite subject?"

"Math."

"Mine too."

We talk a little more about her grades for a few minutes. When we all finish, Jenny helps her dad clear the table. I try to help but they both insist I'm a guest and not to touch anything.

"I have dessert." Jenny brings a box of cupcakes out from a place called Sugar Bliss.

I peel back the wrapper and bite into the vanilla cake with chocolate frosting. "Wow. These are good."

Decker gives his daughter a glass of milk and offers me coffee.

"I know, right? Dad prefers pie, but I told him cupcakes are the way to a girl's heart."

The fact she wants her dad to impress me with cupcakes warms my heart. We sit around and talk a little while longer over dessert. After a few minutes, Jenny gives Decker a hug and a wink she doesn't think I see, then excuses herself to the bedroom. Decker and I move out onto the deck to talk about things.

It's the conversation I've been dreading. I have a suspicion our situation is about to get real, and fast.

DECKER REFILLS my coffee with a carafe he brought out from the kitchen.

I tease him, trying to lighten the mood a little. "Who knew the dirty-talking suit from the office was a good little housewife in disguise?"

He laughs as he sits, and we take in the view of Lake Michigan from his backyard. Not going to lie, it's absolutely gorgeous. The weather is perfect. It's hard to believe we went from such an awkward, intense moment in his office to this, all within a few days.

"I'm sorry I didn't tell you before. When it comes to Jenny, I do everything I can to keep her out of the public eye. I want her to grow up as normal as possible, and my past and my connections at the firm, well..." He trails off for a moment. "It complicates things."

I look over at him, glad I came tonight. Jenny's a sweet kid. I'm still conflicted inside, though. It's just too much information all at once, and I need to take things slow. I have a job to do, and so does Decker. He has two important jobs to do.

I glance around to make sure Jenny isn't eavesdropping on us somehow. "The woman at your office... Monica? Where does she fit into your life?"

Decker winces at the sound of her name, and his face sours like he just sniffed a bottle of vinegar. "That was just bad timing all around. She's been out of the picture a long time. Jenny doesn't know her, and Monica doesn't really want to know her, she just... it's complicated."

I set my coffee down. "I'm here, Decker. You asked me here to lay all this stuff out. Tell me what's so complicated about it."

He sighs. "I met Monica in college, at the height of my baseball career. We weren't even dating seriously. It wasn't a one-night stand, but it wasn't a relationship either. We just had a fling. Things progressed and she told me she was pregnant. I wasn't even sure if the baby was mine, but she swore there was no one else. She can be manipulative sometimes, but she's not a liar.

"Monica wasn't ready for a baby, and I could tell it was tough for her to break the news. I wasn't ready to have a baby either, but I don't know..."

I move my arm forward like *go on*.

"The idea of this baby, this tiny human that was half me... Monica was talking about terminating the pregnancy. She wasn't ready. I wasn't ready. And she knew how important my baseball career was. I mean, everyone did. I was going to be drafted in the first round and offered millions of dollars. It should've been a no-brainer for both of us, but I just had this voice in my head, this feeling. I knew it would be hard being a young parent, but I asked Monica to keep the baby. She was shocked, and gave me the whole 'my body, my decision' speech, which was fine. I told her it wasn't about some political or spiritual belief. I just had a feeling. I told Monica if she would do this for me, if she would have the baby, I'd make sure she was taken care of until the child turned 18, even though she wouldn't have to be a part of the child's life. In fact, that was part of the deal. Monica wasn't allowed to see or come near the kid. When Jenny was born, Monica signed over her parental rights, and we made it all legal. I ended my baseball dreams to be a single father. No matter how good you are, you always spend a few years in the minor leagues, and travel around by bus and plane. There was no way I would put an infant through that. I changed course and went into law. Those years were hard but rewarding. My family helped out a lot while I made it through law school."

The whole thing sounded so crazy. I couldn't imagine basically selling my child off for an annuity, which is what it sounded like. "So, she just gave you Jenny? In exchange for a monthly paycheck?"

"I promised to help her financially if she stayed out of the way. She agreed."

"Wow." I'm speechless. I never really considered having a family, but I could never just walk away from my child. I'm not really in a position to judge. I've never been through anything like that. If both parties were upfront and honest about their needs and wants, it almost sounded like a healthy transaction.

"Yeah." He rubs his jaw. "I wouldn't change my decision for anything in the world. That girl is my life." Decker fidgets with his cup for a second, then sets it down. His smoldering stare lands on me. "Look, I like you, Tate. I want to see where this goes, but at the same time, Jenny is the most important thing to me and will be until she's old enough to go out in the world as an adult."

I nod. "I understand. Honestly, I do. I think it's great you're so involved and take care of your child. Not many people would do what you did. Has dating been an issue for you in the past? I mean with Jenny."

"Nope." He answers the question immediately, without a hint of any doubt.

"Really? Never?"

Decker pauses for a moment, seemingly thinking through what he's about to say next. "I have a confession."

"Okay. Let's have it."

"You're the only woman I've dated that has ever met Jenny. Or been in our home, for that matter."

My heart skips a beat. My eyes feel like they might bug out of my head. Jenny is what, fourteen? And he's never dated another woman or brought her in the house to meet Jenny?

I don't think it's possible for Decker to look more serious than he does now. "I'm extremely guarded and protective when it comes to my daughter. Monica has never met her. I still get attention in the media because of what I do, and because of my past with baseball. I want Jenny to grow up as normal as possible, and I don't want another woman coming in here, getting to know her, then walking out and breaking her heart. You're the first, and to be quite honest, it scares me."

At his confession, I move from my chair and step over him to straddle his lap. My arms cradle his neck and our mouths fuse together.

He pulls me back for a second, his eyes still on mine. "This merger has to happen. It has to work, Tate, I'm serious."

"It will," I whisper, as I kiss along his neck.

He pulls me back away from him, so that we're eye to eye. "No, you don't understand. I have four years left with my daughter before she goes to college. If the merger happens, I'll be able to leave the office at five every day. I'll be able to make her dinner, go to her school functions, be a normal father. If it falls through, I'll be cleaning up the mess forever, and we have new clients that keep signing on, so many we can't keep up with them. I'm already working seventy-hour weeks. This merger is my ticket to a normal life with her. I'll never get these years back."

I put a hand out on his cheek. I don't know if it's too intimate already, but it just feels like the right thing to do. His love for his daughter reminds me of my own dad. The two of them are so different and yet so alike. My dad taught me to shoot guns, and fish, and ride horses, but the universal fatherly sentiment is the same. I remember how special that bond was for me, and I want him to have that with Jenny. It's priceless. "Decker, the merger will happen. We'll both see to it. Nobody can screw it up but us."

"That's what scares me."

I know he's baring his soul to me right now when he doesn't have to. The stakes are at an all-time high for him, and he's still pursuing me. "We won't mess it up. We can't."

Decker holds me close to him and then kisses me so hard it makes me dizzy. I pull back a little, gazing deeply into his eyes, wondering if this is all real or if he's too good to be true. He's smart, successful, talented… and he brought me to his house to cook for me and meet his daughter.

I regard him for a moment and quirk up an eyebrow. "You don't have any other secrets, do you?"

"I have a third nipple." He smirks.

I smack him playfully on the chest and laugh.

"No. I don't." He squeezes my butt and I rock against him, grinding over his erection that popped up during our kiss.

"I've seen your kitchen and eaten your food." I gesture with my head back toward the house. "Now would be a good time to show me your bedroom."

Decker grips my ass with both hands and stands up, carrying me in the process. His eyes turn dark and mischievous. "Oh, I have plenty more to show you."

DECKER

WITH TATE'S legs around my waist and her arms around my neck, I carry her through the back door and down the hall to my bedroom. I'm not worried about Jenny. She's upstairs and sleeps with her TV on. We're downstairs at the opposite end of the house. The only thing on my mind is getting Tate naked, tasting every inch of her, and making her come so many times she passes out.

When we reach my bedroom, she slides down my body and lands on her feet. The complicated straps of her black dress won't deter me from taking what I want. I've been craving her the entire fucking week leading up to this dinner.

It's the edge of twilight and the glow of the moon shines through the blinds. I turn on my playlist and set it to low volume on shuffle. Tate takes a seat on the edge of my bed with a devilish grin, undoing the straps of her shoes. Tonight, I want her completely bare, nothing separating us. No clothes, nothing. I want her naked and panting, begging me to stop, to give her a second of reprieve before she has orgasm after orgasm. Her shoes drop to the hardwood floor and her lashes flutter as she watches me like a cat getting ready to play with its favorite toy.

I smirk at her. She might be used to being the predator but, right now, Tate Reynolds is my prey. I'm going to devour every inch of her until she's begging to submit. I'm the king and this is my castle.

Lifting my shirt over the back of my head, I toss it across the room, and it hits the floor. I reach for my belt, but Tate stops me. "Let me." Her red painted fingernails skim along my chest, tracing the contours of my muscles.

Her lips press to my stomach and she moves to undo my belt buckle. My fingers caress her jaw, moving down her neck to the straps of her dress that criss-cross over her chest and back.

"There's a zipper." She pops the button on my slacks, unzipping them, and shoving them down my thighs. My cock is rock-hard and tents my boxer briefs.

97

Tate runs a finger along my shaft, through the material, and I have to suck in a deep breath and stare up at the ceiling for a moment to collect my thoughts.

I step out of my pants and make good on getting her out of that damn dress. Once it's unzipped, I shimmy it down her ass and thighs and toss it over my head. She laughs as our lips meet and we fall back onto the mattress together. Tonight, I'm taking my time getting personal with every square inch of her. I'm going to worship her like the goddess she is.

Full of fevered kisses and with eager fingers, we collide. Her body melts into mine, molding into me like the missing piece of a puzzle. I kiss her soft and slow, tasting coffee and chocolate on her lips and smelling cinnamon in her hair. She's paradise, a little of heaven and hell. Tate is everything I could want in a woman. I've waited a lifetime to meet someone like her. Now, she's in my bed, mine for the taking. From the moment we first met, this is everything I've wanted.

I'll claim her body and her heart. After tonight, she'll be mine, and anyone who says differently is my enemy.

Her tongue sweeps along my lips and then thrusts inside my mouth. I slide her bra straps down her arms and jerk the lace cups to her stomach, exposing her rose-colored nipples. They're already hard and erect as I trace one of them with my index finger. She shudders at the sensation.

Good.

Her breasts are the perfect size, just enough to fill both hands. I kiss my way down her neck leaving a trail of teeth marks and hickeys low enough on her chest that she'll be able to cover them up at the office. Taking one of her nipples into my mouth, I suck hard then bite down on it while rolling the other between the pads of my thumb and forefinger. I keep repeating the motion, loving the way she gives me full control, opening herself completely to me. A soft purr escapes her lips, signaling her approval. I take her nipple between my front teeth, watching her face to log every reaction of what she likes and what she doesn't. I switch to her other breast and repeat my actions while sliding my free hand between her thighs.

Fuck, she's so wet it drips between her legs.

I take my time kissing my way down her torso, tasting every inch of her skin while my hands stay locked on both her breasts. Her chest rises and falls with labored breaths, each time pressing her tits harder against the grips I have on them.

I look up at her. Those honey-brown eyes lock onto mine.

"These fucking things are in my way." I growl the words and bite at the waistline of her lace thong. Her legs clench together around my face at the sudden intrusion of my head between her thighs. I take both of my hands, place them next to her pussy, and shove her knees apart forcefully.

She moans above me, her legs trying to squeeze back together but unable to break my hold. She gasps out a breath, but manages to say, "Take them off then, fuck." She draws out the last syllable, like she's not totally in control of her body but approves.

I tease at her sweet center with my mouth, kissing over her panties, then run my tongue the length of her pussy, back to front. Burying my face between her tan thighs, I can smell her arousal and my cock aches to be inside her.

Using my teeth, I yank half her thong down one of her legs, then repeat the motion on the other side. My plan is to pull them the rest of the way down with my hands to get them out of the way, but once I spot her glistening, pink cunt I'm like a feral animal.

I dive down onto it with my mouth, spreading her legs once more with my hands on her inner thighs. Her panties go taut and make a ripping sound.

"Jesus, Decker." She pants as she says the words. She doesn't say them like she's upset, more like she's going to come all over my face if I keep this up much longer.

Tate's pussy is sweet like honey and vanilla. I slide my tongue in lazy circles around her clit, then bite the tender part of her inner thigh hard enough to leave a bruise.

Her hands shoot into my hair and her nails dig into my scalp. The insides of her arms squeeze her tits together and, for a second, I think I might blow my load all over the bedsheets. It takes me a second to recover.

Her taut thong is still an obstacle I need out of my way if I'm going to eat her properly. I hook my fingers along the thin straps wrapped tightly around her thighs and tug them down her legs and off her feet.

I pause above her for a moment, her slick folds glistening beneath me, begging for my mouth and my cock. I look her straight in the eyes and say, "When you're getting dressed tomorrow, look at the mark I'm about to leave right here." I trace a finger on the soft flesh of her thigh. "Let it remind you who this pussy belongs to."

"Holy fu—"

She can't even finish her sentence before my mouth is on her. I slide my tongue in a large circle around the tender skin before biting down. Her entire body squirms and she lets out a yelp that carries through the room. Once I'm done, I drop kisses on the area over and over as my index finger circles her clit. Before long, she's bucking her hips at my face, trying to force my mouth back to her.

I put each of my hands behind both of her knees and shove her legs up toward her shoulders, bringing her pussy angled up to my mouth so I can dive straight down on top of it.

"Hold your legs here."

She hooks her arms around her legs, immediately following my order without thinking about it. Good. That's how I want her to react to my commands.

I dip my head down and suckle her clit between my lips, rolling, nibbling, swirling my tongue around it. I have this ability with Tate to be able to sense everything she's feeling. It's like a vibration running through her body that's on a frequency I'm in tune with.

As I continue to tongue her clit, I slide two fingers in and out of her, then curl the tips up to meet the secret spot deep inside that drives her wild.

"I'm about to come, Decker."

At her admission, I slide my thumb into her pussy, just enough to get it wet, then drag it down and press it against her tight little asshole.

She squirms again and her whole body goes tense. She starts to let go of her legs, and I shove them back up against her shoulders with my free hand. "I said hold your legs, Tate."

"So close."

I give her ass a quick smack, trying to introduce a little pleasureful pain to keep her orgasm at bay. It doesn't seem to do much to help. She's coiled up like a spring, like a pressure cooker about to blow its top.

I continue to swirl my thumb against her puckered asshole while I tongue her clit, each moment increasing the intensity, slowly building. Right when I think she can't take it anymore, I look up at her. She's staring back, her eyes straining to focus on me. I give her a nod, and she lets loose right as I bury my entire face in her pussy.

Her toes curl and her feet plant themselves next to me on the bed. Her hips rise and buck as the orgasm rips through her body. I keep my mouth latched onto her the entire time, not giving her one second of reprieve. Her whole body trembles and quivers as her hands fist the sheets into small bunches of Egyptian cotton. She's so fucking hot, and watching her come turns on the animalistic instincts from the ancient part of my brain, where humans were only made to procreate to help the species survive. Evolution turned us into civilized creatures, but one look at Tate right now, and my hips start rutting into the sheets. It's uncontrollable, the urge to fuck her, come inside her, mark her as mine. I keep fucking the covers on the bed as my mouth devours her pussy right as her orgasm crests.

"Fuck, Decker."

I love the way my name rolls off her tongue as she draws it out.

Finally, after a few seconds, she relaxes, her whole body still quaking with post-orgasm ecstasy. I finally regain control of myself and continue to run my tongue up and down her slit as she tries to push my mouth away from her body. She breathes heavily, unable to lift her head from the bed. I work my way back up toward her face, trailing kisses in my wake. I slide my tongue across one of her nipples and she shudders, goosebumps pebbling across her skin.

I smile once I work my way up to her mouth.

"Enjoy that?"

She shakes her head, still panting. "You're so fucking—"

"Good, amazing, incredible?"

She grips the back of my neck like she's pulling me in for a kiss but stops me in front of her face. "Cocky or arrogant would have been my choice of words."

Before I can respond, her mouth crashes into mine. My cock is rock-hard now and pressed up against her entrance, halfway parting her lips. I want nothing more than to shove into her and fuck her so hard she can't walk for a week. But not yet.

I want to take her to the edge of the cliff of another orgasm with nothing but my tongue and fingers and pull her back over and over again until she begs me to let her come again. This is all about pleasing her. Showing her that her needs are important to me... that *she* is important to me.

I work my way back down, so that my mouth is inches from her pussy, and she gives me a look like she can't handle anymore right now. Sliding my fingers through her heat, I watch her reaction, loving the way her mouth parts to let out the most erotic whimpers. I keep doing it, over and over.

"You're making me crazy," she whines, arching her hips up and threading her fingers in my hair. "That tongue has magical powers." After taking a break for a few seconds, she gives me a playful yank and I suck on her clit again. Her body pulses with desire. It doesn't take long before she's coming on my mouth once more. Nothing but frantic hands and deep breaths, before she arches her hips up in the air and says my name over and over.

My cock is so goddamn hard I think I might pass out, and I can't hold back any longer. I need to be inside her. I kiss my way back up her body until our mouths meet and she guides me in. It takes everything I have to hold back and not fuck her so hard my thighs bruise her ass. I want this to be special and intimate, not like the quickie in the office.

I want to take my time and be in the moment, the two of us joined together. As my cock slides in, my eyes roll back in my head at her wet heat squeezing around me. There's something about being inside Tate Reynolds. It just feels like I'm— home. Like everything is right in the world, just how it's supposed to be. I look into her eyes and brush her hair back from her face. "You're perfect, Tate."

"Mmm." She moans into my mouth, arching her back while unable to form words. Our bodies move in tandem in a delicious game of push and pull. Her walls tighten around me as I slide in and out, slow and steady. Gradually, I go deeper with each gentle thrust.

Her body ripples with pleasure and she cries out. I grin at her and roll to my back.

"I want you on top, grinding that pussy on my dick." I slap her ass as she straddles my thighs and I watch as she puts my cock inside her and slowly sinks down on it.

"Fuck," I groan.

Tate rolls her hips, moving from side to side, riding me at a languid pace. She leans down and slides her breasts up my chest so she can kiss me. I grip the back of her hair, and wrap another hand around her waist, just above her ass, then push her down on me as I thrust up.

She moans her approval in my ear, over and over as she rocks back and forth on me.

She finally leans back and straightens so that she's upright. Her hips begin to grind. "Oh my God, Decker." Her body starts to quiver.

I take my thumb and rub circles around her clit as she rocks harder and faster.

"Just like that, Tate. I want to watch you come on my cock."

And I do just that. Within a few seconds she's trembling, and I feel her pussy tighten around me. I'm not sure how much longer I'll be able to last before I blow, but it doesn't matter. I have all night long to do whatever I want to her.

I thrust up in long, hard, sweet strokes, loving the feel of her. Tate crashes forward and I capture her mouth. Her nails dig into my shoulders as she rides out her release.

Once she's done, her head collapses onto my neck and her mouth is next to my ear. "It's your turn to come."

"Don't worry, it's gonna happen any second." I slide up into her hot pussy once more, taking her as deep as possible.

"I bet I can make it happen faster."

"You wish you had that kind of control over me." I smirk, playing her little game. It's quite fun, but she knows who's in charge.

"I'll make you come in five seconds or less, Decker Collins."

I laugh for a quick second, though it's difficult when Tate's hot pussy keeps gliding up and down my dick, and the whole goal is to not come when she wants me to.

"I'll take that bet."

She nods. "Okay, you ready?"

"Whenever you are. Just say when." I immediately start thinking about anything I can that might take my mind off blowing inside her in the next five seconds.

Tate leans down in my ear. "I know what you really want, Decker. What you need to get off."

"And what's that?"

"I want you to fuck me like a dirty little whore and blow deep inside my pussy."

Before I know what's happened, an orgasm rushes to the head of my cock. Tate starts bouncing up and down as hard as she can, right on my cock, her fingers digging into my scalp.

I get two thrusts in, her ass clapping on my thighs, before every muscle in my body constricts and my balls lift high and tight. About three seconds have passed and there's no way I can hold out any longer. My cock kicks deep inside her and hot jets of come shoot into the depths of her pussy.

Once she finishes riding out my orgasm, she presses her forehead against mine. "Told you."

I shake my head at her. "You cheated."

She laughs. "I can't help it if I know what you want. It's the same way you know what I need. We're just like this." She holds up her hand and twists her index and middle finger together. "Can't explain it." She shrugs. "Oh, and Decker?"

"Yeah?"

"Told you I always win." She winks.

I can't help but smile. I brush a few sweaty strands of hair from her cheeks. Her sated eyes meet mine. I stare at her, a hundred percent serious. "I really like you." I can't say I love her, obviously, but fuck me if it doesn't feel that way. I don't know how or why. All I know is, I've never felt this way about another woman, and I want her to know I'm serious. She gets what I'm hinting at judging by the reaction on her face.

"What?" She fights a smile and her cheeks turn a slight shade of pink. Rolling away from me she lets out a breath and looks back over. "You're caught up in the moment."

"I wouldn't have brought you here if I didn't *like* you. I know what I'm saying, what I feel." Sweaty and breathless, I slide closer and pull her into me. Her head falls to my chest. My heartbeat races as she looks at me. But her stare is different. It's like she's looking inside me and can see all my good qualities and all my faults. She looks at me like she knows what I feel, and she feels it too.

"We're doomed, aren't we?"

"Why do you say that?" I let out a light laugh and trace the outline of a circle on her shoulder.

Tate moves up on her elbow and props her chin up on her hand. "Because, I like you too."

I lean over and kiss her, wanting to be inside her again after hearing the words roll off her tongue.

"Where do we go from here? Do you have to go back to Dallas? When the merger is complete?"

Tate's eyes dart to the ceiling, like she's contemplating her answer. "I don't know. I love it here in Chicago. Not just because you're here. It's a beautiful city. I have my family to think about back home, though. My brothers and my nephews."

"You can always go see them or bring them here to visit."

"True." She curls back into me. "I don't know what Weston has planned for me when this is through. We've been laser focused on making it happen. I'm sure we'll figure it out once it's done."

Her ass presses against my cock. Sliding my hand past the curve of her hip down between her thighs, I stroke her clit.

As her legs part, she looks right at me. "Last time started slow and intimate. I really enjoyed it."

"But?" I grin.

"It's time to fuck me the way you want, Decker."

"Might regret that." My eyes narrow.

I only say it to see how she'll react, and she doesn't disappoint. Her pulse speeds up on her neck and she looks—nervous.

Good.

My fingers dig into her hips and I flip her onto her stomach, hard. She lets out a light squeal and I smack her on the ass, hard enough to leave a pink handprint. I run my finger over it lightly, relishing the mark.

Right when she's about to make a smartass remark, I grip the sides of her hips and yank her ass up to my cock. I fist my shaft in my right hand, and use my left to shove her chest down to the mattress.

"Only your ass in the air, sweetheart."

"So demanding."

I reach down and grip a handful of hair, angling her face up toward the ceiling, but keeping her back arched so her chest still presses into the mattress. I line up my cock and slam into her from behind. There's no soft and sweet, this is about showing her who's in charge in the bedroom. I slide my fingers from her hair around to the slender column of her throat as I hammer into her from behind, driving my cock hard and fast. She gasps for air. My thighs smack into her ass so hard the clapping sounds echo through the room.

She tries to say something, but her words vibrate and come out in a jumbled mess that ends in her moaning over and over. Her body trembles, and I know she's about to come again. I have the exact same problem. My balls tighten and swell. I stare down at her small, hourglass figure, and she slams back into me as I thrust into her.

"That's it. Fuck that dick like a dirty little slut."

"Holy shit, Decker." Her words come out on a pant.

Her body quakes, her orgasm coming on quick. She squeezes around me, and I can't take it any longer. Her tight, wet pussy grips down on me and sends me over the edge. I shove her down flat on the bed, pinning her with my hips and chest, and I shove as deep into her as humanly possible. I let loose and come inside her once more as she rides out her orgasm.

We remain joined until her breathing evens out, and I kiss down her neck, shoulders, and back.

"Decker?"

"Yeah?"

"I hate to ruin the mood, but I have to tell you something. You're not gonna like it." Her eyes are half-hooded like she's about to pass out.

"Is it about us?" I sit up, a jolt of fear slamming into my chest.

"It's work."

I breathe a sigh of relief as she goes on to tell me about Donavan's lawsuit against her client.

Fucking Donavan.

I need to go through and review everything in the documents, but I already know it's him trying to tank the merger.

"Don't worry about it right now. I'll take care of it." I pepper kisses all over her, until she falls asleep. I slip out of bed and turn the fan on. It's hot in the room and I want her to be comfortable. I want Tate to know I cherish her, and I'll do whatever it takes to take care of her.

I watch her sleep, hoping like hell when all is said and done, I get to keep her. I want her to be mine. I don't want her going back to Dallas, and I'll fight Weston and my brothers if I have to. I don't want her anywhere else, but with me.

Not now.

Not ever.

I want Tate Reynolds for the rest of my life.

TATE

My body aches as I stretch. I wake up in Decker's king-sized bed, but the other side is empty. My clothing is folded and lying on a chair. There's a note on the pillow.

Tate,

Last night was perfect. I'm in the kitchen. Put these on and join me for breakfast.

Decker

There's a pair of plaid pajama bottoms and a V-neck white tee laid out for me. They're both my size.

Did he go buy pajamas while I was asleep?

I help myself to a shower. His private bath is immaculate. On one side is a clawfoot tub with an adjacent open-door shower with so many heads I don't know if I can figure out how to work the freaking thing. I find towels in his walk-in closet attached to the bathroom. I'm sure Jenny has some girlie shampoo and soap upstairs but I'm not about to ask. I pick up the black bottle and take a whiff. It smells like Decker. I'm not washing my hair here though. I snag a scrunchie from my clutch and sweep my hair up to keep it from getting wet.

I look down as the water cascades over my body and see the bite marks on the insides of my thighs. I think back to what Decker said and a wave of tingling courses through my body.

"When you're getting dressed tomorrow, look at the mark I'm about to leave right here. Let it remind you who this pussy belongs to."

Fuck, he's so damn possessive and just, hot.

After my shower, I slip on the pajamas and walk through the house.

The smell of bacon wafts down the hallway and my stomach growls. Decker worked my body out good last night. I'm a little sore, but in the best way possible. I walk into the kitchen to find him cooking breakfast. He's wearing that goofy apron again. Jenny sits at the breakfast bar with a book, eating a bowl of fruit and yogurt.

"Morning." Jenny smiles at me.

My cheeks must turn some shade of pink. I hope she's okay with me staying over, but I guess it's a little too late for her to complain. She doesn't seem to mind one bit, though, judging by her reactions. She seems genuinely happy her father is happy.

"Hope you're hungry. Dad's cooking enough to feed the neighborhood."

Decker sticks his tongue out at her. He walks over to me with a mixing bowl, stirring pancake batter. His lips meet mine and I pull back to smirk at him. "Show off." I glance at the spread taking up half the counter space. Sitting in front of us are eggs, bacon, fruit, yogurt, sausage, and now the man is making pancakes.

"I wasn't sure what you'd prefer. So, I made a little bit of everything. It's overkill I know." I swear he looks embarrassed by his actions and it's adorable.

"It's sweet. Thank you. I don't eat a heavy breakfast, though." I grab a piece of bacon and help myself to one of the mugs of coffee.

"Told you, Dad."

I listen to the two of them bicker and, oddly, I don't feel out of place. I'm enjoying myself and get the impression Jenny likes having me here too.

I continue sipping my coffee and crunch a piece of bacon between my teeth. It's not lost on me that Decker cooks bacon the appropriate way, crispy.

The two of them go out of their way to make me feel welcome and keep asking me if I need anything else. After the third "no" they take the hint I'm content watching the two of them in their element. Decker finishes making the pancakes and fills his plate when the doorbell rings.

"I'll get it. It's probably, Joselyn." Jenny pushes off from the counter.

"Her *bestie*." Decker sits down on a barstool.

"Bestie, huh?" I laugh at his attempt at teenage vernacular.

"Yep. They're Gucci."

"Okay, just stop, Decker." I put a hand on his forearm.

He grins. God, the first day I walked into his office, I never thought I'd hear him cracking dad jokes. This is all surreal.

"Dad, there's some lady at the door."

Decker groans and drops his fork. When he gets up, he freezes. His hackles rise and his face turns fiery red.

I glance back to see what pissed him off. I've only seen him look this mad once before, and it was at his office.

Sure enough, it's the same reason today. Jenny walks into the kitchen with Monica, and I can see the whole story written on the poor girl's face. She knows Monica's her mother.

I should worry about how Jenny processes the moment, but all I can think about is how this woman ruins every single great moment between Decker and me.

"What the hell, Monica?" Decker's tone is low but deadly.

"I tried calling, but you never answered. Guess I see why. Too busy playing house."

I know it's not my place to get involved but Jenny is on the verge of tears and Decker is about to pop a blood vessel. I feel protective of them even though our relationship—or whatever this is—is still new. "Get out." The words tumble from my mouth before I think them through.

"What?" Monica glares at me and looks to Decker.

"Don't look at him. Look at me." I don't know what I'm doing, but I can't stop speaking. "You shouldn't be here. When Decker is ready to talk, he'll call you." I move toward her and she takes a step back.

"You don't tell me what to do."

"You need to leave. Now."

Jenny rushes to her dad and he wraps her in a hug. He moves her out the back door onto the deck. I'm not sure how he'll feel about me butting in, but this woman is ridiculous.

"He owes me." Monica's bottom lip quivers.

"He owes you?" I laugh. "Decker owes you nothing. If anything, you should be grateful he raised your daughter and doesn't sue your ass for child support. He's a lot nicer than I am, lady. I'm sure he'll get your money for you. He always keeps his word. But you bother him or upset Jenny again, you'll deal with me. Are we clear?"

"Crystal," she murmurs. "Tell him I'll be waiting out front."

I nod and she spins around on her heels and flips her hair, leaving me alone in the kitchen. The backdoor opens and Jenny bolts up the back staircase to her bedroom.

Decker stares at me and, for the first time, I can't read how he's feeling.

"Umm... Monica's waiting out front for you to write her a check."

He nods.

"Is Jenny okay?"

"She'll be fine. She's always known about Monica." He sighs. "Just never met her."

"Sorry I butted in. Figured it'd give you a chance to get Jenny away. I just felt protective of you guys."

"Thank you. I appreciate the sentiment."

I can't tell if he's mad, happy, or just indifferent. He's keeping his cool way better than I would've thought he could. Maybe it's the fact Jenny is here. I admire his restraint at the moment. He's stoic—fatherly. I guess that's what being a good parent means. Not losing your shit in front of your kids, no matter how bad you want to. "If you want me to go, I get it. I know it's not my place."

Decker steps in close. "I care about you, Tate, and I love that you stuck up for Jenny and me." He leans down and gives me a quick kiss.

"Shouldn't you go out there?"

"Let her squirm." He kisses me harder. A few minutes pass and he eventually pulls away to deal with Monica.

DECKER

I CAN'T BELIEVE Monica had the nerve to come here knowing Jenny would probably be home. I walk into the living room and peek out the blinds. She's waiting in the doorway. She has on tight jeans and a purple top cut way too low, showing off the boob job I'm positive I paid for. If not me, some other unsuspecting sap footed the bill. I wonder if the poor bastard she's met has any freaking clue what he signed up for with this piece of work. Looking back, I can't believe I fell into bed with her, but when you're young you do stupid shit.

The worst part is, I know Monica's a good person. I think it's the way she was raised. From what I could gather her parents were both this way. Always looking for a handout, never working for anything. It's hard to assign blame to someone for the way they are, when it's all they've ever known.

There's a black sedan parked on the street with tinted windows. I can't tell if anyone else is in it or not. Monica stares at the front door waiting for me to come out. I need a few minutes to get my temper in control. If I walk out there now who knows what I'll say to her. I don't want to yell loud enough for Jenny to hear. On top of everything, regardless of what Monica does, she's still Jenny's biological mother. My daughter is part her.

I'm glad Tate stepped in so I could get Jenny away from the situation as soon as possible. I know I'm being overprotective; Jenny is fourteen. She's a young woman now, but I don't see myself ever not shielding her from dangerous people. Dangerous in the sense they could harm her emotionally as well as physically. I tried playing it nice in my office when she showed up. It's time to take the gloves off. This shit has to end. We had an arrangement, and Monica broke it coming here.

I honestly thought Jenny would be more upset. All she said to me was, "Is that my mother?" I could've lied to her, but I didn't. We don't lie to each other. I don't keep anything from her, and I won't start now.

Jenny was upset, but she's a tough kid with a good head on her shoulders. She's always known her mother wouldn't be in the picture. I took her to therapy when she was little to make sure it didn't cause any abandonment issues. I rake a hand through my hair and go into my office to grab my checkbook.

Monica doesn't deserve a dime for pulling this shit, but I want her gone from our lives for good. I won't have her setting Jenny back or hurting her more than she already has. Taking a deep breath, I open the door. Monica wipes at her eyes but I don't give a damn if she was crying. I did my best to stay on good terms with her—paid her a ton of money, and this is how she repays me.

I keep my voice down to a whisper, but by the end it's almost a whisper-scream. "What the fuck were you thinking, showing up? At. My. God. Damn. House. We had an arrangement."

"Sorry, Decker, I just started thinking after our talk the other day. I saw that picture in your office and wondered if she thinks about me or asks about me. You know? It was stupid, I know that now. It's just I'm her mom and we've never met. She's beautiful, though, and so polite. I didn't mean to upset her, I swear."

"How selfish can you be? Did you even ask yourself what showing up here might do to her? And for fuck's sake, she's a child. Of course she wondered about you, when she was five years old, but not now. She knows you'll never be part of her life. That was the agreement. You don't get to say, *oh oopsie it's been fourteen years but guess what, I'm your mom.* I know you and, in a month, or hell a week, you'll be with the next man and Jenny will be a fading memory. I'm not having it."

"She probably thinks I'm a monster anyway."

"Don't." I shake my head and point my finger. "Don't pull that shit. Not right now. I'm too upset."

"What shit?"

"That psychological manipulation, where you say things like that. Assume I've painted you in an unflattering way, and that's why she wants nothing to do with you. It's not true. Fact is, we don't talk about you much. But we used to. And I have never uttered one bad thing about you to that girl in there. As a matter of fact, I embellished on the good side. I don't want her thinking her mother is a bad person. Why would I do that? She's half you, you get that, right?"

Monica stares at me with surprise in her eyes. Like she thought this whole time I've told Jenny she's the devil.

I sigh. "Look, you can't be here."

"I understand. I wasn't thinking."

"You never are, are you?"

"That woman seems to care about you guys a lot. It's the same one from your office, isn't it?"

"That's none of your concern." I open the checkbook, but she keeps on.

"I may not be mother of the year, but I still care about you and Jenny."

I snort. Monica's only out for number one. "I guess we're moving on to manipulation tactic number two, where you pretend you care about us now. Look, you're the woman who gave birth to Jenny. Nothing more. So, don't come here acting all righteous like you've ever given a damn about her or me."

"That's not true." She frowns.

"We're done here. Tell me how much so I can sign this check. And once I do, this is it. It's the last one, so make it count. I don't want to see you. I don't want to hear from you. I don't want you to think about Jenny or me again. We're dead to you." I was fine giving her money when she kept away but this stunt today sent me over the edge.

"That's it? You're just buying me off?"

"That was the deal fourteen years ago. I'm just expediting it to a lump sum payout. Give me a number."

She looks at her feet and mumbles, "Fifty."

My jaw ticks but I prop the checkbook on the front door. I fill out the check and rip it from the book. "I give you this money and you promise we're done, or I'll let Tate have a go at you. She's one of the top attorneys in the country and she'd love nothing more than to haul your ass into a courtroom. You don't want to be on the other end of that."

"I promise. I told you I'm leaving Chicago."

"Good."

Monica takes the check and starts for the end of the driveway, then turns back. A tear slides down her cheek. "I'm not a monster, am I?"

I shake my head. There's nothing I'd like more than to shake the shit out of her, but I just can't be cruel. Not too harsh, anyway. I don't know if it's because of our past, or because I see a little bit of Jenny in her. "You're not a monster, Monica. You're just—" I shake my head, searching for the words. "You didn't have the best examples growing up. I'm not blaming your parents for who you are, but it makes a difference. There are a lot of good things about you. I really do wish you the best, and hope you find whatever makes you happy. It just can't be our daughter."

Monica nods. "You really are a great father, and you've been good to me over the years. Can't say the same for myself. I'm sorry."

I walk out to her, because I don't want her to think I hate her. I just want her gone. Once I'm in front of her, I put a hand on her shoulder. "I forgive you, okay?"

She nods and tears stream down her face, even more this time.

"If you show up in Jenny's life without permission again, there will be serious problems. Maybe when she's an adult she'll contact you. That's up to her."

"Okay."

I turn toward the door. "Good luck, Monica."

I walk to the porch and never look back.

TATE

I GO UPSTAIRS and seek out Jenny. She's in the TV room lying on a dark brown leather sectional flipping through the movie channels. I knock gently on the door. "Can I come in?"

She shrugs her shoulders.

I enter and smile when she selects Twilight.

"Team Edward or team Jacob?"

"You like Twilight?" She seems skeptical.

I collapse into the armchair. "Totally. I read the books two times."

"No way."

"Way!"

She laughs.

"I started out team Jacob because I accidentally read New Moon first, but the second time I came around to team Edward."

"I'm team Rosalie."

I freeze. "What?"

"Bella should have chosen herself. She had these two guys who were both right and wrong for her for different reasons, but she should've kicked them to the curb and gone for that nice guy, Mike."

"Smart girl." I know she'll eventually appreciate the brooding bad boys like the rest of us, as long as they turn into redeeming nice guys once their layers are peeled back. Sort of like someone I think about at that exact moment.

We get about ten minutes into the movie when Decker joins us. "There you are."

He comes into the room and grabs my hand. "Come with me."

"No way. Jenny and I are watching a movie. You're welcome to join us."

Decker snorts. "Sorry, I don't do sparkling vampires and teenage angst. Come find me after."

"I will."

He kisses my cheek and Jenny smiles at us.

"If you're not busy, we could use some snacks." I grin.

Jenny nods. "I'm thirsty too."

"How about a pizza?"

"Only if it's homemade," says Jenny.

"I'll need to run to the store for that."

Jenny looks at me then pauses the movie. "If Tate's cool with it can we all go and when we get back, she can help us in the kitchen? You can even pick the movie so we can all watch something together."

A warm tingling rushes through my body. She wants to spend time with me and wants to include me in her time with her dad. I wasn't sure what to expect when Decker said he wanted to see where things go with us. Things are moving pretty fast in a hurry. I know his daughter is his world, but it means so damn much to me that they're trying to make me part of theirs.

I look at Decker and he gives me a smile.

I shrug. "Okay. Let's do it."

The three of us load up in the car and Jenny rides in back even though I offered to.

Decker places a hand on my thigh and gives me a gentle squeeze before we get out.

Jenny pushes the shopping cart and Decker and I follow behind holding hands. I can't help but feel sentimental and a little nostalgic. I remember growing up, most of my friends' moms always did their shopping alone, but not mine. She loved it when my dad went to the store with her, even if he did frown most of the way through the trip. They did everything together, the classic old couple with the serious, grumpy husband who every once in a while cracks a dry joke that has everyone rolling. It makes me miss home a little.

If I moved to Chicago, I'd be leaving all my family behind. I can't recall anyone, even in my extended family, living outside of Texas.

"Okay. Toppings." Jenny grabs sauce, pepperoni, peppers, ham, and lastly pineapple.

My nose scrunches up and my mouth screws into a disgusted pout.

"You don't like pineapple on pizza?" Jenny's green eyes widen.

"Not a fan, sorry."

"That's okay, we can make two. One for me and one for you guys. Dad doesn't like it either, but I usually make him eat it anyway."

I was afraid it would be a strike against me. Monica has no idea what she missed out on with Jenny and Decker. That's okay, though, it left the door open for me to come into their lives.

BACK AT THE HOUSE, Decker wears his ridiculous apron, but it looks so freaking hot on him. No other man could pull off a blue apron with a mustache on it that says—I mustache you a question. Got beef?

I laugh to myself every time I look at the damn thing.

Jenny plays some bubblegum pop music and dances around us, sprinkling toppings over the sauce.

I can see myself wanting this to be my life, spending weekends with the two of them, goofing off, making memories.

Decker pops the pizzas in the oven and sets a timer.

"What are we watching, Dad?"

"Let Tate pick." He smirks at me and my stomach rolls.

"Way to put a girl on the spot, *sweetheart.*" I tap my chin trying to think of something appropriate we'll all enjoy.

"No pressure." Jenny sticks her tongue out at me.

"Um. Have you guys watched the Jurassic Park movies?"

"Not the newest one. Remember, Jenny, you had that science fair project the weekend it came out? The one where you thought it was a good idea to make homemade slime, but it ended up stuck in your hair somehow."

"Oh yeah." She laughs. "That was a terrible idea."

While Jenny finds the movie on Amazon, I walk back to the kitchen to help Decker get the pizzas and grab some plates and drinks.

His arms wrap around my waist from behind as I set the plates on the counter and he kisses my neck. "I like this. Having you here with us. It's nice."

"I like it too." I twist around to face him.

Decker looks at me all sweet. "Jenny likes you. I was worried she wouldn't. Should've known better."

"Me too." I laugh and he kisses me again.

He lowers his voice to where Jenny can't hear. "This is all amazing, Tate. But if I'm being honest, it scares the hell out of me at the same time. Are you scared?"

"Decker…" I touch his face. "This is all new to me too. I've never dated anyone with a kid before."

"You're doing pretty damn amazing so far." He squeezes my butt, and I lean into him. Our mouths inch closer together and I part my lips in invitation for him to kiss me again.

"Is the pizza ready? Movie's about to start." Jenny's voice carries in from the other room.

We break apart and I clear my throat. "Be right there."

Decker winks at me. "We'll finish this later." He glances down to my ass and my breasts. It quickly reminds me he's still the dirty, hot man who put bite marks on my thighs and chest.

I lick my lips and heat flames to life in the pit of my stomach.

This man may very well be the one for me.

The thought terrifies and excites me at the same time.

I grab our drinks and take them to the TV room, placing the glasses on coasters.

"Were you two making out?" Jenny teases and my face goes bright pink. "Oh my God, you totally were." She giggles and I shake my head.

This kid is something else. I have to remind myself I was fourteen once.

DECKER

TATE STRUTS into my office carrying a stack of files.

I arch my brows at her. "What the hell is that?"

"My excuse for coming to your office. Research for a really big case." She slams the files down on my desk and locks my door after turning down the blinds. "I'm afraid we'll have to work through lunch. If we want to finish it all." She starts toward me as I flick through the files full of blank paper. I start to laugh, but my laughter dies when her dress hits the floor.

I move to get up, but she wags a red manicured nail at me. "Nuh uh. Stay right where you are, Mr. Collins. I checked with your assistant, and she assured me you're free until one-thirty. For the next hour, your schedule's full of nothing but me."

She grabs hold of my tie and yanks me forward, thrusting her tongue between my lips. I go rock-hard as she straddles me in my chair. The woman has the art of seduction down that's for damn sure. I look right into her eyes, and give her my best cocky smirk. "You're about to be full of nothing but me."

"He sticks the landing like a pro."

"That layup isn't worthy of a response." The yellow pushup bra she wears corrals her tits. Her nipples show through the thin lace material. I rub one hand over her breasts and cup her tight ass with the other.

"What'd I do before you came into my life?" I growl, nipping at her lips.

"Play shitty golf." She rolls her hips, rubbing her hot pussy over my erection.

I grin. "Gonna get yourself in trouble."

"Mmm." She grinds on me. "That a promise? I could use some discipline."

"Fuck, I need inside you."

"Not yet. I'm in control. I set the meeting, remember?" Her lips curve upward into a mischievous smirk. She gets up from my lap and drops to her knees. "I want these off, Mr. Collins."

Fuck, I can't think of anything I want more than her lips wrapped around my cock, smearing that hooker-red lipstick up and down my shaft. "I like when you call me Mr. Collins. Makes me feel powerful."

"Good. Now shut the fuck up and let me suck your dick, Mr. Collins." She pushes my legs apart and undoes my belt. My cock springs free and Tate licks her red-stained lips. She slips off her bra and tosses it aside. Wrapping a fist around my shaft, she jerks me right between her tits.

Fuck. I knew she was dirty, but this is taking it to a new level. It takes immeasurable restraint not to blow my load all over her chest.

Her mouth comes down on my cock and she licks the tip, swirling her tongue in a circular motion over the head and up and down the shaft. Tate's lips stretch wider accepting me into her mouth while she teases at my balls, rolling them with her fingers.

I thrust my hips and grab her hair, taking over. My restraint only goes so far. I fuck her sweet mouth, pushing farther with every stroke until I hit the back of her throat and she gags. Tears leak from the corners of her eyes, but Tate is no quitter and sucks me harder, flattening her tongue against me, taking every inch.

"You okay?"

She glares at me and takes me even farther into her mouth to prove a point. I love how competitive she is.

Just when I'm about to come, she slips me from her mouth and stands up. She winks then bends over my desk in her best Marilyn Monroe type pose and wiggles her ass at me. Pushing up out of the chair, my pants drop to my ankles and I stand behind her.

The fake files go sailing off the edge of the desk and I splay my fingers across her upper back and shove her down, pressing her tits against the hard wood. Her head lays to the side and she grips the edge for support.

Jerking her panties down her thighs and spreading her legs wide, I slide a finger into her soaked pussy and bring it to my mouth for a pre-fuck taste. It only makes my cock harder in my palm. Without thinking, I fist a handful of her hair, and smack her once across the ass, just to see my handprint.

She lets out a whispered yelp of approval, then smiles back at me.

I cup her pussy from behind. "This is mine, *sweetheart*. You belong to me. Only me."

"God yes." She moans the words on a pant, beneath me as I line my cock up behind her.

I ease into her hot cunt and a shudder rips through me. Gripping her hips, I pump in and out of her tight center, delivering punishing strokes, bringing her close to the edge over and over again. Each time I stop just long enough to leave her hanging. With my free hand, I bend out to the side and wrap my arm under her waist so I can stroke her clit while I pound into her.

I thrust as hard as I can, and the desk moves an inch. The whole office might know we're fucking but right now I don't care. I know I'm falling hard.

Truth be told, I never thought I'd meet anyone who could make me want to commit, but Tate makes me want to try. She's worth it.

I pull out and slam back in. A bead of sweat trickles down her spine and she clenches around me. I lean back and watch myself hammering in and out of her. "Play with your pussy while I fuck you."

"Fuck, your filthy mouth does things to me, Decker." Her hand goes straight to her clit and I feel her fingers brush against my balls every time I slam into her.

My cock glistens as she coats my dick with her juices, and it turns me on even more. After a few more deep strokes, I pull out and grunt, shooting my hot load across her. My orgasm seems to never stop as I stare at her ass and pump my cock with my hand, marking her skin with my release. With ownership.

She smiles back all breathless and sated.

The words I love you hang on the tip of my tongue but I'm afraid it's too soon to say them. So I hold them back, lean over, and place a kiss on her back.

"Let's get you cleaned up." I walk off to my bathroom, my cock still hanging half-mast between my legs. I grab some towels and return to clean her up. She's still bent over my desk showing off her come-covered ass. Sweat rolls down my back and I don't think I've ever been happier.

MY CELL PHONE rings with a call from my daughter.

"Is everything okay?" She never calls from school unless it is an emergency.

"It's fine. I was calling to ask if I can stay over at Joselyn's tonight. Her mom said she would take us to the mall and help us pick out dresses for the father daughter dance. But I wanted to ask you a question."

"Okay, go ahead."

"Do you, um, think Tate would be weirded out if I asked her to meet me at the mall?"

Wow, I don't know if I was ready for that. Things really are moving fast, and it's a reminder of how quick I've brought Tate into our lives. At the same time, it warms my heart that Jenny would think of Tate for something like this. "Umm no, slugger. I think she'd enjoy that."

"Cool. It's just that Mrs. Lykans doesn't have great taste and Tate's a good dresser. She has style."

I laugh. "You want to ask her, or you want me to do it?"

"I can call her, unless you think it'd be better if you did. I know you guys are just starting to get serious. I don't want to scare her off."

I smile at how thoughtful Jenny is. I raised this girl. "I'll text you the number. Tate likes you."

"I like her too. Love you, Dad."

"Love you too, slugger." I smile and text the number after ending the call.

Ten minutes later Tate storms into my office and paces back and forth. Her hair is still a little disheveled, but I don't point it out. "I take it Jenny called you?"

"Yup." She nods clasping her hands together.

"You okay with that? I never would've given her your number if I thought it would be weird for you."

"It's not that." She shakes her head. "I'm nervous. I don't want to mess up. What if she hates whatever I pick out? I'm not experienced in this. Can I buy her makeup and take her to get her nails done? I'll treat her friend too." She rambles on about taking Mrs. Lykans to dinner.

I grab her by the shoulders. "Breathe. It'll be fine."

She sucks in a breath. "Okay. I got this."

"You do."

DONAVAN MARCHES toward my office and he's seething. Thank God Deacon and Dexter at least seem to be on board with the merger. Two out of three is better than I expected, so I still chalk it up as a win.

He yanks the door open and stomps toward my desk. "You dropped my lawsuit? Talked to my client behind my back?"

"It was a loser and you know it."

"I have a responsibility to my client. If someone is stealing…"

I've heard enough. "Oh, shut the fuck up, Donavan." I march up and get right in his face. "I know you're not on board with this merger. I got the memo. But you know why I need it to happen. Think about your niece, at least. Your behavior is reckless."

He paces back and forth. "Your little girlfriend went running to you, didn't she? She knew I'd kick her ass in the courtroom and couldn't take the heat. These are the kind of people you want to work under."

"I won't be under anyone, and neither will you. You're acting like a petulant child. And for the record, Tate would've murdered you in court and you know it. I'm thinking about pulling all your cases, because this was the most irresponsible shit I've ever seen. Which is totally out of character for you. I'd expect something like this from the twins."

"I bet you didn't even review the files. You probably just jumped when she called and took her side immediately. You're fucking whipped."

I let out an exasperated sigh. "Look at me when I'm talking to you."

Donavan glances over.

"You think I'm taking sides? I read the files and reviewed everything before I went to your client, who happens to be my client too. Yeah, I saw your college buddy's name in the documents. The computer science guy you brought home once at Christmas. The guy was always a fucking asshole. You never even liked him. The case is a loser and we don't lose. So yeah, I went to our client and told them I didn't want to keep billing them for it."

"You're tearing our family apart, bro." Donavan walks toward the door. "Hope the pussy is worth it," he says as he leaves my office.

I need a drink.

TATE

How did I get myself roped into this? I agreed to meet up with Jenny, her friend, and her friend's mom at a mall to go dress shopping for a middle-school dance. I don't know a thing about taking girls shopping for dresses, but Jenny reached out to me, and I don't want to let her down.

I've only been seeing Decker a short time, but he and Jenny have become so important to me. I can't believe how protective I feel over them. I never knew I could care this much for two people so quickly. I'm falling in love with Decker. It's obvious even though I don't want to admit it to myself. He's all I ever think about.

The thought of confessing my feelings terrifies me more than shopping with teenage girls. I stare at myself in the mirror as I touch up my makeup in the company bathroom. Decker's going to drop me off at the mall and meet me afterward at my hotel.

I walk to my office, grab my clutch, and shut off the lights. Quinn is still at her desk. "You're here late."

Her cheeks redden. "Oh, umm, just getting things ready for Monday. Gotta think ahead and be prepared."

I observe one of Decker's twin brothers lingering in the doorway of his office but don't point it out. I never can tell them apart. I'm pretty sure she's got something going on with one of them. "What are your plans this weekend?"

"Me?"

I grin at her. "Who else would I be talking to?"

"Right. Umm, probably staying in." Her eyes dart around, then land back on mine.

"I'm having brunch tomorrow with some friends, you should come." If Decker and I become permanent, or serious at least, it would be nice to have more than one friend in this city.

"You want me to come to brunch with you?" Her brows knit. The situation borders on awkward.

"Only if you want to. No pressure. I'll text the address and you can come or not. I'm not the best at making girlfriends."

"Sounds fun. I'll be there."

"Good."

I spy Decker going to the elevator and rush off to join him.

As soon as the door closes, his mouth lands on mine and I'm backed up against the wall. "Somebody's happy to see me." I grab the bulge in his pants.

"What can I say? I'm addicted." He wipes his mouth with the pad of his thumb, but only manages to smear my lipstick across his cheek. I laugh and debate on leaving it there, but considering we're still in his building, I give in and wipe it away with a wet wipe. I keep them in my clutch; with as many hands as I shake, I like to keep my fingers clean. One of my associates back in Dallas once made a comment about how every hand you shake could have been touching a dick or something like that, and ever since then, I've been more mindful of what I touch throughout the day.

Decker drops me off at Water Tower Place but not before groping me like a horny teenager in his car. If I wasn't meeting his daughter, I'd cancel my plans to get him into bed. I tease him but I'm just as infatuated with him as he is with me, if not more. I wake up every morning with a smile on my face thanks to him. I thought I had everything figured out, was content with my career and personal life but now that I've met him… I know I was settling. Coasting through. I don't want to coast anymore. I pull out my phone and fire off a text to Jenny.

Me - I'm here.

Jenny – Meet us in Free People. Third floor.

I find Jenny and her friend, Joselyn, and her mother, Patrice, in the dress section. Jenny's face lights up when she sees me. Her right hand lifts into an eager wave. I smile and wave back, making my way over. Her dark hair is swept up in a high ponytail, and she's dressed in skinny jeans and a graphic tee with strappy low-heeled sandals. Her friend has on a floral-patterned button-down shirt that looks like it belongs on the set of Little House on the Prairie.

I'm not one to be overly judgmental, but based on her friend's mother's style, it's no wonder Jenny called me in for backup. The poor woman dresses like she's going door to door selling bibles in an ankle-length denim skirt and oversized pink smock that does nothing to show her figure. They *all* need me; they need a style intervention. Jenny looks casual cute but still I still have the urge to raid her friend's closet and replace her wardrobe.

"Tate, this is Joselyn and her mom, Patrice. Guys this is my dad's girlfriend, Tate."

It's not lost on me that Jenny just called me her dad's girlfriend, and it's also not lost on me that I love the way she said it. It just rolled off her tongue, like it was a natural part of her vocabulary. "It's nice to meet you." I extend my hand to the mother.

"I've heard so much about you. It's nice to put a face with the name." She accepts my hand, but I feel her assessing me and wondering if I'm good enough for Decker and Jenny. It makes me happy to know she has Jenny's best interests in mind, and I'll show her my intentions with Jenny are pure and not just a means to impress her father. Jenny eyeballs a two-piece called the Thalia. It's cotton-candy-pink with a crumpled top held up with two thin straps and a matching miniskirt that looks crinkled. It's adorable but I think Decker would kill me if we came home with anything that showed Jenny's midriff.

"What about this?" I finger through the rack and hold up a one-piece shoulder-wide legged pant set. It's a rust color that would pair beautifully with her skin tone, green eyes, and dark hair. And it doesn't show so much skin it'd give Decker a heart attack.

Jenny snatches the ensemble and rushes to the dressing room. I look her friend over as her mom holds up something red covered in flowers that would wash the poor girl out completely.

I grab an ivory dress with crochet panels that would be to die for with her dark hair and almond skin. "This would be so adorable on Joselyn." I hold it up and her mom gives me a wry smile.

She accepts the hanger and holds the dress up on her daughter. "I think you're right. You *are* good at this. I've never been very fashionable." As she runs a hand down her denim skirt, I think *oh, honey, don't I know it.*

She's a nice lady, but when it comes to style, I want to give her a good old southern *bless your heart.*

I smile at Patrice. "We could treat ourselves to something while we're here. I was gonna take the girls to get their nails done and thought we could get our toes done while they're doing that."

"Oh." She shakes her head. "I don't think…" She trails off and I can tell she never does things for herself.

"My treat."

"I couldn't."

"It'll be fun. The girls will enjoy it."

After trying two shoe stores, we find the perfect heels for both girls and make our way to the spa on the fourth floor to do a little pampering. Patrice seems to enjoy herself despite her reservations. Her olive eyes roll back in her head as her calves are being massaged.

My phone pings with a text from Decker.

Decker – How's it going?

Me – Checking up on me?

Decker – More like missing you.

Me – The girls want pizza but are afraid of messing up their manicures. I should have fed them first.

Decker – They'll live, but I won't. How much longer till I get you all to myself?

Me – Meet me in an hour.

Decker – Hey, Tate?

Me – Yeah?

Decker – Remember those bite marks?

Me – How could I forget?

Decker – There's going to be more of that.

He adds a little smiling devil emoji at the end of his last text. My heart races. This man is going to be the death of me.

TATE

Patrice drops me at the hotel, and I meet Decker in the lounge for a drink. I slide onto the barstool next to him and I already want to drag him up to my room. The man can rock a suit. That's for damn sure, and I'm used to seeing attractive men wearing suits. Decker puts them all to shame.

As I sidle up next to him, I say, "Come here often?"

He gives me a side eye. "Passing through on business." He plays along with me. "What are you drinking?"

"Something hard." I skim my fingers along his thigh.

"Should probably go easy. Plenty of time for hard stuff later." He shoots me a sly wink and orders me a bourbon drink with a hint of mint.

I take a sip. "Thanks for the drink. Care to join me for a nightcap?"

"I don't think my girlfriend would like that at all."

"I won't tell her." I make the motion of crossing my heart and sticking a needle in my eye.

He grins and slides his card to the bartender. "Can you keep a secret?"

I lean in close and whisper gently, my lips brushing against his earlobe. "What kind of secret keeper would I be if I told you?" I down my drink and grip him by the tie. "Let's go, lover." I move from the stool and sway my hips knowing he's appreciating the view of my ass.

Something about getting him worked up in advance sends heat racing between my thighs. The foreplay with Decker Collins is almost better than the sex.

Almost.

"Hate to kill the mood, but Donavan came by my office earlier."

"Yeah?"

"Wasn't happy about dropping the lawsuit."

I stop and turn to face him. "I don't want to come between you and your family."

"You're not."

I grin. "Yeah, I'm sure he spoke highly of me."

"Absolutely." Decker winks.

I shake my head. "I'm sorry. You don't need the extra stress."

Decker rakes a hand through his hair. "Agreed on that. I don't see any way around it, though."

We arrive in my room and Decker falls back on the couch while I excuse myself to the bathroom for a quick shower. I step under the spray of the water and lather up quickly, opting to wash my hair in the morning. It's our first night alone since we started seeing each other and I have plans for him. I'd planned on revealing my feelings, but after what happened between him and Donavan, I'm not sure it's the right time.

I massage lotion into my skin and put on the sexy underwear set I picked up at the mall while Jenny and her friend tried on dresses. It's a black lace corset and matching thong paired with thigh highs and a garter belt. Slipping on my black pointy toe heels, I stand at the mirror and run my fingers over my loose curls to smooth any strays. I feel sexy and powerful. Decker is getting a night he'll never forget. I step out of the bathroom ready to make my grand entrance only to find him snoring.

To say I'm disappointed would be an understatement, but I know he's been working so hard lately. He wants this merger over with so he can spend more time at home with Jenny, and I get the impression he may ask me to stay when the time comes. I've been trying not to think about that too much. I have so many things to consider. My job. My family. I'd be giving up a lot, but as I run my hand over Decker's head and along his jaw… I think he could be worth the risk.

He's so fiery and intense when he's awake, but when he sleeps, I can see a hint of the boy in him. It's that side of him I love the most. Him wearing his apron and cooking for Jenny or offering to run to the store for snacks while we watch Twilight.

I'm torn between letting him sleep or waking him up. Placing my lips to his and receiving no response, the choice is easy. He needs rest. Quietly, I strip out of my sexy getup and change into a tank top and comfy yoga-style leggings I normally reserve for the gym. I haven't been working out lately and it bothers me a little, but like Decker, I've been working crazy hours too. It's not lost on me that I've been getting in some quality cardio, though. I grab a pillow from the bed, prop his head up, and cover him with a blanket. Once he's taken care of, I turn out the lights and slide into the bed alone.

I'M NOT sure what time it is but I smile when I feel Decker's strong hands part my legs. The leggings I fell asleep in are already missing. His lips meet the sliver of skin between my panties and tank. I thread my fingers through his hair, yawn and simultaneously say, "Good morning."

A lazy grin crosses his face as he looks up to meet my sleepy-eyed gaze.

"Sorry I crashed out last night." He nuzzles my belly with his stubble-lined jaw.

"You were out cold. I started to wake you up, but you seemed so peaceful. You're getting old, Collins."

"Hah! Well, thanks for letting me sleep. I hadn't realized how tired I was until my ass met the couch cushion."

"What time is it?" I can't see the clock but a quick glance at the window lets me know it's still dark out.

"Time for you to get naked and let me make last night up to you. I saw your little outfit in there and cursed myself for falling asleep. Sorry."

"If you're able to please me to my standards, I may model it for you sometime."

"Damn right you will." He kisses my stomach, pushing my top up to pay attention to my breasts. Sucking a nipple into his mouth, he appears to be done talking and focuses on getting down to business.

"Wanna get breakfast when we're done?"

Decker looks up at me like I'm insane for thinking about food while he has my breast in his mouth. "I plan on eating pussy for breakfast. More than one serving."

Only Decker Collins could turn me on with a breakfast metaphor involving my vagina. He quickly snaps me out of my thoughts when his tongue meets my clit. He's relentless and before long I'm squirming as he pulls an orgasm out of me with nothing but his tongue and fingers. My nails drag down his scalp as he raises up and stares at me while I pant for air.

A devilish grin spreads across his face, like he's admiring his handiwork and the way he knows how to press every one of my damn buttons to get me off.

"How'd I do? I think that was a record for time."

I shoot him the bird, but my limbs are so fatigued from the intense orgasm my hand immediately drops back to the bed.

Decker laughs.

"It was a solid six. Not sure if it's worthy of a lingerie show."

He narrows his eyes at me. "Six my ass."

I shrug. "Looks like you may need some practice, champ."

"Oh yeah, do you say, '*Holy fuck, Decker. Right there. Jesus Christ,*' during all solid six performances?"

My cheeks flush and I look away, grinning. "Okay, maybe it was a seven."

He dives on top of me and tickles my ribs, and I can't think of the last time I let my hair down and had this much fun.

I ROLL out of bed looking at the time knowing I need to wash my hair and get ready to meet Alexis and her friends for brunch.

Decker lies there, naked, save for a sheet riding up his hip. He props himself up on an elbow in the Burt Reynolds pose, and it's difficult to look at him without wanting to jump back into bed. "Where you off to?"

"I have brunch plans with Alexis and some of her mommy friends."

Decker watches me dig through my clothes for something to wear. "You don't sound too enthused."

"I'm not."

"So why go? Come back to bed. Jenny won't be home until noon."

"Tempting, but I promised, and I invited Quinn. It'd be rude to bail and leave her on her own with complete strangers."

He gives me a perplexed look. "My assistant?"

I roll my eyes and grab my yellow heels. "*Our* assistant, and yes. She's nice, and I need a non-mommy ally. Someone who won't talk about boogers and puke."

Decker laughs and throws the sheets back exposing his thick erection.

"You can't be hard again?"

He wraps his fingers around his cock and strokes it. "What can I say? Watching you bend over fetching your shoes turned me on."

I try to ignore him, but he lays back on the bed looking like a damn Adonis in the flesh. His abs are like chiseled puzzle pieces and his jaw clenches with sheer determination. Why does he have to look so damn hot while jerking off? His teeth sink into his bottom lips as his mouth curls up in pleasure.

I war with myself for all of three seconds before I cross the room and straddle him. I line up his cock and ease myself down onto it.

His hand smacks my ass and he digs his fingers in. "That's what I thought."

"You're such an arrogant ass—"

He thrusts his hips up into me to cut off my sentence and hits my spot just right. All my smartass remarks fade from my brain and are replaced with nothing but erogenous bliss.

"WHERE HAVE YOU BEEN?" Quinn hisses as I grab the chair next to hers on the rooftop at Cindy's. The restaurant and bar overlooks Millennium Park and Lake Michigan. Alexis grins at me, eyeballing the hickey on my collarbone. I wanted to nut-punch Decker for putting it on me this morning as I got ready. He did it right as I tried to get out of his car when he dropped me off. He's on his way home so he can be there in time for lunch with Jenny.

He attempted to get me to cancel on the girls and go home with him, but I couldn't do that to Quinn. Judging by the uneasy smile on her face it's a good thing I kept my word.

"Sorry. Got held up."

She eyes me with skepticism but doesn't press for information I don't want to share.

"We ordered already but I'm sure you still like pancakes," says Alexis, still seemingly amused at my love bite.

"I do. Thank you."

"So, Quinn says she works with you at the firm."

I nod and Alexis continues.

"I tried to pump her for information about your new boyfriend, but she wouldn't tell me anything."

My cheeks go red and I take a sip of the fruity drink they put in front of me. "Very funny. That's because there's nothing to tell. Aren't you going to introduce me to your friends?" I do my best to change the subject so I don't choke her out later.

She does nothing but sit there and grin. It's like we're in high school all over again, giving each other crap and playing practical jokes.

Alexis finally goes around the table and makes introductions. The other women look like Stepford wives and all they want to talk about are their husbands and children. It's like they have no other interest outside of their family life. I love spending time with Decker and Jenny but that will never be me.

I'm glad Quinn is here as a buffer. The two of us end up in our own conversation about the Collins brothers. "So, all of them are single?"

"Mhmm." She bobs her head.

"Do they ever date within the company?"

"No way, it's against policy. Well, it's against the rules for anyone considered a superior to date a subordinate, and they well, run the company."

"So, for example, if you were to enter into a relationship with Dexter... or say Deacon, you could be fired if it were reported?" I say each of their names slowly trying to gage her response but she's damn good at masking any tells. Usually, I can surmise if someone's lying or not in the first five seconds. It makes sense, though. She works in a law firm and deals with attorneys all day.

"How do you tell those two apart if they aren't in their office? I'm always confusing one for the other."

"Oh easy. Dexter has a scar over his brow and Deacon has a freckle on the pad of his thumb."

Bingo. I knew she was seeing one of them. How else would she know the man has a freckle on his thumb? I've never noticed anything distinguishable about the pair, but then again, my focus has been on Decker from day one.

We finally finish up and, on our way out, Quinn tells me to never make plans for us again. I laugh. She has a dry sense of humor. It's very subtle and you have to really pay attention to pick up on it. I like her a lot.

After parting ways with Quinn, Alexis gives me a ride back to my hotel. I thought about surprising Decker and showing up over there, but he really needs to spend some quality time with Jenny. I've been monopolizing his attention, and it's not very fair, considering how many hours he has to work until the merger is complete.

I need to work on a few things anyway, for when I go into the office on Monday.

TATE

THINGS HAVE BEEN GOING great between Decker and me. For the past three weeks I've spent my free time with him and Jenny, and I can't remember a three-week period in my life where I've been happier. I never stay in my hotel room anymore. Spending the night with him just feels natural.

I make sure to arrive at work separately even though I ride with him. The office doesn't need to know we're together, though I'm sure Quinn figured it out. Bless her for keeping it to herself. Decker needs to give her a raise for not gossiping like some of the women here who spread rumors in the cafeteria.

Quinn has been their target as of late. It hasn't gone unnoticed that an admirer sends her flowers every single Friday. I don't feed into watercooler gossip, but I keep my ears open for signs of trouble that could tank the merger. I trained myself to listen to the same rumor mills back in Dallas. Part of me feels guilty for spying on Decker and his employees but that's why I'm here. Regardless of my feelings, I have a job to do.

I walk down the hallway for my morning coffee while I get dressed. Decker cooks Jenny breakfast before school while she gets ready in her bedroom. She's complained all morning about what to wear. I remember being that age, feeling ugly in everything.

I have their morning routine down to a science at this point, and pretty much know everyone's daily schedule.

The doorbell rings and Jenny shouts from the stairs, "Uncle Weston!"

My face pales and I might vomit right there on the floor. I freeze and my stomach twists in a knot so hard it feels physically painful, even though I know it's all in my mind.

What the hell is he doing here?

I haven't told Weston anything about my personal involvement with Decker.

I'd hoped we could avoid the conversation all together, at least until the merger goes through, but now… here we are.

Jenny tugs Weston around the corner and goes right past me. When his eyes meet mine, I want to dissolve into the hardwood floor. I don't think I've ever seen him this pissed off. I'm standing in Decker's freaking t-shirt and pajama pants. I've gotten used to wearing them when I stay over because they smell like him.

Weston glowers at me, but Jenny keeps moving him toward the kitchen. I don't know what to do. Do I follow them and hope he doesn't make a big scene in front of Jenny?

I know he's irate. He's a ticking time bomb waiting to explode.

He speaks with Decker once he reaches the kitchen, and then he says, "If you'll excuse me, I need to step out and make a call."

"You don't want coffee?"

"Not right now."

Damn. I suck in a breath and hear his footsteps as he searches for me. It's like everything goes into slow motion and I'm in a horror film as the killer creeps through the house. Weston's footsteps grow louder with every second until they pound in my ears.

When he rounds the corner. His mouth forms a tight line and his jaw clenches. "Outside, now."

I nod, feeling like I might throw up. I've never screwed up at work, not once. Something tells me this might be unforgiveable. I knew he'd be upset, but I didn't think he'd be like this. He looks like he might fire me on the spot.

I walk with him out front, grabbing my wristlet as we go. I start to say something but he cuts me off.

"Not yet," he growls, grinding his teeth.

Knowing Weston and the way he keeps up appearances, he may shove me in a car and wait until we get to the hotel.

Instead, the second he's sure nobody can hear, he wheels around on me. "What the fuck's going on here?" He whisper-screams his words and eyes my clothing like he's disgusted with what he sees. He raises a finger. "Hold that thought." He pulls out his phone and calls me a cab, the entire time holding his finger up to let me know not to utter a word. Once finished, he hangs up and says, "You have fifteen minutes. What the hell did I just walk in on?"

"It just happened, okay? But the merger is good to go. The BankIt suit was dropped. No other conflicts. Everything is ahead of schedule."

He sighs.

My temples throb. It's too damn early to have this conversation. I need coffee.

"Great. Since everything is squared away, get your ass back to Dallas. Don't pick up your things. I want you out of here *now*. I'll have my secretary make arrangements. Just show up at the gate. I'll have your stuff sent back."

"We're not finished. I still have matters to go over with Decker and his brothers. Nothing major. I need a few more weeks." I try to buy myself more time. I'm sure Weston sees right through it.

"No need. I'll find someone else. Someone who won't fuck the people we're doing business with."

Finally, the truth comes out.

"Why are you being an asshole about this?"

"Why am *I* being an asshole?" He shakes his head and shoves his hands in his pockets. "You're the smartest lawyer at the firm so I find it hard to believe you suddenly became blind as a fucking bat."

"Humor me."

"You kidding me with this shit? This deal is huge for our firm, and I won't see it fucked into a Chinese circus if you two have a falling out. Christ, look at you." His hand flies from his pocket and waves toward me.

I know I look rough. I'm dressed in Decker's clothes. My hair hasn't been brushed. We had a long night.

"I sent you here because you're the best I have. Who are you? What happened to my ball-busting shark?" He shakes his head like he doesn't even recognize me.

I swallow hard and try to push aside my feelings for Decker. I know some of what Weston says is true. I didn't come here to develop feelings for Decker. I look back at his front door with an uneasy sensation in my gut. "I can handle it." I shut my eyes tight and nod. "I can do this."

His features soften and he gives me a sad smile, almost like he pities me. "It's not personal so don't go full blown pussy on me. How much do I have to kiss your ass and tell you what a great attorney you are? You're my biggest asset. But you need to see this from a big picture perspective. Put yourself in my shoes."

I shift on my feet and keep my mouth closed. He's still my boss. I love my job. I don't argue. I can't, because he's right.

"If you were me, would you risk it? If I wanted to date the partner of a firm you were merging with? With this type of money and all these jobs on the line? Think about all the employees and their families, and you're out here playing Russian Roulette with their livelihoods. Would you be cool with me doing the shit you're doing?" His voice raises up a notch.

I stare at the ground as he chastises me. The truth and weight of his words sink in hard. Decker and I were fooling ourselves.

"No." It guts me to agree with him, but I do. I let out a shaky breath and try to suck it up. This isn't like me.

"So, we're good?"

"We're good." I can't meet his eyes. I'm embarrassed. I'm hurt Decker knows I'm getting my ass chewed and isn't doing anything about it. I wouldn't expect him to change Weston's mind. I just figured he'd go to bat for me. I know Jenny's his main priority but what about me? What about us?

"Go wait for the cab. I'll deal with the rest. Once the merger is complete, I'll send you back. You can work it out. Decker's a great guy. I'm not trying to be a prick."

"I understand."

"Good. Call when you land."

I look back at Decker's front door and feel like I might shatter into a million pieces.

Weston pulls out his cell phone and calls his secretary to make flight arrangements.

I look down at my feet. I'm wearing flip flops, but it doesn't matter. I'll buy something on the way. They have plenty of gift shops at the airport.

As I walk away, part of me hopes this will end like one of those scenes in the movies. Decker will rush out and tell me to stop. He'll tell me he doesn't want me to go, and he'll scoop me in his arms and carry me off to bed. But he doesn't. I reach the end of the driveway and look back one last time. Decker isn't coming and Weston has gone inside. The cab pulls up and all I can do is look at the house and try to lock it in my memory, in case I never make it back.

DECKER

Jenny rushes around grabbing her things, then scarfs down her breakfast.

Why did Weston drop in unannounced? He never stops by without putting something on the books.

I leave Jenny with Weston to check on Tate. I peek in my room and her clothes still hang on the back of my closet door. Her makeup bag is on the counter and the blow dryer is out. I walk through the house to see where she went. My jaw ticks when I come up empty.

Jenny calls out to me, "Dad, I'm leaving. Bus is here."

I meet her in the foyer and kiss her forehead. At the same time, I notice Tate's shoes by the door. "See you tonight. I'm making taco salad."

"Can't wait. Tell Tate I said bye."

I give her a nod. "Will do, slugger."

I wait until she gets on the bus. Once I know she's headed to school, I return to the kitchen to confront Weston. It's no damn coincidence he showed up. Something's going on.

Weston seats himself at the counter and helps himself to coffee and a plate. He grins like an asshole and shovels food into his mouth. Taking his time, he dabs at his face with a napkin. His smile disappears when he sees the glare on my face. "For someone eager to get this merger completed you don't seem very happy to see me."

"Where's Tate? And what the hell are you doing here?"

Weston makes a show of pushing his plate away and standing up. He adjusts his suit and turns to face me. "Got a phone call. Didn't like what I heard. So, I decided to see how things were going. Didn't expect to find my senior attorney playing house with you and Jenny."

I move toward him, fists clenched at my sides. "Don't bring Jenny into this. That's a low fucking blow and you know it."

Weston shakes his head and smirks. "Someone needs to pull your head out of your ass. It's not personal."

"Yeah." I nod. "Business is business. So, you got a call?" *Fucking Donavan.*

He shakes his head like there's no way in hell he'll give up the source. "The phone call isn't important. You wanted this merger, remember? You came to me. Do I need to remind you what was said? Think about Jenny." He takes a second to collect himself. "Look, Tate's my best attorney. I can't afford her juggling all this right now."

I take another step toward him and grit my teeth. "Where is she?"

He scrubs a hand through his hair. "You need to relax."

"The hell I do. Where. Is. She?"

Weston lets out an exasperated breath and walks away, staring up at the ceiling. He finally turns back to face me and shakes his head like he can't believe he's dealing with any of this.

I can't really blame him. If I was in his shoes, I'd do the same thing. But, that's beside the point. This is Tate, and as much as Weston doesn't want it to be personal, it is.

Weston looks me dead in the eye. "You're not going to let this go, are you?"

I shake my head at him, telling him with my stare how determined I am and the lengths I'm willing to go.

"Fuck. I sent her to the airport, okay? I'll have someone else handle the last few things before we finalize our agreement. Once the merger is a done deal, I'll send her back if that's what the two of you want. It'll all work out. Trust me. I know what I'm doing."

I shake my head. It's not good enough. Not for me. Not for Tate. I already feel like I can't breathe without her and she hasn't left Chicago yet. "No."

"No?" Weston raises his eyebrows. He stares at me like I'm from outer space. "What do you mean no?"

I flatten my palms on the counter. "Tate stays or I terminate the merger." I look right at him when I say the words. She's that important to me. I'm willing to walk away from the deal of a lifetime. Jenny will understand. It'll break her heart if Tate leaves.

Weston lets out the most sarcastic laugh I've ever heard, like this all has to be a joke. "You can't be serious."

I step up so that our faces are inches apart. "Look at my eyes. Do I look like I'm joking?"

He stares at me.

I don't budge an inch. "I love her."

Weston scoffs, but I don't give a shit.

"Tate is everything to me. I didn't plan on this, but it happened. I *won't* lose her. Not for a second."

Weston's jaw clenches.

"Weston, you know I wouldn't let her around Jenny if it wasn't serious. How many women have you seen me bring home the last fourteen years?"

"None."

"Exactly. Jenny loves her too."

Weston paces back and forth. He pauses here and there, looks up at me, then glances away. He finally lets out an exasperated sigh and throws his hands up. "Fine. Fuck it. It's your life."

I damn near tackle him I hug him so hard. It wasn't planned, and it's a bit awkward. I finally lean back to maintain some dignity and put a hand on his shoulder. "Thank you. Seriously. You have no idea how much it means."

Weston brushes invisible dust off his shoulder where my hand was resting. "Well, what the hell are you waiting for? Go get the girl. I'm not fucking doing it for you. My generosity for the day has been concluded."

"She's on her way to O'Hare?" I'm damn near bouncing on the balls of my feet as I ask the question, and I'm positive my face is fixed in a permanent smile from ear-to-ear.

"She's probably almost there. Might want to throw your old cleats on and haul ass."

I slap him on the shoulder. "Thanks! I'll see you—fuck, I don't know when, but I'll see you."

"Don't come back without my all-star attorney. And stop acting like a pussy. I might vomit."

I snatch my keys off the hook and slip on the first pair of shoes I find on my way to the garage. I connect my phone to hands free and immediately call Tate, hoping I reach her before she gets on the damn plane.

I hammer the gas and my tires squeal as I get sent to voicemail. The car weaves through the morning traffic, and I curse anyone who gets in my way. "You want to fucking go?" I throw my hands up and bang on the horn.

I try her cell again with no luck. "Fuck." My face heats up to a thousand degrees. I smack the wheel as some asshole cuts me off. I'm going to fucking kill Donavan for calling Weston.

I shake my head to rid my thoughts of revenge and take a few deep breaths to calm down. Being angry will solve nothing. My goal is reaching Tate in time. Nothing else matters. The worst that can happen is she gets on the plane, then immediately gets on another plane back to me. I kick myself for not going to see what her and Weston were discussing in the front yard. If I'd had any idea he was sending her home, I'd have been out there in a heartbeat. I never imagined he'd ship her back to Dallas. She probably sat there wondering why I hadn't gone after her.

Fucking Weston.

It wasn't like that asshole didn't have the woman of his dreams already. I know for a fact one of his partners fell for his assistant, and she was a damn subordinate, not even an attorney.

One thing eats at my gut as my mind wanders to the worst possible places.

What if Tate gets back to Dallas and decides Weston is right? What if she sees her family and realizes how much she'll miss them if she moves to Chicago? There are too many liabilities if she makes it back there. I have to have her, and I have to get to her before she gets on the plane. I wish I'd just told her how I felt before this morning. There's no way she'd leave if I'd just told her the truth.

I love her.

She's the one.

I hammer the gas even harder, and my car rockets down the highway.

TATE

I ARRIVE at the airport feeling like my life is falling apart. I know I screwed up my chance at being named a partner at the firm, but all I can think about is Decker. I'm hurt, embarrassed, lovesick… I reach for my phone and remember I left it on his nightstand. My heart squeezes at the thought of the man. I look down at my haggard appearance, feeling people staring at me—passing judgement. I look like a damn bum.

I make my way to a gift shop and purchase some leggings, a Welcome to Chicago t-shirt, and a pair of flats. It's not perfect, but it's passable for airplane attire.

I find the nearest bathroom to change. At least I have my wristlet with my ID and credit cards. I feel wretched and hope Jenny doesn't think I abandoned her. It sounds insane, but I love that kid to bits—her father too. I wish I'd told him how I felt. Maybe he'd have come after me in the driveway. Maybe he'd have talked some sense into Weston, pleaded with him for me to stay.

I know we haven't been serious for all that long, but I expected him to fight for me. The way he looks at me, the way he fucks me, the way he makes me feel and lets his guard down around me—I know he feels the same way I do about him.

I stop in the bathroom and splash cool water on my face, then dry it with paper towels. I look as rough as I feel. Like I've been run over by a damn semi. I need to slow down for a second, step back, and think things through.

How did my life go from amazing to pure shit in a matter of minutes? I should've gone by the hotel and packed my things, but Weston was insistent I come straight here. I wouldn't feel so lost if I had my stuff.

Why did he rush me out of there anyway? There must be a reason. A small part of me hopes he didn't tell Decker what he was doing. Maybe that's why he hurried me out of there, because he knew Decker would come after me. The probability of Decker chasing me down the driveway was high, but there's no way he'd leave and go to Dallas to find me. He wouldn't leave Jenny and his work at the office behind.

Fucking Weston. I swear that man always thinks three steps ahead when he plans something devious.

It's not like I can defy Weston and head back to Decker's house to see if that's what happened. He'd write me up for insubordination, possibly fire me if he was in a pissed off mood, which he is. And what if I'm wrong? Then I'd look like a complete idiot.

No, I have to get on this plane, head home, keep my nose down, and kick serious ass on whatever Weston assigns me. Once the merger is complete, I can come back. That's what I need to do, and pray Decker's feelings for me don't change in that timeframe.

It's going to be a long couple of months without seeing him and Jenny, but I have to suck it up and get things done.

I check in and receive my boarding pass. Weston wasn't messing around. I'm on the next flight to Dallas. One foot in front of the other, I head toward security. There's nothing I can do, and I feel helpless with each step.

My heart breaks a little more as I near security. A small part of me wishes I'd never come to Chicago. I thought I knew how a broken heart felt when I broke up with my first serious boyfriend at college. Looking back, it doesn't hold a candle this. It doesn't compare to the way my heart pinched in my chest and my stomach tied itself into a knot when Weston let me have it.

It's a shitty emotion—guilt. I'm not too familiar with it because I wall myself off from everyone except my family. Now, I begin to see why. My job is my life and I never fuck up at work, so I never experience the way my hands now tremble and the way every second now seems like an eternity.

Everywhere I look I see smiling faces, and I have this unbelievable urge to scream at the top of my lungs. Right now, I just want one thing. I want to go home, chug a bottle of wine, and wallow in self-pity. I might even shed a few tears. Tomorrow, I'll be back to normal. That's what I tell myself anyway.

I arrive at security and get scanned. Since I don't have any bags, the process doesn't take long. I grab a magazine someone left when I arrive at my gate. I slink down into the seat and flip through the pages. Nothing holds my attention, but it gives me something to do.

A woman and her two kids take up the seats next to me. The baby is red-faced and screams at the top of his lungs.

My temples throb and my chest aches. There's a hole in my heart where Decker belongs. Across from me sits a couple who can't keep their hands off each other. They whisper sweet nothings and talk about the fun stuff they'll do on their honeymoon. My heart sinks further into my stomach. We weren't close to marriage, but I thought someday it could happen. It seems silly, but when you know, you just know.

I grab a coffee and hope the caffeine makes me feel better. More like myself. I'm not used to these emotions. I'm a hard ass. I'm Tate Reynolds. I don't do love and relationships. Maybe it *is* for the best I never told Decker the way I feel. The way I think about him constantly when he's not there. The way I might suffocate if he's not holding me. The way my heart comes alive when he looks in my direction.

"Now boarding flight 292 to Dallas." The loudspeaker interrupts my reverie.

Here goes nothing.

I grab my boarding pass and ID and head toward the gate. The line moves at snail speed.

It amplifies the crushing sensation of my heart being squeezed in a vise. For some reason, the closer I get to the tunnel, the more Decker fades from my life. I just want to get home and pretend none of this ever happened, but how do I let go of the cocky suit who turned my world upside down?

I move up in line behind the woman with the screaming baby and hope he doesn't cry the whole flight. I sound terrible, but my head can't take it. The worst headache of my life approaches at warp speed.

Then, I hear it. It's faint at first, and I barely make it out.

"Tate!"

It comes from far off in the distance, and I wonder if I'm imagining things.

Stop watching Sleepless in Seattle so much, Tate. Your life's not a romantic comedy.

It has to be in my head. I hand the gate attendant my boarding pass.

"Tate, wait!"

I freeze and grip the boarding pass so hard it creases in half. The attendant tries to take it, but I squeeze it harder. My body freezes, locked in time. It's not my imagination. I heard someone shout my name.

"TATE!" The voice booms and people stare and whisper.

I pull myself from a catatonic state and whip my head around.

My heart leaps in my chest, and pure happiness courses through my veins.

It's him.

He came after me.

Decker.

He sprints toward me—faster than I've ever seen any man run—nothing but focus and determination on his face. When he's about fifty feet away he smashes into another man. There's a tangle of limbs and suitcases. It doesn't stop him. He springs to his feet and continues toward me, not bothering to turn and offer an apology.

"Don't you dare get on that damn plane!" He screams the words, but he's panting, and they come out half jumbled.

He gets to the counter and snatches the ticket and shreds it up in front of us.

This can't be real. It's an out-of-body experience. I can't do anything but shake my head. "Wh-what are you doing here?" I know what he's doing here, but I want to hear him say it. I want him to work for it. And part of me knows this can't happen, no matter how bad I want him. Weston gave me strict orders and I can't lose my job.

"You're not going anywhere."

I reach out and grab his forearm. "Look, Decker, I appreciate you coming. It means the world to me, but we have to lay low for a few months until this is worked out. Weston will have my ass if I'm not on this plane." I can't fight back the emotions rushing through my body and I choke up as I say the words. A tear slides down my cheek. I quickly swipe it away hoping Decker doesn't notice. I'm crying. I don't cry. Not where anyone can see, anyway.

"You're not going anywhere, *sweetheart*."

"I have to go, Decker. Please. Don't make this harder than it already is."

He shakes his head and grips me by the shoulders. "You're not listening. I talked to Weston. You're staying."

Before I can respond, Decker sweeps me up into his arms, bridal-style, forcing my arms around his neck.

For some reason, I can't process what he says, but I'll be damned if I ever let him put me down now that I'm in his arms. "What'd you do? Did you get me fired?" My brain isn't firing on all cylinders. My head will explode if I don't get the full story shortly.

Cheering people flank us on both sides. Decker growls his words as he carries me through the airport like a madman. "Stop thinking the worst for five minutes in your life. I wouldn't do that to you."

"What happened?"

"I told Weston, well…"

"Spit it out, Collins."

He stops in the middle of the concourse and his eyes lock onto mine. It's the most serious I've ever seen him look. "I said if you didn't stay the merger was off."

The hackles on the back of my neck rise. "Are you fucking insane? He's going to kill me. Definitely fire me. And you won't be able to hire me if I stay, because he'll own the firm."

Decker laughs. The bastard laughs at me. I want to punch his face.

"You really think Weston is that big of an asshole?"

I raise my brows at him. Did he just ask that? "I thought you two were best friends for fuck's sake." Has he forgotten who we're talking about? Weston is a calculating, hard-nosed bastard when it comes to business.

Decker grins. "Fuck, he cracks the whip on you guys in Dallas, doesn't he?"

"Umm, yes, he does."

Decker plants a kiss on my forehead, then leans back. "Listen, Weston's a good guy. He might run a tight ship, but he's not heartless. He smiled when I left. Told me not to come back without you."

"You're bullshitting me."

"I wouldn't do that. Not about this. He knows I love you, Tate."

I gulp. "You love me?"

I glance around and notice a crowd around us, mostly women clutching their chests.

I stare at Decker for a few moments, our eyes locked. His gaze is nothing but heat, intensity, and adoration. He's telling the truth.

"I should've told you before. I've loved you for a while, Tate Reynolds."

My heart might burst out of my chest. I had a feeling he did, but something about him saying the words sends a torrent of emotions crashing into me. Tears stream down my cheeks and I can't do anything but nod and nuzzle into his shoulder. "I love you too."

His arms tighten around me, then he pulls me up so we're face to face. He kisses me long and hard, with an urgency that says he'll never let go.

I pull back and grin. "Are you really carrying me like this through the airport?"

"Goddamn right I am, all the way to the car." Decker smirks.

God, I missed him so much, and I was only gone for an hour or two. It seems silly, like a teenage crush, but that's what it feels like. I think part of it was the thought I was leaving for good and had no idea if we'd ever be together again.

Not now, though. He's all mine, and I'm all his.

I curl up into his neck and enjoy the moment. "Just don't ever let go."

"Never, sweetheart." He kisses me once more, then carries me through the exit.

DECKER

I GET Tate into my car and can't stop smiling. She has no clue how happy she makes me. From the moment I met her, I knew there was something about her, but I never dreamed she'd fit into my life so perfectly. She's what I've missed all these years. Now that I have her, I'll make every second count. I'm never letting her go again.

"Are we crazy?" She looks over at me. Her honey-brown eyes shimmer.

"Abso-fucking-lutely." I step on the gas. I can't get her home fast enough. I want her to move in. I know it's insane, but it feels right, and she needs a place to stay anyway. I don't want to scare her off, so I bottle the thought up for now, but I'll ask her soon. She can't live in a hotel forever and she's at my place most nights anyway.

She glances over to me. "How'd you get to me anyway?"

Her question takes me by surprise. "What?"

"How'd you get through security? They don't just let you waltz up to the gate."

"I bought a ticket."

Tate straightens up. "You what?"

"Well, if you left, I was going to have to follow you to Dallas."

The corners of her mouth curl up into a huge smile. She shakes her head at me.

"I have something on my face?"

"How could you come after me? You have Jenny and work."

"Didn't I tell you I'm in love with you back at the airport?"

"Yeah."

"There's something you need to know."

"What's that?"

"When I love someone, I go to the end of the earth for them. I already made plans for Molly to stay with Jenny, and I would've handled my management duties remotely. Nothing in this fucking world will keep me from you."

Tate leans over and gives me a peck on the cheek. Then, she slides around to my ear and whispers, "I love you too, Decker Collins." She pauses, and I feel her smile against my cheek. "And if it wasn't so dangerous, I'd suck your dick to show my appreciation." She flops back in her seat, clearly satisfied with herself.

"Fuck, woman." Her words leave me with a raging hard-on. I damn near pull over to the side of the road to remedy the situation.

I finally pull up my driveway and hope like hell Weston has left. I have plans for Tate. I'm going to make her scream my name on a loop. I exit the driver's side and move around to open her door.

"Such a gentleman." She grins her ass off, knowing what's in store.

We walk through the kitchen hand in hand. There's still a mess from breakfast this morning, but it can wait. Fucking Tate to the point of multiple orgasms can't. I want her in every way imaginable. I want her trembling beneath me.

I walk her toward the bedroom, removing her clothes along the way, leaving them behind like breadcrumbs.

Our lips connect. Her tongue flicks inside my mouth and dances with mine. I taste the coffee on her lips as I lick her mouth and neck.

I place my palms on her cheeks and our foreheads meet. "You'll never regret being with me."

"Ditto." Her breath fans over my lips.

Her hands cradle my neck as we do nothing but kiss. I lay her down on the bed. Her fingers tug on the hem of my shirt, lifting the white cotton over my head. I breathe Tate in. She smells like cinnamon and vanilla.

"God, I love you."

"I love you too, Decker."

I'll never get tired of hearing her say those words to me. Her breath hitches when I jerk her bra down and latch onto her nipple with my mouth. I take my time rolling the other between my fingers, teasing her. I repeat the motion, biting at her playfully, loving the sight of my gentle teeth marks engraved on her body.

Her slender fingers stroke through my hair. I see in her eyes how much she loves me as our bodies glide against one another. She skims her fingernails down my back, scratching lightly. She undoes my pants and shoves them down my legs with her feet until they tangle around my ankles.

I kick out of them and pepper kisses down her torso, rolling my tongue along the dip of her bellybutton. Another giggle escapes her lips and she twitches. I file away the ticklish spot for future torture. Gripping her panties, I jerk them to her feet and kiss her inner thigh, teasing her where she wants me most.

I smell her arousal and my cock grows harder. Looking at her folds, I can tell she's wet for me. I shimmy the black lace from her feet and toss it over my shoulder.

I roll over on my back, point to my face, and say, "Your pussy on my mouth, *now*."

There's no hesitation. Tate goes after what she wants, and I love that about her. Moving up the bed, she straddles my face in a reverse cowgirl position. I grip her hips and lower her inches from my mouth, then exhale my warm breath across her clit.

Goosebumps pebble over her ass and thighs and she shudders.

"You want to fuck my face, Tate?"

"God, Decker."

"Tell me you want my mouth on this pussy."

"Please," she moans.

I lick her slow, from clit to asshole, then pull my face back down away from her. She instinctively tries to shove her pussy against my lips, but I grip her ass and hold her away.

"Please, Decker? I'm so close." Her words trail away on a gasp.

That's what I like to hear. Her begging for my tongue. "Tell me who this pussy belongs to."

"It's yours, fu—"

I lick her again, just to interrupt her sentence.

She lets out a frustrated groan and says, "It's so yours. Trust me."

"Goddamn right it is." I shove her onto my mouth so hard it probably leaves a bruise.

She calls out my name as I lick, suck, and nibble.

Tate rocks forward, rolling her hips, riding my tongue and fingers, moaning the entire time.

Her hand wraps around my cock and she slides it up and down. Her tongue dances around my crown as she brushes a thumb over the head.

I groan against her pussy when she wraps her lips around the tip of my dick. She bobs up and down, taking me as far in her throat as possible. The woman is the yin to my yang, her body molding perfectly to mine. We work together like a well-oiled machine. Before long, my cock pistons in and out of her mouth as I thrust up into her.

At the same time, I take two fingers deep in her pussy, pleasuring her g-spot as my tongue flicks over her clit. I don't need her to tell me she's close, I feel the energy radiating through her body.

Trembling over my mouth, she's about to lose it. I wrap my hands around her tiny waist and shove her against my face. My cock slides from her lips and she cries out. Every muscle in her body tenses at once. Her thighs threaten to crush my head as they squeeze together hard enough to crack a walnut. Her orgasm ripples through her body, coating my face with her wetness. I shove her down to the bed and slide out from beneath her. "Keep that fucking ass in the air and your face in the sheets."

Tate complies, gripping the sheets in her hands as she anticipates what's coming next. With one hand on her shoulder and one fisting my cock, I shove into her from behind. Her hot pussy cinches around me and nothing but pure ecstasy courses through my body. A moan tears from deep in her throat and she makes some pleas to the deity. Over and over again I slide in and out of her with deep punishing strokes.

Goddamn, I missed this.

Her ass claps against my thighs and the sounds reverberate through the room. Fuck, her pussy molds to my dick like it was created just for me. I'd planned on fucking her a lot longer, in every position imaginable, but now—watching her petite hourglass body rocking into me, the curls of her hair dancing across her back—I'm not sure how long I'll last.

Just when I think I can hold out a few seconds longer, her small hand reaches between her legs and she cradles my balls. The second she massages them and says, "That's it. Fuck your pussy, Decker," the orgasm I'd been holding rushes up my shaft.

"Fuck, Tate..." My words trail off and my whole body stiffens. I hold back as long as I can, then grab both her hips and yank her as hard as I can back into me.

I want to be buried as deep inside Tate as humanly possible, joined together as one when I explode inside her. Her frantic hands paw at the sheets and I look down as she bites into a pillow.

I groan and let loose, pumping into her sweet cunt. After a few grunts, her pussy contracts around me and she milks the last bit of come from my cock.

I slide out of her and she crawls up next to me as I pull her into a tight embrace, kissing her on the temple. I push a few sweaty strands of hair from her cheek. "Glad I caught you in time."

"Me too." Her arms squeeze tight around my middle, her head resting on my chest. She nuzzles into me and I could seriously lie here like this for the rest of my life.

Words can't adequately describe the pure joy taking over my body right now. It's better than any drug in the world, that's for damn sure.

"Move in with me. With Jenny and me." I don't ask. I tell her.

Pulling away, she looks up at me and smiles big. "Promise you'll never let me go?"

"Never, babe. Never." I bring my mouth down on hers, sealing my promise with a kiss.

DECKER

"It's so hot." Jenny fans a hand in front of her face as we walk to the rental car. I'd laugh but I'm sweating too. Neither of us are used to this heat.

"That's Texas for you."

"Dad, I'm seriously melting."

I unlock the jeep I rented for the weekend and stick our bags in the backseat. It's been a little over three months since the airport rescue, as I like to call it. Tate's been here in Dallas the past two weeks organizing her move to Chicago. I wanted to come down sooner but couldn't get away from the firm.

My phone rings. Speaking of the woman who owns my heart. "Hey."

"When can I see you?"

"Soon. I'm just getting in the rental. I'll be at the hotel within the hour if traffic isn't a nightmare." I didn't tell her Jenny's with me. She was supposed to stay with Joselyn, but they had a fight over a boy, and I decided to bring her along.

"Drive safe. I love you."

"Love you too, sweetheart."

I end the call and tuck the phone back in my pocket. Jenny buckles in on the passenger side and groans for me to get the air conditioning rolling. "Let's go, Dad. I'm dying." She twists the cap off a water bottle and chugs.

I climb into the driver's side, eager to see Tate. Sure, we've video chatted every night but it's not the same.

After fighting traffic for forty-five minutes we arrive at the hotel. We check in and take our bags up to the room. Tate's supposed to meet me here before dinner at her brother's house. She's dying to show me off. Her words not mine. I'm a little nervous. This is a huge step. Being introduced to family makes it all real.

Jenny goes into the bathroom to change and when she comes out, I nearly have a heart attack. My baby girl looks like a woman in a cotton-candy-pink miniskirt and matching top that has the thinnest straps I've ever seen.

"Do you like it?" She twirls around.

"What the hell are you wearing?"

"Dad!" Jenny glares at me.

I never really curse in front of her, even though I don't think hell is actually a curse word. It was probably the way I said it.

"What? Okay, sorry, go back in and come out and try again."

She throws up her hands and huffs her frustration, then goes in the bathroom and walks back out. She plasters the fakest, most sarcastic smile on her face and says, "Do you like it?"

I never really thought Jenny was much like me. She's always so sweet and innocent, but as her teen years continue, I see more of myself in her every day.

I think carefully about what I say next. Fucking women, they cause you to overanalyze everything. "It's umm, you look beautiful in it. Maybe a little, umm, too beautiful, though?"

She shakes her head at me like she wants to say *really*?

I'm sure I fucked up somehow and she'll let me know about it for days.

She twirls around and reveals she's wearing shorts underneath.

Thank fuck, but still… if this is how she plans on dressing I'm going to end up in an early grave or send somebody to one for looking at her. It's too mature.

She grins her ass off and raises her eyebrows. "Tate bought it for me."

My jaw clenches. *Goddamn it, Tate.* I'm going to take her over my knee and spank her ass when I get my hands on her.

There's a knock on the door and I open it. It's Tate. She leaps into my arms. Her legs wrap around my waist and her mouth crashes into mine. She grinds against my cock and I'm met with a raging hard-on coupled with embarrassment.

I pull back and lick my lips, sliding her down to the floor. Maybe it wasn't the greatest idea not telling her Jenny was coming.

Her face goes red when she sees Jenny behind me. "Oh. Hey, sweetie. I had no idea you were coming this weekend." She says the last sentence through gritted teeth as she turns her head to look right into my eyes. She plasters on a fake smile, then turns back to Jenny. "And you look adorable."

Thank God I have the outfit she bought as leverage. "So this was your idea?" I wave a hand in front of my daughter.

"Err… well I thought it was cute and she loved it when we were shopping for her dance."

The vein in my neck starts to pulse. "Jenny, go change."

"But, Dad."

"Now please." I narrow my eyes on Tate.

Jenny stomps back into the bathroom on the verge of tears.

Tate folds her arms and looks up at the ceiling.

"You're in big trouble, *sweetheart*." I step into her space and move her arms away from her body. My mouth goes to her neck and I bite down in a playful way.

"It was a gift." Her tone is soft.

"I know, and she can wear it as a bathing suit cover-up to the pool." I scrub a hand over my face. "I swear to God, are you trying to give me a heart attack? I'm going to spank your ass for this."

"Is that a warning?" She smirks.

"It's a promise."

"I'll tell you what. Let Jenny wear her new outfit, and I'll take the spankings for it."

I lean back and grin my ass off. "It seems like you both win in that scenario."

"I should've never picked a smart one." Tate slides a hand up my chest, obviously trying to butter me up so Jenny can wear her new outfit.

I'm no fool. I know exactly what she's doing, but it still always seems to work somehow.

"I'll never tell you how to parent, Decker. But I am a woman, which means I was a teenage girl once. If you try to force Jenny into doing whatever you want, well..." She whistles as her words trail off. "You're gonna have a rough time, bucko."

"I don't want my daughter dressing like..."

"A slut?"

I point a finger at her, not in a menacing way. "I didn't say that."

"You say it to me in the bedroom all the time." She waggles her eyebrows, clearly enjoying fucking with me.

Goddamn women!

"That's exactly why she shouldn't be wearing that shit."

"Decker, Decker, Decker. Think through this problem like an attorney and not an emotional father. Let's look at the facts, okay?"

I shrug. "Okay." She'll tell me anyway, whether I want her to or not. But she does have a point. I want my relationship with Jenny to stay strong, even though I know she's growing up and becoming more independent.

"Your daughter is the sweetest child. She's smart, funny, adorable, incredibly mature for her age, and she makes fantastic decisions. You trust her, right?"

"Of course I do. I trust her more than I trust me to make good decisions."

"What's it going to hurt for her to wear that outfit while she's down here? Did you feel the heat outside? It's not like she's wearing it to a club or party or down a dark alley late at night."

I hold up a hand because I'm already tired of the conversation, and I don't need her to tell me how wrong I am any longer. "Jenny?" I holler out the side of my mouth.

Jenny walks out in the clothes she wore on the way over. "Yeah?" She does not sound enthusiastic as she asks the question.

"You can wear the outfit here."

Her eyes light up. "I can?"

"Yes, it was a gift. But don't make a habit of this, okay?"

She rushes over and grips me in a bear hug. "Thank you so much, Dad!"

153

"You're welcome, slugger." I plant a kiss on her forehead.

She turns to Tate. "You talked him into it, didn't you?"

Tate glances up at me with an evil grin, like she's about to betray me. We both know she is. "Of course I did, sweetie."

"So, it's really you I should be thanking." They both grin at me, knowing how much they love to get under my skin and see me all riled up.

I just throw my hands up. "Can we get on with our day please? You two are killing me."

"Awww." Tate grabs one of my cheeks and they both wrap their arms around me and hug at the same time. "We love you, Decker."

"Yeah, Dad. You know we love you."

As frustrated as they might make me sometimes, I wouldn't trade these two for anything in the world. This is my life. My family.

EPILOGUE

TATE

Six months later

"You almost ready, babe?" Decker calls to me from the bedroom.

"Just finishing my hair." I look over my reflection and that one curl that always gives me trouble is actually behaving tonight.

Decker walks up behind me. His hands land on my hips and his mouth at my ear. "Fuck, you're beautiful."

"Not looking so bad yourself."

He kisses my neck. "Think anyone will miss us if we show up late?"

"They'd definitely miss *you*. You worked your ass off to make this merger a reality and now it's finally paying dividends."

"Oh, they'd miss you too. How did I get so lucky to secure you in the deal?" He grins at me in the mirror.

"Secure me?" I scoff, twisting around to face him. I put a palm to his chest.

"Damn right. Your ass belongs to me in perpetuity." He knows when he drops his voice down low like that, I can't resist him. It makes me weak in the knees.

"I think you better take me to this party." I wink and start toward the car.

Decker follows me out, dressed in his best suit. My favorite one. It's a dark blue Hugo Boss with a light blue shirt that makes his eyes pop. I'm a lucky woman. We've been living together for the past three months. It took some convincing to get me to agree. I didn't want to jump in too fast although I stayed over nearly every night anyway.

We make it to the firm's cafeteria, and it has been transformed. Everything is so fancy with catered food, linen-covered tables, twinkling lights, champagne, ice sculptures. We enter and Decker is well received. People pull him in ten different directions, but he keeps a tight hold on my hand. The main players from The Hunter Group are all present. Weston is here with his wife, Brooke. She runs a nonprofit for women and children. Brodie has April on his arm; she designed the dress I'm wearing. Jaxson is with his longtime love, Jenna. Maxwell shows off Claire, and I smile to myself. She's wearing a new collar. They're freaks in the sheets, that's for damn sure. The stuff she tells me would make a porn star blush.

Weston and Decker shake hands. Jaxson steals Decker for a minute and Weston leans in and whispers, "You two make a nice couple. Glad you didn't fuck it up."

I shake my head and smile. "Yeah, glad *I* didn't fuck it up. That's a good one, boss."

Weston moves off to mingle, leaving me alone with the rest of the Collins brothers. Some of my female coworkers from Dallas strut past us.

"Maybe this shit show will work out after all..." Donavan trails off, smirking, his gaze following them across the room.

He and Decker have been at war over everything the last six months. I think Decker is more hurt than pissed off, to be honest.

I smile at the brothers. "Told you, boys. The women are better in Texas, and smarter too, so you probably don't stand a chance."

Deacon laughs. "We'll see about that. This ain't golf, darlin'," he says, practicing his southern drawl.

"Yeah, you can't find the hole under any circumstances."

Dexter dies laughing, while Deacon pretends he needs someone to administer CPR.

As they walk off toward the bar, Dexter says to Deacon, "She's the fucking queen of burns. I don't know why you do that to yourself."

I can't help but grin. Decker's brothers—at least the twins—are slowly becoming more tolerable.

I sip on my cocktail and watch the party in motion around me, proud of the work Decker has done.

Decker comes up from behind and wraps his arms around me, interlacing his fingers across my stomach. "Still hate my brothers?"

"They're growing on me."

"Something's growing on me too." His voice is low and seductive in my ear.

"We're at a work party." I spin and smack at his chest.

He puts a palm over my hand and gives me that smoldering stare that sends my heart racing. "Come with me."

I follow, unable to say no.

He escorts me out to the roof deck. The city is lit up with Lake Michigan in the backdrop. Lights reflect off the rippling water. It's beautiful up here at night. Like a scene out of a movie.

"Sweetheart." He takes both my hands in his. "The day we met, I knew there was something special about you. I never imagined what would follow. I never imagined I'd find someone who could fit into mine and Jenny's lives so seamlessly. You put me in my place more times than I can count. You put up with me. You know me better than anyone. You're my best friend. My partner. The only woman…" He pauses and drops to one knee.

Tears stream from my eyes, and I both hate and love that he can turn me into a blubbering mess.

Once down on his knee, Decker continues, "I want to share my life with. Will you marry me?"

He drops my hand and produces a giant diamond solitaire from his pocket.

My hand shoots up over my mouth as I nod through my tears. "Yes. Yes, I'll marry you." I bolt into him, nearly knocking him off balance, but he catches me. He hooks an arm around my waist.

Our mouths collide and I can't stop crying long enough to fully kiss him back.

After a long embrace, Decker pulls back and slips the princess-cut diamond ring on my finger. I can't stop staring at it sparkling in the moonlight.

He looks over my shoulder and says, "Did you get it? Please tell me you got it."

Jenny pops out from behind one of the deck chairs with her phone. She sniffles and has to wipe tears from her eyes as she nods. "Yeah, Dad, I got it all."

"Where did you come from?"

"Uncle Weston snuck me up here." She turns to her father and puts a hand on his chest. "Oh. My. God. Dad, you were amazing. You did it even better than when we practiced."

I turn to Decker. "You practiced this? With Jenny?"

Decker shrugs. "Wanted it to be perfect."

Decker starts to say something, but Jenny squeals and practically tackles me. "I'm so happy for you two."

"Thanks. And thanks for showing your dad how to do that. I'm sure you wrote the speech for him."

Jenny turns to her father and beams with pride. "Actually, he was adamant that I didn't help him with it. He wanted it to come from the heart."

She holds up my hand like it's a display and inspects the ring. "Look how beautiful it looks on her hand, Dad."

Decker nods and they both stare at it.

After a few quick seconds, Decker brings us both in for a hug. "My two ladies. I love you both so much."

Jenny and I in unison say, "We love you too."

The party seems like an afterthought now. I just want to stand here with my two favorite people in Chicago and stare out at Lake Michigan forever. I know without a doubt this is it… this is my happily ever after.

THANK you for reading Cocky Playboy! I hope you loved it as much as we did and because of that, we wrote a BONUS epilogue! You can grab it here → Bonus Epilogue.

HE'S A...

POSSESSIVE
Playboy

—— A COCKY SUITS NOVEL ——

SLOANE HOWELL
ALEX WOLF

QUINN

WHEN I FIRST TOOK A JOB AT a law firm, I never thought I'd end up in a supply closet with a partner balls-deep inside me.

Oh, and it's not just any partner seconds away from curling my toes—it's Deacon Collins. My boss's brother.

The shameful part is, it's not the first time.

Not even close.

I need to put a stop to it. These quickies are becoming more and more frequent, and I tell myself it's the last after each one.

"Fuck, Quinn." His tone is raspy as his lips drag down the side of my neck. He's possessive and hungry, nipping his teeth along my collarbone as he thrusts into me from behind.

A large, firm hand slides up my thigh and yanks my white panties farther across my ass. I wore them for him. There's something about white seeming virginal that turns him on. I shouldn't encourage his fantasies, but I do. We're playing a dangerous game, sneaking around in a place where we could easily be caught. I think that's part of the thrill for both of us.

I inhale a breath, taking in his masculine scent. There's something primal and raw about Deacon Collins.

He slides out of me, and I immediately miss the connection.

My skirt rides farther up my ass as he turns me and lifts me onto the counter. I wrap my legs around his waist and smirk over his shoulder when I spot new storage containers in the corner. They're filled with everything that once occupied the space where I'm sitting. "Clean up for me?"

"Shit was always in my way." His breath fans over my lips as he leans in closer to kiss me.

He gazes at me with gray eyes that remind me of a storm approaching. His torturous fingers rub over my clit, and I don't know how much more I can take. Deacon loves to toy with me—tease me. He always needs to be in complete control.

His favorite thing to do is bring me to the edge of release then yank me back, over and over.

"Gonna come for me, my dirty little office slut?"

I roll my eyes at him, pretending to be annoyed, but my body betrays me, trembling under his touch. Truth is I would kick his smirking ass if he said anything like that to me anywhere else. But when he's buried inside me, there's something about it that drives me insane.

"Less talking, please."

"Keep mouthing off and I won't let you come at all."

"I can get myself off."

Deacon shakes his head and slides a hand up until it's wrapped around my throat.

My eyes widen.

Deacon smirks. "Not like I can."

I can't argue with him, because he's telling the truth.

Right when I start to mouth something back at him, he shoves in deep and hits my spot just right. I have no earthly clue how this man knows how to push my buttons the way he does.

My walls squeeze around him, craving more. I squirm on the counter, a slave to his touch.

Grabbing a fistful of my hair with his free hand, he growls his words. "Not running that mouth, now. Are you?"

"You like my mouth when your dick's in it."

His eyes roll back for a second, then land on mine. "Fuck, woman."

"That's what you need to do, because we're almost out of time."

The cocky bastard slips out of me, yanks my panties down, drops to his knees, and pushes my legs farther apart. I know he does it just because I told him to hurry.

Deacon moves in, flicking his wicked tongue across my clit. "I'll fuck you when I'm damn good and ready."

I rake my nails through his hair. His confidence is off-the-charts hot, but he needs to take care of business. People will come looking for us soon.

Finally, after teasing me for what seems like an eternity, Deacon lines up with my entrance.

My fingernails bite into his sculpted ass as he slides the head over my clit.

"This what you want?" He grins down at me and eases in.

My eyes roll back. When I'm with Deacon all my worries seem to fade away. Maybe it's why I continue to do this—have sex with him in random places around the office. He gives me an escape I can't get anywhere else. Believe me, I've tried.

I've never been this girl. The girl who wears tight skirts because she knows it turns a man on, but I morph into a different person around him.

His thighs smack into my ass. "If you're staring off into space, I'm not fucking you right."

"No, you're perfect. Don't stop." I gasp when he draws out and slams back in harder.

Gripping my hips, Deacon increases the tempo until my mind is nothing but a blur. Thrusting in and out harder and faster, he clearly has his own agenda now, and I happily race him to the finish line. My head bounces off the cabinet behind me, but I don't care. I ride the wave of pleasure coursing through my body.

His stormy eyes sear into me. His stare feels way too intimate for our relationship. Well, our hooking up. I wouldn't call what we have a relationship.

I like his dick, and he's willing to use it on my terms. No strings attached. We both get what we want—the satisfaction of getting off.

I clench around him and a spasm hits me. Deacon's lips find mine and he grunts against them as he comes. We both jolt a few more times—he groans, I moan his name.

Eventually, we're both reduced to nothing but rough pants and smiles.

"Fuck, that was fantastic."

I put a hand on each of his shoulders and push him off me. "Fun's over."

Stepping back, he removes the condom, shoves it in his pocket, and pulls his pants up.

"Gross, Deacon, you're going to ruin your suit." My nose wrinkles.

"Should I carry it out of here in my fingertips?" He shakes his head at me, laughing.

Fair point.

I hop off the counter and pull my skirt down then hold my hand out. "Panties?"

He waggles his eyebrows. "Finders keepers."

I roll my eyes and smooth my hands over my hair. I don't know what his obsession is with my underwear.

"Let's grab dinner tonight."

I freeze. What did he just say? "Like a date?" I snicker. "You *must* be joking."

"Why's that funny?" His brows draw inward as if my words have wounded him.

What the hell?

"Come on, Deacon. We know what this is."

"What's wrong with going on a date with me?"

I exhale a sigh. "Where should I start? You're a player. We both agreed this was casual. Please don't get weird about this. It's fine the way it is."

"Can't two friends share a meal?"

"We're not friends."

Take the hint, sir!

He shrugs. "Colleagues share meals."

"Enough, Deacon." I need this conversation to end. "It's against company policy. You have a meeting to get to."

163

Deacon takes one of my hands in his and he looks more determined than I've ever seen him. "I'm not giving up on this. It *will* happen."

I shake my head. He'll grow tired of me soon enough and move on to the next girl. It's what he does.

He stuffs his shirt back into his pants and adjusts his Hugo Boss jacket.

Reaching out, his fingers stroke my cheek. "You're flushed."

I suck in a deep breath and fight the urge to lean into his hand. There's just something that feels natural about it, but I know better. The man is anything but an adult. There's no way he could handle an actual relationship. He takes nothing seriously. I'm not foolish enough to believe I could be the exception.

With a parting smile he slips through the door quietly, taking what seems like all the air with him.

I inhale a few deep breaths to calm myself. There's too much at stake for me to catch feelings for Deacon Collins. I grab a few pens, Wite-Out, and a pad of legal paper so it looks like I have a legitimate reason for being in here.

My eyes flick back and forth as I walk out. Nobody is around, thank God. The last thing I need is to become the hot gossip item at the office.

I place the stuff from the closet in the bottom drawer of my desk. Deacon exits the bathroom and struts past me wearing a smile so big it might get stuck to his smug face.

"Back to work, slacker."

I scowl at him. *Jerk.*

When he reaches his office, I promise myself I won't give him the satisfaction of catching me staring in his direction.

The heat of his gaze burns into my head, though. I lift my eyes, ever so subtly in his direction, and the bastard winks right at me.

Damn it!

I really need to end this.

DEACON

STEPPING off the elevator after a meeting, I spy Quinn behind her desk. She can play this little game all she wants, in fact, it wouldn't be much fun if she didn't.

We both know how it'll end. Honestly, I thought today would be the day she finally caved and said yes. We've snuck around the office a few months now, fucking like rabbits. The first time it happened she swore it was a moment of weakness, a one-time thing, but now look at us.

I pull her into the supply closet a few times a week, and sometimes even on the roof deck. Ahh, the roof deck. There's nothing better than staring out at Lake Michigan while she squeezes that tight pussy around me. My cock hardens at the memories.

Good times. Great oldies.

I continue past her desk, trail a few fingers along the edge, and knock some papers to the floor, just so I can watch her bend over and pick them up.

We both know she's not wearing panties. They're still tucked away in my pocket.

Part of me respects her reluctance. I know my reputation; everyone does. I never date. Dexter calls me a serial monogamist. According to *Chicago Magazine*, I'm one of the city's most eligible bachelors.

Thinking about that, I realize I'm quite a catch. Quinn should be thrilled at the thought of a relationship with me. There are a lot of single women in this city who would kill for an opportunity to go on a date with yours truly.

Thing is, I've never felt this way about a woman before.

It should bug the shit out of me, but it doesn't. I want to get to know Quinn on a deeper level than just physical. Maybe it's just the challenge. The fact she doesn't give in easily. She confuses the hell out of me, strutting around here in skirts, knowing what her tight little ass and those fucking heels do to me.

I damn near have to bite my knuckle to relieve myself of the thought.

The woman is my damn kryptonite. If I want to be taken seriously, I'm going to need a better plan than fucking her into submission. That much is clear.

I stop just inside my office to enjoy the view.

Right when I'm about to get a nice little show from Quinn, Tate Reynolds comes out of nowhere. "I got it." She bends down and gathers the papers.

Annoyance washes over me at the sight of her, especially when my eyes land on her giant engagement ring she loves to flaunt.

She's the chick Decker hooked up with from Dallas. She's from The Hunter Group, a firm we recently merged with and now she's Decker's fiancée. She's practically the opposite of Quinn in every way imaginable.

Things have smoothed over a little since the merger, but she can still be an uppity bitch who thinks she runs things. Pushy is an understatement with her. The best is when she tries to boss me around.

I'm not Decker and I'll be damned if I let her lead me around by the balls.

"Such a good Samaritan, Tate. I'll put you in for employee of the month."

"I'll be sure your name goes on the plaque for the alternates, down by the ladies room." Tate puts the papers on Quinn's desk and smirks.

Goddamn it.

The *Top Gun* reference would be hilarious if it came from anyone but her.

I walk into my office, over to my desk to check my schedule for next week. I have a court date coming up for a suit against a local heart surgeon named James Flynn. One of his nurses filed a complaint with the court, saying he smacked her on the ass after a procedure and told her, "Well done."

I hate these types of cases. For one, it's he said, she said. Most of the time the accused is a guilty asshole, but I believe Flynn. He's been a surgeon for more than thirty years and everyone raves about the guy, including previous female employees. He doesn't have a single write up on his record. Not to mention he's like sixty and is a family man. The main thing, though, is I've talked to him and sized him up. You can tell he'd never do that shit.

It doesn't matter if I believe him, though. I need a judge to.

I pick up the phone to order Quinn flowers when Tate raps on my door.

I hang the phone up, surprised she actually knocked this time. "Come in."

I really want to ask her if she finished Decker's castration procedure and has his nuts in a jar, but I want her out of here as quickly as possible.

"How are preparations for the Flynn case coming along?"

My jaw clenches. "Just fine, *Tate.*" I grate out her name.

"Doesn't look like it. You have time to run around being a bully and knocking shit on the floor but haven't watched the security video the hospital emailed over."

"I have an idea. Why don't you fetch me a coffee while I have myself a movie night with the video?" I smirk as all the color drains from her face.

That's right, Tate. Fuck off.

"Just watch the damn video. It's a lot like loading male male porn, all you have to do is click the little triangle in the middle. Shouldn't be anything you can't handle."

"That what does it for you and Decker?" I hold up both hands. "Not judging. I think it's great you two found some common ground in the bedroom."

She glares back at me. "Don't fuck this up."

"How about I give you a call the next time something more in your wheelhouse comes along? Like a ranch hand getting mauled by a heifer."

I belt out a moo as she storms out of the office.

Jesus Christ. She deserved that.

I don't take orders from her. She needs to get that shit through her thick head. I do need to review that video though, so I pull up my email. I'm sure there's nothing on it, but it would be really nice to catch a break.

My thoughts drift back to Quinn and how hot she looked with swollen lips and disheveled hair. Her pale skin and petite frame wrapped around me while she milked my cock for every last drop.

The video can wait a minute. I pick up the phone again and dial the florist. All women love flowers. I'd have my secretary handle this shit, but I don't need any gossip getting back to Quinn. She'd end our little fling in a heartbeat.

One thing is certain, though.

Quinn *will* be mine.

QUINN

I GET in line at the cafeteria to grab Decker's coffee and scroll through my task list for the morning. Hopefully, today will go smoothly and I can duck out an hour early to get a head start on my weekend. It doesn't happen often but on rare occasions Decker sends me home before five.

I move up a spot in line and browse the pastries in the display case. I didn't have time for breakfast. My power went out sometime during the night and I overslept. My company cell died, but thankfully my personal phone had a charge and my backup alarm woke me up.

My personal line buzzes inside my bag.

Great.

I can't ignore it. It could be my dad. He only calls for emergencies.

Digging through my wallet, lip gloss, and spare deodorant, I finally find it. My best friend Heather's face lights up on the screen.

"Hey. Everything okay?"

"Yeah. Just the usual. Getting ready to live that luxurious retail life."

"If you hate it so much why don't you quit?"

She works at some swanky store where one skirt costs more than my rent.

"Not everyone is a genius like you."

I can picture her sticking her tongue out at me as she says it. She can be such a brat, but I adore her. And I do enjoy the discount she gets me. I wouldn't have such nice work outfits without it. I make a decent salary but not enough for those kinds of clothes.

"Yeah, yeah. Hold on a second." I mute her and place my order. "Okay, I'm back." I balance the coffee holder with one hand and tuck the phone between my chin and shoulder while I stuff a muffin in my mouth.

She complains about her boss for most of the walk back to my floor. "Anyway, enough about that. What are you doing tonight?"

"Studying."

"C'mon, Quinn. Let's go out. It's Friday." Heather's been after me for weeks to go clubbing with her.

Between work and school, I don't have much time for a social life, which is why closet meetings with Deacon work for me.

"Carter Hughes will be there. He's been asking about you."

I roll my eyes. Carter Hughes is a prick who nails anything that spreads its legs for him. He's like a younger and even more immature version of Deacon. No thanks. One rich asshole is enough for me.

"Can't. I'll call you later. Just got back to my desk." I end the call with Heather when I notice a large bouquet of flowers front and center. They come every Friday like clockwork. I keep throwing them in the trash, but Deacon won't take the hint.

I can't believe he keeps pulling this shit when someone might trace it back to him. I already know how the scenario would play out. He'd get a small reprimand from Decker, and I'd be shown the door.

Sometimes the hushed whispers and stares make me wonder if half the office doesn't already know. I'm almost positive Tate is on to us. I really need to put a complete stop to this madness before it gets out of control. I set the coffee holder on my desk and tuck my bag into the bottom drawer. I pluck the card from the flowers.

I will get a yes.

-D

"Secret admirer?" Decker's deep voice booms in my ear.

"Holy sh—" I clutch the card to my chest, my pulse throbbing in my ears. "Sorry. You scared me." I flip the card face down and hand Decker his coffee.

"How's today look?"

I take a moment to collect my thoughts.

Decker and Deacon are both tall and fit. Where Decker has icy blue eyes, Deacon's are gray and broody. Both men are attractive, but then again, all the Collins brothers are. They're about the same height, but Deacon is way bigger while Decker is lean. Deacon's damn biceps are like basketballs.

My gaze sweeps down the corridor toward Deacon's office out of habit. A habit I need to break but can't seem to. Just like I can't seem to stop sleeping with him.

Decker clears his throat and snaps me out of my reverie.

"Right. You have a meeting with Beckley Brothers. Potential new client. They're a young construction company but growing fast. They need advice on some contracts. They built that new coffee place down the street that looks like a giant cup." I pray he doesn't pile a bunch of work on me for the weekend. I have a big test I need to study for.

"Everything's in order?"

I blink. "I'm sorry, what?"

"For the meeting? I need you focused, Quinn. Something going on with you?"

"No. I mean, right, of course. No worries. I'll have everything ready." I hope that was the answer he was looking for. We work together really well. A lot of people think he's an asshole, but he just likes things to run smoothly and hates repeating himself. Usually, I'm on the ball and anticipate his needs before he asks.

"Great."

I chuck the flowers in the trash once Decker heads toward his office.

Glancing around at my desk, I notice someone has been moving crap around again.

Damn it, Deacon.

This is one of the reasons I can't take his request for a date seriously. He's nothing but an immature office prankster with a big dick who behaves like a teenager.

Why does he get me so flustered?

I'm slipping. I'm off my game and it's all his fault.

I eye the box of chocolates sitting where my phone should be. It really would be a shame to waste them. They look super expensive.

"Who keeps sending the flowers you throw away?" Tate smirks when she walks up. I know she knows.

"This guy Carter. Won't take no for an answer." I roll my eyes, hoping my performance is believable. "Chocolate?" I thrust the box toward her.

"Maybe later."

I shrug. More for me.

I bite into a truffle and nearly have what I could only describe as a chocolategasm.

Man, these are good.

Now, I just need to figure out how to get myself out of this Deacon mess, after I've had a few more chocolates.

DEACON

I SNICKER at the flowers sitting in Quinn's trash can as I head to Decker's office.

I can't help but notice all the gold foil wrappers scattered through the petals.

Didn't throw those fucking chocolates away, did you Quinn?

I'll wear her down, slowly but surely.

She's away from her desk or I'd give her shit about it. I haven't seen her all day.

Dexter and I hit the golf course with some old oil tycoon Dexter's trying to land. Guy has a nine-digit net worth and is on his last legs. It took two hours longer than normal to play eighteen. I don't know how the guy hasn't pickled his goddamn liver. He drank a fifth of whiskey before the turn at hole nine. Even I can't stomach drinking that much that early. I like a good time as much as the next guy, but fuck.

Much respect to him.

When I checked in with my secretary earlier, she let me know Tate dropped off a mountain of files on my desk. The hairs on the back of my neck stand up thinking about it. She does this shit just to piss me off, but I won't give her the satisfaction.

I walk into Decker's office.

His head pops up from whatever he was reading, like a damn meerkat. "You assholes need to start knocking."

"Get your woman on a leash, pussy. Your house is out of order and it's affecting me."

Decker stands up and his jaw flexes. "Watch your mouth." He bows up for a second, then relaxes. "You don't like Tate because she makes you work." Raking a hand through his hair, a smile slowly spreads across his face. "Actually, I have something even you can handle. Easy as shit and you're perfect for it. Do it and I'll tell Tate to ease up."

I rub my hands together. "Now we're talking, brother. Consider it done."

"I need you to speak at a college."

My jaw ticks and I stare at him.

He tries to hold back a laugh at my reaction, but he's damn near trembling.

Finally, I shake my head. "Fuck off. I'm not doing that. Have Dex do it." Decker knows I hate that kind of shit.

"Not up for debate. You already agreed and we might be The Hunter Group now, but I'm still the managing partner in Chicago." His face turns serious as he paces around his desk and leans back against it with his arms crossed. "If you want Tate off your ass, prove to me you can be an asset. Because, if we're being honest here, I'm getting sick of your shit. We're not just accountable to ourselves anymore. You bring in the least amount of clients, log the least amount of billable hours, you're out golfing all morning when Dexter could've gone by himself, and you reek of whiskey. So get your secretary or a paralegal to draft a presentation if you can't come up with one on your own."

I love how he talks shit about me smelling like whiskey when he has a whole goddamn bar in the corner. Regardless, I can see it written on his face that I'm not getting out of this. "Fine." I growl the word, a vein bulging in my neck. "When?"

"Monday night."

I sigh. "You shitting me? Night school? What the fuck, Decker? What if I have plans?"

He smiles. "A Pornhub marathon doesn't count as plans. The professor is a good friend and sends me clients and keeps an eye out for prospective employees. I want you to look for any possible students we might want to offer an internship."

"Night schoolers aren't real lawyers. Why would you hire someone from there?" I groan. I know exactly who goes to night school. People who don't have their lives together and people past their prime. Working adults who have way too much shit going on to be dedicated employees.

I know I'm being harsh, but my brain is searching for any reason it can possibly conjure for me to get out of this.

Decker straightens up in front of me. "Know what your problem is?"

I hold my hands up. "Please tell me, Dad."

"You're incapable of being an adult."

I scoff. "That's not true. I'm always mature."

"Really? How about the time you cut a hole in the bottom of a bag of Doritos, stuck your dick in it, then offered some to Donavan?"

I try to hold back my laugh. Fuck, that was a good one. "He had it coming." I can barely keep a straight face after that magnificent pun. It was a ten if I've ever heard one.

"It was during a staff meeting!"

"Well, he met with the staff, all right. And a lot of people would've been happy with his surprise."

Decker shakes his head and pinches the bridge of his nose. "What about the chart you made in Excel to rate the tits of our hottest clients?"

I point a finger at him, deadpanning a serious glare. "That was an exercise from a training seminar you sent me to. I was practicing pivot tables." I can't even look at him while I finish the last sentence.

"Jesus Christ. Enough. You're speaking at the college and I'll be following up to make sure you represented the firm in a professional manner."

"Fine. Can I fuck off now? Or is there anything else?"

"Go, please. This little chat is giving me a headache."

As I leave his office, Tate saunters by and gives me a side eye. I can practically hear them laughing at me from his office.

Oh, fuck both of you and your missionary sex.

She has him right by the pecker, leading him around and taking over the firm. Decker never had a problem with my performance until she showed up. Donavan told me all about her going to Decker to get one of his lawsuits dropped. Not everyone wants to work their ass off non-stop and never enjoy life like Decker and Tate. They live for their jobs. Some of us have a fucking life and actually enjoy cracking a joke and laughing once in a while.

Bitter old fucks, and they're not even old yet.

Besides, I fill a role and it's perfect for me. I'm the charismatic brother. The one who goes out and drinks with the good ol' boys. I warm them up and then Decker comes in and closes the deal at the end.

The only problem is he takes all the credit for landing them and acts like I don't do shit.

Fuck him.

I go out on the weekends and schmooze while he's at home being a dad in his giant house. I endure countless hangovers for this firm, thank you very much. And I never bitch about my job like Decker. He's turning into a woman. I bet Tate has a bigger dick than his.

I smile at my thoughts, loving the way I rationalize partying as an asset to the company. I am who I am. At least I don't pretend to be something I'm not.

QUINN

DROPPING my bag on the counter, I rifle through it for a tie and pull my hair up into a messy bun. I'm ready to kick my heels off and change out of these stuffy clothes. It's been a long week and I need to make dinner for Dad and settle in to study.

It's just the two of us.

"That you, Quinn?" my father calls from the living room of our two-bedroom apartment. The place has a weird floor plan. The hallway leads past a coat closet then a half bathroom and the kitchen. The living room is just beyond, then a full bath split between two bedrooms. We live on the bottom floor because Dad needs an electric wheelchair to get around. He suffered a stroke a few years ago. It left him with severe nerve damage down his right side and forced him into early retirement. Before that, he drove a bus for the city.

"No, it's Publisher's Clearing House. We won a million bucks." I giggle. It's an ongoing joke between the two of us.

He rolls toward the kitchen using his regular wheelchair, and I smile. He's having a good day if he can wheel himself around, and it's great for his arms to get a workout.

"Heather called. Said you told her you can't go out tonight." His eyes pierce through me.

"Don't start. I have a big exam next week."

"I'm going next door for dinner. Mrs. Waters is making enchiladas." He flashes his crooked grin. The stroke left him with a small droop on the right corner of his mouth.

"You know you'll regret it later when your heartburn hits. You aren't supposed to have that stuff."

"You go out with Heather and I'll lay off the hot sauce. You need to have a life once in a while."

I sit there and mull it over, glancing to the ceiling then back at him. "Fine, old man. I don't appreciate you using your health to hold me hostage."

"Who are you calling old? I'm fit as a fiddle."

"Yeah, yeah." I grab my bag and move around him, so I can call Heather and see what she's dragging me into this time.

———

"DAYUMM. You look hot. If I was into women, I'd be all about this." Heather grins and waves a hand up and down at me.

She's wearing a red dress with see-through mesh that goes up both sides and down the front. She looks fantastic, but her outfit leaves little to the imagination. Her hair is swept up in a high ponytail and sways from side to side as she walks.

"Shut up." I fidget with my hair, smoothing it over my shoulders. "It's not too much?" I don't normally wear clothes this revealing, but Heather snagged the emerald-green dress for me from her store. They were going to toss it because a thread on the hem was frayed and needed replaced.

The front and back has a deep V that runs down to my navel and my rear. I couldn't even wear a bra with it. Paired with my auburn hair, I feel a bit like Poison Ivy.

It's packed wall to wall when we walk inside PRYSM Nightclub. Strobe lights flash off the wall and the thumping bass vibrates in my chest. Being packed in the place makes me a bit claustrophobic but nothing some booze can't handle.

"Let's get a drink." Heather has to yell in my ear.

I nod.

She gestures toward the bar and we navigate our way through the crowd of catcalls and wandering hands. I'm going to regret this tomorrow morning, but I'm already here, so I push the thought from my mind. I've missed hanging out with her and I'm always responsible. I can afford to let my hair down for once and have fun.

Heather goes on dates all the time. She eats up the single life since she ended things with her last boyfriend.

I order a whiskey sour. Heather gets a dirty martini. Drinks in hand, we look for a table, but it doesn't appear promising.

Just have a good time. It'll be fine.

I take a healthy swig from the rocks glass and sway my hips to the music. I should've ordered two drinks, judging by the length of the line at the bar, but I need to pace myself.

We aren't in the club for more than five minutes when my face flushes and a familiar tingling fans out to my extremities.

It's not the alcohol.

I glance up to the second floor that overlooks the main dance area.

178

It's him.

Deacon.

He's chatting up some busty brunette that's fawning all over him. He smiles right at her.

It's a smile some part of my brain hoped was reserved for just me.

I know better but seeing it still stings. He's in his element, doing what he does best—charming women.

I'm an idiot.

I shouldn't feel foolish, but that's exactly how I feel right now. I know he sees other people. I tell myself constantly I hope he finds someone to take his attention away from me. He'll never settle down with one woman.

The music cuts off just as Heather shouts my name. "Quinn!"

His eyes flash in the direction of her voice, but I dart out of his line of sight praying he didn't see me.

"You okay?" Heather eyes me, giving me a once over.

"Good. Just a little overwhelmed." I suck down my drink. "Maybe this wasn't the best idea. I'm not really feeling it."

"Okay." She frowns and knocks her martini back. "Let's get out of here."

I nod.

We place our empty glasses on a nearby table and move toward the exit. The lights dim, and they're replaced with neons strobing across the ceiling.

I turn my head and catch a glimpse at the spot where Deacon stood earlier but he's gone.

"What do we have here?" A deep voice rumbles in my ear, and a hard body presses into me from behind.

For a brief moment, I smile. I shouldn't, but I do. It has to be Deacon.

I turn around and the smile fades immediately. Carter Hughes wraps a hand around my waist like he just won the lottery.

In all honesty, if I didn't know him, I'd probably find him attractive. Unfortunately, I do know him. We fooled around for a bit in high school. Actually, he strung me along under the guise of dating, while he slept with several of my so-called friends.

The joys of high school.

I shoot him a look that says *let go of me now* and move away, but he tightens his grip and pulls me closer. I smell whiskey on his breath, and he slurs his words like he's hammered. Heather is a few feet away talking to one of his friends, Stewart. I already know this is a set up, but I can't be too mad at her. I never really told her about my history with Carter out of embarrassment. I never really tell her about my sex life at all. I thought I'd hinted I wasn't interested in him, but apparently, I didn't communicate it effectively.

I try to squirm my way out of Carter's grip, but Stewart guides Heather toward the bar. She must've seen my initial smile and thought I was okay with Carter. That has to be it.

Great.

Now I'm on my own with this asshole. She better not leave me here alone and go home with Stewart.

"Fuck, you got hot." Carter exhales in my ear, and I shudder.

"Thanks." I sigh and twist out of his grip. "I'm going to the bathroom."

"Want some company in there?"

"That's the exact opposite of what I want."

"Well, don't keep me waiting." He leans in to kiss me, and I duck out of the way.

He damn near stumbles into someone else, and I make my escape.

DEACON

GOD, this place sucks a dick.

This club isn't my style, but I promised to show a client's son a night on the town and he wanted to come here. Wrenley Cooper is new to Chicago. He grew up on the West Coast with his alcoholic former child star mother. His father, Justice Cooper owns one of the biggest recording companies on the planet and he's grooming Wrenley to join the family business.

Good luck with that, Mr. Cooper.

He's fresh out of college and a fucking nerd. He's the exact opposite of his parents, and I can't help but feel bad for the kid, and good for him in a certain way. His dad's an asshole of the highest order, but he's definitely good for padding my billable hours and nets me a nice little bonus each quarter.

The kid looks uncomfortable as fuck in this place, like he'd rather be off playing Call of Duty. Why the hell did he ask to come here? Maybe he's just awkward.

I think Justice hopes I'll get the kid laid. You know the dynamic I'm talking about. Father and son who are night and day different. Kid wants to play computer games. Dad wants him to be a man and live up to the family name, rush a fraternity, run naked through the quad up to the gymnasium type shit.

It's kind of sad, and I can relate to the kid. I know what it's like to live in the shadow of family and not meet expectations.

I chat up this ditzy-ass chick for him. Her tits are about the only thing she has going for her, because the brain cells are lacking. Maybe she's dumb enough to give the kid a blow jay and get his father off both our backs.

Just about the time she starts to regale me with her supreme intelligence, I hear someone shout the name Quinn. My head jerks and I scan the club looking for the auburn-haired woman who loves to tease my cock every chance she gets. It's wishful thinking. There's no way in fuck she'll be caught dead in this place. It's so not—her. Hell, I don't have a clue what she does outside of working at the firm. That's one of the reasons she needs to stop being so goddamn stubborn and go on a date with me. I want to know what she likes to do. I want to get to know her better.

"You're like hot." The chick giggles.

I manage not to roll my eyes. It's all about ol' Wren's dick tonight. I can't be an asshole to her until the mission is accomplished.

"Speaking of hot, you should meet my friend. He could use some company. His girlfriend dumped his ass." I sigh and nod. "Yeah, she really did a number on the poor guy. Dumb decision. He's rich as fuck."

Her nose scrunches up. "What's wrong? Why'd she dump him?"

I lean in close and whisper in her ear. "This is just between us. You can never tell him I told you this."

Her eyes widen. This shit is too fucking easy.

"Okay, I promise."

"She couldn't handle his dick."

She leans back a little, like she's feigning offense.

I shrug and look off at the crowd, scanning for Quinn but putting on a show at the same time. "It's true."

Her eyes dart over to Wrenley.

Fuck, he's standing there looking all pathetic.

"You sure?"

I shrug. "It's always the shy ones. You know this. They don't need to brag."

Her lips curl into a grin. "He *is* kind of cute, but I was hoping you'd take me home." She bumps me with her hip and splays her fingers across my chest over my shirt.

Fucking hell. This chick is thirsty as shit. "Tell you what. You show Wrenley a good time and *maybe* if he reports good things, I'll consider it."

"What?" Her brow wrinkles in disgust.

I can't help but smile on the inside. I'm like a great stand-up comedian. Sometimes you have to lead the audience into dark territory, just to bring them back out of it to make the laughs that much sweeter. "You heard me." I smirk.

"Ugh. You're an…"

"Asshole." I finish the sentence for her. "I know, and you love that about me. Just have a fucking drink with the guy. It's his birthday."

Her brows shoot up. "I thought you said his girlfriend broke up with him?"

Maybe she has a few brain cells after all, but not many. I shake my head. "Terrible isn't it? No guy should get dumped on his birthday because he's packing a huge dick." I shrug and signal for another drink.

I watch the gears turning in this chick's head as she looks over Wrenley.

Fuck, he's a train wreck, but he reeks of money. I already know this chick can smell it on him. She has dollar signs in her eyes.

"I suppose one drink won't kill me." She squares her shoulders, pushes her tits out, and walks over to him. She hooks her arms around his neck and plants a kiss right on his lips, smearing hooker-red lipstick all over his mouth.

It's too fucking easy sometimes.

A hand shoots out behind the woman's back and flashes me a thumbs up.

My work here is done.

Now, what the fuck am I going to do while this kid gets his cock shined?

I scan the dance floor, looking for anyone I might know so I won't be bored out of my mind.

That's when I see her.

My heart tries to pound its way out of my chest.

Quinn walks toward the door in a sinful green dress that hugs her body in all the right places. My cock twitches and starts to rise at the sight. God, I've never seen her look so fucking hot. She's like supermodel fucking beautiful.

Just as my mind races to think of how and where I could fuck her in the club and take our sexcapades to a whole new level, some asshole wraps his arm around her waist and yanks her close to him.

My blood heats to a million degrees and I wouldn't be surprised if steam shoots out of my ears. That son of a bitch is touching what's mine.

I take off for the stairs.

It doesn't take long for me to practically sprint toward her. I knock a few people out of the way and spill their drinks, but I don't give a shit. I move toward the exit, attempting to track her every move but I keep losing sight of her. Just as I start to intervene, she scoffs at the guy and takes off toward the bathroom.

That's my girl.

He stares at her as she navigates through the crowd toward the ladies' room.

"You can fuck right off, sir." I mutter the words under my breath and angle to cut her off before she gets to her destination.

Just as she's about to enter the bathroom, I grip her forearm and pull her over to the corner.

Her eyes dart around for a second, and she looks like she might scream. Then her stare lands on my face. Her tempting lips form an amused grin and she shakes her head. "What are you doing here?"

I rake my eyes up and down her dress and try not to blow a load in my pants just at the sight of her. "Me?" I raise my brows at her.

Our gazes lock and I lick my lips wanting nothing more than to shove her against the wall and have my way with her.

"You on a date?"

"What if I am?"

"I'd want to know his Jedi secrets since you keep turning me down."

She shakes her head in a playful way. "Maybe he's just nice and acts like a grown up."

I shrug and flash her a smile. "Unfortunate for him."

"Oh really?" She grins, clearly amused with our conversation. "Because he landed a date with me and you couldn't?"

"Absolutely."

"And why would that be unfortunate for him? I'm dying to know."

"Because he did all that work. Acted like such an adult. Probably took you to dinner, picked you up, drove you here." I lean in close, so she can feel my warm breath in her ear. "And I'll be the one who takes you home and fucks you."

"Now, that's funny." Quinn tries to play it off like we're joking, but I notice every single one of her reactions when I tell her that. Her breath catches in her throat, her words stammer ever so slightly. The pulse on the side of her neck speeds up, right in the place I want to run my tongue.

I lean back and smile. "It is what it is. Let's get out of here."

"No way. We shouldn't even be seen together."

"Who's going to see? I can have a hotel suite in five minutes."

Quinn laughs. "I'm not going to a hotel with you."

"Oh, but you'll fuck me in a broom closet at work?"

Her eyes narrow. "You're an asshole. Why don't you go find that skank you were flirting with? I'm sure she'd love to go to your hotel suite." She makes air quotes when she says "hotel suite."

"Oh, so you saw me and weren't even going to come say hi? Real mature, Quinn." God, I love it when she gets all worked up. "If I didn't know better, I'd think you're jealous."

"Not even."

"Quinn?" The asshole who had his arm around her walks up. Must've gotten tired of waiting. "Is this guy bothering you?"

I flash him a stare reserved for my worst enemies. "I'm her boss, fuck head. Get lost."

He shrinks back, holding his palms up.

Pussy.

"Real nice." Quinn smacks my arm with her palm.

"I never claimed to be nice." I grin. "Let me at least buy you a drink. I've been trying to get you alone outside the office for months. Don't shit on my one opportunity."

Quinn's eyes dart around the club, then she points a finger at me. "One drink. That's it. No funny business."

Business is the farthest thing from my mind. I wrap an arm around her waist and guide her toward the back. I shoot the asshole a look that says *stay the fuck away from her* as we move to the bar.

When we reach our destination, I move her in front of me. The place is so packed it pushes my cock right up against her ass.

Sliding my arm around her waist, I bury my nose in her hair and inhale. The amount of restraint it takes to not rip her dress off and fuck her on the bar is unworldly.

"Vodka cranberry." I order for her.

"What if I don't like cranberries?"

"You like them." I cage her in at the bar grazing the shell of her ear with my teeth. I love how she pretends I've never seen her drinking cranberry juice at the office. Like I don't pay attention to every goddamn detail when it comes to her.

"This is trouble."

"No one from the office is here. You worry too much." I slide my hand down the front of her dress under the privacy of the bar. I make sure to graze just along her clit, but not quite touching it. It's not my fault the deep v cut in the front of her dress gives me easy access to her pussy.

"Deacon." She lets out a gasp.

I remove my hand quickly when the bartender walks over with her drink.

Quinn drinks faster than she needs to. "Well, we had a drink."

"You made me a happy man." I slide my hand back down the front of her dress and venture a little farther this time.

Her lips part ever so slightly when I circle her clit with the tip of my finger.

I lean in close to her ear. "You can pretend you want to get out of here all you want, Quinn. Your pussy tells a different story."

"God, I really hate you sometimes." She says the words, but her hips grind against my hand at the same time.

Her eyes flash up to mine, but then she looks past me.

Something or someone catches her attention. She jerks away from me and hauls ass through the crowd.

What the fuck?

Quinn stomps off toward the exit.

Like a dog in heat, I give chase. Finally, I grip her by the forearm and spin her around to face me. "Where you going?"

"Home. Alone." She looks away and types furiously on her phone.

"I'll give you a ride."

"No!" She rushes out of the building.

I run after her, but a cab pulls up and Quinn slides inside. She slams the door in my face before I can get to her, and the car speeds off.

What the hell?

QUINN

I sneak off to my favorite coffee shop to nurse my hangover and study for my upcoming test. Dad has a physical therapy appointment and it gives me a few hours to myself. I knew going out last night was a terrible idea.

Any time Deacon's near it's nothing but trouble. The second I let my guard down, I saw two new girls from the Dallas office watching us. At least I think they saw me. I wasn't about to stick around to find out.

No way.

"Refill?"

I smile at the server. "Please and can I get a chocolate scone?"

"Definitely." She takes my cup, and my phone buzzes. I check it, in case it's Dad and something has happened.

It's Heather.

Heather: Holy shit! I went home with Stewart last night after I got your text and let's just say dude has a helicopter for a tongue. You make it home okay? Carter said your boss threatened him. I need details.

I can't help but shake my head as I read over her message. She's so open about her sex life and I'm so guarded with mine. I never told her about Deacon. Part of me feels like a bad friend, but it's my personal information. I don't share it with anyone.

Speaking of Deacon. He won't stop blowing up my phone asking for an explanation. It *was* a little sweet, him constantly texting to see if I made it home okay.

I ignore everyone and try to focus on my notes. I'm ahead of schedule, at least. There's a guest speaker Monday so we won't cover anything new. I decide to fire off a response to Heather as the server sets down my coffee and scone.

Quinn: He thought Carter was bugging me. Which he was. I'm in the middle of cramming for my test. Dinner tonight?

Heather: Depends on if Stewart calls. I think I might like him.

Quinn: Okay, keep me posted. Talk later.

I roll my eyes. She could do so much better than him, but I want to be supportive. Who am I to judge anyway? It's not like I'm killing it in the decision-making department.

My phone pings again. This time it's another message from Deacon.

Deacon: It's Saturday. You should be in my bed, naked.

I try like hell to fight the smile spreading across my face when I read his message. My body screams at me, but I can't risk it. I do find immense pleasure in messing with him, though. I stare at my phone. Should I respond? I fire off a reply before I chicken out.

Quinn: Maybe I'm already naked. Ever consider that?

Deacon: Pictures or it didn't happen.

My cheeks bloom with pink when I read his message.

Know what? To hell with it.

Tucking my laptop in my bag, I gather my things and duck into the bathroom. I can't believe I'm even considering doing this…sending Deacon a picture.

As long as I don't show my face there's no proof it's me and we're texting on my personal phone. I lock the door behind me, place my bag on the sink, and unbutton my shirt, exposing my bra. I've never done anything like this and it's far more awkward than I imagined. Zooming in on my chest, I snap a shot of my cleavage and hit send.

My work cell buzzes in my bag and panic floods my bloodstream. What if it's Deacon messaging me from a company phone? I'm scared to check the message, but I can't be a chicken shit. It's stupid anyway. Deacon wouldn't be that dumb.

I swipe my thumb across the screen and there's an email from Decker. He needs me to come in today and deliver some contracts to the Beckley brothers.

Shit.

It's rare for him to ask for anything on a Saturday, especially after the merger. He never works weekends anymore but I'm already out and it's my job.

I fire off a reply to Decker telling him I'm on it, then call my dad.

"Hey, sweetie."

"I'm going to be a little late. Need to run to the office."

"I'm beat from my appointment. Gonna take a nap."

"You sure you're okay?"

"Stop worrying so much, Mom!" He hangs up on me.

I can't help but smile.

I shouldn't feel guilty for leaving him on his own because it's work related, but I do.

I ARRIVE at the firm twenty minutes later and one of the weekend security guys holds the door for me.

"Mr. Collins is in his office."

I frown but maybe he means one of the other brothers. If Decker was here, he could deliver the contracts himself.

"Thanks. I won't be long."

"Take your time."

I step into the elevator. The doors close and I press the button for my floor. When I get off the elevator, I drop my stuff on my desk. Decker's office is locked, and the lights are shut off. Maybe the security guy was mistaken. I trek back to my desk and fetch my key to Decker's office from the top drawer. Before I stick the key in the lock, I sense a presence and a hand clamps over my mouth.

"Knew I'd get you here." Deacon's voice grates in my ear and the scent of his cologne washes over me. "Such a dedicated little employee."

I spin around ready to smack the piss out of him. "You sent that email, didn't you? Is there even a contract?"

"Yeah, but it's not ready yet." Deacon grins. "I wanted to see you."

"Well you saw me." I stomp toward my desk to grab my stuff and head home.

"Come on, Quinn. Fuck." He takes a step toward me. "You have to appreciate the effort I put in to get you alone." He flashes me his pearly whites with a shit-eating grin.

"You're out of control," I hiss at him.

He shrugs as if my job isn't at stake with his antics. "I asked you out to dinner, but you said no."

I wrap my arms around my waist and look away. "We both know I'll end up hurt. Please, stop doing this to me."

"You don't know that." He steps into my personal space and drags a finger down my throat. He nods down the hall. "Come to my office. Give me five minutes."

I shake my head.

"I won't do anything you don't want me to."

"Deacon, I…"

"Stop thinking so much. It's exhausting."

He grips my hand and pulls me with him. Like an idiot, I follow, knowing I'm making a huge mistake. At the same time, butterflies swarm my stomach, the way they do every time he so much as looks in my direction.

What is wrong with me?

I shouldn't entertain the idea of dating Deacon. We both know what will happen. After the newness and excitement wears off, he'll cheat on me or I'll accidentally end up pregnant.

He's not mature enough to handle a real relationship or responsibility. It's why he always wears a condom, even though I'm on the pill. I'm not taking any chances.

We get to his office and he locks the door behind him but doesn't bother to close the blinds. Not that I'm going to do anything with him. He can have his five minutes then I'm out of here. In fact, as soon as he's done with his little speech, I'm ending this whole thing. It's not worth it. Never was.

He wheels around on me once we're inside and his face is tense. "Why do you keep fighting this?" He wags a finger between us.

"Just stop, okay? This isn't happening in here."

He grins and takes a step toward me. "We both know that's a lie."

"Deacon, I…" I take a step away from him, and my back slams into the door as he stalks toward me like a hungry lion.

I try to think of all the things I want to say to him, to end this little charade, but my brain is a jumbled mess when he stares at me like that.

I start to say something, and he puts his index finger to my lips.

"Shh. We're not here to talk." A devilish smirk crosses his face, and I lose all train of thought when his hand cups my jaw and his lips crash down on mine. He keeps talking as he kisses me. "What do I have to do to show you this is real? Huh, Quinn?" His rough hands grip my ass and yank me into him. His teeth nip at my neck. "I want you. All of you. I want to know what you're thinking." His tongue slides up the side of my neck to beneath my ear. "What you do outside of work."

"Deacon, please…"

"I want you all the time. Not just in a fucking closet."

"We can't." My words come out on a shallow gasp as his hand massages my breast.

He's so hungry and possessive, and sweet and sincere at the same time. How the hell does he do this to me? I allow myself to believe the lie a little longer. That maybe something more is possible. That we could be more than just a fling.

I already know as soon as I step away and analyze the situation, I'll go right back to not trusting him. To wanting to end whatever this is between us, but it's impossible right now with him brooding in front of me.

"We can. Just say yes, goddamn it."

It's impossible to deny the attraction, the way my heart races in my chest. "Why can't I stay away from you?" I grip his shirt in my hands and without thinking, yank it up from his pants. Next, I go to work on the buttons, exposing the chiseled lines of his abs. He definitely works out. He's not as lean as the other Collins brothers. Deacon is thick and strong, but his muscles are still well defined.

"It's cute when you try to take charge." He smiles against my lips, running his finger along the curve of my jaw and down my neck. His fingertip burns a trail along my exposed skin. "I need you naked."

My body reacts to his command before I can even question it. I pull my top over my head and kick off my shoes. Deacon grabs the drawstring of my sweatpants and jerks me forward. He's never seen me dressed this casual before. I'm always in skirts and jackets. I silently pray I'm wearing decent underwear.

After my shower this morning I think I just threw on whatever was clean, and I can't remember what it was. He smirks at me when he pushes my pants to the floor. I look down and realize I'm not wearing any.

His eyebrows lift. "You came prepared." Reaching around my back with one hand and two fingers, Deacon skillfully removes my bra and flings it across the room. "Fuck, you're hot. I've never seen you completely naked before." He steps back and looks me up and down like he's appraising me.

I back up to the wall. "What about security?"

"He won't come up here. Trust me."

Part of me hates Deacon for planning this, and that his plan is clearly working.

I'm already naked and definitely going through with it, so I might as well enjoy myself. I strut past him and bend over his desk. When I know he's looking, I wiggle my ass at him. "Well, what are you waiting for?"

In no time he's behind me, his hard cock pressed up against my ass.

The smug bastard loves taunting me. His teeth sink into my shoulder, and I feel him free his cock. He slides the crown across my clit, and I can already feel the pending orgasm throbbing between my legs. Rocking my hips, I grind against him, craving more.

"You have no idea how bad I want you bare. Fuck."

I glance back and smile when he pulls the condom from his pocket. Some things are non-negotiable, no matter how ridiculous my brain decides to act.

Part of me smiles on the inside that even though Deacon is the most irresponsible human being I've ever met, he doesn't fight me on the issue. It's like he can sense where to press his luck and where not to. Despite his immaturity, he's very intelligent when he needs to be.

Once he's ready, he gives my ass a playful smack.

A light coo escapes my lips.

"I want to take my time with you, but I don't know if I'll be able to." He eases into me from behind. "So. Fucking. Tight."

The suddenness of him filling me from within is almost too much to bear. Why does he have to be so damn good at this? Why do his words do this to me?

"You don't know how long I've wanted you here, just like this." One of his hands grips my hip, the other lands on my shoulder. "Bent over my desk."

His hips speed up as his fingers dig in and yank me back to meet each thrust.

"I'm so close."

Without warning, he lifts one of my legs up onto the desk, and just like that he's even deeper.

So deep.

He's hitting places I didn't know existed and his hand slips around my waist. His finger circles my clit and I'm two seconds away from being in the clouds.

Deacon leans over and his mouth is next to my ear as his thighs crash into me. "I know every button to push. Nobody knows what you like more than I do, Quinn."

"God, Deacon, I'm so…"

"Come for me. I want to feel you."

And just like that, his words send me over the edge and I'm free falling. My thighs quiver and my body shakes. The orgasm rushes through me like a wild, uncontrolled river. Fuzzy stars appear in front of my eyes and I don't know how I'm still able to stand.

Deacon slides out of me, whips me around, and before I know what's happened my ass is on his desk and he's spreading my legs. He drops to his knees and his mouth is on me, his eyes staring up into mine as he suckles my clit between his teeth.

I fall back on my elbows, barely able to support myself.

Deacon pushes a finger slowly inside me while he watches every reaction on my face. I can barely focus on his two gray eyes as he works a second finger in.

Another orgasm builds in my center and it won't be long before I'm coming all over his mouth.

"There's nothing better than watching you come for me."

I grip the edge of the desk, holding on for life. The second I'm about to release, he pulls away and stands back up.

He bends over and presses his forehead to mine, both of us panting, unable to form words, just staring into each other's eyes.

"Nothing better." He slides his cock back into me as he says the words, and a light groan comes from deep in his throat.

It's so sweet and intimate, almost like we're making love instead of just having sex. Deacon's hand cradles the back of my neck, and he pushes in and out, long deep strokes. Staring right at me, he licks the pad of his thumb, then reaches between us and rubs my clit.

Our eyes remain locked as he slowly increases the tempo, and before long we're fucking hard and fast.

His jaw constricts, and every muscle in his body tenses, just as my entire body reciprocates.

His thumb is relentless, right where I need it, and his hips crash into me until the wet slapping sounds of our skin echo through his office. My head falls back and I can't contain it anymore.

Deacon's mouth instinctively moves to my neck and he kisses me in that magic spot halfway between my collar bone and ear.

"Fuck, Quinn…"

My fingers grip the desk just as Deacon grunts. He slams into me as deep as he can go and we both erupt at the same time.

I clench around him so hard I wonder if it's painful for him. If it is, he doesn't show it. His entire body goes rigid as he fills the condom.

After a few long seconds, our foreheads meet again. We both pant, our lips inches apart, eyes locked.

I wait for some smart-ass remark that usually follows, but it doesn't come. He looks out of it, almost like he's in a dream-like state.

Deacon collapses into my neck, his lips on my skin, and I swear he whispers, "You're everything to me."

What the hell was that?

After a few seconds, he straightens up and his breathing returns to normal. "Fuck, I was good, wasn't I?"

That's more like him.

DEACON

"Fuck."

I run my fingers through my hair and rifle through my office for the stupid presentation I had Mary Magdalene, one of the paralegals, draft for me. I don't know her real last name, so that's the name we all gave her. She's always reading a bible at lunch and doesn't booze at all, so I figured she takes pride in her work.

There's a PowerPoint on my laptop, but she printed out the slides and I want to study them at least once. I have the speaking engagement at the college tonight.

Fucking Decker.

I'll get his ass back for this. He should know better. No sleight against me goes unpunished. I really need to read over those slides, so I sound like I know what the fuck I'm talking about. Can't be up there like it's amateur hour.

I should've faked being sick or canceled, but Decker would have my ass. I don't even want to imagine the pleasure it would give Tate.

Oh, no. They expect me to fuck up. They hope I will, to prove them right.

I'm going to crush this presentation and toss it back in their faces. I know exactly how they all see me. The immature brother who doesn't take anything seriously. The class clown. I know my role and I play it well. It is what it is.

One thing bothers me, though—Quinn.

I have this urge to do better, so she'll take me more seriously. It goes against everything I know, who I am.

Get out of your head, bro.

I find the print-out and start toward the elevator. I still have to finish up this contract for the Beckley brothers. I'll have to do it at home. Tate wanted it on her desk this morning, but I had to meet with the doctor over his sexual harassment case. I didn't find shit on the video, so it sucked giving him that news. Still, I know he didn't do anything, and I'll be damned if he pays his accuser a dime.

195

I'm sure I'll hear all about the contract being late. She knows I have a lot of stuff going on, but she won't give a shit.

"Ready for your lecture, professor?" Donavan laughs.

Asshole.

Decker ran his mouth and told everyone apparently.

"You're not going in that suit, are you?"

I stare back at him like *what the fuck are you talking about?*

"Shouldn't it be tweed with some elbow patches, Robert Langdon?"

"How's this for an ancient symbol?" I hold up my middle finger. "What's wrong? Bitter about your soon-to-be sister-in-law putting her dick in your lawsuit?"

Donavan's face steams up and he marches off. Pussy. Don't make jokes if you can't take the heat. I thought it was fantastic. Burned him and Tate at the same time, while calling Decker's masculinity into question. That's the trifecta—a fucking work of art. Layers upon layers of comedy, bitch.

Just when I think I have a second to relax, Dex walks up. "Don't fret, professor. I know what you're worried about."

"What's that?"

He adjusts my tie and tries to maintain a serious face. "Worried you're not qualified to instruct an intro to law class. It's a natural cause for concern, given your background in academia."

"This coming from the guy who made a C in intro to law. You should be mopping floors here."

Dex laughs. At least he doesn't take shit seriously like Donavan. God, he's been a real asshole lately.

"Then I could solve your cases at night on a blackboard, *Good Will Hunting* style."

"Yeah, yeah, I tossed that softball right down the fucking middle. Anyway, enjoy your night beating off to iPad porn while I'm balls-deep in college pussy."

"Nah, something tells me you won't even be looking at any of the chicks in there." An amused smile forms on his face.

What does he know?

I shrug it off. "Probably not. I'm sure it'll be a bunch of old bastards in their forties."

"Dude, you're in your thirties."

I shake my head. "Who the fuck goes to night school to be a lawyer?"

Dexter grins. "Anyway, that's not the reason."

Shit.

"Oh yeah? Enlighten me."

His eyebrows rise. "You're really gonna make me say it?"

I know people always talk about how twins have a connection, like they can sense things. You'd think they'd be full of shit, but they're not. I can take one look at him and see he knows I'm falling for someone. I don't know how, but he does.

I sigh. "No. Don't say it."

"All right, then. Go crush it. Picture your audience naked. I hear it helps."

"I'll picture you naked, big boy." I give a playful slap at his crotch and he leaps backward.

"Over the line."

"Nothing is off limits."

Dexter laughs and walks off. I head to the elevator. As the doors shut, I hear Decker running his mouth off in the background and more raucous laughter.

Assholes.

AT MY APARTMENT, I heat some leftovers from last night and pull the Beckley brothers' contract up on my laptop. They won a bid for a restoration project on a hotel. All the details seem to be in order except for the payment schedule we discussed. I read over the notes of the agreement and shovel a forkful of pasta into my mouth. Sauce splatters on my white Brioni shirt.

Fuck.

I look at the clock and realize I'll be late if I don't get moving. I punch in the number, mark it final, and send it to Quinn so she can get it delivered.

It's supposed to go through review, but I only changed one number and I'm already late getting it out the door.

I breathe a sigh of relief. Tecker (my new name for Tate and Decker) can get off my nuts now.

Typing Quinn's name on the screen brings up familiar feelings all over again. I haven't talked to her since I bent her over my desk.

You don't have time to think about her right now.

The voice in my head is correct for once. I change my shirt and give myself a once over in the mirror.

"Well, damn. You clean up nice, sir, if I do say so myself."

QUINN

I TAKE my usual seat at the front of the class, eager to find out who the guest speaker is.

I've always been a great student, ever since elementary school. If things had gone according to plan, I'd already be on a partner track and not a glorified secretary.

It is what it is. Dad had the stroke. I can't change the past, and I'll never complain about sacrificing my plans to care for him.

It eats at him enough as it is.

Taking care of family is what you do. He raised me by himself, and I would never abandon him for my own selfish reasons. If I have to work twice as hard as everyone else to achieve the same outcome, that's what I'll do.

I never thought I'd be the one taking care of him, though. It's difficult sometimes. Not the work, per se, but seeing him in this condition. He was so damn strong and independent when I was younger.

He'd never brushed a little girl's hair or played with Barbie Dolls, and he never complained once. He took care of me and pushed me to do my best. He still does.

The stroke turned our lives upside down. Taking care of him is hard work. His medications. His diet. Exercise. It's a lot for me to take on while working a full-time job and going to school, but I love the fact he knows I'm in his corner, that he doesn't have to face these challenges alone. Not a lot of people have that type of support system. And I get to hang out with him more than I would've under other circumstances. It helps get through the days to focus on the positive.

"Who do you think it's going to be?" Jillian slides into the seat next to mine.

We're basically the two eggheads who ask a ton of questions. Sometimes it elicits groans from the other students when our discussions push us past the end of class. I don't really care, though. I'm here to learn and get my money's worth.

"Don't have a clue." I smile at her.

She's a recently divorced single mom trying to provide a better future for her kids.

"I hope they're not as boring as the last one."

"Yeah, it's tough to make the tax code interesting, so I can't knock the guy too much."

Professor Billings enters the room and the place grows quiet.

"Good evening, everyone. We have a guest tonight. He's a man who could be your boss someday. Please give a warm welcome to Deacon Collins from The Hunter Group."

What in the fucking fuck? This can't be happening to me.

My mouth goes dry and my stomach twists in a knot. The color drains from my face when I look up and see Deacon.

He spots me on the front row and his eyes widen, then his lips curl into a grin and he winks.

I scowl back.

"Wow. I know where I want to work. Wonder if all the men at their firm are that hot?" Jillian mock fans herself.

If she only knew.

I bite my tongue to keep from saying something I'll regret. Like telling her he's off limits and mine. Or conversely, what a conceited asshole he is, or maybe how well he can use his hips and his tongue.

This can't be happening right now. My chest tightens and my stomach clenches at the thought of him bending me over his desk and making me come repeatedly.

Deacon gets his laptop and PowerPoint all set up. I know for a fact there's no way he put it all together. It looks like Mary's work. Of course, he didn't do the work himself, but he'll pull it all off because he's so damn charming and charismatic.

This is so damn embarrassing. I don't tell anyone in class where I work because my private life is just that... private. Also, I don't tell people from work I'm going to school at night. I don't want them to know that me, the assistant, wants to be a lawyer. A lot of lawyers at The Hunter Group are stuck up and don't think a secretary would be capable of doing their job. I've seen how some of them look down their noses at me.

Deacon starts up his lecture on tort law and how it's applicable in the real world. It's actually very helpful and I could learn a lot from it, but it's impossible to focus. All I keep thinking about is how I'm going to explain this to him later. There's no way he'll let it go.

"Seriously, though. How hot is this guy?" Jillian nudges me with her elbow when he unbuttons his sleeves and rolls them up his muscular forearms. "I wonder if I can get his number and get some help on Wednesday's exam."

Unable to control myself, I shoot her a dirty look when she raises her hand at the end of the lecture to ask questions, and I realize I'm being ridiculous.

I need to get the hell out of here before he talks to me.

I grab my stuff as quickly as I can and head for the door. I'm not sticking around to watch Jillian fawn all over him or hear one of his smart-ass remarks while he flirts with my classmate.

Jealousy courses through me as I rush from the building. I shouldn't feel this way, but this was my space. It was mine, and Deacon came barging through it like a wrecking ball. The thought of him asking Jillian out for drinks makes my blood run hot. I shouldn't care, but deep down I know one thing...

I do care.

A lot.

DEACON

IF QUINN CAN'T SEE the universe pushing us together, she needs her damn eyes examined. When I walked into the classroom and saw the open-toed heels she wore to work today, I couldn't contain the happiness that spread through my chest.

She rushes out of the classroom.

I interrupt some chick mid-sentence to chase after her. I had no idea Quinn wanted to be a lawyer. It makes sense. She'd be a damn good attorney.

I haul ass through the parking lot and catch her arm just as she's about to slide into the driver's side of her car.

"Where you running off to so fast? Going to get me an apple?" I grin. "In case you're wondering, yes, you *can* be the teacher's pet."

Her lips mash into a thin line and her body tenses. Shit. She looks pissed. Maybe it wasn't best to lead with a joke. I'm always fucking things up with her.

We both know she feels this spark between us. Why she continually fights it I'll never know. It would be a hell of a lot easier if she'd just give in to the attraction.

Fuck, it would make me a happy man. The happiest.

She pulls out her keys, unable to say anything, and slides into the driver's seat. Her face is fiery red.

I reach inside and stop her from putting them in the ignition. "Look, I'm sorry. I didn't mean to joke. Let me take you to dinner."

"I'm not hungry." Her words are short and laced with venom.

"Coffee then?" I raise my eyebrows to try and lighten the mood.

It doesn't work.

"I need to study."

"You can study over coffee. Get some coffee with me. Maybe I can help."

She exhales a deep breath. "It's not a good idea. Please, just let me go home."

"I didn't know you want to be a lawyer."

Quinn looks away. "I don't want to talk about it. And please don't say anything to anyone."

I hold up both hands. "Okay, I promise. But let me take you to get a cup of coffee. I won't even bring it up."

She glares up at me. "You're not going to leave me alone until you get your way, are you?"

I shake my head and grin. No words need to be said.

"Ugh. Fine. But I mean it, Deacon, no being a jerk."

I widen my eyes and feign innocence. "I'm never a jerk." Grabbing her bag from the back seat, I lead her to my car and wonder how fast she's going to try to run when she realizes I'm taking her to my place. Better save that news for when she's buckled in the car. I didn't say where we'd be going and coffee at my apartment is the best.

One fact isn't lost on me. I never take women home. She'll be the first.

My place is just that—mine.

I don't want them randomly showing up or leaving their purse or jacket as an excuse to return. It's my lair and it's off limits to women.

Well, it was, it seems.

Quinn is different. The thought of taking her there makes me a little anxious, but I can't help myself.

When I open the passenger door, she sinks down in the seat and her skirt rides up a little on her thigh. My cock attempts to spring to life and I will it to go back down in my pants. Handing her bag off to her, I jog around the back of the car and fold myself into the driver's seat. Quinn's eyebrows shoot up when Dr. Dre's *The Chronic* blares from the speakers.

I look over at her, turning the volume down. "What?"

She shrugs. "Nothing. Just took you as more of an 80s hairband kinda guy. Expected Van Halen."

"Hmm. What kind of shit you listen to? Let me guess. Taylor Swift?"

"No thanks. I'm more of a Foo Fighters kind of girl."

I nod. "Not bad. Not bad. It's kind of punk rock." I drag out the last syllable and it gets a small smile out of her.

One small step for man...

I navigate into the late evening traffic. We pass three coffee shops.

Quinn notices, craning her head to follow each one as we drive by. "Where are you taking us? Canada?"

"It's a great spot. Trust me." I grin and place my hand on the upper part of her leg that's still covered. She doesn't push it away, and I smirk to myself.

One giant leap...

I'm tempted to inch my hand up farther, but I don't want to piss her off...not yet. I'm surprised she even got in the car and I take victories when I can get them.

We arrive outside my building and Quinn wheels around on me. "Is this some kind of joke? I might stab you with my pen."

I bug my eyes at her. "No need to be violent, damn. You'll appreciate the view, and I make a good cup of coffee." I flash her a smile to ease her temper.

She folds her arms across her chest. It pushes her tits together, and I have an unbelievable urge to dive head-first right into them.

"Didn't know you were capable of operating a coffee pot."

"There's more to me than my big dick."

Her cheeks flush pink at the mention of my cock.

It's adorable when I know how dirty she can be.

She smacks my chest with the back of her hand. "Damn it, Deacon. You said you'd behave."

"Oh, please. I'm a perfect gentleman." I exit the car and open her door, grinning my ass off. "It's just anatomy. No need to be shy."

QUINN

"Make yourself comfortable. I'll get the coffee going." Deacon fumbles around his sleek, modern kitchen with stainless steel appliances. He looks clumsy in it, and I wonder if he's ever even made coffee before. It *is* nice to have him waiting on me for once. I've never seen him run his own errands, ever.

Moving through the apartment, I drop my bag on the kitchen counter. His place is the bachelor pad of all bachelor pads, and I wonder if I should sanitize my hands before I touch anything. Everything is oversized, from his giant television mounted on the wall to his black leather sofa that's large enough for three people to sleep on.

I explore the room more, taking in the decor. There are some black and white pictures of him with his brothers. It's when they were kids, and I can barely tell any of them apart. They all wear the same boyish grins on their faces.

I move down the line and there are a few pictures of him and Jenny, his niece. Decker's in a few of them. There are some signed Bears footballs that my dad would go nuts over. Walter Payton and Mike Singletary and Brian Urlacher. I shrug. I recognize the names and have heard them a million times, but that's about it. I'm not big into sports. I watch football with Dad on occasion because he loves it so much and we used to go to games when I was little.

The city slowly lights up below, building by building, as the sun fades over the horizon. Lake Michigan sits to the east and the pretty colors of the sunset play off the waters. Deacon was right about one thing. I do love the view. It's gorgeous. I stare out the floor-to-ceiling window that runs the length of his living room.

The smell of expensive coffee fills the air.

I guess he figured out how to make it. Good for him.

He approaches me from behind. "Be ready in a few minutes." He reaches around me. I'm so relaxed I start to lean back and stumble a little.

"Shit, Quinn." With cat-like reflexes, he catches me and for a long moment has me wrapped up in his arms. We linger for a bit before he stands me upright.

He snickers and reaches over to open a door that leads onto a small terrace.

God, I'm such a klutz around him.

The little balcony is beautiful. Large plants overflow from pots placed equidistant along the wall, and there are a couple huge lounge chairs.

I move onto the patio and take it all in. "Pretty breathtaking."

"Yeah, you are."

My stomach coils into a knot, and I wince internally at the same time. I shouldn't be around him yet I can't stay away.

"I like to sit out here and drink coffee when I work from home."

"I can see why."

He moves past me and flips on the outside light. "Have a seat and get comfortable. I'll grab your bag. There's an ethernet hook-up if you need the internet, or the Wi-Fi password is KimJongTateSucks. No spaces. First letter of each word capitalized."

I shake my head at him.

He shrugs. "What?"

"Nothing. Thanks." I sink down in the thick cushions of one of the chairs and try to imagine Deacon sitting here, mulling over his cases. He returns minutes later with my bag and a steaming mug.

I take a whiff and breathe it in. My eyebrows shoot up. It's hazelnut creamer and two sugars. No wonder he was fussing with it for so long. "How'd you know to make it like this?" I smile over the brim, blowing on the hot liquid before taking a sip.

He takes a seat in one of the other chairs, but his gray eyes fix on mine. "I pay attention more than you think. I notice every little detail about you, Quinn."

My cheeks warm and I'm not sure if it's the coffee or the words coming from Deacon's mouth. Probably both. "I should study." I know it's rude to cut him off when he's being so nice but it's all too much. I'm overwhelmed just being here and I really do need to go over my notes.

"I'll leave you to it. Need to make a phone call." He gets up from the chair and walks back toward the door.

Much to my surprise, Deacon stays true to his word. He leaves me alone for nearly thirty minutes before returning to refill my cup. He takes the pot back to the kitchen and returns with a cinnamon roll that is to die for.

"Now, that's good." I let out a long moan because it's just that delicious.

"I love when you make that sound." His penetrating eyes heat me up from within. Brushing his thumb over my lips, he sweeps some crumbs from my mouth then licks them off.

God, it's so damn sexy. I know he wants me in his bed, and if I don't get out of here quickly, he's going to succeed.

I gather my stuff. Surprisingly, he doesn't try to stop me.

"I should go. You said you'd be on your best behavior. This test is important. This class is crucial for school."

"Umm, okay. Didn't realize I wasn't behaving." He shakes his head like he's confused. "You know the firm offers scholarships for this sort of thing. I could put in a good word for you. We'd pay for your degree."

I shake my head vehemently. It immediately becomes clear in my mind just how different our upbringings were and how many miles apart we are from one another. Or maybe I'm just searching for an excuse to get out of here before his little plan works on me. "I don't take handouts. I'm no charity case. I want to do this on my own for me. You don't understand what that's like because you're used to having everything handed to you." I pause and take a deep breath. He didn't really deserve that but it just kind of slipped out. "Look, Deacon. I'm not like you. Where I come from you have to earn every damn thing you get."

His jaw ticks and he rubs his chin. I can see the intensity burning behind his steely gaze. I don't think he's ever been pissed at me before, but right now, the way he stares at me—he looks the part.

He doesn't explode, though. He sits there, calm. Almost mature, and I don't even know who I'm looking at now. It's like I'm finally staring at an adult.

"So, it's okay for you to just sum me up? Just like that?"

I shrink back in my seat a little. It's the closest we've ever had to a serious conversation and I'm in the wrong. It's unfamiliar territory.

Deacon stands up and paces toward the door. Now, the more the gears in his head spin, the more upset he looks. "Yeah, my life is so fucking easy. You know what it's like being Decker Collins' little brother? The baseball god. I could've been just as good as him, if not better, but I didn't want the pressure of living up to that. I loved baseball, but I played football just to spite him. Just to prove I could do something he couldn't. You think you know me, Quinn, but you don't. You don't even try."

I look down, unable to make eye contact with him.

He walks off toward the door but spins around at the last second. "I try with you. I try to be better. I've never done that for anyone. But I guess I'll never be more than some guy you fuck in the closet at work, right?"

His words are a slap across the face. It hurts—bad. The pain is almost unbearable because he's right. I've never really given him a fair chance. I've been hard on him and maybe I did put him in a box and not bother to look deeper. Maybe the humorous side of him is a defense mechanism he uses to hide who he really is.

I walk over and reach for his forearm.

He won't look at me. I can tell I hurt him, and he doesn't want me to see it. Even now, I get the feeling he's not doing it out of shame. He's trying to protect my feelings, from seeing I've wounded him.

"I'm sorry. You're right."

He finally turns and faces me. "Right about what?"

"Everything you just said."

He leans down and places both palms on my cheeks and stares deep in my eyes. When he looks at me like this all my walls crumble down and I want to let him in. But I'm scared to put my trust in him. I'm scared to fall. Deacon Collins thrills and terrifies me at the same time. He has the ability to hurt me. We both know it. But he's so damn vulnerable right now. He's letting me in, and I get the feeling he's never let anyone else see him like this or told them the things he just told me.

"Look, I like you, Quinn. I don't know what I have to do to make you see that it's real."

Before I can speak, his mouth connects with mine and everything fades away.

Sliding his coffee-stained tongue between my lips, the man makes love to my mouth like he's practiced on me his entire life. Lowering to his knees, he slides a hand up my skirt, teasing his fingers over my panties, but he rests his cheek against my stomach. "I don't want to fight with you."

Instinctively, I reach out and pull him closer to me. I bend down and whisper, "I know," against his jaw and move to unbutton his shirt.

He grabs my hand. "Slow down. We're not at work. We have plenty of time."

He's so sweet and intimate right now. I want it to last forever and at the same time I wish it was just another quickie so I wouldn't have to deal with all these new emotions swarming through me.

My mind races. Deacon makes me feel so damn dizzy and confused.

When we're about to kiss again, my phone buzzes from my bag and it breaks the spell between us. I pull it out and see my father's name light up the screen. "Shit. I gotta go. I'm sorry." I shove past him, nearly tripping over him as I rush to grab my things. My father expected me home an hour ago. He's probably worried.

"Quinn."

His word hits me in my back and I look over my shoulder to get one last look at him. I just want to see his face once more while he's fully exposed to me, showing me who he really is.

It's a mistake. The disappointment in his eyes burns a hole in my chest, but I just can't deal with this right now. I have too much going on with my dad and school.

If only circumstances were different. After everything he just told me, maybe we'd have a chance.

DEACON

A COLD SHOWER isn't enough to ease the pain after Quinn rushed out on me. I don't get her at all. She acts like I'm the one who plays games but she's yanking my strings like a fucking puppet master. I can't get her out of my head. The sugary taste of her lips. Her green eyes and auburn hair.

I completely opened up to her. I've never done that with anyone. It just sort of happened and all spilled out before I could stop it. That's the effect she has on me. But look what happened.

It's why I keep that shit bottled up inside. I hate harboring resentment, and I don't like to look weak. My whole life I've been told not to talk about my feelings. Suck it up and get the job done. Fucking around and joking keeps me from having to face the harsh realities of life and deal with that shit.

What I should do, is give up. But, I can't. I'm not a quitter and I know what the fuck I want.

Her.

I collapse on my bed and look at the clock wondering if she's awake and as horny as I am.

The woman drives me crazy. I want her here right now, next to me, in my arms. Not even necessarily to fuck her. I just love when she's around me, talks to me. Even if it's about real shit.

Yeah, there's no way in hell she's getting rid of me. I'm a persistent son of a bitch when I want something. She'll learn. She'll have dinner with me. I don't care if I have to back her into a corner and grind her down for years.

It's my mission. I'm starting to wonder if there's something wrong with me when it comes to her. I'm acting like a little bitch. It hurts when she constantly turns me down and tosses my flowers in the garbage. Especially when I know she wants me as much as I want her.

What's her fucking deal? If she'd just tell me, maybe I could move on, but she makes no goddamn sense.

At the same time, all of it only makes me want her more. She'll be mine.

I grab my cell phone off the nightstand and look at our last text exchange when she sent me the cleavage shot. It's hot as fuck but doesn't compare to the real thing. My finger hovers over the call button, and my cock grows harder at the thought of her voice and the way she feels when she trembles while I'm inside her. Fuck it. I need to hear her. Even if she yells at me.

"Why are you calling?"

"Why do you think?"

"Deacon…" My name trails away. She's warring with herself, I can tell.

Just talk to me, woman! Let me in that brain of yours.

"I'm trying to study."

"I need you."

"I'm not talking dirty to you over the phone. I'm sure you have a list of women on reserve." She pauses. "Sorry, I didn't mean that. I'm just…"

"No, you're not wrong. But none of them make me feel the way you do. You're the one that does it for me. There's nothing I love more than wrapping my hand around your throat while you come undone."

She breathes heavily into the phone and I make a fist around my dick.

"Come on. At least tell me what you're wearing."

"Fine. You want to know what I'm wearing?"

My cock hardens in my palm. Now, we're getting somewhere. "Hell yes."

"I just took a bath and shaved."

I fight back a groan. "Keep going."

"I shaved everywhere. Completely bare except for a little strip of hair and I can't stop running my fingers over my body wishing they were yours."

"I do believe I like the sound of that. You're pretty good at this." I pump my cock a couple times in my hand. "Keep going."

"Hmm…I want to drag my nails through your hair, pulling and pushing your head between my legs, shoving your mouth on me. I'm imagining your tongue licking me up and down, getting me nice and wet for you."

"God, I'm so close, Quinn." I can already feel a load of epic proportions building in my balls. I didn't expect her to talk so dirty over the phone.

"God, Deacon. You feel so good. I want you inside me right now. I'm using my fingers but it's not enough. I want you to take control. I need you inside me so bad." She lets out a loud moan, but it's too loud. It almost sounds like a shitty porn actress screaming while the dude fucks her.

"You're not really touching yourself, are you?"

She belts out a laugh. "No. I'm sitting here staring at my notes wearing an oversized nightgown, pink fuzzy bunny slippers, and a green mud face mask."

I let out a sigh of disapproval. "All wood gone. Totally deflated."

She giggles, clearly amused with herself, and it's ridiculously cute. "You brought it on yourself, sir."

"If you come over, I could probably tie a stick to it and still get it inside."

"Goodnight, Deacon." She dies laughing and the line goes dead.

My head falls back on my pillow and I stare down at my cock. "Just a minor setback, buddy. It won't stop us." I close my eyes and allow my thoughts to drift back to the fantasy she built moments ago. I imagine Quinn lying on her bed naked with her legs spread, stuffing her pussy with three fingers while thinking about my cock.

My dick rallies in my hand, hard once again.

Told you.

I stroke back and forth, until I'm fucking my hand so hard my arm slaps against my thighs. I'd sum it up as vigorous masturbation. The woman drives me nuts. Her moans play through my mind. I can see it now, a crystal-clear image.

I bet she's touching herself, wishing she hadn't hung up on me. Her fingers are slick and she's thinking about riding me. Fuck. If I knew where she lived, I'd go over there right now and take what I want. If I was there, she'd give in. Quinn thinks she's pushing me away but she's only amping this situation up to eleven.

She knows that smart mouth of hers turns me on.

Sweat beads across my forehead. Quinn has me hot and bothered that's for damn sure.

God.

I let out a groan and jerk harder and faster, thinking about what it'd be like to come inside her, mark her as mine. Fuck, that's like my all-time fantasy rolled into one. Afterward, I'd pull out and put her down on her knees so she could clean her pussy off my cock with her tongue.

The vision loops through my head until I can't take it anymore. Hot spurts of come shoot up onto my stomach. I lie there, breathing heavily, hand all sticky.

I should get myself cleaned up, but just the thought of fucking Quinn totally wipes me out.

I've got it for this woman—bad.

QUINN

My alarm sounds and I groan, covering my head with my pillow. I'm so not ready to get up and get this day started. The first part of my morning is spent getting Dad out of bed and into his chair so he can take care of his morning business. Our bathroom is handicapped accessible so that takes some stress off both of us. Once he's situated and I'm sure he doesn't need my help with anything, I start breakfast and get ready for work. I still have nearly two hours, but the time will fly. I know from experience.

Some days go smoother than others, depending on Dad's strength. On a great day he functions with little help but on a bad day, he can barely hold a cup of water. Today's a good day and I breathe a sigh of relief. A few times he's fallen out of his chair or nearly caught the apartment on fire trying to do too much on his own. He's truly as stubborn as they come.

He wheels himself out of the bathroom and slides into his spot at the table. I notice some small pieces of tissue where he tried to shave and cut himself.

"I could've helped." I motion toward his jaw as I plate his eggs and toast.

"I've been thinking, kiddo."

Here we go. I already know what's coming.

"Yeah? What's that?"

"I should move into one of those assisted living places. You've got enough to worry about without working so damn hard all the time to take care of my old ass. This isn't the life I want for you."

I smile. He brings this up at least once a week. "There's nothing I'd rather be doing. You need to stop. When Mom left, you could've dumped me off with the state. It would've been easier. But, you didn't."

"That's different. That was the best damn day of my life. You gave me purpose. Being your dad made me a better man."

215

I stand up and give him a peck on the cheek. "I love you, Dad. No more talk about you living in a home. Got it?" I point at him with a butter knife.

"Fine. Got it, kiddo. Breakfast is good." His hand trembles as he brings his mug to his lips, and I pretend not to notice. I hate that his health has declined so much these past few years.

"Thanks. Your lunch is in the fridge. Tuna sandwich and fruit salad." I finish my breakfast and rinse our plates in the sink. I glance at the clock and notice I'm making good time.

Before I leave for work, I get the television set up for him. He loves Classic Sports on ESPN and they're airing an old Bears game.

Some of my fondest memories are going to games with him when I was a kid. His buddy Joe always went with us. God rest his soul. I know Dad misses him. I do too. They were like partners in crime. Not a single Sunday night passed by when they didn't go out for a beer and to watch a game, once I was old enough to stay home by myself. I worry about him getting lonely. It's been almost a year since Joe passed. He needs someone his age he can relate to.

I kiss him on the forehead and gather up my stuff. "I should be home for dinner tonight." I point a finger at him. "Stay out of trouble."

"Oh, don't worry about me. Just inviting over a few strippers and the Ronnie kid from down the hall. He has the best weed."

I shake my head. "Don't burn the place down. And no cigars!" I found his new stash hidden down in his recliner last week. Ronnie sneaks them in when I'm at work. Dad has all the neighbors on our floor wrapped around his finger.

As soon as I get to my car Heather calls to tell me about her wild night with Stewart.

"I think he might be the one."

I roll my eyes. "Every man is the one with you."

"Hey, some of us enjoy sex."

"I get plenty of attention. Don't worry about me."

"Is that where you disappeared to Saturday when you stood me up?"

"Got called into work." My cheeks flush thinking about how Deacon bent me over his desk and had his way with me. I wonder if he's pissed I left him hanging after our phone call.

"Is that what the kids are calling it these days?"

"Stop it. We're so not talking about this."

"Killjoy. We *will* talk about this. Soon. Over drinks. You should come by the store this Friday. We're having a big sale."

"Gotta go. I'm driving."

"Bye, bitch."

I drop my cell phone in the passenger seat and focus on the morning commute. I definitely don't think about Deacon Collins at all on the way to work.

DEACON

THE MOMENT I get off the elevator at work, Tecker awaits me with huge smirks on their faces. "Welcome back, professor." Decker snickers.

Tate gives me the evil eye. I swear, Decker needs to fuck her better because she always looks pissed off. It's sad too, because she can hurl insults with the best of them, and they're pretty damn funny.

"You'll be happy to know the lecture was a success. They liked me so much they invited me back next week."

Decker smiles like he's almost proud.

"The offer was later rescinded after I was caught with my pants down and the top student's lips wrapped around my... Well, you get the idea." I wink.

My brother's face hardens, and he narrows his gaze on me. "You better be fucking joking."

I love that he's not sure. I hold my hands up like I'm weighing something with an invisible scale. "Maybe I am maybe I'm not." I shrug. "That's what you want to hear, right? That it was a shitshow."

Asshole.

Truth be told, I crushed that presentation. Every student in that class will be applying at The Hunter Group when they graduate.

So Tecker can eat a shit pie.

I head toward my office as they go into the boardroom for a meeting with Cole Miller, and conference call with Weston Hunter.

Weston's the big swinging dick in Dallas who took over our firm. I shouldn't say he took over. They kept the name, but that's about it. We all work together in a large partnership. Weston is Tate's former boss and one of Decker's old friends.

Tate, God, that woman. We got along for a brief second, but I just find that I don't like her all that much. She's too intense. Her and Decker are a match made in heaven. I bet they sit around and go over their itinerary for the day in the mornings. Probably have a set schedule for every sexual position and have it mapped out to the second.

And my brother is going to marry her. He proposed once our merger with The Hunter Group was complete. I should try harder to get along with her, but she makes it difficult. She thinks she runs this firm and it pisses me off. We've built this thing for a decade and she acts like she can walk up in here and start bossing people around.

Fuck that.

She wasn't even a goddamn partner until the merger went through. When Decker started the firm, it was supposed to be something for us—the Collins brothers. Not the Collins brothers and Tate.

I get why he did it; for Jenny. Part of me is happy he gets more time with her, but we could've figured out a different way without bringing in some ass clowns from Texas. If he'd just sat us down and talked to us instead of making the final decision and ambushing us with it.

I do remember one thing, though. Decker fucked with me by sending me to the college. Thought he got one over on me.

That shall not go unchecked. It's just not my style.

Smirking to myself, I walk into his office and start messing with all his shit like I did when we were kids. I'd rearrange his toys and he'd damn near bust a blood vessel.

I go into Microsoft Office and change all the settings and fonts, then switch the language to Afrikaans. It's the first one I don't recognize. That'll take some time. I'm sure he didn't set it all up himself, so he'll need to get Quinn or someone from IT to fix it.

I plan to do enough damage it keeps him occupied half the afternoon. Once I'm satisfied with his computer, I turn the brightness on his monitor all the way down until his screen is black. His dumb ass will probably think it's not turning on. That'll occupy him for a bit until he figures it out, then he'll have to deal with all his settings.

Next, I start in on his desk and tape all his pens to the underside of his chair. He's going to fucking lose it.

I snicker to myself, mixing his paperclips and extra staples up after I empty the stapler. Yes, it's childish but I don't care. Serves him right for forcing me into that bullshit speaking engagement. Sure, I got to see Quinn out of the deal but that's beside the point.

Decker never takes me seriously. If he wants to treat me like an annoying kid brother, that's how I'll behave. I eye a stack of files that look important and wonder how much shit I'd get in if they were misplaced. Sure, I'm an asshole but that might be pushing things too far and actually hurt a client. I leave them alone and move to his bookshelf instead, rearranging all the titles with the spines facing inward.

Finally finished, I survey my handiwork and smile to myself.

That'll do.

When I exit Decker's office, I spy Quinn at her desk talking to some guy with tattoos up his neck and down to his knuckles. I don't like the way he's looking at her.

Fuck, she looks hot as balls too. She's wearing a navy-blue skirt with a slit on the right side that teases at the lace tops of her thigh-highs.

I have to force down a groan and adjust myself when nobody is watching.

She smiles wide at the man and motions for him to follow her. My jaw ticks as jealousy spikes in my veins. It's a feeling I'm not used to, and one I don't like. I never get jealous. I already had a taste of it with that dipshit at the club, and I don't like it any more today. I never care if women I fuck see other people. Quinn isn't just any other woman, though.

As they near, I recognize the man now. Cole Miller, one of Dex's old buddies. He owns a chain of gyms and used to be a professional MMA fighter. He could probably kick the shit out of me. I wouldn't seek out a fight with him, and he's a client, but I don't give a fuck.

I'd die trying, if it came to that.

Quinn is mine and I don't appreciate the way he's eye-fucking her in that skirt. His gym is being sued in a huge body shaming case. Decker has been working around the clock on it. It's why he stuck me with those contracts for the Beckley brothers.

"Cole Miller, Deacon Collins." Quinn introduces us as she walks past me to get to Decker's office.

I exchange a quick handshake with the guy and his damn grip feels like it might crush a few bones. I don't wince at all, though. Because fuck him.

"They're in the boardroom." I nod toward the hall.

"Thanks." She shoots me a smile and turns to Cole. "If you'll give me a moment, I'll let Mr. Collins know you're here."

He smiles at me then stares at her ass as she walks away. My hands ball into fists at my sides. I want to tell him to wipe that fucking grin off his face, but I know I need to be on my best behavior. Decker really would fire my ass if I fucked this case up for him.

"Good luck with everything." My words come out through gritted teeth.

"Thanks."

I hang back and wait for Quinn to show him in. When she returns to her desk, she's all smiles, and it better not be because Cole was flirting with her.

"Have a hard time getting off last night after our phone call?"

I rub my jaw and grin. "Not at all." I lean in close and whisper in her ear, "Never came so hard in my life, but if you're still in need of some relief I'd be happy to help out. It's getting close to lunch time and I'm starving." My lips brush the shell of her ear.

"Maybe you should get something to eat."

I whisper, "Your pussy is the only thing I'm hungry for."

By the way she just shivered a little at my words, I know I'll be meeting her in the supply closet soon, I just have one thing I need to take care of first.

———

RICK LAWRENCE, our firm's private investigator, knocks on the door to my office.

"Come in." I close out a few windows on my computer and stand to shake his hand.

If anyone can solve my problem, it's him. He might be the cockiest bastard I've ever met, and he's surrounded by the Collins brothers every day. That's saying something. He's early thirties and dressed in some tattered jeans and a Led Zeppelin stretch tee.

He takes a seat and kicks his feet up on my desk. That's how you know he's the best at what he does. Dude has the balls to walk around like he owns the place, and nobody says shit to him about it. He's a fucking magician and about to make my life a lot easier.

"What's up?"

"You know that case I'm dealing with? Flynn? The heart surgeon? Sexual harassment shit?"

"Yeah. Heard he gave some broad a slap on the ass and a 'well done.'" He smirks like he doesn't see anything wrong with that scenario.

I have to fight back a laugh at his nonchalant attitude. "Yeah, it's total bullshit, but it's all he said, she said at this point. What I need from you is to do a full background work up and tail her around. I want to know who she meets with, who she's friends with, everything. Dig hard on it, but don't let her know you're there."

"No problem. I'll be a fucking ninja."

"Perfect. This is top priority; put it ahead of everything else. I don't give a shit what any of my brothers say."

His eyebrows rise. I know exactly what the gesture means.

"Your cooperation will not go unnoticed." Usually, I hook him up with some tickets to the firm's suite at Soldier Field.

He leans in. "I need something a little different this time. Call it alternate consideration."

Interesting.

"What do you have in mind?"

"There's a lot of new Dallas pussy running around this place."

He may be the most misogynistic person I've ever met. "I may have noticed."

"I want first dibs on my choice, above Donavan and Dex."

Fuck, this might be more difficult than I thought.

"I'm not a damn pimp. Won't some football tickets work?"

Rick smirks. "Won't need any help from you. Just keep them out of my way. I can handle the rest. Trust me."

I don't doubt what he's saying. I've never seen him have a problem landing some ass.

"Did you have someone in mind?"

He slow nods. "Oh yeah. Mary."

"Magdalene? The new paralegal who reads a bible during lunch and wears long skirts?"

Rick leans back in his chair. "That's the one."

I shake my head. "Well, I think you're fine on that front. I've seen Dexter ogling Abigail nonstop, and neither of my brothers like to work to get laid. Mary's not really their type."

"Well then. Consider this little problem of yours taken care of."

"Perfect. Let me know as soon as you find something."

He stands up. "No problem. I'll get right on it, as soon as I'm done brushing up on a few bible verses." He tosses me a shit-eating grin. "I'll get out of your way. I know you have somewhere to be."

"Where's that?"

"Supply closet." He walks out the door.

I stare at the door where Rick just walked out, shaking my head.

How the fuck does he know everything?

That guy is a goddamn enigma.

QUINN

THE WORKDAY DRAGS by and Deacon and his not-so-subtle hints don't help matters. I can't get the thought of him going down on me out of my head. It's bad. The man has turned me into a sex addict. How does he know which buttons of mine to press nonstop? He's relentless.

It pisses me off but here I am checking the clock and fidgeting with my pen, knowing I should stay far away from him. My line buzzes with a call from Tate.

"We're taking Mr. Miller out to lunch. I expect it to be a while so if you have anything you need to do, take an extra thirty minutes."

"Um, yeah. Thanks."

Tate is nice.

I know Deacon and her butt heads a lot, but I like her. She's friendly and sometimes we go to lunch together. It's nice to see a strong female lawyer who doesn't take shit from the guys and can hold her own. I hope to be like her once I pass the bar. I can relate to her. She's been here for months and doesn't seem to be great at making work friends. I suspect it has more to do with people thinking she was a spy, and now, she's suddenly Decker's fiancée.

It doesn't bother me. I'm glad to see Decker happy. He's actually loosened up some since she arrived. Tate was exactly what he needed, and speaking of need... I'm in need of some relief.

I should be taking the extra thirty minutes to study but there's always tonight.

Let's see. Study or have Deacon's mouth on me?

The boardroom doors open. Tate smiles at me, and Decker and Mr. Miller follow her to the elevator.

Pulling out my cell phone, I fire off a text to Deacon.

Quinn: You have five minutes. No more.

I make a quick trip to the bathroom to freshen up and decide to mess with

Deacon and take off my panties before he can steal them this time. I've bought more underwear these past few months than I have my entire life. I should hit him up for a gift card to Victoria's Secret the next time he wants to send me flowers. He owes me.

What the hell does he even do with them? Wait, I don't want to know.

By the time I get to the closet more than five minutes has passed and Deacon is waiting.

The irritated look on his face smooths into that devilish smirk of his. Those stormy grays narrow on me. "You're late."

He yanks me inside and shoves my chest flat against the wall, then pins me in from behind. The manly scent of his cologne wraps around me and I breathe him in.

He makes me crazy. I feel so wild and free in the moments we're together. When it's the two of us there are no expectations. No commitments. I'm not running here and there trying to keep up with life. I'm not a student or caregiver or, hell, even a friend. I'm simply me, and Deacon never fails to make me feel a whole lot better.

His mouth connects with my neck with such raw passion it nearly takes my breath away. He sucks at my throat, almost hard enough I'm worried he'll leave marks. I should fight against him, but I can't. I'm a slave to him as his hands roam down my legs and tug my skirt up.

"Thought you were cute with that performance last night, didn't you?"

"Deacon...I'm sorry about..."

"No, you're not." He removes his jacket and tosses it on the floor, then spins me around. "On your knees."

I glare back at him. "Thought you were having me for lunch?"

He shrugs. "Plans change. On your knees, Quinn."

God, he's so commanding.

I kneel in front of him.

When he unzips his pants, his thick cock juts out of his slacks.

Maybe it won't be so bad. He never fails to provide me with orgasms, so it really is only fair, and I don't mind. Licking my lips, I'm eager to taste him. Eager to please him. Gripping his cock, Deacon tilts his hips and feeds it to me slowly. I've only done this for him, but he doesn't know that.

The first time his size terrified me, but I got used to it. I love the sounds he makes when I put him in my mouth. Deacon is all alpha but when I go down on him, I'm the one in control. My lips wrap around the crown and I swirl my tongue along the tip, tasting and teasing him. His fingers dig into my scalp and hold my head in place. Flattening my tongue on his shaft, I take him deeper and suck until my lips stretch and burn to accept more of him. I bob up and down and gag when he begins to fuck my mouth.

"Fuck, Quinn." He groans.

I reach up with my hand and stroke the rest of him that doesn't fit. I may have watched some porn to try and learn how to do it better, after my first time with him.

He finally pulls back and stares down at me, breathing heavily with intense eyes. "You keep that up and this will be over faster than I want."

"You don't have much time left."

"Right." He reaches down and helps me up from my knees.

I watch him go through the motions of putting on a condom and nervously wait for what's to come.

DEACON

QUINN GLANCES over her shoulder at me. She's braced against the back of the supply room door, skirt shoved up to her stomach, her bare ass sticking out, ready and waiting.

Part of me frowns internally, wondering how much better it'd be if she'd at least let me take her someplace nice with a fucking bed. Not that the sex isn't good. It's fucking phenomenal, but she's better than this. I want more with her than to fuck in this closet.

I want to lay her down and take my time instead of being so damn rushed. Not that the thought of getting caught isn't a turn on. It definitely is.

Fuck, I can't stay away from her. I think about her all the time. When I wake up, I can't wait to get to the office just to see what she's wearing, and when I lie down at night, I don't think about fucking her at all.

I picture what it'd be like to take her out to dinner, hold her hand, and show her there's more to me than a childish bastard in a suit who plays games and fucks like a god. Her words not mine, to be fair.

I damn sure won't tell her I don't want to fuck her right now, though. That will never happen. I take what I can get. Stepping up behind her, I line up with her and glide right in because she's so damn wet.

"Fuck, that's nice." Gripping her hips, I slam into her, wishing I could feel her skin to skin. I never fuck without a condom but for her I'd take the risk, just for that deeper connection. I keep that thought to myself. One, because it scares the hell out of me to think like that and two, I don't want to run her off. I don't know when I went from lust to like, but I really like this woman. More than a little. More than a lot, even.

Quinn trembles under my touch when I slide a hand around her waist and stroke her clit.

"Oh, shit." She lets out a whimper, and I cover her mouth to muffle her moans.

I wish I could see her on top of me just once. Lack of space has never permitted her to ride me. I'm tempted to throw her over my shoulder and take her to the couch in my office. Watch her breasts bounce while she grinds on my cock.

There's an old folding chair in the corner. The gears in my brain start to turn. It might just work.

I want to see her face when she comes. As I pull out, she gives me an evil eye. A look that might kill lesser men. I unfold the chair and sit down, holding my cock straight up.

Quinn saunters toward me and she's like all my fantasies rolled into one with each sway of her hips. Lowering herself to my lap she eases herself down onto me, gripping my shoulders. Her tits rub up against my chest, and I love every second of her pressed to me—as close as she can get. She kisses me with an intensity I've never felt before. I'm getting to her. Inch by inch, I know I am.

Hips grinding, bodies rocking, we fuck fast and hard. She bounces up and down as her ass claps on my thighs. The only things passing between us are heavy breaths and stifled moans. Her eyes burn a hole into my retinas. Clenching her muscles tight, she shivers and shakes, mumbling my name against my neck.

I fist a handful of her hair and tug her head back. "Eyes on me when you come."

Once she rides out her orgasm, she looks sated and completely spent. I smack her ass, trying to bring her back to the present, and order her to bend over the counter.

Quinn may have come already, but I haven't. Not that I'm too far behind, though. I'm so damn close. What I want is to rip this condom off and really feel her, but I don't. I shove into her from behind and fuck my frustrations out. A tremble starts in my legs and my balls lift and tighten. I try to hold back as long as I can, but the intensity is too much as the orgasm inches up my shaft.

All I can say is, "Fuck, Quinn," as I blow into the condom.

The whole time I imagine what it'd be like to come inside her. The thought of marking her as mine overwhelms me.

It's an obsession.

One day.

After a few moments of heavy breathing, we both look at each other and smile. Fuck me. I don't know how I'm supposed to go back to work after that.

I feel like a little bitch, because all I want to do is hold her in my arms and sleep. Then fuck her again when I wake up, of course. I've never felt this way with anyone. I've never wanted much of anything until Quinn came along. She makes me feel like I can take over the world. Makes me want to be better for her.

QUINN

WHEN TATE INVITED me to lunch at The Capital Grille, I couldn't say no. I should be studying for my test, but this place is amazing and I'm starving. I was slammed all morning with the Cole Miller case and running errands for Donavan because his secretary called in sick.

"You've been quiet lately." Tate picks at the olives in her salad.

"Just have a lot going on." I sip my water and hope she sticks to talking about her. "Haven't seen you much since you got that giant rock on your finger."

Tate flashes her ring at me and smiles. "It *is* nice, isn't it?"

I nod. "It's gorgeous. Have you set a date?"

"No. We can't even agree on a location right now. My family's in Texas, but Decker's family is here. Well, his parents are in Florida, but all the brothers." I don't miss the disdain in her voice when she mentions the Collins brothers.

It's almost Shakespearean how none of them get along.

I take a piece of bread and slather it with butter. "Jenny still cool with you?"

She leans back and grins. "We get along great. Have a lot of fun going shopping on the weekends. Decker's credit card on the other hand…not so much."

"I can imagine."

"What about you?" She leans in, staring hard, but grins as she speaks. "Anybody special in your life?"

I look up and away before I catch myself. I shrug and try to play it off. "Just my dad." It's not a lie. I'm not dating Deacon.

"Dad sending you all those flowers?"

I swear she gets off on interrogating me. I shake my head. "Nah. Some guy who can't take a hint."

"We have a new employee coming up from Dallas. Well, I've known him for years, but he'll be new here. I could set something up."

229

My cheeks redden and I wonder what Deacon would think of that. "Isn't that against company policy? I don't mean you and Decker obviously but…" God, I want to shove my foot in my mouth.

She tucks a golden curl behind her ear and shrugs. "It's fine as long as he's not your superior and it doesn't get in the way of work. Technically, you work for Decker and well, he's taken." She leans in and lowers her voice. "The latest rumor around the office is either Deacon or Dexter has been taking someone in the supply closet for some extracurricular activities. Would you know anything about that?"

Shit.

My face has to be white as a ghost, but I shovel some food in my mouth and shake my head. "I don't pay attention to those clowns."

Tate grins, and I know she sees right through my bullshit. The woman can read any situation. "You'll keep an eye out and let me know if you see anything? Last thing we need is trouble because those idiots can't keep it in their pants."

"Absolutely." I nod.

This lunch can't end soon enough.

BY THE TIME I get home from my exam, Dad's already asleep. I clean up the remnants of his dinner and tidy the apartment up a little. I crushed my test and feel like a huge weight lifted from my shoulders. I can breathe easy for a bit, until the next one.

Heating up some leftovers, I curl up on the couch and channel surf. I can't remember the last time I watched TV. Ironically, I feel like my only down time is spent with Deacon, which is ten minutes here and there. Even when I tried to go out with Heather, I ended up with him. I know it's pathetic, but the second I think about him, I have this urge to call and tell him about my test. He's the only person I know who can relate and knows I'm going to law school. I should be exhausted, but I'm wired after dumping all that information from my brain. Sleeping is not an option at the moment.

I pull up Deacon's number as I walk to my bedroom, and I'm torn. Should I call him? I want to so damn bad, but I'm not sure it's the greatest idea.

After a quick battle with myself, I collapse onto my bed and hit the send button. He answers on the third ring, and I hope I didn't wake him up.

"What's up?" He doesn't sound tired at all.

I'm not sure if I should be happy or if it should bother me. Is he out with someone? I shouldn't feel jealous. I don't even know if he is, but it's all my brain can focus on. There's only one way to find out.

"Hopefully your dick."

He clears his throat, loud, and doesn't fire back any sarcastic remarks or play along.

Like an idiot, I continue. "Just got home and was thinking about the supply closet yesterday when I had you in my mouth. I was so damn wet."

I'm about to ask why he's so quiet when I hear a woman's voice in the background. "Sir, your table's ready. Will your date be joining you soon?"

"Quinn, I'll have to call..."

"Don't bother." I end the call and bite back the rage building in my chest.

I shouldn't even be upset, and I feel dumb for being hurt when I don't even know what he's doing or who he's with. Not to mention, I knew who Deacon was when we started up this little fling. This is exactly why I've turned him down every time he's asked me out. Still, I can't help the way I feel right now.

Stupid feelings.

Stupid Deacon.

Stupid supply closet.

No more.

I can't go there again with him.

I won't do it to myself.

DEACON

I STARE DOWN at my phone when Quinn hangs up.

What the hell just happened? She didn't even let me finish.

I glare at the hostess for using the word 'date' to describe this meeting, but I know it's not her fault.

Still, I don't even think Quinn heard it and she can't be that pissed off if she did. I'll just tell her what really went down later and everything will be fine.

Karen Richardson called when I left the office and asked to meet. She's the asshole employee in Cole Miller's lawsuit who took the photographs and posted them online. I almost told her to piss off, but maybe she has information I can pass along to Decker, if I can pry it out of her. There's no way in hell I'd ever represent her, but maybe this can get Tecker off my ass.

When she walks in, every male head in the restaurant turns in her direction. She's one of those women who looks like a knockout from far away. She has huge fake tits and probably a plastic ass to match it, platinum blonde hair, tight mini skirt. You know the deal. Up close there's not a natural thing on her body, skin all shiny and stretched across her face.

I turn to the hostess. "Hold on, I think that's her."

She walks up. "Deacon Collins?"

I nod and shake hands with her.

We follow the hostess through the crowded bar to a private table in the back. It's a walled booth with a table and a chair on the other side. I take the booth because I'm Deacon Collins and I like to be comfortable. The crazy bitch slides in next to me.

What the fuck?

My mind immediately flashes to Quinn and my stomach ties in a knot,

233

knowing what she'd think if she saw this. I shake myself from my thoughts, because I need to see if this chick has any information we can use.

Once we order drinks, she snuggles right into my side and it's painfully obvious this woman is coming on to me.

Every other man in the restaurant is probably jealous as shit right now, and until a few months ago, I'd be totally open to this. But not now.

I have to get the hell out of here.

I slide away from her, trying to create some kind of separation between us. "What can I do for you, Ms. Richardson?" Maybe she'll take the hint when I use her last name.

She makes a show of flipping her hair. "I didn't mean for things to get so out of control. Haven't you ever done something you regretted?" She flutters her fake lashes at me.

I want to tell her yeah, I know exactly what she means, like agreeing to meet her for drinks. I can already tell this is a waste of time. Maybe I can salvage something out of it to pass off to Tecker, though. "What was your intention when you posted the photos?"

"It didn't start out malicious. I was taking selfies at work and that cow just happened to be in the background reflected in the mirror. I didn't notice her at first, but my girlfriends pointed it out to me, and we had a laugh. It was just a joke. I don't see what the big deal is. It was harmless. I know I should've taken them down the minute she saw them, but my post was getting so many likes and shares. It felt like I was famous until my account got shutdown and everyone turned on me." She leans in close and presses her cleavage damn near on my arm. "I called you because I'm hoping you can sell the rights or something. I don't know what it's called. Maybe I can get some sort of movie deal out of this. I'd look good on TV, don't you think?"

This woman might be the biggest dipshit I've ever met.

Not only does she want a movie deal out of what she did, she called the fucking attorneys representing her former boss. Her hand on my thigh is a clear indication of exactly what she's willing to do to get it.

I push down the rage building in my chest, and somehow manage to politely remove her hand from my leg. All I can think about is Quinn and how pissed she would be if she saw what was happening.

"Do you practice entertainment law? We'd look great together in the media. I looked up your brother and saw he's engaged but you're better looking anyway."

Part of me is so shocked at this woman, it makes it difficult to stand up and get the fuck out of here. I glance at my watch and down the rest of my drink, trying to play it cool before I make my escape because she's clearly a stage five clinger.

"Do you think Cole would want to team up?"

Is she serious? Cole fired her. "No."

She frowns.

I bite back all the shit I want to say to her. "I apologize, but I won't be able to help you. Good luck, though." I walk from the table without looking back. I don't want to turn around and give her some reason to come chasing after me.

The minute I'm out the door, I already have Quinn's number pulled up. We need to talk. I have to tell her how I feel and make her understand, because I can't keep these emotions in check. She keeps sending me to voicemail and it's really starting to piss me off. If I knew her address, I'd drive straight to her damn house.

QUINN DIDN'T RESPOND to any of my calls or texts all night long or this morning. The second I walk in the office I search for her. She isn't at her desk or in the breakroom. I even check the freaking bathroom. She's clearly going out of her way to avoid me.

Is she that pissed off?

Surely not, but it makes me even more determined to find her. She's going to talk to me one way or the other. When I get to my desk, I call and order her flowers and two boxes of chocolate this time.

It's Friday after all. Some traditions are sacred.

She might throw them away, but she can't hide that quick smile that lights up on her face every time.

She's permanent relationship material. The kind of woman you take home to meet the parents. I never thought I could do the serious thing, but she's it. Deep down, I've known all along. I can't stop thinking about it—about her. Non-stop, twenty-four seven, on a fucking loop, Quinn on the brain. Taking this to the next level is my only option because I can't see myself ever not wanting to be with her.

On my way to lunch, I finally catch her at her desk but the second she sees me she bolts from her chair.

Part of me is flustered, but I'm a competitive son of a bitch. It only fuels the fire.

Two can play this game. Does she really think she can avoid me forever? I pull out my phone and put my plan into action.

Check mate, Quinn.

QUINN

A NOTIFICATION from Outlook pings on my phone.

What the hell?

I open it and the bright red letters jump out at me. It's a meeting request with Deacon and it's marked urgent. It has the exclamation point and everything.

He doesn't set up meetings. I can't believe he even figured out how to work the damn thing.

My face heats up and the hackles on the back of my neck rise. It's just like him to abuse his authority to get his way.

If I don't show for the meeting he could go to Decker and get me in trouble for insubordination. I wouldn't put it past him to make up some reason why he needs to meet and make me look bad for not responding.

The worst part is he knows me damn near as well as I know myself. When I have something on my schedule, I *have* to check it off. It's one of my biggest pet peeves; tasks lingering and not closed out. I grind my teeth as I hit accept on the meeting.

He's a jerk.

THE TIME for us to meet rolls around, and I march into his office—on time—to give him a piece of my mind.

"Shut the door and have a seat." He speaks before I can get a word in and it flusters me even more.

The smug bastard grins from behind his big desk. Man, he looks powerful in his Saint Laurent three-piece suit.

Stay focused.

I remain standing and look away from him just so his smoldering gaze won't get to me. My brain already spent the entire night cursing him, then trying to reason away what he was doing. In a rare turn of events, the part of my brain that tried not to hate him seemed logical. I didn't give him a chance to explain and I should have. I never jump to conclusions about things, except when it comes to Deacon. In fact, I hate when people do it.

After a long self-debate, I realized I was searching for a reason to end things with him, so I wouldn't get hurt. This is the perfect opportunity for it, and I'm not sure when another one might present itself.

"About last night…"

"Save it for someone else." I fold my arms across my chest and shake my head. His lame excuses make no difference—that's what I tell myself—and yet part of me wants to hear every last word. Instead, I convince my brain I deserve better and I'm not going to settle for some asshole player who might screw half of Chicago.

Nothing he says will change my mind. This was good while it lasted, but it can't continue. We need to quit while we're ahead.

Deacon takes a step toward me, reaching for my forearms. "Will you just calm down for two goddamn seconds? Last night when you called, I was in a meeting. It was work related."

Did he just tell me to calm down? Does he not know a damn thing about women?

I yank my arms back. "Sorry, am I being too *hysterical* for you, Deacon?"

He must realize he said the wrong thing, because his eyes widen when he sees the scowl on my face.

I hold up my hand and take a deep breath. "You know what? It's fine. You aren't my boyfriend. You don't owe me an explanation."

"Look." He holds up a notepad as if it's supposed to mean something to me.

God, why can't he just let this go? Why does he have to be so focused on me?

"I was meeting with Karen Richardson."

I didn't realize it was possible to scowl harder than I already was, but I pull it off somehow. Was that supposed to make me feel better? I know who that woman is and what she looks like. Our firm has no reason to meet up with her for business. We're representing Mr. Miller. There's only one reason Deacon would be out with her so damn late. I wasn't born yesterday.

This seals the deal. I convince myself this is the chance I've been looking for to put all this shit in the rearview mirror. Maybe if I make it seem like it was my fault, it'll ease his conscience and he'll finally move on. "Look, Deacon. It's okay, really. We had a good run. It was fun until it wasn't. I've been reckless and stupid to let it continue. It's my fault for letting it go on this long. It was bound to end in disaster so let's just rip the band aid off before it gets any more complicated. Please?"

As I speak, he stands up and pours himself a glass of water at a side table, ignoring my question.

I stand there, waiting for him to say something, but he doesn't. Finally, I nod. "All right, then. Good chat. I'm just going to go…" I trail off when he still doesn't reply and head toward the door.

Right when I'm a few feet from freedom, he grabs my hand and spins me around.

Shit.

Now, his back's to the door blocking my path. "We're not done here."

My pulse hammers at the sight of him. I don't know if I've ever seen his stare this intense. A storm rages behind his gray eyes, and I think I might drown in it. He doesn't even look mad, he's just so—serious.

I expect his eyes to rake up and down my body like they normally do, but they stay locked on mine. He doesn't even blink. "Nothing happened with that idiot last night."

I nod, but it's obviously fake. "Okay."

"You want the truth. I'll give it to you. She called and wanted to meet. I thought maybe I could get some information that could help the Miller case, so I could get Tate and Decker off my ass. That woman slid in next to me in a booth, and the only thing that went through my mind was, 'What if Quinn saw me like this?' And I got the fuck out of there as fast as I could and tried to call you back."

I know he's telling the truth, but this is my one opportunity to stop this madness before it escalates into a situation that hurts me. "You don't owe me an explanation."

"Why can't you just admit this is real between us?"

I feign ignorance. "I, umm…what are you talking about?"

"Stop denying it. You want me to kiss you—right now."

Yes, I want it so damn bad, but we have to end this. "No, I…"

"Bullshit. It's the only fucking thing going on in that head of yours and you hate yourself for it. I have no clue why you're fighting this, but you are." He leans in close, so close I feel his warm breath in my ear. "And if I put my hand up your skirt, we both know what I'd find. Your pussy, wet."

"You're an asshole." I spit the words at him.

The insult doesn't stop his mouth from crashing down on mine, turning my legs into nothing but trembling support beams that could give out any second. For a moment, my weakness almost wins out.

Almost.

Instead, I turn my head, separating our mouths. "Get out of my way."

Deacon's eyes burn into my retinas, but his mouth forms that cocky smirk of his, like he knows something I don't, and he nods lightly. "Okay." He steps out of the way. "I'll give you space for now."

As I walk past him, he leans down to my ear. "But nothing has changed. I *will* have you."

DEACON'S WORDS still ring in my head as I get out of my car and walk down the street to Heather's store. It sends a shiver up my spine just thinking about his voice, and goosebumps pebble down my arms.

My stomach tightens into a nervous knot thinking about what he said to me on my way out.

"Nothing has changed. I will *have you."*

The authority in his voice, and the way he said it—ugh, why can't I stay away from him? There was no mistaking his tone. He meant every last damn word of it. Why does he have to be so—Deacon? It's freaking hot and drives me nuts at the same time, not in a good way. How dare he act like he'll have me? What? Like he'll own me? Is that all I am to him? Some possession, like a toy he can take out and play with whenever he feels like it?

He says he wants a serious relationship, but does he really know what he's asking for? Not to mention, I don't have time for something like that. I just don't. Even if I wanted to give him a chance, I can't make that commitment right now. Even if he's capable of it, which I'm not convinced he is, it's still not possible.

I'm so damn confused, and I hate being confused. I like my life simple. A plus B equals C. Easy and clean. Black and white.

Deacon Collins muddies the waters. Everything is a gray area with him. Part of me is all for it and part of me wants to scream at the top of my lungs.

I could really use some girl talk. Hence, why I'm waiting for Heather to get off work and gathering up the nerve to tell her about my secret fling with Deacon.

Keeping all this in for so long has made me crazy. She's going to be upset I hid it from her, but I hope she'll get over it quickly because I really need her right now. Hopefully, she'll understand, because she knows I like to keep my private life, well, private.

Heather must spot me debating with myself in front of the store. I don't even notice her until she's up in my face, going in for a hug. "Hey. I've missed you." She practically glows as she wraps her arms around me.

That glow can only mean one thing, she's falling for Stewart. He's so wrong for her, but what can I say, really? I've been banging my boss's brother for months. I'm not exactly Dr. Drew.

"Yeah, I had the big test."

"That's right. How'd you do?"

"They're posting grades tomorrow, but I'm pretty sure I nailed it."

"Knew you would. We should go for drinks to celebrate."

"Sounds perfect."

"Let me clock out and grab my purse." Her eyes light up. "Oh, my God. We should do karaoke at the bar down the road. I'll text Stewart."

I roll my eyes when she's not looking. So much for girl talk. I don't want to rain on her parade but hanging out with Stewart is the furthest thing from fun I can imagine. If she tells him I'll be there, Carter will show up too. I don't know if I can handle this, but I go along with it anyway.

She heads inside and returns with her bag. "You hungry? They have appetizers, I think."

I nod. "Sure."

We walk a few blocks down to the bar. A sign out front reads KARAOKE 24/7.

My stomach growls as soon as the fried food smells waft into my nose. After the stressful week I've had I'm game for grease and alcohol. Between the shit with Deacon and worrying about my test I feel like I've been through the wringer.

Thunder rumbles above and a few raindrops plop on my head. It has to be an omen. We make a run for it and manage to dodge the incoming storm. Once we're inside the bar, I duck into the bathroom and dry off with a few paper towels. I remove the mascara from my eyes while Heather grabs us a table. After touching up my makeup, I run my fingers through my tangled hair to prevent knots. My phone pings with a text from Deacon, but I hit delete without even reading it.

Jerk.

I don't know why I let him get to me the way he does.

Because he's hot and funny and relentless.

Shut up, brain.

I fire off a quick text to Dad, so he doesn't worry when I'm not home at my usual time. Now that my reflection in the mirror borders on presentable, I shove my phone in my bag in case Deacon decides to call. I don't want to be tempted to answer.

I walk out and find Heather sitting at a table near the karaoke stage waiting on me with a pitcher of Bud Light and a basket of fried cheese sticks.

"Just us tonight. Stewart's working."

She frowns.

Secretly, I breathe a huge sigh of relief. "Good," I mumble where she can't hear and shove a cheese stick in my mouth. It's like heaven and I must look like I'm enjoying myself too much.

Heather tenses up but she doesn't say anything.

It's probably a good thing because if she starts in on me, I might say something I'll regret. I don't want to argue with her about how ridiculous men are, and I don't want to hear how amazing Stewart is because he's this week's boyfriend. I just want to enjoy myself.

It's not like I can really say much, anyway. This is who Heather is. She's a romantic, always falling hard and fast. I've known that since we were young, so I shouldn't expect anything else from her.

Before long, the topic of conversation shifts to work and school, and we're laughing and cutting up like usual.

I down one beer after another, drinking much faster than I should.

It just feels so good once it hits my lips.

Wow, quoting Old School? Slow down.

The happy hour crowd files in and the music starts up. After a few rounds, we make our way onto the stage to sing every single girl's anthem. *Truth Hurts* by Lizzo.

Heather shakes her ass while I belt out the lyrics. I'm positive I sound much better to myself than I do to everyone else, but who cares? This is exactly what I needed. To cut loose and forget about the world and all my problems for a bit.

Until I have to face Deacon tomorrow at work, anyway.

DEACON

I LEAVE a note with the flowers and chocolate.

If I find these in the trash there'll be two dozen next Friday along with a mariachi band.

-D

I move down the hall and wait for her to arrive. Watching her reaction is the best part, and I never miss it. I peek around the corner when she drops her bag into the bottom drawer of the desk like she always does.

She eyes the flowers and chocolate but doesn't touch them. I watch while she picks up the note. She scans over my handwriting, her lips moving as she reads the words to herself. Her eyes widen and she stares down at the trash can next to her desk.

You don't have it in you, Quinn.

Her lips curl up into a smile, just for a split-second, before a scowl returns.

You're mine and you know it.

She doesn't toss the flowers in the trash. But even if she had, it would've been worth it to see that smile.

It may have been short-lived, but she cares. She feels this between us and she's cracking. I'm wearing her down and I'll win her heart one way or another. I wait for her to head for the breakroom to make coffee. Her routine is so predictable. She's a creature of habit and I'm not above using any intelligence I've gathered over time to my advantage.

The second I spot those peep-toe heels turn the corner, I grab her hand and pull her into the closet. *Our* closet. The place where it all began.

"What the hell are you doing?" She snarls at me and fuck if I don't love the fire in her eyes.

I move in front of the door and lock it before she barrels her way past me.

"You do know what the word 'no' means, don't you?"

"Sure, but we both know it's not a real 'no.' Is it?" I smirk at the way her chest heaves with each breath she takes.

"This is kidnapping. I could scream."

I shrug. "You could, but you won't."

"I really hate you sometimes." Her green eyes blaze a hole in my chest.

"Get your hormones in check, woman. I didn't bring you in here to fuck."

Her eyes widen and then zero in on me. Her brows draw inward. "Do you even listen to the things you say? And why else would you pull me in here?"

I'd be lying if I said I didn't feel like an asshole because she thinks all I want is to put my dick inside her.

The moment gets to me and I freeze up for a few seconds. This unfamiliar feeling gnaws at my stomach, like anxiety times a thousand, coupled with butterflies.

"Well?" She shakes her head like she's gathering her thoughts. "Why am I here?"

You can do this, Deacon.

"I have a question."

"Well, hurry. I'm running behind."

She's not running behind. She's always early for everything, but she has to stick to her routine, or it'll ruin her day. Like I said, I know every damn thing about her.

I suck in a breath. I don't know why this is so goddamn hard, and why I'm suddenly acting like such a pussy. My palms grow clammy and I exhale a long breath.

"Spit it out."

"I know you had a big test the other day and knowing you, I'm sure you killed it. I want to take you to dinner to celebrate."

Fuck, why was that so difficult?

"You sound sincere. Did you just formally ask me out on a date? A *real* date? Like a sit down at a restaurant and talk kind of date?"

"Look, I feel awful about the other night. I want to make it up to you. And I want to hear about your test and…" I fidget with my hands as I trail off and finally have the courage to look her in the eye. "Please?"

Quinn smiles, like she's enjoying this. "You're pale. You look scared shitless." She laughs like she's one part nervous one part elated. "Have you ever asked anyone on a real date before? One where you want to spend time with someone and not because you just want to get laid at the end?"

"No."

Her cheeks turn bright pink.

"I mean not like the way I just asked you. All formal or whatever." I shake my head at myself because I'm acting so ridiculous and flustered. "Fuck, I've never faced rejection before. This shit must be terrifying for normal guys. Doing this all the time."

She grins. "And he's back."

I snicker for a moment, but then narrow my gaze on her. "Look, I don't know how many more ways I can say this, for fuck's sake, but I like you. I've been up front about that from the beginning, and doing this kind of shit isn't easy for me, but I do it because I want you." I step in close, so that we're face to face, and trace her jaw with my finger. "What the hell do I need to do for you to see I mean every word? You think I've sent women flowers before? I don't even send my mother flowers."

She glances away, and I swear I think I might see a tear forming at the corner of her eye. When she turns back, it's gone. "I don't…"

"Stop fucking thinking. Tonight is happening."

QUINN

I FINALLY NOD MY HEAD.

Apparently, that appeases Deacon, because his mouth crashes into mine before I can utter a word. His kiss is different this time. It's not needy and rushed. He doesn't kiss me like he wants to consume me or turn me on. It's gentle and sweet, and I still don't know how to process any of this. He asked me out on an actual date. Not some, "Hey, let's hang out later," after he's done fucking me. And he said it was the first time he's ever asked someone out. I would normally think he was lying about the last part, but I could see the truth in his eyes.

The way he's kissing me is unexpected but nice. When his hand slides to my hip, I know my clothes are about to come off. My whole body warms under his touch and butterflies swarm my belly. I wait for him to strip me naked and shove me against the wall. Flip me around and spank me. Something.

But, he doesn't.

He pulls away, unlocks the door, and starts to walk out.

I glance back and forth, like someone might be coming. "Where the hell are you going?"

He shrugs. "Back to work."

I feel like I'm in *The Twilight Zone*. "Well, we're already in here and it's pretty obvious this is a sure thing." I stare at him like *seriously, you're passing up sex.*

His nostrils flare as he rakes his gaze up and down my body, and it looks like he's debating with himself. Finally, he runs a hand through his hair and frowns. Did I say something wrong? What's his deal?

My pulse races when he storms toward me like a man on a mission. I've never been so confused in my life. Is he going to have his way with me or not?

At the last second, he stops and bends down so we're at eye level. "I won't

247

fuck you in this closet again. I want more, and you deserve better." He brings my knuckles to his lips. "This is real. See you tonight."

I exhale a huge breath I didn't realize I'd been holding and can't seem to find any words as he exits the closet. My body is on fire, my face flushed, and my eyes dart around the room.

What the hell just happened in here?

A small part of me saddens as I look around. If Deacon meant what he said, our exciting closet trysts are finished. I wait a few minutes and grab a stupid pen to cover my ass even though we didn't do anything wrong this time.

My heartbeat drums in my ear and my palms are slick with sweat. My body aches with need after not getting my usual release. I can still feel his intense eyes on me, like he's here, somewhere, staring at me, and every word of what he said replays through my mind.

Eventually, I let out a long exhale, and work up the courage to walk back into the office. The moment I turn the corner, Tate stands there waiting for me.

Her eyes flash to the pen in my hand. "Roof deck. Let's have a chat."

"Umm. Okay." I follow her outside and take in the view of Lake Michigan, still gripping the pen in my palm.

Tate smiles at me over her shoulder. "Get everything you needed back there?"

"Hmm?" I could plead ignorance, but Tate is smart...too smart for me to lie.

Fortunately, she moves on before I can answer. "You didn't throw away the flowers today. Finally give in to the guy who can't take no for an answer?"

"Not exactly."

"You know, I like to think of us as friends. You can talk to me. I know I can be a bit brash. I have to be that way to handle all the egos in this place. I won't run to Decker and throw you under the bus. Out here we're just friends. I promise."

I decide to be honest. I don't want to dig a hole for myself, and I have to get the words out before they consume me from within. Plus, if anyone can relate to dating one of the Collins brothers, it's Tate. As soon as I open my mouth the floodgates open.

For some reason, I can't look at her while I speak. "The flowers are from Deacon."

Tate grins. "I know."

I hang my head in shame, unable to look at her. "How?"

"Remember that time we went to brunch? You mentioned a freckle on his thumb. You only know something like that about someone if you're, well, you know."

"I know he seems immature, but he just turned me down for sex and wants to take me on a date."

Tate let's out a laugh that's a partial gasp. "Did he now?"

I nod.

She mouths the word, "Wow," and puts both hands on her hips. "Well, maybe there's hope for that little shit stain after all. This could be good. Maybe you'll turn him into a functioning adult."

I laugh. "I don't know if *that* will ever happen, but maybe a slightly improved version of him."

"Truer words have never been spoken."

We both laugh for a second. It's hard not to smile at Deacon's boyish nature, even if it's annoying a lot of the time.

"Look, Quinn. All I ever cared about was my career and earning the respect of my peers. A relationship, let alone a marriage, was never really in the cards. But if I've learned one thing since I came to Chicago, it's that anything is possible." She looks down at her diamond engagement ring. "Deacon would be lucky to have you. And as much as it pains me to say this, he's right. You are worth so much more than a quickie in a closet. Make him earn you. *All* of you."

I glance out at the boats in the harbor, then on to the horizon of Lake Michigan. "I'm afraid to get my hopes up. In my experience, this usually plays out the exact opposite. The guy appears to be sweet and caring, but all his actions point the other way. With Deacon, he seems like a player. It's how I perceive him. But all his actions point the other direction, when I really step back and look at them. He's always been honest and up front. He tries to share intimate details with me. He pays attention to everything I enjoy, and not just when it comes to sex. He's sent me flowers every week since the first time we hooked up. He confuses me so much."

"Well I do think he likes you." She pauses for a second and glances around. "This stays between us." She leans in close and lowers her tone. "I personally don't think he's a great attorney." She straightens back up. "*But*, I do think he's a good person."

I want to believe she's right. I want to believe it so damn bad; the part about him being a good person and liking me.

"Now, get back inside. We have work to do."

When I arrive at my desk I can't focus on anything. All my thoughts keep going to Deacon and, if I'm being honest, what I'm going to wear tonight.

I shoot a text to Heather.

Quinn: Emergency. I need a new dress. Got a hot date.

Heather: Done. Come by the store. I know just the one.

I was so excited about Deacon I completely forgot to check my test score. I log into the student portal at the university and wiggle in my seat. When I see my score, I let out a squeal that earns me a few dirty looks from some of the employees passing by, but I don't care.

I aced it. Ninety-eight percent.

The weirdest part of it all...the first urge I have after seeing my score is to run and tell Deacon.

"I SAID A DRESS. NOT A NEW WARDROBE." I shake my head at the rack Heather pulls out for me.

"Shh. Who's the hot date? This is sudden."

"It's Deacon." I purse my lips and wait for her response.

"The asshole from work?" She hands me a black strappy dress. "This is the one." She hurries me into the dressing room but waves her hand forward like *continue*.

I close the door behind me and speak as I wiggle into the dress. "Yep. Same guy. I may have embellished on the asshole part."

"If you say so. I want details tomorrow over brunch."

"Deal. What happened with Stewart last night?"

"Girl, I don't know if you're ready. I'm sure you want to gloat but keep that shit to yourself if you value my discount."

That doesn't sound promising. "Oh no. What'd he do?"

"So, the apartment he's been taking me to isn't even his. He was watching it for a friend who was out of town. He finally came clean and took me to his real place last night."

I have to fight back a laugh. Not at her predicament, but at the fact there's no telling what's coming next.

"Oh, and the best part. I walked out of his room this morning and some older woman was standing there. She called me a whore and told me to put some clothes on. Yeah. It was his mom. He lives with her."

Wow. "Oh man, I'm sorry. Were you naked?"

"Yes!"

I step out of the changing room.

Her entire demeanor changes and her face lights up. "Oh, yeah. That's definitely the one."

I'm a little surprised she's not more upset about the Stewart situation, but the way she bounces around relationships, I guess she's just used to it. I do a little twirl in the mirror. "It's not too much?" I tug on the bottom, pulling it farther down my thighs. I'm afraid my ass will fall out the back, but it does look fantastic.

"Definitely the dress. I won't allow you to say no."

"Fine. So, what happened after his mom saw you naked?"

"The friend he was apartment sitting for was his ex-girlfriend."

"Shut up. You never noticed when you were there? How'd you find out?"

"After I got dressed and headed for the door, the ex showed up with a pair of my panties…"

"No. Way." I cover my mouth and shake my head.

"Yes. Way." She hangs her head, pretending to look sad. "I'm cursed."

I pull her in for a hug. "Maybe you need to try dating outside your usual type."

"What's my type?" She leans back.

"Pretty boys who look rich but might live with their mother."

"You have a valid point."

"You need a working man. Rough hands. Good heart. Humble."

"Too bad your dad isn't younger." She grins.

I smack her shoulder a little harder than intended. "You're terrible."

DEACON

C OLD SWEAT BEADS across my forehead, and it hits me all at once. This shit with Quinn is real. She didn't turn me down.

I've never thought about my future with any woman, but it's all I think about with her. Taking her out on a few dates is the first step but what about everything to follow? Can I live up to that? Am I capable of giving her everything she deserves?

I gaze around my living room. It's manly and awesome. I like things the way they are—toys and gadgets and all my football shit.

What happens when she starts staying over and leaves stuff here?

I'm sure it'll start with a toothbrush or some clothes, maybe something to sleep in. She'll slowly take over my house like a virus until it's full of fruity candles and new curtains. Next thing I know she'll be asking to move in together and leaving wedding magazines on the counter. You know? Dropping subliminal hints like females do.

She'll replace my stuff with cozy little flower arrangements and throw pillows. Will she expect a ring on her finger soon? Will she pack up all my shit and reduce everything I was to nothing but a few boxes in the garage?

Will she start planning our family?

Yeah, she'll definitely do that. She'll use an app to show me what our kids will look like. She'll slowly erode my former life away piece by piece until I'm nothing but a shell of who I once was, floating around offshore, asking permission to buy season tickets to the Bears.

Get out of your head. You're freaking out for no reason.

I shrug, but surprisingly, that nightmare train of thought coursing through my brain doesn't bother me near as much as it should.

Being single has been fun. I can't lie about that. But I want Quinn. Besides,

I'm sure we can take things slow. I know she says she's okay with the way things are, but I need to step up my game. She deserves the world, and if I can't give it to her, as hard as it would be, I need to let her move on.

A knock on my door sends me into a complete panic. I glance at my watch. It's nowhere near time to pick her up and I'm not expecting company.

"Open up, asshole." It's Dex.

I open the door. "The fuck you doing here?"

He breezes past me to the fridge and helps himself to a beer. "Need to plan Decker's bachelor party. I'm thinking big-titted strippers and booze." He waggles his brows and twists the top off a Bud Light.

It sounds like the exact opposite of what Decker would want, but he's been acting like a dick, so it might be fun to watch his uncomfortable ass at a strip club.

"I have plans tonight."

He scoffs. "Plans? What's more important than embarrassing Decker for life?"

I look away and his twin intuition reads me like a book.

"Fucking hell. Remind me not to drink the water at the office. First Decker and now you?" Shaking his head, he takes a swig from the bottle. "Two little lovesick puppies." He points a finger at my face. "That's never happening to me. I need a cornucopia of pussy at my disposal at all times. Who's the lucky lady?"

I swallow, wondering if I should tell him. In the end, I can't keep it from him. He's my twin brother. We don't keep secrets.

Quinn agreed to the date. Surely, she doesn't mind if people find out since we're going to make things official. "Quinn."

Dexter's brows shoot up. "From the office?"

I nod.

"You okay? You look a little pale."

There's something about the way he stares at me. A wave of uncertainty crashes into my chest. Am I fooling myself to think a relationship with Quinn is possible? Judging by Dexter's face, he looks like I just suggested hell might freeze over.

I try to play it off and shrug. "Maybe I should cancel. What's up with the strippers?"

He takes a step back. "Damn, son. You're really twisted up inside."

It's impossible to hide shit from him. I nod, because it's true. I've never felt this way before.

"Look, man. I was just giving you shit. Don't cancel. Quinn's the best. Look how she puts up with all the shit we give her at work." He smirks, like everything makes more sense now. "You've been sending her those flowers and chocolates."

I nod again, waiting for him to call me a little bitch and rank my masculinity somewhere between 0 and 1.

"That chocolate was good, by the way. I stole some of it when she wasn't looking." He grins. "If you like her, fucking go for it, man." He takes a few steps toward the window and mumbles, "Quinn. Who woulda thought?"

"That's it? You're not gonna give me shit about this?"

"Oh, I will. Trust me. But I don't want to get blamed if you fuck it up." He grins. "Besides, you look like you're about to have a breakdown. You need to relax and enjoy the moment if this is your first date."

I'm not sure how to take all this. He's never acted this easygoing before. Something is up with him, but I realize he's right, and my confidence kicks back up to appropriate levels. "Thanks for the advice. You're a great American. Now stop drinking all my fucking beer and get out. I need to get ready and crush this like I do everything else in life. That means better than you."

He sets the beer down and walks to the door, then turns around at the last second. "Then stop being a pussy and live up to your name. You know what they say about the Collins brothers… Nobody fucks you harder, in the courtroom or the bedroom."

QUINN

I sweep my hair up for the millionth time and sigh. I can't decide if I should wear it in an updo or leave it down. I should've gotten ready at Heather's place. This is a disaster. I don't even know where I'm supposed to meet Deacon—or when.

What the hell? Why hasn't he called or texted?

I check my phone again for any messages. Nada. Nothing.

If he stands me up, I *will* kill him. I twist around, eyeing myself in the floor-length mirror on the back of my door. I glance at my phone for the millionth time but check the clock instead of my messages. Fortunately, I still have a few hours, and I need to make sure Dad gets fed before I leave. My mind races about this *date*.

What will happen after?

Will we go back to his place?

Calm down.

Should I take spare clothes?

No way. I don't want to look like I expect to spend the night.

Do I want to spend the night? If that's an option?

Pulling the dress off, I change into yoga pants and a t-shirt to make dinner. I don't want Dad burning the place down. Sometimes he forgets simple things, and I live in a constant state of anxiety. I'm worried he might be showing signs of early onset dementia. In my spare time I spend way too many hours staring at WebMD. I'm no doctor but the signs are present. I tell myself you can drive yourself crazy matching up symptoms on that site, but I'm worried this might be legit.

A few days ago, he was talking about Joe like they were going out for beer and wings like the old days. He played it off like he was reminiscing, but I saw the confusion etched on his face.

I walk into the living room just as he screams at some team on TV. It looks like hockey. Blackhawks maybe? It's difficult to keep up with all the different sports he watches.

My phone buzzes and my heart kicks into fifth gear, but it's a text from Heather wishing me luck tonight. I mentally curse her for a crime she doesn't know she committed.

Send me a damn text, Deacon! You're driving me insane.

Plating the old man's chicken and veggies, I realize he'll be eating alone tonight while I'm out having fun. Guilt creeps into my chest. I shouldn't feel this way, and he'd scold me if he knew about it. Outside our neighbors, nobody knows I take care of him except Heather and Tate, and I haven't told Tate much.

We don't ask for handouts and I don't need anyone thinking we're some charity case. Sure, we struggle to get by here and there, but our life is good. We have each other.

Sometimes Dad tells his doctors about our situation and I see the pity in their eyes. We don't need people feeling sorry for us. I don't take care of him out of obligation. It's because I love him and that's what you do.

He turns to me after I set his dinner on a TV tray. "I'm dining alone I see." His lips turn up into a smile. "Big plans?"

"I have a date."

I toss him a wink and walk to my room to avoid an interrogation. Okay, it's also to see if Deacon replied to my messages yet.

Zero notifications.

I frown but soldier on as planned. I decide to leave my hair down since I always wear it up at work. Once satisfied from the neck up, I wiggle into the form-fitting dress and slip on my shoes. They're wedge peep toes. Heather insisted they went perfect with the dress to show off my legs and add a few inches to my height.

When I walk back to the living room Dad whistles but says, "Where's the rest of your dress?"

I give him a stern look.

"Should probably get a coat on. I have my old trench—"

I cut him off. "Oh stop. It's not that revealing."

His cheeks redden and he lets out a snort of derision. "Who's the guy?"

"Someone from work."

He points at me with his good arm. "Better not lay a hand on you. I mean it." His words come out as a growl, and I haven't seen him look this way in a while.

My heart warms and at the same time I glance down at his wheelchair. "Gonna run over his toes?"

He taps the armrest and grins. "I have a shotgun in the side of this thing that'll pop right out. Ronnie helped me install it."

I shake my head. "You're ridiculous." Secretly, I'm a bit worried he might not be lying.

"Whether I can walk or not, you'll always be my princess."

"I know, Dad." I bend down and plant a kiss on his forehead.

"Seriously though, you look beautiful. You make me proud, kiddo. I hope you know that. This guy better realize how lucky he is. Make sure he treats you right."

"Stop, Dad. You're gonna ruin my makeup."

"Okay, okay. But I mean every word."

"I still have the pepper spray you gave me." I wink.

On the inside, my stomach churns. Deacon still hasn't called or texted and it's only a few minutes before seven and I don't know where the hell I'm going. Surely, he didn't get cold feet. He seemed so determined when he asked me out.

The doorbell rings.

What. The. Hell.

I freeze and glare at Dad. "Plan on having Ronnie over without telling me?"

Dad shakes his head. "No. He's working tonight." He grunts and moves to unlock his chair.

"Stay put. I got it." It's probably one of the neighborhood women he has wrapped around his finger. Who knows what they're going to do when I leave.

I open the door and my face pales.

Shit!

It's Deacon.

How the hell does he know where I live?

DEACON

THE DOOR SWINGS open and Quinn smiles for a brief second—then glares.

What'd she expect?

I told her I was doing this thing the right way. That means I pick her up at her house. She will *not* drive and meet me at our first date. I bribed Rick to find out where she lives and now I owe his ass another favor, but it's worth it. She needs to know I'm serious about dating her. Courting her? Is that what the fuck it's called? Regardless, it will be done correctly, and I will do it better than any other man on the planet.

"Hey."

She lowers her voice and whisper-screams. "What are you doing here?"

"It's not a real date unless I pick you up. That's how the world works." I lean in to kiss her cheek, but she dodges me and moves to block the doorway. She shuts the door behind her when I hear some guy yell in the background. I try to glance over her shoulder, but she gets it shut before I can see inside.

"You live with someone?"

She winces. "My dad."

I rub my chin and glance back to the door. "Are you ashamed of me?"

Her eyes widen. "What? No. It's just, you know?" She hems and haws for a brief second. "Meeting the parents isn't a first date thing, right?"

I brush my lips against hers but quickly stop myself and pull back. I don't want to come on too strong. "God, you look beautiful."

Her cheeks turn a slight shade of pink. "Thanks, you clean up pretty nice yourself." She shakes her head back and forth. "I was really worried there for a while. You could've called."

"I wanted to surprise you, and I knew you wouldn't let me pick you up."

"Yeah, you're right. That's exactly what would've happened."

I gesture toward her apartment. "I want to meet him." I twist the knob and push the door open.

Quinn stiffens. "No, Deacon…"

I'm already past her.

She follows behind, tugging at my bicep. "Just wait…"

"I'll take him out at the knees!" A gruff voice rings through the apartment as I turn the corner.

I stop immediately before I'm in his line of sight and turn to face her.

Quinn's lips curl up into an amused grin. She shrugs. "You wanted to meet him."

I take a deep breath. Fuck it. I want to impress him, and I want him to know his daughter is in safe hands.

I walk around the corner just as he's in the middle of barking another threat.

The moment his gaze meets mine he squints and then his eyes light up. "Deacon fucking Collins?"

I turn and smile just in time to catch Quinn rolling her eyes harder than I've ever seen.

This will be fun.

QUINN

I watch as Dad morphs from threatening to break Deacon's knees to shaking his hand and grinning like a boy on the playground. He's absolutely starstruck, and I have no idea why.

What the hell? Do they know each other?

"Quarterback for Illinois!"

"Yes, sir." Deacon nods.

Great.

Dad is the biggest football fan in the world. If they start chatting, I'll never get Deacon out of here. I leave them alone for a moment to grab Dad something to drink from the kitchen. When I return, he's gushing over a big play Deacon made in some bowl game.

It's simultaneously cute and annoying. I thought dads were supposed to revile the guys who dated their daughters.

"I still can't believe that injury. Man, the Bears were going to take you in the first round."

Deacon smiles like he's had this conversation a thousand times, but doesn't show any signs of irritation. "It was a setback, but things turned out okay."

"Coulda used you out there on Sundays."

"I appreciate the kind words." Deacon looks up at me. "We should get going, but can I have just one minute with him?"

"Sure." I lean up against the wall.

They both stare at me like I'm some kind of disease, like I should know exactly what's going on.

"I meant in private." Deacon's eyes narrow on me.

I glance back and forth between them. "You're banishing me in my own apartment?"

Deacon gives me a look like he's already pleading for my forgiveness. "Please?"

I huff out a sigh and toss my hands up. "Fine." I walk through the hall toward the bedroom but stop where I can still hear their conversation.

"I just wanted to reassure you, sir. I will personally see to your daughter's safety this evening."

Before I can catch myself, my palm is on my chest and my face has to be bright pink. It might be the sweetest damn thing I've ever heard and has totally redeemed him for exiling me to the bedroom.

"Well, look. I like you, kid. And you were a damn good football player. She might look like a woman to you, but she's my little girl and she's my life. I am trusting you. So, I only have one piece of advice."

"Sir?"

"Don't fuck up."

"Yes, sir. She'll be treated with nothing but the respect she deserves."

"All right, then. You take care of her, or I'll take care of your other knee."

"Understood. I suppose I should go get her before she takes care of both of us."

"You catch on quick, son. I think you'll do just fine."

Shit!

I have to speed down the hall as fast as my shoes allow before Deacon catches me. My heart speeds up as he approaches the room. Finally, he opens the door.

I glance up at him and pretend to be irritated when I really want to jump up, wrap my legs around his waist, and kiss him until the sun comes up. "You guys done?"

He takes a step into the room and holds his hand out. "Sorry about that. No more distractions, promise. You ready?"

I take his hand and nod, unable to hold back my smile. "Okay." The second our hands touch, my heart races a million miles-an-hour and adrenaline floods my veins. I can't help but think this is the beginning of something new, something fresh and exciting. It all just feels—right, and I don't know if I've ever felt this way before.

I kiss Dad on the cheek on our way out. "Bye."

"You two have a good time." He gives Deacon a thumbs up.

Classic Dad move.

"Don't worry, sir. I'll have her home at a decent hour." Deacon flashes a mischievous grin my direction as he says it.

On our way to the car, I eye him up and down. He's wearing a suit that probably costs more than my car payment. You wouldn't know it by the way he carries himself, though. He's confident and cocky, but I've never seen him speak to anyone like he's better than them, even at the office with his subordinates.

Part of me worried he would see where I come from and give me the brush off. It's silly, I know, but I've dealt with so many rich clients and attorneys who treat me like I'm nothing more than the help. I don't come from his world of big money. I work hard for everything I have, but I know that trait isn't exclusive to poor people. I've noticed over the past few months there's more to Deacon than I realized.

I really like this side of him. In fact, I like it a lot.

"Where you taking me?"

Deacon walks around and opens my door. It's insanely cute at how attentive he's being to every single detail, to make sure he gets our first date right.

"It's a surprise."

"What if I don't like surprises?"

"Guess I better drop you back at your house and see if your dad wants to go to dinner." He winks.

"Such a comedian."

"If I didn't know better, I'd think you're jealous your old man likes me so much." Deacon pulls out of the apartment complex and hops on a highway.

"You caught me, sir. I'm green with envy." I laugh. "Really, though? That didn't go exactly the way I envisioned."

"So, you envisioned me meeting your dad?"

I smirk and glance at the trees and billboards flying by on the side of the road. "So cocky."

His hand goes to my thigh and engulfs my body in flames. How does he do that? It's a normal gesture. He's not trying anything, but I can't help but notice how every single touch of his sends my body into the stratosphere.

"I enjoyed meeting him. He's a nice guy."

When we pull up to a hotel, my jaw clenches and I shoot Deacon a frown from hell.

He snickers, completely ignoring my reaction. "Oh, wipe that damn look off your face. It's not what you think. Trust me."

"I *do* trust you, Deacon."

That's what scares me.

He opens the door for me and we walk toward the hotel. I can tell Deacon's nervous but he hides it well. It's so cute.

His hand slips down to mine and our fingers interlace. We both look down at our hands at the same time, then back at each other and smile. Everything about this is perfect so far.

He leads me to a private elevator, and I never want him to let go of my hand. When we step out, it's the most beautiful rooftop garden I've ever seen— twinkling lights, flowers, candles, and fancy champagne—swallowed by lit up skyscrapers on all four sides, jutting into the night sky.

I know people always say things take their breath away, but the sight before me truly leaves me breathless.

I smile at Deacon. Everything else in my life—all my worries and fears and stress—fades away in this one moment, and I'm just a girl on a date with a guy who likes me. Deacon has outdone himself.

"Impressed?" He pulls my chair out for me.

"You could say that." I should tease him and make him work a little harder for compliments, but I don't. I've never been on a date like this.

"You seem surprised." He takes a seat across from me and peels back the label from a cork on a bottle of champagne.

"I am. No one has ever done anything like this for me. I just don't understand. Why me?"

He pops the cork from the bottle and fills my glass. "I could sit here and list your good qualities all night long, but it's really pretty simple. I like you. You're worth the effort."

I take a sip and try to absorb everything and live in the moment. When he puts all the focus on me, it makes me a little uncomfortable. I'm not used to people heaping praise. Not that I want it or ask for it, but it *is* really nice. Everyone loves to hear someone appreciate them.

I need to change the subject, though. The spotlight has been on me long enough. "Had no idea you were *that* big of a football star."

He stares off at the surrounding buildings. "It's nothing."

"Don't be modest. My dad's a fanatic and straight shooter. If he didn't think you were any good, he'd have told you."

His gaze lands back on mine. "I was okay. Could have gone pro, but I blew out my knee." He shrugs. "It happens. Just glad I had my family and the firm to fall back on. What about you? I didn't know you lived with your dad."

If there's one thing I've noticed since Deacon showed up at my house, it's that he hasn't shown a hint of judgment for me living with my dad in our tiny apartment. "It's not really something I broadcast to people. Dad was really independent. He drove a bus for the city for like twenty years. My mom dropped me off with him when I was five and I never saw her again. He raised me all by himself. A few years back, he had a stroke and suffered severe nerve damage. Couldn't work anymore. So, it was my time to take care of him."

"But why don't you tell anyone? Maybe people would help out or whatever? He seems like a social guy. I'm sure he's made a lot of friends in his life."

I shake my head. "It's my job, and I don't want anyone feeling sorry for us. When your family needs you, you stick together. I don't know if I'd trust anyone else, anyway."

Deacon gives me a look, like he senses not to press harder. "Well, he seems like a great guy."

I smile.

"I'm sure he has to be."

"Why?"

"He raised a remarkable daughter."

"He's the best…" I shake my head and a million feelings sock me in the chest all at once. *Not now. Not here.* The past plays through my mind, of how Dad was before, and now after.

Deacon takes my hand in his from across the table. "You know you can talk to me. I'm not just saying that to be nice. I *want* to know you and your family."

I let out a breathy exhale. "I'm worried he's showing signs of early onset dementia."

Deacon leans in. "What kind of signs?"

"Little things, like mood swings, short-term memory loss, some days he can almost take care of himself and some days he's almost helpless." I wipe at the corner of my eye.

"Hey, hey, it's fine." His hand covers mine. "Maybe we should talk about something else on our first date. Save the heavy tears for date two." Deacon grins.

I laugh and nod. "Please. That would be great."

"I want to know everything, but you look so beautiful and it's so nice out here. I didn't mean to dig all that up right out the gate." He leans back in his chair and folds his hands behind his head. "Ask anything about me. I'm an open book."

"Favorite movie?"

"*Die Hard.* Next."

I snicker.

"What? Who doesn't love *Die Hard*? It's the greatest Christmas movie of all time."

"Uhh, it's *so* not a Christmas movie."

Deacon's eyebrows shoot up. "It *so* is. Not even just a Christmas movie, the greatest, like I said. Next."

I can't stop laughing then I stop and just look into his eyes and smile.

"What is it?"

"Nothing, you just... you'll get along great with Dad."

"I should hope so. He has excellent taste in cinema and quarterbacks."

How did he take me from the brink of tears to smiling and laughing like a fool within ten seconds?

We drink, eat, and laugh.

The night goes by far too fast and before I know it, he's walking me to my door. I don't know why I feel so nervous right now. Our first date is perfect, and I never want it to end. It's light years beyond any other date I've ever been on, like something from a movie or a book.

"I really enjoyed tonight." His lips brush up against mine as he backs me up against the door. It's not a normal kiss from him, but it still knocks the breath out of me. His mouth moves slowly over mine. No tongue.

My knees go weak at how sensual it is. It's a gentle and dominant kiss at the same time. A kiss that says *you're mine.* It's a kiss that says he cares about me, wants more than just sex in a closet.

Whatever he's doing, it's working because I already feel the familiar throb between my legs, and tingles skittering over my skin.

I'm ready for it. I want him so damn bad right now, and it's not just to get off. I want to feel the connection between us. Something tells me sex with him right now would be on an entirely different plane of existence. Mentally, I'm begging his thick frame to crash into me, pin me up against something.

He pulls back, and I let out a sigh before I can stop it. I can't tell if I'm annoyed or dazed or both, but I instantly miss him pressed up against me.

I gesture toward the apartment. "You know…he's asleep. I could show you my room. You didn't get to see it before."

Deacon lets out a slight groan. "God, don't do this to me right now." His hand shoots out in front of me, palm up. "Sorry, that came out wrong."

I stand there and stare, unable to form words.

Is he really about to turn down sex again? What world am I living in?

Deacon reaches up and tugs at his hair.

He looks so freaking hot in his suit, warring with himself to the point he might pull his hair out. Flames roar through my body and lick down to my fingers and toes at the sight of this gorgeous man who wants me so bad he has to fight it. I want to jump up and wrap my legs around him, refuse to let go until he comes inside.

"I can't believe these words are about to leave my lips, but no."

My eyes widen. "No?"

He places both palms on my cheeks and plants another soft kiss on my lips and I'm not sure how much more I can take.

When he leans back, his eyes plead with me. "Please. All I want is the perfect ending to tonight. I want to watch you go through that door, and I want to miss you like crazy the second it shuts. Then, I want to walk to my car, drive home, and replay the moment over and over in my head until it's seared into my brain. The perfect moment from our perfect first date, so I can tell the story fifty years from now and remember every single vivid detail. The way a first date should be." He reaches out and pulls me in close to him. His hands slide down my dress and cup my rear. "But, so you don't think I've turned into a total pussy, I *will* collect on this offer in the future." He kisses my neck. "Again." He squeezes my ass. "And again." Deacon kisses me once more, hard enough to bruise my lips, and I can tell he's fighting everything in his body to not haul me into the apartment and do unspeakable things.

Holy mother.

When we separate, I give him exactly what he asked for. I turn back and flash him one last smile and an awkward wave before I close the door.

What he doesn't know, is I'm doing the exact same thing he is right now. Taking in the moment, so I can remember it clear as day in the future. It's almost impossible to focus because he looks so damn—just happy, like a young boy after he just gave a girl a flower for the first time. I have to be grinning like a damn idiot. The night was perfect. Absolutely perfect.

Once I close the door, I turn and my back hammers against it and I gasp for air. I press the pad of my fingertips to my swollen lips and whisper, "Wow."

DEACON

QUINN HAS no idea how difficult it was to not throw her over my shoulder and haul her to her bedroom.

I think my dick is still pissed at me about it.

I wanted to so damn bad, but I just couldn't. I promised myself I would do this thing right and treat her with the respect she deserves. I really liked her dad too, and I made a promise to him. There's no way in hell I was going to go into their apartment and fuck her while he was asleep in the next room.

Even though Quinn said it was fine, I would never disrespect him like that. Not going to happen. Her dad was a pleasant surprise. I didn't think it was possible, but now, I admire her even more; the way she takes care of him, goes to law school, and works a full-time job.

She is a total badass and I feel like the ultimate slacker.

I can see now why she was so averse to dating someone, especially me. Look at everything she has going on in her life.

I'm going to have to do better if I want to stay in a relationship with her.

A relationship.

I'm in one now, and it feels awkward and awesome at the same time. I don't think I've ever really been serious with another woman. Sure, I've "dated" or whatever, but it was just hooking up more than once. It's never felt real, until Quinn.

When I pull up the driveway, I can't shake the excitement. I'm practically bouncing on the balls of my feet, ready to hit somebody. It's better than walking through the tunnel at the Rose Bowl in Pasadena or after winning the Big Ten championship my senior year. And that shit was insane. I never thought I'd feel an adrenaline rush like it again.

After a long shower, I crawl into bed and try to watch something on TV.

Nothing holds my interest. I must flip through the channels for like forty-five minutes.

I keep glancing over and staring at my phone. I feel like such a pussy because I want to call a friend and tell them all about my date. Dex is about the only one that'd understand, but I still don't know if he'd *get* it. Really, there's only one person I want to talk to right now.

Fuck it. I'm calling her.

Quinn answers on a yawn after the third ring. "Deacon?"

"Shit, did I wake you up?"

"No. It's fine. I was just getting into bed."

"You don't have to lie. You go to bed early as fuck, don't you?"

"10:42 p.m."

"Huh?"

"Nothing, I was just seeing how long you could go without using profanity. I know you were doing it for our date."

I look at my clock on the nightstand and it's 10:42. I can't do anything but smile and plead ignorance. "I was?"

"Okay, I'll be honest if you will. I was asleep. But it's okay. It's nice to hear your voice."

"Okay, well, when I got home I shouted 'fuck' roughly forty-eight times to make up for any f-bombs I would've normally dropped between the hours of seven and nine."

A laugh comes through the receiver. I've never made her laugh this much in the past. She's warming up to me, a lot.

"Okay, I'm up. What's going on?"

I contemplate making something up, but I just told her we were being honest. "I just promised not to lie, so here it goes. I need to say something, and I don't really have anyone else I can talk to about it. Nobody who won't give me shit, anyway."

"What's up?"

"Well, you're pretty much my best friend, outside of my brothers, and I…"

"Spit it out, Collins."

"Okay. Well, I had an amazing first date with the perfect girl tonight, and I just wanted to tell someone."

She sniffles.

"Fuck, are you crying?"

"No! Don't be ridiculous." She sniffles again. "No…it's just, allergies. And God, you can be really sweet when you want to be. Do you know that?"

"I'm like that candy that's really sour at first then sweet when you get to the middle."

She laughs. "Yes! Perfect analogy. And Deacon…"

"Yeah?"

"I had a really great time too."

"You did?"

"Yeah, see there's this guy…I never really knew what to make of him. We've been sleeping together for months, but I never took him seriously until now."

"Well, he sounds amazing. You should see him again."

"You really think I should? I'm kinda into him."

"Absolutely, I bet his dick is huge."

Quinn bursts into a laugh. "I don't know about the last part. He's pretty average. But maybe I will. He knows how to use his tongue, after all."

I can't stop grinning. "Hey, Quinn?"

"Yeah?"

"Thanks for listening. Goodnight."

"Goodnight, Deacon."

I end the call and feel like I might float up to the ceiling.

Fuck, life is good.

QUINN

I UNROLL my yoga mat next to Heather's.

She nudges me with her elbow. "So, how was it?" She bends down and slips off her shoes.

I take a quick sip from my water bottle before class starts. "Perfect."

"Oh wow, look at you, cheesing like a fool. Must've been damn good." She waggles her eyebrows.

I shake my head at her. "Wasn't like that. He reserved a private rooftop. We had dinner and champagne. The conversation was amazing, then he drove me home and kissed me goodnight."

She stops unrolling her mat and stares at me. "That's it? No foreplay? You *have* already banged this guy, right?"

"I'm serious." I swat at her. "It was nice, perfect even. He called me when he got home because he couldn't stop thinking about me."

"He gonna come over tonight to wash and braid your hair too?" She cackles but clears her throat when the instructor shows up.

I scowl at her and face forward.

"Good morning, class."

"Good morning," everyone says in unison.

"Let's get into position. We'll start with upward facing dog."

"Should be a first for you." Heather makes sure to say it when the instructor isn't watching and shoots out her tongue.

I pretend to scratch my nose and use my middle finger.

After turning my attention back to yoga, I focus on my breathing and relax. I stick to the beginner's class since I rarely have time to come, and feel like a newbie every time.

"Chin up, Quinn," the instructor says.

I do as she says and my muscles strain in the best way possible.

"Hold your position. Good. Now let's get in to downward dog."

The next thirty minutes fly by without Heather yapping in my ear. She's my best friend and I love her dearly, but it's nice to keep some of my feelings about Deacon private. I like having him all to myself.

Heather leaves to get ready for work. They're doing the monthly inventory tonight, but I'm not ready to go home yet. I don't get many free evenings. After I change, I head off down the street with my gym bag.

I duck inside one of my favorite coffee shops and splurge on a white mocha latte with a dash of cinnamon. I pay and grab my drink, then walk through the small park on the way to the apartment, watching the kids play. They're so carefree, without a worry in the world. No crazy course schedule or workload. No bills. No sick parent to take care of.

It's nice to watch them, and I find myself wondering when I went from *that* to my current state. It didn't happen overnight. Adulthood doesn't smack you in the face, it creeps up on you slowly until one day you no longer recognize yourself.

I scroll through my phone and think about sending Deacon a text, but I remember he has Decker's bachelor party today. Wow, finally a free night and Deacon's busy. I could never ask him to skip the party, though. That would be ridiculous and irrational and something I'd never do. But, I can secretly wish he was here, spending time with me. Nothing wrong with that.

Tate flew to Dallas for the weekend to hang out with her friends back home for her bachelorette party. She invited me to go but there was no way I could leave Dad. Who am I kidding? I couldn't afford the flight, even if I'd wanted to go. It was sweet of her to offer, though.

Before I realize, it gets late and I need to head home and make dinner. I try to stick to a routine with Dad as much as I can. As I walk up the sidewalk toward our building, I freeze in my tracks. There's an ambulance out front, and blue and red lights swirl and reflect off the buildings. EMTs wheel someone out the door on a gurney. My coffee hits the sidewalk and explodes into the air. I take off in a dead sprint.

Please, don't let it be him. Please, don't let it be him.

It's him.

Olly, the landlord, meets me at the ambulance. "He had a fall and bumped his head. Ronnie heard him yell for help. He's going to be okay, Quinn. Don't worry."

My head spins so fast I feel dizzy. It's too much to take in all at once. He'll be okay. He *has* to be.

They won't let me in the ambulance with him. There's no room and they're trying to hurry in case he had another stroke.

The EMT guy shouts, "University of Chicago Medical Center."

I rush to my car so I can follow.

DEACON

DECKER ROLLS his eyes and knocks back another shot at the strip club. "You assholes plan this for me or yourselves?" He lets out a derisive snort.

I hold both hands up. "Don't look at me. This was the other two." I point a finger and wave it between Dexter and Donavan. All I want is to hang out with Quinn right now, but I'm stuck here. There's no way I could get out of it and time is dragging ass.

A brunette with giant fake tits takes to the pole. Her ass cheeks clap against a dental-floss thong as our idiot brothers throw wads of dollar bills at her. They both have unlit cigars hanging from their mouths and laugh it up. I can't help but think only a few months ago I'd have been right there with them. That was the old Deacon, though.

Part of me smiles at the sight. At least Decker and Donavan are in the same room together. Shit has been tense between them ever since Donavan called Weston and told him about Tecker. They need to kiss and make up. I've never seen my brothers pissed at each other for longer than a day or two.

"I'd have been happy with a night of poker." Decker downs another drink. "Fuck, imagine all the germs in this shit hole."

I nod. "I hear you."

Decker rolls his eyes. I know he doesn't believe me, but he doesn't know about Quinn and me. I haven't told anyone but Dex. I don't want to make shit weird for her at work and Dex won't say anything. There's no way she'd be fired. I'd make sure of that, but she doesn't need the added anxiety. She has enough to worry about as it is.

"You seeing this shit?" Dex howls and points at the stage. The stripper is picking up dollar bills with the ol' downstairs.

"Fuck." I look away.

This is not my damn scene at all. In fact, it's a little repulsive. I can't believe I used to enjoy this kind of shit.

I would rather be anywhere in the world but here. What I'd love most, is to take Quinn to dinner, or just hang out and watch a movie.

I know I sound like a pussy, but I don't give a single fuck. I wonder if Decker would kill me if I left early? I glance at my phone to see if Quinn has texted.

"What's with you? You seem distracted. Somewhere else you'd rather be?"

"Who me?"

"Yeah, you, dipshit. What's her name?"

"Who?"

"Whoever's call you're expecting on your phone. You can't stop staring at it."

Before I can answer, my phone rings and Quinn's name flashes on the screen.

"Don't think I don't know it was you who messed with all the shit in my…"

His words trail off and everything else fades away when I swipe the screen. "Gotta take this." I cover the receiver until I'm outside. "Hey."

"Deacon." My name filters through the speaker on a sob.

My hand grips the phone so tight my knuckles turn white and my stomach twists. "What's wrong?"

"It's my dad… he umm, fell. I'm on my way to the hospital and I didn't know who else to call. I couldn't ride with him. They wouldn't let—"

"What hospital? I'm on my way."

"No, you have Decker's thing. I'm being selfish. I just wanted to hear your voice for a second."

She sounds like she's about to have a breakdown and all I want to do is hold her in my arms.

"Decker will understand. What hospital?"

"University of Chicago Medical Center."

"Everything will be fine. He'll be okay. Just drive safe, I'm on my way." I take off in a dead sprint for the street. The only thing that matters right now is how fast I can get to her. I hail a cab and must scare the shit out of the cabbie when I leap in.

"University of Chicago Medical Center! Now!" I pull three hundred bucks from my wallet and toss it up in his seat. "As fast as you can."

I ARRIVE at the hospital and see Quinn alone in the waiting area. I rush up to the desk before she can cut me off.

"Why the hell isn't she back there with her dad?"

The lady behind the counter holds her hands up and her eyes turn into two huge white orbs.

I point back at Quinn, but don't even turn. "This shit is unacceptable. I want her back there. *Now!*"

Quinn puts her hand on my arm and turns me to face her. "It's okay. I saw him already." She bolts into my arms. I yank her close to me and run my hand up and down her back, then hold the back of her head in my palm and smooth her hair with it. I should feel terrible about her father, but at the same time I can't help but think this is what I'm meant to do. Be there for her when she needs me. Everything in my world feels right again.

I pull back from her, place both palms on her cheeks, and swipe her tears away with my thumbs. "What happened?"

"God, I don't know, just...thank you for coming. I would've called Heather but she's working and I..."

"Just, slow down. It's going to be fine. I'm glad you called."

Her bloodshot eyes meet mine. "You are?"

"Of course I am. So what's going on?"

"I wasn't home. I was walking through the park and saw the ambulance and it all happened so fast. They took me back to see him right when we got here, but now they're doing some kind of scan and making sure he didn't have another stroke. I guess he tried to change chairs but forgot to lock his wheels in place. He hit his head on the corner of the entertainment stand."

I breathe a sigh of relief. Sounds like a bump on the head, but I make sure not to downplay anything. "I'm sure everything will be fine. He's tough as nails."

Quinn shakes her head. "I should've been there."

"It's not your fault. Accidents happen."

"I know, but still. He's my responsibility. If I'd been there..."

"You can't hover over him twenty-four seven. You could've been in the shower or the kitchen. He won't blame you." I kiss her temple and hold her against me.

The nurse comes through the double doors and calls Quinn over.

I follow.

"He didn't have another stroke but we're going to keep him overnight to monitor for signs of a concussion. Sorry, I know you were worried out here. You can go back in and see him now."

I shoo Quinn away when she glances back at me. "Go. I'll wait out here."

She follows the nurse.

I walk over to the desk. The woman looks like she might have a panic attack with me standing there.

"I'm very sorry. I didn't know she'd already been back to see him."

The woman nods. "It's okay. No problem."

"No, it's not okay. I should've had all the facts before I started in on you. I apologize."

"Okay, well, apology accepted, sir."

"Thank you." I step outside for some fresh air and text Decker.

Deacon: Sorry. Had to bounce. Something important came up.

Decker: Something or someone?

Deacon: Both.

Decker: Everything okay?

Deacon: It will be, but I can't make it back out. I'm sorry.
Decker: It's fine. You owe me.

WHEN QUINN finally returns from the room, she's smiling. "Thanks for coming and waiting. Sorry if I was a little dramatic on the phone."

He must be doing okay if she's smiling.

"Don't mention it. Is he okay?"

"I think so. He's a little shaken up, but everything is normal."

"Good. So, you heading out?"

"Yeah. For a bit. Dad said we both need rest and he'd have them throw me out if I didn't go get some sleep."

"I'll drive you home."

Quinn shakes her head. "That's not—"

"Quinn, I'm driving."

She nods and hands over the keys. We walk out through the ER and into the parking lot to her car. I open the passenger door for her, then walk around and climb in the driver's side.

The whole ride home I don't say much. I know she has a lot on her mind.

When we arrive, I walk her to the door. I give her a kiss, but I don't want her to think I want more, with everything going on.

When our lips part ways, her eyes roam up to mine. "Stay with me? Please."

I know I told her we needed to take this slow, but fuck she's making it a torturous journey.

How the hell can I tell her no? It's impossible. There's nothing I want more than to hold her and comfort her—take care of her and make sure she has everything she needs. I give her a nod.

We both walk inside, and she heads to her bedroom. "Make yourself comfortable. I'm gonna change clothes."

"Sure." I pretend like I'm about to sit down, but once she's in her room I walk to the bathroom and start a bath for her. I find some lavender bath salts under the sink and dump them in. Once that's started, I pull out my phone to order a pizza. When that's done, I start back for the living room, but she appears in front of the bedroom door.

"Thought you were making yourself comfortable on the couch?"

I move out of her way and point to the tub. "Get in there. I don't want to hear from you for thirty minutes. I'll let you know when the food gets here."

"What kind of food?"

"Pizza."

She shakes her head. "I don't know how, but it seems like you can read my mind sometimes."

"I pay attention."

"Oh yeah? What kind of pizza did you get?"

"Mushroom and extra cheese." I walk past her and give her a playful little slap on the ass, coupled with a wink. "You're welcome."

"Glad to see you're still as cocky as ever." The way she smiles as she says the words tells me I'm knocking it out of the park right now.

"Thirty minutes. No sooner. Relax. I'll hold down the fort."

———

FORTY-FIVE MINUTES LATER, she comes out of the bathroom wearing silly pajama pants with rubber ducks on them and a matching tank top. I can see her nipples through the thin material and my cock takes notice.

I tug on her pantleg as she sits down on the couch. "Nice pants."

"Wore them just for you." Quinn curls into me and it feels so fucking good to just hold her. "Thank you for the bath. It was perfect. You always know just what I need."

A movie plays in the background on the TV but I can't stop staring at her.

She wiggles her ass against me to get comfortable and it's a little bit of heaven and hell at the same time. "I'm glad you're here. Thank you."

I push a few strands of hair behind her ear. "Nowhere I'd rather be." I tilt her chin up and kiss her softly on the lips. This is fucking perfect.

The door buzzes. It must be the pizza.

Quinn starts to get up.

I stop her. "I got it. Just lie there and relax."

"Yes, sir." She grins.

Fuck, even the way she calls me "sir" makes my dick hard.

I walk back with the pizza and set it on the coffee table. "I still don't know what kind of normal human being from Chicago doesn't like deep dish."

Quinn shrugs. "Can't help what I like." She takes a piece straight out of the box like *fuck plates*. "And I can't believe you remembered my favorite place, and the exact pizza I always order."

"I've seen you haul in leftovers to the office. I notice everything about you."

Quinn takes a huge bite and her eyes roll back like she's in heaven. "I can't argue with you. You're batting one hundred."

I laugh. "That's actually a baseball stat, and one hundred is piss poor. One thousand is perfect."

She shrugs, not even remotely interested in anything but her pizza. "Well, I gave it my all."

"I applaud your effort."

QUINN

IT'S UNDERSTATING things to say I'm nervous about leaving Dad on his own today, but he did fine the last few days when I finally went back to work. I really didn't need to take two days off last week, but Deacon went over my head to Decker and insisted they give me the time. It's been one week since the fall.

I'm still surprised Deacon didn't try anything while we were alone at the house. All he did was hover over me and rush to get anything I needed. It was sweet and cute and so not how I imagined him handling any kind of crisis.

Nerves flutter through my stomach thinking about him. I'm heading to his apartment; we still haven't had sex since we started dating. It's been nice getting to know him, but I'd be lying if I said I didn't miss the sex. A girl has needs. I'm afraid it'll be different, now that there's an emotional connection there. Still, if there's one thing I do know, it's that I want sex. I want sex with Deacon, bad.

When I arrive at his apartment, he greets me with a kiss. "I'm almost ready."

"Okay." I grin at the walls. It seriously looks like he hired my dad to decorate.

"That helmet's signed by Tom Brady."

"Who?" I smile. It's fun messing with him. Even I know who Tom Brady is.

"You're joking right?"

I laugh. "Yeah. He's married to Gisele."

Deacon shoots me a playful glare. "That the only reason you know who he is?"

I shrug. "Is there anything else important about him?"

He strolls over and takes my hands in his. "Did you know you're perfect?"

"I am? What am I doing here with you then?" I smirk.

He hooks an arm around my waist and tickles my ribs. Our lips meet and going out to lunch just became an afterthought.

"Fuck, I've missed your smart-ass mouth. Nice to have you back."

"That all you missed?" I whisper.

"No. I missed these too." His lips pepper sweet kisses down my throat as his hands slide down to my breasts over my t-shirt.

Finally!

Deacon wastes no time gripping the hem of my shirt and pulling it over my head. A groan strains from his throat when he gets a full look at the white sheer lace bra I'm wearing.

"These. Off." He fumbles with the button of my jeans, and I kick off the red leather heels I wore just for him. The moment my jeans are off, Deacon lifts me to his chest.

My legs hook around his waist, and he carries me to his bedroom.

"Your clothes are in my way now, Mr. Collins."

"We should do something about that."

"Yes, we should."

"Someone wants to get laid."

I shake my head and kiss him again. "You have no idea."

"Well, well, my dirty little office slut is still in there."

Any other man would get kneed in the balls for talking to me like that, but right now, in the moment, it's hot as all hell. Excitement swirls down and pools between my thighs at his filthy mouth. He heaves me onto the bed, and I realize something. Not only is this my first time in *his* bed, but it's our first time in a bed at all.

It feels like we should celebrate or something. I suppose the sex will be enough of a reward, but there's something special about the moment.

I'm not sure how, but his clothes are off in an instant, as if they've magically disappeared.

He hovers over me and brushes a lock of hair behind my ear. "You have no idea how many times I've imagined this." His strong hands roam my body as he looms above, staring into my eyes. "Alone. In my room. No time constraints."

I gulp at the look in his eyes right now. He looks one part wolf, one part lion.

He traces a finger along the curve of my shoulder. "Do you have any idea how beautiful you are?"

"I enjoy hearing you tell me."

"Most beautiful woman I've ever seen." His lips land on mine.

It's soft and slow at first, but I need more than that. "Thank you, Mr. Collins." I bat my eyelashes at him, reach between his legs, and stroke his cock. It grows harder against my palm.

"Fuck, I'm going to enjoy this."

"I sure hope so, big guy." I smirk but all silliness leaves my face when those stormy eyes narrow on me.

His hand slides between my thighs. "Plenty big, but you already know that." His voice is coarse and laced with raw need. It's primal and makes my blood hum with desire.

My back arches into him, eager for his touch, longing for any kind of friction I can get.

Sliding down my body, his mouth replaces his hand between my legs. His nose presses against my panties and he breathes me in. "I like these. Too bad they're in my way." Deacon snaps the waistband in one possessive movement.

I let out a gasp before I can stop myself.

If I thought he was sexy and dominating in the supply closet...he's a whole other level of alpha in his bedroom. The look in his eyes tells me everything he wants to do to me, and I'd be lying if I said my heart rate doesn't redline at the sight of him.

I glance around the room. There's nothing personal on display other than a black and white photograph of him and his brothers. I almost ask him to turn it around. It's like their eyes are watching—judging—and waiting to score his performance.

If I say it he might think I'm crazy, but right now, I might just be crazy the way he's teasing me.

Slow and methodical, he kisses the tops of my thighs, taking his sweet-ass time. I need more of him, now, but he knows exactly what I want and withholds like he always does, teasing me into a frenzy. He bites down on my skin hard enough to leave a mark.

I let out a small yelp of approval and rake my nails through his hair.

Looking up at me he says, "This is mine." He flicks his tongue across my clit, his eyes fixed on me, watching every reaction. "Only mine, Quinn."

His words turn my insides to Jell-O. When he says things like that all my thoughts and reservations drift away. All I can do is nod in surrender.

"Fingers or mouth?" He teases at my clit with his tongue and slides a finger inside me.

I nod furiously.

"Use your words, Quinn." He slips the finger out, and I clench around nothing the second it leaves me.

My hips lift instinctively, practically begging for his touch, and all the breath steals from my lungs. "Both." It's the only word I can manage.

"So fucking greedy." His mouth latches onto my clit and the man is relentless. This time he pushes two fingers in deep and with more force.

Right when I'm on the edge of an epic orgasm, he lifts up, not letting me finish. "There's nothing better than watching you get off." He presses his mouth against my inner thigh and brushes his hands over my nipples. With one swift motion, he reaches up with both hands and jerks the cups of my bra down, leaving me exposed. His fingers grow possessive and dig into my hips as he yanks me against his face, over and over. "I could fuck this pussy with my mouth all goddamn day."

"I. No. Complain." The man turns my words to gibberish, and a light moan parts my lips.

He slides up my body, slanting over me.

His lips meet mine and against my mouth he whispers, "Can you taste yourself on my tongue?"

Oh. My. God.

Can he get any dirtier?

Yes. Yes he can. It's a ridiculous question.

Rocking back on his calves he pulls a condom from the nightstand drawer.

Pre-come beads on the head of his cock and I want to lick it off.

Deacon takes his time rolling the condom on. I watch the whole time, praying for him to hurry up and get me off. I'm practically writhing on his bed. If he so much as breathes on me I'll combust immediately.

There's something between us and we both feel it. I need to just give in and embrace it, put all my chips on the table, because not being serious with Deacon doesn't seem like an option.

He lies back and fists his dick so that it's pointed up at the ceiling.

I crawl toward him, unable to resist the pull vibrating through every atom of my body. I lift one leg and slowly slide down on him, until I've taken every last inch.

He groans as I squeeze around him, and his eyes roll back for a brief second. "I've been dying for this. To have you in my bed, on top of me."

"Well, you have me." Our bodies move together in perfect rhythm, like we've done this a million times. In a way, it feels like we have. Right now, we're two old souls who've always shared a connection. I grind my hips in small circles, loving what it does to him.

His thumb goes straight to my clit, stroking back and forth across it while he watches my face. His other palm smacks my ass and he groans. "Fuck. Right there."

I shudder at his words, his thumb, his cock—all of him. As much as I love the way I feel when he's inside me, I also love knowing how crazy I drive him. That I can satisfy him as much as he satisfies me.

"That's it. Come on my dick. I want to feel you."

"Oh God, Deacon." My orgasm crashes through me, spinning and whirling like a hurricane.

His thumb speeds up on my clit and I ride the undulating waves until I'm breathless. I don't know how I manage not to collapse onto him. I'm running on pure determination and willpower right now.

"So. Close. Too." His eyes stay locked on mine the entire time, watching me come undone on top of him.

He finally places both hands on my hips and presses me down, so I take every bit of him as deep as possible. At the same time he grunts. His cock twitches inside me.

"Fuck, Quinn."

My eyes flutter open at the sight of him emptying himself, and for a brief second I wish he wasn't wearing the condom. I want to feel him bare inside me, filling me.

I shouldn't think that. It would be incredibly reckless and stupid, but I can't help myself. I want to know what it'd feel like, what it'd be like. It should scare the hell out of me, but it doesn't. I can't form rational thoughts right now. My brain is a jumbled mess of exposed wires.

When he finishes, I collapse on top of him, and he holds me to his chest for what seems like an eternity, but probably isn't more than a few seconds. Then, I remember he's still inside me with a full condom and I roll off to his side.

We both lie there, panting, staring up at the ceiling. At the same time, we both turn over to face each other.

Through several labored breaths I say, "That was…"

"Incredible." He finishes the sentence for me.

I never want to get up. Never want to leave his bed again.

Eventually, my brain resumes its regular function, and I excuse myself to the bathroom.

Staring in the mirror, I splash cold water on my face.

Glancing around, I still can't believe I'm here with Deacon in his apartment. It's surreal after months of hooking up at work. Three months ago, if someone had told me I'd be dating one of the Collins brothers, I'd have died laughing. I'd have written them off as a crazy person.

But, here I am.

When I return to the room, Deacon's in front of his dresser pulling some clothes out. He tosses me an oversized t-shirt as he walks toward me. He stops and plants a kiss on my forehead, then shoulders past into the bathroom.

I have to stop and ogle him as he walks away. He's so—perfect, and male, and manly as all hell. His broad shoulders and thigh muscles expand and contract with each step. The way he walks almost looks like he's strutting, but it's not because he's some douche trying to look tough. It's because his chest is so damn wide it forces his arms out at an angle. I can't help myself and glance down from his back to between his legs. His thick cock hangs down, bouncing from side to side.

I can't help but give him a little catcall whistle.

"Enjoying the view?" he calls over his shoulder.

I bite my lower lip between my front teeth. "I am actually."

"Gonna end up in HR for sexual harassment." He closes the door to the bathroom, laughing on his way in.

"Worth it," I whisper to myself.

My body already starts to thrum with desire once more, just picturing him walking away from me. I pull his shirt over my head loving how it smells exactly like him.

He exits the bathroom still fully naked.

My cheeks pink at the sight of him from the front.

We just had sex in his bed.

"I love it when you blush." He walks up and traces my jaw with his finger. "Hungry?"

"Starving."

"Well then, how do you like your eggs?"

I smack at his chest, then grab it a little because it's hard as granite and I can't help myself. "Shut up. You cook?"

"I can do lots of things." He slips on his boxer briefs.

I follow him to the kitchen. "What can I do to help?"

He points at a bar stool along the kitchen island. "Just sit your hot little ass there and look pretty. I got this." He kisses my nose.

"Okay then, hotshot. Let's see what ya got." I cringe at my awkward, accidental rhyme, and take a seat on the stool.

"Okay, Funkmaster Flex." He laughs. "I see you're sitting in the front row. Big shocker. Might wanna grab your notebook and pencil."

"So I can write a Yelp review trashing your eggs?"

"You're gonna regret that in a few minutes. Just wait." He pulls down a spatula from a hanging pot rack and points it at me. "You'll see."

I laugh and watch him go to work. God what a view. There's something inherently sexy about a man cooking in nothing but boxer briefs. His muscles expand and constrict at the slightest movements as he strolls around the kitchen. I swear he looks like a breathing Michelangelo sculpture.

He grins at me as he pulls bacon and eggs from the refrigerator. "Like omelets?"

"Yeah." Anything with Deacon sounds good. Why does it feel like all the air leaves the room when he's around? He makes me insane.

I can't believe he's cooking in his kitchen for me. It feels like a dream. This whole day has been amazing so far. I never want it to end, but I know as the sun inches down on the horizon, reality awaits. At some point, I'll need to go home and take care of Dad. I don't mind *that*. I just wish there was some way I could have everything I want all at once. My life seems like a zero-sum game. If I want time with Deacon, it has to come out of time with Dad. And if I want time with Dad, it has to come out of time with Deacon.

I allow myself to briefly think about what it'd be like if we all lived together. It's insane, I know. But I wouldn't have to feel so torn between the two of them. Trying to be two places at once is exhausting. I'm allowed to think about what it'd be like, even if it would never happen.

"What's going on in that brain of yours?" He must notice the far-off look in my eyes.

"Wondering how terrible this omelet will be." I laugh and breathe a sigh of relief when he chuckles at my terrible joke.

There's no way in hell I'll tell him I was fantasizing about him living with Dad and me. It's so hilarious I almost laugh out loud but catch myself. I have this vivid picture of his reaction in my mind. It consists of his silhouette sprinting over the horizon, growing tiny in the sunset. He's in nothing but his boxer briefs, and he doesn't look back. Nope. Not once. There's nothing but a trail of dust kicked up in his wake.

284

I don't want to scare him off, but my feelings for Deacon are so intense. He makes me so happy. Happier than I've ever been.

"My lady." He does some medieval curtsy and slides a plate in front of me, then retrieves a glass of orange juice.

It looks so damn good I almost want to take a picture of it with my phone. I take a bite of the fluffy eggs, cheese, and crunchy bacon, and I damn near have another orgasm. Okay, not really, but it's incredible. Incredible enough I let out a slight moan. Did he really just cook this? I'm so caught up in the moment of enjoying the omelet, I don't realize he sidles up next to me with a plate for him.

His warm breath exhales straight into my ear. "I love when you make that sound but it's usually because I'm inside you."

Heat blooms across my cheeks; they must be ten different shades of pink. How does he still find ways to make me blush? I should see these things coming, but secretly I hope he never stops. I also can't help but notice how he almost sounded jealous of the eggs. He's so damn—I don't know. He's just Deacon. I've never met anyone like him.

"Don't be shy." He digs into his plate, eating faster than I've ever seen anyone eat in my life.

He must catch me staring at him, because he pauses from inhaling his food and asks, "What?" with a mouthful of eggs.

I grin and shake my head. There are no words.

"You've never been in a cafeteria with eighty college football players. You eat when you fucking can or the linemen take all the damn food."

Well, that makes more sense. It also explains a lot of the practical jokes and his sense of humor. Dad always called it locker-room talk.

Deacon resumes annihilating his food, and I can't help but stare at his body. It must take a lot of protein to stay in that type of shape. I'm starting to think his suits don't actually do him justice. All the Collins men are tall, but Deacon is definitely thicker and more muscular than all of them. Football makes sense.

His eyes roll over to meet mine. "What's up?"

"All I can think about is getting you back in bed and getting these off you." I tug on the waistband of his boxers.

He takes a gigantic drink of juice and starts shoveling eggs into his mouth.

I stare at him with wide eyes. His damn fork looks like the Roadrunner's legs.

His hand shoots out with the fork in it and he taps it on my plate. "Eat up." It sounds like a drill instructor barking orders.

I continue to just gape at him.

He stops for a second, turns, and says, "You're gonna need the calories, Quinn."

I shake my head and laugh. "You're crazy."

"Crazy about you."

DEACON

GROANING AND STRETCHING, I move to roll out of bed and realize Quinn's head is on my chest. We took a nap after we finished eating. I look around the room, taking in the scene, and run my fingers through her hair. It's perfect.

Life is perfect.

I lie there, thinking about her living with me. A few months ago, I'd have dry-heaved at the thought of a woman moving in, but now, I think I could get used to waking up next to Quinn every morning.

I pull the sheet back and stare at the curve of her hip pressed up against me. There's a dusting of freckles on her right shoulder. It's impossible to see and not want to kiss them.

My eyes roam to the teeth marks on her left breast. Something primal stirs in me, in the unevolved part of my brain, back when cavemen would mark their territory. It doesn't bother me, though. There's nothing I want more than to protect her—take care of her, even though I know she can fend for herself.

To say I'm turned on right now is the understatement of the century. I'm like a damn addict. Just watching her is like a narcotic flooding my veins.

My cock hardens at the sight of her pale skin and smooth legs. I look at the clock and know her dad probably expects her home soon. I slip out of bed, thinking what I'm about to do might be a mistake, but I can't stop myself. I snatch her phone off the coffee table and press the call button.

"Hello." His voice is gruff.

"Mr. Richards, it's Deacon Collins."

"Is Quinn okay?"

"She's fine. I just wanted to let you know she fell asleep. I know she's normally home by now. I didn't want you to worry, but if there's anything you need, I'll do whatever I can."

"I'm good for a few more hours."

"Great. Thank you, sir." I end the call and grab a glass of water then slide back into bed.

Quinn rolls to her side, hugging my pillow. The urge to reach out and touch her is unbearable and I give in. I trace her curves with the tip of my index finger, down her hip toward her thigh, inching my way between her legs. She's about to get the wake-up call of her life; a Deacon Collins alarm clock special.

I can't imagine what it'd be like to sink my cock into her every morning.

It'd be perfect. We'd get up and fuck. Go to work, come home, have dinner, and fuck again.

I take one of her nipples between my fingers and slide my head down her stomach. She needs to know what it's like to wake up to my tongue every morning.

I don't make it down in time.

Quinn lets out a soft yawn and her eyes flutter open. They dart down and land on my head between her thighs, staring back up at her.

"Hi," she whispers.

"Hi." I slide back up and brush some hair from her cheek. "Sleep good?"

"Like a baby. I think I'm in love with your bed." She stretches her arms up behind her head.

I take the opportunity to grab her wrists and pin them there. We sit there a moment, faces inches apart. I want to ask her if that's all she loves, my bed, but I choke the words down. It's way too soon for that kind of talk.

"What time is it?" Her eyes widen with panic etched across her face.

"Five-thirty."

"Shit!" She breaks free and shoves past me. Her feet drop to the floor. "I need to get going. My dad."

I watch her from the bed. "Don't worry." I hook my arms around her waist and pull her back into the covers with me. "He's fine. I called him."

Quinn's eyes turn into two huge orbs. "You called him?" Then, a smile spreads across her face. "And how'd that go?"

I shrug like it was no biggie. "He said he's good for an hour or two."

Quinn falls into my arms and breathes a sigh of relief.

I rest my chin on her shoulder where it meets her neck.

"You two besties now? Should I worry you'll be texting and trading football stories?" She laughs at herself and I love hearing that sound. The sound of her happiness.

"Come here," I growl. "We only have two hours and I don't know if we'll have enough time."

Her eyebrows rise as her head falls back on my chest. "Time for what?"

"Time to fuck each other with our mouths."

She squeals my name as I flip her over. "Deacon!"

"Got something against a proper sixty-nine?" I lean down and capture her nipple between my teeth.

288

She lets out a soft moan, more like a purr, and my cock hardens at the sound. I go back and forth between her tits trying to decide which one I like best. It's an impossible chore. I tease her repeatedly until she spreads her legs and says, "Fine. Do what you must, sir. I'll endure it."

"I like when you call me sir. Makes me feel powerful and shit."

"Does it now?"

"Goddamn right it does." I roll next to her, abandoning the idea of taking my time. I can't keep my hands off her. "I need you here."

She squeals when I grip her hips and yank her to my mouth. She's facing away from me and straddling my face. I exhale warm breath across her clit, knowing it'll drive her crazy. Like I expected, her thighs quiver against my cheeks.

Her pussy lowers to my mouth, and I dig my fingers into her thighs so she can't scurry away if things get too intense. I bury my tongue in her, licking, sucking, and teasing.

Soft coos of approval fall from her lips, and then I feel her mouth on me.

"Fuck."

She stops to say something, and I fight the urge to grab her head and shove her back down. "Sounds like I'm doing a good job on my end."

I laugh. "Oh, you want this to be a competition?"

"First one to come loses."

"Deal." I smack her on the ass playfully to seal the agreement.

Her lips meet my cock once more, and I already know I'm at risk of losing this bet. Her hot mouth sucks around my shaft taking me as far as she can.

I flatten my tongue on her pussy and tease her clit with the tip of my tongue. She squirms immediately and her cheeks suck tighter around me.

This is heaven. Pure fucking heaven right here.

I always operated under the assumption I could eat pussy better than I could play football, but Quinn is a worthy opponent.

I sink a finger inside her while I tongue her clit. The angle damn near makes my hand cramp up, but I'm not about to lose. Her wetness streams down her thighs and lands on my tongue and she tastes like…mine.

All fucking mine.

It does nothing but fuel me, and I speed up the tempo. Her legs tremble, more and more, amping up in intensity, and I know she's fucking close. I slide a finger down to collect some lube from her hot cunt, then tease the rim of her ass with it.

Her hips start to buck, and I know I have this thing won now. In fact, I'm so confident, I take my mouth from her for a moment to do a little mid-game shit talking. "It's all over for you, Quinn." I watch my finger press tighter against her and smile when she shakes even harder at the sensation. "Who knew the innocent girl at the office was such a filthy little slut in the bedroom."

She always comes fast when I talk dirty to her.

I hum against her clit and tease both of her holes.

Her pussy clenches tight around my finger and I can tell she's fighting it back with everything she has. Her hips buck against my mouth until she's full on fucking my face and fingers. I love every second of it. I add a second finger to her pussy and tease her ass with my thumb.

One day I'll fuck her there.

Suddenly, I notice I've been so concentrated on pleasing her, I didn't realize my own hips were thrusting up and down, fucking her mouth.

"Dea-con." She pulls her mouth away from my dick, and her entire body quakes. "Oh God."

I yank her into me, and the orgasm pulses through her, from her hips down to her curled toes. She's like a live wire, short-circuiting all over the place.

While she rides my face, my balls lift high and tight.

Uh oh! What the hell?

Then, I feel it. Her fingers, stroking my cock up and down. Everything goes blurry for a split second, almost like an out-of-body experience, then I blow all over her hand.

I can't stop panting. Two-a-day practices in hundred-degree weather my whole life, and I've never been as spent as I am right now. Just as I'm catching my breath, Quinn's mouth is on my cock.

I lean out around her ass and she's cleaning me up with her tongue. I already have the urge to fuck her again. I'm not going soft anytime soon, not with her licking around my shaft.

"I'd call it a draw."

She doesn't see me watching her, and she smiles against my dick. "I was still going after you tapped out."

"Oh bullshit. Remind me to have cameras installed. In case we need an official review in the future to keep you from cheating."

"I'm sure that's exactly why you'd want a camera in here."

I grin. Fuck, she's perfect.

I'm nowhere near done with her, so I flip her around and lift her on top of me.

She doesn't miss a beat. Her hot pussy slides down on my cock, and I nearly lose it. God, she's so hot and wet. I'm not wearing a condom and I never imagined her feeling this goddamn amazing.

She starts to move up and down, but I grip her by the hips and stop her. I stare up into her eyes. "You sure?"

Her cheeks flush and she nods.

Holy fuck.

Quinn takes me all the way to the base, and I groan when she squeezes tight around me. It's so much better this way, bare, skin to skin. I palm her ass and spread her cheeks apart. After her little show earlier, I'm not about to let up on pressing that button. I slip my pinky up against her puckered ass as she rides me. It doesn't take long. Another orgasm rocks through her. It's so intense I can barely hang on.

Her hot pussy clenches around me, and without the condom between us I don't know how much more I can take. Everything about her intensifies to eleven.

She doesn't know, but Quinn's the only woman I've ever fucked without protection. In a way, I feel like she's my first. It's so much more than sex. It's real and passionate and emotional. It's everything, and I can't let go of it now that I've experienced it with her.

My eyes roll back in my head and I want to come inside her so bad it aches down to my bones. I hold back, knowing I shouldn't.

My brain goes to war, because I don't want to fucking hold back. I want it more than anything I've ever wanted in my life. The thought alone should terrify me, but with Quinn it feels so fucking right and the rest of the world fades away, leaving nothing but the two of us here in this moment.

I lean up and push her back, breaking our connection for a split-second before I slide right back in.

Her ankles hook around my waist and I slant over her mouth and kiss the shit out of her. I know I said I'm possessive, that Quinn is mine, but she owns me just as much, if not more. Nothing has ever felt more right than this, than us.

Our tongues intertwine as I take her as deep as I can. Our foreheads press together, and I lock eyes with her. I swear I can see everything about her in them, all her thoughts and feelings, her goals and desires.

I slide into her over and over, long deep strokes. She gives me everything I want and more. Things I never knew I wanted or needed but I want and need them from her.

Only her.

So.

Fucking.

Intense.

I bite down on her shoulder as my balls tighten. The war rages in my brain as an orgasm inches up my shaft, but at the last second, I pull out and come all over her stomach. Using the head of my cock, I sign my name in it, right there on her belly, my eyes never leaving hers.

Through my rough pants, the only word that escapes my lips is, "Mine."

Quinn hooks her arms around my neck, pulling my mouth to hers for a kiss.

After we catch our breaths, I grin down lazily at her flushed expression. "We need a shower. You can't go home like this."

We both laugh while she shakes her head.

"Definitely not. I don't care how good you were at football."

It's hard as hell to keep my hands off her in the shower. It's equally difficult to keep my dick from getting hard, but I know if I touch her right now it'll send me on a mission to convince her to spend the night. That's a position I refuse to put her in, regardless of how many positions I'd like to put her in. Her dad needs her, and she has to get home.

I know without a doubt I'll be jerking off later to the image of her all soaped up in my shower.

Once we're toweled off and dressed, and it's time for her to leave, I pull her back one more time for a kiss. Who am I kidding? I pull her back four times, promising each one is the last. I can't remember ever feeling this carefree in my life. Colors are more vibrant and sounds more vivid. It feels like I'm floating in the clouds, completely weightless.

She breaks away from my last kiss far too soon.

My hands instinctively roam her hips.

"Deacon, I gotta go." She pulls away, still grinning.

"Text me when you get home."

"I will." She stops to get on the elevator, but before I close my door, she sprints back for one more kiss, then finally breaks free and leaves.

When she disappears into the elevator an emptiness settles over me and I don't like it at all.

She's the only one who can soothe this ache deep inside me. Not seeing her face is torture.

My phone rings from the other room and it's a welcome distraction from thinking about Quinn walking away. I jog back to the bedroom and Rick Lawrence's name lights up on the screen.

About fucking time.

I've been waiting on this call. I swipe my finger across the screen and place the phone next to my ear. "Tell me something good, bitch."

"Better than good. We need to meet."

"The Gage?" It's a restaurant with a nice bar over by Millennium Park. Everyone from the office hangs out there after work sometimes.

"Fifteen minutes."

"Perfect timing. See you there."

I HOP out of a cab on Michigan Avenue, across the street from the park. I didn't feel like driving and parking downtown, and I wanted to be able to think freely about Quinn without dealing with traffic. Walking through the glass door, I spot Rick at the bar knocking back a rocks glass that's most likely filled with expensive whiskey.

I take the stool next to him and order a scotch.

He doesn't say a word, just slides a file in front of me. "I smell virgin pussy in my future."

Jesus, this guy.

I crane my head around to make sure nobody is within earshot.

Rick grins wide as hell but stares straight ahead, clearly amused with how uncomfortable he makes people. The guy has no filter. It's one thing to talk that way with the guys in a fucking locker room, but he lets it fly no matter where he's at.

"Depends on what you have here." I flip through the folder and my eyes widen. My hands speed up on the papers, my eyes scanning the pages. "Fuck, can I use any of this? How the hell did you get it?"

"First, we have something more important to discuss."

"Okay?"

"I saw Donavan looking at my sweet, innocent Mary the other day. You're going to take care of that, right?"

I wave a flippant hand in his direction, my eyes still roaming the evidence he brought. "Yeah, yeah. Consider it done. Can I fucking use this shit?"

"All admissible. Didn't have to do anything shady."

I turn and give him a stare that says *don't fuck with me.*

He holds both hands up and laughs. "I'm not bullshitting. Nobody knows. I kept up my end of the bargain."

I slide my rocks glass over and bump his with it, unable to peel my eyes away from the documents in front of me. "I'll talk to Donavan." There's no way I'll talk to Donavan, because then he might actually take an interest if he knows there's competition. I already know there's no way in hell he wants Mary and her ankle-length skirts. I'm sure he just glanced in her direction or ordered her to do something for him.

Rick knocks back his whiskey and stands up. "Well then, I gotta go to mass or whatever it's called. Have to get right with the Lord. Jesus won't be the only one getting nailed in church this week." He tosses me a grin and heads out before I can reply to his blasphemy.

My eyes glance once more to the papers. I'm about to score a game-winning touchdown for the firm, and I'm going to rub that shit right in Tecker's smug faces.

DEACON

It's early Monday morning and I couldn't feel better.

Dr. James Flynn stands in front of the building as I hop out of a cab.

"Mr. Flynn."

"Deacon." He reaches out and shakes my hand.

Dude has a decent grip for being in his sixties. He looks confused.

I hold up the file Rick gave me. "It'll all make sense in a minute. Thanks for coming on such short notice."

We walk into the building and head to the receptionist's desk.

Dr. Flynn's eyes roam around, taking in the surroundings. "Why are we meeting at her lawyer's office?"

"I'm about to put this whole ordeal behind us. Trust me."

"Can I help you?" asks the receptionist.

"We have a meeting with Chauncey." He's the lawyer representing the woman who accused Dr. Flynn.

"Oh yes, right this way."

She leads us down a long hallway, the clacking of her heels amplified by the tile and twelve-foot ceiling. At the end, we walk into a conference room surrounded by four glass walls.

It's nice, but not as nice as my firm's building. Their shit is on the first floor, and I'm about to remind Chauncey and his client they fucked with the wrong people.

"Mr. Collins, Dr. Flynn." Chauncey shakes both our hands. He's about Dr. Flynn's age and probably thinks he's about to steamroll a young hotshot attorney into a settlement.

I told him on the phone we were ready to talk about making a deal, but it was really just laying a trap for an ambush.

His client sits there with a cocky grin on her face. I can practically see the dollar signs in her eyes.

Despite that, I can't help but notice Dr. Flynn doesn't look angry. He has no idea what I have in my file, but he doesn't look emotional at all. His demeanor is friendly even.

Fuck, this guy has way more composure than I do. If some woman tried to ruin my career I'd burn her house to the ground. There's no way I'd smile and be nice. I wouldn't even pretend.

We all sit down, and Chauncey starts in, "So, we have matters to discuss."

"Yes, we do." I pull the manila folder out and set it in front of me.

Every eye in the room lands on it.

"What's that?" asks Chauncey.

"Just some research." I open it up and rifle through the pages, pretending to read them even though I have them pretty much memorized. "Has your client ever lived in Phoenix?"

The smug grin disappears from her face, and her eyes widen.

"Maybe worked for a…" I pause, for dramatic effect. "Dr. Lancaster?"

Now, her face turns red with rage. Her entire body tenses and her hands grip the arms of her chair.

"What is this?" Chauncey reaches over for her forearm. "I thought we were discussing a settlement?"

I ignore his question and keep going, staring right at her. "Of course, you weren't using the name Bridgette Smith at that time, were you? How about New Orleans and a Dr. Markwardt? That ring a bell?"

Chauncey looks at Bridgette, then back at me. "What's going on here?"

"Well, it seems your client has a pattern. Job as a nurse. Sexual harassment suit. Payday. Moves on when the money runs out, I'm guessing. It's a clever little cycle, until you get caught."

"Let me see those."

I slide the papers over to him but keep some in front of me.

He fumbles through the pages. "Even if you can prove this is her, it doesn't mean your client didn't do what she's accused him of."

Bridgette, or whatever her real name is, perks up in her seat, like maybe there's still some hope.

Surprisingly, Dr. Flynn remains calm and collected, like he doesn't have a care in the world. He hasn't said a word and hasn't looked worried the entire time this case has developed. All he ever insisted on was a fair defense, from the beginning.

I glare at the woman across from me, because the shit she does undermines every real victim of harassment and sexual assault and makes it difficult for them to come forward. There's a fear they won't be believed, because it's rare for concrete evidence to be present in these cases. Not to mention, I just don't like her.

"Let me just squash any hope you have of getting paid today." I keep my eyes locked on her. "These…" I slide more papers out into the middle of the table. "Are text messages to and from your friend, Crystal."

Her face heats up again and her jaw sets firm. She knows I have her.

"If you'd kept quiet, we might be cutting you a check. But you had to go brag, didn't you? And I'm guessing, since you like to screw people over, none of your friends are actually loyal friends. Yet, you spilled your guts to Crystal about how you were about to get a huge settlement from Dr. Flynn." I slide another sheet of paper out. "This is a sworn affidavit from Crystal stating you also told her you made it all up. You can read it if you want. You go into a lot of detail."

I push the papers toward her and she shoves them back at me.

I snicker and gesture toward the affidavit. "Know what that cost me? All your messages and emails and that affidavit?"

Bridgette glares. "I don't know. What?"

"Five hundred bucks. That's how easy your friend rolled over on you."

"Well, I think we all need to step back a moment…" Chauncey backpedals in a hurry. I can't tell if he's pissed or embarrassed by us blindsiding him.

"That won't be necessary." All eyes go to Dr. Flynn. He stares right at Bridgette.

She's moved past anger, and I swear it looks like she's about to cry now. It has to be an act. She's a damn con artist.

Dr. Flynn looks across the table at her with soft eyes. "Do you still want your job at the hospital?"

What the fuck?

I put a hand on his arm. "Doctor, I would strongly advise—"

He holds up his other hand to cut me off, but doesn't break eye contact with her. "Would you like your job back, Bridgette?"

The tears flow down her cheeks and she sniffles. "Yes, please. I'm sorry."

"Well, then. It looks like we have a settlement after all." He stands from his chair, walks around the large conference table, and holds his hand out in front of her. "See you at work Monday."

She looks up at him and takes his hand, nodding. "Yes. I-I'll be there."

"Sounds great. Can't wait to have you back." He looks at me and gestures with his head toward the door. "Let's go, son."

I don't know what the fuck just happened, but I gather up everything and head out with him. We make our way to the front of the building and I turn to face him.

"I have to advise that this is a terrible idea. I mean, I would understand if you don't want to go after her for defamation of character, but hiring her back..."

"Did you see that woman in there?"

I shrug. "Sure."

He sighs. "She didn't just start doing the things she does one day out of the blue. Someone taught it to her. She grew up with that. It's all she knows."

"I mean, okay? That's not a good reason to ruin people's lives for her own gain. Have you seen the things they've said about you on the internet? Even when we dismiss this case, the stigma will still be there. It's all over Twitter. 'High profile heart surgeon sexually assaults nurse.' All it takes is being accused. They won't publicize them dropping the suit because it's boring. It'll be back-page news."

"Do you have good parents? Do they love you unconditionally?"

What the hell is he talking about? "Sure. I mean, my mom would tell us she loved us no matter what. I always knew my dad felt that way, even if he didn't say it."

He points back at the building. "She's never known that. She's never had anyone care about her, even after she made a mistake. This is an opportunity to show her what that's like. If she continues the same behavior, then so be it. But I won't be the one who perpetuates it."

"I just… Okay. Fine. You're the client. If that's what you want to do, go for it."

I sigh.

He puts a hand on my shoulder. "You're a good kid, Deacon. It's why I like you. I can see you care about those close to you and your clients more than you care about money. I know you think you're looking out for me, and I appreciate that. People need to step back and see the big picture, though, before rushing to condemn someone. Nobody is perfect, I don't care who you are." He stares off across the street. "God knows I'm not, even if I didn't do this. The world needs a lot more empathy and a lot less judgment."

He climbs into a cab and I wave. It wasn't exactly how I saw this thing playing out, but it's still a win for the firm. Also, in roughly a decade of being a lawyer, I don't think I've ever seen anything like that happen.

Regardless, I can't wait to see Tecker's face when I shove this up their ass.

QUINN

I CAN'T STOP GLOWING from my time with Deacon. It's nothing like what I expected a relationship with him would be like. He leaves me breathless with the things he says and the sweet things he does.

I still can't believe he called Dad to check in on him. I mean, who the hell does that? I can't remember any guy I've dated taking that kind of initiative. The old man was impressed.

Like it wasn't already bad enough he worships Deacon as a football god. Dad keeps mumbling things like, "That boy is perfect."

The funny thing is, I can't argue with him.

He freaking cooked for me!

Maybe I'm a little jaded from years of preparing every meal, but I can't remember a man ever cooking for me, other than Dad, and that seems like ages ago.

My only complaint about the weekend is it went by too fast. I didn't want it to end. I spent most of yesterday studying and texting back and forth with Heather. She must've thought I was insane, because I never share intimate details of my dating life, not even with her.

But I couldn't help myself. Maybe I've never opened up to her because I've never dated anyone worth mentioning. I didn't share everything, of course, but I'm pretty sure I gushed non-stop to the point she likely rolled her eyes and wanted the conversation over. It was payback for all the times she's done it to me.

Now, it's Monday, and I'm already looking forward to Friday.

I get to my desk and don't even have to look; the sound of Tate's heels clacking on the floor is unmistakable. I glance in that direction just in time to catch her curly blonde head of hair turn the corner. I swear she's always so put together and dresses like she stepped out of a fashion spread in a magazine.

299

She starts to pass me, then stops, turns, and smirks. "Someone had a good weekend."

How the hell does she do that?

I must've been cheesing like a fool at my desk. Yes, Tate, it was in fact the best weekend I've had in a long time. I still can't believe I had unprotected sex with Deacon Collins. He's the first man I've ever let do that. I'm on birth control and he pulled out, but pregnancy isn't something I want to worry about anytime soon.

It was so damn intense, bare, skin to skin. I'm pretty sure I could have sex with him twenty-four seven the rest of my life and die happy. I'd probably live to be a hundred. Sometimes I feel like sex is all I think about now that I'm with him.

I'm with him.

Shit, Tate's still standing there.

"It was kind of perfect. How was yours?"

"Crazy. I spent both days with a wedding planner and centerpieces." She rolls her eyes.

I kind of feel sorry for the wedding planners. I wouldn't expect Tate to be a bridezilla because she's nuts about her wedding being perfect, I'd expect her to be one because she's nuts about *everything* in her life being perfect.

"Well, you only do it once." Hopefully.

"If I'd known it would eat so much time, I might've suggested we elope instead." She takes a deep breath and it's rare for her to look flustered. "It's all to spend the rest of my life with Decker. That's the only thing that keeps me from shoving a candelabra up someone's ass." She gets this faraway look in her eyes, though, when she mentions Decker. I want that for me.

Could I have that with Deacon? *Do* I already have that look with Deacon?

The answer in my mind is a resounding yes. I don't even have to think about it.

"You've got it bad," Tate mumbles.

I laugh and the phone rings.

I hold up a finger to Tate and answer. "Decker Collins' office. How may I help you?"

"I need your boss now."

"He's in a meeting. Can I give him a message?"

"Someone at your office fucked up my contract. I only received one percent of the payment. I can't purchase any materials for the job." The angry voice booms on the line and I realize it's one of the Beckley brothers.

"I'll look into it right away, Mr. Beckley. If you could just give me the specifics for Mr. Collins."

I take down the information, and Tate peeks at my notes, clearly taking an interest in what's going on.

I hold up a finger at her as the man screams a few more expletives before slamming the phone down. I feel awful for him but yelling at me won't fix his problem. Decker's going to blow his top when he hears. It won't be pretty around the office.

I cradle the phone and pull the Beckley contract up on my computer. I scan through the pages, looking for the section on payment terms.

Uh oh.

"Erm, Tate…this contract on that hotel renovation. Shouldn't this be ten percent instead of one? I'm no expert or anything but I…" I catch myself before I tell her about my class on contracts at school.

"Let me see it." She spins my monitor toward her, narrowing her eyes on the text I highlighted. "Yep." Her lips mash into a thin line and her jaw flexes. Someone is going to be up shit creek. I would not want to be on the other end of that conversation. Tate writes down something on a Post-it and storms toward Decker's office.

I close out the contract and hope whoever messed this up doesn't get in too much trouble. That's a significant error to overlook, though, and I have no idea how that could happen. There's a review process to prevent these types of things.

I keep myself occupied going through my schedule and making sure I'm ahead on my tasks for the day. I've learned the best thing to do when Decker is on the warpath is to have my head down and look busy. If I can have whatever he's after waiting for him before he asks, even better.

Where the hell is Deacon? He's normally in by now.

My phone buzzes with a text, like he can read my mind.

Deacon: Good morning, beautiful.

I grin at the screen then catch him stepping off the elevator.

I give him a small wave. It's awkward as hell, but he looks so cute with his sheepish grin when he sees me.

He lifts his hand to reciprocate, but immediately drops it when Decker hauls ass toward him.

Oh no.

Deacon, what'd you do?

Maybe Decker's pissed, and just wants to tell Deacon someone made a mistake and he needs to go have them fix it. That has to be it. At least, I hope that's it. It's probably wishful thinking.

The more heated Decker looks, the more my stomach twists into a knot.

Within a few seconds it's clear Deacon handled the contract. I wish I had known it was him. Maybe I could've gone to him after the phone call and given him a chance to correct it before anyone found out. But Tate was right there, and I couldn't lie to her.

Decker and Deacon both stomp toward a conference room once they notice all the associates and paralegals staring at them. What if Decker and Tate tell Deacon I'm the one who told them about the error in the contract?

Say goodbye to this fantastic Monday.

DEACON

I FIRE off a text to Quinn, then walk off the elevator feeling on top of the world. I spot her right as she gets my text and I smile and wave.

I'm a little late getting to the office after my meeting with Dr. Flynn, but I called ahead and told my secretary I'd be in by ten.

It doesn't take long for Decker to ruin my fantastic morning.

He heads right at me with a scowl on his face. "Conference room, now."

I glance around and the entire office stares at us. "Okay." I look back at Quinn, but her head's down. The uneasy look on her face makes me frown.

What the fuck just happened in here? I just won. A huge goddamn win and they're coming at me?

I follow Decker to the conference room and take a seat. Tate walks in a few seconds later.

Fucking wonderful.

"Someone piss in your oatmeal?" I grin.

"How about you explain this to me." Decker slams a contract down on the table.

I glance at it. It's the construction contract for the Beckley brothers. "What about it? Sent that off a long time ago."

"Look. At. It."

"You made a huge error." Tate stares at me with a smug grin, like she's pleased I made a mistake.

I can't think with her eyeing me while I try and read over the contract. My face heats up as I scan the words. I can't believe I just went through all that shit, murdering the Flynn case like a goddamn champion, and they have the balls to sit here and waterboard me over a fucking contract.

Tate lingers closer, almost at my side.

"Jesus Christ, would you get her the fuck out of here, Decker?"

"Excuse me?" Tate starts toward me like she might get in my face, all five foot nothing of her in heels.

I glare back at her. "You heard me. I don't need you running your yap at me non-stop. This shit doesn't concern you."

Her hands go to her hips. "I'm a partner just like you. Everything concerns me."

"Yeah, you had to fuck the boss to get the title, too. Now, what? You fucked Donavan over and that wasn't good enough? You gotta start in on me?"

"You little motherfucker." She takes off toward me once more and Decker grabs her by the waist and yanks her back. She doesn't stop yelling at me over his shoulder. "You had to share a mom with the boss to get your title, you ungrateful little—"

Decker puts himself between us and wheels around on her, then glares back at me. His face is fire-engine red. "Enough! Goddamn it!" He paces back and forth and clutches his temple like he might have an aneurysm. "Both of you are giving me a fucking headache with your crybaby bullshit."

Tate glares at me. I knew I'd hit a nerve, but I don't give a shit. She's not even thirty and struts around like she's a fucking manager. She ran off to Decker and made him drop Donavan's suit against one of her clients. Decker did exactly what she told him to do. He's like a puppy following her ass around.

Pussy-whipped bastard. It'd be understandable if she was cool like Quinn, but I don't know what the fuck he sees in her. Every once in a while, I think we're on good terms, then she does shit like this. Decker and Donavan barely talk anymore. She's ripping our family apart.

My hands ball into fists, and I know I need to keep my shit together and just ignore Tate and fix the problem. I'd love to throw the Flynn case right back at them, but they won't care. They only focus on the fuck-ups when it comes to me. Everything else gets swept under the rug or glossed over. I won't give them the satisfaction of downplaying my success.

I take a few deep breaths and skim over the contract, finally able to think. It doesn't take long to spot the mistake.

Yeah, I fucked up. So what? I typed one percent instead of ten. It's my fault. I know it is. It wouldn't have been a big deal if I hadn't ignored the review process and sent it through. It's no excuse for them to scold me like a child instead of treating me like an adult colleague.

I shake my head. Jesus, the one time I skip a step, this shit happens. It's like the universe hates me.

"I'll take care of it."

Decker takes a step toward me. Clearly, he's not going to let me do my job and fix the problem without running his mouth about how irresponsible I am. "Do you know how much money this cost a brand-new client? He's pissed and threatening litigation."

"Fuck, I said I'd fix it. Calm down and I'll smooth it over."

Tate pops off from the corner of the room. "I'm not comfortable with him doing—"

I cut her off, speaking through gritted teeth. "Decker, if you don't shut her up, I'm going to choke slam her on this table Undertaker-style."

Decker's eyes get wide and he shoots a glare at Tate like, *I don't know if he's serious, but please just shut up for five seconds.*

His scowl returns when he turns back to me. "This is rookie shit, Deacon. You shouldn't have been making changes on this contract. You should've been reviewing the fucking thing after an associate handled it."

"You done yet? I'll fucking fix it. How many times do I need to say it?"

"Oh yeah, maybe you should have your girlfriend review it this time around. She's the one who found your mistake." His words are like a slap to my face.

What the hell was Quinn doing looking at my contracts? Then she ran off to Tate and Decker and ratted me out?

"The fuck did you say?" When I glance up, I see something I don't expect.

Tate's practically shooting lasers out her eyes, but they're aimed right at Decker. Her gaze rolls back over to me and her eyes soften. It's maybe the kindest look she's ever given me.

I shake my head. I don't need this shit. I don't want Tate's goddamn pity, either.

Decker doesn't know when to quit, though. It's his opportunity to pile it on and he doesn't miss a beat. "Maybe we should give her your office. Put you out on the phones and running errands."

He's taking this shit too far, and I can't bottle the rage coursing through my veins any longer.

I fly out of my chair.

Tate's eyes bug out of her head.

In two long strides, I'm right in Decker's grill. "Keep pushing me." I lean in so close we're inches apart. "I fucking dare you."

Decker gulps a little. We're about the same height but I have at least thirty pounds on him and didn't play a pussy sport like baseball. He takes a step back and waves me off with a flippant hand, trying to save face. "Just get it handled, goddamn it."

"Yeah." I glare at both of them then step into the hall before I do something ridiculous like throw Decker through the window. I can't remember ever being this angry and I don't like it. It's not me. My chest heaves up and down and I want to rip the fucking walls of this place down.

I don't even have a bad temper, but when he mentioned Quinn I just about lost my shit. I've never felt this way, never flown off the handle like that. I need to get out of this place for a while. Just to calm down.

As soon as I walk past Quinn's desk, Dexter appears right next to me. "Drinks tonight at The Gage, you in? I'm taking out some new girls from the Dallas office." He punches me in the shoulder, oblivious to what just went down.

I scowl at Quinn and she shrinks back in her seat.

I don't even know why, but without thinking I say, "Yeah. I'll be there."

Her face pales, and I immediately regret the words, but I'm too pissed to talk to her right now. I'll say things I don't mean, like I just did. I need to get away from everyone.

Fuck. I hate Tecker. I hate the whole world right now. Most of all I hate myself because I know I just hurt Quinn.

I didn't just hurt her. I could tell by the look on her face, I crushed her.

I head to my office feeling like the world's biggest asshole.

I've never seen anyone make a situation better when they're pissed off.

I get to my desk and flop down in my chair. It's not like the problem is hard to solve. Add a goddamn zero and draft a new contract, kiss a little ass and wipe my hands of this mess.

Fuck the client for not reading the shit he signed anyway. I could never say that to his face, but he's the biggest dumb fuck in this whole ordeal. Who signs something they haven't read?

I drop my head into my hands and close my eyes.

Quinn.

Why did I say that shit in front of her? Am I sabotaging myself? She didn't deserve that. I don't even know what really happened and now she probably hates me.

I just don't understand. If she knew, why didn't she come to me? Why go behind my back to Tate and Decker?

I know Tate and Quinn are friends, but Quinn knows I don't get along with her. She knows every detail about every person in the office. She's well aware how my brothers—outside of Decker—feel about Kim Jong Tate.

Regardless, I can't focus on my personal shit right now. I have to get this contract situation smoothed over in a hurry. Quinn will have to wait, and it'll do some good to step back like Dr. Flynn said. Empathize instead of judge.

That's what I need to do.

QUINN

I don't know if I've ever felt as stupid as I do right now. I thought Deacon cared about me; we were moving forward and starting a serious relationship that meant something to him. Meant something to both of us.

Maybe it was all me and I was seeing what I wanted to see or building up a fantasy in my head that didn't reflect reality.

The Deacon I was with all day Saturday isn't the Deacon who showed up after he left the conference room.

I can't breathe. My chest burns and my stomach twists into a pretzel. Was it all a game? Was he building me up just to rip my heart out?

"Just the person I was looking for." Decker smiles.

Tate shoots him a death stare that even makes my fingers tremble.

"Oh yeah?" I squeak the words out and my throat burns tight.

Tears attempt to gather in the corners of my eyes, and I fight them back. I won't cry in front of my boss. I can't break, but all I want to do is crumble right here on the spot. Deacon's words play on a loop through my head and I can't rid the dark expression in his eyes from my brain.

"What's wrong?" He shoots Tate a *what the fuck* look, but she ignores him. "I'll, uhh, come back."

When he's gone, Tate grabs me by the shoulders. "Let's go to my office."

I nod, biting back my tears. I don't know if I'm about to cry because I'm pissed and want to punch Deacon in the balls or because I'm hurt. Maybe it's a little of both. This is exactly what I was afraid would happen. He'd get me to trust him. I'd let him in, and he'd jump on the first opportunity to crush me.

He can have his drinks with the new employees from Dallas. I won't be sitting around waiting for his empty promises.

It will pass.

I feel completely empty, like a shell. Used? Confused? I want to hit something.

Tate leads me to the leather couch in her office. I'm too upset to sit but I do it anyway to keep myself from going after Deacon and screaming in his face. My bottom lip quivers and I sink my teeth into it, trying anything that might replace the pain in my heart. It doesn't help. I don't think anything will.

"Quinn," Tate whispers. "I'm sorry."

"Why are you sorry? You didn't do anything, did you?"

"Decker wasn't supposed to bring your name up. He told me he wouldn't but the two egomaniacs in there got pissed off at each other, and personal shit started flying around the room. You did the right thing pointing it out." She reaches out for my hand. "You know how they get. It was ugly and I'm sure Deacon didn't mean whatever he said out there just now. He's pissed off and embarrassed."

"Makes two of us."

Tate did her job, but I feel betrayed by her too. She told Decker about me and Deacon. I know how Decker is when he gets pissed.

I'm sure he loved rubbing Deacon's nose in the mud, just because he could. "Maybe I should look for a job somewhere else."

"That seems pretty hasty." Tate leans back, clearly surprised.

"Tate, I've been going to law school at night for three years. I'm almost finished."

Her frown turns to a smile. "Really? Good for you. That's awesome."

"I keep thinking. You know how it'll look if I'm dating a partner when I'm done. People will think I slept my way into a position I didn't earn. I've worked so hard for this firm."

"If anyone can relate, I can. I had to scratch and claw for everything I have. I'd probably tell you to do just that; go to another firm and start fresh, but we need you here. You're irreplaceable. I have no doubt you'll be a great attorney."

"Nobody will look at me as anything but Decker's glorified assistant and Deacon's ex-girlfriend."

Tate huffs out a long sigh. "You have to do what's best for you. There are plenty of great firms out there and I'll personally write you a letter of recommendation. But right now, don't do anything sudden. Men expect us to act emotionally because that's all they think we are, a big ball of emotions waiting to explode. Step back and get out of your head. Make sound, logical decisions. Sit down and do what you do best; analyze. Trust me. I've been there."

I nod. I know she's right. When men act petty or get angry, everyone just brushes it off. Like Decker and Deacon fighting like children in the conference room. It won't be brought up in reviews or management discussions. But everyone remembers when a woman does it and she's seen as a time bomb waiting to go off. "I'll think about it."

"It'll be a real shame if we lose you. I mean that as a colleague and as a friend."

"Thanks."

"Anytime." She glances at her watch. "Why don't you take an early lunch. Let the temperature cool a little around here."

I leave her office feeling a bit better, but I still can't shake Deacon's hateful stare from my mind. I walk past his office and start to knock but my pride won't let me. I didn't do anything wrong. If his first reaction is to throw other women in my face instead of talking to me like an adult, he's not mature enough for a relationship.

Tears burn in my eyes once more when I pass the supply closet. Our closet.

I do need to get the hell out of here for a while. I make it to my desk and fire off a text to Heather asking if she can meet for lunch.

QUINN

IT'S BEEN two days and I can't stop thinking about Deacon. I miss him more than I should. More than I realized I ever could. I miss his smile and his random texts. I miss him yanking me into the closet.

Neither of us have made an attempt to reach out, and he hasn't been in the office. I have no idea if he went out for drinks with Dexter or not. I tell myself I don't care, but I do. Which eats me up because I don't have time to worry about him or be jealous.

I have school and my father to think about. The one thing I'm certain of is I'm glad I listened to Tate about taking my time to think things through. I haven't decided what to do about my job yet. I would love to resign if Dad and I could afford it. It would free up time to be home with him and study.

It makes me hate Decker even more for paying me so well. I'm dependent on him now. I have to think about our bills and Dad's medical care. However, I know I'll never be taken seriously at The Hunter Group. I'll always be the girl who hooked up with Deacon Collins in the supply closet and slept her way to the top, or the girl who was the best at fetching Decker's coffee.

Even if it's not true, perception trumps reality, always. Once people know Deacon and I were together, it'll be all anyone talks about at the office. I could transfer to Dallas, but then I'd have to move Dad across the country. There's no way in hell he'd go for that. He's a Chicagoan, born and bred.

My chest squeezes tight at the thought of Deacon and I let out a sigh.

Dad glances over at me. "What's the matter, kiddo?" His eyes crinkle at the sides, showing his age.

I haven't said anything to him about Deacon. Regardless of how pissed I am, I can't bring myself to say anything bad about him. I don't know if it's to protect

Dad or Deacon. Probably both. I can't keep this charade up forever, though. My dad can read me better than anyone.

I get about halfway through the story and trail off, no longer wanting to think about everything. It hurts too much.

My dad snickers.

I glare at him. "Why are you laughing?" How is any of this remotely funny to him? Can't he see I'm hurting and conflicted? My damn life is at a crossroads and I have no idea what I should do.

"I'm not laughing at you. I just remember those feelings."

"Huh?"

"Being in love."

I roll my eyes. "I am *not* in love."

"Sure." He snickers again.

My face heats up, but deep down I know he's right. I do love Deacon and that's why this hurts so damn bad.

Dad gets this far off look in his eye, like he's reliving the past. "When I met your mom, she was the prettiest thing I'd ever seen. She had your big green eyes. Of course, back then I still had my red hair." He pats his bald head and laughs.

I smile.

He never talks about my mom…about before.

"I made a lot of mistakes with her. But God did I love her and wish I could've been the man she wanted me to be. I miss that feeling. I miss her smile and sometimes I see it when you laugh."

"You think she ever thinks about us?" I've never allowed myself to truly miss her. I mean, you can't miss something you never had, but I had a small sliver of Deacon and I miss him so damn much.

The jerk.

"Maybe. I know I think about her and wonder if I should have gone after her. Or asked her to stay. Things were complicated, kiddo. She had dreams she wanted to go after, and she did. I think I got the better end of the deal." He winks at me.

"Gee, thanks." I nudge him with my elbow.

"Do you love this guy? Be honest with yourself."

For some reason, everything crashes into me at once. Maybe it's just me admitting to myself I'm in love, and all the hurt that follows knowing he must not feel the same way. He'd have come after me already. My hands shoot up to cover my face and tears stream down my cheeks as I nod at my dad.

"Oh, sweetie." He wraps an arm around my shoulder, and I collapse right into him.

He smooths the hair on my head as I cry into his shoulder. When I finally rise, he's smiling.

"God, I really wish you would stop smiling at me right now."

"Oh, honey. It's not because you're having problems with the guy, or because you're hurting. I know you're in pain."

"What is it then?"

"It's because I haven't been able to do this in years."

"Do what?"

"Be the one taking care of you."

Well, if I was crying hard before, the floodgates open up now.

"And don't worry. I've got a shotgun shell down there with Deacon's name written all over it. I don't care how good he was at football; nobody messes with my baby girl."

"Thanks, Daddy." I curl up into his side again.

"Joking aside, sweetheart. I've seen the way that boy looks at you. You may not think it, but he's suffering right now. Bad. Trust me, I know things."

"I don't know what to do. It's complicated. He probably hates me."

"As much as I still dislike some of your mother's choices, I still love her. I think I always will. Finish law school and go work at a different firm. He'll come running, begging for forgiveness."

"When did you get so wise?"

Dad belts out a laugh. "I'm not wise. Just been through a lot of shit. Experience has its merits."

I shake my head at him. This talk was nice, and I feel a little better.

My heart hurts a little less.

But I still miss Deacon and I can't see that feeling ever going away.

DEACON

"Good job getting that contract shit squared away. I know you've been working around the clock. Everyone was happy with the terms. Don't fucking do it again." Decker semi-smiles at me as his eyes dart over to a picture of him and Tate. After a few long seconds he says, "It may have been a mistake to bring up Quinn. And I shouldn't have said all that other shit."

I smirk. "Almost sounds like an apology." Yeah, I did work my ass off, you prick. I had to draft an entire new contract and get it negotiated between the parties, then had to offer a hundred free legal hours to each of them to keep them from going elsewhere.

"You fucked up. Don't press your luck." He shuffles some papers on his desk and I can't help but glance over at them. He mumbles, "Sorry."

"What was that?"

"Don't make me kick your ass. I'm your big brother; I don't give a fuck how many extra pounds of gut you're rocking under that suit."

"Hard as granite, bitch." I rub my abs and laugh. "I shouldn't have yelled at Tate that way, either. It was purely from a professional standpoint and not personal. But, she's your fiancée and I feel bad about it."

"I appreciate that. It's like a daycare around here trying to deal with all of you."

This is how it's always been between all of us. One minute we're about to fight, the next second we're best friends. It is what it is. Although, Donavan and Decker's little feud is still ongoing and worries the shit out of me.

"By the way, I fixed the Dr. Flynn problem. Would've told you sooner, but you ripped my ass about the contract."

Decker's eyes dart up to mine. "Really? You made it go away?"

"Yeah, I do a lot more than just party with clients. I work hard around here, even if I fuck off sometimes."

"How'd you get it taken care of?"

I tell him everything that happened and by the end he's grinning like a madman.

"Well, fuck. Good work." His eyes roam over to the wall. "Maybe I'm too hard on you sometimes, but it's only because I know how good you could be."

"Yeah. Anyway, I have some shit to take care of." I stand up from the chair.

Decker slides some papers off to the corner of his desk.

I notice Quinn's name and bend down so I can read it.

"Shit." Decker tries to cover it up but I'm faster.

I snatch it off his desk.

"Don't…"

I hold a hand up and start reading. By the end, the paper is balled up in my fist and my eyes dart around his office.

I haven't spoken to her since everything blew up a few days ago. I know she probably thinks I'm an asshole, but I had to fix this mess and it's taken up all my time. I figured she was mad as fuck and I just didn't know what to say to her. I thought I'd give her a few days to cool off then reach out. But now…

"You weren't supposed to see that." Decker runs a hand through his hair and cups the back of his neck. "God, I wish everyone would keep their personal shit out of the office. I'm no good at dealing with it."

"I'm your brother." I shake the paper in front of his face. "You should have told me Quinn was resigning. Tate told you about us. You know how I feel about her."

"Are you sure she knows how you feel about her?" He glances to the paper in my hand.

I rush out of his office on a goddamn mission, ignoring the question.

Fucking women.

Two days and she already resigned.

I head to her desk and she's not there.

Fuck.

She can run but she can't hide from me forever. The contract shit is done, and I have nothing but time on my hands. We're going to talk about this whether she likes it or not and it's not going to be pretty.

I pause to think through the problem. If anyone knows where she is it'll be her little buddy Tate. This was probably her idea, anyway. I swear that woman wants to ruin my life. If Decker had any clue what was about to happen, it'd be world war three, because I know Tate is still seething from everything I said to her, but I don't give a fuck.

I may have promised to be nice to her, but that was before I knew about this.

I barge into her office without knocking. She ends her phone call and looks up at me with wide eyes. Her face slowly morphs to red and I'm begging for her to give me a reason to take out all this frustration on her.

"Where is she?"

"How about you fuck off out of my office then come back and ask nicely." She folds her hands neatly on her desk and continues to stare at me.

My jaw ticks. Does she really expect me to say please? I've about had it with this chick, but I'll be damned if I don't walk out of her office, swallow my pride and the desire to rip the door off the goddamn hinges. I want answers, and this is the best way to accomplish it, but inside I'm raging. I do my best to hide it behind my eyes and walk back in. "Will you please tell me where Quinn is?"

I expect Tate to laugh hysterically at me, but she doesn't.

What the fuck?

"It's real, isn't it?"

"What? I don't know what you're saying. Can you please just tell me where she is?"

"You're in love with her." She eyes me from head to toe. "Like, batshit crazy in love. I've never seen you look mad a day I've known you, and now you're about to rage on anything in sight."

I stand there, unable to form any words. I just look at the ground and nod.

"You know what, Deacon? You might not believe this, but I actually like you."

"Huh?" I huff out half a laugh. I'm more surprised than anything.

"Yeah. And I think you and Quinn are great for each other. Even though I shouldn't break the girl code, I'm going to tell you where she is. But hear this and listen up. If you piss her off, hurt her more than she's already hurting, I'll take that golf club from your office. You know the one I showed you how to use when I first came to the firm, because you *suck* at golf... remember that?"

I grind my teeth and ignore her insult because I want to know where Quinn is more than anything in the world. "I remember."

"And do you remember all that shit you said to me in the conference room?"

"I'm..."

"Don't apologize for it. You didn't mean any of that shit. You were pissed off at Decker and took it out on me."

"That's correct."

"Okay, so yeah, the golf club..."

"Fuck, I remember, okay? Jesus Christ."

Tate smiles. "Well, you talk to me that way again, or tell Quinn how you found out where she was...I'll shove it so far up your ass it'll knock your goddamn head to the eighteenth green. We clear?"

"Yeah, yeah. I get it. You're a badass and I'm an asshole, so just tell me where she is."

Tate takes in a deep breath and looks away at the wall. "She went to a coffee shop to study on her lunch break. The one two blocks over is her favorite."

I nod and head toward the elevators.

"You're welcome."

I swear to God I hear her mumble, "Asshole," as I turn the corner.

I don't give a shit.

QUINN

I DIDN'T EXPECT to be so sad when I turned in my resignation letter, but I feel deflated, like a balloon after a date with a needle. I'm still struggling with what to say to Deacon and when to talk to him.

My dad was right. I do love him. I loved him the second we started dating, I just couldn't admit it to myself. I want to tell him, but I'm scared. Half of me loves him with every fiber in my body and wants to chase after him. The other half screams to cut my losses and go on with life.

I take a sip of coffee and flip through my study notes. I can't concentrate. About the time I decide to get up and leave, I glance toward the entrance.

This can't be happening.

Not now. I'm not ready.

Deacon walks through the door and damn near collides with a hipster. His jaw is set, and his eyes scan the room, until they land on me.

What the hell?

I've given him space. I sat around waiting for him to make a move and just say something. Anything. He's given me silence in return and now he wants to look at me like he's irritated?

"Were you going to tell me?" He marches toward me and looks down his nose, right into my eyes.

I blink a few times.

This is all wrong.

I was supposed to have time to prepare before I talked to him. "Deacon... I—"

"I've been working my ass off fixing that contract and I kept thinking, Quinn will come talk to me. Surely, she'll come to me and explain why she went behind my back and threw me under the bus to my brother and..." He stares out the

319

window, unable to even look at me. "God, I don't even want to say her name, but *Tate* of all people. Instead you give me the cold shoulder and pretend like nothing happened." His eyes land on me once more and his voice rises a little more. "I was going to apologize for everything I said that day in the hall." His jaw ticks and everyone in the place stares at us, but he doesn't seem to care. "I didn't mean it. I didn't go anywhere with any girls. All I've done is work my ass off."

"Deacon, if you just—"

He cuts me off and talks over me, shaking his head. "Never took you for a quitter, though. I thought you were tough, all that stuff about earning everything you get. Thought maybe I meant something to you, but I guess I was wrong."

Tears form in the corners of my eyes and the back of my throat burns. "I've been wanting—"

"Just don't, Quinn. Save it for the next guy who loves you and break his heart."

I can't stop shaking. I want to say so many things, but he won't let me, and I'm not even sure they'd come out of my mouth if I wanted them to.

Deacon takes one final look at me and says, "Good luck with your law career."

He's already out the door before I can process what just happened. I don't even know what to think right now as I wipe my eyes and hurry to collect my things.

A barista comes over with some tissues. God, he's made me cry twice this week already. How could he possibly think any of this is my fault?

"Honey, are you okay?"

"I'm fine. Thanks." I gather my stuff in my arms and quietly slip out the door as fast as possible. He didn't even give me a chance to explain. Why would he think I would get him in trouble on purpose?

Then he basically says he loves me while insulting me at the same time.

You made the right decision. You don't need that in your life.

I curse the tears that won't stop coming and walk toward my car. Once I'm inside I call Heather. I need her more than anyone. "Hey." The word comes out as a croak.

"Everything okay? You sound sick."

"Everything is completely fucked."

"Want me to bury that son of a bitch? I totally know someone. Mafia guys come into the store all the time."

I can't even bring myself to laugh at her joke. "No. It's even worse because I don't want you to and I should."

"Are you good to drive?"

I sniffle. "Yeah. I'll be fine. I just need to breathe."

"Okay, well come over. I have wine and cheesecake. We can cry it out of your system."

"I'm getting in my car now."

"See you soon."

"Yeah." I hang up the phone and see the screensaver I snapped of Deacon and me when I was over at his place. Everything filters up through my chest again. I dump my books in the backseat and lay my head on the steering wheel and try to breathe.

Fuck being in love. It's the worst thing I've ever experienced.

DEACON

AFTER THE CONFRONTATION WITH QUINN, I came straight home. I couldn't go back to the office and stare at her, sitting at her desk, knowing I can't have her. She gave up, quit before we ever really began. In the beginning she always had one foot out the door, but it didn't feel that way toward the end.

I guess I should be thankful it ended now before I got even more serious about her. Who the fuck am I kidding? I've been serious about her since the first time I saw her. She's the only woman I've ever been serious about, that's ever made me feel something.

I knock back a drink and stare out at the skyline from my patio, wondering if things would have gone differently had I talked to her sooner.

It was two fucking days! Two days and she quits her job?

I'm a grown child and even I'm more mature than that. Another thing she and Tate always get wrong about me. I bet Tate isn't running off telling everyone how irresponsible and immature Quinn is.

I replay the situation from every scenario in my head, second-guessing every single decision I've made the past few days, including ambushing her at the coffee shop. Fuck, I was pretty mean to her. She deserved to know how I felt, but not like that.

That's the kind of shit that happens when you bury thirty years of emotional baggage and hide behind practical jokes. Finally find someone I care about, have a real connection to, and I sabotage the relationship.

Most of all, I can't stop thinking how good we were together. I was insane for her. Fuck. I still am. I don't know what to even do right now. It's like my skin itches everywhere and I don't know where to scratch.

I hear footsteps behind me and turn around half expecting to see Quinn even though I know there's no way in hell she'll show up here.

"The fuck you doing out here? Looks like you're about to have a mid-life crisis, buy a Harley, and marry a stripper." Dexter laughs.

"Look, I'm not really in the mood. So..."

"What the hell did you do to Quinn?"

"What?" My jaw ticks.

"I was in Decker's office and Tate busted in like Pontius Pilate, ready to crucify you. Decker kicked me out before I could hear the whole story. All I made out was something about a golf club and Quinn never came back from lunch."

"What the fuck does it matter? She quit."

Dexter shakes his head. "Sometimes I think you're a bigger idiot than me. And sometimes you prove me right. Today is one of those days, bitch."

I stand up. "I said I'm not in the mood. Please don't make me be an asshole to you too."

He nods and takes a step toward the patio door. "You do realize it was a letter of resignation that doesn't take effect until after she graduates from school, right? She wasn't quitting anytime soon."

My eyes roam up to meet his, then I drop my head in my hands.

"You didn't know, did you?" Dexter takes a step into my apartment, then seems to change his mind and walks back out. "Decker just wanted it as a formality so he could look for someone to train alongside her. Shit even I knew that, and I don't pay attention to anything." He stares out at the lake in the distance. "The way you look, I'm guessing she's gone for real now, though."

"Fuck!" I beat my fist on the chair.

Looking up at Dexter, my chest heaves in huge waves, and I try to just breathe. My face has to be redder than hell, but I know losing my cool is what caused all my problems in the first place. It's not even anger, really. I just hate myself and it's hard to breathe. I think I might be having a panic attack.

She just makes me so damn crazy. All I want is her. It's the only thing I want in my life. I would give up everything for one more day with her. I want her so bad it physically hurts inside, an ache that runs bone-deep, everywhere at once.

"What'd you do?"

I scrub a hand over my face and pour myself another drink. A tear slides down the side of my cheek and I freeze when it happens. It's something I've never felt before, not since I was a child anyway. I turn my head and wipe it away with my shoulder, so Dexter won't see. I've humiliated myself enough for one day. "I found her at the coffee shop."

"And?"

"You know those big machines that raze parking lots?"

"Jesus."

"It was a little like that. I couldn't stop myself. I was hurting so damn bad, man. I think subconsciously, I just wanted her to feel what I was feeling."

"Well, that's not good."

I don't know whether to laugh or hit him in the face for his nonchalant reaction. It's just how we talk to each other. Nothing is off limits from a good joke. "I made her cry. Not a single tear sliding down the cheek, either. Like, the floodgates opened, and she's tough as nails. Guarded. Called her a quitter, blamed her for ratting me out. Then I wished her luck with her career. I don't even think it was so much what I said to her, but how I said it." I shake my head. "Fuck, I even told her I loved her, but somehow twisted it into an insult in the same sentence. Like for her to save her bullshit for the next guy who loves her and crush his heart with it." I exhale, now even more ashamed than I was before. "There's no recovering from this. She's never going to speak to me again. *I* wouldn't speak to me again."

Dexter stares at me blankly for a while and pours a rocks glass for himself. He takes a long sip and groans. "Fuck me."

"What?"

"Are you a hundred percent sure you love her? That she's the one?"

My eyes narrow on him for even questioning my feelings for Quinn. "What the fuck do you think? Of course I'm crazy in love with her. What else would explain all that shit I told you? Does any of that sound like me?"

"No, actually. I've seen you take ass chewings from the meanest coaches in the country and just smile like you could do it all day." He sighs loudly. "Jesus. I mean, I could fix this for you. Quinn's such a great girl and could do so much better, though."

I start toward him and he laughs and holds his hands up in surrender.

"Look, I got you, man. You'll get her back. You just have to do every fucking thing I say, exactly how I say to do it."

I stand there, shaking my head, not even believing I'm considering whatever he's about to say. It's so absurd, and yet, at the same time I know I'd do anything for just ten more seconds with Quinn. "What exactly do you know about romance, Sir Fucksalot?"

He pretends to clutch his heart. "You wound me." He laughs. "I watch romance movies."

I snort. "Yeah. Okay. Whatever."

His face tightens. "I'm fucking serious. Haven't you ever had to watch chick flicks to get pussy? You know Netflix and chill stuff? Hallmark channel?"

"No way. I draw a hard line on girl movies. I can't handle them. Even the comedy ones suck."

"No wonder you can't keep a woman."

I roll my eyes.

"Okay, fine. It's whatever. I was just trying to help but if you don't need any…" He starts to walk off.

Before I know what I'm doing, I spin him back around by the forearm. "Let's not do anything hasty now. You have a plan or what?"

He pretends to brush some imaginary dirt off his sleeve where my fingers touched it. "Unlike you, I *do* watch those movies, and I pay attention to that shit, making notes in my head as I go along. In case I need to talk a chick into ass to mouth, dirty sanchez, the donkey punch, you know? The regular."

I shake my head at him.

"But to answer your question... yes. To fully understand, you have to grasp the big picture, then work out the details. You have to break down the romance into its basic structure. There's the meet-cute in the beginning. You know? Some over-the-top way in which the two people bump into each other that's a nearly impossible coincidence. Then they date for a while. That's when the first problem comes in. Something to throw a wrench into their lives to push them apart. They come back together. Another bigger problem pushes them apart. This repeats, amplifying in intensity, until the epic conflict arises, usually where the man does some shit that seems unforgiveable in the audience's eyes. Because the target audience is female, the guy has to be the problem. It's like a law of romance. He has to get on his knees and grovel to win her back. Women go insane for it." He pokes me with a finger. "And that's where *you* are right now."

I can't help but shake my head that he thinks about this shit. I'd laugh if I wasn't so damn desperate. What's even worse is he's actually making some sense. "So how the fuck does he fix it? The guy in the movie?"

Dexter holds up his index finger and his eyes widen. "Ahh, this is the part I call the over-the-top redeeming gesture." He waggles his eyebrows.

"Well what the fuck does that entail?"

"Take a seat, rook. I'm gonna need some markers and a dry erase board to map out something spectacular after your epic fuck-up."

QUINN

I PULL out my study guide. It's Sunday, and it's been the longest week of my life. Four days have passed since Deacon ripped my heart out and stomped on it. I feel guilty for leaving everyone at the office hanging all week. It's not like me to not show up.

I managed to call Tate later on Wednesday, after the coffee shop incident, and told her I wasn't feeling well. She saw right through it, but she was nothing but kind and said she understood.

It's not even so much the words Deacon said but the way he looked at me. It was like he loved me and hated me at the same time.

I can't focus. I can't eat. I can't sleep.

Finally, I give up on studying and join Dad in the living room. He's watching the early football games.

I collapse on the couch. "The Bears play tonight?"

"Oh yeah. Primetime."

I don't get to ask who they're playing against because the doorbell rings. It's probably Heather coming to check on me. She invited me out last night, but I couldn't bring myself to get off the couch. Not yet, anyway. It's too soon, and last time I went out with her I ran into Deacon. I need a few days to mope around and feel sorry for myself, then I'll brush my shoulders off and get back to life. "I'll get it."

I open the door without bothering to check the peephole. I damn near have a heart attack as rage, humiliation, and then relief all wash over me within approximately two seconds. I blink and realize it's Dexter. "What the hell are you doing here?" The sound of a diesel engine lands in my ears. I move to look around him and see a white transport van parked out front. There's a small ramp lowering off the side for a wheelchair. I shake my head furiously, right at Dexter. "No." I wave a hand out at the van. "Whatever that is the answer is no."

I turn around to shut the door in his face, but he breezes past me like I'm not even there.

Ugh! Collins brothers!

"Mr. Richards, you've been watching games on this TV for far too long. That changes today." He tosses a Bears jersey in Dad's lap.

I stand in the hallway, dumbfounded, staring at the living room.

"You've got a brass set of balls showing up here, son!" Dad stares at Dexter for a second. "Who the fuck is this clown, Quinn? He looks just like Deacon, but it ain't him."

Dexter doesn't miss a beat, like he's a high-pressure marketer. "I'm the goddamn clown who's going to make all your dreams come true today, sir." Dexter pulls tickets from his pocket and fans them out in front of Dad.

Dad's eyes go wide. Fast. "Well okay then. Tell me more." He looks over at me and shrugs, then points at Dexter. "I mean, he's not Deacon."

This is going downhill fast, past the point of recovery. I might as well just not even be here.

Dexter looks like he's on *The Price is Right*, rattling off a prize package. "Well, tell me how this sounds, sir." He pauses to flash a smile right at me, and I swear to God his tooth sparkles.

I have to be in a dream right now. This can't be happening.

"Tailgating on the upper level of the Waldron Deck. You'll hang out with Mike Ditka and Brian Urlacher for one hour. We'll float a keg together then have a meal at The Chicago Firehouse Restaurant. Followed with a VIP suite to watch the game."

I know Deacon put him up to this but why? The things he said to me at the coffee shop made it sound pretty final. Why the hell is he going out of his way for my dad?

None of this makes sense.

"I know it sounds amazing, Dad, but there's no way you can handle all that." I hate to crush my old man's heart but it's true.

"No worries." Dexter smirks at me. "Sir, I have a nurse waiting outside with a fully handicap-accessible van to provide you with transportation and healthcare should the need arise." He leans down to Dad and whispers something, but then holds his hands out in front of his chest suggesting the nurse may be well endowed too.

These assholes thought of everything.

Dexter walks over to the window near Dad and pulls back the curtain. Dad leans forward slightly and sees the same thing I do. There's a blonde girl dressed in tight jeans with a Bears jersey tied up at her waist showing off her midriff.

I pull Dexter back by the collar. "That's Abigail from the Dallas office." I hiss the words at him.

He shrugs. "She went to nursing school for a semester. It's totally fine and she's hot. Look how happy he is. Don't be a dick. You're ruining his moment."

I scowl at him. He thinks I'm being a dick. He came over here and got my dad all excited about this game.

Dad stares at Abigail then looks back at me, raises his eyebrows, and says, "Oh, we're going to have some fun today, baby girl."

"Excellent choice, Mr. Richards. Please allow me." Dexter moves past me and grabs the back of his wheelchair.

Dad pats him on the arm as they head to the door. "You may just be my new best friend."

Dexter looks back at me and says, "You comin'?"

I sigh and grab my bag. It's not like they're giving me much of a choice. There's no way in hell I'm turning Dexter loose with my dad for the whole day.

The driver loads Dad into the van, and I yank Dexter back by the sleeve of his shirt. "I know Deacon put you up to this and it's not going to work. Even if you get my dad to the game and he has the time of his life…" My heart stutters in my chest when Dexter smirks at me. He looks so much like Deacon it's painful to see his smile.

Dexter puts his palms on my cheeks, and I wonder what the hell he's doing until he pinches both of them and grins wider. "Well, aren't you adorable. I see why Deacon likes you. But guess what?"

"What?" I put both hands on my hips, but I can't even look at him.

"It's already working."

My confidence falters a little as he steps away. I inhale a deep breath and get my shit together. God, every one of those brothers is so damn cocky. We'll see if it works.

Before Dexter can climb in, I tap him on the shoulder, less forceful this time around.

He spins around but doesn't look annoyed. "What's up?"

I look down at the ground because I don't want him to see the shame I know is plastered to my face. "Is he going to be there?"

Dexter puts a hand on my shoulder, and I'll be damned if he doesn't actually look sincere this time. "When the time is right. Not before."

I nod and climb into the van. Dad's smiling so big it's kind of contagious. It's freaking impossible to be upset when he's having possibly the greatest day of his life.

Abigail has her paws all over him, helping him get his jersey on.

Dad's in heaven and it feels like a little piece of my heart might have stitched itself back together.

———

DEXTER LIVES UP to his word. The day has been amazing so far. Dad got to hang out with Mike Ditka and Brian Urlacher, and they talked football the entire hour.

They didn't even act embarrassed at all Dad's questions. They all just sat there like they've been friends their entire lives.

We had great food. God, the food was incredible. It hits me in the chest how much Dad needed this, and I've never had the time or the financial support to do it for him.

Deacon made this happen. He did this for me. It means more to me than he'll ever know, and my heart feels like it's slowly coming back together again, because he really does pay attention to every little detail and knows every little gear and pulley that makes me tick. I know somewhere in my heart I have it in me to forgive him, but I'm still not sold on the idea. He hurt me so bad, even thinking about him right now is painful. If I just give in, what kind of precedent does that set for any possible relationship? That he can just walk all over me when he feels like it, then stroll through the front door the next day?

No, he needs to beg and plead. I need to look in his eyes and see if he's sincere or not.

All the same, I glance around, missing him more than ever and wishing he was here and things between us were okay again.

It pains me to say it, but Dexter was right. Their plan is working, slowly but surely. This morning I wouldn't have given Deacon the time of day, and now I already find myself willing to hear him out.

Stupid men!

Now, we're up in the VIP suite. Dad's drinking non-alcoholic beer because of his medications but he doesn't mind. He's doing what he loves. He's living again, and I have to bite back the emotions swirling inside me.

"Enjoying yourself?" Dexter nudges up against me.

"Okay. I'll admit, this is incredible. Thank you so much for making him happy." I gesture toward Dad.

Dexter shrugs. "Don't mention it. It's nothing. We do it every Sunday when there's a home game. He's always welcome."

Several seconds pass between us and I twiddle my thumbs. "Where is he?" The question comes out before I can stop it.

Dexter turns. "He didn't want to cause a scene or interrupt you and your Dad having a great time. He only cares that you two enjoy yourselves and he thought that might not happen if he showed up. He knows between the medical condition and work, school..." He pauses. "Shit. Sorry, he told me about law school."

I shrug. "It doesn't matter now. I'm sure he needed someone to talk to and it sounds like you were it. Which makes sense, twins and all that, right?"

Dexter nods. "Anyway, he knows you guys don't get to go out and do stuff like this. Believe it or not, it's not just some thing to win you back. His number one priority today is for you and your dad to have the best day ever. That's all he cares about right now. I'm sure you guys have a ton of shit to work out, but it can wait."

I wrap my arms around my center and wish Deacon was here so I could at least thank him.

"Stop overthinking this. Let your hair down and pretend you like football. Here, have a beer." He hands me a bottle.

I try to do what he says and just enjoy this day for what it is and relax, but I can't just turn off the way I feel like that. There's no on and off switch.

Dexter grins. "I'm not normally this nice, so you could at least pretend to enjoy hanging out with me too."

"Yeah, yeah." I clink my bottle with his and take a big sip.

It does taste really good. I walk over to Dad, put my arm around his neck, and give him a gentle squeeze. "You having the best time ever or what?"

"Yeah, kiddo. I am."

"Me too."

I'm so in love with Deacon, but I just don't know what to do. One question lingers at the back of my mind.

Is he doing this out of guilt or because he wants to make this work?

DEACON

I'VE HUNG back at a safe distance all day watching Quinn and her dad. There were a few moments where I swore she was looking around, trying to spot me. Maybe that's wishful thinking on my part, but I'm going to believe it's true.

It was damn near impossible not to run to her, wrap her in my arms, beg for her forgiveness, and tell her everything would be okay. I know it's just my mind playing tricks on me. I doubt this plan has a single fucking chance of working after the way I treated her, but once Dexter told me his general idea—*"Give Quinn the best day of her life without you there."*—I knew exactly what to do.

I didn't even have to think twice. Even if she doesn't take me back, I want her and her dad to have the best day ever. They deserve it after all the shit they've been through. This won't be the last, either. Just like the flowers every Friday, I'll never stop doing nice things for her.

I don't want Quinn to work anywhere else. She belongs with me, every fucking day. I want to go to work with her and go home with her. We'll have the American dream. She'll move in with me, we'll get married, and start making babies, if that's what she wants. If she doesn't want kids, I'll get a damn vasectomy. I don't give a shit. I just want to give her everything she wants for the rest of our lives.

I can see it all so vividly inside my head. Nothing will feel right again if Quinn doesn't take me back. Nothing will matter if I don't have her to share it with.

I'm not very religious but fuck me if I haven't been saying silent prayers all damn day, making God all kinds of impossible promises I probably couldn't live up to, if I could just get her back.

The fourth quarter ends but they haven't left the suite yet. It's time to make my move. My hands tremble like a rookie at the Super Bowl and my palms clam up. I

333

played football at some of the highest levels possible and never got nervous, but now, I'm about to die.

The stakes have never been higher in my life. Because it's my future on the line. I can't live without her.

It's now or never with Quinn and I can't live with never. I walk to the entrance and give Dex the signal he came up with. I scratch my nose with my middle finger and roll my eyes at the same time.

He makes a circle with his index finger and thumb on his leg, then laughs when I look at it, because he'll get to punch me in the arm later. He taps Abigail on the shoulder, and she wheels Mr. Richards toward the exit. After that, Dex smiles and actually gives me a thumbs up.

Maybe he has a heart after all.

Quinn hasn't noticed me yet. I hear her voice call out from inside the room. "Where the hell are you taking him now?"

"After party with the players. Dad's gonna be up late tonight. Don't worry. He's in good hands."

I'm standing right outside the door as they wheel him out.

Abigail and Mr. Richards stop next to me.

I hold out my hand. "Hope you had a good time today, sir."

"Yes, I did." He holds his hand out, but scowls at me. He motions for me to lean down and I do. He grits in my ear, mustering up the most menacing tone he can, "Tread lightly. Hurt my daughter again and you'll lose a knee. We understand each other?"

"Yes, sir."

He straightens up and grins, like that's all taken care of. "All right, then. If you'll excuse me, this pretty lady is taking me to a party."

Dex gives me a fist bump as he follows them out.

I step inside just as Quinn starts toward the door. She freezes in place and her face pales. Fuck, she looks like she's about to cry, and I think my heart shatters into a million pieces, just watching her about to crumble.

Without hesitation, I run toward her, afraid she's about to break down.

She holds up a hand before I get there and I stop in my tracks, holding my hands up.

"Sorry, I just, you looked…"

"It's okay."

I hook a thumb over my shoulder. "Look, I can go. It just seemed like…"

She shakes her head. "No, it's okay. Now is good."

"Look, Quinn, I've tried to think of the right things to say all day long. How, I mean what… God, this is hard. Just, nothing seemed good enough. I don't think there are any words that are good enough."

She stares down at the floor and I think it's because she's about to cry and doesn't want me to see.

Fuck, I'm ruining this.

"Quinn, please, can you look at me?" Then, I feel it again, a fucking tear running down *my* cheek. I don't try to hide it, though. I don't try to push all the hurt back inside, because I don't give a shit what anyone else thinks. I want her to know that seeing her in pain, pain that I caused, is the most excruciating experience of my life.

Her head tilts up and her eyes land on my cheek.

My voice starts to crack as I speak. "I-I'm sorry."

Her face is pink, and I can't tell if her tears are angry or if she's just hurt.

"I overreacted. I just… I could rattle off a thousand excuses about shit, but I won't. I don't want to make any excuses. I've never done anything like that in my life. It's not who I am, and I am truly sorry that I put you through that and humiliated you the way I did."

"I would never go behind your back, Deacon." She wipes a tear from her eye. "I was at my desk talking to Tate when Beckley called. She was standing right there when I pulled up the contract. There was nothing I could do. I didn't even realize you were the one who handled it until Decker pulled you into the conference room. You hurt me, Deacon. Crushed me. You broke my heart."

It's hard to look her in the eyes because I'm so ashamed, but I don't dare look away because I deserve every bit of the pain. "I'm sorry. I'll do whatever it takes. If you don't want anything to do with me, I understand, and I'll stay away. I just want you to be happy, even if that doesn't include me." I sniff again. "It will be absolute hell. Torture, even. But I'll leave you alone." Then, I do something I never thought I'd do in my entire life. It's like my body has a mind of its own. I fall down on my knees in front of her.

Her eyes widen.

"I'm begging you, though. Please. I want another chance. It doesn't have to be today, or tomorrow, or even a month from now. If you'll just promise to give me one more chance, I swear I will make it up to you a thousand times over. I've never begged in my life, never asked anyone for anything, but a sliver of hope with you is worth a lifetime of begging."

Her eyes soften a hint and more tears flow down her cheeks.

I want nothing more than to wrap her in my arms and kiss her so hard she's dizzy, but I can't. Not anymore. I gaze up at her green eyes and it's hard not to get lost in them. "I love you, Quinn. I've been in love with you for a long time. As long as I've been sending you flowers. I should've told you sooner."

Her eyes narrow. "Don't say things you don't mean, Deacon. We were just a fling back then."

"No." I shake my head. "I loved you the first time I saw you. I know it sounds ridiculous, but it's the truth. I knew the only way you'd give me any type of chance was if it was casual. I know what you thought of me, my reputation, but you're the only woman I've been with since you started at the firm. That's where the closet came in. I've learned every detail I could about you from the beginning, and I loved you so damn hard the whole time. I was just too scared to tell you, because I thought I'd run you off. I used sex as a reason just to be near you because you kept turning me down and throwing the flowers away. But I didn't give up then, and I won't give up now. I fucked up. I know that. It won't happen again. You're it for me, just let me prove it to you. The only way you're getting rid of me is if you tell me to leave you alone. And the only reason I'd leave you alone then, is because I love you so fucking much, and I never want to see you hurting because of something I did."

Tears stream down her cheeks, and I want nothing more than to just wipe them away, just hold her and promise over and over this will never happen again.

"I love you too, Deacon. I just…"

I rise to my feet. She said the words I've waited a lifetime to hear.

I hold my arms out, letting her make the decision for herself. I don't want to force anything on her this time. I want it to be purely her decision. "Come back to me, please. Quinn, I'm nothing without you."

She stands there for a moment, staring at my outstretched arms.

Tears slide down her cheeks, then she rushes into me, burying her face in my chest.

I wrap her up in a hug and squeeze her against me so hard I worry she might not be able to breathe. "Thank God." I look down at her. "Thank God." I drop a kiss on top of her hair and run a hand up and down her back.

Just feeling her up against me, her heart thudding against my ribs, everything in life is perfect again, even if it's only for a moment. I just sit there and hold her, praying it never ends. Praying that it's real.

Finally, her chin tilts up and she looks at me once more, only this time there's a smile on her face. "Hi."

"Hi." I lean down and kiss her, because it just feels like the right thing to do. Everything clicks. The moment our lips touch, heat blooms in my chest again and colors grow vibrant. That feeling of floating on the clouds returns.

We continue to kiss, like two old souls reunited after decades. That's what it feels like, even though it's only been a few days.

"I need you so damn bad." I whisper the words against her neck, backing her up to the glass of the suite window that overlooks the Soldier Field. "Need you in my life. I can't fucking breathe without you."

"I need you too, Deacon." This time Quinn is the one who kisses me.

It turns passionate quickly, her needy hands roaming my chest.

I grab her by each wrist and pin them above her head on the glass, then rake my eyes up and down her body as her chest heaves with deep, labored breaths. When my mouth hits her ear, I whisper, "You have no idea how bad I want you. Right here. Right now. But we need to go spend time with your dad at the party. And it's too soon. When I'm with you I want to move at the speed of light, but I know going slow is better for us."

Quinn's eyebrows rise. "You're turning down sex with me, again, at Soldier Field, to go hang out with my dad?"

"Well…" My eyes narrow on her. "I have one thing I could do that would be acceptable."

"What's that?"

336

"A proper apology."

Quinn stares at me like I'm an alien from another planet. "Isn't that, like, what all this was?"

"I said a proper apology, Quinn." I flip her around and press her up against the glass.

"Ohh."

My mouth is right in her ear. "One that's tailored specifically for your own benefit."

"Well, I do like the sound of that."

I reach around and unbutton her jeans, then yank them down to the floor. "An apology that leaves my balls aching all night as punishment."

"Tell me more, sir."

I pull her panties down to the floor and she steps out of them and her jeans. "It requires a demonstration."

I bend down and shove her panties in my pocket. Some traditions must continue. I rise and cup her pussy in my hand. "So. Fucking. Wet."

Quinn's mouth moves to say something, and I slide a finger in. It turns her sentence into a soft moan. There's something about watching her squirm and writhe under my touch that just does it for me, every single time. She's like an instrument I've already mastered. I love playing it more than anything in the world and can't wait to perform the rest of my life.

I lower myself to my knees behind her, spread her ass, and sit back on my heels, just to stare at her slick, glistening folds. "I need to work fast, since we have somewhere to be."

Quinn nods.

I always love doing the opposite of what she thinks, catching her by surprise. So, I slowly kiss up the backs of her legs, all the way to the bottom of her ass. I take my time working to her inner thighs, teasing closer and closer to where she needs my mouth. She tries to push back into me, but I have my hands on her ass and keep her from getting what she wants.

"Thought you were going to be fast." Her words come out on several pants.

Teasing her is the best part. "Don't rush an artist."

"So damn cocky."

I grin, my mouth just inches from her pussy, wanting to taste it more than anything in the world. I plan to work fast, when the time is right, but amping her up with anticipation is vital to the process. It has to be a slow build to the crescendo.

My tongue darts out and grazes her clit. It sends a shudder down the back of her legs.

That's right.

I slide my thumb down and work lazy circles around it while I take my tongue as deep as it will go. One of her hands flies back and paws at the side of my head, looking for anything to grab hold of. She's already so close, I can feel it in the tiny vibrations of her body. Before long, I have two fingers teasing the secret spot deep inside her while my tongue flicks across her clit.

"God, Deacon." Her fingernails dig into my scalp and she pulls my face into her as she releases. Her thighs tremble and there's no better feeling in the world than satisfying her, giving her exactly what she needs when she needs it.

Her hips buck and she jolts a few more times, then her muscles relax. I slowly work her jeans back up around her waist and button them in the front, kissing up the side of her neck as I do it.

"My panties?"

I love it when she's so worn out she speaks in sentence fragments. "They belong to me, just like you."

Quinn falls back into my arms and shakes her head, both of us staring out at the field. "I can't believe you did all this for us."

"I can't take all the credit. It was Dexter's idea."

"I know. He told me."

I spin her around to face me. "Of course he did." I snicker.

"It's not like that. Believe it or not, he was sweet and told me you thought of all the details. He just shoved you in the right direction."

"He watches romantic comedies."

We both laugh.

"Really?"

"He claims it's to get laid, but I think he watches them alone at night eating ice cream."

Quinn shakes her head. "Who would've thought…"

"So did it work?" I grin to lighten the mood, but inside I'm trembling in equal parts anticipation and fear of her response.

She smacks at my shoulder. "Yeah, dickhead. It worked. You got the girl." She leans up on her tiptoes bringing her mouth to mine for a soft kiss. "Just don't ever put me through that again. Promise?"

There's not a doubt in my mind. I will never lose her again. "I promise."

EPILOGUE

Quinn

"I'M SO PROUD OF YOU." Deacon opens the car door and ushers me into the passenger seat. "Time to celebrate. I made reservations."

"Okay." I smirk and buckle my seatbelt as he goes around to the driver's side. "Where you taking me?"

"It's a surprise." He starts up the car and backs out of his parking space.

"I have a surprise for you too."

"Oh yeah? What is it?"

"If I told you, I'd have to kill you."

"You've been watching too many action movies with your dad."

"You're one to talk. I heard the two of you up late last weekend."

"Guilty. We were watching porn, though."

"Deacon Collins!" I smack his arm and laugh at the same time.

Some things never change.

"We were studying the cinematography. It was incredible. You should've seen the lighting, and they got this one shot…"

"Just stop before you dig yourself a hole."

Deacon puts his hands up in mock surrender, holding back a laugh.

It took some convincing to get Dad to move in with us. He pleaded for us to put him in assisted living when I told him I was moving in with Deacon, but neither one of us were having that. Deacon goes out of his way to spend time with him. They watched sports nonstop while I studied for finals and I'm sure it'll continue as I study for the bar.

We go to all the Bears home games and Deacon is slowly teaching me everything he knows about football. I usually fall asleep while Dad sits there absorbing every little detail of Deacon's stories.

He had his place completely renovated to accommodate Dad. Everything is handicap accessible, and Dad can nearly function on his own when we aren't there.

Sometimes it doesn't even seem real, that I'm with him.

"You going to at least give me a hint?"

I can't keep it in any longer. I'm about to burst at the seams. "I wanted to discuss a career choice with you."

"Oh yeah?" His knuckles grip the steering wheel a little tighter, but he doesn't overreact and keeps a smile plastered to his face.

"Yeah. I think it's best for all of us if I stay at The Hunter Group. What are your thoughts?" I watch his reaction in my peripheral vision.

"Seriously? Don't toy with me, woman."

"Yeah, I want to end where I started."

"That makes me so damn happy." He pulls into a parking space near the restaurant. Before we exit the car, Deacon takes my hand and leans across the console. "You won't regret it. I promise."

"I know." I touch his face then kiss his lips.

"Mmm." He leans back and gazes into my eyes. "Come on we better get inside before I bend you over the hood of my car."

Deacon leads me through the front door and the moment we enter the dining room everyone from work jumps out and yells, "Surprise!" There's a huge banner that reads CONGRATULATIONS, QUINN.

"What is this?"

He cocks an eyebrow up at me. "I don't know. A center for ants? What's it look like?"

I shake my head. "Point taken." I give him a huge hug, then move through the room to thank everyone for coming.

Even when we're separated, I can't stop craning my neck back to smile at him, though. It's hard to take my eyes off the man I love.

EPILOGUE

Deacon

I stand next to Quinn, watching her scan the room. I know who she's looking for and there's no way I wouldn't make sure he's here. When she doesn't see him, her smile fades.

I whisper in her ear, "I have another surprise for you." I nod to Abigail and she walks through a side door and then returns, wheeling in Mr. Richards.

"Dad!" She sprints over to him.

I walk behind, slowly soaking up the moment and taking videos and pictures with my phone, so she'll have them later.

"I'm so damn proud of you, kiddo."

She bends down and gives him a kiss on the cheek. "I love you."

He shoots me a wink and we all make our way to the huge table in the middle of the room. Over the course of the evening, everyone takes turns going around telling stories about how Quinn has bailed them out of a jam or gone above and beyond at work. Her Dad grins the entire time, loving the praise being heaped on his daughter. The goal was to have her feel like she was on top of the world and I'm positive I've succeeded.

"I think I speak for everyone when I say we wouldn't know our heads from our asses without you, Quinn." Tate raises her glass.

"That's exactly right. I'd be completely lost without you and I know you'll be just as effective as an attorney. So proud that you'll be one of ours." Decker winks at her.

When we arrived earlier, I told him she was staying at the firm.

"Quinn, you definitely keep my brothers in check." Donavan grins his ass off, like she doesn't save his ass as much as anybody's, but it's clear he's joking.

"Quinn, I know all about your secret stash of pens and office supplies." Dex laughs and Abigail smacks the back of his head, Gibbs-style. "Ow! Damn. Okay. You're awesome, Quinn. Thanks for everything." He grins and nods to me. "Your turn, big boy."

There's just one more thing that will make today perfect.

I scoot my chair back and hold my hand out to her.

"Umm. Okay. What's this?" She takes my hand and rises from her seat. "What are you doing?"

The confusion on her face makes this so much better. I walk over to her dad and hold out my hand. He smiles as he reaches into his pocket and pulls out a black box.

I turn back to Quinn. I'm doing this the right way. Like in the romance movies I've watched with her. Clearly that shit works, and I want every tool in my arsenal to make Quinn happy the rest of her life. I stare deeply into the same green eyes I fell in love with the first time I saw them, knowing without a doubt she's the one.

I take her left hand in mine and drop to a knee.

"Quinn, you're the most beautiful woman I've ever met, inside and out. The first time I saw you, I knew. I can't explain how or why, I just felt it in every cell of my body. And I want to tell you something in front of everyone tonight." I look back over my shoulder at my brothers and our closest friends.

Tate, who never cries, dabs a napkin at the corner of her eyes.

"Words don't exist to accurately express how much I love you. You're my best friend. Every morning, when I wake up next to you, I feel like the luckiest man alive. But there's one thing missing. A promise that you'll be mine forever. So, I'm lowering myself before you today to ask you one question. Will you marry me?"

Her head bobs up and down. "Yes, Deacon. Yes! A thousand times yes!" Her entire body trembles as she leans down to kiss me.

I slide the ring on her finger. It's an emerald-green princess cut that matches her eyes.

"I love you so much. I had no idea you were going to do this." Her eyes keep darting from the ring then back to me. The largest smile I've ever seen spreads across her face.

She's absolutely glowing, and I plan to work my ass off every day to keep it that way.

When our moment is over, everyone makes their rounds congratulating us.

I look at Dex and Donavan, wondering which poor bastard will be next, now that Decker and I are off the market.

Once everyone has told us how happy they are for us, I take Quinn's hands in mine and just stare into her eyes. "Fiancée."

"Fiancé." She does a little fancy curtsy and we both laugh.

I take her in my arms and hold her close to me, never wanting to let go. I kiss her forehead, then pull her back to me once more.

EPILOGUE

I can't think of anything in the world better than this moment, right here, right now, and I know the future will only be better.

Because she's all mine.

———

Want a little more of Quinn and Deacon? Grab it here —> Bonus epilogue!

HE'S A...

FILTHY
Playboy

— A COCKY SUITS NOVEL —

SLOANE HOWELL
ALEX WOLF

DEXTER

Two things matter in this world—pussy and money.

There's plenty of both on display tonight.

Navigating through PRYSM night club, the bass thumps in my chest when I spot Wells Covington. He's difficult to miss at six-four in his Brunello Cucinelli suit. I head up the stairs.

"Collins!" He tosses me a head nod as I round the corner, like he already knew I was here and expected me right at that moment. He leans over the railing, observing the dance floor from above.

I glance around. The place is anything but optimal for discussing business. This is casual, though. I use the term 'casual' loosely because I'm always on the hunt for a new whale to add to our client roster. Wells is the top of the food chain and Tecker (my brother Decker and his fiancée Tate) would be all up on my nuts if I wrap him up in a nice bow for the firm.

"Hope you haven't been waiting long." I grip his hand firm after I make my way over.

He's constantly back and forth between Manhattan and Chicago. We were tight back at college, then drifted apart. I've been trying to meet with him for months. Our schedules never permitted a get together until tonight. One look at this bastard and I see nothing but dollar signs. It's almost enough for me to ignore all the hot ass strutting half-naked around the club.

Almost.

"Nah. Haven't ordered a drink yet."

"What do you want? It's on me."

He eyes me up and down, grinning his ass off. I know he's about to ask for something ridiculous. "Clase Azul. For old time's sake."

Hmm. He's being nostalgic. We used to chug that shit in Cancun on spring break in college. Last time I saw him he ordered twenty-one-year-old Suntory Hibiki, an eight-hundred-dollar bottle of Japanese whiskey.

"Sounds like a party." I motion a waitress over.

A brunette in tight-fitting black jeans and a vee-cut top saunters our way. One look at us and she grins her ass off. She knows she's just hit the lottery waiting on us. "What can I get you?"

"Clase Azul Reposado. Bring the bottle."

Wells smirks.

"You got it." The girl wanders off through the crowd.

"I'd much rather be having her." Wells looks toward the crowd on the dance floor below.

I follow his gaze to see who he's leering at. I need to make sure he's taken care of tonight. Shouldn't be a problem.

We may go way back, but time has passed. If I can get our relationship back on a personal level, he'll be more apt to do business with the firm. Being the ultimate wingman is a specialty of mine, and I'm not above making sure he gets to fuck whoever he wants, if it comes to that.

My tie feels like it tightens around my neck and the hair on the back of my neck stands up when my eyes land on his target. She's hard to miss.

Abigail.

Fuck. Why did she have to be here?

Her long blonde curls bounce as she sways her hips to the music and waves her arms up in the air. The bright red dress she's wearing clings tight to her curves.

Of all the women in all the goddamn clubs in Chicago…

It's like the world hates me.

Fuck, she's hot.

My nostrils flare when the asshole she's dancing with grabs her hips from behind. He's pawing all over her, and she doesn't seem to mind one bit. In fact, I think she enjoys the attention.

I'm not used to this feeling—jealousy. It's totally foreign to me. I do my best to tame my reaction, but Wells is a goddamn shark and I'm sure he notices. You don't become a billionaire in your thirties by not reading people like a book, and he's the fucking Tony Stark of hedge funds.

I'm seeing red.

Not good.

Why do I even give a shit? I don't get hung up on chicks. Women chase me, not the other way around.

Abigail is different, though.

She's not like the usual women I date—or fuck. She's independent, young, and carefree. No baggage. Which is highly attractive.

Wells grins, suddenly taking more of an interest. "You know her, don't you?"

"Yeah." I let go of the railing after I look down and see the whites of my knuckles. "She works for the firm. Transferred from Dallas after the merger. You don't want anything to do with her, trust me. She's a stage five clinger. I'll introduce you, though. If you want."

A devilish smile forms on his lips when the waitress returns with the tall, slender bottle of tequila and two shot glasses. I silently pray he'll forget about Abigail as I snag the bottle and don't bother with the glasses. I tip it up, and it burns in my throat.

"Well fuck. I guess it's like college all over again tonight." Wells grins and takes a drink straight from the bottle too.

I rub the back of my neck, unable to keep my eyes from darting to Abigail on the dance floor. It's not like we're dating. We've hung out a few times after work, totally casual. Okay, we made out once when we were hammered after a Bears game when she did me a huge favor for Deacon's dumb ass; which he still owes me for.

Still, there's nothing going on with Abby and yet I have this unbelievable urge to grip that guy by the back of his neck and shove his face into a bucket of water. Nothing life threatening, just enough to feel his fear course through my palm.

I want to stake my claim on her like a caveman. Brand her ass with my handprint.

Wells leans over. "No need for an introduction. Plenty of women here tonight, Collins."

"Yeah." I nod. He keeps calling me by my last name. That's a good sign. It *should* make me happy.

None of the women here compare to Abby, though. I glance around the bar and notice she has quite the group of admirers. Every fucker in the place stares at her from afar, and I know exactly what's on all their minds.

They're all pounding booze and watching her shake her ass. The back of her dress rides her thighs, coming dangerously close to showing her panties, if she's even wearing any.

I can't fight my smile, despite the irritation coursing through my limbs. She has this spark about her that lights up the room with energy. She's magnetic, like a tractor beam that reels you in. I get why these assholes are staring, and at the same time, I want to let every one of them know she's off limits.

I take another pull from the bottle when she walks off the dance floor toward the bathrooms. "Be right back."

Wells waves me off with a flippant hand and strikes up a conversation with a leggy brunette.

I take the stairs two at a time to the lower level, losing sight of Abigail momentarily.

The last thing I want to look like is a stalker, so I pull out my phone and do the ol' 'fake call' routine. I shuffle down the narrow corridor toward the women's bathroom, hoping I time this shit just right.

I watch in a mirror and wait for her reflection, then I turn the corner just in time so Abigail bumps into me.

"I'm so sorry. Are you okay?"

I huff out a fake sigh, staring in the other direction. "I'll call you back." I make a show of pocketing my phone and glance up to meet her stunned gaze. "Don't worry about... Abby?"

"Oh my God, Dex!" She goes in for a hug, and I'm pretty sure it's heaven with her tits pressed up against me.

Fuck, I never want to let go of her. I'm close enough to smell her fruity body wash and the effect she has on me is damn near hypnotic.

I have to compose myself and will my cock not to get hard up against her stomach.

"Sorry, I wasn't paying attention." Her hand slides down my arm.

"It's fine."

"What are you...," we both say at the same time.

I hold out a palm. "Ladies first."

"Out with friends. You?"

"Here with a client. Hedge fund manager."

"Cool, well, I should..." She hooks a thumb over her shoulder toward the bathroom.

"Right. Was good to see you."

"You too!" she yells over her shoulder, and I can still barely make out the words as she disappears through the door.

Look at yourself for fuck's sake. What's wrong with you?

We only made out the one time. We were both wasted, and I don't know if she even remembers it. I'd be lying if I said I didn't remember every minute detail of the kiss, though. Not a damn day goes by I don't think about it.

I decide to take a piss, since I'm already down here, so I walk through the door. That idiot she was dancing with primps himself in the mirror, fixing his hair. The guy is pathetic. He's wearing a fucking Winnie the Pooh shirt and corduroy pants.

I thought this place had standards and a dress code. Fuck.

I cannot believe I seriously have to compete with this ass basket.

I take a piss in the urinal, unlike bitch boy over there who probably squatted in the stall. Afterward, I wash my hands, and he's still there, checking himself out. Of course, as soon as I walk out of the bathroom, he decides to leave at the same time. I open the door and he speeds up to follow, but I let it fall right in his face.

Stay away from what's mine, pussy.

As I walk out, Abigail leaves the women's bathroom at the same time and we nearly collide again, this time not by design.

I catch her in an awkward hug and do my best to try and pull her off to the side, so Pooh Bear doesn't see us.

Of course, he heads in our direction, and I pray for him to do something that makes it acceptable for me to kick the piss out of him.

"Abby, you okay?"

Fuck you for calling her Abby. I call her that.

She's still staring up at me with wide eyes, and I slowly stand her upright.

350

I don't ever want to let go of her and at the same time my palm twitches with the need to choke this asshole until he passes out.

"Yeah, I'm good." She smiles and it's ridiculously cute. "This is Dex. He's a partner at the firm and we've literally almost ran each other over twice in the last five minutes." Her head tilts in my direction.

Her friend shoves his hands in his pockets and shuffles his feet around like pussies do. "Oh, well, uhh... Chuck and Barbie got us a table."

What in the holy fuck kind of names are those? Chuck and Barbie? I scoff under my breath where Abigail doesn't notice.

Her hand flies out. "Dex, this is my friend Kyle. He lives in my building."

"Good to meet you." I hold out my hand and resist the urge to crush this guy's metacarpals so he never puts them on Abigail again. It's absolutely *not* good to meet him, at all. He needs to piss off.

He barely squeezes my hand back. It's like shaking hands with a wet noodle. *Jesus.*

You can tell a lot about a man by the strength of his handshake and this guy is just as I thought, soft as fuck.

I glance up to the balcony and Wells has two brunettes on his arm, and I'm almost positive one of them is supposed to be for me. He chats them up, but it seems like he's watching me out of his peripheral vision.

Abigail looks at me, and I swear there's a sparkle in her eye. "Okay. Well, I should get back."

"Sure, see you at the office." I watch her go and barely refrain from scowling at Kyle when he glances back at me.

Once I'm back up to the balcony, Wells leans in and his voice lowers. "Don't worry. I found us some ass." He says it like I just struck out and nods to the two brunettes a few feet away.

It makes my blood boil even hotter. If I want Abigail, I'll have her. I always get what I want.

I scan the room and watch Abigail meet up with her friends. Our eyes lock for a moment, but I quickly turn toward the table and sit next to the other brunette.

"I'm Sandra." She holds her hand out and sinks her teeth into her bottom lip.

I take her hand. "Dexter. Call me Dex."

"I've never fucked a Dexter before."

What the hell did Wells just get us into?

He leans back with a satisfied grin.

Sandra smirks and slides her hand up my thigh. Her red fingernails give me a squeeze. Any other night I might enjoy a woman being so direct, but the one I want is across the room with some fuckbags named Kyle, Chuck, and Barbie.

"Let's get out of here," says Wells. "I have the top-floor suite at The Peninsula."

I shouldn't be surprised. That room only goes for eight grand a night. The bastard has a new mansion on Lake Michigan, but it's about a forty-five-minute drive away. I give him a head nod, letting him know I'm on board so we can get the fuck out of here. I'm ready to call it a night even though I'm leaving without Abby. It's still a success. I'll have Wells as a client before the weekend is up so I'm still batting .500.

Like a true asshole, I can't let it go, though. I make a point to parade Sandra and her big tits right past Abigail's table. She needs to know what she's missing out on. I want her to be just as jealous as when I saw her on the dance floor grinding with that limp-handed cock boy.

Instead, she just smiles and waves, like she doesn't have a care in the world.

Goddamn it.

We finally make it outside to the sidewalk.

Sandra leans in close and whispers, "Your place or mine?"

Her friend slides into the back of a black Mercedes with Wells. Of course, he has a car and a driver. Why wouldn't you on a random night out in Chicago?

Man, I *have* to bring his business to the firm.

"Neither."

"Hotel? With those two?" She nods toward Wells and her friend.

"I'm going home, alone."

She frowns.

I lift my chin in Wells' direction. "He has enough dick for both of you. Enjoy yourselves."

Wells smiles, then shrugs. "He's not lying."

Sandra walks over and climbs in.

Wells tells the driver where to take them then turns back toward me. "My life doesn't suck at all and I appreciate the generosity." He pats Sandra on the leg, like she was my possession and I'm sharing her with him for the night. "I'll call you tomorrow."

"Yeah, you will, bitch. Have fun."

He shoots me a middle finger and they speed off down the road.

I glance back at the front of PRYSM once more, then start down Kingsbury street, looking for a cab. Jerking off to the thought of Abigail is a million times better than putting my dick in that thirsty chick.

ABIGAIL

MY ALARM BLARES way too early. It definitely feels like a Monday already.

I stretch and yawn.

Staying up late watching scary movies with Kyle and Nick was a bad idea. I know better than to do that when I have to work the next morning.

I rub the pad of my finger over the creases of my eyes. It's like my head just landed on my pillow and I could easily go back to sleep for another four hours, but I roll over and sit up. The minute my feet touch the cold floor I regret not turning the heat on last night. I was exhausted when I got in, and Barbie, the ice Queen, is anal about the thermostat. I think her real name might be Elsa because my room is a damn ice box.

Yes, we're roommates, but it's very much *her* apartment. I needed a place to stay and she had one. No way was I going to move in with some random man in Chicago. Grabbing my bathroom caddy, it's like being back at summer camp. Barbie's a neat freak and bitches any time I leave things scattered about. To be fair, she keeps her stuff put away so I can't really complain.

Leaving my bedroom, I head to the bathroom, but the door's locked.

"Just a minute."

Great.

Chuck, Barbie's boyfriend, apparently stayed over—again.

He's probably in there taking a dump. Talk about lousy luck this morning.

I set my stuff by the bathroom door and shuffle down the hall to the kitchen. I need coffee or I might turn murderous. I grab my favorite mug from the dishwasher.

Opening the refrigerator, I pull out my hazelnut creamer and scowl. I shake the bottle and my face heats. It's empty.

I open it up and tip it upside down over my mug and bang on the bottom.

Not a drop.

If I did this to her I'd have to hear about it for a week. Now, I have to stop off on my way to work and pay a small fortune for what I could've enjoyed at home for free. I press the button for the lid to the trash can with my right foot and toss in the bottle along with my disappointment.

I glare toward the bathroom. I know he's the one who finished it off, and I hope it gave him the coffee shits.

I mentally smack myself. I still haven't taken a shower, and I don't want to go anywhere near where he's been. I need a new roommate. One who doesn't come with an annoying hairy boyfriend named Chuck.

The bathroom door opens and to no one in particular, he says, "Whew. Someone light a match."

This is your life right now. You need to get it together, Abby.

The sound of the aerosol lands in my ears, hissing as he sprays it around.

My nose scrunches in disgust.

Gross.

I hate to skip my shower, but after this, I have to risk it.

He struts past me in the kitchen, looking like a damn yeti in his boxer briefs and no shirt.

Maybe it's a good thing I don't have my coffee, or I might spew it everywhere. I can deal with the hairy, shirtless act, but the rest is a big fat no.

I quickly move down the hall, scooping my caddy on the way to my room and slam my door a little louder than I need to, but screw that guy. I light one of my Bath & Body Works candles and pray it works its magic quickly. Sitting cross-legged on the floor in front of the mirror on the back of my bedroom door, I twist my hair up into a bun. Today will be a light makeup day. A few swipes of mascara and cherry lip gloss. I smooth my eyebrows and pop up to get dressed.

After throwing on my work outfit, I blow the candle out and make a wish. It's a silly ritual that should be reserved for birthdays, but it makes me happy. Plugging my nose, I brave the bathroom long enough to brush my teeth. I gasp for air once I stumble into the living room and manage not to inhale anything toxic.

Once I escape the apartment, I head to my favorite coffee shop down by the L-train station.

Grabbing my white chocolate mocha from the barista, I board the train, throw on my Beats, and crank up *Everyday People* by Sly and the Family Stone.

Just another day in paradise.

MY MORNING GOT off to a shitty start, pun intended, and it seems my bad fortune will carry on through the workday. I've already had trouble tracking down three associates for important depositions. I screwed up and set up two meetings at the same time for Donavan. Fortunately, he hated one of them and rescheduled, then thanked me for the blunder.

That's the totality of my good luck, and I'm starting to think the candle wish from earlier was nothing but a curse.

I walk by Dexter, hoping maybe he can turn around this disaster of a day. "Hey, how was your weekend?" I didn't think he was going to let go of me when we ran into each other at the club, and part of me secretly wished he hadn't.

He barely looks in my direction. "Fine."

Oh my God, what's his deal? The world hates me.

Come on, Dex, just give me that smile of yours once. I need it so bad. I'm drowning over here. Help a girl out. "Do anything fun?" Surely that'll be a good ice breaker to talk about running into each other.

He shakes his head. "Nope." Then, he just walks off, leaving me hanging.

Ugh!

I head back to my desk. I just need to embrace the fact it's not my day; just get through this one and start fresh tomorrow. I don't have the faintest clue what crawled up Dex's ass. He was so flirty at the club. Maybe Mondays aren't for him either.

I consider us friends in a way. We've met up for drinks a few times after work and it always goes well, despite the intimidation factor because hello, he's a partner. It's never anything too casual. I try to hold back on the flirting and keep the conversations about work considering he's a boss, even though I don't report directly to him. I don't want him to think I'm coming on to him, even though if the roles reversed it might be impossible to resist. He's freaking gorgeous.

He doesn't act like a boss, though. I know for a fact him and Deacon are practical jokers of the highest order and Decker always wants to wring their necks. I think it's cute and fun. They know when to be professional and when they can let their guard down.

I pass by Quinn and she gives me a wry smile, like she knows I'm thinking about Dexter. I know it's just my brain playing tricks, but it feels like everybody is watching me, judging.

The tattoos are the only way I can tell Dexter apart from Deacon. Well, that and he's way leaner. Deacon is big because he played football. Oh, and the scar. Dexter has this scar right above his left eyebrow. It's not huge but it gives him this edgy, bad boy look.

And the kiss. God, I'll never forget it. That whole day was incredible. When Dex told me what he was doing for Deacon, helping him win Quinn back, I couldn't say no. And okay, maybe just maybe, Dexter and I made out in the bar that night to raucous cheers from professional football players.

I don't even remember exactly how it came about, but he just fixed his gaze on me and I was done for.

We were so drunk I don't think he remembers doing it, but I will never forget the way I floated into the clouds when we parted ways that night.

Dex is smoking hot, and I'd be a liar if I said I wasn't attracted to him. Every woman in the office practically drools over him and his brothers. Anytime he's nearby I get this sensation deep in my belly. My heartrate spikes and I feel on edge.

This attraction is insane because I'm not looking to date anyone. I'm twenty-four, just out of school and beginning my career. I tried nursing school for a year but switched to paralegal and I love it. It's the first job I've really felt was meant for me.

No, I need to rid myself of these thoughts of Dex and focus on my job.

At the same time, as I sit down at my desk, I can't stop thinking about his foul mood. I don't know if I'll be able to focus on anything until I get him to smile again.

I need to hit up the breakroom and get my head in the game before I start my afternoon.

Perfect.

He walks in there just as I stand up and stroll that way. He keeps chocolate pudding cups hidden in the back of the refrigerator, practically daring someone to eat them. Nobody in their right mind would do it, but it's cute. He has this boyish charm about him, but he's anything but a boy in that Dolce and Gabbana suit.

No, Dexter Collins is all man and he knows it.

I march over, intent on finding out what crawled up his ass. He's got a big stick up there, and I need to yank it out. I pass by Quinn's desk, and she shoots me this mischievous smirk like she knows exactly what I'm up to. I don't know how to process her grin, so I shove it to the back of my mind.

I don't usually hit it off with women, but Quinn is very likeable, and I could see us being friends. I give her a small wave then feel stupid when I realize she wasn't smiling at me at all. She was looking at Deacon, her fiancé and Dexter's twin who strolls up to her desk.

You're so awkward.

My cheeks pink with embarrassment as I enter the breakroom. Dexter leans up against the dark counter next to the refrigerator. His ankles are crossed, and I can see a hint of his charcoal-gray plaid socks. I didn't take him for a patterned socks kind of guy, but they're perfect with those shoes and that suit. His jacket is draped over a chair, like he didn't want to get it dirty, and the sleeves of his button-down are rolled up on his forearms.

It's arm porn to the nth degree. Ink snakes down his forearms. My chest grows warm. Electricity jolts through my veins along with curious thoughts of what the rest of those tattoos look like under his shirt on his chiseled frame. I blink at the sight, and his gaze meets mine and snaps me out of my daydreams.

I can't tell, but it's almost like he's halfway scowling while he takes an angry bite of pudding.

"You ever going to try something besides chocolate?"

His brows shoot up, but he doesn't reply.

I'm not giving up that easy, Dex. "I went through a butterscotch phase once, but banana is the dom of pudding flavors."

He sighs. "Cool."

What the hell? He'd usually smile at a joke with sexual undertones.

Thought you didn't flirt with him, Abby?

Okay, maybe I do a little. I'd do anything right about now. My brows furrow. "You upset with me or need to talk? I mean, I'm a good listener." I sidle up next to him and give him a bump with my hip. I don't know how much more obvious I can be, and I'm getting nowhere.

"Nah. I'm fine."

I stare down at the floor, like maybe he'll have some pity and actually talk to me. "Don't sound fine."

He drops his empty pudding cup into the trash. He licks the spoon, slowly, for good measure before tossing it in too. And holy shit the way he wrapped his tongue around the white plastic sends a current between my thighs, and for the first time in my life I find myself jealous of a freaking spoon.

He starts for the door, not bothering to look back. "I'm fine. Why you on my case?"

I follow and grip his forearm.

He turns back to me.

I shrug and can't stop the frown that forms on my face. "I don't know. I guess you just seem different. You're not very talkative." The guy isn't usually a chatterbox, but I can always coax more than a few words out of him.

He plasters on the fakest smile I've ever seen. "I'm fine. Promise." He turns and coolly says, "See ya," over his shoulder.

I frown again. I just want one real smile. It could totally turn around this shit day of mine. "Hey, um, Dex?"

Pivoting slowly, the darkened color in his eyes pins me in place and steals my breath away. He sighs again, like I'm his little sister and he *has* to deal with me. "What is it? I've got a lot of paperwork."

I don't know why I won't let this go. Maybe I'm just competitive and have to get my way. I shrug. "Right... me too. I just..."

He looks like he wants to be anywhere but here right now. I have to look sad, because that's the way I feel inside, and Dex must take notice because he actually attempts a real smile this time, even though I know he doesn't want to do it.

Spit it out, Abby.

"I'm going to The Gage for a drink after work. Maybe we could meet up?" I try to hide the hope in my voice. I know I said he's hot, but that three-letter word doesn't really do him justice. Like the dude could be on the cover of GQ Magazine. I'd put that poster on my wall. And if I'm being honest, I'd so pull out my vibrator and chase more than one big O staring at said poster.

This is bad. Way bad.

I didn't realize how attracted to him I was until just now. I don't need to be having these feelings about Sex...

Shit.

I mean Dexter.

Oh boy.

I let out a breath as he stares me down, and I hope like hell he can't read my thoughts.

His lips curl up into a bit more of a smile, and my stomach rolls in a good way. Maybe my day is turning around after all.

"Sounds fun. I'll be there."

"Grood." *What the hell, Abby?* "I mean, yeah, I was going to say great, then switched to good. You know what? I'll see you there."

This time he gives me a genuine smile, and my whole world lights up.

Then, it simultaneously crashes. I watch him go and already wonder if I should cancel. I shake my head. I'm being stupid. He thinks I just want to hang out, nothing more. Dexter and I can totally be friends.

It's fine.

I'm fine.

There's that stupid word again. I am *so* not fine. I am anything *but* fine.

Stupid Sex...

Hell! Dexter.

I scoff out loud at how ridiculous I am, and I wish my brain would sort itself out. I need some kind of buffer to control myself around him, so I don't get drunk and make out with him again. Or worse, end up in his bed for the night.

Would that really be so bad?

Stop it, brain!

When I get back to my desk, I send a text to Kyle.

Me: Hey, drinks at The Gage after work. Invite a friend.

Kyle: See you there.

Me: Perfect.

If we all hang out as a group, I won't be tempted to flirt with Dex. I'll have at least one distraction I can turn to if he does that smoldering gaze thing at me or rolls up his sleeves and I see his tattoos. This is perfect. I mentally congratulate myself for coming up with it on the fly.

My brain might be cursing me right now, but my body didn't get the memo.

I do know one thing, though.

I got my smile.

DEXTER

COVINGTON MUST'VE ENJOYED himself the other night, judging by this afternoon's phone conversation. Wish the same could be said for me. I went home alone and rubbed one out in my bed thinking about Abigail. Fuck, the way her tits bounced in my little fantasy as she rode my cock. I don't know if I've ever come that hard in my life.

Then, my thoughts went rogue on me. I couldn't stop wondering if she went home with that pussy friend of hers. I got so fucking mad thinking about it I had to go for a run along the lake at two in the morning. It was cold as tits, and I ended up even more pissed than I was before.

Covington drones on in my ear about the brunettes and the freaky shit he made them do. Fuck, this dude is into some crazy stuff. Something about spreader bars and nipple clamps.

His goddamn sex life sounds like he lives in a torture dungeon. Not my thing, but it's whatever. As long as they were both into it, who gives a shit if they like to put on dog collars and hang from the ceiling while they fuck?

For some godforsaken reason, though, I can't stop thinking about Abigail and that prick friend of hers. It's stupid. It's not my business if she takes some asshole home from the bar, but the thought of her with another man has me all twisted up. I grip the phone tight in my palm and let out a long, frustrated sigh, trying anything to get the tension to leave my body.

Eventually, the conversation comes full circle and returns to business at hand. I'm ready to get out of here. It's been a long and frustrating day, but this is the conversation I've been waiting for, and I can't let all my hard work warming him up go to waste.

"All right, Collins. Give me the fucking pitch. You've worked hard all weekend for this opportunity like a patient little boy."

I laugh. Nothing gets past this guy, no matter how laid back he seems. I can practically hear him smirk on the other end, and I have to appreciate how fucking cocky he is. Some things never change. In fact, some things get worse over time, and Covington is the most arrogant motherfucker ever. I like that about him. "Look, bitch."

He laughs loud enough it booms through the phone. "Oh, I'm going to enjoy this. Fuck, I miss the shit out of you. We spend too much time in boardrooms these days and not enough time at the bar."

"You gonna let me pitch or what, asshole?"

He's dying now. "Please proceed."

I'm like a goddamn sales magician. "I'll cut to the chase and save both of us the time. I head up finance and tax. We specialize in dealings with the SEC and IRS." I tuck my phone between my cheek and shoulder as I exit my office for the day. I told Abby I'd meet her for drinks at The Gage.

"I'm aware. But you know this, so carry on."

Biggest pitch of my life and I can't stop thinking about Abigail.

Fuck. Get out of my head for two minutes, woman!

"I think we should have a discussion about what we can offer you. I know what you're about to say... Bennett Cooper, blah blah..."

He cuts me off. "Absolutely. Let's get something on the books for you to swing by the new place on the lake. We can try out the golf course I have on the property. I'll have my people get in touch and see what we can set up."

My eyebrows raise. "That's it, asshole? You don't want any specifics right now?"

He laughs again. "No, I'm good. Would've set this up over the phone if you'd asked, but it was good drinking tequila straight from the bottle with you."

"Yeah, it was fun."

"Hey, Collins?"

"Yeah?"

"You know I'm not loyal to Cooper. I go where the numbers take me. Everyone else follows. Bring your A game when we set a meeting."

Adrenaline floods my veins and I'm on top of the world. This will be huge.

"Oh, and Collins?"

"Yeah?"

"Full disclosure, I have a meeting already set with Cooper when I get back to Manhattan, to discuss expanding his representation of my new holdings. He's fucking good and business is business. It's not personal, so if you want me, make it worth my time."

Fuck! Fuck Bennett Cooper.

Bennett Cooper is the most pompous prick of all time. He represents damn near every heavy hitter on Wall Street, including Wells right now, and everyone in the industry lives in the shadows of Cooper and Associates. Not for long, after I'm done pilfering his clients.

I need Wells on board, bad. He'll double the firm's revenue. It could mean raises and bonuses for a lot of people, not just the partners. It could be life-changing for a lot of employees around here.

I set my worries aside. Wells will sniff weakness through the phone. "No problem. I welcome the competition."

"That's what I like to hear. Fuck, my life is good."

"Oh yeah?"

"Of course, best attorneys in the world fighting over me. I can't wait to see what the future holds. Better start getting creative. Cooper doesn't fuck around and everyone in New York is aware of you gunning for his clients. I've heard the grumblings."

"They should be grumbling. Maybe he should get better."

Covington laughs. "There ya go. Looking forward to our meeting. Thanks for the eventful weekend."

"No problem. Talk soon, pussy."

I end the call and walk straight toward the elevator.

Fuck. Tecker is in there.

I groan inwardly. I love my brother, but Tate is a tough pill to swallow sometimes, and sometimes she's awesome. Just depends on the day. I probably get along with her better than any of my brothers, besides Decker, of course. It's my job. I'm the goddamn peacekeeper in the family. Always have been.

My brothers argue and give each other shit better than anyone, but Decker and Donavan have been at it for months. Usually, these little family altercations regarding business resolve themselves within a day or two. I'm going to have to do something soon because they're both acting like petty assholes.

"Just the two people I wanted to see." I smile at Tate. Someone has to combat all the glares she gets from Deacon and Donavan.

"Can't wait to hear this," says Decker.

"Just got off the phone with Covington. Wants me to swing by his new pad and talk shop. Maybe play a round of golf on his new course."

Decker grins his ass off. It's a sly grin. The one that forms on his face when big money is involved.

"Maybe I should go so you don't embarrass yourself off the tee." Tate smiles like she got me. "I'm sure he'll show you his one wood over a nice dinner."

Decker laughs. He loves it when she talks shit to us. This is probably foreplay for the two of them.

I laugh because it was pretty funny, and I can appreciate a good joke. "Tate, for Wells Covington's business, I would wash his balls personally and take the one wood in all eighteen holes."

She grins her ass off. "Nicely-played with the self-deprecation. Always a good defense tactic."

I give her a little nod. "Thank you."

As the elevator makes its way down, Decker attempts to change the subject. "How's the rest of the new client roster shaping up?"

Did he not hear me? I'm about to land Wells Covington. "Fuck the rest of those minnows. I'm doing minimum maintenance on them. Covington is my priority right now."

He shakes his head. "You're putting too much time and risk into one potential client."

"Yep." Tate pops the p when she says it.

Just like that, the lighthearted mood of the elevator evaporates.

Fuck these two. I'm thinking about the firm and all the direct and indirect revenue Wells would bring in. That could be a lot of Christmas bonuses for a lot of employees who don't live in a fucking mansion off Lake Michigan like these two. "Look, I don't tell you how to do your jobs. Don't tell me how to do mine."

Decker's eyes narrow. "I'm the managing partner. I tell everyone how to do their goddamn jobs."

My hands ball into fists. I need to control this anger rising up in me, but I just can't leave it alone. "Then leave your little echo chamber in her office when you discuss mine with me. I don't need her sitting back there making snide remarks."

Tate's mouth drops open. I'm not usually so harsh with her, and I feel a little bad about it, but fuck, I can see why Donavan and Deacon get flustered around her sometimes. She doesn't know where her authority lies.

She folds her arms over her chest. "I'm a partner too, dickhead."

"Yeah, there are lots of partners, yet you're the only one here commenting on things that don't concern you. I run finance. You don't know a damn thing about it. You can go back to leading Decker around by the balls as soon as I get off the elevator."

Decker gets in my face and grits his teeth. "You're talking about the overall wellbeing of the firm. We're not discussing SEC and tax dealings, we're discussing client relations, which all partners are privy to be in on those strategies. And I'm telling you, you're putting all your eggs in one basket and it's reckless. It would create a high concentration on our books from one source of revenue."

"Jesus Christ, what a terrible problem to have. And once Covington brings in more clients, which he would, that risk would disappear. As long as we don't take out idiotic loans against future revenue or buy another fucking building, we'd be fine. He can open up a lot of new avenues."

"Look, I hear you, asshole. It's just my job to be skeptical and protect what we have. Covington is a whale. Dedicate some time to him, sure, but do *not* neglect anyone else at his expense. Is that understood?"

I shrug. "Fine, Dad. Anything else?"

"Yes. Apologize to Tate."

I laugh.

He looks serious.

"Decker, don't…" Tate grabs him by the forearm. "I was talking shit first. I thought it was lighthearted and fun, but the conversation took a turn."

I glance over at Tate. She looks sincere. I know she cares. I'm sure she's dealt with assholes talking down to her ever since she became an attorney. "No, he's right, Tate. Sorry. I shouldn't have made things personal."

"Apology accepted."

Decker glares back and forth at Tate and me. "Fuck, I can't with this place. Bunch of children." The elevator dings and Decker scurries out like he wants far away from everyone.

Tate grins at me. "I think we just aged him five years. He's gonna go gray up top before long."

"Down below too. Ol' silver crotch."

We both die laughing.

"I can hear you assholes!" Decker shoots a middle finger up at us and doesn't bother to turn around.

I drop by my place to change into something more casual and then head to The Gage.

When I arrive, I find Abigail at a table drinking whiskey. It's weird and, at the same time, I have to smile. I'm surprised to see her sitting alone, and I wonder how many men she's waved off since she got here. Judging by some of the dirty looks as I walk up, I'd say a few.

Eat shit, assholes. She's mine.

She looks up from her drink and smirks. "You came."

Her reaction makes me feel a little assholish. I was pretty short with her at work, but I had a lot going on, and I didn't appreciate being kept up all night with thoughts of her fucking some other guy. It wasn't her fault my mind was being a dick, but still.

"Said I'd be here. Getting started without me?"

"It was a long day, and I *really* needed this drink. Some guy was being a jerk at work."

"Give me his name and I'll write his ass up."

She grins and takes another drink as I slide into the empty seat to her left. I order a Booker's bourbon neat and an intense silence stretches between us.

"So, banana pudding? That's your go to?"

"Hah!" She slaps her palm down on the table. "You *were* listening."

"I was in a mood."

"Because…"

I trace a finger along the rim of the rocks glass. "Not important. Back to this pudding phase. I'm sure butterscotch and banana are fantastic, but chocolate is king. Everyone knows this."

"You ever had homemade banana pudding?"

I shake my head. "No."

"Then, it's settled. I'll make it for you, and it'll blow your mind."

I can think of another thing I'd like her to blow with those cherry-red lips. Wrap them around my cock while I make a fist in her hair.

"Dex?"

I snap out of my fantastic thoughts. "Sorry. What were you saying?"

"I'll make some pudding and bring it to work for you."

"Oh yeah. That'd be nice." Why are we talking about pudding so much?

"Don't doubt my pudding skills. I work magic with bananas."

Fuck.

I'm going to need to adjust my dick if she keeps talking like this. I know she did it on purpose.

"Abigail!"

The high-pitched voice comes out of nowhere and the masculinity held within is questionable at best. What the fuck?

"Kyle!" Abigail waves at him, practically bouncing in her seat.

What. The. Fuck.

Is she trying to piss me off on purpose? Is this payback for earlier at work?

I glance over my shoulder and the bitch from the club the other night pulls up a chair along with two other guys, and the fact I refer to them as 'guys' is extremely polite.

"Hey, man." He sticks his hand across the table.

I leave his hand hanging in the air because fuck him and fuck this.

Abigail's brows knit together. "Dex, you remember Kyle, right? You met at PRYSM, before you left with your friend and a couple of women."

So she *was* paying attention.

"Sorry." I shake my head right at Kyle. "Wasn't a very memorable night."

Man, I need to get out of here. My heartbeat pounds in my ears every time Kyle and his friends so much as breathe in my direction.

And the hell it wasn't a memorable night. I can't stop thinking about her tight body and that clingy red dress riding up her damn thighs. How bad I wanted to bury my face between them and get a taste. I want to fuck her in that dress so bad my balls ache thinking about it.

Kyle interrupts our conversation. "This is Craig and Seth. Some of my work buddies."

"You're old enough to drink?" I take a sip of my one-hundred and twenty-five proof bourbon. It slides down my throat and heats up my chest.

"Dude, I'm like twenty-seven." He scoffs and rolls his eyes.

I feel like a goddamn babysitter. I bet they still live at home with their parents. Why in the fuck do I even need to compete with these jerk offs? This is a total waste of my time. I'm better than this.

Abigail.

"Can I talk to you for a minute?" Abigail slides out of her seat and jerks on my arm.

"If you'll excuse me, ladies." I give them a head nod, coupled with a smile, and down the rest of my drink.

Abigail grabs my arm and tugs, leading me toward the bathrooms away from her little reverse harem I've been made a part of. I don't compete for a woman's attention and I'm not about to start now. She invited that fucker who was grinding all over her the other night. That's some bullshit. I thought it would be the two of us. She never mentioned Kyle and his piss pot friends tagging along, or I'd have told her to kick rocks.

"What the heck was that back there?"

I shrug. "What?"

She throws her hands up and gets all animated.

Fuck, she's even cuter when she's irritated. I stare at her lips, and it's hard to concentrate on her words.

"You know exactly what I'm talking about. You're being rude to my friends." Her manicured nail pokes into my chest.

I glance at my watch like I'm late for a meeting. "You finished?" I don't do dramatics and bullshit either. I'm not playing these games. That's what I tell myself, even though I'm clearly entertaining them. It's about to end soon, though. If she wants to have a bunch of pussies fawning all over her and hanging onto every word she says she can have it. I thought she was cool, but maybe I had her all wrong. I'm starting to think she gets off on male attention. Maybe she has self-esteem issues or something, and I hope she gets it worked out if she does, but I won't be part of the solution.

"Somewhere else you'd rather be?"

"I gotta go." I don't wait for her to respond. I stop off at the bar and pay for our drinks.

Jimmy, the bartender says, "And theirs?" He gestures to the three ass clowns.

"They can buy their own. Here, this is extra for you because I'm sure they don't tip for shit." I slide a twenty across the bar.

"Thanks, Dex."

"No prob. See you later."

Sliding quickly through the crowd, I make my exit. Out on the sidewalk I scrub a hand over my face and let out a sigh. Fuck this fucking day.

"Hey!" Abigail comes out of the shadows, ninja-style, like she just teleported in front of me, and flies up in my face.

What the hell?

I stumble back for a second before I catch my balance. "You trying to give me a fucking heart attack? Christ!"

There's a fire in her eyes that turns me on like no other. She's practically seething, her arms flying around all animated as she lets me have it. "What the hell is your problem?"

My eyes widen and I just stare at her. She must be blind as a goddamn bat if she doesn't know what's going on here. "What's *my* problem?"

"Yeah, that's what I said, dickhead." Both her hands go to her hips.

"Dickhead?"

"That's what I said, isn't it?"

Fuck this.

I'll show her the answer to her question.

I close the distance between us and cup her face with both palms, then stare straight into her fiery eyes. Before she can pull away, I slant my mouth over hers and kiss the ever-loving shit out of her.

Her lips are even softer than I remember. I slide a hand down her neck, along her curves, all the way to her ass, then yank her hard against me.

That's my fucking problem. I'm a goddamn man.

I don't play little boy games.

When I want something, I take it.

The kiss is sweet and faster than I'd like but it is what it is. Now she knows and she can quit toying with me like I'm on the same level as those shit birds in the bar.

I'm interested.

Her eyelashes flutter for a moment, and she's in a daze.

She leans toward my mouth, but I pull away, even though it's the last thing I ever want to do.

What I want to do and what I need to do are two different things. I *want* to pull her tight little ass into a cab, take her back to my place, and bury my face between her thighs until she comes so many times she can't breathe.

Abigail stares back at me with her baby blues, seemingly in a trance. I may have kissed her so hard she went catatonic. Her fingers move to her lips.

"*That's* what the hell my problem is." I walk away instead of kissing her again.

I don't look back when I hear my name come from her lips. She can think about shit for a while.

Nope, I keep walking down Michigan Avenue until I find myself at the gym.

I swipe my card and grab the spare clothes I keep in my locker. I need to burn off all this frustration and pent up energy before I do something stupid.

Fuck, she has me so wound up.

I want to take it out on someone, and I definitely don't want it to be her. As enjoyable as it might've been, I didn't want to take it out on her friends either.

Friends.

She really needs to get rid of those guys. You can tell by looking at them they're hanging onto a dream, that someday she'll get too drunk or have a really bad day, and they'll slide in when she's vulnerable and get to put their little baby dicks inside her one time. I know how those fuckers operate. They'll waste months, clinging to someone who has no interest in them, in hopes of taking advantage of them just once. How pathetic can you be?

It was only a matter of time before I blew up on one of them. It's not like I can really blame them for wanting to hang out around her. Abigail is gorgeous. She's funny and a little bit of a goof when she wants to be. She makes me smile.

As I start my workout, my brain settles down and I do what I do best; analyze. There are more than a few problems at play here. For one, she's young. Too damn young for me but I can't help the attraction. She's twenty-four, but she's way more mature than I was at that age. That's not saying much. She's probably more mature than I am now, if I'm being honest.

Another problem; she's one of Tate's Dallas transfers, and I'm sure Tate would not approve, and Abigail probably listens to her more than anyone. I get along with Tate better than any of my brothers, but we both know it's just to keep the peace and for Decker. I'm sure if given the opportunity, Tate would tell Abigail what a player I am if she finds out we're seeing each other. She wouldn't be wrong for doing it either.

I can't help the fact I like women. I like fucking them and I like making them come. It's just what I do. I've never been so fixated on one, though. The more I think about it, the more I realize I haven't even thought about sleeping with another woman since I met Abby.

I throw two twenty-five on the bench press, trying to rid myself of this confusion. I don't have time for it. The biggest client of my life is within reach and I should be devoting a hundred percent of my time to getting that signature on the dotted line.

After three sets on the bench, I hit the treadmill, my feet racing against my thoughts in a battle to see who'll win as music from my phone filters through my headphones and pounds in my ears. These Abigail-induced runs need to stop. This shit is bleeding over to work, and I can't have it become a problem. At least this time I won't be cold as fuck and get pissed off all over again, after going on an Abigail run at night. The music is an epic fail. I couldn't tell you the last five songs I listened to. All I can think about is her and how I can still taste her on my lips.

The worst part is, I want to taste her again.

ABIGAIL

IT'S BEEN two days since Dexter stunned me with that kiss. It wasn't a good kiss. It was a smack-you-in-the-face, steal-your-breath-away kind of kiss. It was deep and passionate and forceful, and God, possessive. The way his rough hands and fingers dug into my ass and yanked me into him, like I was his and only his.

Then he just walks away without even looking back?

I've never had a guy kiss me then just leave me hanging. How do I even interpret that? It makes no sense. I don't know what to make of the situation or him.

I've never been one of those girls who gets excited when men fight over her, but I'd be lying if I said it didn't turn me on like no other, how jealous Dex looked. I don't know what he has to be jealous of. It's not like I have feelings for Kyle or any of the other guys. They're completely harmless.

Kyle thinks Dex is a smug bastard, but he doesn't know him the way I do. He doesn't know him at all.

I apologized when I went back inside and said it was a rough day at work.

The more I looked at Kyle and his reactions, the more I tried to figure things out. Could Kyle possibly want more than friendship? No way. He's just a friendly neighbor. He's never once tried to make a move or ask me out or anything like that.

I'm so conflicted right now. I could fall for Dexter, that's for sure. What's not to like about that situation? He's successful, handsome, and charming but he's also older than me and we work together.

I need to step back and just slow down. I moved to Chicago to have fun. Get in life experiences before thinking of settling down with anyone. I've seen so many friends get married right out of high school, settle down, and start having babies, and never really go out and live at all.

There's nothing wrong with that lifestyle, it's just not for me. I want to travel and see the world and have fun before I get married and have those types of responsibilities. I don't want to be accountable to another person right now. I'm in the prime of my life and I want to enjoy it, get everything I can out of every day.

There's only one problem, though. Dexter has me questioning my entire life plan after that dang kiss. That ridiculous, pulse-shattering kiss that threw my world off its axis.

I shuffle my fork through my salad looking for a piece of grilled chicken. I'm eating in the cafeteria today instead of going out for lunch. If I want to move out, I need to save some money. Originally, I was saving for a car, so I wouldn't have to rely on public transportation, but I find I don't mind the train at all. It's actually kind of nice.

What I do mind, is my nutty roommate and her boyfriend. He slept over every day this week.

"You look deep in thought." Quinn slides into the chair across from me. "Mind if I join you?" She has law books with her.

I can't help but notice the huge emerald engagement ring on her finger. It's freaking gorgeous and perfect for her. It makes me want to swoon, just thinking about the night Deacon gave it to her. I still can't believe I smacked Dex in the back of the head. It was playful, like Gibbs on NCIS, but I'll admit, I had a few cocktails in me at the time.

I glance up and Quinn's probably making conversation so she can get out of studying. It's what I'd do. She's sitting for the bar exam soon, and I'll feel horrible for her and Deacon if she doesn't pass. I'm sure she will, though. She's crazy smart and probably the hardest worker I've ever met. I definitely look up to her when it comes to professional conduct. She's always put together and one step ahead of everyone.

"Sure, have a seat."

"Good." She unpacks her lunch. It looks like a container of soup and a sandwich. "So what are you debating with yourself?"

"I'm... I'm not... I was just thinking about some stuff."

"Stuff that had you looking like you were about to murder your salad?" Quinn grins as she crumbles crackers into her bowl of soup.

I don't really have anyone to talk about relationship stuff with. I mean I live with Barbie, but we're not friends. She'd find a way to make the conversation about her. There's Kyle, but I could never talk to him about Dexter. He made his feelings about Dex perfectly clear.

I have to get these thoughts out of my head. "What's the deal with Dexter?" I cringe as I ask the question. Well, it's out in the open now.

"What do you mean? Like as a boss, coworker, friend, or like as in a boyfriend?"

"I don't know." I bury my face in my palms and think maybe the world will disappear along with this conversation. I'm so bad at this. "I don't know anything right now."

"I'm just giving you a hard time." She blows on her spoonful of soup. "Dexter's a good guy. Obviously, he did something, though. Just get it out. You'll feel better."

I still can't look at her. "This stays between us, right?" I'm so terrible at this gossip thing and I have to be super careful. Quinn's not just any girl. She's Deacon's fiancée. As in she lives with Dexter's twin brother. I don't want her running behind my back and spilling this conversation to Deacon. It might get back to Dex.

"You can trust me."

"Okay." I suck in a breath then exhale, because I really want the information she has to offer. "Dexter and I have hung out a few times after work. Nothing major, just grabbing a drink at The Gage, normal stuff people at the firm do. I invited him out the other day to meet up with me and some friends and he was rude to them for no reason."

"Were they guys?"

"Who?"

"The other friends you invited."

"Yeah, why?"

She stares at me like I'm from outer space. "I know you're younger but come on. Men love to piss on everything in the room, to mark their territory. The Collins brothers more than anyone. He likes you. Honestly, the other day I told Tate I thought you guys were secretly dating because he never shuts up about you. Him and Deacon are like this, so I overhear everything." She crosses two of her fingers. "It's the whole twin thing."

"Really? He talks about me?"

"Yeah. I mean, he tries to not make it obvious, keeps it subtle. But he always finds a way to bring you up in conversations."

"Huh." I had never thought about Dex having conversations with his brother outside of work, and I definitely wouldn't have thought he'd talk about me.

"Was that all he did?"

"Well, umm…"

She leans in and grins. "Come on, give it up."

"Well, there was a kiss." My cheeks must be ten shades of pink. I can't remember ever doing this before, talking to another woman other than my mom about a guy. Even that is rare because I've never dated anyone seriously.

"Nice." She slow nods. "Tell me more."

"Okay fine. There have been two, but I don't know if the first one really counts."

"Why wouldn't it count?"

"It was the night at the Bears game, when he got me to take care of your dad."

"So… we both got a little lucky that day, huh?" She jabs me with her elbow.

"Well, we were both hammered. I don't even know if he remembers doing it. We were with all the football players after you'd left. God, it's all so blurry."

"What about the second time?"

371

"When we were at the bar the other day, he was really shitty to my friends. So, I pulled him aside to ask what his deal was, and he blew me off saying he had to go. I got pissed and ambushed him outside. There was this intense moment and he just kissed me, and I mean he kissed me good."

Quinn nods. "They do that. The Collins boys. They sure do."

I snap my fingers in front of her face when she gets this far-off look in her eye, like she's reliving every kiss ever with Deacon. "We're talking about me here."

Quinn laughs. "Sorry, continue."

"Well, afterward he didn't say anything. He just walked off. No look back. No nothing. I just stood there in a daze. And the past few days he's avoided me, and I don't know what to do or what to say. It's driving me insane."

"Do you like him?"

"I mean... I don't know, I'm so confused. I just... don't like feeling awkward, and that's what everything feels like right now."

"Well, I have experience dating a Collins brother, and my advice is to track him down and make him talk. Yes, they act like boys, but they're calculated. Whatever he's doing, it's for a reason. You have to keep them on their heels."

She makes it sound so easy. I don't even know what I'd say and I'm probably reading way too much into it. He probably just got caught up in the moment.

She looks at her phone. "Oh shoot. We better get back."

I get up to leave and she grabs me lightly by the forearm.

"We'll talk soon. I want a follow up."

"Yeah. Okay. I need to head your way. Decker wants to see me." I gather up my stuff and toss what's left of my salad in the trash.

We walk back to the elevator and get off on our floor.

"I think he's in there alone for another few minutes. Good timing." Quinn nods to his office.

I walk through the doors and Decker's head pops up from behind his computer. "Perfect. I have something for you. Have a seat."

Decker rifles through some folders, and I can't help but appreciate how neat and exact he is about everything. He always gives very specific instructions, and I love these special projects he assigns me. There's always a clear task and a deadline. If I could only have that type of order in my personal life, I'd be in heaven. I always feel like I'm spiraling out of control outside of these walls. The job keeps me centered, like I have a purpose.

He finally finds what he's looking for but pushes it to the side. "Sorry, had to get that separated or it would drive me nuts."

"What can I do for you, Mr. Collins?"

"I need you to do some research. You're the best I've got at this kind of shit."

I nod, my chest swelling with pride. I don't know if anyone, other than my parents, has ever told me I'm the best at something, and it feels amazing to hear it from the managing partner. "Thank you, sir. What am I researching?"

"Not what, who. I need you to have a look at Wells Covington. He's a hedge fund manager. Has a residence in Chicago, but splits time with Manhattan. I'm sure he has real estate there as well."

"Anything specific you're looking for?"

Decker stands and walks around his desk, then leans back against it and folds his arms over his chest. I can't help but notice how much him and all the other brothers look alike. Not just their looks, either, their mannerisms and the way they speak and phrase things. It's like I'm staring at an older, more mature Dexter; like what he'll be like in five or six years.

"I just want to know if he has any secrets. Don't focus on his work and that type of thing. I want to know about his personal life, hobbies, etc."

"So extracurricular activities outside of work?"

"Exactly."

"When do you need this by?"

"Make it a priority. As soon as possible."

I nod once more. "Okay. I'll get started right away."

"Thanks, Abigail."

I stand up and walk out of the office. It's nice to be sought after for special jobs like this, especially from the head of the firm. Plus, the research isn't that difficult. You can find out anything about anyone on social media. They all think I'm a genius at using it. Maybe it's because I'm younger than most of the other paralegals, but I grew up with it and know how to navigate all the platforms.

WHEN I GET HOME from work, there's a note from Barbie on the fridge.

Please be considerate when you get ready in the morning. I'm on night shift tonight and will be going to bed when you wake up.

–Barbie

Ugh!

She's so annoying. I'm not even loud. She works at the hospital assigning patients to beds or something. I can't remember what she told me exactly. I wasn't really listening. I'm terrible, but it was when I first moved in and I was so tired. She's like a female Sheldon Cooper with a normal IQ. I should leave her a note that says tell your boyfriend to take his morning dump at his own house.

I shove my stuff onto the counter and trudge down the hall after crumpling her note up. I kick my heels off and shimmy out of my skirt and hose in exchange for a pair of sweats and a tee. After letting my hair down, I toss the bra aside since I don't have to worry about Chuck showing up.

My stomach growls, voicing its disapproval of half a chicken salad in the cafeteria this afternoon. I'm starving, but I don't want to cook anything. I should since I need to save money, but it's been a long day, and I just want to curl up on the sofa and veg out while I have the apartment to myself.

Barbie doesn't like anyone eating on the couch. She acts like it's a five-thousand-dollar leather sectional. It's a Walmart special, but the last thing I want is to be on her radar, then suffer her on the warpath.

I grab the stack of takeout menus from a kitchen drawer and collapse onto the sofa, sinking down while I make a dinner decision. I'm not in the mood for Chinese or Thai. I could go for a pizza, but I know if I get one most will get thrown away, unless I invite Kyle over.

I'm not exactly up for his company tonight and there's really no reason I shouldn't be.

You're lying to yourself.

Of course I am. I know exactly why I don't want his company, and the name starts with a big fat D.

Gah, Dexter is so frustrating. I know we need to talk about that dang kiss. I don't want it to ruin our friendship, though. He's one of my favorite people at work. Okay, he's the best, with his pudding cups and broody stare he reserves for everyone but me, until lately.

Stupid hormones.

I'm about to give up on the menus and just walk to the store when a knock sounds at the door. I don't want to get off the couch to answer but I need to. What if Barbie is expecting a package or something? I'll never hear the end of it.

I begrudgingly stomp to the front of the apartment.

When I open the door, Kyle stands on the other side holding up a bag of fast food.

"Stopped on my way home. Thought you might be hungry." He flashes me a big cheesy grin.

He's so goofy but in a cute way. He is a bit of a dork in his tan Dockers and plaid shirt that's untucked and unbuttoned. He has on a Mickey Mouse t-shirt underneath. He's a manager at some video game store chain his dad owns.

"Is it safe?" He scans the room behind me searching for Barbie. I'm surprised he even comes over here at all after some of the encounters he's had with her.

He only agreed to go out to PRYSM with us because it was so loud he wouldn't be able to hear her talk most of the night.

"Yes. And I'm starving." I wave him in and close the door behind him. I know I said I didn't really want his company right now, but I am so hungry. Plus, it's silly. Kyle's my friend. It shouldn't matter what Dexter thinks. We're not together. I just need to steer the conversation away from Dexter and it'll be fine.

Kyle places the bag on the kitchen counter and pulls out two steak sandwiches and two orders of fries.

"You're the best."

"I always come through."

"This is true." I grab us some plates, cups, and pull a two liter of Pepsi from the fridge.

The two of us settle in on the couch with our food, and I start flipping through Netflix. It's my turn to pick.

Kyle exhales an audible sigh when I make my choice.

"Labyrinth is a cult classic. Who the hell doesn't love David Bowie?"

"You're so weird."

"Says the grown man in his Mickey Mouse shirt."

"Pfft, whatever. I have great style."

I snicker. "Sure."

"You're just used to being around suits all day, like that asshole you're always fawning over."

No, we're not supposed to talk about this. "I do not fawn over Se— Dexter." Damn it! I've got to stop doing that.

Kyle has this weird look on his face.

Fine, I guess we're doing this. I shrug. "What? He's hot."

Kyle rolls his eyes. "Whatever. I don't care who you date."

"I'm not dating him. We work together."

He smiles when he hears that. "Good. You're too good for him."

"I'm not interested in dating anyone. You know that." Even as the words leave my mouth, they sound weak.

"So you say."

I pause the movie and turn to him. "What's that supposed to mean?"

He shrugs. "Nothing, damn. Let's just eat and watch your movie." He bites into his sandwich.

I decide to let it go.

I don't want to argue with Kyle, but the room seems like it just cooled off about twenty degrees. I pick at my food. My mind drifts back to my conversation with Quinn. *He likes you. I thought the two of you were secretly dating.*

"Hey." Kyle taps my knee.

I jolt before I can stop myself. "Sorry. Just have a lot on my mind."

"Yeah. I see that. If you want to talk or whatever..." He scratches at the back of his neck.

I don't say anything because I don't want to talk to him about Dexter.

"Okay, well, I think I'm going to call it a night. I've got some stuff to do."

"Oh, okay. Thanks again for dinner. Next time it's my treat."

"Sounds like a plan." He moves to the door and gives me a wave.

Once he's gone, I turn off the TV and clean up our mess. Last thing I need is a passive aggressive note from Barbie reminding me no food on the couch. It's still too early to go to bed so I pick out my work clothes for tomorrow and treat myself to a bubble bath.

Sinking down in the warm water I try to clear my head and relax. Laying back with my head against the wall, I close my eyes. My thoughts find their way to that damn kiss all over again. Only this time I imagine what might have happened had Dex not walked away. Maybe the two of us would have gotten a cab back to his place or even a hotel room.

Maybe that's what we both need. Just have sex and get whatever this is out of our systems. I play the fantasy out in my mind, picturing Dex leading me into the hotel room, his mouth fused to mine. Trailing my fingers down my neck, I rub and tweak my nipple, touching myself lower and lower as the dream plays out.

I wonder if he would go fast or slow? I bet Dex is a man who goes all out with the foreplay. Takes his time and teases like a maniac. He'd want me begging for it, begging for him. I imagine him sitting there all powerful in his suit, ordering me to get undressed while his broody eyes never leave mine. He just has this vibe about him that is a hundred percent male, pure sex and power. He's older, but not too old, just right. Experienced. That's what he is.

I'm all kinds of worked up after I finish my bath.

When I make it to my room, my eyes flick back and forth between the bed and the drawer where I keep my vibrator. It doesn't take much to convince me I should go ahead and finish what I started.

DEXTER

It's Thursday, and I'm on my way back to the office after a business lunch that about did my head in. An old friend is going through a divorce and owns stock in several corporations. Both him and his spouse have assets. He wanted my advice about his financial options, and while he's a great guy, he's a total moron when it comes to business. He threw so much money at MLM and other shitty investments. The guy blew through everything and racked up some incredible debt. No wonder his marriage didn't work out.

However, his soon-to-be ex-wife is a trust fund baby with her own healthy portfolio that's managed by competent people. She's worth more than him. He needs her to cover some of his debt. The poor dumb bastard cheated with their nanny. The whole thing is a clusterfuck and emotional as all hell, something money should never be. He's going to be on his ass with nothing. I would feel sorry for him, but he had it made. All he had to do was keep his dick in his pants. The whole situation damn near gives me a migraine.

I'm almost to my office. I think I have some painkillers in my desk, and I plan to eat a couple, sit back, and have myself a nice little stress-free afternoon after that shitshow of a morning.

Turning the corner, I bump into Cole Miller. We go way back, all the way to our days at the University of Illinois. The two of us and Wells were inseparable at college but gradually grew apart as our careers took off. He was a professional MMA fighter for a while and now he owns a nationwide chain of fitness centers. He's a billionaire, but as humble as they come.

He's been in and out of the office a lot the past year. One of his employees took a selfie with one of the members in the background, put it up on social media, then her and her friends started making all kinds of jokes about the woman's weight and appearance.

ALEX WOLF & SLOANE HOWELL

It blew up and went viral, all over Twitter and Facebook. The member sued his company and now our firm is representing them. Decker's running point on it since media relations is one of his specialties.

"Just the guy I was looking for." Cole holds out a hand.

I take it, and his fucking grip damn near makes me wince, even though I'd never show it. "How's it going? You about to get out from under all that bullshit?"

"Things are shaping up. Decker thinks it'll be dismissed. You guys have worked your asses off for me. Don't think it hasn't gone unnoticed."

"It's what we do. You know this. You were looking for me?"

"I wanted to give you these. Decker mentioned something a while back. Said you're a huge fan." He reaches into his inner jacket pocket and slaps two tickets in my palm for the big MMA championship fight this weekend at the United Center.

Fuck yes. My luck just did a one-eighty. I've been trying to get tickets, used up every connection I could think of, besides Cole, of course. Last thing I wanted was to bother him with a ticket request when he's getting his tits sued off. "Hell yeah. Thanks." I fan them out in front of me. "I've been looking forward to this shit. Didn't want to bother you with it with everything on your plate."

He waves me off like it's nothing. "Don't be ridiculous. Hit me up anytime. It's gonna be a bloodbath. Mandez is a beast."

"I'm sure he is, considering you trained him. Does he have the speed, though?"

He slow nods. "Nice, Collins, you know your shit. And I don't know, but it's gonna be good."

"See you there."

"Yeah." He takes a step toward the conference room. "Gotta get in there and meet with your brother."

"Good luck, man."

We part ways and I smile to myself. It's been a few days, and I do believe Abby has had enough time to stew on that kiss and what she's missing out on. Now, it's time for the next step in my plan. I've seen how this shit works in their little romance movies. Always leave them wanting more. Never look too desperate. The hero always kills when he abides by these principles. I go by her desk, but she isn't there.

Well fuck a goddamn duck.

ABIGAIL

"HEY, Quinn. Is Mr. Collins available? I have some research I was doing for him."

"Yeah. He's not with anyone right now. You talk to you know who yet?" She smirks and tucks her red hair behind her ear.

I sigh and stare off at the wall. "No. Haven't really had a chance." I don't tell her he's still been avoiding me like the damn plague since that stupid kiss. I'm completely over it. That's what I keep telling myself, anyway. No matter how many batteries I've burned through with my vibrator, I'm sticking to it. I'm over Dexter Collins and his little games.

"Better get on it." Her cheeks pink a little and she grins at her computer screen.

"I have work to do." I wave my file at her and smile. Going back and forth with Quinn is fun and helps take my mind off things. Maybe I should have more girlfriends, and the ones in the past have just been unlucky experiences.

"Fine." She fakes a frown at me, like she's disappointed in my response. "I'll let him know you're here. Have a seat." She points to the waiting area for Decker's clients.

I sit down and flip through my papers trying to recall where I've seen this dude before. He looks vaguely familiar.

Quinn picks up her phone. "Abigail is out here. Okay. I'll send her on in."

I meet Quinn's gaze and she waves her hand motioning for me to go ahead.

I know I'm coming back earlier than Decker would've expected, but there's still something about walking into the boss's office that has my stomach in a knot. It's like when you were in elementary school and knew you weren't in trouble, but still had to walk into the principal's office. The room just always seems ominous.

"Got something? That was quick."

I set the file down. "Combed through his social media and online. Nothing criminal or anything. I did find some connections to some umm…" I wince a little because people shouldn't really be judged on this type of thing, but they are. It almost feels wrong bringing it to him, but I know he'll want to know.

"What is it?" Decker leans in, taking a sudden interest.

"Umm, some kinky sex club type stuff."

Decker rubs his chin and twists in his chair, seemingly mulling over what to do. "Take it to Rick. Tell him I want him to dig deep on this guy. I want it all, work and personal."

I nod. It's not my job to question the boss. "Okay. Did you want to read over all this before I…"

"No need." He makes a face that tells me he wants nothing to do with what I found on the Covington dude. "Tell Rick I need this off the record and to keep it discreet. Only the three of us need to know anything."

"Will do."

"Thanks, Abigail. You're killing it. Keep doing what you're doing."

Getting the compliment leaves me on cloud nine. Decker seems pretty cold and all business, but he always gives me compliments. There are so many stories floating around about what an asshole he was before the merger. I wonder if he learned this new technique in a management seminar? Maybe Tate makes him do it. That'd be hilarious. They're so cute together.

At the same time, I feel a little bad about digging through this guy's personal life, regardless of how much money he has. I really need to get over this feeling if I want to succeed at this job, because there will likely be a lot of this type of work in the future.

I leave Decker's office and make my way to Rick's, even though he's never there. I pause and look around before I get to his door, anything to take my mind off this encounter. He's quite possibly the most chauvinistic asshole I've ever met. It's probably why Decker keeps him out of the office on assignment twenty-four seven. As I walk up, I say a silent prayer, begging over and over for him not to be there so I can just send him an email with the instructions.

When I get there, the door is open and he's sitting at his desk reading the Bible.

What the heck? The irony of this situation is almost too much to bear.

And what the hell is going on in here?

He's wearing this all-black suit and hat that makes him look like he's going to an Amish funeral or something. I nearly burst into laughter but manage to swallow it down.

I knock lightly on his door, trying not to grin at his outfit. "Hey, Rick?" I wince, just waiting for him to say something about some new hire's ass or tits. It's par for the course with him.

"Come on in."

"Sorry to interrupt." I hesitate.

"It's fine. Close the door." He doesn't look up from the Bible.

I don't *want* to close the door, but Decker did say this needs to be discreet.

"Right." I close it almost all the way but leave it cracked just a hair. I hold out the file, but he doesn't take it, just keeps reading. "Okay, so Decker has a job for you. He wants you to dig up everything you can on this Wells Covington guy. This is what I have on him so far from my social media research. He said to stress that this needs to be super discreet. You should only communicate your findings to one of us."

He nods toward the desk, indicating for me to leave the file there.

I set it down and quickly take a step back.

"You and Decker. Wells Covington. Got it."

"Great." I turn to leave.

"Hey, what do you know about Mary?"

I stop and have to think for a second. "Magdalene? The paralegal?" What in the ever-loving hell is going on here? Is that why he's reading the Bible?

"Yeah, the one with the curly brown hair. Didn't you work together in Dallas? You paralegals all talk to each other, right? She ever mention me?"

"We, umm, don't really talk much. She keeps to herself a lot."

"You guys don't hang out and braid your hair and gossip and all that shit?"

I damn near start laughing. Is that what he thinks all the women in the office do in their spare time?

"No, she does a lot of stuff at her church, I think. That's about it, I guess. She's kind of quiet and we don't talk much."

He still hasn't looked up and his lips mouth the words like he's reading Bible verses. "Okay, thanks. I'll let you know what I find out about the asshole in the file."

"Umm… Okay then. I gotta get going." I grab the door handle.

"Yes, he likes you."

I turn back to him. "Sorry, what?"

Still hasn't looked up. "Dex, after the kiss. And Kyle wants more than friendship."

"Excuse me?" How the hell does he know any of that stuff? I've heard he's legendary about knowing everything, but what the hell?

"You heard me." He finally looks up. "I have to go plan for a nativity scene at the church. Peace be with you, Abigail." He walks by and I stand there with my mouth wide open. "And your social media research is always top notch. Great job."

Once he's gone, I scurry out of his office and into the breakroom.

A shiver goes up my spine. That was too weird. And what the hell did he mean when he said Kyle wants to be more than friends? How does he even know who Kyle is? That's absurd. Seems the mighty Rick Lawrence failed in his intelligence gathering, for once.

When I open the fridge there's a package of banana pudding next to Dexter's chocolate ones. I smile but it still doesn't make up for the way he's been so back and forth with me. One day he's kissing me and the next he's avoiding me. Am I that bad of a kisser? No way. I know I'm not. I don't want to sound conceited, but

I can kiss above average at the least. He wanted that kiss and enjoyed it as much as I did.

I open up a pudding cup and lick the lid before tossing it in the trash.

"Don't let Dexter catch you eating those." Brenda, Dexter's paralegal walks around the corner. "He had me pick them up this morning. Said they were the most important thing on my to-do list."

"Oops." I grin. That familiar warmth spreads through my veins again. I refrain from telling her I'm almost certain he got them for me. Maybe he did it to be a jerk and eat them in front of me. Maybe I'm searching for a reason to still be irritated with him, because I don't need to be involved with any man right now. Either way it doesn't matter. I'm going to enjoy the hell out of this pudding cup.

"I've never seen a grown man act the way he does over some pudding, but I swear he's obsessed."

"I've noticed."

"Well I won't tell him it was you if he asks." She winks and steals one of the chocolate ones. "If you don't tell him I swiped one too."

"I will take our secret to the grave."

"There ya go. Us girls have to stick together against the evil overlords."

I grin. "Right." I never had any idea what other women meant when they would talk about sisterhood or girlfriends sticking together, but I'm starting to catch on. I've never had a 'tribe' or whatever the cool kids call it these days, but I'm starting to wish I did.

I WALK out the front of the office when my cell phone rings with a call from Kyle. We haven't spoken since things got all tense and awkward. Now, it's even worse after the shit Rick pulled out of his magic hat in his office.

Damn him!

I start to ignore the call, but I don't want to be like Dexter and blow him off. I know how it feels to be ignored, and it's not pleasant. Especially when Kyle's one of the best friends I've had since moving here. Not to mention the fact we're neighbors and he'd be hard to avoid.

"Hey, what's up?"

"Just clocked out. Wanna meet up for pizza and beer with me and Nick before he goes in for his shift?"

No, I want Dexter to talk to me. I don't have anything else to do on a weeknight, though. "Sure. The usual place?"

"Meet you in fifteen?"

"Okay." I end the call.

A text from Barbie pings on my phone the second I hang up.

Barbie: You off work? I need you to do something for me.

I love how she doesn't even ask, just demands things.

Me: Just leaving.

With her I never know what kind of favor she'll ask. Learned that one the hard way. One time I ended up attending a baby shower for some girl I didn't know and had to buy a joint gift with Barbie because she couldn't afford what she agreed to buy off the registry. I'm clearly still not over that.

Barbie: I need jumbo tampons. I'll pay you back.

Me: I can but it'll be a while because I have dinner plans.

Barbie: Can you hurry?

I scrunch my nose at my phone. Can I hurry? Do I look like her assistant? I would be inclined to hurry if she wasn't crazy and the biggest narcissist I've ever met.

Man, she makes me want to punch something, and I am *not* a violent person. Or maybe something else has me on edge and her text is just the catalyst. No, Dexter Collins has nothing to do with it at all. I'm sure of that.

Even my heart knows I'm full of it.

I take two steps, look up, and holy hell…

DEXTER

I'VE BEEN TRYING to track down Abigail all afternoon to ask her to the fight this weekend. She was nowhere to be found. I did notice someone ate one of the banana pudding cups I left for her. Like I said, I know how to deal with women in their own language, *P.S. I Love You* style. Deacon talked some shit about my methods too, until I showed him how it's done. You're welcome, brother. Enjoy one fiancée, courtesy of Dexter.

I hang out by the corner and wait for her to come out of the building because I don't have a clue where she lives.

Finally, I breathe a sigh of relief when she walks out the front door.

"Hey." I step right in her path. It's been twenty minutes and it's starting to get cold as hell. I was beginning to think she caught on to my stalkerish ways and slipped out the back.

Her face lights up and then hardens. "Oh, Dexter, right? That's your name, isn't it? I feel like we met once or twice."

"Come on, Abby. It's been a stressful week."

She continues her little act. "Ohh, you remember my name? Wasn't sure." She starts down the sidewalk.

I can't remember the last time I chased a damn female, but I do it anyway because—it's Abigail. "Hey, just stop for a damn second, woman. Jesus."

She whips around and points a finger at my face. Not in a menacing way. It's more in a *I'm pretending I'm mad at you, so you know not to do this to me again* kind of way. "Just so you know. I'm not making you banana pudding."

I smile really big; bigger than I've smiled in a while, come to think of it. "I'm pretty stocked up on pudding right now, even with someone coming in and stealing them."

She shows me that cute-as-hell grin of hers that says *I'm busted.*

"I've got two tickets to the fight Saturday night. I want you to go with me."

Her grin widens, but she pretends to mull it over. "I don't know."

"Yes you do. I know you ate the damn pudding. This is happening."

She lets out a fake sigh. "Fine. Hot as hell half-naked dudes beating the crap out of each other. Count me in."

My jaw ticks at her comment about hot naked dudes but I refrain from saying anything. "Great. I'll pick you up Saturday. Just give me your address."

"I'll just meet you there. I'm starting to like taking the train around town."

I start to argue but think better of it. She said yes. That's the important part.

"Well give me your number so I can text you the details later."

"Okay cool, Sex... I mean Dexter." Her face goes pale and she can't even look at me.

"Sex, huh?" I grin. It's going to happen sometime, Abigail. Don't you worry your little heart.

She finally glances back. "Shit. Sorry. I meant Dexter. I don't know why your name came out like that. Been a long day for me too. Anyway." She pulls out her phone and calls me real quick so I'll have her number.

I save it in my phone.

She darts off before I can say anything else. "See you there."

"Absolutely." I stand there, admiring her as she walks away.

I can't do anything but smile like a little boy. The way she shakes her ass as she walks down the street; she knows I'm watching, the little tease. I instinctively reach up to pull my hair but stop before she can turn around and see me. The way she said the word "Sex." That tells me a few things. One, I make her nervous. Two, she's been thinking about me...

And sex.

I've got it bad for this girl.

The thought terrifies me. I don't know if I keep pursuing her because I'm obsessed or because the chase is phenomenal. I've never had to work this hard for a woman's attention. Never wanted to, before her.

I need to talk to Deacon. He can help me sort this shit out, and he owes me one. More than one, in fact.

AN HOUR LATER, I let myself into Deacon's apartment and head directly to the fridge and grab myself a beer. I twist the cap off, fling it in the general direction of the trash can, and down the whole thing.

It tastes incredible. A little Abigail-said-yes celebration chug.

"They went to dinner." Mr. Richards' voice echoes off the walls of the living room.

I walk in and he's kicked back in the recliner watching some documentary about the greatest boxers of all time. He needs a wheelchair to get around because he had a stroke a few years ago, so he spends most of his time in the La-Z-Boy.

Shit.

I always forget Quinn's old man moved into Deacon's apartment when Quinn did.

There goes my game plan. Deacon's probably getting his dick wet in a coat closet somewhere. That's their thing.

"Bring me one of those, kid?"

I snort. "All right." Fuck it, I need a refill anyway.

I grab a couple bottles and join him. I twist the caps off both beers and pocket them, then go pick up the other one I slung on the floor. I know how anal chicks get about leaving shit around the house, and Deacon would love to throw me under the bus for making a mess. Anything to take some blame off his ass.

Never in my life would I have pictured this for Deacon. Totally pussy whipped.

He loves the shit out of her, though, and I suppose things could be worse. They balance each other out. Quinn is cool too, so that helps. She's way less intense than the other fiancée in the family, that's for damn sure.

I never saw myself wanting something like this. The whole love and commitment thing. That shit has never been for me.

For a brief moment, I allow myself to fantasize what a life like this would be like with Abigail. Coming home to her every day, waking up in bed next to her every morning. Surprisingly, it doesn't make me want to run for the hills.

I glance around Deacon's apartment to see if much has changed but it's really about the same as before.

Sure, there are some flowers and shit, but it's not too bad. She let Deacon keep all his stuff.

Interesting.

"Thanks, son."

"No problem. You know if they'll be out late?"

"Not sure. You need something important? I can call Quinn and get them back here."

"Nah. I'll live."

Quinn's old man is cool as hell. We have a blast at Bears games.

He looks over at me and his eyebrows rise.

"Okay, so I got these tickets for the big fight coming up and... it's just—" I wave him off with a hand. "It's nothing. Forget it." I shake my head and let out a sigh.

"You got tickets?" He looks like he might come out of his chair. "Lucky son of a bitch."

I laugh. "Yeah."

"Your brother watches football with me, but he's not big into boxing and MMA."

"I love that shit. My buddy Cole hooked me up. He used to fight."

"Cole Miller? Damn, your family knows everyone."

I kick back. Mr. Richards really is awesome. I try to stop thinking about my situation with Abigail, but I can't get her out of my head. Mr. Richards and I fall into an easy conversation about our favorite fighters for a bit. I drink a few more beers with him.

He must sense something is going on, though. "You look flustered, kid."

Flustered doesn't come close to what I'm feeling.

Finally, I decide fuck it. I need to talk to someone. He's here and the dude looks like he knows some shit. He has life experience.

———

"I DON'T KNOW if I like her or if it's chasing her that's driving me up the goddamn wall." I'm lying on the couch, staring up at the ceiling like I'm in a counseling session when the front door opens and shuts.

Quinn and Deacon walk in.

I don't even bother to stop. "I mean, she's everything I could see myself wanting. Smart, gorgeous, funny... she's a damn challenge. Tits are outta this world." I hold my hands out in front of my chest to make my point. "Know what I mean?"

Mr. Richards nods and grins like he knows what's up.

I shake my head. "She just frustrates the hell out of me sometimes. I think it's because she's so young."

"What the hell is this?" Deacon marches into the living room. "You should charge his ass by the hour." He looks to Mr. Richards and shakes his head, then stares at me like I'm pathetic.

I shrug like *what the fuck?* "You weren't here. I needed advice."

Deacon snickers. "What's wrong? Still stuck in the friend zone?" A smile plasters across his face. "She's never gonna date you. Way too hot for your ugly ass."

Quinn swats him in the chest. "I fell for you and I'm *way* out of your league."

These two make me nauseous sometimes. They're still in the honeymoon phase of their relationship. Always touching, can't keep their hands off each other. I don't know how her dad puts up with their PDA shit all the time.

"You were *not* out of my league. More like the other way around."

Quinn scowls. "You need to help him. Do I need to remind you it was Dex who saved your sorry ass? You wouldn't have me if it weren't for him."

"She ain't wrong," Mr. Richards says out the side of his mouth, not bothering to turn from the TV.

Deacon frowns but Quinn ignores him and walks over and sits next to my feet.

She turns to face me. "Why don't you work your movie magic on her? One of those grand gestures like the romantic comedies you secretly love." She smirks.

I groan. "I don't *love* those movies. I don't know where you guys got that shit from. I pay attention to them, there *is* a difference."

"You're so full of shit," says Deacon. "We all know you like watching them, just admit it."

"Do not, fucker."

"Boys!" Quinn snaps her fingers. "Back to Abigail."

I sit up. "Abigail isn't like you or other girls. That shit won't work on her. She's too smart." She deserved that dig for suggesting I like those movies. "She'll see it coming from a mile away. It's not her style, anyway. She doesn't get caught up in her feelings. We need to address the elephant in the room. I'm afraid Deacon was right for once. She's put me in the goddamn friend zone. I kissed the shit out of her the other day, and she didn't even seem fazed by it when I asked her out. Said she wants to meet me there and talked about the hot dudes who were going to fight. What kind of shit is that? The guy never gets out of the fucking friend zone. Rarely in the movies, and never in real life. I know things."

"Move over and listen up." Quinn shoves my legs off the couch.

It forces me to sit up.

She takes a seat and Deacon slides down on to the couch and pulls her into his lap.

Could they not touch each other for two goddamn seconds while I'm in a crisis? He leans in, sweeps her hair to the side, and kisses the back of her neck.

I might hurl.

Quinn wags a finger at me. "Listen good because I'm only going to tell you this once in a language you'll understand. Abigail may try to come off cool, like one of the guys, but deep down she's a girly girl who wants the same stuff as the rest of us. All women want romance and to be swept off their feet. We want to be independent and respected, but we also want that take-charge macho shit, even if we roll our eyes at it. You can't be the junior varsity, half-assing everything and expect a keeper to fall in your lap with minimal effort. You gotta step up to the plate and woo her. So, stop acting like a pussy, crying on the couch to my dad and do something about it or yeah, you'll stay in the damn friend zone. If you think that's where you are, that's where you'll be."

Mr. Richards chuckles.

I turn to him. "What's so funny?"

"You, still sitting there. What the hell you doing, son? You heard my daughter. Get your ass up."

I jump up off the couch and look back and forth between all of them, then stare at Quinn. "You know what? You're right. Fuck this." I'm tired of pussyfooting around with Abigail; like she's going to take the train to our first date.

"Of course I am. I'm a woman."

I walk by the end table and sweep a pile of magazines onto the floor. They fly everywhere, making a huge mess.

"What the fuck?" yells Deacon.

"I do what I want, bitches. Dexter Collins runs shit!" I yell the words over my shoulder as I storm to the front door.

I swear I hear Quinn mumble, "What the hell did we just do?" as I yank the door open and walk out.

Fuck this. Abigail *will* be mine.

ABIGAIL

I WALK in the door after meeting up with Kyle and Nick and toss the tampons on the counter. I ate a piece of pizza, but I left early because all I could think about was Dexter. Barbie doesn't even say thank you, and I just walk to the living room, still in my own little world thinking about Dexter.

I can't believe I did that. I said Sex to his face, instead of his name. He heard me say the word—out loud.

How am I ever going to look at him without turning bright pink? This is a Private Santiago code red—a DEFCON one situation. That was utterly humiliating. Now, he'll think I daydream about him and sex.

Well, you do.

That's beside the point!

I'm almost tempted to talk to Barbie but I'm not that desperate yet. This would be one of those rare occasions where I could use a girlfriend. I walk into the kitchen while she hems and haws over some dish she's trying to cook for Chuck. Thankfully, she's taking it to his place.

Honestly, she's not even that bad. We're just a bad match. I think I exhaust her as much as she exhausts me. It's just awkward and uncomfortable. It's a square peg, round hole situation.

I've tried being friends with her, but it's just never going to happen. We're complete opposites one-hundred percent of the time, and not in the good way when friends balance each other out.

We're like a bomb, slowly ticking down to the day one of us explodes.

I lay down on the couch and flip through channels, doing my best to ignore her banging around in the kitchen, while simultaneously trying to rid my mind of me making an ass of myself in front of Dexter.

"Do you know how long to bake lasagna?" The words fly out from the kitchen.

How the hell should I know? I don't want to fight with her, though. "Is it frozen?"

"Uhh yeah. I don't know how to make it myself!"

Her nasal voice is like nails dragging down a chalkboard in slow motion.

I pop up from the couch.

I don't want to make dinner for Chuck, but the sooner I get her ass out the door the better. I'm a terrible roommate."What does the back of the box say?"

"I don't know. I threw it away."

Jesus. How can she be so anal and picky, and still have no common sense? "Okay." I march to the trash and dig out the box. It looks like a child opened it on Christmas morning. She ripped right through the directions. "It says here..." I fold the flimsy cardboard back together. "Bake it at three seventy-five for two hours."

Shit! Two hours?

"Two hours!" She stomps her foot like a toddler throwing a tantrum. "I'm supposed to be there in an hour."

My mind races for a solution to both of our problems. "Maybe you can bake it until you leave then microwave it the rest of the way? It's already pre-baked, right?"

She huffs out a sigh and stares up at the ceiling, rolling her eyes as if I'm the one who screwed this whole thing up. "I don't know. This is a disaster. It's our three-month anniversary and he said to make something special, but I don't cook. I'm a fraud. I think he might pop the question, but not if I bring him frozen dinner."

Wow, what a way to get engaged, and after three whole months. She thinks pretty highly of herself expecting him to pop the freaking question, but I don't mention she may just be being a little unrealistic. It's difficult, but I manage to fight back a laugh. Who the hell would date a guy who would demand they cook him dinner on their anniversary? Especially a hairy-ass, disgusting slob like Chuck? You have to be Dexter Collins-level hot to make those sorts of demands and have them taken seriously. I'd cook him the best damn lasagna he's ever tasted.

Stop it, Abigail.

My eyes roam back to Barbie and she's staring at me like her entire life depends on me. I can't help but feel bad for her. I don't want to, but I do. "Listen, Chuck loves you. If you're that worried, order carryout and put it in your own container before you get there."

"That's not a terrible idea." She taps her chin. "Yeah." She nods her head as if she just came up with it. "I like it. You can have this one if you want."

"Okay, thanks." Sweet, free food.

"It was twelve bucks." She stands there, staring like a salesman making a deal and settling on the terms like I didn't just buy her tampons.

Jesus.

I bite my tongue and nod. "I'll Apple Pay it to you later."

"Perfect." She claps her hands together.

I turn the oven on. If I'm paying twelve bucks, I'm definitely cooking this damn thing, and eating every last bit of it. I'm not really that hungry, but I can take it to work and get a couple lunches out of it. Anything to save some money.

That day can't come soon enough, when I can move out.

Barbie grabs her cell phone and taps the screen furiously. "Hey." She looks up. "Thanks for, well, just thanks."

"Sure." My lips move upward and curve into a half smile.

It's almost like we just had a moment and it was kind of nice.

She goes off to get ready in her room.

I pull out a cookie sheet and load the lasagna onto it. My mom would have a coronary. She's all about home-cooked meals from scratch. Buying frozen dinners is a sin in the south. Good thing what she doesn't know won't hurt her.

After the oven preheats and I toss the lasagna in, I move back to the couch and pick up where I left off, scrolling for something I haven't seen a million times.

Barbie struts out of her room a few minutes later with her hair teased up wearing enough perfume I can taste it in the back of my throat. I let out a small cough as she twirls around in a black sequin dress with a bow on the shoulder. It reminds me of my eighth-grade snowball formal.

"How do I look?"

The snarky side of my brain says ask if she wants honesty, but I settle for a white lie. "Awesome. Chuck will love it."

I wish Kyle and Nick were here to see this but it's probably better this way. I should try to snap a picture, but there's no way to do it without being caught. Instead, I snatch my phone off the coffee table, intending to text them. That would be mean. It's no secret I don't like Barbie, but I'm not that person, so I pretend to check my messages and put the phone back down.

"Don't wait up. I think tonight's going to be the night. Eek!"

"Good luck. I hope it goes well."

Just like that, her face goes ice cold. "I don't need luck."

I fight the urge to roll my eyes. She goes out the door and my phone rings.

"Ugh!" My entire body tenses when I see "unknown caller" flash on the screen. I hope this isn't a work emergency or a bill collector. That seems like the only two possible options.

I really hope it's not work. I'm already in my comfy clothes and the smell of the lasagna isn't half bad.

I slide my thumb across the screen. "Hello."

"Hey, it's Dexter."

It's Sex!

Dexter.

Damn.

I seriously need to break that habit. "What's up?" I frown and wonder why he's calling, and at the same time tingles shiver across my arms and goosebumps pebble all over.

"So, Saturday..." He pauses.

My pulse spikes. Is he going to cancel? I bet I freaked him out when I did the whole Sex thing. He probably just didn't have anyone to go with him. Deacon probably canceled and I was an afterthought and then I acted all weird and got excited for nothing. I bet I was just the first person he saw after he got the news.

"I'm taking you to dinner. Before the fight. And I'm picking you up."

What? The? Hell?

I want to scream my address at him through the phone, but I have to stay calm and play it cool. "Umm... that makes it sound like a date."

"It *is* a damn date. What's your address?"

What the hell is happening right now? His confidence is off the charts. More than usual. I don't know if I could say no if I wanted to. It's so damn sexy. "Dex... I-I... are you sure? 'Cause I mean..." I trail off.

I sound like a babbling idiot. I mean holy shit. Dexter wants to take me out on a date? This is too much to process right now. I thought he only asked me to the fight to try to make up for ignoring me after our kiss. I mean after the kiss I was all about it and had tons of confidence that he liked me, but then he ignored me for several days, and it confused the hell out of me.

"It's happening. Give me your address."

I give in to his demand and shoot off the building name and apartment number before I can stop my mouth from doing it.

"Wasn't so hard, was it? See you at five on Saturday."

The call ends and I stare at my phone in disbelief.

What the hell just happened?

I agreed to go on a date with Dexter, that's what happened.

I promised myself no dating, just casual fun. I thought I could handle this attraction to him but apparently, I can't. I'm screwed. Going out on a real date goes against everything I said I wouldn't do when I moved to Chicago. As conflicted as I feel, I can't help but notice the gigantic cheesy smile staring back at me when I look over at my reflection in the TV screen.

Will it really be so bad? He's hot and successful. If there was a man I wanted to be serious about, it would be Dexter. He's pretty much perfect.

I should find a reason to cancel but I'm too damn excited about this fight. I've always wanted to go to an MMA event, ever since I saw one on TV.

The real question is...

What the hell am I going to wear?

I toss my phone aside and leap up from the couch. Once in my room, I rifle through my closet for the perfect outfit. This would be another time when a female friend would come in handy. About now, I'd settle for Barbie. I laugh at myself and remember the dress she wore to Chuck's. No, maybe I wouldn't settle for Barbie.

I pull out my favorite jeans and spiked heels. I need a new shirt. Maybe I can make a mall run tomorrow after work. I want to wow Dexter. If I'm going to go on a date with him, I need to do it right.

LATER THAT EVENING, as I shovel lasagna into my mouth much faster than I should, Barbie bursts through the door in tears. My eyes widen, and I freeze like a deer in headlights, because I know I'm not supposed to eat on the couch. She said not to wait up, though. What the hell is she doing here?

She sobs so hard it sends a shiver through her. Black mascara snakes down her cheeks.

I sit up and nonchalantly slide the plate underneath the couch to hide my crimes against her. "Hey." I drag out the syllable. "What's wrong?"

"Chuck... he... he..." She sniffles and wipes her arm over her nose. At the same time, she kicks her shoes across the room. "He broke up with me. Said we aren't on the same page right now. That things were getting too serious for him. He's too young to be tied down and wants to date other people. Can you believe that asshole?"

I feel bad for her, and at the same time I can't help but feel bad for myself. I'm going to have to deal with this all night now. "No way." She was so excited when she left. Who the hell dumps someone on their anniversary, even if it's a three-month one? You have to be a major-league asshole to make me feel sorry for Barbie. "Here." I pour her a glass of my wine and shove it toward her.

"Thanks." She takes a long drink. "I thought he was going to propose." She smacks a palm to her forehead. "How could I be so stupid?"

Well, I mean... No, you need to comfort her. "He's a dipshit if he didn't appreciate you."

"We should go out and get drunk. Pick up the first guys we see and bring them back here. Then I could accidentally video call Chuck right in the middle of it."

My eyes bug out. *That escalated quickly.*

I pat her on the forearm. "How about we hold off on that? We can watch a movie. There's plenty of lasagna and wine."

She nods. "You're probably right." She walks into the kitchen and eats lasagna straight from the pan like an animal. After a few gulps from the glass, she ditches it and goes straight to drinking from the bottle. After a few more seconds, she lets out a long sigh. "Be glad you're not that pretty."

My brows shoot up.

Did she really just say that? Out loud?

She shakes a finger at no one in particular. "That's what it was. He was intimidated. Scared because I'm out of his league. Be glad you don't have that problem."

I was being nice to her!

I stand up, put my hands on my hips, and shake my head. "I know. You're right." I let out the most sarcastic sigh I can muster to rival hers. "The wine was twenty bucks, by the way. You can Apple Pay me." I walk off and leave her to clean up and be miserable by herself.

To hell with her. I'm not going to sit around and be her punching bag. Screw that. This is exactly why my friends are dudes. I can't stand catty-ass women. I slam the bathroom door a little harder than needed. I genuinely attempted to console her. Hell, I even felt bad for her. I should've known better.

I decide to just call it a night and go to bed early. I want to look extra hot tomorrow at work, no bags under my eyes.

I need to talk to someone, though. I don't want to go to bed pissed off. I should be ecstatic about my date and instead I'm brooding around my room like an angry teenager. There's one woman I can count on, though, and that's my mom.

I walk into my room, flop down on my bed, and call her.

"Hey, Mom."

"You being safe?"

"Yes, I'm at home."

"You still have that pepper spray?"

"Yeah, on my keychain." I can't help but smile every time she nags me.

"I was watching the news."

She means Fox News, obviously.

"Oh yeah?" I grin even wider. Here comes a diatribe about gun violence in Chicago.

"Yep, all kinds of murders in Chicago. All those gun laws are just doing wonders up there. You sure you don't want to take a pistol with you next time you're home? You can ship them on the plane. I was looking at the rules…"

"Mom, I'm fine. I live in a nice part of town." It's not super nice, but she doesn't need to know that. There definitely aren't many murders around here.

"Oh, well okay. I have it here, if you ever want it."

"I'm going on a date this weekend."

"Oh, sweetie. That's wonderful!" I swear I hear her mutter, "Sure you don't want the gun?"

"I'm really excited. He's super cute." It's amazing how ten seconds of talking to my mom can make me feel like I'm back at home. How it can make me forget about Barbie and all my other worries. Her voice is like being wrapped up in a warm hug. "You need to make a trip up here. I could show you around."

"Honey, you know I can't…" She's scared of flying. It's one of her greatest fears, but I'm determined to get her up here one weekend for a visit.

"You could drive. I could fly home and ride up with you, then ride back to Texas."

"I don't know. I'd love to see where you live, so maybe… Anyway, tell me more about this guy."

I grin. "He's funny, and cute, I already mentioned that, but it's worth saying twice. He has a great job…"

"Will he treat you right? I worry about those boys in the north. They don't have manners like the men down here."

I can't help but notice she called them boys up here and men down there. It makes me smile even harder. She is who she is, and I wouldn't change her for the world.

"He's a man, trust me. And yeah, I think he'll treat me right."

"Okay then. We raised you to make good decisions, so if you're all right with him, so are we. You know that."

I lean my head back on my pillow. "Thanks, Mom. That's all I needed to hear. I'm going to get some rest."

"Good idea. Me too. I'm glad you called and I'm happy you found yourself a hot date."

"Me too."

"I love you, sweetie."

"Love you too. Give Daddy a kiss for me."

"I will, and you stop eating frozen dinners. Cook yourself a damn meal. It'll impress that boy up there too."

How the hell does she do that? Always know everything? I laugh at her intuition, and the fact she called Dexter a boy. "Okay, I will. Promise."

"Goodnight."

"Night."

I fall into my pillow and hug it tight to me. I bury my face in it, kick my legs, and just grin. I'm going out with Dexter Collins, and he's about as far from a boy as you can get.

DEXTER

It's Friday morning and I feel on top of the world.

Tomorrow night, Abigail is all mine.

I feel much better after talking to Quinn. I like Abigail. She's exactly the kind of woman I want.

Quinn's right, I can't do this shit halfway. Not a fucking chance.

Abby deserves the best and that's what she'll get, goddamn it.

I walk into the breakroom and snag one of my puddings. Unwrapping the plastic spoon, I toss the wrapper in the trash. I peel the lid back and lick the excess chocolate from the foil.

When I look up, Abigail struts past the doorway looking sexy as fuck. She has on this charcoal-gray dress that clings to her curves—no jacket. The dress squeezes her tits together, and I groan internally. My thoughts immediately move to yanking her into a supply closet and having my way with her, Deacon and Quinn style.

Can't do it.

It's too soon, and even if I wanted to, Decker installed cameras after word got out about all the extracurricular activities that used to go down in there. Said it was because people were stealing stuff. Yeah right, big bro. I swallow some pudding, and Abigail's eyes shift over my direction. Those baby blues pierce straight through me, and I'm worried I just went from six to midnight in my pants.

She's a damn ten and she knows it. Fuck, I want to taste those cherry lips again.

I pause for a split second to see if she'll walk over, but she doesn't break stride. My eyes roam down to the strappy heels she's wearing. They wrap around her ankles and part way up her calves.

399

She goes on like business as usual and my heart sinks for a brief moment, but then she looks back over her shoulder with a cute-as-hell smirk.

Yep, definitely hard as a rock. You're so mine.

Tomorrow night.

No work. No jackass friends coming between us. Just her and me.

I can't wait to have her all to myself. I never can seem to get her alone.

I finish off my pudding and grab a bottled water. When I return to my desk, Brenda doesn't look up from the files she's rifling through.

"Decker wants to see you."

I roll my eyes. "Wonderful."

She snickers but keeps toiling away with the files.

I take a few sips of water and stop off in the bathroom. I take my sweet-ass time, hoping I might bump into Abigail on her way back to her desk.

No dice.

Not all is lost, though. I love making Decker wait for me when he calls these little impromptu meetings, probably to micromanage every little thing I'm doing. He called me in last week to bitch about the way some files were paperclipped together; like I bother myself with shit like that. I didn't have the heart to scold Brenda for it. She works her ass off, so I just took the blame and nodded my head, promising it wouldn't happen again.

I finally stroll on over like I don't have a care in the world. Donavan is here too.

What the hell?

This better not be an ambush about something trivial, but I'd almost suffer through it to see them get along for five minutes. It's about damn time. We're all getting sick of this petty war over some shit that went down with Donavan and Tate. It happened a long time ago.

Business is business, but their two egos are too goddamn big to put it behind them.

Tate walks in and the familiar tension fills the air.

The second she takes a seat, Donavan pops up. "Got work to do." He hauls ass out the door.

I shake my head glancing back and forth between Decker and the door. "Would you assholes work your shit out? You're acting like children. That's saying something, coming from me."

Tate nods her head slowly but doesn't look up from her files.

Decker waves me off with a flippant hand, like nothing is wrong and he has it all under control. "It's fine. We have other things to discuss. I'll worry about Donavan."

"It's been like six months. I'm losing confidence."

"That's enough. It's not why you're here."

I shrug. "Whatever, Dad. What's up?"

"We need to talk about Wells Covington."

My eyebrows rise. "Umm, okay. What about him?"

"His extracurriculars don't align with our image."

"What the hell does that mean?"

Decker straightens up and adjusts his tie. "He's into some weird shit. Underground sex clubs. BDSM-type stuff. He has a reputation for being a sexual deviant."

"Deviant." I laugh and shrug. "Check out Father Collins over here. Who the fuck cares? I give a shit about the commas on his net worth. So what if he likes his dick poked with toothpicks or clamped off with clothespins, whatever the fuck they do in those places. It's none of our business. He wouldn't be the first or last client we have that's into that kind of thing. Hell, I bet half our roster does shit that'd make your head spin. We've never cared before."

Decker takes a step toward me. "Look, just do yourself and the firm a favor and don't be seen going to those clubs with the guy. The last thing we need is a PR nightmare, especially after just merging with Dallas. You know how the media gets with Deacon and me when they smell a scandal."

Going to a sex club with Covington is at the bottom of my to-do list, so whatever, if it gets me out of this room faster. "Won't be a problem. Is there anything else?"

"You ask Abigail out?" Tate still hasn't looked up from her files. It's obvious she's as tired of Decker railing on about Covington's secret sex life as I am, and I'm pretty sure she asked the question just to give him shit, because he tries to ignore anything beyond business that happens between these walls.

Decker's hands go straight to his temples like he has a migraine coming on. "Please tell me you didn't. I'd almost rather you be seen with Covington at a sex club." His hands fall and he glares lasers back and forth at Tate and me.

I can't help but snicker at how uncomfortable he is, and Tate looks like she's biting back a laugh as well.

He shakes his head at both of us. "Are we a law firm or a fucking dating agency? Maybe I'll have the sign out front changed. Tell Weston we're switching our focus from law to helping singles find their special someone. Fuck."

Well, he's in a mood today. Better pile it on in retaliation for him giving me shit about Covington. "So, let me get this straight, so I have all the facts... It's okay for you and Deacon to fuck whoever you want at the office but the minute I take an interest in Abigail it's not a good idea?" I turn to Tate. "No offense."

She still hasn't looked up. I swear to God, she has ridiculous multitasking skills. She's probably reviewed an entire contract while carrying on this conversation. "None taken. I think Decker's rule is idiotic. As long as it doesn't affect your work, I don't give a shit, personally."

"It's company policy," Decker groans. "Rules are in place for a reason. What if she decides to sue us for sexual harassment?"

"You're being unrealistic as hell. You put a bunch of people in a building and have them working together all the time, they're gonna wanna fuck, okay? That's the natural order of things."

Decker shakes his head. "Your intuition is pure fucking Shakespeare, you know that?"

I bite back a laugh. "I'll take that as a compliment."

"You would."

I swear Tate just giggled. I didn't know she was capable.

"Look, Cole hooked me up with some tickets to the fight tomorrow. I'm taking Abigail to dinner then to the fight."

"Fine, whatever. Just don't tell me about it." Decker turns his back. "I don't want to know. It helps me sleep at night."

Tate gives me a thumbs up where Decker can't see her. That's a good thing. I thought Tate might warn Abigail off from dating me. Being nice to her has its perks it seems.

"Then we're hitting up the Sex Dungeon afterward for a little bondage and fire play..."

He points to the door without looking. "Just get the fuck out."

Tate's about to die.

I can't stop snickering as I head toward the door.

"I swear to Christ, between this place and Jenny's teenage hormones, I'm not going to make it to forty."

"I think you'll make it, you're not too far away."

He spins around, his face heats up. "You about done?"

I hold both hands up. "I'm done, I swear."

"Good."

"Might be time to update the will, though. Good to take precautions. Be sure to list me as..."

His face tenses. "Just go." He fights back a laugh and points to the door. "I might be pushing forty, but I'm the big brother and I'll kick the piss out of all of you, including Deacon's fat ass."

I grin and walk out, tossing Tate a fist bump along the way. I'm glad her and I have been getting along better. It just took some time. Giving Decker shit has brought us closer together, and I think it was just the merger and all the emotions that came along with that. We all got started on the wrong foot, but one thing is certain, she's perfect for my big brother. Believe it or not, he has mellowed out a ton since they got together.

AFTER WORK, I head straight to the gym. I may not be a world-class athlete like Decker and Deacon, but I like to keep myself in shape. I was good at sports, but they never interested me much, so I quit by the time I was in middle school. I tried it out, but at the end told my dad I didn't like it. He never took me back to another practice.

"You always finish something when you start it. Honor your commitments and give it a fair chance. But after that, if you don't like it, don't do it. Life's too short

to do things you don't enjoy." He told me that when I was ten, and it just stuck with me.

Deacon and I have always been super close, because of the twin thing, but it's weird. We both kind of do our own things to separate us from always being lumped together. At least I think so. He'll always be my best friend, but I'm my own person.

Deacon was into sports and always looked up to Decker. I was into comic books and stories and art and shit. I'm a daydreamer. I like to get caught up in my imagination, have since I was a kid.

When I walk in, there are a few gym bunnies hanging around the front, but I ignore them. Normally, I might sit back and enjoy the view for a bit, maybe even strike up a conversation, but I have no inclination to do that today.

I haven't for a while, actually. Now that I think about it. Ever since…

Abigail.

Ever since she transferred to the firm, I haven't looked at other women the same way. I never even noticed until recently. She might not realize she's mine yet, but she will.

After my workout, I grab a quick shower and head over to pick up Jenny, my niece. I promised her I'd take her and her friends to some trampoline place. They're almost old enough to drive, and almost old enough to start drinking and doing all kinds of shit that really would send Decker to an early grave. They might even already be doing it. If they want to go to a trampoline place, I'm all about it. I miss her being younger; it's difficult watching her innocence fade. I can't imagine what that's like for Decker. Maybe it's why he's so stressed out.

When Decker became a single dad, us other brothers made it our mission to give him at least one Friday night a month to himself.

It's a tradition that stuck. I love it. She's a good kid. When she was younger, I'd feed her a bunch of junk then drop her back at home.

He'd get mad as fuck, but hey, that's what uncles do. They spoil the shit out of their niece. I'm not trying to be her parent. I'm a goddamn funcle, and we have fun when we hang out.

Parents have to be responsible, not me.

He always says he's going to pay me back, but the joke's on him. I don't plan on having kids. Being Uncle Dex is fine by me.

I park my car on the street for a minute so I can wait for Decker to back his piece-of-shit SUV out of the garage. Decker traded in his Audi after Tate moved in, and they got matching vehicles. I'll be damned if I park my baby out on the road all night. It needs to go in his garage.

Yes, I'm that douche who treats his car like it's his child. Blow me.

It's a 1970 Chevelle SS and it's a goddamn work of art. I restored it all myself and there's no way I could fit a bunch of teenagers in it, nor would I want to.

"Uncle Dex!" Jenny rushes down the driveway. Her arms wrap around me as she barrels into my chest.

"Hey, kid. You all set to go?"

"Almost. Beth's on her way." She looks at my car. "You have to let me take that to prom in a few years. Please!"

I waggle my eyebrows at her. "Yeah, right. Tell your dad to buy you one. He makes all the money."

"Pfffft. He's already talking about how I need to get a job and pay for my own car."

"Not a bad idea."

"Hey!" She punches me in the arm.

I pretend like it hurt and rub it for a second. "Ow. What was that for?"

"You're supposed to always take my side..." She pauses. "I mean, if you want to be the *coolest* uncle and all that. There's a lot of competition for that title."

I point a finger at her and laugh. "You're a little shit, you know that? You're more like your dad than you think."

We both laugh and walk back up the driveway. I give my car a little glance over my shoulder and tell her with my thoughts that she'll be okay out there until I can get her in the garage.

"Dad ordered pizza for us if you're hungry."

I follow Jenny into the house.

There are three other giddy teenage girls seated at the kitchen counter scarfing down pizza and chugging soda. I can already feel the headache coming on, but traditions are traditions.

"You sure you're up for this?" Tate grins as I walk up.

"I can handle them. Though, I will admit it was easier when they were eight. They'd get hopped up on sugar and crash. They never shut the fuck up once they're teenagers."

Tate laughs. "Well, if you need backup don't call. Decker's taking me to the movies."

"I'll call their asses an Uber if they don't act right, or stick them on the train."

"Jesus." Tate shakes her head. "I can never tell when you and Deacon are joking. So, when's the big date with Abigail?"

"Who's Abigail?" Jenny cuts in. "Uncle Dex, you have a girlfriend? When can I meet her? Is she pretty? What's she look like?"

There is entirely too much estrogen in my presence. "Easy, killer. I'm sure I have all night to tell you about her."

"Cool."

Decker walks in from the garage. "What's cool?"

"Uncle Dex has a hot date tomorrow night with Abigail."

Decker glares. "I know." He shakes his head like he's trying to rid his brain of the thought. "The truck's ready to go. You need anything?"

I shake my head right back at him and grin my ass off. "How many times do I have to tell you that's not a truck. It's barely an SUV and might as well be a soccer mom van."

His jaw ticks a little, like he's trying to bite back whatever sarcastic remark he's thinking of, because he knows it'll give Jenny a reason to sass his ass twenty-four seven. He finally just shoves Tate's keys into my chest. "Don't call for anything." Then he whispers, "And stay away for a while."

I pat him on the back and toss him a wink. "Don't worry, bro. I got you. Probably been a while. You need to clean the ol' pipes out. I'm sure they're rusty."

"Jesus Christ." He grabs Tate by the arm. "Time to go."

"For real, we'll be fine. Going to the trampoline place then maybe hit up the arcade and ice cream. It'll wear them out."

"Perfect. Thanks. I mean it."

"Yes, thank you," says Tate.

"No worries."

"Beth!" the girls all squeal when their other friend arrives.

Fuck, this is going to be a long night.

ABIGAIL

MY STOMACH FLUTTERS. I'm anxious and excited.

"I mean look at Kyle and me. We hang out all the time and it's never been awkward. He's a good friend…"

Barbie rolls her eyes from the chair next to mine as the stylist goes all scissor crazy on her hair.

I brought her with me to the salon, despite her being so damn rude, because I felt bad she was moping around about Chuck nonstop. It was probably a mistake, but she looked so damn happy when I asked if she wanted to come.

I mean, who can't be in a good mood after a nice cut and color?

She glances over. "Because you put him in the friend zone. Trust me, he's sitting there biding his time, just waiting for an opportunity."

What? Why does everyone think Kyle wants to be more than friends? That's insane. He's never once acted interested in me in that way. "Kyle? No way."

I swear if someone wasn't cutting her hair, her nose would go straight up to the ceiling. "Bury your head in the sand all you want. Just wait until he finds out you're dating the hot lawyer. He's going to turn into a different person. He hangs out with you because you're single. Chuck and I talked about it all the time. We were betting how long it'd be before you got drunk and he made his move."

"What?" I'm already regretting inviting her here. I'm only entertaining this conversation to keep her mind off the breakup, and because I don't want to hear her cry again. I can't imagine myself ever crying as much as she has, but I've never been through a bad breakup. I've never really had a serious relationship. I dated one guy for a few months in high school, but we broke up when he went off to college my junior year. He's married with two kids, and I'm happy for him. In college I dated a bit but never anything hot and heavy. I've definitely never been with anyone I could see spending the rest of my life with. The thought of it sends a shudder through me.

I mean, over half of marriages fail. Why would I ever want to roll those dice? I've seen couples I thought would last forever turn a one-eighty and hate each other after a year.

Maybe that's why I'm so damn nervous about this date with Dex. I've never felt this way about someone else, but I know it's just physical attraction. We don't even really know each other all that well, and I won't just be handing my heart to someone with nice eyes and a little ink snaking down out of their suit.

What if we turn into more? I don't want to end up all sad and pathetic like Barbie.

My usual hair lady moves me back under the dryer for my lowlights while Barbie gets her color done.

She's going darker and I think it's a smart choice. It fits her personality better, makes her seem more adult and serious, which is perfect for her.

While I'm under the dryer, my thoughts return to Dex. There's nothing worse than a date filled with awkward silence. What if we have nothing to talk about? What if I bore him? I'm young, in my early twenties, and he's a decade older than me and has an important job. How could we possibly relate to each other? For some reason, the thought of us not clicking, once we get to know each other, turns my stomach.

Once Barbie and I finish, I rush home to get ready. Thankfully, I shaved my legs this morning when I took a shower. Barbie's going out with some work friends to drink her heartache away, and I'm happy to dump her problems off on them. I did my good deed for the day with minimal confrontation. Score.

With any luck she'll crash somewhere else if things go well with Dex.

Unless he invites me back to his place. Wow, what if he *does* invite me back? What if he wants more?

Should I take a toothbrush? I don't think we'll have sex, but you never know.

Would I have sex with him tonight?

My brain screams no, but my body screams yes. Damn, he has me all worked up again and he's not even here.

Right as I slip on my jean jacket, the doorbell rings.

Shit.

He's here.

I suck in a deep breath, pop a piece of gum in my mouth, and open the door.

Mother of God.

He's dressed casual, and I swear it's even hotter than him in a damn suit. He has on dark jeans and a graphic stretch tee that hugs his biceps and shows off even more of his ink than I usually get a peek at.

His gaze rakes up and down, taking me in. His eyes travel from my peep toe, leopard-print heels, up the legs of my tattered dark jeans, to the bare midriff where my black halter begins. It has sexy straps that cross over my back. There was no wearing a bra with this thing. It's like a black silky hanky that leaves little to the imagination.

My hair is blown out in soft waves that curve around my shoulders. I've got the vintage Pam Anderson look going on, perfect for an MMA fight.

"Wow, you look… incredible."

Don't blush. Don't blush. Why does he make me want to smile like an idiot?

Pretty sure I blush. "Thanks, you look… great too."

Stop being awkward.

"You have a bigger jacket?"

What the hell? "Uh, no."

He smirks. "It's gonna get cold."

I shrug and it's hard to focus on the words with how hot he looks. "I'll be okay, promise."

He shakes his head, then smiles at me. "Texas girls," he mumbles.

He looks different without his suit on. I've only seen him without one a few times. His demeanor is different outside of work, like he lets his guard down and doesn't have to be so serious around me.

As I walk out, the smell of his cologne hits me and makes me want to jerk him through the doorway and climb his ass like a damn tree. I manage to keep my hormones in check and grab my clutch.

"Come on. I know a great place to eat."

I manage not to tell him he can have me for dinner *and* dessert if he wants. "Sounds perfect. I'm starving."

He smirks. It's the sexiest of all smirks. "Good. Was afraid you'd be one of those girls who orders a salad then shuffles it around on her plate." He grins and puts a hand to my lower back and guides me to the elevator.

His hand. It shoots flames up my spine. This is going to be a long night, and I don't mind one bit.

"No way. We know how to eat in Texas."

"Atta girl, Whitley."

We make our way down the elevator, and Dex leads me through the front door.

"Holy shit…" My hands shoot over my mouth. I can't believe I just said that out loud. I seem to do that a lot around him. "Sorry, I just have a thing for cars." There's a Chevelle parked by the curb. It's the mother of all badass cars. It's a dark blue color with white racing stripes. It looks completely restored, like it's brand new.

"What?" Dex shrugs half-heartedly.

"What do you mean *what*? Do you not see that Chevelle?"

"Yeah, I see it every day." He holds up his keys and jiggles them at me.

No way is that his car. How have I never seen it? Maybe because I take the train everywhere and never go near the parking garage.

"Her name is Betsy and ogle her when I'm not looking. She's all mine."

We walk over and he opens the door for me. I slide in onto the vinyl seats, and damn, it just smells like raw power.

Dex folds himself into the driver's seat. He fumbles for his keys, and I get a better peek at his tattoos as his sleeve slides up his arm. Butterflies go crazy in my stomach as he turns the key and the car rumbles to life.

It's so freaking hot. Like James Dean, *Rebel Without a Cause*, hot. I peek into the back seat, and holy hell, he has the leather jacket and everything.

Dex slouches back in the seat with one hand on the wheel, and I just take a mental snapshot of him while the vibrations run through my body.

It's like we're setting off on a journey together, and I've never seen a man look so damn sexy in all my life.

I really did pick out a great outfit and it's not lost on me that we look like a perfect couple together.

Dex looks over and winks, and before I know it he backs out and we're flying down the street.

DINNER'S GOING GREAT.

We're in this hip little place with a name I can't pronounce and would butcher if I tried, but it's intimate and fancy. It's perfect for a first date. No having to talk over a crowd. We're at a table in the back that's very private. The ambience screams romantic, but not over the top. It's very subtle. A dainty chandelier hangs over our table and we're seated on brown leather chairs that curve slightly toward each other.

He clearly put a lot of thought into choosing this restaurant. Chalk another one up in the win column for Dexter Collins.

"So, what was it like in your house with all those boys? I've always wondered about that."

Dexter laughs and takes a drink of his beer. "Utter chaos. Rough housing nonstop that drove our mom crazy. I don't know how she put up with us. Someone was always breaking something or bleeding."

"So… you're a mama's boy?" I tease him.

Dex picks at the label on his bottle of beer. "What makes you say that?"

Damn, did I say something wrong? God, am I ruining the moment? "Nothing, I just… You made the question all about her. It seemed like you had empathy for her situation, mentioning her raising all those boys, you guys driving her nuts."

He smiles, like he can sense my discomfort. "Can you keep a secret?"

"Sure." All feels right once again when he smiles at me.

"Total mama's boy." He leans back. "There, I said it and I'm not ashamed at all." He pauses. "But seriously, don't tell anyone."

I laugh. He's so relaxed right now. I'm really digging this playful side of him. "I would never." I stare at him long and hard for a few seconds.

"What?"

"Can I tell you a secret too?"

He straightens up. "Absolutely."

"Total mama's girl over here too. I call her almost every night. I told her about you." I fidget with my hands on the table and break eye contact.

His lips curl into a sly smirk. "Only good things, I hope."

"She called you a boy." I laugh.

He frowns.

I hold a hand up. "Oh no, don't worry. She thinks all the men who aren't southern are boys without manners. She's kind of partial to the south."

He reaches out for my hand, and it's like a jolt of electricity flashes through me when our fingers connect. "I'll just have to change her mind, won't I?"

You're blushing again. Knock it off, Abby!

"Tell me more about your mom."

Dex leans back in his chair, and both of us completely ignore the food in front of us. "I don't know, she just always got me, you know?"

I nod, almost furiously. He has no idea how much I can relate.

"Decker and Deacon were good at sports, like my dad. It wasn't my thing." He pauses like he's holding back.

"What is it?"

"Okay, so you know… No, I don't know if I…"

I grip his hand a little tighter. "Tell me. I want to know."

"Well, everyone thinks I love pudding at the office."

I shake my head. "Would've never thought that." Oh goodie, the mystery of the pudding is about to unfold. I've always been curious what his deal is with it. It's like a ritual for him.

He laughs. "The truth is, that was mine and my mom's thing. She always kept them hidden in the house and told me where they were when I was a boy. It was *our* secret, you know? Four boys and I had a twin brother, so we had to share everything, but it was something just for me. I think it all started when I got this scar." He points to his face. "Crashed on my skateboard when I was young. Decker was supposed to be watching me and I had to go get stitched up. Mom would bring me pudding because it was all I would eat. I was milking it for all it was worth, but it just continued, all the way through high school, and even when I moved out. Hell, sometimes I'd show up to the old house before they moved, when something was bothering me, or I had a problem. She always had them there, and we'd sit down and talk and eat pudding together… It sounds stupid."

I shake my head. "It's not stupid at all. I understand, trust me."

"Well, her and Dad moved down to Florida, and she sends me those in the mail and always has a note with them, telling me what's going on with her and asking me about life. I send some to her with notes from me. It's our thing, still. And I take them to work and keep them up there anytime I have a case that's gnawing at me. It's like I can't think if I don't have them there. It's why I get pissed when people steal them, and why I put a sign on them in the fridge. People think I'm just being anal like Decker, but it really is important to me."

I think my heart might've just melted away. I can't believe he just told me all that, and it makes so much sense. I don't know what I'd do if I didn't always have my mom one click away on my phone.

For some reason, I just sit there, staring like an idiot. I must look so dumb.

"Sorry, I shouldn't have dropped all that on you. You just asked, and I..." He starts to move his hand away, and my fingers tighten around it, almost to the point I might be digging my nails into his skin.

Don't you ever move that hand, Dexter Collins!

"No, thanks for telling me. I'm serious. And I won't ever say a word to anyone else, promise."

Dex nods and snaps out of his thoughts. "What about you? Any siblings?"

I nod. "Yep. I have a younger sister. She was a surprise baby. She's ten years younger than me so we aren't super close. It's weird. I almost feel like half parent, half sibling. I never was great at the whole getting along with other girls thing, but I do miss her like crazy. I never really had girlfriends growing up. I went to a small school in Texas. It was all about football and you were pretty much a cheerleader or you weren't, and I didn't like cheerleading. So, I didn't have anyone, you know, to spill all my secrets to or have sleepovers with. My roommate for instance. I never know how to take her. I can't tell if she's just being a bitch or if she's half joking sometimes when she says things. I think I need to live on my own. I can't wait to find a new place. One that will let me have a dog."

"A dog lover, huh? Totally had you pegged as a cat person."

"No way. Cats are assholes. I want a husky. One with big blue eyes. Growing up I never could have one because my dad was allergic."

"So, you love banana pudding, your mom, and dogs... what else?"

I laugh, and I love that he wants to know more about me. The feeling is mutual. "I don't know if I should tell you this next one. It *is* a first date after all. I won't be mysterious and interesting if I tell you everything."

He leans in like *now we're getting to the good stuff.* "Tell me. Can't leave me on a cliffhanger like that."

I draw out a sigh, just to tease him a little longer. "Well it's bound to come out sooner or later since we work together. I'm Christmas obsessed. Like, I get crazy. Ugly sweaters, decorations, the movies. I love the classics and all the romantic movies that come on the Hallmark channel. Actually, I love pretty much every movie ever made. I can have an entire conversation in movie quotes. But Christmas is my big thing, above all else."

Dex rubs his hands together. "Okay, most important question of your life, Whitley."

Oh no. I hope I don't say the wrong thing. "Is this a test?"

"Yeah, the biggest one of your life." He grins. "*Die Hard;* Christmas movie or no?"

"Definitely a Christmas movie," I say without thinking.

Dex grins like his day just got a lot better.

I try to hide the large breath I exhale. "Thank God I passed the *Die Hard* test."

"With flying colors. Didn't even have to think about it. I like it."

"That could've been a deal breaker for me too."

"Glad we're on the same page."

I nod. "Yep, you got lucky there."

"Oh, *I* got lucky?" Dex laughs.

"You did."

"Did you know Quinn doesn't think *Die Hard* is a Christmas movie? Deacon looked like he was going to die when he told me."

"What? I thought for sure Quinn would be pro-*Die Hard*."

Dexter shrugs. "What can I say? You're better than her already." He glances away, like he's having a little too much fun. "Okay, crazy Christmas lady. I take it you like hot chocolate?"

"Duh! I make the best hot chocolate ever. I learned it from one of my teachers when I was like eight. Every year in my hometown they have a festival. They go all out with a tree-lighting ceremony and Santa parade. It's a big deal."

"You're adorable." He winks.

I fake-scowl. "Shut up. I'm not cute."

"No, you're right, you're a big Christmas clown."

I lightly rap my fingers on the tabletop and try to suppress a grin. Dexter's sweet. He makes me smile a lot, and there haven't been any weird or tense moments. I haven't felt this relaxed in a long time, longer than I can remember. I feel weightless, like I could float off into the clouds. My guard is totally down and that should scare the hell out of me, but it doesn't. Not at all. "Well, I was going for sexy tonight." I say it right as he takes a sip of his beer.

He damn near starts to choke but manages to compose himself. "Well, you nailed it. Trust me."

I'm not usually one to fish for compliments, but I could listen to them come from Dexter Collins all night long. "Don't lie."

"Not a lie. You could dress up like Mrs. Claus and I'd put your poster on my wall. True story."

I laugh at the thought, then heat flushes through my face, thinking about dressing up in a sexy Christmas outfit for Dex. That could be a lot of fun. "Maybe I will sometime. You have to do the classic Chevy Chase rant from *Christmas Vacation*, though. Word for word, Collins."

Dex laughs. "Oh, I'd nail it. You bring Frank Shirley into my living room and I'd tell him what a dog-kissing, brainless, dickless, hopeless, heartless, fat-ass, bug-eyed, stiff-legged, spotty-lipped, worm-headed sack of monkey shit he is."

Oh my God, he just quoted it without even trying. Why is him quoting Christmas movies so freaking hot? "I'm impressed, sir."

I hold up my beer, and he taps the bottle with his.

I don't know if this date can go any better. It's seriously perfect.

I grin. "So, about my poster on the wall? What would you be doing when looking at said poster?"

"It's classified. I could tell you but then I'd have to kill you."

Did he just quote *Top Gun*? "It's not your flying, it's your attitude."

"Nice, you weren't lying."

"You can't stump me. I'll quote any movie. The great ones anyway."

"Tell me something else about you. I could listen to your stories all night long. What's on your bucket list?"

I tap my chin. "Okay, well, I've always wanted to go ice skating. It's not real big in Texas and we lived like an hour outside of Fort Worth. I almost got to go once, though. I begged my dad over and over and he found this outdoor skating rink in the city. We drove all the way there, and I was so excited, but when we got there it was closed for maintenance or something. Dad was furious. Tried to call the manager and didn't get an answer. He apologized to me a million times and looked like he'd let me down. I felt awful for him and told him it was okay. I know he tried his best. But the story is just as good as getting to ice skate. It really showed me how much he cared and stuff, you know? I'm pretty lucky to have two amazing parents."

Dex nods. "Sounds like a great guy. And as far as ice skating goes, well, you moved to the right city for that." He glances to his watch. "Okay, one more Abigail fun fact, then we need to get going."

"That one's easy. Roller coasters. I love them. We used to go to Six Flags every summer and I'd ride them until I couldn't walk straight."

Dex's face pales a little, and he takes a sip of water. "Awesome. Love roller coasters."

He almost sounds like he's mocking me. "What? You don't like them?"

He shakes his head. "No, they're fine."

Shit, did I say something wrong?

Dex signs the air at the waitress and she brings the check over. He tosses some cash on the table and winks at me. "Let's get out of here."

Normally, I'd find a guy winking cheesy as hell, or goofy, but Dex somehow pulls it off. I think it's because he's not taking himself seriously when he does it.

"All right, Collins." I give him an obviously sarcastic wink. "You're one for one so far, let's see how you do next. I'm ready to watch those hot, naked, sweaty dudes pound on each other."

Dex snickers and starts to say something but pauses and shakes his head. "Damn Christmas clown."

"I'm not a clown. Christmas crazy but not a clown." I point at him.

He catches my hand and wraps his around mine. Our fingers interlace like we've done it a million times before.

"Keep telling yourself that..." He leans in close and whispers, "My little sexy Christmas clown."

His hand moves to the small of my back, and I fight the urge to lean into it.

It's so gentle and possessive at the same time.

It's like a warning to everyone around, *she's mine*, but at the same time I'm leading the way. Maybe I'm just overanalyzing this whole situation. That's probably it.

Before I know what's happened, he's draped his leather jacket over my shoulders and we're headed toward the door.

"Sun went down. You're gonna freeze."

I seriously might combust. It smells just like him and his cologne and there's something incredibly intimate about the moment.

Do not sniff his jacket!

I lean into him while we wait for the valet to pull his car around and inhale the intoxicating scent of his cologne once more. It's late October and he wasn't lying. I'm cold through both layers and he has to be dying in just his tee shirt, but he doesn't show it. I've never lived anywhere that gets this cold, but it gives me an excuse to lean into him and let him and his jacket keep me warm. I just hope he doesn't notice me constantly sniffing. He's definitely ticking off all the boxes. I mean, damn. This date is perfect so far.

DEXTER

WE RUMBLE down Madison in the Chevelle toward the United Center.

I can't stop stealing glances over at Abigail. I think she might be more into my car than me.

Things seem to be going too good to be true. I didn't mean to drop all that stuff about me and my mom on her, but she seemed to get it. She seems to just get *me*, more than I thought she would. Some part of my brain kept telling me she was too young, and this date would show me why we're not compatible, then I could get her out of my mind. I mean, I still planned on trying to get laid. Let's not be ridiculous here. The exact opposite has happened, though.

I'm drawn to her, like a moth to a fucking flame, and I don't know how I'll deal with it if this doesn't work out. The feelings are already there. There's a connection that already runs deep and we haven't done anything more than kiss twice.

I keep trying to hold back but it's not working. I don't want to come on too strong, but every time I see her, I have this unbelievable urge to tell her everything on my mind and kiss the breath from her lungs.

She's so confident and sexy, not afraid to show her true self. The more she talks, the more I want to know even more about her. We get to the arena, and I don't know what to do. I should drop her off up front, but no way do I want to leave her up there alone while I park the car.

Why didn't I think about this beforehand? I should've hired a car and a driver. Then it wouldn't be as intimate, though. I wouldn't have her all alone.

I drive around the block once and my hands tighten around the steering wheel. What the hell am I going to do? She's gonna freeze in her little jacket she's wearing.

Finally, I decide to just go park and then let her use my jacket again. I don't ask because I know she'll refuse it. It's cold as balls out here. The wind cuts through the buildings and it's like daggers on bare skin.

I drape it around her shoulders as soon as we're out of the car.

"Dex, you're gonna freeze."

"I don't get cold. I'm fine." I toss her another wink, but inside I'm shivering my damn tits off. Fuck, I should've worn a long-sleeve shirt. I don't let my teeth so much as chatter, though, because I'm no pussy, and there's no way I'll let her know I'm cold.

She's warm and that's all that matters.

I walk next to her and our hands brush up against each other. If I was cold before, I'm not now. Even the slightest touch sends heat rushing through my veins.

The second time our fingers graze, they interlace, and we hold hands the rest of the way to the arena.

Her hand fits perfectly in mine and she doesn't pull away. By the time we get to the gate, my lips mash together in a thin line because I have to let go of her. The moment we pass through, our hands naturally gravitate back together. We make our way in and head down toward the octagon, ringside. There's media everywhere. Some chick who was obsessed with Decker years ago flies out of nowhere and snaps our picture, damn near blinding us with the flash.

Once her eyes pop out from behind the camera, her shoulders slump and she lowers her head slightly. She was probably expecting Decker and Tate.

Finally, we make it down. Cole wasn't fucking around. We're on the front row next to a shit ton of celebrities and families of the fighters.

Abigail's hand grips mine a little tighter. "Holy…"

"Yeah, it's a different world down here."

She grins back and I pull her closer to me.

"There's Cole. Let's go say hi."

"Okay."

Our heads crane around, taking in the packed arena as we make our way over to him.

My eyes roam down to her. She's so small and petite. "Ready to see some naked dudes kick the shit out of each other?"

Abby blushes and looks away. "Nah."

I raise my eyebrows. "What? Thought that's why you came?"

"No, I came because some cute guy asked me to." Her teeth sink into her bottom lip.

I want nothing more than to kiss her right now, but it'd be too forward, and we need to go make appearances. It'd be rude not to. "Good answer. C'mon."

We navigate through a sea of people on our way over to Cole.

"You made it. Nice." He holds out a hand.

I shake it. "Wouldn't miss it. Was that 50 Cent back there?"

"Yeah, man. He loves this shit."

"This is Abigail. Abigail, Cole."

He reaches a hand out. "Of course. I think we met at the office. Great to see you again." He flashes his million-dollar smile at her.

I scowl.

Abigail takes his hand in hers, and I really want to smack his damn hand away from her, but I know I'm being ridiculous. "Oh yeah. I remember you. You offered me a discount at your gym." She smiles.

"Hey, filling the place with beautiful women is good for business."

"Well, if you guys will excuse me, I'm going to hit the ladies' room." Abigail turns back to me. "See you at our seats?"

I nod. "Sure."

Cole and I both watch her melt into the crowd.

He turns and slaps my chest. "Holy shit, son. She's hot as fuck."

I narrow my brows. "Hell yeah she is, and she's all mine so don't get any fucking ideas." My words come out on a growl before I can stop them. What is this woman doing to me?

He holds both his hands up and laughs. "Jesus fuck. Calm down, caveman. I got you. Look around. There's plenty of women here tonight." He shakes his head. "I swear to god, you Collins assholes. Quinn led me to a meeting a few months back at the office, and I thought Deacon was going to crush my goddamn fingers when I shook his hand on the way out."

I grin. "We do like our women, don't we?"

"If I couldn't kick all your asses with ease, I might actually be intimidated."

He's got a point. We'd go down swinging, though.

I nod and try to cool it. I don't know what it is about Abigail, but she has me ready to fight any man who even looks in her direction.

Cole straightens up and his brow furrows. "On a serious note, I've been meaning to set up a meeting. I know you handle the finance stuff at the firm, right?"

"Yeah. You need a consult?"

He nods. "Once this bullshit with the lawsuit is done, I'd like to have a face-to-face and talk shop. I'm looking for some angel investors or VC for an infusion. I know a few, but I want to exhaust all my options. Or look at franchising options. We're starting to stagnate and I'm looking for new growth and capital to make that happen, know what I'm saying? Merchandising and product too. I'm looking to do my own bottled water, protein, and workout gear. It's one of the reasons 50 is here, he did the Vitamin Water thing and made millions. Hell, I may even do my own workout equipment if I can get the capital. I'm not above Chuck Norris-ing my ass on some Total Gym informercials."

I'm surprised he hasn't had a sit down with Covington. Maybe he doesn't know he's in town. "Absolutely. Have you called Wells?"

"No, I think it'd be too weird. I don't like mixing friendship and money."

Makes sense. "Okay, well we can run an analysis and I can put you in touch with the right people. With your connections we could get you new capital easy. I don't handle marketing, but we have a department and I can set up a meeting with my cousin Harlow. She just opened a firm in town. In the meantime, just keep networking with all these celebrities. Do them as many favors as they want and get them in your gyms. When the time comes, they'll return the favor. Like Dre and Jimmy Iovine did with Beats. It's free exposure. Send these celebrities and influencers free shit and have them post pictures with it on their Instagram. Make your stuff the next cool thing and stay relevant."

"I like the sound of that. You know your shit. Always have. Speaking of favors, you think Decker would be into some kind of trade for services? I can get your employees a discounted rate at the gym."

"Definitely, he's been on this big wellness kick anyway. It's all the rage in corporate America right now, keeping employees healthy and happy. Cuts down on healthcare costs, which reduces insurance rates. Preventative health. I'm sure you could work something out."

"Great. I'll call the office. Enjoy the fight. And you better get over there. Some asshole is chatting up your woman. Maybe we'll get an undercard fight in the stands before this starts. You might even win this one." He laughs then walks off.

I look over at our seats and Abigail is laughing at something the old man seated beside her says. He looks old enough to be her grandpa.

Fucking Cole.

I hang back a second to watch her. I swear she could make a new best friend anywhere. Everyone is drawn to her. Now, she's striking up a conversation with the guy next to her. I can't see his face because she's blocking the view.

I strut over there toward my woman. Fuck. I'm already thinking shit like that.

It's too soon.

I know it's a first date, but I just want to zoom a hundred miles an hour into the sunset with her.

Her gaze meets mine and she smiles.

My heart squeezes in my chest at the sight. That's a smile that's only for me. There's this sparkle in her blue eyes as I get closer, and I can't remember ever feeling this way before her.

I take my seat and realize she's sitting next to J.B. Pritzker, the Governor of Illinois.

I stand up and shake his hand. "Governor." We've met once or twice at a few functions and at the Capitol building.

"I was just telling your girlfriend here I don't usually come to these things, but I couldn't say no. It's quite the turnout."

Abigail's eyes go big when he says *girlfriend* but neither of us correct him. Not that I want to. I like the sound of it.

No, if I'm being honest, I *love* the sound of it.

I love that he immediately thought that.

"Yes, sir. Great for tourism and the local economy. Lots of tax revenue."

We have a seat and I take her hand on my thigh, giving her a gentle squeeze.

The main lights go down and colored lasers dance around the arena. Music

420

fires up and Abigail leans into my shoulder. She smells amazing, like strawberries and vanilla.

"Who should I be rooting for? I don't know any of them."

I tell her about each fighter. Of course, she picks all the underdogs. Chicks usually do.

We fall into easy conversation during the undercard fights, and Abigail winces a few times when dudes knock the hell out of each other about ten feet from us. We're so damn close you can see blood and sweat on the concrete around the octagon.

Finally, it's time for the main event.

Bruce Buffer announces the first fighter. "Hailing from the southside of Miami, for Team Takedown, weighing in at one hundred sixty-nine and a half pounds, Callum Black." The crowd goes crazy.

This fight is a big deal.

Cole trained Pedro so I have to root for him.

"And your hometown hero, fighting out of Team Miller, weighing in at one hundred seventy pounds, the undefeated, welterweight champion, Pedro Mandez." The dude is a damn beast.

This will be his toughest fight, though.

Abigail's eyes are trained on the octagon and right now I only have eyes for her. I have to force myself to watch what's going on, because all I want to do is stare at her.

The referee calls them to the center and they tap gloves, then the fight is underway.

Pedro comes in strong, working Black with jabs. He's a striker so he's trying to stay off the mat. He'll have to do that if he wants to win. They fall into the fence locked together.

Abigail is practically bouncing out of her seat as she cheers. She's such an adorable goof. I take that back; she's a sexy Christmas clown.

"This is awesome. Thank you for bringing me. I'm having a great time."

"No one else I'd rather be with."

"Now who's being an adorable little clown?" Her teeth graze her lip.

I lean in about to claim those tempting cherry lips. The crowd roars and Abigail squeals. The moment is lost but I know she felt it too. Fuck she's incredible, and I'm glad to see her cutting loose and having a good time.

"Oh shit!" The words come out before I can stop them. I'm obviously rooting for Pedro. He's Cole's boy. Abigail is cheering for Callum, since he's the underdog.

Callum takes him down, and the crowd goes deathly quiet. Pedro is the hometown boy.

Callum has Pedro on the mat, hammering his head with his fist, legs pinning him down. He moves with lightning speed and wraps him up in a hold.

Abigail is the only one around us cheering Callum on. "Tap him out!"

Somehow Pedro breaks free and scrambles, rolling away from him. The crowd surges to life.

The bell rings, just when they're about to obliterate each other.

"That was freaking intense."

I look over and Abigail is breathing heavily. Her breasts are expanding and contracting in her halter top, and fuck, I gotta get out of here for a second, before I put on a real show for these people, in my pants.

"I'm going to go grab us a couple beers."

Abigail grabs my forearm and her eyes are dilated, face flushed. "Hurry back, okay."

I smile. "Be back before you know it."

Holy shit.

I need her, right here, right now. It's bad.

ABIGAIL

DEXTER KEEPS his hand on my thigh the whole drive back to my apartment.

The holes in my tattered jeans allow his fingers to brush across my skin, and my entire body is on fire.

I had no idea I'd get so worked up watching grown men beat the crap out of each other. There's just something so manly and primal about it. My adrenaline spiked, and it hasn't come down at all. I'm one-hundred percent sure the reason is sitting right next to me, driving a manly car, looking manly as hell. He had to be freezing his ass off when he gave me his jacket, wearing nothing but that thin t-shirt the whole way, but he didn't so much as shiver once.

It's hard to put into words what walking into a room with Dexter Collins is like. I just feel—safe, invincible even.

Tonight has been perfect. I can't remember the last time I had this much fun. He's a true gentleman, but part of me wishes he wasn't. I keep getting this feeling like he wants to kiss me but he's holding back. There was a moment during the fight when I thought he was going to. I don't get it at all. I've thrown out every signal in the book, short of taking out a billboard ad. I lie my head back at a red light and look at him with my lips parted hoping he takes the hint, but he just grins at me and squeezes my thigh.

"What'd you think about Callum getting knocked out at the last minute?"

"That was freaking insane. I thought for sure my guy was going to win. Pedro looked dead on his feet."

"Yeah, I thought he was done for. He dug down deep for that knockout."

"I wanted the underdog to win, but it was fun either way."

"Honestly, I didn't think he'd pull it off. I thought it'd be close though."

Dexter and his beast of a car rumble down my street, and I don't want this to end. It's been perfect. I wonder if Dex is going to walk me to my door. Is he finally going to kiss me again? Should I invite him in? Why did I not think about any of this until just now? I don't go around sleeping with every guy who takes me on a date or anything, but I'm attracted to Dex and if he wanted to… I don't know. I guess I'll have to see where things go.

I'm like ninety-nine percent sure he's into me, like a lot, but I'm still young and don't know *that* much about guys. Dex and his brothers are mysteries too and intimidating. Maybe he just likes hanging out with me. Which will suck because I really like him more than I should.

The Chevelle rolls to a stop and Dex parks along the curb. He slides out and holds his hand out to me. Before I know it, his jacket is on me again.

I pull my keys out as we get into the elevator, and I wonder if Barbie's home. Even if he does want to come in, she might ruin the whole damn thing. We get to my door and Dex hasn't even tried to make a move to kiss me in the elevator. Maybe he's just waiting until the timing is perfect. He's been super fidgety ever since we got out of the car.

We pause in front of my door. I wish I could just read his damn thoughts. I want to know what to do, because I want him to kiss me more than anything in the world. I want him to crash into me, and shove me up against the wall, and do whatever the hell he wants. Anything other than staring at me and saying nothing.

He takes his jacket back, and I stick my keys in and twist the knob.

I turn to face him, and his hands are shoved in his pockets like he's scared to touch me after he held my hand all night and rubbed on my leg. What the hell is going on here? "Well thanks. I, umm, had a great time. We should hang out again. If you want to."

His eyes say he wants to eat me alive, the way he's leaned against the wall next to the door, practically searing a hole in my chest with his gaze, but he's still holding back. I feel like a crazy person. I'm going to explode if he doesn't do something.

His jaw ticks and he swallows hard. "Yeah. I had a great time too. See you soon, Abby."

I blink. "Okay, umm, goodnight." I don't know what else to say and I'm not going to act like an idiot and throw myself at him. That would make work weird as hell come Monday, especially if he rejects me.

I open the door and quickly close it behind me.

My entire mood deflates like a balloon. How the hell did I go from being on top of the world to feeling like absolute shit? My heart pinches in my chest. I don't think I realized just how much I like Dexter Collins until right now.

I kick off my shoes wondering what in the hell that was. I sling my purse to the couch as the doorbell rings. My blood heats to a million degrees, and I think I just switched from confusion to rage in two point two seconds.

I swear, if that's Kyle I will punch him in the face if he gives me any lip for going out with Dex. He probably walked past him in the hallway and is coming to give me shit.

It's the last thing I need when my ego just took a beating. I'm not vain, but I know I looked as hot as I could for our date, I gave off all the signs saying I was interested. I dressed sexy. I shaved my legs and trimmed up the rest nice and neat just in case...not that I thought we'd have sex, but I wanted to be prepared. What did I do wrong?

I march to the door and throw it open.

Dex barrels into me and the door closes behind him.

His intense stare is on me and his arms move around my waist. I start to ask what he's doing but his mouth crashes down on mine, and I'm floating. Just floating on the damn clouds, electricity flooding my veins. A wildfire burns through me and funnels down between my legs. My body just—needs, it needs Dex. It's a want so intense I may burst into flames.

Sweet lord can this man kiss too. His tongue thrusts into my mouth and consumes me from within. He pins me to the wall, kissing me so deep and hard it's a good thing he's pressed up against me or I might melt into the floor.

I whisper against his lips, "About time."

"Should've done that a few minutes ago. Wanted to do it all night." His words come out against my lips as a growl.

"I'm glad you did."

His hand grazes my jaw, and his forehead rests against mine. His breath fans over my lips. "Is your roommate home?"

"No. You'd definitely know if she was."

"Good." His lips claim my mouth once more and I don't hold back.

I give as good as I'm getting, running my hand up under his shirt feeling the hard wall of muscle there.

His lips meet my neck and I might just die. "Which way?"

I tilt my head toward the hall and Dex lifts me into his arms, his hands gripping my ass. My legs instinctively wrap around his waist, my arms cradling his neck.

Our mouths remain fused together as he hauls me down the hallway to my room.

Once we're inside, I slide down the front of his body and lift his shirt over his head because I want him to know without a doubt that he can do whatever he wants to me.

Holy crap, I'm about to have sex with Dexter Collins.

Once his shirt is off, I pause for a split-second, just to take him in. The man is beautiful with his razor-sharp jawline, and neatly trimmed stubble. His eyes are a dark blue that could melt steel.

He unties the back of my top and we fall onto the bed together, tongues and fingers moving a million directions. Exploring and touching each other anywhere and everywhere at once. God he's a ridiculous kisser. My shirt comes off and he rubs a hand over my breast, looking at me all sweet but with a wolfish grin that says he's going to devour me.

Man do I want that. I do but this is going fast and it's only our first date.

Now, who's giving off mixed signals, Abigail?

425

"Wait." I brace my hands against his shoulders.

His eyes widen, but he doesn't look angry that I stopped us, just confused.

"I want this so damn bad, but I don't want to be that girl. I just, I really feel something between us, and I don't want to look back..."

Dex cuts me off. "It's not like that." His hand slides inside my jeans, rubbing over my clit.

I gasp. I don't know if any other man has ever even found it, let alone automatically.

God, he feels so good. Too good. I couldn't make him stop if I wanted to.

He rises up and slides his body down, taking one of my breasts in his mouth. "I just want to make you feel good, Abigail."

His teeth graze my nipple and my toes curl into the mattress.

I can't believe this is happening. I can't believe Dexter Collins, a partner at the firm, is half naked in my bed, fooling around with me.

I glance down and my God, he might be the hottest thing I've ever seen. His muscles expand and contract at the slightest movements, and I finally see all his tattoos. They roam up both his arms and snake across his chest and back.

Dex trails his tongue down lower, closer and closer to where I need him the most, but I squirm because it's almost too damn intense.

"Relax. Just let me take care of you, Abby."

Even his voice is hot as sin. If he so much as grazes my clit again, I might come undone.

He unbuttons my jeans and slides them down. Next come the panties and oh my god, I'm totally bare in front of him. He leans back on his heels for a moment, and just sits there, staring at me, completely naked.

He rakes a hand up through his hair and his fingers ball into a fist as he stares at me, first my pussy, then my breasts, and then at my eyes. "God, you're a work of art."

Before I can respond, his face is between my legs, and I feel his scruff rub up against the insides of my thighs. He's licking and sucking and nipping, teasing me everywhere. One of his large, rough hands roams up my stomach and he rolls my nipple between his thumb and forefinger.

My legs instinctively try to squeeze together because the sensations are almost too much to bear, but Dex places both hands on my inner thighs and spreads them apart.

He spreads my legs so hard it burns, but in a good way, like a nice deep stretch.

"I've dreamed about this pussy."

Holy shit. He has a filthy mouth.

I've never had a man say anything like that to me. It's still so surreal. Dexter Collins, in my bedroom, talking about my pussy, and I'll be damned if his dirty talk isn't on point.

He keeps teasing and licking everywhere but right where I want his mouth. It's torturous.

"Tell me you want this, Abby."

I look down and his eyes are locked on mine, his mouth inches away from me, so close I can feel his exhales brush across my skin.

"Please."

"Tell me *what* you want." He flicks his tongue across my clit, one time.

Mother of God.

My hands reach out and claw into the sheets.

The only word I can muster is, "You."

I glance down in time to see the devilish smirk on his face.

"Fingers, mouth, or both?"

I don't even know what I say in response to that. It probably sounds like groaned out gibberish. I'm coiled so damn tight and the only thing my body is focused on is the most intense sexual release of my life.

I nod furiously.

Dexter slides one finger in slowly and my back arches off the bed. He's just —intense.

"So fucking greedy, and wet."

I glance back down and he's taking his sweet time, grinning, like he knows he can make me come any second he wants to, like he's in total control.

"Give me thirty seconds and you'll be bucking these hips, fucking my hand."

Another finger slides in and I'm about to lose control. He pushes them in deep and curls his fingers somehow to hit a spot I didn't even know existed.

My whole body tenses, and I reach up for the headboard, panting out labored breaths. "I'm so close, Dex. You have no idea."

"Want me to stop?"

"I'll kill you." I stare daggers at him.

Dex snickers and his fingers speed up. Just when I think I can't handle anymore, his mouth clamps down on my clit.

"Ohhh, God. Dex…"

Every ounce of energy in my body funnels straight down between my legs. I hold back as long as I can, trying to savor this moment, lock it in my brain for a rainy day with my vibrator, because holy hell it's unlike anything I've ever experienced.

No man has ever gotten me off before.

Dex suckles my clit and does the curl thing with his fingers again, and before I know it, fuzzy stars dance behind my eyelids, and I'm doing exactly what he said I'd do. My hips are bucking against his mouth and hand, and the best damn orgasm of my life rips through my body in gigantic, undulating waves. My ass comes up off the bed, back arched, toes curling. Dex stays latched onto me, riding out the pleasure with me, his tongue relentless on my clit.

My hands fly down to his hair and I grab two handfuls so hard, I wonder if it's hurting him. "Oh God, Dexter." It's the only thing I can say.

Once my hips decide to come back down to the mattress, I feel tingly all over, like I just huffed a bunch of nitrous at the dentist office. Everything is sensitive, everywhere. Dex trails a finger across my inner thigh and goosebumps break out up and down my body.

"There's nothing better than you moaning my name while you get off." Dex leans up and kisses me full on the mouth but doesn't linger. It's like he's trying to make his escape before we both do more than we should.

I can't be bothered to do much of anything. I just want to lie here until I pass out. I feel like I just sprinted a marathon in three minutes.

How the hell did he make me come that fast? I can't even do that to myself.

Dex hops up and pulls his shirt on.

"I really had a great time tonight. Not just because of..." I trail off, already needing to yawn because he just pulled every ounce of energy from my body. Part of me feels bad. He made me feel so damn good and now he's about to bounce. I should at least give him a hand job or something, help the guy out. But I'm so damn spent, I don't know if I could, even if I wanted to.

When he walks back over, I catch a glimpse of the outline of his hard cock against his jeans. God, he's big. Of course he is. And I got him all worked up and now he's just going to leave.

When he makes it back to the side of the bed, I instinctively reach out and touch it.

His eyes roll back for a second, then come down and land on mine. He leans over and his lips brush up against mine. He nonchalantly moves my hand away. "Another time. Tonight was all about you. See you soon, Abigail."

And with that, he turns and walks right out the door.

I listen for him to leave the apartment, then kick my legs and let out a squeal that comes out of nowhere. But, damn. That was just—wow. Dexter Collins has skills. His damn tongue is magic.

I want to just pass out, but I need to get my phone and do a few things before I go to sleep. I grab my robe and wrap myself up in it. I need to take a shower, but I don't want to, because I smell like Dexter after he rubbed all up on me. I check my phone a few minutes later and I have four messages.

Kyle: Hey, where are you?
Kyle: You should come out to The Gage.
Kyle: Barbie and Nick are totally making out.
Kyle: Where the hell are you? I miss you.

I laugh about Barbie and Nick. How drunk did they get?

I should text Kyle back, but my mind is still on Dex. It just feels wrong to message Kyle right now. The worst part is it shouldn't. Ugh, I know it sounds corny as hell, but I don't get why people can't just get along.

DEXTER

I NAB Abigail as she walks outside the office. It's been exactly two days and twenty hours since I ate her pussy on her bed, not that I'm keeping track or anything. "Excuse me? You work in that big building right there?"

She looks gorgeous. I didn't talk to her Sunday and I was out of the office yesterday.

"Yeah. You better watch out. The boss is pretty cute, and he doesn't let us fraternize with strangers."

"Dating the boss, huh? Sounds like trouble."

"Something like that."

"Man, and here I was about to ask you to dinner. Doesn't look good for me."

She hems and haws for a few long seconds, staring up at the sky, pretending to think it over. "Maybe I can pencil you in. The boss had a big evening planned, though."

I slide a hand to her hip, yank her closer to me, and pin her with my gaze. "I'll show you a much better time."

Her eyelashes flutter for a split-second. "Well, I just, that's some offer. I don't know. I mean I was really looking forward to some takeout and all the Hallmark Christmas movies."

"Thought you had a big evening planned with the boss?" I clutch my hand to my heart like I'm wounded.

Abigail grins like an idiot.

I grab her hand, finally ending our little game. "Where you headed? I'll walk you."

She holds a hand out and hails a cab like it's nothing. Must be nice to be smoking hot in a city full of male cab drivers. I've never seen anyone get a cab that fast and now I'm definitely riding with her in case this asshole gets any ideas.

429

"Right here. That's my cab."

"Perfect. We'll get some drinks then go to dinner. I know a great place."

"Dex?"

"It's gonna happen, so just agree."

She grits her teeth. "You're not gonna let me leave by myself, are you?"

I shake my head slowly.

Her head cranes around and I wonder what she's looking for but don't comment. Finally, she huffs out a sigh and grins. "Fine. Come on. This food better be amazing."

"Don't ever doubt me, Whitley. You're better than that." I open the door for her.

She slides in. "Yeah, yeah. We'll see how you do on my rating scale."

"Wait, you rank your dates?" I slide in next to her, my curiosity piqued. "How does that work?" My thigh brushes up against her leg and my dick takes notice immediately.

"It's a secret."

"How am I doing so far?"

"Meh... I don't know, depends on dinner."

"We both know I'm the opposite of meh."

"Someone's full of themselves."

Someone's going to be full of me if she keeps lacing her words with innuendo. "It's not cocky if it's true."

"Oh really?"

"Yes, really." I fire off the name of the place to the driver. He better keep his eyes front and fucking center. Wells owns one of the hottest new restaurants in Chicago. He told me to stop by anytime I want, and I can't think of a better time than this.

Abigail smiles over the brim of her wine glass. She's next to me in a private booth. Wells isn't here, but that's not surprising. The hostess seemed like she knew who I was the second we walked in.

"This place is amazing." She gazes around the opulent dining room taking the scenery in. Everything is white. Except for the walls. They're a slate gray, but the tables and chairs are all white. A silver candelabra hangs over the table and there's a red rose arrangement between us with a few tealight candles. Our first date was casual, and now I'm slowly building up the romance, just like in the movies. Can't blow your load and go full-on romantic on the first date.

Of course, I have to give her the obligatory modest reaction. "It's okay."

"Are you kidding?" She grins. "Anyway, I enjoy being wined and dined, sir."

I have to stifle a groan when she calls me 'sir.' Fuck, it's hot. "What else do you enjoy?"

Her tongue peeks over her bottom lip, and I lean forward and kiss her before she can answer the question. Her cheeks bloom a soft shade of pink.

As I pull away, she sits there, momentarily stunned before her eyes open.

"I enjoyed that kiss. I like spontaneous things like that."

I lean in next to her ear. "I'll make a note." My hand slides up her leg. Personally, I'm thoroughly enjoying the way her skirt rides up her thigh.

"Dex." Her word comes out on a sigh, but she doesn't try to squirm away. In fact, it feels like she's fighting the urge to roll her hips toward my fingers.

My mouth remains next to her ear, and I exhale warm breath down her neck when I speak. "I could fucking devour you right here on this table."

Goosebumps pebble down her arms and I feel them along the bare skin of her leg. "You're making things very hard for me."

"That's my line, Abby."

"You're driving me..."

My hand roams farther up her leg, until I'm inches from her panties.

"Insane," she finally huffs the last word out on a labored breath. "And nervous." Her eyes dart around the room, then roll back when I slide my hand a little farther up to where she wants it.

I lean in closer, close enough I could easily brush her blonde curls away and kiss that spot halfway between her ear and collar bone. "Good." I graze her earlobe with my teeth.

A shiver runs through her entire body and she tenses for a brief moment. "Someone could see," she whispers. She paws at my hand but it's a half-assed attempt at best.

We both know what she wants and where she wants it.

I grin against her neck. "Let them see."

"Dex." She pushes against my hand again.

I start to pull it away and she grips me with her fingers, keeping it right where it was.

That's what I thought, Abigail.

"Can I ask you something?"

"No. I'm afraid of what I'll say with your hand right there."

I smirk and continue my line of inquiry. "Have you seen anyone come near us? Since they dropped off the wine?"

Abigail shakes her head.

"There's a reason for that." I hook a finger in her panties and slide them to the side, exposing her pussy under the table.

"Oh my God." Her breasts rise and fall in her top with each of her deep breaths.

I love every second of how bad she wants this, how much she's trying to fight it, but she just can't. She wants me just as bad as I want her. It takes an act of sheer willpower and determination not to bend her over this table, eat her pussy until she moans my name on repeat, and then fuck her so hard she can't stand up straight.

I slide one finger across her clit, and she lets out a light gasp. "Still want me to stop?" Her pussy is so hot and wet I can feel it on my hand. I rake my gaze up and down her face and body, taking in every single reaction, every bit of data I can gather for future use.

"No." The word comes out on a whisper.

"Didn't think so." I know exactly how to make her come all over my hand without causing a scene. It has to be a gradual ascent, like a good symphony. Start slow, then build to the climax. Unlike last time when I just had to prove I could get her off anytime I damn well pleased. I continue to work her, rubbing lazy circles over her clit. It's only a matter of time before she claws at the linen tablecloth.

Her lips part ever so slightly, and I don't need a better invitation.

It's time.

I slant my mouth over her cherry-red lips and push two fingers inside her sweet, hot pussy. Fucking hell, she's soaked, and my dick rages against my slacks, jealous of my fingers.

Pure, untamed sexual energy courses through her body. I can feel it up against me, feel it in my fingers, in the air around us. She's so damn close, but she's holding back, most likely because we're in public.

I press my forehead against hers, so that we're eye to eye. And fuck if I couldn't get lost in her eyes. They're so innocent and helpless as she stares at me, completely vulnerable in the moment. It's a stare that says, *I want to give myself to you, but please don't hurt me.*

Right then, something stirs deep inside me, and it's not even one-hundred percent sexual. It's just a deeper connection, on a molecular level, a force that can't be described, pulling me closer to her soul.

"Just let go, Abby. You can trust me."

I take two fingers deep and curl them inside her, hitting that deep spot nobody else knows about. At the same time, my thumb strokes over her clit.

Her eyes lock on mine, inches apart, for another brief second. It's like I'm having an entire conversation with her and no words are being spoken. Then, all at once, her hips rise and her hand grips my forearm.

Her pussy clenches and a tremor rips through her body. I move my other hand over her mouth to stifle her moans, our foreheads still pressed together. Her eyes roll back into her head and I ride out the waves from her orgasm.

After one last, quick shudder, I move my hand from her mouth and kiss her full on the lips.

Her whole body relaxes so much, I almost think I need to hold her up, so she doesn't just slide down the booth and onto the floor.

She looks completely sated, just relaxed. Almost like she's in another world right now.

"That was..."

I slide my hand out of her gently and adjust her panties back. "Just the beginning."

"You're dangerous," she whispers, her eyes still half-hooded.

I lean in next to her again. "You're right..." I look her up and down and pretend to adjust a non-existent flight suit. "Abby, I *am* dangerous."

She comes out of her orgasm coma and laughs. "You're not a bad Maverick. Actually, you're better because you have the height to go with the cocky attitude."

"That's what I like to hear."

"Gonna take me to bed or lose me forever?"

"Hell. Yes."

I almost don't even want to bother with dinner, but I hate to come here and not take advantage. I'm pretty sure Abigail is starving too. I know how long the days can be at the office.

The rest of dinner goes perfectly, just like our first date. We slip in and out of easy conversations like two people who have known each other our whole lives. Right before we leave, she leans over and blows out one of the little candles on the table. Just one.

After dinner, when we get back to her place, I escort her to the door of her apartment. It almost feels like a glitch in the *Matrix* because I just did this a few days ago.

I know she was just quoting *Top Gun* back at the restaurant, and it's too soon, but words can't express how bad my cock wants to know what it feels like to be inside her. It feels right, and if she wants to fuck, I'm not going to say no, but something about this whole thing with her... I don't know. I just want every moment to be special—memorable. I want us to have a highlight reel of memories, including the first time we have sex. This feels like a normal weekday night after a nice dinner.

Abigail presses a palm to my chest when we get to her door. "I would invite you in, but my roommate is home and she's not great company."

I don't want the night to end, but I don't let it show. I might not want to fuck her right now, but I could still eat her pussy and make out with her until the sun comes up. Or just sit around and talk. I just want to be near her.

"Maybe you should come see my place sometime."

She nods. "I wouldn't mind that. I had a good time tonight, Dex." Abigail leans forward and kisses me then pulls back. "In case you chicken out like you did last time."

I nod, smiling. "Oh, it's like that?"

She laughs. "Yep. It's like that, Collins."

I yank her harder into me, digging my fingers into her hips. "Be mindful of your provocations. I fulfill all verbal contracts."

She hooks both arms around my neck. "Why is it so hot when you talk like a fancy lawyer?"

I kiss down her neck. "Why is it so hot when you come all over my hand in a restaurant?"

Her cheeks go pink. "Dexter Collins, my mom would wash your dirty mouth out with soap."

I grin back at her. She's something else, I've never met anyone like her. "I had a great time tonight too, Abby."

"Likewise, sir." She pulls me into her for another kiss, then leans to my ear. "Yeah, I know you like it when I call you that."

I back her up against the door and press into her, my knee separating her legs in her skirt. I kiss down the side of her neck. "You have no idea, Abby."

"I might have an idea."

"Is that so?"

She nods seductively.

"What was that all about back at the restaurant?" I say.

"What?"

"When you blew out the candle. You had your eyes closed."

"It's nothing. It's dumb."

I brush some hair behind her ear. "Tell me. I want to know, even if you think it's dumb."

Her lips curl up into a smile. "I like to blow out candles and make a wish, even when it's not my birthday."

"What'd you wish for?"

She shakes her head. "I can't tell you or it won't come true."

I kiss her on the forehead. "Okay." Then I work my way down, peppering kisses on her cheek and then her neck. She presses her chest into me when I hit the spot halfway between her ear and collar bone.

Always leave them wanting.

I slide my hand up her skirt once more, through her panties, and graze her clit. She's as wet as she was at the restaurant.

Abigail's head looks back and forth in the hall, like she's checking to make sure nobody is going to walk up on us. I slide my fingers through her slick folds, just enough to give her a little tease, then pull my hand out and back away from her.

"A little taste to remember you by until we do this again." I slide both fingers in my mouth and it immediately brings back the memory of going down on her two days and twenty-two hours ago. "Night, Abby."

Then, I walk off.

DEXTER

THINGS HAVE BEEN phenomenal the last few weeks with Abigail.

Except at work. It's driving me nuts. It's like she changes into a different person at the office.

We still haven't had sex. Just more fooling around and light petting, nothing major. She's holding back and taking things so damn slow my balls might shrivel up, but I don't mind.

I mean, I like her. I like her a lot.

She makes me smile and I think about her nonstop. Don't get me wrong, there's nothing I want more than to fuck her, over and over.

But, the timing hasn't been right. I'll wait as long as she wants me to. I want it to be perfect when we finally take that step.

Something just feels, off when we're at work. We don't have that rhythm, you know? That natural melody that carries us along and makes conversations and actions effortless.

I'm on my way back from court when I spot her by herself in the breakroom. My gaze immediately goes to her ass in the black skirt hugging her hips. How does she look so fucking hot every single day of the year? She's wearing black stilettos with animal print on them. My mind immediately imagines her in nothing but those, legs spread on my desk, heels digging into my ass while I'm balls-deep in her.

"You eating my pudding, knowing my mom sends them to me?" I sneak up behind her, wrap an arm around her waist, and move in for a kiss.

The moment my lips graze hers, she yanks away, like she's on fire or something. It's harsh. Super harsh.

I take a step back and narrow my gaze on hers. "The hell is that all about?"

Her eyes dart around. "You can't be doing that here."

I frown. "What? Why? You ashamed of me?"

She glances around like someone might be watching us and lowers her voice. "Of course not. Why would you say that?" She wraps her arms around her waist and hugs herself, like she's putting up some kind of wall I can't break through.

"You're pulling away and looking around like someone might see. You don't want me to meet your roommate. You seeing someone else?"

She shakes her head like I'm an idiot or something. "It's nothing like that. Calm down. I'm just not a fan of public affection."

"Didn't mind in the restaurant."

She whisper-screams, "I don't *work* in that restaurant. I don't want people to think differently of me."

I take a step toward her, and she takes a step back. "People are going to find out about us."

Her eyes narrow into slits, and I can't believe she's actually upset about this. I don't get her. We're great together. She wants me. It's obvious, and I feel the exact same way.

She moves to go around me.

Get your goddamn house in order, Dexter. This is ridiculous. You can land 10-figure clients but can't handle a twenty-four-year-old paralegal?

As she walks by, she stops, and her voice softens. "I want to talk about this with you, just not here at the office. Is that okay?"

"Sure. Whatever."

I immediately feel like a dickhead, but fuck that. What if I want to talk about it here? Does she think I just want to mess around and have a middle school romance with her? We sneak off and fool around under the bleachers and then move on when we go to separate high schools? I'm not messing around with her. I want her, and I'm not putting on an act while I'm at work.

I'm not going to walk around and pretend everything is platonic, then as soon as we leave the office where nobody can see she gets to turn into a new person and fuck my mouth and my fingers. That's not how this works. People need to know she's off limits, at least the men around here do.

She frowns, almost looks hurt.

I don't think I have any reason to feel bad, but I do. I don't like it when she's upset. What the hell is wrong with me? Shit.

She starts to walk off, and I narrow my eyes on her. "Hey, Abby." I reach down and grip her forearm, stopping her in her tracks.

Her gaze tilts up to meet mine. "Yeah?"

"This thing here." I motion back and forth between us. "It's real. You can pretend all you want, for now, but you're not fooling anybody. You're mine."

"You're ridiculous." She scowls and stomps off.

I don't even try to hide my amusement. She can be as stubborn as she wants, it only makes my dick harder.

When she turns the corner, I catch her profile, and she's glaring even harder.

Fuck, she makes me crazy.

Now I want to go after her and kiss the shit out of her in front of the whole goddamn office.

Just to show her I can, and I will.

ABIGAIL

Ugh!

How is Dexter so cute and annoying at the same time?

He looks so hot in his three-piece suit today, and I have to remind myself it's no excuse for him to act like a damn caveman.

Cornering me in the breakroom and trying to make out with me? What's that all about?

I honestly don't know what I'm more upset about—the fact he damn near groped me at work—or the fact that deep down I really liked it. What the hell is wrong with me? It was so inappropriate and yet I wanted to lean into him, kiss him back.

I shake my head at my ridiculous thoughts. I go out of my way to avoid office drama and politics. The Chicago firm is just as bad as Dallas.

What I do on my own time is my business, and if people want to speculate about that, whatever. But I *will* be professional at all times at work.

People still talk about Quinn and Deacon banging like rabbits in the supply room.

It's not that I don't want Dex. We have great chemistry, and yeah, I feel something there, but I'm not ready to settle down and get serious. I'm just not. I'm too young. He needs to slow down.

Dexter is amazing but the way he spoke to me in the breakroom, it's like he thinks I'm his property.

If I'm honest with myself, though—it's hot. It makes me want him even more.

I have to wonder if I'm actually irritated, or if my brain is just being a dick and telling me I *should* be irritated, and that's what's wrong. I'm so confused about this whole situation.

Dex makes me feel so damn safe around him, and I don't want to want a man to make me feel safe, if that makes any sense?

Gah, I'm so confused right now.

He has me spinning a thousand different directions, like a tornado blowing through my life and scattering things everywhere.

He needs to get it through his thick head that I don't belong to him before this gets even more out of control. I can already see this all playing out. I fall head over heels, he continues this behavior until I'm afraid to even talk to another man without him being petty and jealous. It all culminates with him breaking my heart and judging by the way I already feel when I'm around him, it will take a long time to get over it.

I'm in a really good place right now. Well, other than needing to get a *place* of my own, but still. Professionally, I'm killing it. Decker hands me important projects and puts his full trust in me. Multiple partners praise me for doing a good job all the time. It's the one place in the world where I have everything in order.

I've made a life for myself here. I feel wanted and respected. I have friends.

Some of them are guy friends and ugh, Dexter has a serious problem with that, I can already tell. I'm not going to ditch my friends and be a jerk because Dexter doesn't approve.

I've been blowing Kyle off ever since Dex and I started this up, dodging him in the hall of my building like a chicken shit. All because him and Dex don't get along. That's not like me. It's not who I am. Even Barbie asked me what crawled up my ass the other day. For her to take notice of something I'm doing means it must be obvious as hell because she lives in her own little Barbie world every minute of the day.

I pull out my phone and scroll through all the texts I've been avoiding.

Kyle: Hey, just got off work. Wanna split a pizza?

Kyle: Drinks after work, you in?

Kyle: Where are you? I knocked earlier. Nick got Chinese if you want to come over.

Right when I'm about to type out a reply, Rick Lawrence knocks on the edge of my desk. He has that same mischievous smirk across his smug face as always. He's such an asshole, and I have to refrain from taking all my frustrations out on him.

What the hell?

He's wearing rosary beads around his neck.

Can the day get any weirder?

"Got a minute?"

I shake my head. "Not really."

"Great." He cranes his head around, looking at the other paralegals. "You seen Mary?"

I fidget with some files, pretending like I'm reading them and about to get up and leave, hoping he'll take the hint and go away. "Did you try her desk?"

"Yeah. Even checked under mine but she wasn't there, where she belongs."

What is it with the male egos in this place?

He stands there, staring at me, like this is an everyday conversation and he's done nothing wrong.

I sigh, because he won't leave. "Haven't seen her. Did you need something, *Rick*?" I think about calling him "Dick" instead, but he'd wear it as a badge of honor and stick around and make it even more awkward. Or actually comment on his dick and send me sprinting to HR.

He leans in toward me.

I immediately lean back because I don't want him near me, and part of me knows Dex might come out of nowhere with a Macho Man elbow drop if he sees another man in my vicinity.

Rick's voice lowers. "Got new info on that secret shit for you and Decker. How would you like to proceed?"

"Can you email it to me?"

"Will do." He takes one final glance around the paralegal bullpen. "You see Mary around, you tell her Rick says hey."

I roll my eyes. "Will do." I'd agree to just about anything to get him out of here.

"Peace be with you, sister." He grins his ass off and kisses the cross hanging around his neck, then makes a cross with his finger over his chest. As he's walking away, he hollers over his shoulder, "You both love your mothers. He loves Christmas too. Stop fighting it. You have a lot in common."

What. The. Hell.

He never turns around, just disappears through one of the side doors.

I swear to God he's a damn soothsayer. If he warns me about the Ides of March, I'm finding a bunker, removing every sharp object, and locking myself in it. Finally, I shake my head and finish typing out my text.

Me: Sorry about the last few weeks. I've been super busy with work and just life. Wanna meet up for drinks later?

Kyle: Wrong number.

The bubbles immediately start bouncing around before I can type out something snarky.

Kyle: Kidding. Drinks sound good. We need to catch up. The Gage tonight?

I lean back in my chair, already worried that it's a bad idea. Dex goes there sometimes. Hell, it's where everyone from work always hangs out.

I shake my head at myself. I can have friends. I shouldn't have to sit here and stew about this. I never had to before. I'm an independent woman and I can do whatever the hell I want. Dex doesn't own me. Worrying about his fragile ego is not my concern.

Kyle's my friend. Nothing more. He's never given me a reason to think he wants anything more than friendship and I'm not going to shit all over him because Dexter doesn't like him.

If he would stop acting like a Neanderthal around him, I think they'd actually get along.

Me: Does 7 work?
Kyle: See you there.

"Do I KNOW YOU?" Kyle grins when I walk up to the bar.

"Stop. I said I was sorry. I was busy with work and Barbie has been nuts since the whole Chuck thing." Most of that is true, but I still feel bad, knowing the reason I haven't been around is because of Dexter.

"You get a pass this one time." He grins at me. "Nick has a table already. I ordered you a shot."

"Awesome, thanks."

The bartender walks over and hands us the drinks.

I take the shot and knock it back. It tastes like heaven after the day I've had.

Kyle loops his arm through mine as we head toward the table. It's Friday night and everyone is ready to unwind after a long week it seems. The place is packed.

"Hey," I say to Nick as I sit down.

"Hey, stranger." Nick gives me a head nod. "Tell me you didn't invite Barbie."

"Actually, she's on her way. I told her I was meeting up with Kyle and you'd be here all alone. Hope you don't mind. She said she thinks you're the one." I give him a smirk as his face pales. "Feeling okay? You don't look so hot."

He glances to the door, looking for Barbie, then shakes his head. "Please tell me you're joking."

I finally can't contain myself and burst into a laugh. Kyle follows suit.

"I hate all of you." Nick takes a huge swig of beer and fights back a grin.

"Okay, yeah, I'm joking, but I do need all the details of you making out with her."

Kyle laughs. "Oh, man, we missed you. We were starting to think your boyfriend had you chained up somewhere."

What the hell? "Boyfriend?"

Kyle sighs. "Dude, the real reason you haven't been hanging out with us. We're not dumb. We know you've been seeing that douche in a suit."

I shake my head. "I never said you were dumb, I just don't have a boyfriend. And he's not a douche."

Nick jumps in. "Oh come on, Abby, we saw you making out with him in the hallway. Thought Kyle was going to cry himself to sleep because you've been ignoring him."

I take a drink of the beer Kyle brought over, then wave a hand out at both of them. "Oh what the hell ever, you guys. Stop trying to change the subject. We were talking about your make out session with Barbie, not mine, and I would hardly call a kiss making out."

Kyle doesn't seem fazed one bit by my attempt to deflect. "So, you guys getting serious?"

Ugh, what is their deal? They're acting like a bunch of girls. I came here to escape thinking about Dexter.

"Look, no offense, but I don't want to talk about him. I want to hear about Nick getting hammered and making out with the ice queen. I'll buy a round of shots for details."

"Deal." They both say at the same time.

"The sacrifices I make for inebriation," says Nick.

"Oh, poor baby." I fake-pout my lips and reach across the table to ruffle his hair.

"You owe me two shots for reliving the torture."

I crack up laughing. "Was it that painful?"

"It was pretty crazy." Kyle straightens up in his chair like he's getting ready for story time.

"Enough, please." Nick shoots me a pleading look. "I'll tell you everything, for shots, of course. But it really wasn't as bad as Kyle makes it out to be."

Kyle stares at him. "Dude."

"Okay, fine." He turns to me. "So, first off, I was crazy hammered. Like, beyond-all-rational-thought drunk."

I nod. "Duly noted."

He looks up toward the corner of the ceiling, searching for the right words. "You know when you had to watch those nature videos in science class, and they show like a boa constrictor swallowing a rat?"

I can barely contain the laughter building in my chest and roll my hand forward like *continue.*

"Kissing her was how I always envisioned that rat's point of view, like what he would see right before the snake swallowed him."

"Keep going," says Kyle.

"Yeah, so we were in a cab when it happened, and the worst part is…"

"Wait for it." Kyle nudges me, already about to die.

"Well, like, right after we, umm, parted ways, so to speak, she gets this look on her face, like, I don't know how to describe it, but she tilts her head down and projectile vomits all over my chest, right there in the cab."

"Ewwww!" I squeal.

Kyle bursts into laughter. He's so loud everyone in the bar turns to look at us.

"You were right, I didn't need details. Can we please never discuss this again?" I can't imagine how mortified Barbie must've been. I mean, I feel bad for Nick and everything, but damn.

"I'm quite all right with that arrangement." Nick bumps fists with me.

I shake my head, trying to rid myself of the thought of that cab ride. "All right. I'll order shots. What do you guys want?"

"Tequila," they both say at the same time.

Uh oh. This could be a long night and a morning headache. I take a deep breath. "Okay, let's do it."

443

DEXTER

I PULL up to the entrance at Covington's mansion that sits right on Lake Michigan. He bought the land last year, but I haven't been over since he built everything. The black wrought-iron gates have a solid-gold WC right in the middle, and I'm almost positive it's twenty-four karat.

I laugh to myself. How gaudy can this motherfucker get? It's hilarious because I know he's self-aware and does this shit just for that reason.

The man is a troll one-hundred percent of the time, only he buys companies just to fuck with people and piss them off. I guess when you have "fuck you" money, you can do those types of things. The security camera zooms in on my face as I roll my driver's side window down. I press the intercom button and wait.

"Can I help you, sir?"

I'm still laughing, barely able to get the words out. "Tell Covington to open this monstrosity."

The man doesn't show one hint of irritation. He sounds British too. Of course he does. "One moment, sir."

What the hell? I shake my head and can't quit snickering.

The gates part and I drive up, snaking around a few hills, not believing my eyes. I knew this bastard was loaded but holy hell. When I finally reach the main drive, the house is massive. The front is a mix between brick and rock with floor-to-ceiling windows between that look like they're three stories high. I don't even want to know how he had those fuckers hauled in here. Okay, maybe I do want to know.

I bet he rides around on a Segway with a little helmet barking orders at people.

Decker is out of his fucking mind if he doesn't want this guy for a client. I don't give a shit what kind of kinks he's into. Bet he has a damn sex room ten times bigger than the one in that *Fifty Shades* movie. Yeah, I watched it to get laid. I've made worse sacrifices and Dakota Johnson is hot.

Anyway, what Wells does is none of my business, but I'd be curious to see a giant torture fuck chamber. Who wouldn't want to sneak a peek at that?

I snake around to the side and there's a damn helicopter landing pad. I pass by the eighteenth green of his golf course that's on the property. This guy has it all.

I pull up to the roundabout that circles the front entrance and park Betsy.

The front door swings open.

I exit the car and tuck some confidentiality paperwork he asked me to bring under my arm. Covington has a rocks glass in one hand and a cigar in the other. The British butler guy follows him, but he waves him off.

"You like?" He holds his hands out, barely keeping a straight face while he asks the question.

He's in a black silk robe, and all he needs is a few blondes with fake tits on his arm and he'd put Hugh Hefner to shame.

"It's gaudy as fuck and you look ridiculous."

"Good, that means I'm winning at life." He bursts into a laugh. "Fucking Collins, the straightest shooter I know. You're as honest as they come, and that makes you a great friend." He glances over at some lights right off the lake. "Building this pissed off everyone in a two mile radius. It was glorious. Should've seen all the petitions filed."

I shake his hand and he pulls me in close and leans down to my ear.

"From overhead, the house looks like a giant cock and the landscaping is a giant middle finger to anyone flying overhead."

"You'll always be a ten-year-old boy at heart."

"Pissing off people with opulence and some nice pussy are the two things that do it for me. No point in having money if you can't enjoy yourself."

I follow him up to the door. "Indeed."

The front entrance opens into a large foyer with twin staircases that spiral up both sides of the room to the upper level. We pass through a breezeway underneath the staircase. The hall splits three ways and we go to the left to his den. Rich brown couches and a ton of leather-bound first editions throw off a historic vibe. You'd think they'd all be for show, but underneath the shit-eating grins and practical jokes, Covington is a genius. He's a shark and I know for a fact he's read every book in this room, and more than that, understood what the hell he was reading. He's the kind of guy who does keg stands while quoting *Wealth of Nations* and arguing the merits of supply-side economics.

"You like cigars?"

"I don't turn them down."

"Come on." He takes a puff and pats me on the back.

We pass into an anteroom that's a giant humidor. There's a huge display on the wall showing humidity levels and temperatures.

"You've never had one like this before."

"Oh yeah? Why's that?"

"They were a gift."

"From who?"

"Raul Castro."

I raise a brow. "No shit?"

He shrugs like it's nothing. "Had some business in Cuba."

I don't even want to know. I laugh and shake my head. Dude is whack and eccentric as fuck. Of course he only smokes the best cigars in the world.

He punches in a code and pulls a cigar from a drawer, then shuts it and an electronic bolt retracts into place.

He pushes two more doors open and it leads into what I can only describe as the most elegant sports bar in the world. There are flat-screen televisions everywhere, and a giant screen with a projector on one side. They're all tuned to sports, C-Span, and stock market channels.

"I do my best thinking in here, come on." He motions me over to a long bar with a marble top that runs along one side of the room.

I take a seat on a leather barstool.

He opens a box and pulls out a bottle of fifty-year Glenfiddich like it's no big deal. I accept a rocks glass with it poured neat and take a sniff. You can't just throw back a twenty-five-thousand-dollar bottle of scotch, though Covington probably goes through one a week.

He takes his time cutting the end of the cigar and hands it over. "Can't drink that swill you're used to with this cigar. This shit is an experience."

I lift my chin and take a sip. It's fantastic. I can taste notes of vanilla and toffee. I don't know if it's worth twenty-five grand, but fuck it, I'm not buying.

"It's orgasmic, right? Now for the cigar." He pulls out a lighter that looks like a small welding torch.

I decide fuck it, I trust him. I puff as he holds the blue flame to the end.

As soon as I taste the smoke and take a few more puffs I immediately relax.

Look, I'm a man who has a lot of money, an important job—I'm happy. But right now, I feel like a fucking titan, like a peasant made into a king for the day. Covington operates on an entirely different level of wealth than my family does.

We bullshit a bit more and he takes me on a tour of the bottom floor. I keep bracing myself for it, almost a little excited, but there's no sex dungeon in sight, yet. I find myself a little disappointed, but I'm not going to ask him to fucking see it. There's an indoor pool, a bowling alley, two movie theaters, and a gym that would make Cole Miller's dick harder than a diamond in a hailstorm.

Covington pauses randomly, in the middle of a normal hallway. "Did you sign the paperwork?"

"Of course." I pull out the accordion folder I've been toting around.

"Let me see it."

I pull out the non-disclosure shit and hand it over.

Covington looks relaxed, but his eyes work the pages over, a million calculations running through his brain. Finally, he hands it back. "Okay, so look, Collins, I like you. We'll start with a trial run. I'll hand over a few of my newer entities, still nothing to balk at for someone like you. They require quite a bit of start-up administration-type work, instead of usual legal maintenance, so it should net some decent billable hours for your firm. They're a healthy mix of different industries. The rest will remain in care of Cooper and Associates, but that's a temporary situation for now. You outperform, you get the rest."

I know I secretly hoped he'd want to shift everything over but that's a pipe dream. If I was him, I'd do the exact same thing, throw me a wide range of entities and make sure I nailed each one. This is a test; one I will not fail. "No problem. I don't mind kicking a little ass to prove myself."

"That's what I like to hear. Let's go celebrate. You're driving."

Oh shit. Tomorrow is going to be a long-ass day.

Fuck it.

"Let's do it."

I hang out for a bit and Wells gets dressed. He's gone for roughly five minutes and comes back looking like he just stepped out of a GQ spread.

It makes me wonder if he has a personal stylist back there on call to get him ready at a moment's notice.

The two of us walk outside and Wells has to fold himself into the Chevelle. The fucker is like six-four and he's not a twig.

He definitely looks intrigued by the car. "Nice. I like it."

"Restored her myself. Took five years."

"No shit? Why so long?"

"Some of us work for a living, asshole."

He laughs. "I know. Being me is pretty awesome."

I nod. "Pompous motherfucker."

"Always. You ever do any racing?"

"Nah, not since my college days. Got busted and ticketed. Parents were pissed."

Wells nods. "Yeah, that happens when you get caught." He grins and turns to face me. "I never learned my lesson."

This fucking guy. Just when I think he can't get any more arrogant, he outdoes himself.

"We'll go sometime. Friend of mine owns a few stock cars for Nascar and has a private track. You could bring this beauty out there if you want. Open her up a little."

"Sounds awesome."

"What's under the hood?"

"All original, four-fifty-four."

"She purrs like a kitten."

"Damn right she does. Her name is Betsy." I pat the dashboard lovingly.

Wells nods. "Nice to meet you, Betsy. Hopefully, this won't be our last encounter."

We blast off into the night and forty minutes later arrive at The Gage and head straight to the bar. I hadn't planned on coming out at all tonight. I was hoping to convince Abigail to come over to my place for a movie. After the way we left things at the office, I want to make it up to her. I was kind of a dick, but I'm tired of all her mixed signals. Wells called and I couldn't pass up the opportunity to sneak in and meet with him earlier than expected. She didn't act like she'd be up for anything anyway. Maybe it's for the better. Let shit cool down a little.

I lean on the bar while Covington orders a few drinks.

I glance around and quickly jerk my head back.

What the fucking fuck?

Abigail is at a table with those two friends of hers. She's slouched in her seat a little and laughing like an idiot. Her eyes are all glossed over and judging by her mannerisms and the wild way she flings her hands around, she's wasted.

"Gotta be fucking kidding me," I growl. My face heats a million degrees with every second I see her there.

Wells leans over, clearly intrigued. "Ahh, the girl from the club. The one you're falling for."

I whip around to Wells. "I'm not..." I see it in his eyes and can't even finish my sentence.

He knows. Fuck, the whole world probably knows, but Wells *definitely* knows. The fucker can read any situation, probably knew it that night at the bar.

"We've been dating." I pound my drink and set my glass down a little harder than needed.

Wells seems amused, like he's just waiting for something to happen. Like he *wants* something interesting to happen. It's how he is. "Does she know that?"

I fire off a glare in his direction.

It only makes my blood run hotter. Is he testing me? Seeing how far I'll go to defend something important to me? Is it a metaphor for his companies?

He glances over at the table and snickers again, shaking his head. "Christ, Collins. I don't know how to offer you any counsel. My experience doesn't extend to this type of situation. My women don't pull stunts like this." He leans in closer. "What are you going to do about it?"

Just as he says it, Abigail dies laughing and reaches over for Kyle. Her hand drags down his forearm and my hands ball into fists.

"Fuck this shit."

"Atta boy." He leans back, highly interested, as I shove off from the bar.

I glare back at him, scowling. "You can shut the fuck up too."

It only makes him grin wider.

I storm over to Abigail's table.

Lifting her head up, Abigail meets my gaze. "Heyyyy, Dex!" She lets out a giggle and slurs the shit out of her words. She turns to her dumb fucking friends. "You remember Kyle." Her arm shoots out and she nearly falls off her damn chair.

I grab her arm to steady her, then lift her up so she's standing.

Kyle starts to get up and say something.

I wheel around on him. "Fuckin' do something, kid."

He sits back down but glares at me. I glance over and his buddy's eyes are two giant white orbs.

"Sex-Dexter, you need to stop!" Abigail slurs her words again and smacks at my hand.

How can she be this fucking irresponsible? Usually she's the more mature one out of the two of us. I have to remind myself she's only twenty-four.

"I'm taking you home. Grab your shit, let's go."

"No you're not." She points a finger in my face. "You're not my boss." She waves the finger around, trying to finish her thought. "Here, anyway. I'm my own boss. I do what I want when I want. You don't own me, asshole."

I now understand why Decker is always getting migraines dealing with our childish shit all the time. I point to the door. "Go to the car, now!" I bark the words at her.

"Fuck you!" She yanks her arm away from me and moves toward the bar.

"What the hell is your problem, man?" The other guy stands up this time. He must've sat there and worked up some courage.

"You better sit the fuck down, piss pot." I take a step in his direction. "Try something and I'll put you through that goddamn window." I turn and point right at Kyle. "My *problem* is *him*."

Kyle shrugs and leans back, trying to look cool. "She said you guys aren't together, man."

He's pretending to not look scared, but he's practically quaking in his fucking Dockers and Bugs Bunny shit. Who the fuck dresses this ass basket? His mother?

I lean down and get right in his face. "You listen to me and listen good."

He starts to say something, and I grip the collar of his shirt, just hard enough to choke him a little. I really need to calm the fuck down, but I've had it with this piece of shit. I already know he'll play the victim to Abigail after this, but I don't give a fuck.

"I know the fucking game you're running, and it ends tonight. You pretend to be her friend when we both know what you're really up to. You play the nice neighbor and listen to her problems, but all you're doing is waiting for her to get so drunk she touches that little toddler dick of yours just one time."

His eyes move to the ground, then he glares back up at me. It tells me everything I need to know.

I let go of his shirt and he gasps for air. I point in his face. "Stay the fuck away from her or the only way you'll get laid is up in a goddamn hospital bed."

His buddy steps over and gets in my face. "How about you go fuck yourself. You think you're better than us in your expensive suit acting all tough? Maybe she likes the attention, and did you ever think maybe she wants one of us to take her home and fuck her? She was pretty flirty before you got here. Yeah, really slutty. I wouldn't be surprised if she wants both of us to take her home and…"

I don't hear the rest of his sentence because everything sort of fades off for a second. So much rage consumes me all I see is red and hear people scream and yell.

450

I ram my forehead straight into his nose and hear the sound of bone crunching against me. Blood spurts down his face.

His voice goes up about four octaves and I'm pretty sure he's crying, but it's hard to tell with the blood running down his mouth. He clutches both palms over his nose. "Oww! What the fuck, man?"

Kyle's eyes go big and he stares up at me. His hands tremble on the table.

Good.

I glare right at him. Fuck it, I already broke his buddy's nose, I'd better squeeze every ounce of intimidation I can out of the moment. "How about you? You want to try to fuck my girl too?"

He shakes his head back and forth so hard I worry he might injure his neck. "Sh-she's all y-yours."

"What I fucking thought."

ABIGAIL

I DON'T KNOW what the hell just happened, but my blood is boiling so hot I can't see straight. You ever get so damn angry because other people are acting like idiots that it sobers you up instantly?

Suddenly, my thoughts are clear as day and none of them are good.

What the hell is Dexter's problem? Oh yeah, he has caveman syndrome. He thinks I'm his property.

To hell with men!

I'm going to have to find a new job. I should've known better than to get involved with someone at work, let alone a damn partner.

Just as I step outside, the cold air socks me in the face, sobering me up even more. People start shouting inside and there are screams.

Oh my God, what just happened? I start back for the door just as Dexter walks out.

His hands are balled up in fists and a vein bulges on the side of his neck. His friend is practically bouncing on the balls of his feet behind him, like he's all amped up on adrenaline.

I immediately recognize the guy from his social media pages when I was doing research for Decker. It's Wells Covington. What the hell does Decker have me doing?

I don't know if I should say something to Dexter about it. Decker was very explicit in his instructions—although now he's on my shit list too, for putting me in this situation. I finally decide it's best to keep my mouth shut; I'm not losing my job to go along with this shit storm of an evening.

Wells follows behind Dex and smirks at me. They stop for a moment and Wells talks loud enough for both of us to hear.

"Thanks for the fun. I'll find my own way home so you can tend to your situation over there." He nods directly at me and heat rushes into my face.

I shoot him a scowl I thought only Dexter could deserve tonight. What an asshole.

My nostrils flare and my nails dig into my palms. "Oh, so I'm a *situation*, Dexter?" I throw my hands up and try to ignore the people now gathering around us on the sidewalk to take in the rest of the show. I spin around and yell at all of them, "What are you looking at? Mind your freaking business!"

"Get in the damn car!"

I start to protest, just because I'm sick of him telling me what to do, until I see the harsh lines on his face. His eyes narrow into two dark, cold slits.

Dexter is being a complete buzz kill.

Yes, I drank more than I should have, but he's not my father. I can drink if I want to. I don't have to work tomorrow.

I stomp over and get in the Chevelle, just to get away from all the people on the sidewalk. It's so damn embarrassing. I lie my head back on the vinyl seat. More and more people are walking out of the bar and staring around.

Why the hell was he so upset? Okay, yeah, I was drunk, but it's a damn bar and I was with my friends. People from work get hammered there all the time. I've gotten drunk with Dexter on more than one occasion, including the time we made out in front of the Chicago Bears.

But if there's one thing I do know, it's this: I don't like Dexter being mad at me.

As much as I know I didn't do anything wrong, clearly, I did in his mind. My stomach sours at the thought I made him so mad he acted like that. I refuse to take the blame for his bullshit but all I want for now is to get him to calm down. I do know I never want to show my face in The Gage again. It's completely humiliating. I throw my hands up. And of course that's exactly what he wants to happen. He'll be getting his way if I don't go back there, or go out drinking.

Oh God, and there's Kyle.

He already hated Dexter. Did Dex punch him? From the sounds of all the hollering, I wouldn't be surprised. Do I have to choose one of them over the other? Why is Dexter putting me in this position? It's not right.

We need to get on the same page and fast. This type of thing cannot happen.

Dexter parts ways with Wells Covington and walks over.

He opens the door and slides into the driver's side. "Buckle your seatbelt." It's a command, not a request.

I grind my teeth together. "Stop telling me what to do."

"Stop acting like an idiot."

My pulse is running a two-minute mile and I'm about to snap. I whip my head over to him. "You're the one telling me obvious shit, like to buckle my seatbelt."

He starts the car and takes off so fast the tires squeal on the pavement. "I'm sorry for being concerned about your safety."

"You're insecure and concerned about your ego. Those are your only concerns."

He snickers, but the vein on his neck is still bulging and I can hear him breathing heavily. He zooms in and out of cars, his fingers white-knuckling the steering wheel. Classic rock filters through the speakers.

I've never dealt with this type of situation, outside of seeing it in movies and reading about it in books. I've never been in a serious relationship and Dexter is definitely giving off jealous boyfriend vibes. Does he think he's my boyfriend? We've never discussed that. What the hell makes him think he can tell me what to do?

For some reason, everything just filters up to the surface at once and smacks me in the face. Every emotion in the damn book. Shame, embarrassment, anger, hurt. "Take me home." I growl the words at him, as harsh as I can.

A tingling feeling spreads across the bridge of my nose. Tears threaten to fall, burning in the creases of my eyes. He's made me mad enough to cry. That alone tells me something. I care about him. I want to say it's my reputation I'm so upset about, the relationship with my friends, the embarrassment, but I know it's not. I'm pissed at Dexter and it hurts because I want him, and I won't be with him if this is how he is. I just won't.

He shakes his head and gives me what I can only describe as a parental-like stare. "Fine."

I steal a glance over at him and notice a dark crimson blotch on the collar of his shirt. "Is that blood?"

He glances down at his shirt then back up to the road. "Fuck."

"What the hell happened to you?"

"It's not mine."

My eyes bulge and I bare my teeth at him. "What the hell did you do?" Oh my God, is Kyle hurt? Does he need medical attention?

"Nothing, everything's fine."

"Tell me what happened, or I'll jump out of this damn car. Is Kyle okay?"

His face goes red the second I say Kyle's name, but he takes a deep breath before he responds. "Wasn't Kyle. His friend said things I didn't like. My head met his nose. He'll live, trust me. His pride is the only thing wounded."

I shake my head. Hearing it was a million times worse than thinking it. "Take me home *right now*." My jaw clenches and my fingers tremble against my legs. I'm from Texas and I'm used to men getting in fights, but it doesn't mean it's not childish and stupid.

"Getting you there as fast as I can. Trust me." He snorts. "At least I know you'll be safe in your own bed and not acting like a goddamn moron." He grips the wheel even harder.

I scoff. "Classic. Coming from the guy who just headbutted someone in a fucking bar."

"You know what? That's fair." He points a finger at me. "But you were sitting there shitfaced, alone with two dudes who only want to take advantage of you."

"You don't know what you're talking about." He's so ridiculous, this is insanity. "They're my *friends*. At least they *were* until you showed up. I'm sure they'll want nothing to do with me now, which is exactly why you did what you did. Congratulations, you got what you wanted."

"You don't know why I did what I did because your head is up your ass."

"They're nice to me. And I'm nice to them in return. That's how society works. It's called friendship. You should try it sometime."

"Christ, you're so naïve. It would almost be cute if it wasn't so dangerous."

"Well, it's no longer your concern. This isn't going to work so you don't have to worry about it happening again. I won't be with someone who goes around beating up anyone who talks to me."

"Would you listen to yourself? I'm not a fucking animal. I didn't headbutt that douchebag because he was hanging out with you."

"Why'd you do it then? Enlighten me."

Dexter shakes his head. "I had reasons, okay?"

I turn in my seat and glare at him. "No, tell me. Don't hide behind your actions like a chicken shit now."

His voice kicks up an octave. "Okay, fine. Your *friends* want to take advantage of you. I know this because I was a guy their age once. I know how they are. They're bad fucking news and you're too blind to see it."

I shake my head. "You're so full of shit. You were jealous and went into a rage because I was drinking with my friends. The same way you threw a little tantrum when I didn't want you to kiss me at the office. You're a grown toddler who kicks and screams when he doesn't get his way."

"Oh bullshit, I know that's all they want from you because they fucking told me."

I feel the color drain from my face. More tears come and I don't know what to do because I've never felt this way and they won't stop. My jaw clenches. "You're lying."

His eyes dart over my direction and his glare softens. "I got up in Kyle's face and told him I knew exactly what he was up to and that it was going to end. His buddy got pissed and stood up and told me maybe they'd both go back to your apartment and fuck you, that you'd been all over them all night acting like a slut. That's when I lost it and headbutted him. He was disrespecting you and he wanted to take advantage of you. Look, Abby, there are women across the country getting shit slipped into their drinks by smarmy little cocksuckers like those two every damn day. I haven't punched anyone in ten years. I'm not a violent person. Think whatever you want, though. I knew what they were up to from day one, that's why I've been an asshole to them. They're not your friends, no matter how bad you want to believe they are."

"Maybe I am naïve, but so what? You have to trust me or this, whatever, between us will never work. You should know me well enough to know I wouldn't go home and sleep with them. I'm young. I moved to the city to live my life the way I want to live it, to have fun."

Suddenly, Dexter swerves the car to the shoulder of the road and slams the gearshift into park. He turns and he stares at me so intensely it steals all the air from my lungs. His gaze is different, and I've never seen him look like this before. It's like he's in pain, on the verge of tears even. He's totally vulnerable right now, the way he was when he told me about his mom and the pudding. His face is a hundred percent sincere. It's so intimate and just, I don't even know how to describe the way he's looking at me. It's a look that says, *I care about you so damn much it physically hurts.* His voice lowers and changes into a pleading tone. "If you want to have fun..." He swallows like he's choking on his words. "Have fun with *me.*"

He reaches out with his hand and cups my face and no matter how bad I want to fight it, I can't. There's something about him, some cosmic force yanking us together no matter how much I want to resist. I lean into his hand.

"I want you safe."

"I know, it's just..."

"I don't want to argue. I just want *you.*"

My body takes over and I can't even think right now. The moment just overwhelms me, and I think part of me just wants to forget everything that happened back at the bar, but at the same time all I can focus on is the truth I can see in Dexter's eyes. I thought he was just doing the macho, petty jealous guy bullshit, but I can see it all happened because he cares so damn much. And I haven't ever seen him act violent toward other men. In fact, I've only ever seen him be an asshole to Kyle and Nick. Other men have talked to me in Dexter's presence, and he hasn't snapped on them. The exact opposite in fact. Maybe he stiffens a little, but nothing more than that, even when Cole Miller shook my hand, or when I talk to other men at the office. The old man and some of the other guys at the MMA fight flirted with me right in front of him and he just grinned, even though I'm sure it irked him a little.

He must be telling the truth about Kyle, but it's a tough pill to swallow. What a freaking night. Dexter has no reason to lie, and he has no reason to be jealous. I mean, look at him. He could have his pick of the women in Chicago. They'd line up at his doorstep.

I undo my seatbelt, and without a second thought, I slide across the console to his lap. I straddle his thighs and our mouths meet. The temperature in the car doubles instantly. Dexter kisses me deep and hard, but it's full of emotion. There's no denying this connection between us, no matter how hard I want to fight against it sometimes. Caressing his hair, I breathe him in as our tongues roll and dance.

"I'm sorry." Dexter puts both palms on my face and holds me away from him so he can stare into my eyes. "I lost it when he said that shit, but it wasn't jealousy. It was your safety. I just want you safe, even if you end up not wanting anything to do with me."

I nod. "Okay."

His eyebrows quirk up. "Okay?"

"I believe you. Just please don't hit anyone again, even if they say something about me. I don't like it. I don't like this."

"Okay, I won't. I promise."

Gripping my thighs, Dexter gives me a squeeze. A possessive squeeze that says *I want you and I will have you.* I grind against his cock over his slacks, seeking more friction. All this energy between us from the fight has me so damn turned on I don't even know if I can wait to get home.

I want this. I want *him.* So damn bad it aches.

We finally part and Dexter's half-hooded eyes sear into me. "Two weeks has been a long enough wait, right?"

I nod furiously. "It's torture."

His eyes rake up and down my body as I slide back to the passenger side. Dexter puts the car in gear and floors it back onto the highway.

My entire body heats up and I squirm in my seat.

Holy hell, I'm about to have sex.

DEXTER

I PUT my car in park and go around to the passenger side to open Abigail's door. I hold my hand out to her and the minute her feet touch the pavement, I flip her up over my shoulder and carry her through the entrance of my building.

The automatic front door syncs to the Bluetooth on my phone and opens for me as I walk up. For once, I start to see some real value from that feature. I haul ass through the foyer. I need in my apartment yesterday.

Abigail laughs as I step into the elevator, careful not to hit her head on the ceiling. "Are you going to put me down?"

"Nope. I'm carrying you the whole way, like they do in your little chick movies."

"Hallmark."

"What's that?"

"The Hallmark romances. Those are the best because they're so cheesy it's funny."

"You calling this cheesy?" I smack her on the ass.

She gasps.

When we get to my door, it automatically unlocks with the app on my phone, but I have to actually turn the handle on this one. We walk through the apartment, and I can tell she wants me to put her down so she can look around the place, but there's no time for that. She can get a tour later. I want her in my bed right now.

"I can walk you know?"

"Yeah, but I'm having so much fun."

"You're crazy."

"Crazy about you." I take her straight to my bedroom. Once we're through the door, I flip the lights on and set her down on the mattress. "I need to ask you

459

something serious. And I need you to be one hundred percent honest with me, okay?"

Abigail nods, no longer joking. "Sure, what is it?"

"How drunk are you?"

She looks up at me and pulls her bottom lip between her teeth. "Sober enough to know I've wanted you for weeks." She makes a "come here" motion with her finger.

I don't miss a beat.

She stands up next to my bed before I can make it over, and I kiss her harder than I've ever kissed a woman in my life. At the same time, I unzip her dress and slide it past the curve of her hips.

This is happening.

My mouth goes dry and all my senses are heightened. It's like I'm sixteen again, about to get laid for the first time.

When her dress puddles around her feet, I appraise her from head to toe. She's in a red lace bra and matching panties. I take a mental snapshot because she's just —perfection, inside and out. She uses her foot and kicks her dress across the room. It hits the wall and slides down to the floor.

I reach for the hem of my shirt and peel it up over my head, my eyes locked on Abigail the entire time. She does that sexy shit where she bites her lip again, and if she's not careful I might bite it for her.

"I think we need to take these off." She takes a step toward me and reaches for my pants.

"Agreed."

She fumbles with the button on my pants. I can't remember my cock being this hard, ever. She doesn't even get to the zipper before her hand is down the front.

My head tilts up to the ceiling for a split-second, because fuck, her soft hand on my dick is heaven. My entire body is on fire for her, immolating from within. I want everything, her mouth, her pussy. All of it.

More than that, I just want her.

She's mine.

Her hand is still down my pants when I fist her hair and tilt her head up to face me.

Her eyes widen in shock, then the corners of her mouth turn up into a sly grin. A slight gasp parts her lips and I can't help myself. She needs to know who's in charge in the bedroom, and she doesn't seem to mind one bit. I claim her mouth once more, licking and exploring. Her hand strokes back and forth on my dick, and I groan against her lips.

She takes her free hand and shoves my pants and boxer briefs down my legs, freeing my cock. "I can't believe I just came to your apartment."

I shove her down onto my bed and a soft coo parts her lips. Before she can recover, I spread her legs and stare right at her pussy. "You're about to come in my apartment, repeatedly."

"Holy shit, Dex." She moans when my mouth dives straight between her thighs.

I glance up at her face and her eyes are heavy and sated. They widen when I grip her panties with both hands and rip them apart for getting between me and what I want.

"Holy sh—" Her back arches her tits up into the air.

I reach up and grab both of them, feeling her hard nipples brush against my palms.

I lick all around her pussy, tracing an outline around the edges, just enough to tease her relentlessly. She instinctively tries to close her legs, and I dig my fingertips into the insides of her thighs and keep them spread apart. I exhale warm breath over her clit and lick all the way up her slick folds and end at that sensitive bundle of nerves.

Goosebumps break out all over her tan skin, telling me I'm doing my job correctly. Just when she's about to come, I pull away, put my hands on the backs of her knees, and shove them up to her shoulders. It lifts her ass from the bed and angles her pussy straight up to my face.

Before she can say or do anything, I dive back down and stroke her clit with the tip of my tongue.

"So. Close." The words are barely audible over her labored breaths.

I lean back and fist my cock, then rub the head back and forth over her clit to feel how wet she is.

She stares up at me and our eyes lock. I watch every expression on her face, note every muscle in her body that tenses when I touch her a certain way. Her body is perfect, and I plan to master it, learn every way possible to give her more pleasure than she's ever had in her life.

"How close are you?"

"God." She drags out the syllable. "So close, please."

"Good, beg me to let you come."

"Please, Dex. I want it so bad." Her words come out on a whimper.

I use my thumb to rub lazy circles around her clit, then line my cock up and barely push the head in, back and forth. "Not yet. I want to feel it with my cock." I reach for my drawer and pull a condom out, then roll it on, my hand never leaving her.

"I'm on the pill."

For some reason I frown. Fuck, how does she make me so damn jealous? Why is she on the pill? For whose benefit?

She shakes her head immediately like she can read my thoughts. "I just started two weeks ago, after our first date." She looks away, damn near blushing. "Just in case."

Euphoria shoots through my veins at her admission. I stare back at her, the head of my dick lined up with her warm, slick entrance. I wanted our first time to be special, and while earlier in the evening wasn't my finest moment, I can't think of anything more special than her, here in my room, saying these things to me. Not to mention that moment in the car, on the side of the road. I just cracked. Something stirred deep inside me and I couldn't hold back my feelings.

I gesture toward my open drawer. "I bought these two weeks ago too, just in case." I hope she doesn't think I'm just saying that, because I'm not. It's true. I lean over to her and our mouths lock. I still can't believe how soft her lips are, how phenomenal she tastes.

I want nothing more than to just shove into her and fuck her so hard she can't walk straight, but I don't. I slide into her and, oh my God, I'm falling, falling hard. She's hot and tight, but having sex with her feels more like a warm hug than just a reason to get off. We fit together perfectly.

Her legs spread apart, and I push deeper and kiss her harder, rocking back and forth. Our foreheads meet and her eyes flutter. She bites her bottom lip between her teeth and soft moans escape her lips each time I push farther into her.

I slide a hand down and circle her clit with my index finger while I push in and out, harder and faster, ramping up in intensity. "Look at me when you come. I want to see *you*."

I'd be lying if I said I hadn't fantasized about fucking Abigail nonstop, since the first time she walked into the office and was introduced with the new Dallas transfers. In my mind, I bent her over, pulled her hair, spanked her ass. Made her go to her knees and beg for my cock in her mouth.

But right now, it's so different. We're not fucking, we're making love and it's perfect; the perfect moment. I feel so connected. Maybe it's because I've told her things I've never told anyone else. The world just feels right when I'm inside her.

"Dex." Her voice snaps me from the moment, just being submerged in the experience of her wrapped around me.

"Yeah?"

"Please let me come."

"Okay. Come for me, baby."

She nods against my forehead once more, and I watch her eyes as they roll back in her head. Her entire body tenses and I speed my finger up on her clit and drive into her as deep as I can. She clenches around me and it feels so damn phenomenal words can't describe it.

"Oh, God, Dex…" Her words trail off when she bites down on my collar bone.

Fuck, it hurts so damn good. Something about it awakens the primal part of my brain, when men evolved to hunt and conquer. I want to own her, every fucking inch of her body. My hips speed up as the orgasm crests through her body and her low groans turn into audible moans.

"Oh God. Oh God."

I'm about to blow, so I pull out and stare at Abigail, nostrils flared, trying to keep my own orgasm at bay. Her eyes widen and they're two parts excitement one part nervous; the perfect ratio.

I dive down on her pussy again and lick and suck, my fingers digging into her hips, yanking her up against my mouth. Her hands fly out and my sheets rumple between her fists.

I take two fingers in deep and hit the secret spot inside her while my tongue lashes at her clit. At the last second, I flip her onto her stomach and pull her ass up into the air.

"Oh my God."

I fist a handful of her hair and lean down to her ear. "What's that? Want me to stop?"

"No." She damn near barks the word at me. "Don't you dare."

I grin against her neck. "Good answer." I line my cock back up with her from behind. "Are you nervous?"

She nods toward the headboard. "A little."

I push into her and tighten my fist in her hair. "Good, you should be. I'm going to fuck you so hard you feel me inside you a month from now."

"Holy sh—"

I speed up my hips, pounding into her from behind. Her pussy is so wet it streams down her thighs onto the sheets. "So. Fucking. Tight." I groan out the words.

I expected Abigail to be more submissive than she is, but she's not. Her hips buck back into me and she gives just as good as she takes. It's hot as shit. I don't know how much longer I'll be able to last.

"God, Dex, don't stop."

I let go of her hair and grip both her hips, yanking her back into me as her words fuel my hips forward. The sound of our skin slapping together echoes through the room, and I wouldn't be surprised if she has bruises on her ass tomorrow from my hips crashing into her.

I don't want to finish too early, not before she gets off again, so I pull out and spread her ass with my palms. I dive into her pussy from behind and fuck her with my tongue, licking and sucking.

Abigail let's out a squeal and covers her mouth when it comes out. I lean back and slam back into her and resume where we left off.

"Again. Soon." It's all she can manage to get out.

I know exactly what she means, she's about to come again. I reach forward and wrap a hand lightly around her throat and pull her head back toward me as I drive into her over and over. I slide my free hand around the curve of her hip and reach down so I can stroke her clit while we crash into each other.

"Shit, Dexxx."

The orgasm rolls through her and she clamps down on my cock so hard I can't hold back now. I ride it out long enough for her to finish, then pull out and yank the condom off. I don't know what comes over me, but I have this unbelievable urge to mark her, brand her as mine.

My hand flies over my cock, stroking furiously and my balls tighten. I splay my fingers across her upper back, shoving her chest down to the mattress. It angles her ass up in the air. I hold my cock inches from her and grunt. Every muscle in my body contracts at once, and I shoot hot spurts of come all over her ass, then lash her hot cunt with the rest.

When I'm finished, I can barely breathe. I pant uncontrollably, trying to catch my breath, then stare down at my orgasm as it rolls down her thighs. It's fucking perfect. She's mine. The proof is right there.

She stares back at me, a huge smile on her face. "That was amazing."

I nod. "Yeah." That's all I can say at the moment. I feel like I'm floating on the clouds. Like the strongest narcotic just shot through my veins. It was far and away the best sex I've ever had in my life.

Finally, I shake my head to snap out of my euphoric daydream. "Shit, sorry. Hang on." I get up and walk off to the bathroom, then return with a towel. I stop halfway into the room and just stare at Abigail.

Her long blonde curls drape over her shoulders and frame her perfect face. She's still on all fours, ass up in the air.

"Dex?"

I shake my head again. "Yeah?"

She laughs and glances around. "You gonna clean me up?"

"Shit, yeah, sorry. I was just... I don't know." I walk over and bend down, then drop a soft kiss right on her cherry-red lips. "You're just perfect. I can't stop staring at you."

Her eyelashes do the flutter thing again. "Thank you." I swear she blushes at the compliment.

I grin and move back to clean myself off her.

"Why are you grinning?"

I shrug. "Nothing. Just you blush at that compliment, but two minutes before you were throwing that ass back at me and begging me to fuck you harder."

Now, her face turns full-on pink and she buries it in the covers. "Oh my God. You're not supposed to say stuff like that. I'm so embarrassed."

I can't stop laughing. Once she's cleaned up, I crawl into bed with her and kiss her a few more times, then push a few wayward strands of hair from her face. I swear I could stare at her blue eyes all night. I slide a palm onto her cheek and cup her face in my hand.

She leans into it and does a long, slow blink, like she's about to pass out.

"Don't ever be embarrassed. You're gorgeous and it was hot as hell."

"It was?"

"Fuck yeah." I slide my hand under her chin and lift her face up so we're eye to eye. "Don't be afraid to tell me what you like and what you don't. I want to make you happy, out there." I gesture toward the wall. "And in here. I'd try anything for you."

She grins. "Anything, huh?"

My eyebrows rise. "Within reason, of course."

She taps her chin, pretending she's deep in thought. "Well, I mean all of it was perfect. It started so sensual and slow, and that was amazing. And then you got this look in your eye and I thought my heart was going to beat out of my chest. It was all a blur after that, but it was incredible."

"Anything else?"

Her cheeks turn pink again. "Okay, come here."

I lean in and she pulls my neck over so that her mouth is next to my ear. She licks slowly up my neck to my ear and whispers, "I really liked when you pulled my hair."

I grin like the devil. "Good." I snake my hand up into her hair and give it a light tug. I smile against her lips and say, "I like pulling your hair. And I like you saying my name when you come on my dick."

"You have the filthiest mouth I've ever heard."

"Get used to it, Christmas clown."

She smacks at my chest. "Maybe I will. I kinda like that too."

We both laugh and she curls up against my chest. I stare around the room and up at the ceiling as she falls asleep on me.

I could get used to this. Going to bed and waking up next to Abigail every morning. I kiss her on the forehead. I don't want to go to sleep. I don't want this night to ever end.

ABIGAIL

GROANING AND STRETCHING, I come to and look around the room. The smell of fresh coffee wafts into my nose. I smile as memories of last night play through my mind. I spent the night with Dexter.

Holy crap.

And we had sex. Not just any sex, but like the whole spectrum from making love to hardcore banging, for lack of a better phrase. Phenomenal freaking sex.

The ache between my thighs reminds me just how good he was, and his words filter through my brain. *"I'm going to fuck you so hard you still feel me inside you a month from now."*

I squirm in his bed just thinking about it. He wasn't lying. He has magical powers. I'm convinced of it.

My cell phone beeps from somewhere in the room. I rub my eyes and slide out of bed. I help myself to a t-shirt from Dex's drawer and find my way to his bathroom. I go through the motions of washing my face and brushing my teeth with my finger. It's not the best method but I don't want to have horrible morning breath if he kisses me. It should work.

I find my purse on a chair along with my dress. Pulling out my phone, I scroll through my missed texts while the sound and smell of bacon frying sweeps into the room.

Kyle: Wow. That guy is a fucking asshole.

Kyle: He headbutted Nick.

Kyle: Do you even give a shit?

Kyle: Did you really go home with him?

Kyle: Nick saw you get in his car.

Kyle: I don't know if we can hang out anymore if you're going to date that guy.

I shake my head. He's not sure if we can hang out? I don't even know how to respond to that. I don't like ultimatums, and I believe what Dexter said. It hurts like hell, but I feel like Kyle played me like a fool.

I was nice to him. I genuinely thought he was my friend. I don't know what to do. He's still my neighbor and it'll be impossible to avoid him until I can move out. I'll just have to nod and smile in the hallway until I can find a way to deal with it somehow.

I stop in the living room and cover my mouth when I glance in the kitchen. Dexter is completely naked, dancing around and singing, using the spatula as a microphone. He pauses during the chorus, between flipping two eggs, and does a little helicopter twirl with his dick, then goes right back to cooking.

Laughter erupts from somewhere deep inside me. I don't even know how I laugh that hard, but I can't freaking breathe.

Dex sees me and shoots me that boyish grin of his, then shrugs. "Tha fuck ya gonna do?" he says in some kind of Boston accent.

I shake my head and finally manage to control myself. To his credit, he stops dancing after he sees me. I wonder if he's embarrassed he got caught and is playing it cool.

I walk over as he puts everything onto two plates. He's acting so sweet. I can't believe he cooked for me, and I'd be lying if I said he didn't look incredibly hot while he did it, dancing and everything. He reaches up into the cabinet for something and muscles upon muscles ripple. He's not huge like Deacon, but he's lean and cut. The ink comes to life all over his torso as he moves around, hell, even when he just breathes.

I finally get a look at his tattoos and they're so interesting. It looks like some ancient Greek buildings, like the Acropolis or one of those things, along with a few philosophers. There is writing. Then some music notes fill in the background along with a few more sayings in what looks like Latin.

"What do your tattoos mean? I've never seen anything like that."

He turns around slowly and does a three-sixty to let me get a look at them. "They're everything that makes me, well me."

"Elaborate, sir."

"Well, I have stuff that symbolizes the Hammurabi code, the Old Testament, Lady Justice. Because I'm a lawyer and it's a huge part of my life. Then I have the musical notes and work from some of my favorite artists, then the double helix DNA structure and some binary code. It's all sort of an amalgamation of me trying to reconcile science and art, the subjective and the objective. Those are things I struggle with internally."

"Well, aren't you just a riddle, wrapped in a mystery, inside an enigma."

"Nice, Churchill. One of my favorite quotes." He eyes me for a long moment, like we're still figuring each other out.

I do a fake little curtsy. "I know things on occasion. So, what'd you cook for me? I'm starving."

"You know I was actually planning to surprise you with breakfast in bed. But this is good. Less crumbs on the sheets."

I walk up, trying to look as sexy as I can, and wrap my arms around his waist. "You cooked for me." I peck him on the cheek. "I don't care where we eat. That's enough for me."

His rough hands dig into my hips again. "Is that so?"

I press a finger to his lips, silencing him. "I have a much better idea." I drop to my knees on the dark, hardwood floors. My knees may hate me later, but Dexter is worth it. Eye level with his cock, I smirk up at him.

His brows shoot up. "Food's gonna get cold."

I wrap a hand around the base of his shaft and stare at it. Wow, it's even bigger than I remember. "Not *my* breakfast." I flick my tongue out, swirling it around the tip. "You were saying?" I bat my lashes at him, sliding my fist up and down him.

His eyes roll back and he groans. "Breakfast can fucking wait."

Dex is big and thick. I take him into my mouth, and I can't fit all of it. I suck my cheeks around him, even harder, just to hear him groan again. It's so damn hot, knowing I can have that effect on him. I wrap my hand around the base and stroke him in a circular motion as I take him in and out of my mouth.

He fists the back of my hair, and I have to fight the urge to lean back into his hand.

Why the hell do I love him pulling my hair so much? It feels incredible, especially when his knuckles press up against my scalp. He holds my head in place, and before long, his hips start to move, slowly at first. I swirl my tongue around him and after a few seconds he's thrusting into my mouth.

I stare up at him with wide eyes and love how he's about to lose control. Tears burn at the corner of my eyes, but it's only fair. He's gone down on me twice and I haven't done anything just for him.

The tighter he squeezes his fingers in my hair, the harder he strains to hold my head in place—it's just raw, and possessive, like he never wants to let go of me.

"Fuck, Abby."

I want to smile at his reaction, but it's impossible with his thick cock in my mouth. The way his face tenses, screws up tight, like he's about to release sends a shudder through me. I love knowing I can get him off this fast. It means I'm doing something right.

It's only like my third time total doing this, but I've watched enough porn to know what guys like while I got myself off with my vibrator.

I stare up at him once more and his jaw clenches.

He moves to pull out of my mouth, and I latch onto him and shake my head back and forth.

His eyes widen. "Fuck."

I want to taste him. I want to make him as happy as he made me, and there's something about girls swallowing that just does it for guys; so I've heard anyway. I have no clue what I'm in store for, because I've never done it, but I don't show it. This is his fantasy and I want to do it for *him*.

His hand tightens in my hair and the burning against my scalp has my senses on high alert. He grunts. "Shit, Abigail."

His cock twitches and he comes in the back of my throat. I gag for a quick moment but do my best to just leave it in my mouth and keep my throat in check.

My fingers dig into his ass with my free hand, and his whole body tenses. His ass and legs are rock-hard, and I keep stroking him as he fills up my mouth.

Finally, he pulls my head back from him and stares down at me.

This is the moment of truth, Abby. Just be sexy. Be sexy.

Our eyes lock, and I open my mouth and show it to him on my tongue. His eyes widen again, and I close my mouth and swallow it all like a shot of tequila, just as quick as possible.

Not gonna lie, it's not awesome. But, it's not the worst thing I've ever done.

Once I swallow, I open my mouth and stick out my tongue at him, just like the girls always do in the videos.

He's grinning like an idiot, his eyes bugged out. "Holy. Fucking. Shit."

I smile at his reaction. For some reason, all I want to do is make Dex happy and he's smiling like a little boy again. My heart warms and comes alive at the sight.

"That was some next level shit. So fucking hot."

I take his cock in my hand. "Oops, I think I missed some." I clean the rest of him up with my tongue and he's still rock-hard.

He could easily have sex with me for another thirty minutes, especially after I just got one out of the way with that blowjob, but I'd hate to ruin breakfast for him. He worked so hard on it.

Maybe afterward. God, I hope so.

Dex scoops me up by my arms and lifts me to my feet.

He immediately goes for a kiss and I pull away. "Gross, I just…"

"I don't give a fuck." He puts both palms on my cheeks and plants a kiss right on my lips. I don't know what it is, but it's hot once he does it. Like he doesn't give one shit, he just wants to kiss me and that's what he's going to do.

He walks to his bedroom and slips on some boxer briefs, then walks back out.

I can't help but stare down between his legs. He's still hard and it's corralled against his thigh.

He catches me looking. "Later."

"Huh?" I mumble, still in a trance just staring at his sculpted body.

He glances down at his crotch. "There'll be more fun later. We need to eat. Need some energy so we can fuck like rabbits later tonight."

Why tonight? Why not all day? I shake my head and grin back at him. "Okay, Dickens."

He does the worst British accent I've ever heard. "Thou est well versed, is he not?"

I burst out laughing and dig into my omelet. Damn, this dude has skills in the kitchen too. Mushrooms, onion, cheese, and sausage—it's perfect, everything I like. I sip on my coffee.

"Listen." Dex sits down, taking up the stool next to mine. "I know I might have overreacted a bit last night."

I put a hand on his forearm. "We don't have to do this right now. I'm actually enjoying myself."

"No." He shakes his head and puts his fork down. "I don't want shit between us. I don't want things like last night happening again." He wags a finger back and forth at us. "This is serious to me. I'm serious about you and I want to do it right, clear lines of communication."

I set my fork down. "Maybe you overreacted a little."

His brow furrows.

"Those were my friends. Maybe they still are, maybe they aren't anymore, I don't know yet. But, if you want to be with me, Dex, you need to trust me."

His jaw clenches a little tighter and he starts to say something, but I cut him off.

"I know my limits, okay? I'm an adult."

Dex's fingers tighten around his fork. "I just want you to be careful. You don't know guys like I do. There are a lot of assholes just looking for someone to get drunk and take advantage of. And I know you're smart and you think those guys are your friends, but they aren't. You wouldn't believe the types of cases I've seen. The women we represent and the shit that's been done to them."

"I know. I get it. I appreciate you having my back and looking out for me, but I have to know. What exactly did you say to them? I have messages this morning saying we can't hang out anymore."

"Good. Fuck those guys." He shovels a forkful of egg into his mouth. "I'm sorry if I made you uncomfortable. Or made things difficult for you, but I'm telling you." He huffs out an irritated sigh. "Yeah, I could've handled it differently. I was pissed." He points the fork at me. "Someone needed to give them a kick in the ass. Even if they didn't try something with you, they'd pull it on someone else. You're better off without them. And that Nick guy deserved what he got. I won't apologize for wanting to protect you. If you're pissed at me about it, fine. I can live with that, knowing you're safe."

"I'm just… I don't know, it does put me in an uncomfortable position."

Dex mumbles, "Better than you getting hurt."

"Okay, well, can you just not headbutt anyone else? Please?" I grin to try and lighten the mood.

"I would never do that to anyone who respects you. And I promised you I wouldn't do it again. When I promise something, I follow through, always."

"Okay. Fair enough. But for the record, I will have to have a conversation with them at some point. They're my neighbors and I have to figure out what to do."

Dex glares at his eggs. I know this a tough pill for him to swallow, but to his credit he doesn't blow up like he did last night. Through gritted teeth he says, "Fine."

"You know I mean without you present, right?"

His lips mash together in a fine line and he looks like he wants to explode, but he finally nods. "I understand."

It's almost funny, but it's really not. He's trying, though, so I have to give him that. I finish my food and my coffee. While Dex finishes eating, I walk over and start on the dishes.

He comes up behind me. "You don't need to do that. I have a cleaning lady."

"I want to." I lay my head back on his shoulder as he wraps his arms around my center. "Thank you for breakfast. This is nice. I feel so domesticated."

"Don't get too comfortable. I ain't put a ring on it yet." He laughs.

I smack playfully at his shoulder. "Jerk. I'm trying to say I'm enjoying spending time with you."

He squeezes his arms tighter around me. "I know. It is really nice. Amazing actually. We work together pretty well."

"Oh yeah? Me doing the dishes while you cop a feel?"

He moves my hair away and drops a kiss on my collar bone. "If I copped a feel, you'd know it."

I snicker. "Totally believe you."

"I don't think you do." His hand works up under the shirt I'm wearing and he squeezes my breast.

His hand feels so damn good. It burns a trail of flames up my skin, every time he touches me. When he presses against me, his hard cock rubs up against my ass.

How the hell does he take me from zero to horny faster than his car runs the quarter mile?

"I'll be right back."

I don't want to let go of him. Don't want him going anywhere. "Where you going?"

He whispers, "Protection," in my ear. "Just a sec."

My nails dig into his thigh and pull him back to me as I grind my ass up against him. Shit, he feels so good right there. "I told you, I'm on the pill."

His eyes widen. "You sure?"

I nod.

What the hell is wrong with you, Abigail? My body rationalizes it, but my brain isn't sold. In fact, it's screaming "No!" with big red warning signs. "I'm sure."

Before I know what's happened, Dex shoves me over the counter and yanks the t-shirt I stole from his drawer halfway up my back. One of his large hands kneads my ass, and then out of nowhere he smacks it. The stinging pain radiates up my spine, but it doesn't hurt. It just burns in the most delicious of ways.

I've never been spanked before, but a coo parts my lips and I think I actually enjoyed it. What is this man doing to me?

"What are you doing, Dex?"

"Wanted to see my handprint. It looks amazing."

Before I can get another word out, he's inside me. I'd never truly been filled until I was with Dex. His cock is thick and stretches me in ways I've never been stretched before. I back into him and moan out my approval.

"Fuck, Abby, you keep doing that and this is going to be over fast."

I smile at the counter. He pushes into me harder, each thrust more and more intense until I'm throwing my hips back into him as he pounds into me. It feels so much more intimate when it's bare, skin to skin. I don't know how to explain what it's like being with Dex, but we just have this connection that hums between us on a microscopic level.

I'm so close, and he keeps pushing me higher and higher until my vision starts to blur. Right when I think I can't take it anymore, one of his hands grips my hip, and the other goes straight to my hair.

Damn, when he pulls on my hair, I think I'd do anything to make him happy. It's heaven, pure heaven.

"You gonna come on my dick?" He grunts out the words.

I nod against his hand. "Very. Soon."

When he reaches around and strokes my clit, I lose control. My legs quiver and my body quakes. I clench around him. There's nowhere in the world I want to be but in this moment as the orgasm rolls through my limbs like an electric current, buzzing through my veins.

Once I release, I feel like Jell-O, like I might melt into a puddle on the floor. Dex slips out of me and picks me up, carrying me toward the table.

I half giggle, still in a partial orgasm coma. "Where are you taking me."

"I want you on top of me." He yanks one of the heavy chairs from the table with one hand, moving it like it's nothing.

He sits down and pulls me to him, so that I'm straddled over each of his legs. I stare into his eyes as I lower down onto him, watching his face the whole time.

I trace the curve of his jawline with my hand as I take every inch of him.

He's so deep. Deeper than deep. The angle of his cock hits my spot perfectly, and a small shudder rips from the base of my spine up to my neck and goosebumps pebble all over my skin.

"That's it, fuck me, Abby."

Between his mouth and his cock, I'm already on the verge of another big O. I wrap my arms around his neck and ride him up and down.

He has that young boy look about him again, like he's so excited I'm riding him like a roller coaster. He has these flashes where he's so cute and innocent sometimes.

"Fuck, it's so good when you ride my dick like that. You have no idea."

And then he opens his dirty mouth and all innocence is lost. I nod against his forehead. "It's just as good for me, I promise." I smile at him until he thrusts up and hits my spot again. "Shit, right there. God, Dexter, don't stop doing that." This time my hands grip his hair and it's like someone possesses my body, because I ride him harder and faster. "Don't. Ever. Stop."

Before long, my ass is clapping on his thighs and I can feel my wetness stream down into his lap, but I don't care. It feels incredible. I don't know if I've ever been this wet before.

"Abby, fuck. I'm so…"

An orgasm hits me at the same time and I bite down on his shoulder because it's too much to bear all at once, the intense feeling pooling low between my thighs. "Holy shit, Dex, Dex…"

I seize up on him, clamping down as another one rocks through me. At the same time Dex's cock kicks deep inside me and he lets loose. Hot jets of come shoot into the depths of my pussy and it streams out around the base of his shaft and down my legs.

I stare into his eyes and get lost for a second. I don't want to get up. I don't want to do anything but sit there and feel him inside me, feel this connection between us I've never experienced before. It's just so *real*.

Finally, our foreheads touch and we grin like big cheesing idiots at each other.

"That was incredible." He cradles my cheek in his palm like he did last night.

I lean into it and close my eyes, nuzzling his hand. "Agreed." I nod, unable to form any words. "We should probably go shower."

"Okay, then I have to go in and work for a while this afternoon."

I can't hide the frown on my face. I don't want to do anything but stay here with him.

As if reading my thoughts, he says, "You can stay here if you want, but we need to go by your house tonight or sometime tomorrow morning."

"What for?"

Dex waggles his eyebrows. "It's a surprise."

DEXTER

ABIGAIL STAYED over at my place last night too, and we fucked nonstop until we passed out. It was incredible. She's so damn young she might wear me out, but I'll go down fighting.

We cruise by her apartment this morning so she can grab warmer clothes.

It's cold as tits outside.

There's no way she'll go for it if I told her what we're doing, so I keep telling her it's a surprise.

Finally, we pull up to Harry Caray's Tavern on Navy Pier.

She looks over at me with a quizzical glance. "A bar? At this time of day?"

I shrug. "It'll be fun. Trust me."

As soon as we walk in, she freezes, and her shoulders tighten. She starts to turn around but I nudge her toward the table. "You're fine. Just smile."

Everyone else is already here, sitting around with beers wearing their Bears gear. Deacon, Decker, Tate, Quinn, Cole Miller, and Mr. Richards.

"About time," says Decker.

Abigail turns to me and glares. She lowers her voice where nobody can hear. "A heads up would've been nice."

Deacon must've read her lips or something because he turns to Cole and says, "Shit."

Cole grins as Deacon pulls out his wallet and hands him a twenty.

I point at both of them. "What's that all about?"

Cole says, "Bet him a twenty spot you wouldn't tell her she was hanging out with the family."

Deacon shrugs at Quinn. "I didn't think he'd be that big of a dumbass."

Abigail laughs at that then turns to me. "See, you should've told me."

I stare at her like she just sprouted three heads. "You wouldn't have come."

Abigail sits there, thinking over what she wants to say. "Okay that's true, just…" She motions with her head like *can we please speak out of earshot of everyone?*

I follow her over by the bar.

"Seriously, what are we doing? I work with most of the people at that table."

"Oh stop. It'll be fine. This isn't work. You already know everyone except for Mr. Richards. He's good people. It's not like they don't already know about us."

"You told them?"

I shrug. "Well yeah, they're my family. I tell them everything. Especially Deacon."

She finally sighs. "Okay. I just wish you would've warned me."

"Come on, it'll be great." I squeeze her hand and she doesn't protest as I pull her along to join the group.

Tate smiles, trying to lighten the mood a little, and latches onto Abigail. She hands her a Bud Light from one of the buckets in the center of the table.

"I see you stopped being a bitch." Quinn hands me a bottle.

I glance down and Mr. Richards gives me a thumbs up. When nobody is looking, he holds his hands out from his chest, suggesting Abigail has a nice rack and he winks. I shake my head. I did the same thing to him when I had Abigail help out getting him to the Bears game after Deacon royally fucked up and had to win Quinn back, and then again during our little counseling session on the couch.

I excuse myself while Abigail chats winter work outfits with Quinn and Tate.

I walk down and have a seat next to Mr. Richards.

"Don't worry, son. She's a great date. I should know." His gaze moves over to my girl.

I laugh. "Yeah, you would, you old shit."

He dies laughing. "I'm happy for you, kid."

Decker smacks me on the back, a little too hard, and speaks through his teeth. "*So*, this is happening." To his credit he doesn't reach for his temples like he's about to have an aneurysm.

"Yeah. Get used to it. I like her a lot."

Decker sighs. "All we need are some cameras in the office and for Donavan to start nailing interns and we can film the fucking Jerry Springer show."

"He's already fucked like three interns." I turn to Deacon. "Or is it four?"

"Might be four," says Deacon.

"And we already have the cameras ready. Just have to go in the supply—"

"I fucking hate all of you." Decker bites back a grin.

A waitress brings out our food. It's chilaquiles and some bean dip.

I turn to Decker and lower my voice. "Donavan not coming?"

Decker takes a long drink of a beer and glares at me. "Fuck, man. Please don't start. I'm actually enjoying this, and Jenny is off with her friends right now. I'm trying not to worry about that. I know they're talking to boys and shit."

"Will you just talk to him? Fuck man, it's brutal not having the whole family together. The holidays are coming up."

"I know, okay. I fucking know. It's just..." His jaw clenches. "Look, I've been trying, the timing just hasn't been right. It's not my job to kiss his ass and be his mother. He's acting like a baby, because he is a goddamn baby."

"I know you're marrying Tate, and I expect you to have her back a hundred percent, Decker." I shake my head. "It's a tough spot but it's family too. So, apologize or whatever you have to do, even if you don't mean it. If Mom and Dad still lived here, this shit wouldn't be happening, and you know it. So work it out as if they're here. Find a compromise. Does he even spend time with Jenny anymore?"

"He calls. They talk on the phone and he's picked her up a few Fridays but doesn't speak to me much. Just the bare minimum. From what I can gather from Jenny, he doesn't say anything about me, but I don't press her about it. I don't want her caught in the middle of anything. It's just me he's freezing out."

"Well, good." I nod. All of us are close with Jenny. We all helped raise her.

"You happy now? I want to enjoy my Sunday."

I grip his shoulder. "It'll work out. Don't worry, we're pressing him as hard as we're pressing you. It doesn't all fall on your shoulders."

Decker looks over at me. "At the risk of sounding like a total bitch, thanks. That means a lot."

"And don't worry about Jenny. She might be dealing with teenager shit, but she's a great kid. The attitude is normal."

"How the hell would you know?" Decker laughs.

I shrug. "I don't but I thought it'd make your anxious ass feel better. Eat a goddamn Xanax like an adult, fuck."

"There he is. You were acting too mature there for a moment."

We clink our bottles together and I look down the table.

Abigail blends in perfectly with the group just like I knew she would. Tate and Quinn are doing their best to make her feel welcome. She glances at me and smiles. Fuck, I can get lost in that smile.

Decker turns to me and Deacon. "So hey, I meant to tell you two. Mom and Dad are flying up for Thanksgiving. We're doing it at my place."

"Awesome." Man, I can't wait. It sounds corny as fuck, but I love everyone getting together at the holidays, especially when Mom and Dad come into town. All of us do. It gutted me moving Mom to Florida. I miss her constantly.

I grin over at Abigail and can't take my eyes off her.

"You two getting serious?" Cole nudges me with his elbow.

I do my best impression of Kip from *Napoleon Dynamite*. "Yeah, man. She accepted my friend request on Facebook, so I guess you could say things are getting pretty serious."

He dies laughing. "She have any single friends?"

"A roommate from hell."

"Crazy, huh?"

"From what I hear."

"I don't know, I like 'em a little nuts. Psychos are good between the sheets."

477

"Not this kind of crazy. You don't wanna go there, man."

"Go where?" Abigail asks as she walks to our end of the table.

"Nothing," we both say at the same time.

"Mmhmm." Abigail stares.

We finally finish off our food and drinks, then everyone files out the front door.

There's a charter bus parked in front.

"What's that?" asks Abigail.

I nudge her. "To take us to the game."

She shakes her head. "I should've known."

"Yeah, you should've." I lean down in her ear. "Don't worry, we've already made out in front of the team once, so it won't be a big deal when we do it again."

She pinches my arm.

"Ow, woman!"

"You deserved that." She walks in front of me, swaying her ass. "You coming or what, clown?"

I run up behind her. "You're the Christmas clown, not me."

"Mmhmm, let's go, *clownboy*."

AFTER THE GAME, the charter bus takes us back to Harry Caray's, and I drive Abigail home. I don't want to, but the weekend is almost over, and we have to work tomorrow. It was awesome spending the last two days with her. I'm a little behind on some work I need to do, even after going in on Saturday, but nothing major.

As I walk her to her door, that Kyle prick leaves his apartment. Abigail tenses up immediately. I swear to God that smarmy bastard probably sat there and watched out his window like a loser and timed it so he'd leave right when we walked up. I know how dipshits like him operate.

He stares at the ground and ignores us as he power-walks by.

Good. I want that son of a bitch to be afraid to even talk to Abigail.

She stays tense until he's in the elevator and the door closes.

I grab each of her shoulders. "You okay?" I glance around at her dilapidated building. She really does need to move out of this shit hole. That would solve all my problems. I know Abby, though. She'd never let me pay for it or accept any kind of help. I'll think of something to get her out of here.

She shakes her head. "No. Yeah. Totally fine. I was just worried he might say something to piss you off."

"He pisses me off by existing, but you don't have to worry about anything happening. I promised you."

"Dex?" She stares at me like I'm full of shit.

"I would never do anything." I hold up both hands and mumble, "In front of you."

She pushes at my shoulder. "Stop, you're terrible."

"I'm fine, okay. I don't get pissed off very often. That was a fluke deal. Bad timing and his friend said the wrong thing. That's all." I push her up against the wall next to her door. "I meant what I said about my promise. Though I do feel like Johnny Lawrence, not allowed to touch Daniel Larusso until the tournament."

"That makes you sound like the villain."

I scoff. "Uhh, Johnny was the hero. Daniel was an arrogant dickhead."

She laughs, then her eyes lock onto mine. "I had a really great time this weekend." She strokes my jaw with her petite fingers.

"You could have a great time with me tomorrow night at dinner too?"

She grins. "I'll think about it. I can't always let you get your way, though, you know? Have to keep you on your toes."

"Yeah you can." I move in for what is supposed to be a quick kiss, but it turns intense in a hurry. "You drive me crazy."

Abigail grins against my lips then bites the lower one. "Ditto."

The moment is nice, and it's hot as hell. If she keeps looking at me like that, I may have to kick the door down and haul her to her room, because who has time to use a key?

Out of nowhere, the door to her apartment flies open.

"There you are." This chick's voice is as nasal as a voice can get.

What the hell? Just be nice. "You must be Barbie." I hold out my hand. "Dexter."

Her nose goes up in the air. "Funny. Abigail's never mentioned you."

I can't help but snicker. Jesus fuck, Abby wasn't kidding at all.

I flash her a smile. "No worries, you'll be seeing a lot of me."

Abigail shakes her head, and I lean in for one more kiss, right in front of Barbie.

I squeeze Abigail's hip. "Call me later before you go to bed."

"Okay."

"Barbie." I give her a weird salute. "Say hi to Ken for me. Night ladies."

As I walk toward the elevator, I hear Barbie pissing and moaning about a guy named Nick.

I wonder if it was her boyfriend I headbutted in the face? Interesting.

I glance around on my way down the elevator. Yeah, I have to get Abigail the fuck out of this place. She deserves way better.

On the way to my car outside, Kyle creeps out of the shadows and saunters up the sidewalk. He's such an idiot in his little Pokémon t-shirt. It looks like something one of Jenny's friends from school would wear.

He starts toward me but abruptly stops and scowls when he sees me.

I sigh. Fucking perfect, just what I need. I know he's been out here waiting on me. Guys like him never learn and they don't handle rejection. They're dangerous for women. I've seen it a million times.

Stay calm.

The last thing I need is this twerp mouthing off and me sticking my foot up his ass. Shoving his hands in his pockets he shuffles awkwardly.

I can't believe how pathetic he is. Who raised him? If he wasn't such a conniving little asshole, I'd feel sorry for him.

I try to ghost him, just walk right past.

But, he turns around the second I walk by. "Hey!"

I stop and exhale a large breath. Silence would've been too easy it seems. "What?"

He shakes his head in the most condescending fashion possible and snorts. "Women are all the same."

I laugh at that one and eye him up and down, knowing exactly what he means by it. "It's not the women who are the problem."

I turn and walk off.

"The hell is that supposed to mean?"

I toss up a middle finger without turning back. "That means you're the problem, Kyle. And don't go near Abigail or I'll rip your legs off and kick your ass with them."

I glance back in time to see his eyes get big, then he power-walks all the way back to his apartment.

I get in my car and rev the engine then pull out onto the road. The entire drive to my place I try to think about Abigail but can't get that smarmy asshole out of my head. I have to get Abigail away from her roommate and that guy. What did she get herself caught up in? The people in her life give me anxiety, and I rarely have to be around them.

At my apartment, I go through the motions of getting everything ready for the week. I check my calendar and get my schedule up to date. Brenda's always on top of things but I like to double check. I hate being caught off guard with last-minute changes. Nothing irks Decker more than incompetence, and I don't need to give him any more petty reasons to fuck with me over the Wells Covington situation.

After a quick shower, I crawl into bed just in time to get a text from Abigail.

Abigail: I had a great time today.

Me: Me too, miss you though.

Abigail: Wow, did you just say something sweet?

Me: I have a problem over here.

Abigail: What's that?

Me: Cold bed and my dick is lonely.

Abigail: There's Dexter, I was wondering who was texting me. And poor little guy, hope he'll be okay without me.

Me: Nothing poor or little about my dick.

Abigail: SMH. I wasn't being literal.

Me: Sounded literal. Afraid I'll need to prove myself again. Come on over.

Abigail: Some of us have to be at work on time.

Me: All right, then. No more pudding and a spanking is in order.

Abigail: Hmm, I may need to misbehave more often.

Me: Careful, Abby. You're making my poor little dick hard.

Abigail: I'm sure he misses me. What are you going to do to him?

I stare at the message. Shit, is she really going there? Fuck it. I'm not passing this up.

Me: It's not so much what I'll do to him as what I'm going to think about while I do it.

I can't get the image out of my mind of her squirming on her bed, touching herself as she reads my messages. I need to perform at my best here.

Abigail: What are you going to think about?

Me: Bending you over the bed, and spanking your ass just to see the outline of my hand.

Abigail: Then what?

Me: Tease all around your pussy with my tongue, until you beg me to touch you.

Abigail: Maybe I'm already touching myself.

Fuck. She has me so wound up I might explode. I stare down at my lap and my dick is pointing up at the sky, the only thing on my mind is feeling Abigail's tight pussy wrapped around it.

Me: You're definitely getting spanked for that.

Abigail: That a promise or a threat?

Me: Both.

Abigail: While you figure it out, I'll be here all alone with my vibrator, dreaming of being punished for my insubordination.

A close-up photo comes through of her slender hand shoved down the front of her white lace panties.

Fuck texting. I try to Facetime her, but she rejects the call.

Me: Pick up the damn phone, woman!

I'm so hard it aches as I stare at the picture.

Fuck it.

Two can play at this game. I send her a picture of me fisting my dick. Obviously, I angle the camera just right so it looks gigantic. Minutes go by and there's no response. I try to call three times and it just rings and goes to voicemail.

You dirty little girl, Abigail. I can't believe this.

I'm going to think up some way to get revenge, as soon as I finish jerking off to her picture.

ABIGAIL

"OH HEY! WHAT'S UP?" I stare at Mary as she hovers near the edge of my desk. We don't usually talk much, even though I've worked with her longer than anyone here.

She transferred from Dallas at the same time I did. From what little I could gather, it was to do some work for her church up here.

She has on a terrible brown sweater that completely washes out her complexion. It's paired with navy blue dress pants and black leather flats. She could be so cute and adorable if she'd let me dress her or take her shopping, but I don't want to be rude and suggest it.

She fidgets, reaching up and fumbling with the rosary beads around her neck. I don't know how she survived the interview process because she's incredibly shy. She knows the law like nobody's business, though, and is always putting together presentations for partners. We call her the Power Point wizard.

"I was just over near the partners' offices and Dexter needs you. Said it's urgent. I hope you're not in trouble. He seemed really mad."

"Did he now?"

She grimaces. "I don't think he's had any coffee. He was grumpy." Her voice drops down low and she glances around to see if anyone is listening. She makes a twisted-up face and does her best Dexter impersonation and reenacts the whole scene for me.

I bite back a laugh. I can picture it all playing out in my mind perfectly. "Thanks for letting me know. I'll go see what he wants."

"No problem." She smiles and goes to her little cubicle. "Good luck," she whispers as I shove my chair back to go see what Dexter is up to.

This better be work related.

I walk over to his office and stop in front of Brenda. "Hi. Mary said Mr. Collins needed to see me."

"Yeah, go on in. He's waiting." She waves me forward.

I smooth my hand over my skirt before knocking on the door. I don't want to just barge in even though she said to.

"Come in." His voice is smooth and deep, and I feel it reverberate through my body. I blink a few times. Things are different now. We've spent the night together more than once. We've been intimate.

I take a deep breath and walk in.

"Close the door." He says it like it's a request, but we both know it's an order.

I close the door behind me.

I don't know why, but for some reason I lock it too. Okay, I know exactly why I lock it. Because I know exactly what Dexter is up to and I don't want to look intimidated. I want to look confident and sexy. The lock clicks and the sound of the bolt echoes through the room. Or maybe I just imagine it did. It sounded so loud inside my head I could swear the whole office heard the noise.

You're being paranoid.

I gingerly step toward Dexter who still hasn't looked up. "You wanted to see me?"

I can't read him. He's emotionless, staring down at some papers on his desk. "Come here."

I shuffle forward and start to take a seat in front of his desk, but he shakes his head at me with that devilish smirk.

"Abigail, I said come here. You're over there. I want you over here."

I sigh. "Dex."

His voice goes low and he speaks slowly, enunciating each syllable. "I said come here. *Now.*"

Something flashes in his eyes, a primal hunger that ties my stomach in a knot. He has his damn jacket off, and the whole sleeves-rolled-up thing again too. I think he does it on purpose to torture me. Does he just accidentally look this hot and commanding, or does he practice it in the mirror at home?

My feet urge me forward though my head screams no. I know what he wants to do and it's completely inappropriate. "I've told you. Not at the office."

"Don't make me get up."

I want him so bad I can't see straight. My entire body is on fire. I know I locked the door and nobody can see in here, but still.

I shake my head at him but bite my lower lip at the same time. I shouldn't tease him because it's so not cool, but it's like my actions are completely separate from my brain at this point.

"It's gonna be worse." He starts to get up and I walk over to him.

I can't believe you're doing this.

Every time I think Dex can't turn me on more than he has before, he proves me wrong.

"What are you going to do?" I inch my way around his desk.

He doesn't respond and my heart is about to redline its way out of my chest.

As soon as I'm in front of him, he reaches out and snatches my forearm. I don't even know what happens, because it's all a blur, but suddenly I'm bent across his lap and he has me pinned down with one arm.

Holy. Shit.

I'm on fire inside, and for two different reasons. I'm so into this, but it's so wrong. "We're at work." I hiss the words out at him, knowing it's only goading him even more.

His hand slides up the back of my thigh and scorches a trail of fire up my leg. "Why'd you lock the door then?" His voice comes out all gravelly.

Warmth spreads through my veins and I soften to him automatically. I have no answer. "I... I don't know."

"Strike one." His firm hand squeezes my ass over my skirt. It feels so damn good I have to bite back a soft moan in my throat. I'm so damn weak for him, not myself at all when he's around.

"Don't lie to me."

"I'm not."

"Strike two."

"What are you talking about, strikes?"

"Too much talking. Strike three." Dexter yanks my skirt up and his strong fingers knead my ass over my panties.

My eyes dart around the room, making sure all the shades are drawn. If someone saw this, I would never be able to show my face in this office again. "What the hell, *Dexter*?" At the same time I say the words, I close my eyes because it feels so damn good.

I squirm in anticipation because I know he's about to spank me and ever since he did it the first time at his apartment, I've wanted him to do it again.

He shakes his head back and forth. "Fight this all you want. I told you what was going to happen."

"I fell asleep," I say in the most innocent tone I can muster while his fingertips dig into my ass.

"Is that so?"

"Uh huh." I nod my head.

"That's the story you're going with?"

"Yeah."

He laughs. "Okay, maybe I'll let you off the hook this one time."

Disappointment washes over me at once. He's such a tease.

His hold loosens for a second, and then his hand grips my hair.

Whack!

The pain radiates from my ass straight up my spine, and God, it stings so good. I let out a gasp.

"That one is for lying. Tell me the truth, Abby."

"I-I did." I can barely get the words out because I'm so damn aroused and out of breath.

485

His palm rubs over me, like he's warming me up for another one.

Whack!

"Okay, okay!" I grin and huff out a breath. "Fine. If you must know…"

"The truth this time. I'll know if you're lying."

I crane my neck around and fake-scowl back at him. "I got… distracted."

"How?"

My cheeks must turn a bright shade of pink. "I, umm, I was taking care of myself."

"You finished without me?" He growls the words and nips at my ear lobe. His tongue traces the shell of my ear.

Holy shit. The sex at his apartment was phenomenal but this dominant, possessive side of Dexter is heating me up in all kinds of new ways I didn't know I enjoyed until just now.

"I like these." He runs his fingers along each one of my garter belts that ride halfway up my thighs. He snaps them against my skin one at a time, like he has all day to mess with me.

I yelp.

"Shh. Don't want anyone hearing you alone in here with me, with the door locked and the shades drawn. What would people around the office think?"

"Oh my God." I exhale the words.

His hand slides over my mouth while his free hand continues to massage my ass. He continues to take his time, enjoying playing with me like I'm some kind of toy put here for his amusement.

I bite his palm but it's useless. He only tightens his grip.

One. Two. Three. Four.

The swats come in quick succession and I gasp into his palm.

The outline of his hand throbs on my ass, and I feel the heat rush back into my rear.

Dexter releases his palm from my mouth, and I look over my shoulder at him. My eyes narrow on his.

"Want a few more?" He smirks.

"What if I do?" I mumble.

I'm at his mercy and it's impossible to resist him, and judging by the look on his face, he knows it.

He leans down to my ear and growls, "That can be arranged."

"I'm gonna get even for this."

He smirks. "We'll see." He pats me on the ass, gently this time. "Oh, we'll see about that."

"Don't threaten me with a good time." I slide down from his lap, then make my way up and straddle him. Grabbing his hand, I suck two of his fingers into my mouth getting them good and wet.

His gaze pierces through me and his breaths grow ragged at the sight. His eyes go half-hooded.

"Touch me, Dex." I lean next to his head and lick around his ear. "Fuck me

486

with these fingers." I push his hand down between my legs. "I've never been this wet for you before. See for yourself."

As his fingers rub up against me and he feels my heat, his eyes roll back. "Fuck, Abby. I won't be gentle."

I grind against his hand. "I don't want you to be."

He grips my panties and yanks them to the side.

I wrap my arms around his neck. "Please, I need it so bad."

"This what you want?" Dex forces two fingers inside me.

Holy shit. It hurts so damn good.

"You want to fuck my fingers while you're at work? Like a dirty little office slut?"

Oh. My. God.

I can't believe he just said that, and I can't believe how much I liked it.

I nod and purr against his lips. "I've been bad. I deserve to be punished."

His thumb slides up to my clit and he does exactly what I asked for, pumps two fingers in and out. "Yes, you do." He cups me in his palm and squeezes hard, digging his fingers into me. "This pussy is mine. Nobody touches it unless I say they can. That includes you. Is that understood?"

"Yes."

"Say it, Abigail. Tell me who this belongs to." He grips me harder and digs his fingers in.

I whimper through a shaky breath. "It's yours."

He shoves two fingers back in me and his thumb moves back to my clit.

I'm so close already, it's not going to take long. Before I know it, I'm riding his hand while he stares into my eyes. My center coils tight like a spring and I'm on the edge, so damn close. An intense heat funnels between my legs and I gasp in his ear. "Let me come, please."

His free hand massages my breast through my top, then he pinches one of my nipples so hard it yanks my mind out of the clouds.

"You have my permission to come on my fingers like a little whore."

And I'm done for.

I buck and thrash on his hand, every muscle in my body constricting and contracting as the orgasm fires through every nerve ending in my body. "Oh God, Dex."

"Yeah, say my name. Tell me who owns this." He shoves his fingers in deeper.

I shudder a few more times. "Dexter Collins, it's his."

"Goddamn right it is."

I exhale a huge breath. Once I'm finished, I stand up in front of him and straighten my skirt.

Dex stares down at his tented slacks, then back up at me.

I pat him on the shoulder. "Sorry my little office manwhore, I need to get back to work."

"What the fu—"

I'm already almost to his door before he can stand up and turn to face me.

I smirk. "Told you I'd get even." I unlock the door and open it halfway, then turn back. "Maybe I'll make it up to you later, if you take me to dinner."

He smirks his ass off right back. "You're in a lot of trouble."

"A lot?" I grin.

"That's strike twenty-three. Better pack a fucking lunch tonight, Whitley."

A tingle rips up my spine at the thought of what he'll do to me. Mission accomplished. My entire day is going to be amazing now, anticipating tonight.

"See you later, Mr. Collins." I sway my hips as I walk out the door.

I step off the train and head a block toward Dex's apartment, hurrying as fast as I can. It's difficult carrying the casserole dish with me. I had to rush around my apartment while Barbie whined nonstop while I made it.

I pray it's a sufficient peace offering because I have no idea what Dex will have in store for me when I get there. I left him hanging and even felt a little guilty, but it's so much fun. I've never played these little sex games like this. It's so hot. When he finally gets what he wants, it'll be that much better for both of us. That's what I tell myself, but secretly, I worry I pushed things too far. Somehow, he just makes me feel so damn comfortable and sexy around him, that I'm not afraid to do anything I want. The more I think about it, the more I think that's the way it should be.

I love how confident he makes me feel in the bedroom, or the office, when the doors are locked and nobody can see, obviously.

I walk through the front of the building and hop on the elevator up to his floor. When I get to his front door, I ring the doorbell.

The door opens but nobody is in front of it.

"You're late." His voice echoes through the entryway, but I still don't see him anywhere.

"I brought…"

"Get your ass in here."

My heartbeat kicks up about twenty notches.

I take a few tentative steps through the door and I feel a presence slide in behind me. I start to turn.

"Don't fucking turn around, Ms. Whitley."

My breath hitches. "So, we're keeping things formal are—"

Something wraps around my face, cutting off my sentence, and I realize it's one of Dexter's silk ties from work. He covers my eyes and ties it off in the back, a little more forcefully than needed.

"What's this?" He takes the dish from my hand.

"Umm, h-homemade banana pudding."

There's complete silence and I can't see. It's a little disorienting to say the least.

"Dex, what are you doing?"

His finger slides up to my lips. "Shh. You just do what the fuck I say, understand?"

This is so freaking intense. I don't know if I should be scared or elated. Does he have one of those red rooms in his apartment I don't know about? I don't know how I'd feel about *all that*, but something inside me really wants to see where this goes.

"Follow me." He takes me by the hand and leads me down the hall.

At least, that's where I think I'm going. I have no earthly clue where I'm at in his apartment at this point. He turns me into a room then releases my hand.

"Stay there."

I do as he says, then hear him set the dish down on something.

I hear his feet on the wood floor as he walks back over. His hands go to the buttons on my jeans and instinctively I squirm.

He grips both of my hips and digs his fingers in. "Hold still, or you'll only make this worse for yourself."

For some reason I can feel the grin on his face, like I can sense that he's enjoying this immensely.

"Would that be so bad?"

"Probably not." He pops the buttons on my jeans. "For me, anyway."

He slides my pants down and I kick my heels off then step out of them. Next, he grips the hem on my top and lifts it slowly over my head.

"Fuck, your body belongs in the Louvre."

"Thank you, sir."

He hisses out a breath. "You have no idea what it does to me when you call me that."

His hands roam my body, caressing and massaging every square inch of me up and down, until I feel his face right in front of mine and his warm breath plays across my lips.

He doesn't kiss me, though. Just teases the hell out of me like he might do it.

I'm already wet for him. My panties are soaked through.

He slowly inches me back with nothing but his hard frame pressed against my chest until I run into what I assume is the bed. I jolt at the sudden impact.

His hand slides up my stomach to one of my breasts and he grips it tight over my bra, then all at once, his fingers splay across my chest and he shoves me backward.

Panic rips through my body while I fall until my back makes contact with his mattress.

I pant uncontrollably, my heart racing. "Holy shit."

I hear him walk around the bed as I scoot to the middle.

"Lay down." His voice booms through the room.

I do exactly what he says because holy hell is this hot. My senses are dialed up to eleven. Sound, smell, touch… Everything is so intense.

He takes one of my hands in his and ever so delicately, I feel him slip something around my wrist and he ties it off. Then as my brain processes what he's doing, he yanks my arm back and ties me to the bedpost.

"Oh wow, I've never been tied up before."

"Good." He leans over in front of my face, so that I can feel him inches from me. "I'll be your first for everything from here on out." There is zero uncertainty in his voice as he says it.

He does the same thing with my other arm and both of my legs, until I'm stationary in the center of his bed, all four limbs stretched out, in nothing but my bra and panties.

Dexter climbs up on the bed. I feel his weight shifting around on the side of me.

"Look at this fucking body." His hand glides along my ribs and he traces a finger down my shoulder. "So helpless. Nowhere for you to go."

I squirm but it's no use. I can't move at all.

"I could do whatever the fuck I wanted to you right now, Abigail."

Be sexy. For the love of God, be sexy and turn him on more right now.

"Do it then." I spit the words at him.

He snickers. His hand travels over both of my breasts. "I could fuck your tits." His fingers slide up and he shoves two of them in my mouth so hard I nearly choke, but his words remain calm and composed. "Could fuck this pretty mouth."

Oh my God, I might die.

His hand slowly makes its way down my stomach and he cups me in his palm. "This pussy." Two fingers slip down lower and he presses them hard up against my ass.

I squirm on the bed, but oh my God, it feels kind of nice.

"So fucking dirty. Look at you. You're enjoying yourself." He applies even more pressure and I hear his breath go ragged. "I could definitely fuck this ass. I could shove my cock anywhere it'll fit in you."

My thoughts race, but I don't even have time to process all the filthy things he's telling me because his hand slides up around my throat.

It's extremely possessive, but he doesn't choke me, just grips tight enough for me to know his hand is there. I gasp out a breath because I don't know how much longer I can stand all this anticipation.

"Don't worry. I have you for the entire night. I think I'll take my time."

His hand slides down to my breast and in one violent motion he yanks the cup down, exposing me to the air. My nipples harden at his touch. He reaches over and yanks the other down the same way. Ever so slowly, he leans down and grazes my nipples with the tip of his tongue.

I shudder and fight against the restraints for a quick second, before I relax again. I want to grab his head and put it between my legs, but I can't do a damn thing all tied up like this. It's agony.

His hand slides down and he caresses my pussy over my panties. "Look how wet you are, Abby. You get off on this dirty shit, don't you?"

"No." I shake my head. "It's not doing it for me."

He doesn't fall for it at all. Just snickers. "Sure. Sure. You fucking hate this, don't you?" He slips a finger inside my panties and rubs it over my clit. "Yeah, look how fast you're breathing. I can hear your damn heart racing. You definitely want me to stop."

My hips betray me and lift against his hand.

"So responsive." Then, his finger slides down farther and he presses it up against my ass again.

This time, I roll my hips and push my ass up against his hand.

He snickers again. "Just like I thought. You want to be my filthy little whore, Abigail?"

I nod furiously, unable to play this game anymore. "I'll do whatever you want. Just don't stop touching me, please."

He immediately gets up off the bed and it's like I can feel it when his presence is gone.

I writhe against my restraints. "Dex, please. I'm so close. Come back, I need it." Hell, I'd settle for straddling his damn pillow at this point and trying to ride one out.

His door closes and he leaves me there. Dude freaking leaves me alone, tied up to his bed!

"Dex! Dex!" I keep shouting.

He makes me wait for a good three minutes, then walks back in. I only know because I hear the hinges on the door and then his feet on the hardwood floor.

"I'm going to *kill* you when you let me up."

"Highly doubtful. You'll be begging for more, trust me."

"You wish." I hold my head up as far as it'll go, trying to get a sense of where he is.

It's completely silent.

His hand grips my hair and yanks me down to the bed. I gasp as his knuckles dig into my scalp. How did he get over here so quickly? I didn't even hear him.

He leans over, and I can feel his mouth inches from mine. "Your pussy is wet. Your body tells me when you lie."

I start to say something and oh my goodness.

Something ice cold makes contact with my nipple and the delicious chill tears through my limbs.

What the hell is that? It feels like a spoon flipped upside down.

He rubs it over both of my nipples, and it feels so damn amazing.

Then, he slides the curved part down my stomach. When he gets to my pelvis, he pulls my panties halfway down my legs.

Holy shit, he's not...

He does.

He rubs the back of the spoon across me, then presses it down on my clit.

Never in my life did I think a man would get me off with a spoon, but Dex has me damn near there and he's barely even touched me.

He rubs the spoon in small circles all over me.

His fingers trace a line up my jaw, and then he pulls the tie back from my eyes.

When my eyes adjust to the darkness of the room, I spot Dex next to me, completely naked.

He has the pudding I brought, and he scoops some out and makes a show of savoring his first bite, right in front of me, with the spoon he just rubbed all over me.

It might be the hottest damn thing I've ever seen in my life.

He licks it, taking his sweet time, curling his tongue around it. Then, his eyes land on mine and he heats my entire body with nothing but his stare. "Best fucking pudding I've ever had in my life." He scoops another bite and shovels it in his mouth. "Tastes like bananas." He leans down to my ear. "And *you.*"

My chest heaves up and down with deep breaths, watching him eat the damn pudding right in front of me. I need him so damn bad right now. My body is in flames. I ache just watching him, and when I think it can't get any hotter, he spoons some pudding out and dumps it right above my pussy, then spreads it around slowly with the spoon, his eyes never leaving mine the whole time.

Next, he does the same, right on each of my breasts. Then each side of my neck. He smears pudding on the insides of my thighs and makes a little trail from my breasts down to my stomach.

"That should be enough. I have quite an appetite."

His fan is on above us, and I can feel the chill everywhere he has the pudding on me.

He takes his sweet-ass time, walking over and setting the dish on his nightstand, along with the spoon. The wait is killing me. I writhe on the bed, covered in the pudding I hauled ass to make after work. It might be the best peace offering of all time.

He moves the tie back over my eyes until everything goes black again. "I'll be back shortly, and I'm going to have you for dessert."

I don't know how much more I can take. It's excruciating.

He walks off and he's gone for like another five minutes that seems like an hour. This time, I don't even hear him come again. I don't know what's happened until two hands spread my thighs apart as far as they'll go and then it happens all at once.

His tongue makes contact with my skin and he laps up the pudding from the insides of my thighs, constantly grazing the edges of where I need his mouth, but not making direct contact.

I move against the restraints in agony, trying to get him to speed up but he doesn't. "I can't hold it, Dex, you have no idea."

"Don't fucking come until I'm finished. Or I'll leave you tied up all goddamn night."

I nod furiously. "Okay."

I can do this. I can do this. There's no way in hell you'll last until he's done. It's impossible.

Dex ignores my pussy, once he's done with my thighs, and hovers over me up to my neck. He cleans both sides of it with his tongue, and I fight the urge to arch my chest up into him. His hard cock drags across my stomach, and I know he just got pudding all over it. I can feel it smeared up to my chest.

"You made me make a mess." His hand cups my jaw and his fingers squeeze my cheeks until my mouth forms a big O. "Gonna need you to take care of that for me."

I nod, eager to do anything to relieve myself of this torturous foreplay that I secretly want to never end.

He presses the head of his cock to my lips, and I open immediately and take him in.

Sure enough, as soon as he pushes into my mouth, I taste the pudding all up and down him. I'm not one to be outdone, and I want to be sexy for him, so as soon as he pulls his dick away from my mouth, I say, "Your balls too, sir."

He groans, loud, and breaks character for a brief moment. "Fuck, Abby. You're killing me."

He lowers his balls and I lick and suck each one of them, until I'm sure I got every speck of banana pudding off them.

Dex hovers back down and licks across both my breasts. He bites down on my nipples and sucks until I'm writhing in agony.

"You're gonna have to hurry. I'm not going to last."

He spreads my legs apart and his tongue connects with my clit. I buck my hips as hard as I can at him as he fucks me with his mouth.

"Please, Dexter. Please." I drag out the last word on a whimper. My hands grip his headboard, and I'm about to shatter into a million pieces.

"Okay." As he says it, he shoves his thick cock inside me, and I come undone all over it. "Fuck, Abby." He groans the words as I clamp down on him and have the most intense orgasm of my life.

In my limited sexual experience, there have been self-induced orgasms, regular Dexter-induced orgasms, and then *this* orgasm. It's on another plane of existence.

My mind is a blur, my arms and legs trembling, my entire body seizing as I writhe against the restraints. His headboard thrashes against the wall, banging loud enough anyone in a three-block radius might hear. I squeeze around him while my hips buck uncontrollably.

"Dexter." I groan out his name.

I'm in a fog, floating around on the clouds and it's like a strong drug flows through my veins down to my fingertips and toes. I don't know how long it lasts, but it's pure euphoria. Fuzzy stars firework in front of my eyelids. After a few long seconds, hell, it might even be minutes, my brain returns from a temporary fog and I crane my head around, the room still completely black.

I shake my hands and legs, panting uncontrollably. "Get this shit off me, now."

He slides the blindfold down and his eyes widen when he sees me, and he furiously unties all the ties. The second my arms and legs are free I dive into him and knock him onto his back. Before he can recover, I straddle him and put his cock back inside me. I start rolling my hips, riding him as hard as I can.

"Fucking hell." His eyes roll back then narrow on mine.

Before I know it, he's flipped me to my back and he's on top, pumping into me. I'm not even sure I know what happens after that, but we're a mess of tangled arms and limbs. Dex fucks me so hard, I come again without notice and my whole body spasms underneath him.

"God, Abby, fuck." He grunts and groans. His whole body stiffens, and he comes deep inside me. It's like it never ends as he fills me up so much it streams out around his cock and down my thighs.

We both pant heavily, staring into each other's eyes, then we both grin at each other.

He lingers above me for a long moment and brushes a wayward, sweaty strand of hair from my face. "You're mine." It's the only two words he says and then he collapses onto my shoulder and nuzzles into my neck, his arms wrapped tight around me.

Yep. He's not wrong.

ABIGAIL

IT'S BEEN EXACTLY four days since the pudding incident. That's what I'm calling it, anyway, and it's been impossible to think about anything else.

I gather all the information Rick Lawrence gave me on Wells Covington. I haven't looked at any of it yet and Decker asked for it ASAP. I glance down at the top page and see his picture. His dark eyes stare back at me, and for some reason it sends a shiver up my spine.

It's probably because he was there the night Dexter and I had the huge fight. I think he just reminds me of a shit memory, but I can't help the effect his picture has on me. He stood there and basically cheered Dexter on, jumping around, voicing his approval. Asshole.

I still wonder why Decker is looking into his background. He's done it for a few other clients, but they're usually criminal cases, not for potential financial clients. It seems weird but I'm sure Decker has a reason. You don't build a firm this size without being smart and careful.

I'm sure Dex knows about it by now, but I don't like talking about work when I'm with him. I get enough of that here, and we have plenty of other things to do. Not to mention when you bring up money or work with Dexter, he gets that shark look on his face, like it's all that matters. I love possessive Dexter, but I like a nice mix of that guy and the boyish one who tells me about phone calls with his mom.

I do my best to remain professional at work, well, other than the time he spanked me in his office, but other than that, my willpower has kept me in check since. He's always trying to sneak kisses and touch me in front of people whenever he gets the chance, and I still have to tell him to knock it off.

I hurry to Decker's office to get the file to him. He's about to leave for the day and I want to catch him before he takes off for the weekend. I heard Tate mention something at lunch about them going away to do wedding plans and she was sneaking out of the office early. When is their wedding, anyway? It must be coming up soon, but they still haven't announced a date, even though they already did the bachelor and bachelorette parties. Tate's was back in Dallas a while ago. I went home that weekend and went out with them.

When I get to Decker's office, he walks out the door with Tate.

I put myself right in their path. "Hey, Mr. Collins, I have that uhh, project you had me working on." I glance around because I'm not sure Tate is supposed to know, and I like to follow instructions to the letter when I get an assignment.

"Is it top secret or something?" says Tate.

Decker ignores her. "Thanks. Great work." He snatches it from my hand. "Enjoy your weekend."

"You too." Tate winks at me like she knows something I don't.

I watch them leave totally smitten with one another. She teases him about the file, he whispers something in her ear, and she laughs. Decker is a complete hard ass. Tate too, but something about the two of them together, they mellow each other out. The man is head over heels in love with her. I see it in the way he looks at her when he thinks no one is watching. He looks at her like Deacon looks at Quinn and like—oh my God.

It's the exact same way Dexter looks at me.

I don't know why the thought hits me right then, on a Friday, in the middle of the office. But it slams into my chest like a Mack truck.

I suck in a breath. Holy shit. I mean I don't think Dexter is in love with me. That's crazy, but he definitely *likes* me a lot. I know the look and I'm stupid for not recognizing it sooner.

When I get back to my desk, Dexter is waiting for me. I take a seat as he leans over the cubicle. "Hey, you. What are you doing?"

He has that boyish grin on his face and gives me that look I just saw on Decker when he stared at Tate. "Don't make any plans for tonight. I have a surprise. Pick you up at seven."

I don't get a chance to contest because he immediately turns and struts down the hall.

Okay, I sneak a look at his ass when nobody is watching. Just one though.

Damn, it's a fine ass too.

DEXTER

I swing by my apartment and grab a quick shower before my date with Abigail. For some reason, moments of clarity always come to me in the shower. It's where I do my best thinking outside the office. It's usually about work, but not so in this case.

I'm either nuts or I'm fucking falling in love. I never go this above and beyond planning dates for women I'm with. I may help my brothers out when they need it, because they're clueless and I'm awesome, but I make fun of them for doing this shit.

What does that mean? I know I'm not in love with Abigail. It's too soon and falling in love is for pussies. I do love burying my cock inside her, though. Thank God she's on the pill because I've been reckless. Coming inside her like an idiot; I just can't help myself. The moments are so intense and it's just… It's never been like this with anyone else. There's a connection there. A force I can't pull away from.

I can definitely see a future with her. I know she has reservations about getting serious with anyone. She's mentioned it multiple times, and it heats my blood anytime I hear her say it.

You'd have to be blind to not see we just work together. We fit. She may be young and not want to settle down, but I know she feels it too. It's more than lust. I thought that was all it was at first, and once I fucked her, I'd have it out of my system and want to move on, but I can't. It runs much deeper than getting her into my bed. It's bone-deep, and I feel the pull every goddamn day. I just want to wake up and see her face. It's painful when she's not around me.

I shoot Abigail a quick text to let her know I'm on my way. When I arrive at her building, I spot her watching for me in her window. I take the stairs two at a time instead of the elevator.

She opens the door before I get there, and I walk right past her.

"Dex, what the…"

"You need an overnight bag."

"Oh." She grins before the recognition sets in. "Ohh." She draws the syllable out this time.

Her roommate rounds the corner in a robe, then shrieks when she sees me.

"Abigail, why the hell is he—"

I hold up a hand. "Save it. I'll be gone in two seconds. Go back to your room."

"You don't tell me what…"

I glare right at her. The stare I reserve for opposing counsel and my worst enemies, back when I used to try criminal cases right out of law school.

She immediately turns on a dime and walks to her room.

"Holy cow. How did you do that?" Abigail gawks at me like I'm some kind of magician.

"Doesn't matter. Hurry up before she changes her mind and comes back out here. I want to stay in a good mood."

"Good idea." Abigail rifles through her armoire and grabs a few things and shoves them in a bag. "You *have* to teach me your Jedi ways, Obi-Wan. It would drastically improve my standard of living."

I reach out a hand. "Join me, and together we can rule the galaxy as… Shit, that doesn't work, does it?"

She shakes her head like I'm an idiot. "Was that some weird attempt to get me to call you daddy?"

I burst into a laugh. "No, actually, I'm not much of a fan. It's weird."

She nods. "Agreed, I'll never call you that."

"Thanks." I kiss her on the forehead. "And, I don't know if the death stare can be taught. It's just a natural talent."

She does this fake glare at me, a terrible imitation of my courtroom scowl.

I can't stop laughing and hold out my hand again. "Come on, crazy. Let's go on an adventure."

She looks around and giggles like a girl sneaking out of her parents' house late at night. "Okay. Let's do it."

We both run down the stairs, even though there's no hurry, and exit out into the freezing cold night, laughing like kids.

I didn't think I could ever have this much fun again. It's even better than I thought, like playing hide and seek with my brothers when we were little at my Uncle's house outside the city.

I open the passenger door for her and take her bag and stick it in the trunk.

I return to the driver's seat. "You ready?"

Abigail smiles. "Hell yes. Barbie is a nightmare, alternating between raging and crying."

"That bad?"

Abigail rolls her eyes and groans. "You have no idea. I don't know how women do this whole girlfriend thing. I'm exhausted."

The hairs on the back of my neck stand up at attention. "What?"

She reaches for my forearm and laughs. "I didn't mean, like *girlfriend* girlfriend, I mean like, being friends with a girl. I don't mind being *your* girlfriend at all."

My heart warms immediately. We've never really discussed our relationship status. We just sort of went from zero to sixty in a matter of weeks. I keep glancing over at her and smiling.

"I have something on my face?"

I shake my head. "No, we just haven't really talked about, *us*, you know? You called yourself my girlfriend."

"Oh." She looks away. "Was I being presumptuous?"

I squeeze her hand tight. "Hell no. Not at all. I loved hearing you say it. I've been so caught up in work, and, well, you..." I shake my head and my jaw clenches. "I didn't do it right. Fuck." I glare out the window. "I should've asked you. It should've been a thing. It feels like it should've been a big romantic..."

"Dex?" She shakes my arm.

I turn to her and can't help the shame coursing through me. "Yeah?"

"The answer is yes, okay?"

I don't think I could want to kiss her any more than I do right now, but instead I decide to tease her a little. "Yes what?"

She fights to hold back a smile. "You know *what*, you big idiot." She smacks me on the arm.

I can't take it anymore and the first thing that pops in my head is to tell her I love her.

Whoa! What the fuck?

My palms get slick on the steering wheel and my shoulders stiffen.

"You okay?"

I look past her and play it off. "It's nothing." I try to shake the thought out of my head. If I was driving alone, I'd roll the window down and shout it right out of my head. I smile. "We're gonna have fun tonight. Deal?" I hold out my fist.

She bumps it and her smile returns. "Deal."

"You're gonna love it."

"I'm excited." She's practically bouncing in her seat.

Abigail is so beautiful. I'm so damn lucky. I'm going to prove to her this shit is real between us. She might say she's my girlfriend, but that lingering tension is still there, like she's going against her own wishes. I need to get rid of that quick before it poisons things.

"Do I at least get a hint?"

"Nope. But trust me. You'll love it."

"All right."

A few minutes later I pull up for the valet.

Abigail glances around. "A hotel?" Her eyes widen and she mumbles, "A very *nice* hotel. Holy..."

"Yeah."

The valets open both our doors. One of them takes my keys and opens the trunk.

We walk inside and get checked into our room. The valets carry our bags and lead us up to the elevators and into the suite.

The phone rings and the manager tells me everything is set while Abigail walks around, scoping the place out. It's not the top floor like Wells normally reserves, but it's nice as fuck. It's a corner suite with fantastic views of the city.

"This is incredible, Dexter."

"Haven't seen anything yet." I hold out my hand. "You ready?"

"Almost." Her arms go around me and she brings me in for a deep, passionate kiss. After a few long seconds, she lets go. "Okay. Now I'm ready."

I swat her on the ass playfully as she walks toward the door.

We take the elevator up to the rooftop.

"This way." I take her by the hand, and I'm so excited I'm damn near shaking.

"Oh my God, I love how excited you are. You look like a little boy on Christmas."

"I don't want to build up the hype too much, but you're going to love it."

The wind whips up from between the skyscrapers. "Where are you taking me? It's freezing!"

"Don't worry. You'll warm up fast. Come on." I think I might be more excited than she is.

Right when we're about to turn the corner, I stop us. "Hang on, I'm not sure you're ready. Maybe we should…"

She flies right past me. "Dexter Collins I'm going to—" She stops on a dime as soon as she sees it. Her hand covers her mouth for a second, and then a tear slides down her cheek.

Oh God, did I screw this up? Maybe it was too much.

She's practically shaking, and I don't know whether I should turn and run for the hills or what. I slowly walk over to her with caution in every step.

She looks over at me and smiles so damn big through the tears. She waves me over to her, and I jog the last four steps.

She wraps her arms around my neck. "Oh my God, it's… You…" She leans up and kisses me, then pulls back. "I can't even talk I'm such a mess right now."

I spin her back around to face it and wrap my arms around her from behind.

"I can't believe you did this. How…"

"I know the manager. Come on, follow me." I take her by the hand.

Abigail can't peel her eyes away from the rooftop ice-skating rink. Tall skyscrapers shoot up all around us and evergreen Christmas trees form a perimeter around the outside. They're covered with red bows and Christmas decorations.

We get our skates all laced up, and I hold out my arm. "You ready? Got the place to ourselves for the next few hours. Did I do good or what?"

"Yeah, you… It's just perfect, and you surprised me, as usual." She cranes her head around, taking it all in. "It's amazing." She looks like she might cry again and wipes at the corner of her eye. "No one has ever done something like this for me before. Not for a date."

I take her hands in mine and look down at her. "I know I have some rough patches to work on. I'm not perfect." I gesture out toward the ice. "This is just the beginning."

She hooks an arm in mine and she can't stop grinning. I don't think it could get any more perfect, but once we're out in the open, ever so slowly, large snowflakes start floating down all around us. If this isn't meant to be, I don't know what the hell is.

We get to the edge and I help her onto the ice. Her knees wobble and shake.

"Easy. I've got you." I grip her waist and guide her until she gets balanced.

Abigail laughs. "I look like a newborn calf finding its legs."

I shake my head. Southern girls. "I'll have to take your word for it."

She looks totally relaxed; despite the fact her legs are working overtime to keep her balance. "They look just like me; awkward."

"You're doing great, come on."

I lead her around the rink slowly.

She keeps looking over. "Seriously, Dex. Thank you for this. It's so much fun. I had no idea this is what we'd do."

"I have more planned tomorrow."

"What more could there be?"

"You'll see." I skate off and cut around the ice a couple times, then head over to her and spin around backward, grab her hands, and pull her along with me.

"Okay, hotshot. Now I'm impressed. Where'd you learn how to do that?"

"Everyone up here can skate. It's like playing football down in Texas. I played some hockey when I was younger. My mom said I needed a healthy outlet to burn off energy and take out some aggression."

"I could help you with some of that aggression."

My cock strains against my zipper when she says stuff like that. "Don't be a tease. I still owe you one more. We're not even yet."

"I have no idea what you're talking about." She feigns innocence. "We're totally even."

"Oh, Christmas clown. Don't act all innocent. You know exactly what you did. Got me all worked up on two different occasions and then ghosted me." I slow to a stop, pulling her to me for a kiss.

"I would never. I'm a southern lady." She uses a fake southern drawl that's way over the top.

Truth be told, it's kind of hot. I wouldn't mind her doing it again.

Our lips meet, and her mouth parts, inviting me in for a deep kiss.

It sets me on fire inside. I need her, like now. Once we part, I give her a smirk. "We better calm down, don't want to melt the ice."

"Okay, that was corny." She shakes her head, laughing.

"I thought it was pretty smooth. Kissing me, is like…"

She puts a hand on my chest. "Just stop, Dex. You're embarrassing yourself."

I yank her into me and lift her up off the ice. Our mouths connect again, and I twirl us around in a slow spin while I kiss her. It's fucking incredible. Maybe the most perfect moment of my life with the Christmas trees and skyscrapers and snow falling all around us.

After we part, I cradle Abigail in my arms and skate us around for a few laps. She nuzzles up next to me and she just looks—safe, like she feels right at home. It's amazing. I could do this shit for hours.

Finally, out of nowhere, she says, "Keep this up and I'm gonna suck your dick so hard you can't breathe."

"What the...?" It takes me by surprise and my feet fly out from under me.

All I can hear is the sound of Abigail shriek and then her laughing as she comes down right on top of me.

"Are you okay? Are you hurt?" I scramble to try and get up, but she straddles me and pins me down.

She's dying laughing. "I'm sorry, I just..." She mimes what just happened, with half sentences that make no sense, and she laughs so hard reenacting it she can't breathe. "You were just, so... And then I said..."

I nod, trying to hold in a laugh. "You don't say shit like that when someone's skating you around on a block of ice."

She's damn near hyperventilating. Her cheeks are bright pink. Finally, she collapses onto me and we're lying there on the ice, like a couple of fools, me on my back and her on top of me.

Before I can think, I say, "I'm falling for you, Abby."

I expect her to take off so fast she leaves a vapor trail behind. But, she doesn't. She presses her lips to mine for a long second, then sighs. "I know."

I flip her over and tickle her ribs. "Seriously, you're gonna Han Solo me like that?"

She's laughing so hard she can barely breathe again. "Yeah, I mean, we were on the ice and I started thinking of carbonite then Harrison Ford and it just kind of..."

I stop tickling her for a second, then push a strand of hair from her face. She stares up at me with those baby blue eyes that could stop a man's heart. "I'm falling for you too, Dex. Hard." She looks away. "It's bad. It scares me."

I cup her cheek in my palm. "Why?"

She puts her hand on mine and leans into it. Fuck I love when she does that. She's so vulnerable right now, her feelings totally exposed. "Because you could hurt me. Like, you could really hurt me bad."

I shake my head. "I'll never hurt you, Abby. I promise."

She stares at me. Her face hardens, then she reaches up and cups my cheek. "Please don't make promises you can't keep."

"I'll never break that promise. I won't."

She nods. "Okay."

I still can't tell if she believes me or not, but I don't care. I won't ever break her heart, so I have nothing to worry about. We're perfect together.

"Come on. You're getting cold. Let's warm you up with some hot chocolate." We skate over to the benches and change into our shoes, then go into the heated lounge. I had hot chocolate brought in from Lavazza and Chicago-style hot dogs from Hot Doug's, both the best in the city.

"Jesus how many marshmallows you put in there?" I laugh at the mountain toppling over the brim of her mug.

"What are you talking about? So sue me. I like a little hot cocoa with my marshmallows." She flings one at me.

"God, you're adorable." I scoop whipped cream off the top of mine and dollop her nose with it.

"You're so dead for that." She doesn't wipe it away.

"Did I ruin your makeup?" I grin.

Her mouth drops. "I'm not wearing makeup."

I squint. "You sure?"

"Yes, I'm sure."

I look down at my cup. "They're going to fire you from being the Christmas clown if you don't keep your makeup on."

"Oh, now you're really a dead man."

"Yeah right, come here." I hug her into my side and kiss the top of her hair. "You ready to go to our room?"

"That depends."

"On what?"

"You gonna stop being mean to me?"

"Oh quit playing the victim. You love it." I squeeze her hip and slide my palm up under her sweater.

"Holy sh... Your hand is cold."

"So warm me up then."

Abigail stares up at me with a goofy grin.

I kiss her once more and slide my hand up farther and tweak one of her nipples.

She pulls back and nods. "Yep, let's go to the room."

ABIGAIL RUSHES AROUND the hotel room, throwing clothes on, even more excited than she was last night. "I didn't know there would be a Christmas parade. Are you freaking serious? It's not even Thanksgiving yet."

Every year they have the Magnificent Mile Christmas Parade and tree lighting ceremony. It's the week before Thanksgiving this year, but when Abigail told me how crazy she gets for Christmas I knew I'd have to take her.

"I'd never joke about Christmas." I glance off at the corner of the ceiling. "Not around you anyway."

"Damn right. You better not when I'm not around either. It's not a joking matter, Collins." She wags a finger at me with fake anger. "I don't know why I put up with you."

I hold up my hand as I count the reasons on each finger. "You like to fuck me. I take you on amazing dates. I make you feel wanted. I pay attention to details."

"Damn you're good." She laughs. "I noticed you listed me getting to fuck you first."

"It *was* in order of importance, yes."

She shakes her head. "You're so damn cocky."

"I know." I smack her playfully on the ass. "Get dressed or I'm going to chain you to the bed and eat your pussy all day."

She shrugs. "Can we compromise?"

I quirk an eyebrow up. "How so?"

"You can do what you just said, as long as we're at the parade on time."

My cock goes hard at the thought and I smile at how cute she is. "I suppose your needs can be accommodated."

She smiles, but then scoots back on the bed when she sees the hungry look in my eyes. "Uh oh. What did I just agree to?"

"You wanted this, Abigail." I crawl up over her and use one of my ties to bind her wrists together over her head. It's not as good as having her completely subdued like she was in my room, but it'll do. I roll her tank top up over her shoulders and neck, leaving it over her eyes like a blindfold.

"Dex!" She squirms beneath me.

"Be still." I drag my tongue between the valley of her breasts, pinching both nipples between my fingers.

I slide farther down her and rip her panties in half because they get in my way.

"Hey, I liked those."

"You'll like this more." I flick my tongue across her clit and her thighs squeeze around my head.

Life is good.

I could stay buried between Abigail's legs the rest of my life if she'd let me. I'd get down on my knees and worship her pussy every damn day.

It doesn't take long and she's moaning out my name as an orgasm rocks through her. When she's done, I pull her shirt back down.

"Okay for real, now. We need to hurry."

"What about you?"

I love how considerate she always is. Like she always wants things to be fair. But I love going down on her. I love making her feel good, even when I don't get anything out of it. I really don't mind it at all.

"Don't worry about me. We can take care of me later. This weekend is about you."

"Hey, Dex?"

"Yeah?"

"I'm falling a little more."

I smile. "I know."

ABIGAIL

THIS WEEKEND HAS BEEN TOO good to be true, and we're still not done yet. It's Sunday, and I'm definitely falling for Dex and I don't know how I feel about that, other than the fact that I can't help myself. You don't get to pick and choose when and who it happens with, the heart just knows when it knows.

It's scary how much I like him. Ninety-five percent of the time, he's too good to be true. He took me freaking ice skating and then took me to the Christmas parade and the tree lighting yesterday. The way Dex looked at me under all the twinkling lights... He says he's falling for me, but it's more than that. He's fallen already. I just know. I feel it deep inside me, and if I'm being honest with myself, I'm right there with him.

My two biggest reservations are how he handled the Kyle/Nick situation, and that he's demolishing my plans. Finding myself a Dexter Collins was not supposed to be in the cards for three to five years max, according to my life plan. I always stick to my plans. If I set out to do something, I do it.

It's so hard to make that adjustment. What happens after this happy phase when things get serious? How will Dex handle a high-pressure situation when things aren't all sunshine and rainbows? These are things I need to know, regardless of how well put together he seems in his professional life. That doesn't necessarily equate to personal life where the emotional stakes are much higher.

I'm reckless around him. I'm on the pill but I should still make him wear a condom and I don't. The worst part is I know he'd do it for me without question, and I don't even ask him to.

I look over the red sparkly dress he gave me in the mirror one more time. He told me to put it on and get ready to go to dinner. It fits perfectly. How the hell did he pull that off? Did he go through my closet when I wasn't looking and find my size?

I smooth my hair over my shoulder and apply some lipstick and mascara. This is as good as I'm going to get, but I don't think Dex would care one way or the other.

I walk out of the bathroom and do a little twirl for him. "How do I look?"

"Gorgeous." He helps me into my jacket. "There's a car waiting for us downstairs."

We get down to the lobby of the hotel and there's a limousine and a driver. When he said a car was waiting, I thought he'd called us a cab. I glance over at him all dressed up in his Marc Jacobs suit and Saint Laurent dress shoes. He looks refined with his perfectly slicked-back hair, like he just stepped out of a magazine. All these dates and the way he looks, if Mom ever meets him, she's going to eat her words. He is *all* man. I know she always pictured me staying in Texas and marrying a local boy like she did, but she never seems to judge my life decisions. If she was here, she'd be pushing me toward him.

She's old fashioned and thinks the man should take care of the woman. I like that to some degree, but I'm much more modern. I like having a job and making my own money, making my own way. It's empowering. I don't like being dependent on anyone. Even if this works out with Dex, I'll still always feel that way. Staying at home and taking care of kids and a house is not for me. That doesn't mean I don't like it when he gets all forceful and takes charge, though. It's just a situational thing.

We climb into the back where a tray of champagne flutes and strawberries await us.

"Where we going?"

"Another surprise." He feeds me a strawberry to silence me.

We ride a little ways and I sip some champagne. The car comes to a stop. I try to look out the window, but Dexter stops me.

"No peeking. Just trust me."

"I do trust you." I try to steal a glance over his shoulder. "The suspense is killing me, though."

He shakes his head. "Looks like we're doing this again, since I can't trust you to keep your eyes closed." He sighs, grinning the whole time, and pulls his tie off and wraps it around my eyes.

"Damn it, Dex."

"You only have yourself to blame."

"Fine."

He finishes and I hear the car door open. I get that tingly feeling all over my body because there's no clue what he has planned this time. I could end up naked or in the middle of a football stadium, I just don't know.

Dex leads me from the car then swoops me into his arms, cradling me. I hook my arms around his neck and inhale. I smell water and the sound of boats.

"Ohh, are we going on a boat?" I move to take the blindfold off.

Dex sighs. "Would you stop? You're ruining this shit. I'm doing a whole thing here... Just, okay?"

I smile. I love when he gets all frustrated while he's trying to be sweet. "Fine, grumpy."

He ignores me and keeps walking for a while. Finally, he gently slides me down his chest and spins me around. My back to his front. "Keep your eyes closed, promise?"

I nod.

He lifts the blindfold, but I keep my eyes closed since I did promise him, and I know he put a lot of effort into this.

"Okay, open your eyes."

I slowly open them and stare out at the water surrounding us. "Holy shit," I whisper.

"Right?"

"This is a yacht. Like not even a yacht." I spin around. "This is a damn mansion on water." I turn and get a glimpse of the Chicago skyline and the harbor.

Dex hugs me as the boat slowly eases farther out in the lake and the skyscrapers melt into the horizon behind us. "This is just... wow. How did you? It must cost..." Why am I always bringing up how much everything costs like an idiot? It's so rude, but I'm not used to being spoiled like this. I didn't grow up with much, but we were always happy and that's all that matters to me. It's so nice, though. All of this. I won't lie.

"Easy, killer. It belongs to a friend."

I start to ask if it belongs to Wells Covington, but I think better of it. Tomorrow is the start of another work week and I don't want to talk about work. I just want to live in the moment.

"What are you grinning like an idiot about? I can see it on your face."

I turn to him, trying not to laugh. "Nothing. It's nothing."

"No, spit it out, Whitley. You're giggling like a schoolgirl."

"Okay." I take his hand. "Follow me." I take off running down the deck and he follows behind. I head toward the very front of the boat.

"Oh God."

I turn back and laugh at him. "What?"

"I know what you're doing. You're out of your mind."

My breaths become labored because this freaking boat is big as hell and it's taking much longer than I thought it would to get to the end of it. "You're doing it with me, Jack!"

"My name is not Jack! And that movie sucks!"

"Don't ruin my moment, Collins!"

I swear I hear him mumble, "Fine," as he chases after me.

When we get to the very front of the boat, I hold my hands out to the side, just like in *Titanic*.

Dex wraps his arms around me and I can barely keep a straight face because I know he thinks we look like idiots.

"Jack, I'm flying!"

I don't have to look back to know Dex is smiling; I can feel his chest rising and falling with laughter.

"If you ask me to draw you like one of my French girls, you're getting a stick figure and then I'm fucking you while you're still naked."

I lean my head back on his shoulder. "My boyfriend is so romantic. Jack would draw me perfectly." Finally, I turn back to him. "And what do you mean that movie sucks? It might be the most romantic film ever."

"Maybe for you."

"Why don't you like it?"

His eyes bug out. "Because all the men die, Abigail!"

I can't stop laughing at how serious he looks, like he's really thought this all through. "Yeah, but he loves her."

"Yeah, and she gets to live and bang other dudes the rest of her life while he freezes to death." His hand flies out and he points at me. "And she had room on that thing!"

Finally, we both stare at each other and then burst into laughter.

"Look, I'll do whatever I can for you, Abby. But you're scooting your hot ass over on that board and we're both floating to land if this yacht goes down."

I hook my arms around his neck and plant a kiss on his lips. "Deal. And thanks for indulging me, for a while anyway."

He drops a sweet kiss on my forehead. "No problem, babe. And for the record, I would draw you as good as I could, but nothing would do you justice."

"Ohh, he recovers just like that. Very smooth, Mr. Collins."

"Come on, we're going to freeze to death out here." He leads me by the hand, giddy with excitement and takes me inside to meet the captain. It hadn't even dawned on me other people would be on the boat to operate it, and I just acted like a fool in front of everyone. My cheeks are pink the entire time Dex introduces us and it's not from the freezing wind outside.

Once that's done, the chief steward gives us the grand tour. I can't get over the size of this thing. People actually live like this. It's mind blowing. There're several bedrooms, an office, media room, fully staffed kitchen with a private chef, who happens to be cooking us dinner, I'm told.

The intricate woodwork detail in the bar is out of this world. I feel like I'm on an episode of *Lifestyles of The Rich and Famous* or *MTV Cribs*. We used to watch those shows at home and talk about what it'd be like to actually live in those houses or have all those cars.

This whole world is so alien to me. It's like I'm floating overhead watching this fabulous dream play out.

There's a guy behind the bar making me a drink as Dexter sips on a beer.

"So, how did I do?"

I cup his jaw. "At the risk of sounding ridiculously cheesy, so, sounding like you…"

He laughs.

"You've taken my breath away more in the last two days than anyone has my entire life. I don't know how to repay you for this weekend."

"Easy over there, Texas. Not everything is a business exchange. You don't owe me anything." He flashes me that million-dollar smile. "Just be happy." He cups my face again, like he always does. "Just smile for me every day. It's all I want." He kisses the corner of my mouth. "You're worth more than any of this."

How does he make me forget the damn world outside of us exists? I love the fact he's so damn confident, and not afraid to say cheesy things to make me smile. He makes it hard for me to keep my walls up. I'm playing Russian roulette with my heart, but even if I get burned, these experiences almost make me think it'll be worth it. We're past go and I've collected the two hundred dollars anyway. If he hurts me now, it's going to destroy me. I have no choice but to drop my guard and plow forward.

I accept my drink from the bartender and take a sip. It's like heaven in my mouth. "This tastes like sex with you."

Dexter laughs.

"I'm serious, it's incredible. They should call it Dex sex."

He flashes me a blank stare then raises his brows. "Guess you foreshadowed the drink the first time I asked you out."

"Stop! That was so embarrassing." I smack at his chest. "Was mortified the rest of the day when I did that." I hold up my drink. "You should have one of these, though. A Dex sex."

"Wouldn't want to masturbate at the bar. It's not civil, Abigail."

I damn near spit the liquor out and choke for a second. We're both dying laughing when the steward returns to show us to the dining room. He leads us to the upper deck where a candlelit table is set up in a room with a glass dome ceiling and fireplace. Off to the side there's a hot tub and a small pool.

"In the summer this ceiling retracts."

"I could get used to this."

"Don't." Dex cracks up.

I return his laugh with one of my own.

"I'm serious. I'll do whatever I can to impress you, but I'll never have this kind of money."

I reach for his forearm. "I don't care. I'd be happy in a shack with you, freezing cold with no heater."

"Okay, Texas." He laughs. "You've never been through a Chicago winter with no heater, obviously."

"Oh, and you have, Mr. Designer Suits?"

It's meant as a joke but Dex's jaw clenches a little. "Yeah." He doesn't say it mean or anything, but I can tell it bothered him.

"Dex, I didn't... It was just a joke, sorry."

He winks. "It's okay. I know."

I set my drink down and stop eating. "Don't do that, babe."

"Do what?"

"The guy thing where you pretend like I didn't just hit a nerve in your wisdom tooth with an ice pick."

He rubs his jaw. "Fucking hell, woman. Could you find a little less direct metaphor?"

I grin and shrug. "I am who I am."

He finally says, "Fine, I just… People always assume we grew up rich, because we have the firm and everything, but it wasn't like that. We weren't poor, but for a while our parents lived paycheck to paycheck. One year, they didn't pay the gas bill on time and we were without heat for three days, in the middle of winter."

"I can't imagine. That must've been awful."

"Actually, it was kind of nice. We all huddled in the middle of the living room in sleeping bags. I don't know. I thought it brought me and my brothers even closer together. Mom took care of us. We had a space heater and we went to school during the day. I thought it was going to kill my dad, though."

"Why?"

He traces the rim of his glass with his index finger. "It was the only time in my life I've seen him look ashamed. Like he couldn't provide what his family needed. Family is big with him and he's traditional, old school. Like it's his job to take care of everyone, you know?"

"I know exactly what you mean. My parents are the same."

"My mom talked about getting a part-time job and he wouldn't have it. He got a second job after that and I guess, maybe that's why I'm closer to my mom. Dad wasn't around as much then. When he did have time off work, he was always taking Decker and Deacon to sports stuff. I don't knock him for it. He did the best he could, you know?"

He hasn't really opened up this much to me since our first date, so I want to keep him going.

"I love hearing about you and your mom and your dad and your brothers. It's so hard to picture you all as kids."

"We were ornery little shits. Always playing pranks, getting into trouble." He smiles like he's reliving his childhood. "We fought nonstop, but if anyone outside the family started any shit, we all finished it. Like we could fight with each other, but once an outside party jumped in, we ganged up on them and made sure they never did it again."

"I think that's a universal family code. I don't know much about it, but my friends were that way."

Dex sighs. "It's why I'm so worried about Decker and Donavan."

"Why would you be worried?"

Dex takes a drink of his beer. "That's right, you weren't here when the shit went down before the merger was finished. Did they not talk about it in Dallas?"

"I guess not. What happened?"

"Well, Donavan… ehh, that's not fair. None of us were really on board with the merger. No offense."

"I heard whispers about that from some partners, like everything wasn't going smoothly. Tate reported back to Weston but people talked."

"Well, Decker didn't tell any of us about it and had already signed a letter of intent before discussing it with anyone."

"Really? Wow."

"Yeah. Me and Deacon were opposed but came around. He did it to free up some time to spend with Jenny. Which was great. It really has been best for everyone. Last year I wouldn't have been able to date you like this. I rarely had nights off. But Donavan just snapped, out of nowhere. Didn't like it. Wasn't having it. He's always been that way, goes against the grain. I think it's because he's the baby and always feels like he has to prove himself. They can be in the same room now and be civil, but if Tate comes around, he's gone. Him and Decker rarely speak. He won't even talk to Tate. Donavan hates her."

"You know, I noticed they'd give each other dirty looks when they pass, but I kind of keep my head down at work. I just want to do a good job and be taken seriously."

How did we end up talking about work? I guess it was inevitable we would have to do it at some point. I should get used to it. I need to get this rolling before he ends up bringing up Wells Covington. I don't know what he knows, and I don't want to be put in a position between him and Decker, and I wouldn't put it past Decker to keep it from him. Especially after hearing how things went before the merger.

"So, you were saying about them not getting along." I roll my arm forward like *continue*.

"Long story short, Donavan tried to sue one of Tate's clients, knowing it was her client and knowing it would cause a conflict of interest while merging the firms. She told Decker. Decker squashed his lawsuit behind his back. They had a huge blowout and things haven't been the same in the family since."

I glance out at the lake. "Wow."

"Yeah, anyway, enough about that shit. They'll work it out. They have to. He's marrying Tate. There's no chance that won't happen. Donavan will have to get over it, eventually. If he makes a scene at the wedding, my dad will kick his ass so hard he won't sit down for a week."

"I think I like your dad."

"He's a great guy. I wish they still lived here, but they're really happy in Florida."

The stars shine above us and I feel like I'm at the top of the world.

I look down and realize I've taken about two bites of food. I'm just so enamored with Dex and hearing about him as a boy. I glance over at the pool. "That hot tub looks amazing."

"Better put it to good use."

I eat a few more bites and finish off my drink, then Dex and I go change into bathing suits. I don't know how he found time to get me a bikini and in the right size. He must've spent a lot of time planning this, like he does with everything.

ALEX WOLF & SLOANE HOWELL

I'm really enjoying how calculated he is. He must be a shark as an attorney if he puts this much effort into his work.

I think he likes me in red because my dress is red and the bikini is red too. I make a mental note to wear more of it.

I can pay attention to details too, Dexter Collins.

Dex sneaks up behind me and runs a hand over my ass. "I don't know if we're going to make it to the hot tub."

"Why's that?"

"All I want to do is watch this bikini fall to the floor." His hand glides up my back and with an expert twist of his fingers, my top comes undone from around my neck and falls in front of me. The red triangles fall to my waist and his mouth crashes into mine. I climb him without even thinking, legs wrapped around his waist.

Dex kisses me deep and our tongues roll in unison, like we've done it a thousand times before. Warmth pools between my legs. Thoughts of the hot tub fade away as we fall to the bed.

We're nothing but a tangle of limbs. He yanks off my bottoms and flings them against the wall. Dex sucks a nipple into his mouth and I let out a low moan and rake my nails through his hair. He knows just how to touch me. Which buttons to push to drive me wild.

I use my foot to shove his shorts down his hips, wanting nothing but him, inside me. His stiff cock pulses between my legs. It's so close and I need it closer. The tip parts my lips, teasing me just enough to drive me mad.

I groan in his ear. "I need you, Dex."

"You have me." He guides himself into me, thrusting in long, deep strokes.

I hook my ankles around his backside, pulling me up into him, angled just right to feel him deeper. Dex's forehead presses up against mine and our eyes lock.

It's so intimate and perfect. He doesn't choke me or spank me this time. He's tender and loving and it's exactly what I need in this moment. His hands stroke my cheeks and rake through my hair, until he's kissing me deep and soft. It's so sweet, I don't ever want him to let me go. I don't ever want to be apart from him.

He hits my spot perfectly and I shudder beneath him, right on the edge, where he likes to keep me.

His hips speed up a little and he hooks an arm in the crook of my knee and pushes harder.

"Come for me, babe."

I nod against his forehead and he takes me higher, higher, higher, until I'm breaking apart beneath him.

"It feels so damn good when you come while I'm inside you." He thrusts a few more times and then his eyes roll back as he groans and blows deep inside me.

Once we're finished, we're both reduced to heavy pants. He collapses to his side on his back, and I snuggle up next to him, resting my head on his shoulder.

His hand caresses my hair. "You're my world, Abby."

I nuzzle into his shoulder, loving how safe he makes me feel.

He rolls to his side and his palm rests on my cheek. "I mean it. I love you, Abigail Whitley."

Holy crap! Dexter Collins just said he loves me!

I should be scared out of my mind right now, but I'm not. I'm not because it's Dexter and I can see he means it with every fiber of his soul. And the scariest part is, I love him too. I love him so much. To hell with my plans, when you find the right person, you just know. And I just know. We were meant to be together from day one. I could feel it then, and I feel it now, I just wouldn't admit it to myself.

"I love you too, Dexter Collins."

I wish I had a camera to capture the smile on his face right now. He looks like I just made him the happiest man on earth. I take a mental snapshot, because I never want to forget the way I feel and the way he looks.

He reaches over and puts my hand on his chest, right over his heart. "You own this. It's yours. And as long as I'm breathing, I'll fight every day the rest of my life for you."

I blush. What else can you do when the man of your dreams says something like that to you?

He reaches over and lifts my chin so I'm looking right in his eyes. "I mean every damn word. You can trust me with your heart. I promise."

We kiss once more and then I snuggle back up on his shoulder.

This is all too good to be true.

I EASE out from underneath Dex, wondering what time it is. There's a cart at the end of the bed with breakfast on it. I grab a mug and pour myself a coffee then start looking for my phone.

I find my purse and blink when I see the time. Oh no. "Dex." I put a hand on his shoulder and shake him.

He stirs, mumbling under his breath as he squints and glares at me. "What?"

"I don't mean to panic but how the hell are we getting to work?"

"You worry too much." He smirks and rolls out of bed.

My eyes naturally roam south, where his thick cock swings between his legs like a pendulum. Dex sees where my gaze is trained and grins. "Didn't get enough last night?"

My cheeks flush. He woke me up in the middle of the night with his face buried between my legs. "Stop distracting me. How are we getting to work? We're on a boat in the middle of the lake."

"Stop stressing. I took care of everything. It's covered." He yawns.

"Okay, well get your dick covered too, or we won't make it there in time and I need my job."

"Fine. You're no fun."

We both scurry around and get dressed. I stare out the window and it doesn't look like we've moved an inch. "We haven't gone anywhere. The boat's not moving."

He grins like he's amused with the whole situation. "Will you stop freaking out? Come on."

I've never been late to work a day in my life and I don't plan on starting today. "Umm, okay." I take his hand and follow him up some stairs.

Then, I hear it. *Whop whop whop.*

Dex opens a door that leads out to the helicopter landing pad.

I can't help but feel a little like a Bond girl, going on crazy adventures with a suave man in suits.

The cold air whips all around us as we walk hand in hand over to the chopper. The pilot takes our bags and puts them in a compartment, then makes sure we're both buckled in. Once everyone's secure, he straps himself in and we lift off.

I can't stop going back and forth between me and Dex, looking out my window then leaning across him and looking out his. The yacht turns into a speck on the horizon.

"Enjoying the view?" Dex asks, laughing his ass off at how excited I am.

I've never flown in a helicopter before, not that it matters *how* we're flying. "I really am the worst. You always want to give me the window seat if we fly on a plane. This is even worse because of windows on both sides."

He smiles and takes a sip of coffee that I have no idea where it even came from. He looks like he's done this a million times. "I see that."

I give him a smack at his chest, then gaze out the front of the helicopter where the Chicago skyline grows bigger and bigger as we head right toward it. It's so beautiful. My eyes roam back and forth between the lake and Dexter.

Chicago is growing on me, fast. It's starting to feel like home, and I know it's a beautiful city with amazing food and culture and nightlife. But, part of me knows Dex is the biggest reason I have these feelings. He's anchoring me to his city, and I clearly don't seem to mind one bit.

The helicopter makes a large loop around the city, giving us a view of downtown from all angles. I wonder if the pilot did it to be nice and show us the city, or if it's because of some air traffic rules from O'Hare. Regardless, it's incredible. Finally, we hover the pier, and the pilot drops us off right where the yacht picked us up yesterday.

Once we're in the limo again, I curl into Dex in the back and fall asleep until we arrive at my apartment. Dexter carries my bag and walks me to my door, lingering long enough to kiss me. When we're done, he gives one of my breasts a quick squeeze. "One for the road."

I shake my head and can't stop cheesing like an idiot as I watch him walk to the elevator.

I can't believe this is all happening. It's totally surreal.

DEXTER

ABIGAIL SNUGGLES UP next to me on the couch. There's nothing better than having a fire going and wrapping my arm around her. It's perfect.

I talked her into staying in at my apartment tonight. I ordered takeout because it's colder than fucking Hoth outside. She giggles when I pull out a tauntaun blanket I ordered when I saw it on a Facebook ad. You can unzip it, crawl inside, then zip it up around you.

We share one container of twice-baked spaghetti I ordered from a place down the road on DoorDash. The fireplace crackles and spits a few sparks when I adjust the logs. The night couldn't be more perfect. We watch two girly Hallmark Christmas movies even though it's still not even Thanksgiving yet. Multiple glasses of wine are had by both of us.

I shake my head at her after the last movie, even though I know this will work in my favor in the future. I know these movies like the back of my hand. "You have to admit the plots are almost identical. There's always a catastrophe that robs her of her Christmas spirit, and the hero always has some tragedy that's caused him to lose hope in humanity and become a loner. He springs into action and his name is always Nick and her name is always something like Holly. He does something monumentally stupid that seems unredeemable, then makes a huge gesture and begs for forgiveness. They share a wonderful PG-rated kiss, Christmas is saved, the end."

"Wow." She laughs. "You've really done your homework on this." She takes another drink, finishing her third glass of wine.

"I want to see one where they break up. Or it looks like they're about to kiss and make up and instead he fucks her brains out. Or one where it doesn't work out and he just lives his days hating Christmas even more. It'd keep me on my toes, not knowing if the happy ending was coming or not."

Abigail glares. "It's not romance if they don't end up together."

"Okay, well how about one where *she* screws up and has to beg *him* to take her back for fuck's sake? We need more equality in Christmas movies."

"Eww, no. Nobody would watch that."

"Why? It's the same shit, just gender reverse the plot."

"Because, Dex." She grabs my chin and gives it a shake like I'm a puppy who just got caught digging. "The hero has to mess up and redeem himself. It's the natural order of things. Women don't do stupid stuff like men do."

I laugh. "Oh really?"

She shrugs, biting back a smile. "Yep. We're perfect and you guys need to beg for our affection. That's how the world works."

"I'll show you how the world works." I tickle her ribs then plant a kiss on her mouth.

"Mmm, show me more." She purrs the words against my lips.

Abigail switches the channel and a rerun of Jeopardy is on the TV.

I slip my hand between her legs. "I'll take Abigail's pussy for five hundred, Alex."

She smacks at my chest. "You're terrible."

"You like it."

"You're not wrong. But you know what I like even more?"

"What's that?"

She slides down to her knees, situating herself between my legs, and fumbles with my zipper. "Your dick."

"I do not mind this at all." My head falls back against the cushion.

Abigail tugs my pants down. "You did so well, indulging me in my cheesy movies. I feel I should return the favor."

I lift my hips as she slides my pants down to my ankles and my hard cock springs free. She strokes her hand up and down my shaft and I already feel like I might pass out. She drives me crazy with even the slightest touch. I'm addicted to her. Every time she walks out of the room withdrawal sets in. When I'm with her, all I can think about is burying myself inside her.

"Mmm, I missed you." She smiles at my dick, fist wrapped around my shaft. She kisses the tip, her eyes locked on mine, savoring every second she gets to tease me. Her lips part and she slowly slides me into her mouth.

My fingers go straight to her hair and I make a fist. Abigail sucks me deeper, swirling her tongue around me.

When she takes more of me, my eyes roll up to the ceiling then land back on hers. Her hand grips me at the base and she pumps up and down while taking the rest of me in her mouth.

It's so fucking good, but I want her pussy. I'll go crazy if I don't get it soon.

I tug her head back, sliding myself from her soft lips. "Need you naked, now." I stand up and make quick work of undressing her and then myself. I lay her on the couch, ready to eat her pussy until she hollers my name then fuck her senseless. I'm about to dive in right when my phone rings.

"Shit."

"What's wrong?" Abigail glares at me like *don't you dare answer that right now*.

"It's my mom. I have to take it."

She covers herself up like my mom might see then nods. "Okay."

"I'm sorry." I hold up a finger. "Just give me a second." I grab my phone off the coffee table. "Hey, Mom." I could say it nicer, but my balls ache like a motherfucker.

"Hey, Dex. We're gonna be there in a few days for Thanksgiving."

"I know. I'll see you then." I keep my eyes locked on Abby while I try to get Mom off the phone.

She starts in on some story about what her and Dad did today.

"Now's not a great time, Mom, can I call you back?"

"Why, what's going on? Are you working late?"

I never lie to my mom but I'm not about to tell her my girlfriend is spread eagle in front of me, covering her tits with her hands. "No, no, nothing like that."

"Well I feel like I never get to talk to you or any of my boys for that matter. Deacon is always busy with Quinn or her dad. Decker is always running around taking Jenny to something or sneaking away with Tate. I just love Tate, she's perfect for him." She yells in the background. "Yeah, Tate. Decker's fiancée! That's what I said. Decker and Tate. Deacon and Quinn. I said it right, you don't know what you're talking about."

"Mom!"

"Yeah, honey?"

"You gonna talk to me or Dad?"

"Oh, yeah, sorry. Did you get the pudding I sent?"

I grin, then look down and remember everything I did to Abigail with the pudding she made me. It's ridiculously awkward talking to my mom with Abigail's pussy staring me in the face. "Yeah, I got it. It was great. Thank you."

"You already finished it? I'll get you—"

"Mom, I'm not done. I just had some and it was great so far. Anyway…"

"I miss seeing you. You know I don't play favorites, but still… You'll always be my little Dex, even with the tattoos and the suits."

"Mom, I love you. You know this. But I—"

"Deacon said you have a new girlfriend. Why am I hearing it from him and not you? You used to tell me everything. Is something going on with you?"

I sigh and I think Abigail can hear Mom through the speaker because she's covering her mouth and trying not to laugh so hard it's shaking her breasts. And if I don't stop staring at them, I'll have to mute Mom and put them in my mouth. "Of course not. I meant to tell you, I've just been…"

She feigns being upset and teases. "For years I want you boys to settle down and get your lives in order. Then you all get girlfriends and forget all about the woman who gave birth to you."

I laugh. "I still call you all the time."

"Yeah, yeah. Can't even tell me about your new girlfriend."

I glance down and Abigail is still grinning her ass off like she's enjoying this more than my mouth.

"Have to hear all about it from your twin brother. Maybe I should be sending him pudding in the mail."

"You're being a little dramatic, don't you think?"

She laughs. "I'm so excited for Thanksgiving. I'll have everyone together again. All my boys."

"We're excited too." Deacon and I haven't had the heart to tell her Decker and Donavan are barely talking. We both keep hoping it'll resolve itself before she finds out.

"Well anyway, I expect to meet her on Thanksgiving. Is she coming to Decker's?"

"No. She's probably going home to spend time with her family. She's from Dallas. Can we talk about it later? I really need to go."

Abigail raises a brow at me.

I shrug like *I'm so sorry.*

"Well, ask her what she's doing."

"What?"

"Ask her."

"I will, okay? I'll call her as soon as I get off the phone."

"Dexter, it's not polite to lie to your mother. Just go ahead and ask her right now."

"What lie? You want me to call her then call you back?"

"No, I know she's right there. It's the only acceptable reason you'd have for hurrying me off the phone at this hour." I can't fight back a smile. She knows me too well. I should know better.

Abigail's grinning from ear-to-ear when I glance at her.

"My mom wants to know what you're doing for Thanksgiving?"

She leans forward, like she's talking directly to my mom instead of relaying the answer to me.

I finally just sigh and put it on speakerphone.

"Hi, Mrs. Collins. I was planning on staying in town. My roommate is going to her family's house, so I figured I'd just volunteer at a shelter or something."

"Oh no. That's not happening, sweetie."

I mouth "I'm sorry" to Abigail over and over, but she seems amused. I don't know if it's because of my discomfort or because my mom is well, Mom.

Mom shouts into the phone and it blares through the speaker. "Dexter, you're bringing her to Decker's for dinner. That's final. And you know when I say final that's it."

"If she says yes will you hang up?"

"Yes."

I glance to Abigail and shrug like, *this is the only way we're getting rid of her right now.*

518

Abigail grins wide and looks at the phone. "I'd love to, Mrs. Collins. Thank you for thinking of me."

"You're welcome, sweetie. And you let me know if my boy is anything less than a perfect gentleman. I'll drag him out of the room by his ear if—"

"Mom!" I holler the word before I can stop myself.

Abigail dies laughing.

"Okay, I'll leave you two alone now after Dex does one thing. He knows what it is."

My eyes roll up to the ceiling then land back on the phone. "Sorry for lying, Mom."

"That's a good boy. Can't wait to meet you, Abigail. Love you, Dex."

"Love you too." I say the words as fast as possible and Mom laughs right into the speaker before it cuts off.

I grin at Abigail as I move back between her thighs. "You're in for a treat."

"I'm so nervous."

My eyes widen. "Why? I've eaten your pussy half a dozen times at least."

She smacks at my chest. "I mean about meeting your entire family at Thanksgiving. Were you talking about going down on me when you said I'm in for a treat?"

I smirk. "Of course, what else would I be talking about?"

She laughs and shakes her head at me. "You are the most arrogant—"

I dive down and flick my tongue across her clit.

"Phenomenal man on the planet."

I grin against her slick wet heat. "What I thought." I lick the length of her slit, then go back to focusing on her clit. "Don't be nervous. It'll be fine. You'll love my parents."

"Mmhmm. Oh, God. Whatever you say. Just don't stop what you're doing right now." Her fingers tighten in my hair as her hips grind against my face.

I take two fingers to the hilt and curl them up to her favorite spot. Her greedy pussy squeezes tight around them. I make a 'come here' motion inside her, hitting the mark over and over again while my tongue works lazy circles.

Abigail makes this cute whimper sound that tells me she's about to come.

"You want me to keep going or you want my dick?" I glance up at her.

"I need you inside me."

I shove off from the couch and pick Abigail up. Her legs wrap around me and her hot, wet pussy grinds against my shaft. We make it halfway to the bedroom and I can't take it anymore. I slam her back up against the wall and it knocks a picture frame to the ground. Fortunately, it doesn't shatter everywhere.

"Can't wait." Before she can respond, I shove my cock into her. Her head smacks back against the wall.

Before I can stop myself, my hips are a blur, bouncing her up and down on me as I thrust deep into her. She bites down on my shoulder, like she always does when she's about to come.

"Fuck, Abby." I groan out her name just as she clamps down on me.

ALEX WOLF & SLOANE HOWELL

My cock kicks and I shove her down on me, as deep as humanly possible before I blow inside her sweet cunt.

Her forehead falls onto my shoulder. A few seconds pass and her eyes drift up to mine. We both turn and look down the hallway to my bedroom.

Through rough pants, I say, "We almost made it."

She nods in agreement. "Almost."

"There's always next time."

"Indeed, sir."

ABIGAIL

I'm on my third outfit change this morning. I don't know what I was thinking agreeing to go to the Collins family Thanksgiving. What if I screw up? What if the food I made is terrible and gives them all food poisoning? What if I make a complete ass of myself and say the wrong thing or do the wrong thing? What if Dexter decides he doesn't like me as much as he thought he did?

Thanksgiving is for family. Everyone will be there. It's too much.

We haven't been dating *that* long. I mean, we're both obviously in love, but it's still too soon. I told him I loved him too early and now I'm about to lose my sanity.

You're psyching yourself out. Stop being ridiculous.

I glance at the clock and wonder if it's too early to start drinking. It's a holiday. Day drinking is acceptable. At least I think it is. I need a Xanax because my anxiety is off the charts. I almost wish Barbie was here to talk me down from the ledge, but she left last night to stay at her parents. They live about two hours away in Indiana.

Pull yourself together, Abby.

Dexter is going to be here soon and I'm a damn mess.

My cell rings and I pick it up. "Hey, Mom. Happy Thanksgiving." Perfect. I should've already called her. If anyone can get me through this, she can.

"Hey, sweetheart. I wanted to check in on you. Did you make plans?"

"I'm going to Dexter's to meet his family and I'm freaking out a little, to be honest." I yank a casserole dish out of the oven with the phone clutched between my cheek and shoulder.

"It'll be fine, baby girl. Just be yourself. They'll love you."

"I wish I was at home with you and Dad. I should be there."

"Nonsense, you're coming home for Christmas and that's enough for us."

"Thanks, Mom." There's a knock at the door. It's probably Dexter. "Shit," I mumble.

"Abigail Louise!"

"Sorry, Mom. I just. I'm all over the place. I gotta go. He's here. I'll call you tonight if it's not too late when I get in."

"Okay. I love you."

"Love you too." I end the call and open the door.

It's Kyle.

We haven't spoken since the night at the bar when Dex headbutted Nick.

"Wow. You look great."

I glance down at the tan wrap sweater dress I settled on and raise an eyebrow. "Umm, thanks. What are you doing here?"

He scratches the back of his neck and rocks back on the heels of his feet. "I know things have been weird, but I wasn't sure if you had plans or anyone to spend Thanksgiving with. Barbie told me she was going to her parents last night and I just wanted to invite you to go down to the mission with Nick and me." He holds up a hand. "If you want to. I'm sure you made plans already."

"I appreciate the invite, but I'm actually waiting on Dexter. We're going to his brother's. His parents are in town."

"Meeting the family." He mumbles something else I can't hear under his breath. "Sounds like things are getting pretty serious."

I glance down at the floor, I don't know why I feel so ashamed. I don't know why I feel any kind of way. Kyle and I are friends, at least I think we are, but I won't sit around and listen to him badmouth my boyfriend. I can do whatever I want.. "Yeah. We are."

He kicks at an imaginary rock. "Cool."

"I really like him. I'm sorry if you don't get along, but he's going to be around. If that's going to be a problem…"

"I just miss hanging out with you. I still want to be friends. We just won't talk about your boyfriend, okay?"

"Sure." I agree even though I know it'll never be how it was. Too much has changed and even though Dex headbutted Nick, I don't know what Kyle said in the bar. I just don't want to be rude. We'll see each other in passing and say hi until I finally move out, then I'll probably never hear from him again. It makes me sad, but I love Dex and I just need to keep the peace a little while longer. I already have half a security deposit saved up and I'm sure my parents will give me money at Christmas time, even though I tell them not to.

"Guess I'll see you around then."

"Yeah, see ya." I close the door and pull a few other dishes out of the fridge and set them on the counter. I made pecan pie, caramel drizzle cheesecake, and banana pudding for Dex, plus sweet potato pie because even if they made it you can never have enough, and I don't know if they make it right up here.

A few minutes later, Dexter shows up. He kisses me good and deep, grabbing my ass in the process.

"What's all this?" He motions to all the dishes on the counter.

I pace back and forth, trying to calm myself down. "I'm an idiot. It's so dumb. I just didn't know what to make and where I'm from you don't show up empty-handed when someone invites you over."

"This all looks amazing." He starts to dip his finger in my pudding.

I smack at his hand. "Don't you dare touch that food, Dexter Collins. I slaved all night making these for your *family*. Not just for you." Wow, we sound so domesticated already, and it's actually nice. It warms my heart and makes this whole thing easier. We just work together.

"You're gonna make me fat if you keep cooking like this."

I wag a finger at him. "Well keep your fat fingers out of it, okay?"

He holds his hands up in surrender. "Okay, Betty Crocker. Damn."

When I look away, he gets a finger full of pudding and shoves it in his mouth, grinning his ass off.

I scowl at him. "No more for you today. You're in a timeout."

He grabs me by the hip and yanks me into him. "Abigail, you love me because I don't give a shit about rules. You did this to yourself."

I shake my head at him. "I *will* tame you."

He laughs at that. "For real, though. That pudding is amazing." He leans forward into my ear. "I'll have to get a spoon from my brother's house, for later."

He always knows how to make me blush.

WE GET to Decker's and the moment we walk through the front door his daughter, Jenny, and Tate snatch the food I brought and take it into the kitchen.

A woman, who I assume is Dex's mom, launches herself at us, hugging us both tight. "You must be Abigail. Let me get a look at you." She holds my hands and pulls back assessing me from head to toe. "Gorgeous." She drops my hands and smiles, then turns to Dexter.

She's a thick woman. Tall, like an athlete, but very graceful. She's wearing this goofy sweater that reminds me of Dexter's sense of humor, and I start to see where he gets his silliness from. There's a cartoonish turkey on the front in a suggestive pose and it says 'Pour some gravy on me' above it. I think we're going to get along just fine.

"Jesus," Dex mumbles.

She smacks his arm. "You watch your mouth, Dexter Harrison Collins."

I glance up at him. "Harrison?" I grin.

"She says it's after the president, but we all know she had a crush on Harrison Ford when I was born." He turns to her. "Because there's no way she'd name me after a president who died a month into his term, right, Mom?"

She giggles and gives him a big hug. "I love you, baby boy."

"Love you too, Mom."

She takes me by the hands. "Now, Abigail, has Dex cooked you breakfast yet?"

"Oh my God, yes. And it was fantastic."

Quinn and Tate walk up about the same time.

Quinn says, "Deacon cooks amazing breakfast too."

Tate nods, like she's in a trance. "So does Decker."

"You're welcome, ladies." Mom grins at all of them. "I taught all my boys to cook breakfast and told them that's the secret to keeping a good woman, because I always wished *someone* would cook breakfast once in a while." She flashes a dirty look across the room like she's looking for her husband.

He's oblivious, talking to someone else.

All the boys turn around, suddenly interested, and Dex glares in a playful way. "Wait, that was just a trick to get us to cook?"

"Dexter Harrison Collins, the girls are talking. You mind your business."

"Someone's in trouble." Donavan laughs and walks up behind us. "I heard the middle name come out."

She wheels around on him. "Don't you start getting mouthy, Donny, or I'll go around the room asking why you can't keep a woman happy like my other boys. At least they have someone to cook breakfast for." She shakes her head and looks at me again. "Four boys and only one grandbaby to spoil. You see what I'm dealing with here?" She turns to Deacon. "You should think about getting your sperm tested."

Decker damn near shoots whiskey out of his nose. "Mom!"

Quinn turns bright pink and smiles up at Deacon. Deacon's eyes bulge and he freezes up.

I've never seen the Collins brothers look so nervous in my entire life. They usually walk around with scowls while employees scurry around trying to look busy.

She turns back to me. "You and Dexter are going to make beautiful babies. I know these things."

I try not to gape at her, but holy crap we just started dating. Babies? I don't even know if I want kids, but there's no way I'm going to admit that here. My face must say it all.

She smiles and runs a hand across my forearm. "I'm not trying to scare you off. I'm just armed with a mother's intuition."

An older man walks into the room and damn near takes all the air with him. He has on a collared shirt with a sweater pulled over it and looks like he could've stepped out of a Calvin Klein catalog. He looks regal and stately, with silver hair slicked back perfectly. He leans down and pecks Mrs. Collins on the cheek. "Give the girl room to breathe, honey. Let them get their coats off before you start counting future grandchildren." He turns and holds a hand out to me. "Nice to meet you. I'm David." He leans in close. "The father of all these little shits running around here."

Great, another D name to remember!

I laugh. "It's nice to meet you both. Thank you so much for having me."

"Don't mind Donna. She gets excited about grandkids. We have Jenny, but she's older and chasing boys around now."

Decker glares in his direction when he hears it but doesn't say anything.

I follow Quinn and Tate into the kitchen and politely make my escape from the family craziness for a few minutes.

"I'm so glad you came." Quinn smiles.

"Thank fuck you brought pecan pie," Tate mutters, eyeing my desserts. "Man, I miss the food back home. And my mom's cooking. And Daddy's fried turkey. They don't do Thanksgiving for shit up here."

I laugh. She's probably right. You can't beat Thanksgiving in the south. "How do you and Decker handle holidays with your families in different states?" I ask because I'm curious, but I also want to see what the future might be like for Dex and me.

"We're flying down in the morning. We couldn't leave knowing that his folks were coming from Florida. Did you see Jenny invited her boyfriend? Decker's shitting bricks but trying to be nice. It's hilarious."

I follow Tate's gaze to the dining room where Jenny and a boy are seated next to each other looking at something on her phone.

"Oh, she went for the bad boy right out the gate. Well played." He has dark shaggy hair that lays to the left side and his bottom lip is pierced. He's wearing a hat turned backward. Decker is in major trouble.

"Right? Boys did *not* look like that when I was in school. Just saying," says Quinn.

"Amen to that." Tate grins. "All we had were jocks and country boys. Trucks full of shoulder pads or rifles. No angsty artists and tortured souls in leather jackets."

"Babe, come here I want you to meet someone." Dex practically yanks me into the other room and thrusts me in front of a man who looks almost identical to David Collins, and a young woman, maybe mid-twenties. Wow, she's beautiful. She has tattoos up her ripped arms, just like Dex, and jet-black hair with icy blue eyes. "This is my uncle, Damian, and my cousin Harlow."

I hold out my hand to both of them. "It's nice to meet you."

They're both super nice even though Harlow looks like she could beat the hell out of anyone in the house. She's seriously intimidating, the way she carries herself, but she's as nice as can be and stunning.

Dex can't stop singing her praises; they must be really close. "She works in digital marketing. She's been killing it too, ever since she graduated. Just started her own firm here in Chicago."

"Speaking of that, I wanted to talk to you. We need to set up a meeting."

"What for?"

"Work."

"Might want to talk to Decker about that, if it's about marketing…"

"Look, you hire my firm for the financial services division. I'll have you kicking everyone else's ass and make you look like a fucking hero at your firm."

"Harlow, language," says Damian.

"Oh fuck that. We're all family."

"What kind of shit do you do?" asks Dex. "I don't handle marketing much. Haven't studied it since undergrad."

"I'm sure you pussies probably have billboards and other lame shit, sponsor events, things that get you a bullshit ROI. I'll install pixels on your website, launch Facebook and Google adword campaigns. Highly targeted with warm audiences to get your ads in front of the right eyeballs."

Dex looks like a deer in headlights but shrugs. "All right, fuck it. Let's get something on the books."

Harlow smiles. "You were always my favorite cousin." She dives into Dex and wraps her arms around him. "My pitch kicked ass, didn't it?"

He kisses her on top of the head; they look more like brother and sister than cousins. "Kicked all the ass."

She leans up and whispers something in his ear, and he stares right at me and grins wide. I want to ask Dex what she said, but Decker walks into the room.

"Okay, we're ready to eat. File in, ya bunch of animals." Decker's voice booms through the house.

Everyone moves to the dining room to find their seats. Their dad says a prayer over the food and then everyone jumps up to go fill their plates.

I lean over to Dexter. "What'd Harlow whisper to you?"

"That I'm lucky you didn't go to college with her when she went through her phase."

I damn near choke on the water I was taking a sip of.

The four brothers start for the food, looking like ravenous wolves, and their dad glares right at them. They freeze in their tracks, and I'm starting to see where they get their commanding presence from. Hell, he stared at them and I shrank back in my seat a little.

He turns to the rest of us. "Ladies, go ahead." He turns to the boys and I hear him grumble as we walk by, "Act like you have some damn manners."

After everyone fills their plates, I sit next to Dexter, and Donavan takes a seat on the other side of me. Jenny and her boyfriend sit at the kitchen island on barstools, secretly holding hands where they don't think anyone can see.

The food is fantastic. Tate baked a ham. She said she marinated it in Coca Cola. Everyone eats and makes small talk at the table.

Dexter's parents crack me up. I was expecting them to be more, I don't know, not how they are. They're both really down to earth, but Mr. Collins seems like he's mellowed out a lot from how he probably was. He definitely fits the hard-worker personality type. Man of few words, but when he does speak, it matters, and everyone listens.

One thing I do notice, that sends a warmth spreading through my veins, is that he looks at his wife the way I've seen the Collins brothers look at all of us. I think the way a man treats a woman is learned behavior; his experiences watching his parents interact shapes the way he'll be one day. Mr. Collins might look hard and no-nonsense, but his face lights up, even when his wife tells an embarrassing story in front of him. He changes when she walks into the room, and that's really what it's all about, having that effect on the man you end up with.

"It's just a beach we go to. It's no big deal." Dex's Mom says it proudly, and all the color drains from the boys' faces.

I lean over to Tate and Quinn, because I was daydreaming, waxing poetical about how I think Dex will treat me. "What was that? About a beach?"

Tate grins her ass off. "They go to a nude beach."

Mr. Collins shrugs when all the boys, his brother, and Harlow look at him like there's no way he'd ever do anything like that. He takes a huge bite of turkey. "Don't knock it 'til you try it. It's quite liberating, actually."

"Jesus Christ, like I don't get enough of this shit at work," Decker mumbles and buries his face in his palm.

DEXTER

I LOOK over at Abigail and can't stop grinning like a complete idiot. She fits in like she's been coming to these things for years.

Mom walks up while I'm spying on her helping with the dishes. "I know that look." She bumps me with her hip.

I inhale a huge breath. "So, what's the verdict?"

Mom narrows her eyes, then she puts her arm around me. She says, "Are you kidding? You haven't brought a girl to meet us since high school, and that was for prom."

"I'm nervous. What if I screw things up? What if I hurt her?"

"If you're concerned about hurting her, you won't."

"I don't know."

"Dex, look at me."

I turn to face her.

"You're not perfect, kiddo. Nobody is. You're gonna screw up." She gestures toward the kitchen. "She's gonna screw up. It's how you deal with the screw-ups that defines the relationship. If you love each other, nothing is irreparable."

"So… verdict?"

"If she makes you happy, she makes me happy. But I do like her. So you can relax. You and your brothers are so high strung. I worry about you boys."

I bend down and kiss her on the forehead. "Thanks. I'm glad you like her."

Mom bumps me with her hip again. "Noticed she made you pudding."

"Yeah, sorry, I know that's our thing, and I told her about it. I kinda felt like I betrayed you a little."

"Don't apologize. I'll keep sending it. I like that you want to share our little thing with the woman you love."

"Really, I thought, I don't know. Thought you'd react different. Like maybe, I don't know, like she was moving in on your territory or something. This is all new to me. I've never felt this way before."

She gives me another hug and does her best to get her arms all the way around me, like she always does. She whispers, "You'll always be my little boy. But I can relinquish being the number one woman in your life with grace. That's how it's supposed to be. I'll always love you, no matter what."

"I love you too." I look out at Abigail. "I love her. So much it hurts."

"I know." She winks. "Moms always know."

I smile as she walks off and Dad wraps her in his arms. They sit back, watching everything unfold in front of them. When I glance back to Abigail, I wonder if that'll be us someday, watching all our kids as adults.

"You boys got any other women around the office for Donavan?" Dad grins his ass off. "Looks like he could use some pointers."

Donavan rolls his eyes. "You guys keep this shit up and I'm leaving."

Mom glares. "Language, son. There are ladies present."

"Sorry, Mom. I forgot Deacon was here."

"So you could ask me for my number, big boy?" Deacon laughs.

Without thinking, Donavan says, "Fu—" He looks at Mom. "Uhh, screw you guys." He shakes his head and mumbles. "A-holes."

"A-holes. Well done on that one," says Deacon.

I can't stop laughing. "Hey, Abigail has a crazy-ass roommate. I can hook you up. Just let me know." I slap him on the back, and apparently he's had enough because he yanks me into a headlock and down to the floor.

We go at it like we're ten years old all over again. Decker and Deacon take bets on who will tap out first and egg us on.

"You see how they act?" Mom says to Tate, Quinn, and Abigail. "I raised a bunch of animals. Boys! Knock that crap off!"

We get up and I dust myself off. "Totally won."

"Like hell you did."

"All right, that's enough." Dad gestures toward the hall. "Let's go to the study. I brought cigars."

"He was *not* talking to you." Decker holds his arm out in front of Jenny's date as he starts to follow.

Fuck, that kid has balls.

I glance back to the kid and shrug. "Sorry, ol' smoke crotch isn't any fun, is he?"

Decker glares lasers at me.

I hold my hands up. "Hey, just saying. The ol' rug is getting a little silvery up there."

"I'm not Donavan, I'll lay your ass out for good."

"Please. Snap those brittle bones like twigs if you come at me."

"All right." Dad looks back to make sure Mom is out of earshot. "Knock the shit off."

We get into Decker's study and Dad leans against the desk after passing out cigars and lights his first. The rest of us follow suit.

Dad has that serious stare on his face, like he did when we'd get in trouble as kids. Fuck. I have no idea what this is about, but it's not good. An ominous feeling fills the room.

He glares back and forth at Decker and Donavan and points a finger at each one of them. "Front and center, *now*."

They both glance at each other and for a brief moment in time, we're kids again and not high-powered attorneys. They both know what's up.

"What the hell is this?" says Decker.

"Boy, I will knock your fucking dick in the dirt you talk to me that way again. This shit has gone on long enough. You're lucky I didn't fly my ass up here a long time ago. Your mother has been a wreck for months. You know how she gets when you're not getting along."

We all stare at him like we can't believe they know.

"Yeah, she knows. That woman knows everything going on with her boys at all times." He stares around at all of us, pointing his cigar. "This is family. You don't have anything but each other, and you'd better not fucking forget it. This shit gets aired out and resolved *right now*. I won't have your mother endure another minute."

Donavan stares at Decker, then at Dad. "He merged the goddamn firm without discussing it with us first. I have to share my criminal law department with a bunch of incompetent assholes out of Dallas. Then, he took Tate's side over mine with a client and fucked up—"

"Enough." Dad turns to Decker. "Well?"

"The shit wasn't personal. It was business. I built the firm. I run the firm. I make the decisions. Nothing changed other than a lighter workload for all of us. Excuse me if I didn't want to be a piece-of-shit absent father to my only daughter. I was thinking about Jenny when I made the decision to merge the firm and now the bonuses are bigger and the hours are less for everyone."

Donavan looks away, shaking his head when he mentions Jenny. "I get the dad stuff, but fuck, man. You let Tate waltz in here like she owned our damn firm, boss people around, all because you fell in love with her."

Decker shakes his head. "It had nothing to do with my feelings for Tate or you for that matter. You're my brother and I'll always have your fucking back, always. But when you're wrong, I'll call you out on that shit. I have to. At work I'm the boss, and family shit comes second. As soon as we walk out the door, it's family first."

"It sure fucking felt like you were picking her over us."

"Look, maybe…"

Dad glares at Decker.

Decker holds up both hands. "Okay, I maybe could have communicated things better. It was never my intention to piss you off. I knew you'd throw a fit and I'd have to deal with all of you for months to get you on board and I didn't have that kind of time. Every minute I didn't get with my daughter was torture for me, don't you get that? But regardless of your feelings for Tate, that lawsuit was petty as fuck and you know it. It was a frivolous loser. You wanted to tank a nine-figure business deal because you were up in your feelings. I couldn't have that. Too many jobs on the line and people who aren't in our family would be affected by it."

Dad turns to Donavan. "Donny?"

He shrugs. "Okay, maybe the lawsuit was bullshit. And yeah, it did hurt when you ignored us for a woman. I'm glad you found someone and I'm happy for you, I just…" He sighs in frustration. "It was our thing. The firm. It was ours. Our name was on the wall and now it's gone and we'll never get it back."

Decker's glare softens. "Isn't it better, though?" He raises his shoulders like, *come on, man.* "It was just a name on a wall. It doesn't take away who we are or where we come from."

Donavan looks away. "Yeah, I mean, I guess it is. I just… I wish you'd done it differently and I'd have been on board, maybe. But fuck, why does your fiancée…"

"She's the way she is because she won't get any fucking respect if she isn't. You know this. We all know how women associates get treated. Fuck, we're all guilty of doing it. Do you know how many times she's begged me outside of work to reach out to you? That she *hates* being a wedge between us. It keeps her up at night. Do you know how many fake promises I've made to reach out to you to try and resolve this? I've just been too damn proud to do it and no time ever seems like the right time. You know how I get." A tear slides down Decker's cheek. "It's why our fucking wedding has been delayed, because she refuses to marry me while I'm pissed off at you! You don't know her. Not like you think you do."

"I-I didn't know she felt that way."

Decker finally cracks. He walks over and puts a hand on Donavan's shoulder. "Look, maybe we can talk when we get back to the office after Thanksgiving. If you want a more managerial role all you have to do is say something. I think you'd be great for it and I have a ton of shit on my plate I'd gladly farm out if I could."

Donavan's eyes light up, but he tries to play it cool. He nods. "Yeah, *maybe,* I'd be interested in something like that."

Decker glances to Deacon and me with his eyebrows raised.

At the same time, we both hold our hands up. "Fuck that," says Deacon.

"Yeah, you guys can have that stress." I grin.

Simultaneously, it feels like a weight just lifted off all our shoulders. Like every burden in the world just removed itself from the room. For the first time in months, it feels amazing to have them getting along. It just took Dad putting his foot down.

"You two know what to do." Dad waves his cigar hand between the two of them.

They both hug it out and they're actually smiling. It feels surreal. I didn't think it was possible at this point.

"Work your problems out from now on." Dad throws an arm around me and Deacon and moves us in closer to Decker and Donavan, almost like a football huddle. "I don't want to see this shit happen again. You're fucking Collins's. That's not a light responsibility, I raised you better than that. Honor, integrity, respect. You have responsibilities and duties to your family. I'm proud of all you boys. You've all amassed more than I ever dreamed for you when I was working two jobs to get you all the way to college while your mom took care of you. It's the only thing that got me through it, knowing I was providing, and your mother was making sure you didn't kill each other, so you could have better lives than we did. So you could accomplish everything you wanted." He leans back and takes a puff off his cigar. "Respect and love for your family is the glue that holds it all together. We have a role to play and when one cog in the wheel isn't functioning right, it's up to all of you to get off your asses and fix it." He turns to Donavan and me. "Tate and Quinn are already part of this family because your brothers have made promises to them." He turns to Deacon and Decker. "And when a Collins man gives his word, he follows through." He grits his teeth and gets that angry-as-hell look on his face that sends a shiver up my spine. "Tate and Quinn are to be treated like you would treat your mother. They are to be protected at all costs and they will *NOT* be disrespected in any fucking way. Or if I hear about it, I will fly up here and kick every ass in this room personally. Is that understood?"

"Yes, sir," we all say in unison.

He smiles. "Good. There will be peace in this family, as long as I'm breathing. Now, let's finish this little get together with me sharing a cigar with my boys. It's been too fucking long."

"Amen to that," says Decker.

I grin. "Where do you keep the whiskey in here?"

"Great idea, son. I like the sound of that."

Decker and I pour everyone a glass and things go right back to normal, just like that. No more fighting, no more tension.

We laugh and joke and bust each other's balls. It's perfect. I glance over at Dad, laughing and cutting up. I haven't always agreed with him on everything, but he's a good father and I hope I can be somewhat like him one day, with the things that matter anyway. I could imagine it eating me up inside if my sons weren't getting along, whether they're rich or poor. Some things are more important than money and status, and he's right, at the end of the day, the people you love are all that matter.

"This is how family is supposed to be." Dad stamps out his cigar in an ashtray, wearing a satisfied grin. "I don't know about you fucking clowns but I'm ready for some dessert. Tone down the goddamn language in front of the ladies. It bothers your mother."

We all file back toward the kitchen when Decker puts his arm across my chest. "We need to talk shop for a second, while I've got you here."

"Dude, it's Thanksgiving. What the hell? Can't we forget about business for a few hours and enjoy everyone getting along?"

"It's about Covington."

"Seriously? You're still on that shit? Let it go. I already secured part of his business, and I'll have it all by the end of the quarter. It'll be a big fuck you to Cooper and all those pompous pricks in midtown Manhattan."

He shakes his head. "Not gonna happen. I had Rick look into him."

"You what? What is the goddamn deal? You don't do this type of due diligence with any other white-collar clients."

"You don't know what I do. There's a lot I don't tell you guys and there are reasons for it."

"Why are you trying to fuck this deal in the ass? Where Covington goes, the money follows. Do I need to spell it out for you? This is what you pay me huge bonuses for. I can't do my goddamn job with you hamstringing me behind my back."

"Will you just cool your temper for two seconds and listen to me? Jesus Christ."

I wave an arm out. "Well go on. You're going to anyway."

"I run a clean house. I had Abigail and Rick both look into him. It's all bad."

My face heats up and it's not good. I can already feel the rage building in my chest. "Abigail knew about this?"

"Shit." Decker looks away then back at me. "You two weren't really, *serious*, when I put her on it. And I told her to only report to Rick and me, nobody else."

"Why the fuck wasn't I read in? I'm the one dealing with him." He's always pulling this clandestine shit and I'm sick of it. And him and Abigail are keeping secrets from me?

"It was need-to-know and your emotions are clouding your judgment. Look, your buddy owns a few corporations with ties to cartels and organized crime shit. They're money washing operations. He also owns a large portion of a shipping company, and we think they may be involved in human trafficking."

"Does it tie back to him? *Legally*?" I have to put an emphasis on that, because he's speculating right now.

"None of it ties back to him, legally, but I don't want him on our roster. Do you really want your name associated with that shit?"

"Fuck you. Our criminal law department defends murderers. Do you want our name associated with *that*? Money is money and we don't know for a fact that he's doing any of that shit, or if he's aware of any of it. He's at such a high level he looks at spreadsheets and data. He owns interests in thousands of companies. I know him personally. You're biased because he likes all that BDSM shit and you're looking for a reason to fuck this deal up." I shake my head and all I can think about is how Abigail didn't say anything. "No. I know what's motivating this. Fear. You're pulling this shit because you're afraid of ruffling feathers in New York. Cooper has you scared like a little bitch."

He gets up in my face. "I will say this once and it's final. Fuck Bennett

Cooper. And Covington is done, so get him out of your thick fucking head and move on."

"Fuck you. He's my client. I've been working on this for months if not years. It's happening. We don't need to know about any shady shit he has on the side. We have plausible deniability. When did you become such a fucking saint? Tate put you up to this or something?"

He points a finger in my face. "Don't bring my fiancée into this because you're pissed off about being wrong and because I gave your girlfriend an assignment. Business is business and she was just doing her damn job. Covington's not to set foot in our fucking offices until I say so."

"Fuck this. I don't need it. Not from you. Not from anyone." I throw a shoulder into him as I storm out of the study.

ABIGAIL

I'm in the kitchen helping Tate serve dessert as the guys stroll in from the study with Mr. Collins leading the way.

Donovan and Deacon fall in behind him and grab a plate.

"This pudding is amazing." Jenny beams at me and gets a second helping.

"Thank you." I turn to Deacon. "Where's the other half of you?"

He shrugs. "I don't know, he stayed behind with Decker for a minute. Maybe something with work?"

"Holy… this pecan pie reminds me of home," says Tate, trying to make idle conversation, but I see her keep glancing toward the study too.

I slide into a seat next to her where nobody else can hear. "Thanks again for having me. I know Decker wasn't thrilled at the thought of Dexter and me. I hope it's not a problem. I don't want to cause tension in the family."

"Oh, trust me. Whatever is happening in there right now… It has nothing to do with you. All these boys like to act tough, but inside they're all softies. You just have to be around them outside of work to get to the good stuff. I think they're at each other over a potential client."

My stomach drops and I wonder if this is to do with the file I gave Decker about Wells Covington.

Finally, I see Dexter and I know the look on his face immediately. I've seen it once before and it wasn't a good outcome.

Decker storms in right behind him, looking just as pissed off, if not more.

"Oh shit," Tate whisper-sighs the second she sees them.

Dexter doesn't slow down at all as he marches past me. He shoots me an angry scowl and goes straight out the front door.

"What the hell?" I look at Tate.

Decker goes to the fridge and yanks the door open so hard I'm surprised it doesn't fly off the hinges, then takes out a beer.

I stand up. "I'm going to go check on Dex."

Quinn steps in my way. Her eyes are wide. "Don't. Trust me. Whatever it is let him cool down and work through it. If you go out there it'll be worse. Seriously. Him and Deacon are exactly alike."

"I'd listen to Quinn," says Tate.

"No." I shake my head. "He can be pissed at Decker all he wants but he has no business treating me that way. I didn't do anything."

I grab my coat from the hall closet and find him outside pacing on the sidewalk. "What the hell happened back there? You don't just shoot me dirty looks and walk out on your family and me with no explanation."

His hands are trembling and not from the cold. "Just let me be, Abby. Fuck! I just need five minutes."

I shake my head. "No, if you want us to work, you talk to me."

He points a finger in my face. "You mean the way you came and talked to me when you were doing research on my friend?"

Shit. It *was* about Covington. "I was doing my job. What my boss told me to do."

"Horse shit! You knew Decker was working behind my back, but you said nothing. Not one word. You knew about Wells. You saw us at the bar, you knew who he was so don't act all innocent now. You went behind my back with my brother to sabotage me." His hands ball into fists and his face is bright pink. "Were you even going to tell me at all?"

"Oh, can I speak now? Or would you like to keep screaming at me like a child throwing a tantrum?"

"I told you to leave me alone for five minutes and you didn't listen. What you see is what you get."

"I didn't know what was going on, *Dexter*." I point at him. "This is why I knew we were a bad idea." A tear slides down my cheek as I say the words, because I knew this was coming. I knew something like this was going to happen. "I told you we wouldn't be able to keep business and personal separate, but you kept at me, kept pressing, until I gave in and now look at us. Is this what you wanted? You're breaking my heart right now and you promised me you wouldn't."

"Just doing your job?" He scoffs. "Rationalize it and play the victim all you want. You betrayed me. You didn't come talk to me. You hid things from me and now you act like it's my fault. I don't need this shit."

I'm not going to sit here and be his punching bag. I don't have to put up with this. Not from him. Not from any man. Maybe my mom was right, and he is just a boy, throwing a hissy fit, all up in his emotions like women supposedly get.

"Yeah. My job."

"That's what everyone around here says. I'm just doing my job but when I'm the one doing mine, I get fucked."

"I didn't do this to you."

"Right. You just fed the information to Decker during the day and fucked me at night. You know what, Abigail? Why don't you go back in the house with my brother and enjoy the holiday. He's the one who pays your fucking bills. Business is business, right?"

Tears burn in my eyes as he climbs in his car and squeals the tires, leaving a trail of smoke behind them.

I cover my face with my hands and the back of my throat burns. He just left me here, knowing I'd be alone with his family after what just happened.

I don't know if I've ever been so ashamed in my life.

I wipe the tears from my eyes.

Fuck you, Dexter!

I start toward the end of the driveway with my phone in my hand, because there's no way in hell I'm going back in that house after what just happened. It's too humiliating.

The front door opens, and Tate and Quinn come rushing out. They probably heard Dexter peel out of the driveway like an idiot.

"Just come back inside, please?" Tate wraps her arms around my shoulders.

I shake my head. I can't. And if I see Decker, I might blow up at him and lose my job. "I'm fine. I'll call an Uber. Really."

"I'll drive you home," says Quinn.

I can't even look at her, I just nod.

"Just let me tell Deacon and grab the keys. Did you bring a purse?"

"I'll grab it." Tate gives me another squeeze on the shoulder.

I sniffle and try to dry my eyes on my sleeve where they can't see. I'm a mess, crying in front of all my coworkers.

A few minutes later, I'm in the car with Quinn.

She turns the radio down. "You don't have to talk about it if you don't want." Her gaze and tone softens. "But I'm here if you need me. Those boys can act like idiots sometimes."

"I appreciate the offer, but I'm fine, really." I'm not fine. I'm anything but fine right now. I can't be with someone who doesn't respect me. The only good thing about today is that Barbie is at her parents' house, so I can't explode on her and end up homeless.

Quinn pulls down my street in front of my building.

"If you need anything call me. We can grab lunch one day next week."

"Sure. That'd be great." I know it won't happen, but Quinn is nice, and I don't want to be a bitch to someone who doesn't deserve it. I know her loyalty is with Dexter. She's engaged to his twin brother. Anything I say to her will get back to him.

She drops me off and I walk inside. The apartment is quiet and cold. I turn the heat up and sulk down the hall to my bedroom and change into sweats and a t-shirt. I put on fuzzy socks and twist my hair up into a messy bun.

Finally, I settle in on the couch and watch the Hallmark Movie Channel with a pint of sea salt caramel ice cream.

I'm halfway into my movie when someone bangs on my door.

I don't want to answer. It's most likely Dex and he's either here to be a bigger asshole or to get on his knees and grovel. I don't have the patience for either of those scenarios tonight.

I do walk over to the door though, my curiosity getting the best of me. I look out the peephole and it's Kyle.

I open the door and he takes one look at me, then pulls me in for a hug. "Are you okay?"

I shake my head. "No, my life is shit right now."

"What happened?" He takes a step inside and I close the door. "Were you crying?"

I look in the mirror and my eyes are still red as hell. "No. It's... I'm fine."

"Did he do this?"

"I don't want to talk about it."

He hems and haws for a second, but surprisingly he doesn't mention Dexter again. "Well, come to the apartment. We have chocolate cake and shots. Nick brought a bunch of food from his family's get together. We're just chilling. Don't sit here all alone on Thanksgiving."

I glance around my apartment. He's right. I shouldn't have to sit here all alone, miserable. "Okay." I grab my keys and leave my phone. "Just for a bit, though."

DEXTER

I'VE DRIVEN AROUND AIMLESSLY for about half an hour trying to cool off. I know I shouldn't have exploded on Abigail the way I did. I was pissed at Decker mostly. Yeah, I'm upset with her, but I shouldn't have taken off like I did and left her alone at Decker's house. If she would've just given me five fucking minutes by myself, it's usually all I need to cool down. But when I'm like that and people don't leave me alone, I say and do hateful shit. She wouldn't stop pressing and I just lost it.

I don't know what I'm doing. I'm too mad to see Decker right now, but I need to at least go back and drive Abigail home. Then she can tell me she never wants to see me again and scream in my face or whatever she needs to do. I'm in the right frame of mind and won't act like a maniac this time. I deserve it, whatever she does. Who knows what the hell everyone else is saying to her about me.

Fuck!

I turn my car back around and head to Decker's house as much as I don't want to. I pull up and leave the Chevelle running in the driveway and jog to the door. Tate comes to the front and glares like I'm the world's biggest asshole.

That's fair.

She steps outside and lowers her voice like someone might be listening in on us. "She's not here. What the fuck is wrong with you, Dexter?"

I inhale a deep cold breath. "I don't know. Your goddamn fiancé was acting like an idiot and he had Abigail running research projects on Covington behind my back, telling her not to report to anyone but him. I'm sure you were read in on it, but Wells is my friend. Not just a client. And he had my girlfriend investigating him and nobody told me shit."

"Did he now?"

"What, you didn't even know?" I shake my head. "Fucking figures."

541

"I'll handle Decker. Just go patch things up with Abigail. She was really upset."

"I told her to leave me alone for five minutes, she didn't listen."

Tate points a finger up at my face. "Listen up, short stack. It doesn't fucking matter who started it or who didn't do what or who was wrong. You assholes get to rule the workplace with an iron fist, women rule everywhere else. Get your shit together, snapping at her like that. You're the man, now go apologize. Those are the goddamn rules of the universe if you like to get laid and be with a badass like Abigail. So suck it up."

"Where is she?"

"Quinn drove her home."

"Thanks."

"Hey, Dex?"

"Yeah?"

"Please work things out with her. She really loves you, and you two are perfect for each other."

I walk back to my car and say over my shoulder, "I'll do my best."

When I'm back in the Chevelle, I grab my phone and dial Abigail. There's no answer. No surprise. She's no pushover. It's one of the many things I love about her.

I drive straight to her place but there's no answer when I call again from the car.

I make my way up her stairs, dreading every step, wondering what the hell I'm going to say. Finally, I stop in front of her apartment door.

I knock.

No answer.

I knock again, "Come on, Abigail. I know you're there."

A door down the hall opens and that prick Kyle walks out of his apartment. He spots me and has a smug grin plastered across his face.

Don't say shit to him, Dexter. Don't do a damn thing or you'll never get her back.

He takes a few steps toward me. "She's not home."

"How the fuck do you know?"

Damn it, just be civil to this prick. Turn the other cheek.

He smirks at me. "Because she's in *my* apartment." He hooks a thumb behind him. "And she doesn't want shit to do with you."

I shake my head at him. "You're pathetic. Your manipulation bullshit won't work, kid. Go fuck yourself."

"I might fuck someone else who's sitting on my couch. Because I'm not lying."

To hell with being nice.

"I'm getting sick of your shit, you smug little prick." I start toward him, fist clenched.

542

His eyes get big. "I'm calling the cops if you don't get the hell out of here." He yanks his phone out of his pocket.

"You don't own the building. I'll bring a sleeping bag and camp out in the goddamn hallway if I want to, dipshit."

"No, but you're walking toward my apartment threatening me."

"I don't need to threaten you before I kick your ass. Now get out of my face before I punt you out a fucking window."

"Fuck you." He flips me off, but damn near stumbles over his feet as he backs up toward his door.

"Kyle? Where'd you go?" Abigail steps out into the hallway in her damn pajamas with a beer in her hand.

I don't know if I've ever felt so fucking stupid in my life. I thought for sure he was lying. No way would she be in his apartment. Less than an hour and she already ran off and started drinking with him. Everything in my body aches, all over. My heart feels like it was just ripped out of my chest. I keep waiting for anger and rage to consume me, but it doesn't. It feels like my body might collapse on itself. I have to get the fuck out of here.

Kyle stands there with a cocky, 'I told you so' smirk on his face, and I've never felt so emasculated.

I shake my head right at her. "Unbelievable."

"Dex?"

"I can't believe I came here to apologize. Enjoy your evening."

"Dex!"

Her word hits me in the back and I just keep walking.

To hell with everything.

ABIGAIL

I CAN'T STOP CRYING and I don't remember ever being this upset in my life. Dexter was a total asshole, but I can't get the look on his face out of my head. I didn't make him mad, I hurt him. The worst part is I don't know if I should feel bad or not. I don't know how to feel.

Yeah, I probably shouldn't have come to Kyle's, but I was so upset, and I just didn't want to be alone. I know how it looked to Dexter but it wasn't what he thinks. He'd never listen to me if I tried to tell him and I shouldn't have to explain myself anyway. He's supposed to trust me. He's the one who blew up and acted like a damn idiot. If he hadn't done that, I wouldn't have been back at my apartment all alone, eating ice cream.

Kyle walks up with two full shot glasses. "Here, it'll help."

I shake my head. I shouldn't even still be here, but my feet feel like concrete and I just can't move. Nick is in the bedroom playing some video game so I'm all alone with Kyle in the living room.

Get up and leave.

Kyle plops down next to me. "More for me then." He takes both shots, back to back. When he's done, his eyes dart over to me. "You're better off."

"Don't. Please. I need to go."

I start to get up and his hand moves to my thigh.

I glare down at it. "What are you doing?"

He leans up. "Oh come on, you deserve better than him. Someone who knows how you should be treated."

I shove his hand off me. "What the hell are you even saying?"

His jaw ticks. "You know what I'm saying. You have a guy right here in the same hallway who cares about you and you're off messing around with some asshole twice your age."

545

"He's not twice my age and you're supposed to be my friend." I stand up. "Dexter was right. What did you say to him that night in the bar?"

He remains silent, sitting there, brooding.

"I'm out of here."

When I take two steps, Kyle leaps up from the couch.

"Of course you are, you fucking tease. Go on, run back to him. It's what you bitches do best."

My face heats up and every muscle in my body constricts, partly because I'm pissed at Kyle and partly because Dexter was telling the truth and was right. I was stupid not to listen to him. I wheel around on Kyle. I want to say mean things to him, but I don't want to stoop to his level. I'm tired of being angry today. Everything hurts. My heart aches for Dexter. A real friend would be comforting me right now and not because they wanted to get me drunk and get laid.

"You're pathetic."

"Don't, Abigail. Just stop with the whole pity thing." He waves a finger up and down. "It doesn't suit you. You're just like all the pretty girls in high school, running after the hottest dude you can find, even if he's a total prick to you."

"It's true, I do pity you, Kyle. You know why?"

"Why?"

"Because you were nice to me when I moved in. I liked you and Nick. I thought you were actually my friends. And if you'd asked me out on a date before Dexter did, I would've said yes. You were too insecure to even try. But now, I wouldn't pour water on you if you were on fire. Have a great Thanksgiving."

I storm out while he stands there, staring at the ground.

You did the right thing.

I could've gotten into a shouting match with him, but what would that have done? It feels so much better knowing I was the bigger person. And I wasn't lying. I would've gone out with him, but now I won't, ever.

Now, I just have a broken heart I need to get over. I'm so done with relationships, for a long time.

ABIGAIL

It's been two weeks and Dexter and I haven't spoken since he saw me in the hallway. I know it didn't look good, but what the hell? It wasn't what it looked like and I'm not going to chase him down and apologize when he's the one who acted like an idiot.

It's been tense and awkward at work. I go out of my way to not cross paths with him. Not because I don't want to see him. I do. I miss him like crazy, but it's just not worth it. He hasn't even said he's sorry and I'm sure he won't. All he'll remember is seeing me in the hallway and forget everything he did before that. I need to get out of this city. I don't want to be at work around Dexter and I damn sure don't want to be around Kyle or Barbie.

It'll take some time to get used to being single after Dexter, but once I'm over it, I'll be happy again.

Any time I do happen to see Dexter, it's like I don't exist. He doesn't glare, doesn't look frustrated, just carries on like I'm nothing to him.

I can't believe I put myself in this position. He promised me he wouldn't do this to me. I don't know what to do.

Living with Barbie has been unbearable. She's back to being a total bitch. She hates the world thanks to Chuck and wants to make everyone as miserable as she is, not that she didn't before, but it's worse now.

Tate and Quinn have reached out multiple times, but I'm just not good at this stuff. I don't want to talk about my problems with them. I know where their loyalties lie.

I wouldn't expect anything less, either. They're both engaged to his brothers. If I was in their shoes, I'd report back everything I heard. It makes me feel so out of place. I can't wait to go home to Texas for Christmas. It's my favorite thing in the world and I refuse to let Dexter ruin it for me.

I turn the corner and catch him walking a female client to the elevator. My heart sinks when I see his hand at the small of her back. I'm sure it's nothing. He's probably just being polite, but it's like a knife to the heart. That was something I thought he only did for me. Every feeling I have is amplified by a thousand any time he's near me. Just seeing him hurts.

He smiles and jokes like nothing is wrong in his world and I feel like I'm slowly cracking. Like my entire life might just crumble down any second. I hate it. I hate this. I hate being in this office breathing the same air as him. I hate feeling this way. Being angry and still wanting him. I want out of my head for just five minutes.

I exhale a long breath and do what I should have done two weeks ago. I march to Decker's office.

"Is he in there?"

Quinn nods. "I'll let him know you're here." She picks up her phone. "Abigail is out here. Do you have a minute?" She hangs up the phone. "You okay?"

"I'm fine." I plaster a fake smile to my face and hope it's convincing.

"You sure?"

The pity in her eyes has my skin crawling, but I know she's just being nice. "I'm good."

"You can go on in. He's waiting."

"Thank you."

I walk in.

Decker leans back in his chair and looks intimidating as hell, but I square my shoulders and push all my anxiety away.

"Abigail." He gestures to the seat in front of his desk. "Look, I'm sorry about—"

"It's fine. It's done. That's not why I'm here."

His glance turns quizzical. "Okay, so what can I do for you?" He's being way nicer than usual, which tells me he knows he fucked up, but he probably won't apologize.

I don't want him to anyway. I meant what I said. I just want to forget it ever happened. I don't want to hold grudges or blame anyone. I just want to put this all in the rearview mirror.

I take a seat. "I was, umm, I don't really know how to say this, but is it possible for me to transfer back to Dallas?"

"Is this because of Dex?"

I shake my head. Of course it is, Decker, Jesus. How can you run this firm and be so blind sometimes? "No, I just miss home. I want to be back near my family." I'm sure he probably sees right through the lie. If he doesn't, he's oblivious.

"You sure it's not about Dexter and the Covington thing?"

I really don't want to get into this again. It'll bring back too much pain. "I don't know, Mr. Collins. Probably some of it. I do miss my family. I just feel awkward, like I don't belong here."

"You're a great employee. I had really high hopes for you. Have you talked to him?"

"No." I have to choose my words carefully. For all I know he's recording the damn conversation. "There's not really anything he can say or do. Things just didn't work out between us."

He glances off at the ceiling, then his eyes fall back on mine. "If that's what you want then I don't see why not. I'm sure Weston would love to have you back. Do you have any work that needs transitioned?"

"No. I got everything wrapped up. I was going home to visit for Christmas before any of, well, you know... It should go pretty smooth."

"Okay, well, when do you want to go back?"

"I'm leaving for Dallas tomorrow. It would make it easier if I could just stay there."

"Wow. Okay, I'll call him this afternoon. You sure you're okay? You've thought about this?"

I nod. "Yes, sir."

"Okay, well I'll make the call."

"Thank you, Mr. Collins. I really appreciate the opportunities you gave me here. I learned so much."

"The pleasure was ours, even if we only had you a short time."

I turn to walk out.

"Abigail?"

I stop and face him. "Yeah?"

"It's Decker, okay?"

I nod. "Okay, thank you, Decker." It feels so weird calling him by his first name, but I don't want to be rude and I really do appreciate everything he's done for me, professionally. I could stomp a hole in his chest for mixing business with my personal life, but I love my job and going off on him in his office would be stupid. It would be something Dexter would do and I'm better than that.

I walk through the door and let out a deep breath. I'm not going to cry. I'm doing the right thing.

As soon as I look up, Dexter is standing right there.

Shit.

DEXTER

I HEAD toward Decker's office. I need to talk to him about Wells Covington. He's going to get on board or I'm finding a new job. He's making a monumental fuck up, the way he's handling this. I've had to meet with Rick twice already to go over stuff when I've had far more important things to be dealing with.

It already destroyed my relationship. It's not going to ruin me professionally too. I've had to meet with clients and work a ton the past two weeks. I still met with Covington twice, but I'm not about to tell Decker that.

I know I should apologize to Abigail, but I don't know what to say to her, so I bury myself in work, meeting with potential clients. I tried to reach out a couple times and my calls went straight to voicemail. I sent two texts and they went unanswered.

I need to clear all my work off my plate and then I'll deal with her before she leaves for Christmas. If there's one thing I know about her and me, it's that we need to cool off. I can sit down and talk to her now that all the anger is out of our systems and at least give her something to think about while she's there. I can't do two things at once and be in two places at once and it's driving me insane.

As soon as I walk up to tell Quinn I need to talk to him, Abigail walks out of his office. Fuck, it's too soon. I'm not prepared to say anything, but I have to say something.

She eyes me and tries to speed past, but I step in her way. "Hey, I really need to talk to you. I've been slammed with work, but I tried calling a few times. I just really want to sit down and talk face to face. Please?"

She shakes her head. "Don't bother. It's too late for that."

Before I can respond she just walks past me.

What the fuck? I didn't yell at her. Can she not even talk to me now? I know I screwed up, but she was at that asshole's apartment and I didn't even blow up on her. I kept my cool.

I keep glancing back and forth between Decker's office and Abigail walking away and I want to scream. My whole life is out of order and I'm going to die if I don't get all this shit figured out soon. Fuck it, she needs to cool down a little more apparently. She looked like she was about to rip my head off. I'll just wait it out another day or two. She can't stay pissed-off forever.

Or can she? That's what worries me. Fucking women. They know how to hold a grudge. Jesus.

I walk into Decker's office.

The second his eyes come up from whatever he's reading, he lets out an exasperated sigh and holds up a hand. "Not more personal shit. I can't fucking deal with it right now."

My eyebrows rise. "What?"

"Yeah, your little girlfriend was in here wanting a transfer back to Dallas. She's my best researcher out of all the paralegals and she wants out of here, because of you. I'm sure you're coming in here to stop it from happening. I can't deal with all this shit. Not right now."

I swear my heart stops beating. All the air sucks out of my lungs, and then my face heats to a million degrees. It's even worse than at Thanksgiving. And fuck Decker for wanting to blame all of this on me. He's guilty too.

Decker turns around and his eyes widen when he sees me. "Just calm down for a minute, okay?" He takes a step toward me.

"She's not fucking going anywhere." I haul ass toward the door.

"Dex! Get your ass back…"

I fly out of the room before he can finish his sentence.

The whole office is a blur. People try to say shit to me, but I don't hear a word. I sprint down the stairs and out the front just in time to see Abigail slide into a cab.

"Fuck!"

Everyone on the sidewalk turns and stares at me after I scream the word. My head is on a swivel, craning around, and I see the parking garage. Thank God I drove today. I take off running through the street and a couple cars screech to a halt and lay on their horns, but to hell with them. I fish for my keys as I slalom between a couple pillars in the parking garage over to my car.

It fires up and I haul ass out into Chicago traffic. The skyscrapers float by overhead and the engine rumbles under my feet as I zoom in and out between cars, going as fast as I can through downtown.

At the last second the car in front of me slams to a halt while the light is still yellow.

"Fucking pussy, go!" I beat on the horn.

A middle finger flies up and I halfway start to unbuckle my seatbelt, but I can't chase Abigail down and tell her to stop being an idiot from a jail cell. So, I just sit there, breathing heavily, brooding.

What the fuck? Yeah, I was an asshole but you're just going to up and move across the country over it? Why the hell did I have to fall in love with a twenty-four-year-old? This is the type of shit they do. The sky is falling anytime someone makes one little mistake. It's not like I fucked someone else. I can't even think about anyone else but her and she won't give me the time of day?

You were a dick, man. It was a major screw up. Don't rationalize it. You need to calm down.

I want to do anything but listen to my brain right now, even though I know I should. My fingers grip the wheel. I shouldn't be going to talk to her right now, not like this. It's what got me in trouble the last time, but I can't help myself. I just want to grab her by the shoulders, shake her, and make her listen to reason. I want to promise I won't ever fuck up like that again. My heart just aches. I've never experienced anything like it.

It's my fault. All my fault.

I just want to scream at the top of my lungs.

I don't think you can ever really appreciate how much you love someone, until they're taken away from you.

Finally, the light turns green and I fly down Abigail's street. I catch a glimpse of yellow and her getting out of the cab, just as I pull up. I throw the Chevelle in park, right in the middle of the road because I don't give a shit about a car or a job or anything else. I just want her.

I rip open the door to my car and take off running to cut her off before she can make it inside her building. Horns blare and people shout all kinds of shit because my car is blocking the road, but I don't pay any attention to it. I run up the steps and grip her forearm and spin her around.

Her eyes go wide at first, then narrow in on me. "Go away. I don't want to talk to you right now."

I throw my hands up. "Seriously, Abby. We need to talk."

"It's not the time. Like I said, not right now."

"Oh, would tomorrow be better, when you're in Texas?"

She grits her teeth. "I said not right now. I don't want to talk to you."

"You're acting like an idiot."

Her face tenses. "Me! I'm an idiot? Are you kidding me right now?"

I shake my head. "You're not going back to Texas. What's wrong with you?"

She shoves a finger in my face. "You don't tell me what I can and can't do. You're not my father. You were supposed to be my partner, but you're not anything to me anymore!"

Her words are like a slap to my face. Fuck, it hurts so damn bad.

She stares down at the concrete. "I didn't… I didn't mean that, Dex. I'm just hurt, and…"

"Well, you said it. I'm here. I'm trying. I wish you'd just talk to me. I just need to hear your voice or be around you or something, I don't know."

She looks up and there are tears in her eyes. Her voice lowers an octave and her words slow down, like she's having trouble getting them out without having a break down. "You left me. At your brother's house, with your whole family, on

Thanksgiving. And I work with all of them. They're my bosses. Do you have any idea how humiliating that was? Do you really have any idea? You acted like a child. In fact, all of you act like children. And that's saying something, considering it's coming from a twenty-four-year-old who is actively trying to have fun and be irresponsible at this stage in her life."

I nod. "You're right. I know."

She reaches out and grabs my forearm.

I just want to hold her so fucking bad and make a million promises to her, but I can't. She won't let me. And I can't really blame her when I step back and look at everything I did. I broke the one promise I made to her. The one that mattered the most.

"I really, really love you, Dexter. It's why this is so hard. If you were any other guy, I wouldn't even talk to you. I had an amazing time, being with you, and I'll never forget it. But I can't be near you right now. I just... can't." Her voice cracks a little. "It physically hurts, so much, even being in the same building as you. I have to go back home and get away from this place. I'm sorry."

Before I can say anything else, she turns and walks through the door. I want to run after her, but I don't. Seeing her in that kind of pain was the worst thing I've ever experienced. I don't want to make it worse.

I finally make my way back out to the car. I don't know what to do. I've never felt the way I do right now.

It feels like my life is over. Like there's nothing worth living for.

DEXTER

Iт's a week before Christmas and I can't concentrate for shit. Work sucks. I see Abigail everywhere, even though she already left for Texas like a week ago. Life is dull, colors are drab. Going for runs, working out, driving along the lake in the Chevelle—none of it helps. All I think about is *her*. I see Christmas displays everywhere and I just want to light the fucking things on fire.

I should throw myself into work and focus on managing this Covington situation, but I can't think. I finally got Decker to listen to reason for two fucking minutes and we're assessing things with Covington on a day-to-day basis. It's the one highlight of the last week, but even that feels insignificant. I think he only did it because he felt bad. That's how he apologizes for shit, by not being an asshole about something for two seconds but leaving it open-ended so he can still get his way.

I barely eat anything. Can't sleep. I want her back so goddamn bad. All I think about is her meeting some asshole in Texas. Smiling at some other guy at one of those line-dancing bars where they ride bulls and shit, whatever they do down there. He has a big belt buckle and talks like a fucking moron with his pussy cowboy hat. The entire scenario plays out in my mind over and over. It's fucking torture, and I did it to myself.

I'm sure she's probably doing the same thing as me, judging by her reaction outside her apartment. I'm sure she's talking to her mom and lamenting ever giving me the time of day. But in my brain, she's moved on with someone else, because the mind is a dick like that.

How could I have been so stupid? I pushed her away and acted like a total asshole.

I head up the elevator in Deacon's building. I know him and Quinn are off doing some stupid romantic shit and it reminds me of ice skating and the yacht.

The whole time Deacon told me about his big plans for Quinn tonight, my heart squeezed tighter in my chest and I damn near had a panic attack. I managed to escape without him noticing. How? I have no idea.

Mr. Richards is home, though, and he's a good listener. At least last time I talked to him I ended up going and asking Abigail out. It turned my luck around and fuck if I wouldn't try anything right now. I'm desperate. I've never been superstitious in my life. I've always left that to my idiot brothers, but here I am. I'd go see a fucking psychic at this point if I thought there was an inkling of a chance of it working.

I walk through the door without knocking, like I own the place, and he's faced toward the TV in his electric wheelchair.

"Come on in, son."

"How do you know I'm not here to rob the place?"

"I figured you'd be here sooner or later. Quinn told me what happened."

I shrug. "Fair enough."

His hand points to the couch, but his eyes never leave the TV. "Well, lie down. I'm thinking about starting a side business, imparting wisdom to all you pompous rich bastards."

I snicker. He's probably right. It'd make Decker happy if he could take care of all the personal shit around the office. I walk over and lay down on my back, staring up at the ceiling. It really does feel like a counseling session all over again.

I don't even wait for him to ask, I just launch into it. "I messed up, bad, Mr. Richards. Got pissed off about some work stuff. I mean, it was a huge deal, but it wasn't her fault. I just got so damn, angry, all at once. And I never get pissed. I'm always the one keeping the peace with everyone else, staying neutral, level-headed and all that bullshit. Like fucking Switzerland or whatever."

"Yeah, you Collins brothers do get angry like that under certain conditions."

"What? Really?"

He nods slowly, still staring at the TV. "Yep. You guys are a weird bunch when it comes to your damn women. Always fucking it up, flying off the handle." He does that whistle thing that trails off.

"This was about work, though."

"Involves your women when it happens. Deacon did the same thing, didn't he? He ever blow up about 'work shit' before then?"

I think back. "No. Never." Interesting. I never put two and two together. I mean, I know Abby was involved, but I just thought it was work-related because I always compartmentalize everything. Abby and I rarely ever even talked about work. When Deacon blew up it was because Quinn was involved too.

"Look, son. There's nothing wrong with being passionate about your woman. Fuck, you should be, otherwise what's the damn point? It's why some places have rules and it's definitely an unwritten rule that you shouldn't date people at the office." He shakes his head. "Stupid, though. You can't help who you fall in love with."

"Yeah." I sigh.

"So she went back to Texas?"

"Yeah, she's gone."

The old man snickers.

What the fuck? Doesn't he see me pouring my damn heart out here? I don't make it my business to share my personal life with just anyone.

"Something amusing? What the hell? I'm dying over here."

"Oh cut the shit. You ain't dying."

I sit up on the couch. "Is this some kind of mindfuck you're pulling on me right now? Of course I'm dying."

"Men overseas are dying, away from their families, wishing they could hold the people they love. You're acting like a pussy. Talking instead of doing. Feeling sorry for yourself. And I must say." He finally turns and eyes me up and down. "It's not a good look."

I halfway want to punch his ass, but he's in a damn wheelchair for fuck's sake. Not to mention, I can't really argue with him. I *am* feeling sorry for myself.

Before I can say anything, he says, "Maybe that's a little harsh, but you're thinking about this thing all wrong, kid. When Deacon fucked up, what'd you do? He was probably looking the exact way you are right now, wasn't he?"

I hold my face in my hands. "Yeah, he was in bad shape. A fucking mess."

He spins his chair around. "Well, what did you do? You were on the outside looking in. That's how you need to approach your little problem here. You smacked him around a little, I'm sure, to get him out of his own head. Then you guys came and took me to the Bears game, Deacon begged and pleaded until she couldn't say no. He refused to let her go. He made his move. He did something instead of crying on a couch about his problems. Why aren't you taking your own advice right now? You watch all those damn romance movies and shit. Wasn't that how you came up with it?"

Jesus fucking Christ, I could kiss this old bastard.

I jump up to my feet. "You're right. I've been caught up in my emotions like a little bitch, wallowing in self-pity. I'm not a damn woman like Deacon."

"Well, I wouldn't exactly put it like…"

He sounds like he's in a tunnel a million miles away right now. My brain is spinning, scheming. Concocting a web of ideas like John Nash in *A Beautiful Mind*. The light bulb goes off. "Fucking hell." I shake my head. It's all so obvious now. I can still have her. I snap my fingers and point right at him. "The over-the-top redeeming gesture. I need one, bad. And it needs to be way better than Deacon's because he's a bitch and I'm the pioneer of this shit."

Mr. Richards laughs. "Well, hell, there ya go, son."

"Gotta get out of here. I have work to do. Thanks, Mr. Richards."

He waves me off with a hand and goes back to watching TV. "Anytime, kid. Good luck."

I haul ass toward the door and damn near barrel over Deacon and Quinn as they walk in.

557

"What the fuck, bro?" Deacon yanks Quinn to the side so I don't level them to the ground.

"Outta my way!" I grin at both of them. "I need a dry-erase board and some markers. Gonna draw up a plan that shits all over yours."

They both stare at each other as I haul ass to the elevator.

"What just happened?"

Deacon shrugs. "I think he's going after Abigail."

Quinn clutches her chest. "Finally. I wish I could be there. I bet it's amazing."

Deacon grins at Quinn. "Bet mine still ends up being better."

The elevator doors open, and I step in and turn back to them. "You wish, dick breath." I hold up a middle finger at him as the doors shut.

ABIGAIL

It's Christmas Eve and I've sulked nonstop for the last twelve days since I got back to Dallas. Weston told me I didn't have to start until after the new year, and to enjoy a break before I came back to the firm.

I glance around the room and I should be happy right now. It's freaking Christmas, my favorite time of the year. Dad's legs are shot out perpendicular to the floor in the recliner and his snores echo through the house. He has a Dallas Cowboys blanket draped over his Longhorns hoodie because Mom keeps the house cold and he just deals with it and never complains. I smile at him. I know it drives him up the wall, but he always shrugs and says, "Happy wife. Happy life."

Mom's in the kitchen, baking a turkey she'll use for turkey and noodles tomorrow. It's our tradition. My sister is back in her room, doing God knows what. She's fourteen and at that angsty teen stage where she listens to her headphones all day and wants nothing to do with anyone. *National Lampoon's Christmas Vacation* is on the TV and all I can think about is Dexter quoting it word for word on our first date.

I start to laugh at the thought, then stop myself. Part of me wishes Cousin Eddie would drag Dex to the house so I could give him my own version of a Clark Griswold Christmas diatribe, but the rational part of my brain knows I need to just mope around for a bit longer and then forget about him.

Dexter.

My favorite Christmas movie is on, the house smells amazing, and yet all I can do is think about him. What's he doing? Who's he doing it with? I know he's probably with his family but all I can seem to imagine is him finding someone else and moving on already. She's probably older, more mature, more beautiful, more experienced in the bedroom. Better for him.

You did the right thing.

I know my brain is right, but my heart doesn't agree one bit. Why does this hurt so damn bad?

Mom walks into the living room and gives me the obligatory *I'm sorry you're in pain, sweetheart* look. "Honey, why don't you come help me in the kitchen? Take your mind off things."

I shrug. It can't make anything worse.

I sulk into the kitchen behind her and she reaches into the very back of the fridge and comes out with a bottle of wine.

"Mom!" My eyebrows rise.

She waves me off like it's nothing, but then peeks around the corner to make sure Dad is still asleep. "It's this or the gun. Which one do you want to use to fix this problem of yours?"

I can't tell if she's joking or not. Finally, I nod at the bottle. "The wine, please."

"Nothing wrong with it on a holiday." She pauses and points a finger at me. "In moderation of course." She pours us both a glass.

This is hilarious. I've never seen her drink a day in her life. I wiggle my eyebrows at her. "So, does Dad know you like to get all sauced up?"

She glares. "I do *not* get all sauced up." Mom stops and sighs long and hard. "Look, nobody is perfect. Not me. Not your dad. Not you. And not your boyfriend you're getting over, okay?"

I nod.

"It's hard to watch you going through this, especially since we just got you back home, and because I know how much you love Christmas."

I feel like I might tear up. This is the part where we finally talk about everything, like we always do, and for some reason my throat is scratchy, and I don't know if I can get any words out to my mom. And we talk about everything.

"This is a part of life though, sweetie. Everyone has their heart broken by someone. It might sound, I don't know, insensitive, but I promise you something…"

"What's that?"

"It's going to make you a stronger woman. It will hurt and you'll cry, and I'll be here every step of the way to comfort you, but you'll eventually look back at it, learn from it, and it'll lead you to the man who ends up with your heart one day." She walks over and pulls me in close to her chest.

I finally break. The tears start to flow as she smooths down the back of my hair.

"Mom, I know I'm still young, and I didn't plan on meeting the right guy for a long time." I sniffle and bury my face into her shoulder. "I just… For some reason, I just knew he was the one. I don't know how to explain it. He just got me. And I got him. We were just… right."

Her grip tightens around me, and I know she's having murderous thoughts about Dexter right now. It's what I'd do if someone caused my child any emotional pain. "If he loves you the way you love him, he'll come crawling back. Trust me, they always do."

"I don't think so. He would've done it already. He's older and has a good job. He won't have any problem moving on. It was stupid. I think I just read too much into it." I can't believe I'm in my kitchen, crying to my mom over a guy. I've never been that kind of girl. I can't believe Dexter Collins turned me into this.

I wipe away at my tears and pull back.

Mom grabs her glass of wine and glances out into the living room at Dad, then back at me, and her voice lowers. "You never tell another living soul what I'm about to tell you, okay?"

I take a sip and nod. "Umm, okay."

"Your dad screwed up really bad once too, back at the very beginning. It was our first anniversary and you weren't born yet. Our *first* wedding anniversary, and he stood me up, didn't show. Who the hell does that? I could still wring his damn neck. We were supposed to go to dinner. His friends got tickets to the Cowboys and Giants game. He went. Didn't tell me he was going. Didn't say anything about it."

"Oh. My. God." I almost want to laugh because it's so Dad, and it was so long ago, but I bet she was furious when it happened.

"Yeah." Her eyes bug out. "I sat at the restaurant and he never showed. We didn't have cell phones yet. I had no way to get hold of him. I just sat there, seething, then crying, turning my wedding ring over and over on my finger, wondering if we were going to work. So, I went to Grandma's. He got home. Didn't know where I was. Didn't know what was going on." She pauses and looks like she's getting worked up about something that happened more than twenty-five years ago all over again. "Geez, that big idiot, I swear. It was our first anniversary as a married couple. Anyway, so, he shows up at Grandma's at almost midnight and bangs on the door."

"Uh oh."

Mom nods. "Yeah. Right? At your grandma's house. Your father is a lot of things, but he does not lack testicular fortitude, at all. We made it a point to never argue in front of you girls, but we're not perfect at all. We can have blowouts with the best of them when you kids aren't around, still do on occasion. So, anyway, he's upset. I'm even more upset and the dummy doesn't know why, and I have to finally tell him. Things get really heated. He's telling me to stop acting so dramatic and being stupid. I tell him to just go home. I don't want to see his dumb face and I'll come back to the house when I don't want to tear his head off."

This is so surreal. I can't even picture them arguing like this.

"And I sat up, and I cried to your grandma, looking the same way you look right now. She pulled a bottle of wine from the back of the fridge and shocked me the same way I shocked you just now when I did it. That bottle's been sitting back there waiting for this moment for years, honey. I bought it the day you went on your first date, knowing this day would come at some point."

I laugh and cheers her glass, somehow feeling a little better because I know the HEA is coming soon. "So, what happened with you and Dad?"

She smiles toward the living room, the smile she reserves just for him and nobody else. "The big goof didn't even make it until the morning on his own." She laughs and leans in. "He was back within an hour, begging and pleading and apologizing."

I almost want to swoon. Good for Daddy.

"Look, Abigail, the moral is, if you screw up in a relationship, you own it. You ask for forgiveness. That's all you can do. I don't know all the details of what happened with you and that boy up north. But I know you're a good judge of character. We raised you to be. If he's any kind of a man, he'll be back, and he'll fight for you. If he doesn't, you don't need his sorry ass." She covers her mouth. "I swear, this is why you shouldn't drink. This stuff turns you into a heathen."

I laugh and cheers her glass one more time. "Thanks, Mom. You're right." I reach for her glass. "Should probably let me have this then, so you don't turn into more of a heathen."

She smacks my hand away playfully. "I didn't say it was a bad thing to be a heathen once in a while. I've waited years for this wine."

We both laugh.

Dad's snores eventually echo into the kitchen while I help Mom with some of the side dishes. She just shakes her head and keeps baking. "Maybe I should've stayed at Grandma's house forever."

A WHILE LATER, we're still in the kitchen and the doorbell rings.

I look up from a mixing bowl. "You expecting company?"

Mom shakes her head. "Not at this hour. Maybe it's Lorraine next door. She's baking too and all the stores are closed. Probably needs something." She continues to knead a pie crust. "Can you grab it? My hands are all doughy."

"Sure."

I push away from the counter and walk past Dad. He's still completely out of it, probably asleep for the night. *A Christmas Story* is on the TV now and I curse myself for missing part of it.

As soon as I open the door, about ten carolers start singing *We Wish you a Merry Christmas*. My face lights up for the first time in weeks, since I left Chicago. It's my favorite Christmas carol of all time because it's so simple and to the point.

The carolers are adorable too. They're all boys and girls ranging in age from about six to twelve.

I stand there, basking in it, just remembering why I love the holidays so much and being with my family. I glance back and Mom, Dad, and my sister are fanned out behind me, smiling at the carolers. Mom must have rustled them up and hauled them to the door.

When they sing the verse about figgy pudding, they part in the middle and Dexter rises from a knee and starts toward me.

Figgy *pudding*. Of course, he planned out every damn detail.

Mom's hand grips my forearm and her fingers are trembling. Not in a protective way, but in a way that says *oh my God, what did I tell you?*

I don't even have to look back to know she's grinning like an idiot. It looks like a scene right out of the Hallmark Christmas movies.

As much as I want to stare at Dexter's face, and read every single one of his expressions, I can't, because he's holding a Husky puppy with the brightest blue eyes I've ever seen. My brain tells me I should scream at him to get away, do something. Tell him off in front of everyone. Let him know how stupid he is for what he did. I should do anything but gush at the puppy in his arms, but I can't.

It's the most beautiful dog I've ever seen in my life. If any man on this godforsaken planet knows how to buy my affection, it's freaking Dexter Collins. Ugh!

"Merry Christmas, Abby."

I fold my arms over my chest. All I want to do is grab that puppy from him and bury my nose in its fur, but I know I can't just let Dex off the hook like that. He hurt me, bad. He can't buy his way out of it by flying to Dallas with the cutest puppy in the world, but it might get me to listen to him for two seconds and no more.

I can't be bought, and I don't know if I want to forgive him anyway. I already moved across the country because of him.

"Dexter, I…"

He cuts me off. "Look, Abby, I was an idiot. I know there aren't words that can make up for what I did." He glances down at the ground, but then angles his gaze back up at me.

I can see the shame written across his features. He looks like he genuinely feels remorse, but it's still not enough. I was doing my job back in Chicago and I won't apologize for it. My career means a lot to me and I will always work my ass off. That's how my parents raised me. I didn't keep any personal secrets from him.

He hands the dog to my mom and I immediately want to snatch it away from her, but I don't. All I can do is stare at Dexter. He has that little boy look about him again, the one where he shows me his vulnerable side. It's the Dex I fell in love with.

Then, he does something I don't expect. He takes both my hands and drops to his knees in front of me. Why does it feel so good when he touches me? Why does it send warmth rushing through my veins and make me want to forget all our problems and rush into his arms? I've missed him touching me so much.

"I'm not perfect, Abigail. I never will be. I'm an idiot. I do stupid things all the time and I won't promise I won't screw up again. I should've never made that promise to you in the first place. But I'm begging you. Please, I want another chance. I was always content being on my own, doing whatever I wanted, until I met you. You deserve the truth and the truth is, I'm going to screw up again. And

563

again. But what I will promise you is that I'll always come back, and I'll always apologize, and I'll always make it up to you."

A tear slides down my cheek. Everything hits me at once, all the pain and all the happiness. Dexter just makes me—feel things, emotions I didn't know I had inside me. "Dex, I can't…"

"Yes you can."

I look away because staring at him like this in front of me is too much to bear.

"Abby, look at me."

I glance back to him and his eyes are glassy, tears forming in the corners. His voice cracks when he tries to speak. "I'm miserable without you. I can't eat. I can't sleep. My whole world is gray. There's no color in my life without you. I'm blind, stumbling around, lost."

If I wasn't turning into a blubbering mess before, I am now. "I just can't, Dex. You hurt me so damn bad."

He uses his shoulder to wipe away some of his tears. "I know. I don't know much, but I know I hurt you and I know I screwed up. I know one other thing, though."

"What's that?"

"I know I love you." He glances down. "I'm down on my knees, in front of your family, risking the worst rejection of all time, begging for you. I've never begged a day in my life. It's the hardest thing I've ever had to do, but I'd beg for eternity just for one more chance to show you how much I love you. I'm not going away, not now and not ever. I'll fight for you every day the rest of my life if I have to." He shakes his head. "I just need one more chance. Please don't leave me. I'll do anything."

I glance back at Mom and she has a hand over her mouth like she can't believe she's seeing what's taking place in front of her. Dad's smiling, like he can relate to Dexter's predicament. He's clearly been in that position a time or two in his life. It makes me smile on the inside. What would their life have been like if my mom hadn't forgiven him over and over? Dexter is a good man. I know it in my heart. I know he means what he says. I could see myself spending the rest of my life with him, and when I picture it, I'm always happy. It's the best life I could hope for and I really want that. I really want him. My life is also gray without him in it and I hate wallowing in all this pain nonstop, and it doesn't feel like it will ever go away.

"Abigail Whitley, come back. We want you to move in with us."

My head whips back to Dexter. "We?"

He gestures toward the puppy. "Me and Max."

My face softens when I see the dog, because how can it not? "You named him Max? After the dog in the Grinch?"

Dex nods. "Yeah, but we can change it. You can name him whatever you want…"

I shake my head. "No!" More tears stream down my face. "No, it's the perfect name for him."

"Abby, please. Just give me one more chance." He stands up and holds my hands in front of him. "Take a leap of faith with us. We won't disappoint you."

I glance back at Mom and she has tears in her eyes. She's snuggled up with Max and nodding her approval. I glance to Dad and he's practically a mirror of Mom.

"Oh for fuck's sake, take him back before I do," hollers my sister. It's one of the few sentences she's uttered since I've been home.

"Hey! Language! There are children out here." Mom scowls at her.

I can't fight the smile that spreads across my face.

I turn back to Dex and rush into his arms.

I think it takes him by surprise because he almost stumbles backward, but his big, strong arms wrap around me and for the first time in weeks, I feel safe again. I feel like I have a body of armor around me and nothing in the world can hurt me.

His hand caresses my hair and he pulls my face into his broad chest. "Thank God, Abby. Just, thank you." He kisses the top of my head, over and over, then puts his palms on both my cheeks and angles my face up to his. "You won't regret this."

Before I can say anything, his lips meet mine. He doesn't overdo it. I assume it's because we're in front of my parents and he hasn't even formally met them yet, but I can tell he doesn't ever want to let go.

And I don't want him to. I lean into him and resist the urge to melt into a puddle on the ground. After a few long seconds, he pulls back a few inches and smiles so damn big it could light up the whole block. "Good to have you back, Christmas clown."

I want to give him a smack to the chest, but I can't fight back my smile. "I haven't been much of a Christmas clown lately, but I'm sure I'll turn it around soon."

"Abby?"

"Yeah?"

"I'll always do my best for you, I promise. I'll give it everything I have."

I nod. "So will I. Promise."

"I guess I'll let go of you now."

"What? Why?"

He tilts his head toward Mom. "I know there's someone you want to meet."

I immediately jerk away from him once I remember. "Max!" I rush over to Mom and snatch my new puppy out of her hands so hard she gasps. "Oh, how's my new big boy?" I shake my head at him and do the silly baby-talk faces at him. His head tilts to the side like *is this lady serious? Is this my life now?*

I hug him close to me and pepper his snout with kisses, then bury my nose in his fur, all the while grinning up at Dex. "Bribery won't work on me again."

"I know." Dex smirks as he pulls out his wallet and hands a twenty-dollar bill to each of the kids standing around.

They all take their money and take off running to their parents out by the road.

He turns and grins. "Totally, can't ever bribe you again."

"Oh, it's like that?" I laugh. "Good to see you're still as cocky as ever." My eyes widen when I remember I've forgotten my manners. Mom is going to kill me later. "Crap, I'm sorry, Dex. This is my mom and dad." I glance back. "And my sister."

Dex walks over and shakes hands with Dad. He holds his hand out to Mom and she yanks him in and wraps her arms around him. Dex's eyes widen, but he quickly reciprocates. She leans up and whispers something in his ear that sends pure panic across his face. Then she says something else and that mischievous grin of his appears.

"Yes, ma'am." He nods.

Holy cow. I've never heard Dexter say "ma'am" before, like ever. He definitely learns fast. He starts toward my sister and she immediately backs away like *don't touch me.*

"Uhh, nice to meet you." Dex holds his hand up in an awkward wave.

"Good job with all… *that.*" She waves her arm out at the scene in front of her then takes off back for her room.

Dex mumbles, "Um, thanks, I think," to her back as she walks away.

"Come on. Come on. Let's get out of the cold." Mom ushers us in.

"Give me just a second." Dexter walks out to what must be a rental car. He turns back and sees us waiting on him. "Go on inside and get warm, I'll be right there."

I walk in next to Mom, hugging Max so hard to my chest I worry he can't breathe but I don't care because I already love him so much. He's the best dog in the world. I keep him away from Dad since he's allergic, but Dad doesn't complain. He just keeps smiling at me.

"Well, I like him. The boy grovels like a champion." Mom laughs and gives Dad a pat on the back. "Could give you a few pointers."

"I'd take 'em. No stranger to screw-ups. It's why you love me."

"I don't know if I'd go that far." Mom scoffs. "Best just stay out of trouble, mister."

Dad holds up both hands and goes back to his recliner.

Max and I sit down and he sprawls out and rests his head on my lap. When I stop petting him to adjust myself on the couch, he whines and shoves his snout back into my hand.

"Aww, are you co-dependent on mommy already? That's a good thing, because I love you so much. Yes I do." I scratch him behind the ears.

"God, what have I done?"

I look up and Dex is standing there, staring at Max like a jealous lover, probably wondering if he's ever going to get any attention. He has a bag of dog food cradled in one arm and some puppy toys in his other hand.

It's so freaking adorable how sad he looks.

I pat the cushion next to me. "Don't worry, there's plenty of me to go around."

Dex doesn't hesitate and rushes over to sit down next to me.

Max glares right at Dex the second he slides a hand on my thigh. He even growls a little while he does it.

Dex's eyes go wide.

"Someone's protective already, isn't he?" I scratch behind Max's ears to show him I approve of his behavior. "Such a good boy."

"Third wheel Dex. That's my new nickname. I can see it already."

I reach up and scratch behind Dex's ear with my other free hand. He makes a show of closing his eyes and leaning into it the way a puppy would.

Everyone laughs, even Dad. "Know your place in the pecking order, son. That's what I always say."

I scratch a little harder behind Dex's ear and he starts kicking his leg out in the air.

Mom dies laughing.

I look around the house, and it just feels like Christmas again.

It's perfect.

My two boys, my family, and the holidays. What more could I ask for? It's the perfect happy ending.

I glance over at Dex. "Hey, remember that time you asked about my wish? After I blew out the candle at the restaurant?"

"Yeah."

"It came true."

He smiles for a brief moment, then stares blankly. "Wait, that we would end up together, or you would get your dog?"

I scratch Max behind the ears and pet his sweet little head. "Guess you'll always wonder about that, won't you?"

EPILOGUE

Dexter
Three Months Later

"You excited?"

Abigail nods, practically bouncing in her seat. "Freaking giddy."

We're on our way to Six Flags Great America for Employee Family Appreciation Day. The firm does it every year and it really is a lot of fun. They rent out the whole park and we get it to ourselves. Abigail hasn't shut up about it since she found out about it last month.

"I can't wait to ride Goliath. I looked all of them up online. It reminded me of the Texas Giant back at Six Flags Over Texas. That one was always my favorite when I was a kid. I like the wooden roller coasters the best. They have this vintage feel to them and really toss you around."

I shake my head at her. "Just glad you're excited."

I love going fast in my car, but heights aren't my thing. In fact, I'm terrified of them. I've ridden a roller coaster once when I was about eleven, and that was enough for me. It was the worst experience of my life.

My stomach has been in a knot for days, actually, but I don't have the heart to tell Abigail I don't want to ride roller coasters with her. Plus, I'm no pussy. I'll never tell her that. I just have to man up and do it. Hopefully, my brothers don't say shit to her.

We arrive and pull into the private parking lot up close. For once in my life, I wish the place was packed with people, so we'd have to wait in line and wouldn't have time to go on that many, but only the people from the firm and their families are here.

I park the Chevelle and we walk in holding hands. To take my mind off the damn roller coasters, I focus on the past few months with Abigail. It's been fantastic. Her and Max moved into my place and it's awesome. Max is a total mama's boy. He's always crawling up in her lap and nudging me away from her. I still take his ungrateful ass for walks in the park sometimes. He's a really good dog and we've bonded some, even if I do have to fight for Abigail's attention on occasion.

Work was the one thing I was worried about, but it's actually been great. Since Abigail does mostly research stuff, we're always working on different cases. She always has the craziest stories. There's not a lot of weird shit when it comes to finance, unless Decker is looking into Covington's sex life.

We're still on a trial run with Covington and I'm taking care of his legal needs for a few of his smaller entities. It looks promising now that Donavan is a managing partner too. He's not nearly as conservative as Decker. He doesn't give a shit about the firm's image, just the bank account. The situation with Covington will change soon. I can feel it. I've been knocking shit out the park and already restructured his companies and saved him seven figures in income and capital gains taxes. He knows what that means if he gives me the reins on all his holdings. Bennett Cooper is about to eat a dick, and then I'm coming for the rest of his big-name clients.

"About time!" Decker glances at his watch and shakes his head.

I can't tell if he's just giving me shit or serious, probably a little of both.

Tate nudges him with her elbow, telling him to knock it off. "Hey guys!"

Abigail walks straight over to her and they start talking about the Six Flags back in Arlington and how Jenny already ran off with her boyfriend, probably to make out somewhere.

Decker glares right at them when they bring up Jenny.

"You look nervous as shit," says Deacon.

Quinn walks over to the girls to get away from us. I don't blame her. I'd do the same probably.

Mr. Richards wheels himself up. "Lucky sons of bitches, I can't ride shit. Anyone wanna take my seat and let me have theirs? I used to love roller coasters."

"Shit, I would if I could," I say to him.

"Sure you wanna go through with this?" Decker gives me a sly grin.

I slowly nod.

"Way to sell the jury. Let's go, pussy, before you change your mind."

I gesture toward Goliath, the big wooden fuck towering into the sky. "She wants to ride that one. Better make it that one."

Decker and Deacon both look up at it as Donavan walks up.

"He's really gonna do it?" says Donavan.

"That's what he says," says Deacon. "We'll see."

"Anyone tell Abigail about the last time he rode a roller coaster and pissed his pants, then had to walk through the crowd?" Decker's about to die laughing.

I wheel around on all of them. "Nobody is saying shit, assholes. It's not gonna happen this time. I was like eleven."

"Sure, maybe we should grab you one of those souvenir drinks to take with you. You can 'accidentally' spill it in your lap, Miles Davis." Deacon's cheeks are at full capacity and pink as shit, like he might explode any minute.

"Probably the best plan on short notice. I doubt they sell Depends around here," says Donavan.

My middle finger comes up before I can stop it.

"You guys coming or what?" Abigail hollers from twenty feet in front of us.

"On our way, babe." I turn to my brothers. "Do what you're told and keep your mouths shut. Got me?"

"Yeah, yeah, little bro. We won't let you down." Decker throws an arm around my shoulder, and the rest of us follow suit.

Other than the gigantic roller coaster in my future, this day is perfect, this moment right now. It's like we're kids again, arm in arm, walking through the amusement park. I'm so glad Decker and Donavan put their shit aside back at Thanksgiving. Life has been a million times better, once Abigail took me back anyway.

We get to the roller coaster and the girls walk up to get on.

I take a deep breath and try not to look up at the fucking thing.

"We're all set. You sure you're good?" says Deacon.

I nod.

I'm not fucking good at all. I should've eaten a goddamn Xanax earlier. I want my mind to be clear, though.

I walk in front and the guys fall in behind me. Abigail is in the front seat waiting. Perfect.

I climb in and hear the muffled laughter behind me from my brothers, but my stomach is in my throat and my palms are sweaty as hell. Front seat. Front row view, all the way down.

Abigail's hand slides into my lap and she squeezes my leg. "You okay? You look really pale."

"I'm fine." I do my best to smile at her. I really am excited about today, but roller coasters are like my biggest damn fear. I really should get off this thing.

Abigail looks so carefree and happy, though. I'd never ruin this for her. She's ecstatic, practically bouncing up and down in her seat.

The worker guy walks up to the platform and he looks nothing like an engineer or someone who would be qualified to work this thing. He's a fucking pimple-faced teenager. My fingers grip the bar in our lap so hard my knuckles turn white. My whole body is tense.

You can do this. You can do this. God, you're such a bitch, saying you can do this over and over.

"So, uhh, yeah dude, keep your hands in the car and hold onto the bar at all times. Here we go."

That's it? What the fuck? I'm going to die.

My body involuntarily starts rocking back and forth and it's like the sky is falling in on me, like I'm in the trash compactor in *Star Wars*. Black spots dance in my vision like I'm about to black out.

"Enjoy the ride." The kid hits a button and a buzzer sounds.

Bolts retract and we start rolling.

"Oh shit." Fuck, did I just say that out loud? "Oh shit." Yep, definitely said that one.

"Babe, are you okay?" Abigail leans over and puts a palm on my forehead. "You're sweating, like bad."

I nod furiously. "I'm fine, babe. I promise I'm fine."

"No, you're not. I'm going to holler for them to stop this thing. Look at you."

I grip her forearm. "No!" I nod again for the thousandth time. "I'm fine. I promise."

"Babe, what's going on? You keep saying you're fine. Over and over."

Deacon leans forward from the seat behind us. "He's scared shitless of roller coasters. It's basically his biggest fear in life."

We go around a turn and a chain jerks us up the steepest fucking hill I've ever seen in my life.

"Oh, Dexter." Abigail wraps me up in her arms.

I feel like the biggest bitch in the world right now, but I don't give a shit what I look like. It feels good when she squeezes me into her. I didn't realize how bad I was shaking until she hugged me. I turn into a stuttering asshole and I can't stop myself, no matter how bad I want to. "I-I-I'm okay. I promise."

"Stay away from his lap." Deacon laughs from behind, then says, "Ow!"

I assume Quinn smacked the shit out of him.

"What?" says Abigail.

"Nothing." I glance over at her. "If you don't know how much I love you, now you do." I shoot a glare back at Deacon and see how far up we've already gone. "Oh fuck."

"Look forward. Don't look down, Dex."

I glance over to make sure she's looking straight ahead, and I turn back and raise my eyebrows at my brothers. We're almost to the top of the hill.

They all flash me a thumbs up.

"It's all good, brother!" Decker hollers.

Okay. It's gonna be worth it. Another five minutes and it'll be done.

We start to crest the hill and Abigail looks over at me. "I'm so sorry. I would've never asked you…"

I shake my head. "Don't be sorry. Don't worry about me. Just enjoy this. I'm serious."

She gives me a worrisome nod, then holds her hands up.

And fuck, fuck, fuck, fuck, we're at the top.

The roller coaster stalls out for a split second. I look around and the view would be gorgeous from an enclosed room or an airplane, but not with my torso hanging out in the damn open.

We slowly pull forward, heading down the hill, and I think my heart might explode it's beating so fast. Then, it happens…

We roll over the edge and my stomach leaps into my throat. I close my eyes and say about ten million prayers in the span of two seconds.

My body vibrates all over the place while Abigail and everyone else screams their asses off. We fly down the hill, then through a tunnel and once we're at the bottom, relief washes over me and I open my eyes. I can't believe I didn't pass out.

"Oh fuck!" I scream.

Just as everything gets a little calm, we're yanked up a second hill. I was so focused on making it through the big one I didn't bother to think about the rest of the roller coaster.

"Fuck! Fuck! Fuck!"

The thing tosses us back and forth, jarring my neck and my back all over the goddamn place. I grip Abigail's leg so hard I worry I might be cutting off her circulation. It's two minutes of hell. That's exactly what the fuck it is. By the time we come to a stop, I exhale a gigantic breath I didn't realize I'd been holding.

Abigail leaps out of her seat, and I slowly stand up and make sure I didn't, in fact, piss all over myself again. I hobble out of the fucking death trap from hell and Abby spins around.

"Oh, babe, I'm so sorry." She dives into me and hugs me.

I wrap my arms around her. "It wasn't that bad."

She glances up at me and flutters her eyelashes the way she always does, like she's swooning over a romance movie. She leans up and pecks me on the cheek and whispers, "Thank you." Then, she leans back and stares for a long second. "You're never going on a roller coaster with me again."

I laugh as Decker, Deacon, and Donavan walk past and smack me on the back. "You didn't do too bad," says Decker.

I snicker. "Yeah, right. You know what they say about facing your fears?"

"Yeah."

"It's total bullshit. I'm never getting on one of those things again."

They all start laughing and we walk off.

Everyone falls behind Abigail and me and I grin my ass off at Deacon.

He gives me a fist bump on the sly, when nobody is watching. "It's done."

I nod at him.

"Oh my God, the pictures!" Abigail starts toward the little kiosk where they sell the photos of people going down the first big hill. You know, where everyone is making stupid faces and screaming their tits off on the big displays, then you can buy them for like fifty bucks.

We walk up and Abigail is bouncing up and down. "I can't wait to see your face in this picture, Dex. We're blowing it up and framing it on our wall."

I snicker. "Thanks, babe. You always got my back."

She leans up and pecks me on the cheek. "You know you love me."

"Yeah, yeah. Go on, check them out." On the inside my heart is still beating like a damn hummingbird's wings.

She's grinning so wide her face might get stuck that way. I love how happy I just made her. I've pretty much forgotten about all the anxiety from the ride, but my stomach is still all twisted up.

I take a few deep breaths as Abigail stares at the photo screen.

Her hand shoots over her mouth and tears well up in her eyes. I walk over to see my brothers didn't let me down. I look at me in the photo first, and it looks like I'm about to vomit everywhere with my eyes squeezed shut. Abigail has her hands in the air screaming and smiling.

Behind her in the photo, Donavan holds up a sign at the rear that says, "Abigail."

Next is Decker and Tate, holding one up that says, "Will you."

Then Deacon and Quinn are holding the last one that says, "Marry me?"

I already have the bright blue box out of my pocket, and I drop to a knee next to her. I open it up and reveal a princess-cut Tiffany solitaire in a platinum setting. She's still staring at the photo on the screen, her whole body trembling, tears streaming down her cheeks.

She turns and glances down to me on the ground, then looks around at everyone else. Tate and Quinn have their hands on their chest. My brothers are all grinning, along with Mr. Richards. Jenny flashes me a smile while her boyfriend stares down at his phone.

"Oh my God," says Abigail, when she sees Mr. Richards has a leash and Max is sitting on the ground next to him, watching us. She whips back around and stares down at me.

"Abigail Whitley, I love you more than anything. There's nothing I want in this world more than to ride the roller coaster of life with you. Will you marry me?"

She nods so hard she might break her neck. "Yes! Of course, yes!"

I take her hand and slide the ring onto her finger, then stand up and pick her up in my arms. Her legs wrap around me and I kiss the softest lips I've ever felt.

"Someone's chopping a damn onion out here," says Tate.

"Are you chopping it by Decker too?" says Donavan.

"Oh fuck off, I'm not crying," says Decker.

I grin right at Abigail and press my forehead against hers. "I love you. I always will, no matter what."

"I love you too." She shakes her head.

"What?"

"I cannot believe you rode that damn thing, knowing what it would do to you."

I glance around at our family and friends, then turn back to Abby. "Worth it."

"You're always full of surprises."

"Speaking of surprises, hold that thought." I glance around the corner of the roller coaster, set Abigail down, and yell, "Did you get it?"

"Wait, what?" Abigail's head flies around.

"We definitely got it!" Mr. Whitley hollers with his phone in his hand as Mrs. Whitley comes sprinting over, barely able to control herself.

"Mom!" Abigail takes off in a sprint and the two of them damn near tackle each other to the ground.

Mr. Whitley walks up in his Texas Longhorns shirt and shakes my hand. "Congratulations, son. You did good."

"Thank you, sir."

He tightens his grip on my hand. "Take care of my little girl."

"I absolutely will, sir."

He walks over and starts up a conversation with Mr. Richards, probably about dad stuff.

My brothers, Tate, and Quinn walk up. Tate and Quinn both hug me at the same time. "You did so good! We're so proud of you."

I give them a little squeeze then shrug them off me. "All right. All right. I'd love to remember this last part, but we can all forget about the minutes leading up to it, right?"

"Oh fuck off," says Deacon. "That ain't happenin'."

I laugh when Jenny nearly tackles me and wraps her arms around my waist. "You're the coolest uncle," she whispers.

I drop a kiss on top of her head. "And you're the coolest niece. Best ever."

"Congratulations, Uncle Dex."

"Thanks, kiddo." I turn to all of them. "You guys did great. It was perfect. Thank you."

Quinn shakes her head. "You really are a master at the over-the-top romantic gestures. You could write this stuff in Hollywood, you know?"

I buff my nails on my shirt. "I have a particular set of skills."

"Damn right you do," says Tate.

I glance over and Abigail is talking to her mom a million miles an hour and keeps showing her the engagement ring.

We all turn to Donavan at once.

I smile big as hell. "Looks like you're up next, asshole."

Donavan smirks. "Not a goddamn chance. You bitches are gonna hate me the rest of your lives, while I'm out doing whatever the hell I want, and whoever the hell I want."

I see Abigail in my peripheral vision, smiling her ass off. "Nope, got everything I need."

"Me too." Decker wraps an arm around Tate.

"Me three. Fuck that was lame as shit, but you know what I mean." Deacon wraps his arm around Quinn.

Donavan shakes his head. "Whatever, let's go get hammered and celebrate."

"Sounds good." I walk over to Abigail and her mom.

"Oh, Dexter, I'm so proud of you." She goes in for a hug. Once she has me in tight, she whispers in my ear, "We have a lot of guns, boy."

I laugh, but secretly I'm a little nervous. I'm not quite sure if she's joking or not.

"I can't believe you got her here. I've been trying to get her to come visit for like a year."

"You know when I was away on business last Wednesday?"

Abigail nods.

I shrug. "It was family business."

Abigail's eyes widen. "You went down and picked up my parents and drove them here?"

"Yeah." I smile. "They're staying for the week then we're going to rent an SUV and drive them back. Stay for a few days in Texas. I have a little work to do at the Dallas office. Then we'll fly back out of DFW. Already booked the vacation time at work for both of us."

Abigail flies into my arms again. I don't think I'll ever get tired of making her happy.

Fuck, my life is awesome.

THANK you so much for reading Filthy Playboy, we hope you loved it! But don't go yet! We have a BONUS epilogue for you!

Give me my BONUS epilogue please!

Grab your copy of **Arrogant Playboy**, book four in the Cocky Suits Chicago Series, where we introduce you to Donavan and Paisley!

HE'S AN...

ARROGANT
Playboy

—— A COCKY SUITS NOVEL ——

SLOANE HOWELL
ALEX WOLF

DONAVAN

RESPECT MAKES MY DICK HARD.

There's nothing on this earth better than destroying an opponent in a courtroom, and I'm the king of doing just that. Now, it's time to reap my rewards.

I'm in Manhattan and I miss it here.

The walk down Broadway in the spring sends memories flooding in. So much has changed and yet it hasn't. Busy streets. Busy people. I throw on my Beats and it's like I'm transported to the past as *Blitzkrieg Bop* by the Ramones filters into my ears.

It's been seven years since I graduated from Columbia Law School, but it feels like I walked across the stage yesterday.

The bar I'm looking for, The Heights, comes into view as I stride up the sidewalk. The alumni meeting last night was the same as always, a room full of lawyers and someone from administration asking for money. I cut the check because that's what you do.

But the moment right now is what I've been looking forward to. Seeing the guys. Most of them work for Cooper and Associates here in the city. The firm in Chicago I run with my brothers was just named the number one criminal defense practice in the country. It's time to gloat. That being said, my brothers may hate Cooper's guts, and I do as well, but I was in the trenches with these guys for three hard years at Columbia. I'll never disown them, even if Cooper can eat a dick sandwich on rye. They're great friends.

I take off my headphones, shove them in my bag, and walk inside. It's like old times already. My best friend, who I don't see nearly enough, Penn Hargrove, greets me with a beer.

"About time, Collins, fuck."

"I know, bitch. I walked. It was nostalgic."

"Find any ass on the way in?" says Mason as he leans out.

I jolt, thinking only Penn was here right now. "Jesus Christ."

He laughs and I notice Jacob hiding with him on the other side of Penn.

I grin. "Any ass? Just your mom's. It's gotten bigger but give me a few more of these." I hold up the beer Penn just handed me.

He shakes his head. "Still a dick."

"Some things never change." I walk over and grip both of them by their necks. "Missed you fuckers."

"Yeah, yeah," says Jacob.

I glance down to the bar top between them. There's a legal magazine and it says, "The Hunter Group – Voted Number One for Criminal Law."

I pick it up.

"What, you didn't see yet?" says Penn.

I shake my head, thumbing through the pages.

Penn tries to snatch it from me, but I turn away and box him out.

"Don't read it right now. We're trying to have a good time."

What the hell?

Why would I not read it? They're talking about my department. Criminal and family law belong to me and I'm the goddamn king. We've won it three years in a row, since I made partner and took over. Of course, this year it says The Hunter Group because my idiot brother merged us with a firm out of Dallas.

I get to the article and immediately realize why Penn didn't want me to read it yet. There's a giant picture of Weston Hunter. My fingers grip the magazine a little tighter as my eyes scan the pages.

"Don't do it to yourself, bro."

I can't stop. The more I read, the more my collar tightens around my neck. There's not one mention of the Chicago office in it.

Not. One.

All he's talking about is his firm in Dallas, his brother, and all the work they're doing. It has to be a mistake. This cocksucker wasn't even on a radar for any awards until he inherited my departments.

Goddamn it. This is supposed to be my moment to brag on my people. It's why I work so hard, so I can come back to New York and talk shit to my buddies. I love my friends to death, but it's a war out here and to the victor go the spoils.

I keep waiting for the hammer to drop, for Weston to finally tell the interviewer the reason why The Hunter Group is suddenly the best criminal law firm in the country.

It doesn't happen.

I look up, and Penn's eyes are wide. Mason and Jacob both have smirks on their faces.

My jaw flexes. "He didn't mention Chicago once. He rode in, took the title on a merger, and doesn't even have the courtesy to give my department one goddamn sentence?"

"Chiseled your name right off the wall too," says Mason.

Penn glares at him.

I take a couple deep breaths. No, fuck it. I came here to have a good time. Penn told me not to read it. I'm not giving Weston Hunter's bitch ass the satisfaction of ruining my weekend.

"What's your name on, Mase?" I laugh, but it still feels like bugs are crawling all over my skin. "Cooper even give you a desk yet, or do you just stay under his all day?"

Mason grins and shrugs. "First of all, I'd stay on my knees in perpetuity for the checks he writes. And I don't give a fuck about my name on the wall. The money works for me."

Sure. He's so full of shit.

Who wouldn't want their name on the wall? That's respect. Fuck a paycheck; anyone can make money. Your name on the wall is like being a made man in the field of law. People look at you differently. Treat you differently. You're a man with authority. Being a name partner is the goal of practically every attorney on the planet.

How the hell did my life get reduced to this in the last year? All that shit my dad preached about working hard, going into the world and taking everything you get, and Decker sold us all out.

"Oh shit," Penn mumbles.

"What?" I turn the direction he's looking and... *fuck my ass.* This day can't get any worse.

Paisley Williams.

The universe is shaming me. What the hell did I do to deserve this karma?

I haven't seen her in seven years.

Not since *it* went down.

She never comes to this alumni stuff. Christ, she looks even hotter than she was in law school.

She walks up with a smug grin, until she sees me, then her face pales. The next second it heats up with a light shade of pink. Any other man would think she was blushing, but she's not.

She's seething at the sight of me.

I have that effect on women sometimes, her more than most.

Usually, it's because I've kicked their ass out of bed before the sun comes up. With Paisley, it's a little more than that. We have a past, and it's not pretty.

"Number two," she says, with a little nod to me, then walks by and gives the other guys hugs.

My hackles are up, but I can't let her get the best of me. She wins if I give in. "Nice to see you, Pais. Still living in the past, I see?" I spin around, and she has that look; like she's ready for verbal warfare. If we were a movie, her face would be painted blue and she'd be giving the William Wallace speech.

She eyes the magazine and her smirk grows.

Fuck. She's read it.

She picks it up and pretends to flip through the pages. Mason and Jacob look like they're about to die of laughter. Penn has this look on his face that says *please don't flip the fuck out, we're trying to have fun here.*

I can deal with Mason and Jacob. It's not personal with them. With Paisley, it is.

"Has to hurt," says Paisley. She tsks me. "The Hunter Group." She shakes her head and smirks. "This Weston Hunter is pretty hot for the number one criminal attorney in the country. Much better looking than the last guy."

Penn gives me a side eye.

I finally just turn and walk away.

Fuck this.

I damn near plow straight through some guy who steps in my way. It knocks him over onto a table and his beer explodes everywhere.

"Hey!"

I keep walking.

No turning around. No apology.

I want on a plane, now.

When I step out onto the street, the sunlight socks me in the face. I pull out my phone. My plane doesn't leave LaGuardia for another eight hours.

Goddamn it.

I scan the streets, looking for a taxi. Part of me doesn't even want to stop off at the hotel and grab my shit. I just want away from these skyscrapers, and far away from that woman inside the bar.

As I wait for a cab, Penn walks up from behind.

"You're gonna bail without saying bye?"

I wheel around on him. "How could you invite her? What would go through your head that would make you think I wanted to see her?"

He holds up his hands in surrender. "I didn't know she was coming. Okay? I'm sure Mase or Jake did it, and honestly, I don't think they were being malicious. They work with her." He takes a step closer and lowers his voice, his eyes pleading. "And we all used to be close, remember? They don't know everything that went down."

I shake my head. "Still. Fuck." I look up at the sky and try to take a few deep breaths. I'm sure he's being honest.

Penn is a great guy. The best, really. And he doesn't sugarcoat anything.

But goddamn, I knew I'd see her again someday, even though I hoped I wouldn't. I didn't think it would still hurt like that when I looked at her, knowing what I did to her. Everything comes back to the surface and I just need to get the hell out of here.

"Why are you torturing yourself, man? It's not good for you. You always do this. You're so fucking high strung."

"I know, it was just… everything all at once back there." I need to change the subject or I'm going to take this all out on a flight attendant later and end up kicked off the plane. I'm off my game and I need to get it back. "What's going on with you? It's been a minute. I was looking forward to catching up."

He sighs. "Shit's good, man. I'm just kinda doing whatever right now. You know I left Cooper a month ago, right?"

"Yeah, we talked about it on the phone, right after. So, you're not doing anything? Practicing?"

"I don't really know if law is for me. Have the trust from my family, and a shitload of money socked away from working at Cooper. I'm still pretty young. Just figuring some stuff out."

I raise an eyebrow at him.

"Oh, I'm definitely chasing pussy. It's the beautiful thing about Manhattan, the surplus of ass."

An old lady gives us a dirty look when she hears Penn say that, and I laugh.

"So what? You're staying at your apartment? Upper East Side?"

He shakes his head. "No, I sold it. Got a price I couldn't pass up. Made off nice on that too."

"So, you're homeless?"

He laughs again and holds his arms out at the buildings around us. "Richest homeless guy in New York City."

"Well, fuck, come to Chicago for a while, if you don't have anywhere to be. Midwest pussy is sweeter and doesn't talk back as much."

Another dirty look from the old lady.

Penn laughs, then looks around and shrugs. "Hell. Why not? Little change of scenery might be good. And we can catch up like old times."

"Let's get a cab." I hold out my hand. "I have plenty of time to hang out, now that Decker sold the firm. This will be awesome, and I'm telling you. Chicago girls fuck way better."

Another dirty look.

A cab rolls up to the curb and we hop in.

I roll down the window and glance to the old lady. "Have a nice day, ma'am."

She shoots us a middle finger.

God, I do miss New York.

PAISLEY

I'T'S BEEN EXACTLY one week since I saw Donavan Collins in Manhattan and it hasn't made what I'm about to do any easier. I wanted to break a beer bottle and stick it in his neck, but that would've been uncivilized. I imagine they'd revoke my license to practice law for something like that, so I had to resort to verbal emasculation. Not my favorite thing to do, but if anyone deserves it, it's him.

Despite the seven years, and the bullshit he put me through, my body still wanted to betray me, and it's eaten at me all week. How does he do that to me just by existing? Standing there in his Hugo Boss suit and perfectly slicked-back hair, looking even better than before. How was that even possible? I'd secretly prayed, the few times I'd thought about him, that when I saw him again, he'd be fat and balding. Nope, the years have been excellent to him.

Fuck men.

And now, it's really going to hit the fan.

Standing outside The Hunter Group building, I take a deep breath, compose myself, and walk inside.

Maybe *he* won't be here today.

You will never get that lucky.

I don't even know why I wanted to hurt him so bad when I saw him. When he's not around, and I think about him, I have empathy. It's almost to the point where I think we could get along. Then, I saw him. His smug face, his sneer, his disdain for everyone and everything—I just turned into a different person. It's like he burrowed right under my skin and I wanted to claw myself to death to get him out.

How the hell is he even hotter? It's the stubble, has to be. Baby face—gone. Where the hell did that smoldering stare come from? At college his face was so boyish and cute, now it's rugged and fierce.

He's not why you're here. Get your head out of your ass.

I make my way to a security station when I first walk in and give them my name and tell them why I'm here, nothing out of the ordinary. I look around while they find me a badge.

The building is nice. Really nice.

It's not Cooper and Associates in Manhattan, but damn, I could get used to it. I'll have to, for a while anyway.

The security people point me to an elevator, and I make my way up to the correct floor. When I step out, it's not how I envisioned the place at all. I expected classic, sophisticated, old school. What lies in front of me is a modern office. Big glass walls, sharp lines, and a lot less mahogany than in New York.

I think I like it. It feels new and shiny, hip.

A woman named Quinn greets me as I step off the elevator.

"You must be Paisley Williams. Come with me."

Quinn's beautiful. She has auburn hair and green eyes. We walk past her desk and she has me take a seat outside Decker Collins' office.

"Can I get you anything? Water, tea, soda?"

"No, I'm fine. Thank you." I wave her off and try to be as nice and casual as I can.

Reading people is what I do, and I'm surprised Quinn's a secretary and not at least a paralegal. She's relatively young, but she looks like she has her shit together. Her engagement ring is gorgeous. It's an emerald solitaire you could spot from across the room.

I start to think her fiancé must have money, when I see a picture of her and a man who looks like a bulked-up version of Donavan in a picture. Holy hell, it looks just like Donavan if he did two cycles of steroids and power lifted for ten years.

So, she got herself engaged to a Collins brother. Good for her. At least, maybe it is. I wouldn't know. I've only met one Collins brother and he's the biggest asshole I've ever encountered.

Speaking of that, I forget I'm supposed to be avoiding him right now.

"Should only be another minute or two," says Quinn. "He's finishing up a quick meeting. It wasn't on the books."

"It's fine."

She apologizes again. "We don't normally operate this way, but it was… umm, urgent."

"It's really okay. I promise."

The voices inside the office grow loud, like the conversation is heated.

I look over at Quinn and she winces, then goes back to her computer screen and clacks away on the keyboard.

I look around her desk, underneath Quinn's monitor. Her eyes keep darting over there, like she wants to look at something, but maybe she's not supposed to. As an attorney, you train yourself to pick up on every single detail—movements, surroundings, body language. Anything that can give you an edge.

586

Quinn is tense. She's trying to hide it. The lines around her eyes are a little more pronounced than they should be. She keeps reaching up and tugging a small strand of hair, probably a nervous tic.

When I see what's beneath her monitor, I immediately respect her even more.

"When do you sit?"

Quinn's eyes dart over to mine. "Huh?"

"For the bar?"

Quinn's eyebrows rise for a split second. "How did you…"

"Strategies and Tactics for the MBE." I gesture to her book. "It's out of the way, but I'm guessing you look at it every chance you get, when nobody's around and your work is done. When's the test?"

Quinn finally lets out a long sigh. "Too soon. I'm not ready."

I give her a warm smile. "Everyone feels that way. It's normal, I promise."

"Do you mind?" She nods to the book.

"Please, go ahead, and good luck. I can entertain myself. No worries at all."

"Thank you." Quinn flips through several pages with color-coded tabs all over them.

She's going to do just fine.

The voices in the office go back to a normal decibel level, meaning I can't hear them.

I wait another five minutes, which is fine, I don't have anywhere to be. The legs of a chair squeak against tile, and I hear rustling from inside the office. Quinn and I both bolt upright the second we hear it, and Quinn slaps the book closed and shoves it away.

I stand up before the door opens, because there's no way I want Decker Collins looking down on me the first time I meet him. Butterflies swim through my stomach and it has nothing to do with this interview. Okay, maybe a little, but I know the real reason.

Stop it, Pais.

Decker walks out and right behind him…

Shit. Shit. Shit.

It's Donavan. His eyes widen when he sees me, and then I swear they turn a fiery red. Okay, maybe they don't, but in my mind they do. I will never give him the satisfaction of showing him any kind of fear in his presence, though, so my brows knit together, and I send the scowl right back in his direction.

"What's going on *here*?" He waves an arm out to me and turns to Decker. The look on his face says it all.

Decker's right hand goes up to his temple, like he just had a headache smash into him like a freight train. "Not now," he says to Donavan. "We'll talk about it later."

Donavan takes his sweet time, looks me up and down, head to toe, then shakes his head and snarls in disgust. He walks away, and I feel a little bad for whoever he crosses paths with.

587

"Sorry about that." Decker holds his hand out in a welcoming gesture. "After you, Ms. Williams."

I walk in and he closes the door behind me.

"It's Ms., right?"

"Yes, it is, thanks."

He walks up behind a chair in front of his desk and places a hand on top as if saying *take a seat*.

I do and he walks around his desk. *Damn the Collins boys know how to wear suits.* If Donavan wasn't here, I might actually consider all these handsome men a perk, and I'm no stranger to powerful men in suits.

Decker waits for me to have a seat and then does the same. "So, I looked over the resume you sent us. I was going to ask if you knew Donavan at Columbia, but I think you two already answered my question."

"Yeah, about that, I'm…"

He holds up a hand. "Don't worry. He pretty much hates everyone."

My heart drops into my stomach for a moment. As much as Donavan hates me, I kind of hoped he reserved it all for me, like I was special somehow. I've wondered for years what kind of man Donavan became, and so far, I don't really like what I see, although deep down I think I knew he'd turn out this way.

"Let's cut the shit and get to the heart of things here. Why us? Clearly you and Donavan don't like each other. There are thousands of law firms in Chicago. Dozens that would welcome you with a compensation package, partner opportunities, and a million perks that would be competitive with what we'll offer."

"That's true. But they all lack one thing."

"What's that?"

"You're the best in the city. Obviously, working at Cooper and Associates, we keep an eye on everything. It's part of my job and I want to be straightforward. We watch what Dexter is doing with the finance division. He's the best in Chicago and I want to work with him."

Decker leans back, like he's amused. But is it a double bluff? Is he secretly worried and pretending to be amused? Projecting power and confidence? Or is it legitimate? "Yeah, I noticed you specialize in finance. I would imagine you're number two, beneath Bennett. Which means you do most of the work and management."

"Your assessment is correct."

"Why are you leaving Cooper?"

"Personal reasons. I'm from Chicago. I need to handle things with my family, and it requires I be here on a permanent basis."

Decker leans in. "Why doesn't Cooper have an office here for you to transfer to? Let you work remotely? I know he has clients in Chicago, although we've managed to secure most of them."

I need to be careful here. I technically still work for Cooper and Associates, and there are clauses in my employment contract. "Cooper is selective about where he sets up shop."

"That's all I'm going to get?"

I smile. "Until you hire me."

Decker's lips curl up into the devilish grin I've seen a thousand times on a thousand different men when they think about power and money.

"Look," I say. "I just want to have a job lined up before I move back. It needs to be soon, too." Always put some pressure on them. Don't give them time to think too much.

Decker stands up as if the meeting is concluded. I follow suit. He walks around and holds a hand out.

"We'll be in touch soon. End of the week at the latest."

I shake his hand. "Works for me. Thank you for the opportunity."

He leads me out of the office and walks me all the way to the elevator. As I step on, I look past him, and Donavan's standing there.

His fists are clenched at his sides, and he's breathing heavily. He's intimidating, I'll give him that. I might even be a little nervous, if he still didn't turn me on with that death stare of his. They'll call within the week. I'll have the job. I'm too good for them to pass up. They know it and I know it.

All I have to do is avoid Donavan at all costs. Easier said than done.

DONAVAN

I WALK to the conference room and my defenses are already up. Why was she even in the building? How the hell did I not know about this? I would've had security escort her straight back to the parking garage.

Yeah, right. You wouldn't do shit.

When I walk in, everyone else is already there, like they've been discussing this without me. I just scoff and shake my head. What else can I do? Decker does whatever he wants, despite me being a managing partner now.

"Go ahead and have a seat and we'll get started." Decker points at the one empty chair at the table.

I walk over and probably yank on it a little harder than I need to.

The twins look amused, Tate looks down at a folder in front of her, and Decker glares right at me.

"Have you calmed down yet?"

"I'm perfectly calm. Why wouldn't I be?"

"Right. What's your problem with her?" asks Decker.

The other eyes at the table land on mine.

I inhale a deep breath. "Well, she works for Cooper." There's no way I'll tell them the real reason, but my excuse sounds good enough to me.

"Yeah, that seems like a problem on the surface, but are there possibilities there?"

I shake my head just slightly as he starts to speak.

"What?"

"Nothing, it's just reckless." I don't know why I'm even wasting my breath with him. He's going to do whatever he wants.

Dexter straightens up in his seat. "She could have a lot of valuable information. And she's a fucking rockstar in finance. I follow her, read her articles. She's a badass."

"She says she needs to move home for personal reasons. Any idea what that might be, Donavan?" asks Decker.

I shrug. "No idea. But Dex is killing it already. He doesn't need any help." Maybe if I get Dex on my side that'll help, so stroking his ego is a good move.

Decker shrugs. "So, we hire her for a probationary period and see how it goes for a while. No harm done. I think she's a good fit."

Dexter glances down at me and I know the look already. "I agree with Decker. I think the pros outweigh the cons."

"It seems like a decision for the managing partners, and I'm wondering why this wasn't discussed with me before the interview stage."

Dexter sighs. "Whatever, Donavan. This directly involves finance. Has nothing to do with you and your precious criminal department. I have more of a say in this than you do."

"What do you think, Deacon?" I glance down at him, hoping to get some support. It feels like I'm drowning right now. I can't believe this is even up for debate.

He shrugs. "Whatever you guys decide. I'm indifferent."

"Tate?" Decker glances to his fiancée.

I try to bite back the anger building in my chest and remain professional. Jesus, I can't believe this decision rests in the hands of the woman who hates me more than Paisley probably does. I'm fucked.

She glances to Decker, then to me, then back to Decker. "It doesn't sit right with me, if I'm being honest."

All the air leaves my lungs. I can't believe that just happened. It surprises me so much I can't even think for a few seconds. I mean, I still hate her, but maybe I misjudged her a little. Maybe there is a hint of objectivity in there somewhere. Maybe she's just trying to win brownie points, so I'll stop being an asshole to her. Whatever the reason, I'll take it.

I wave a hand out at her. "At least someone has a fucking brain."

"Would you stop with the ad hominems, asshole."

I hold up both hands. "Do whatever you want. You will anyway. But I'm telling you. It's a bad idea. There are a dozen firms she can work at. Dex is kicking ass without her. We don't need the drama."

Decker glares. "I don't know what personal shit you have going on with her, but it has no bearing on this decision. You don't have to work near her. She's in a different department. Grow up."

I shake my head and half-snicker. "So that's it? Making me a manager was meaningless, just a way to squash family beef? My input doesn't count?"

Decker shakes his head. "You're acting like a child."

"Decker." Tate glares at him.

Decker stands up. "You know what? I know how to decide. There are three managing partners."

Goddamn it, don't say his name.

"Weston can be the tie breaker."

A wave of heat sparks in my chest and travels straight to my face. My jaw clenches tight and I have to force myself to smile. "Whatever you think, boss."

"I give up." Decker's hands go to his temples.

"I said do whatever you want."

"You don't fucking mean it, though. What's your problem with Weston?"

I need to let this shit go. I need to just get out of this conference room, but I can't. Why is he hellbent on destroying this place we've worked so hard for?

"Did you not see the magazine article?"

Decker glares right at me. "This is over an article in a magazine? Because your feelings got hurt and you didn't get the recognition you *think* you deserve?"

"It's not about the article, or hiring someone, Decker. It's about... No, just forget it. I told you my thoughts, can we just end this damn meeting please?"

Decker exhales a sigh, hellbent on not letting this go. "It's an article in a magazine."

I stand up and walk out the door. I'm done discussing this shit and receiving zero respect in return. He's going to burn this firm to the ground by the time he's done with it.

PAISLEY

"WHAT?" I glance over at Dad and the huge cheesy grin he has on his face.

"Nothing, baby girl. It's just good to have you back."

"I'm just moving a few things right now. I don't know if it's going to be permanent. We'll see."

"They call you back with an offer yet?"

"No." I shake my head.

"Because of *him*?" Dad won't even look at me, and I notice he refuses to say Donavan's name.

"I'm sure it has something to do with it. It won't be long, though."

Dad walks over and takes a seat in the recliner. I do the same on the couch.

"How do you know?"

I shrug. "I know men, especially rich ones. They're motivated by money and power, and they can't pass up opportunities like this."

Dad leans back, resting his head on the cushion. "I still don't know how I raised you."

"That an insult?" I grin.

He shakes his head. "Of course not. I just don't know where that brain of yours comes from. Able to read people, know what they'll do before they do it. What they'll say before they say it. I could've used some of that in my own life."

I reach over for his forearm. "Dad, it could've happened to anyone."

"Yeah." He sighs. "But, it didn't."

My heart pinches in my chest. "I'm sorry I didn't do more."

"You couldn't have."

"I could always do more, especially for family. I should've been here instead of sending associates to work on your case. I should've made sure you were protected from the beginning."

595

"Nonsense, you had to deal with billionaires and their money. The guys you sent did the same things you would've."

"I'd have found something. Dug harder. I will, now that I'm back. It's not over yet."

He holds his arms out. "Look at me. I'm living in this little house, no way to take care of my parents. My daughter had to move home to save the day. My business is now nonexistent."

I want to cry, but I can't. I've only cried once in my life and I doubt it'll ever happen again. Still, seeing Dad like this, it's torture. He looks at me like he's a total failure. No parent should ever have to look at their child that way. He was my hero growing up; still is, but he'd never let me call him that now. When I was young, I thought he could do anything, he was larger than life. It's a cold reminder that the world can crush you in an instant, and nobody is off limits.

"You get a fresh start. You can build it back up. I'll help, Dad."

"I'm pushing sixty, with a bad back and aging parents." He shakes his head and sighs. "I hate you seeing me like this."

I stand and pull him up into a hug. "I know you do, but there's nothing wrong with humility. It makes you stronger."

He grins. "I think someone said that once."

I nod, happy to see him smiling again. "I think they did. A wise man who is stronger than anyone I've ever met."

He hugs me again and kisses my forehead, the same way he has since I was a child. "Thanks, sweetie."

"I love you, Dad."

"I love you too." I don't want to let go. I don't care what's happened, what I've been through, how strong I have to be in front of attorneys and powerful men, there's still something special when Dad hugs me. I feel safe, transported to another place entirely. The world fades away and nothing can touch me. I felt that way with another man once, but not anymore. "We're gonna be all right. I promise."

"I hope so, kiddo. I hope so."

"Well, the same wise man once said, make your own luck and work hard. So, hand it over."

"It's done, Paisley. Just…"

"Hand it over."

He walks off to a file cabinet and comes back with a manila envelope full of legal documents. "Fine, I have dinner plans anyway."

I raise my eyebrows. "Ohh, a hot date?"

"Something like that." He winks.

The old man still has it. I take the folder from him. It holds all the court documents from the lawsuit that tanked his business. I've studied them a million times on my computer, but there's something about thumbing through physical papers that turns the wheels in the brain a different way. If there's something in there, I'll find it.

"Well, good luck. I'm heading to Giordano's and I'll look through this."

"Malnati's is better."

I fake a look of horrifying disgust. "Go on your date, and hope she has better taste in pizza than you."

He laughs. "Don't work too hard. You need to relax some too."

I have to laugh at that one. "Yeah, whatever you say."

He gets to the door and turns back. "It really is good to have you back, Pais. Even if it's for a short time."

I nod. "It's good to be back, even if it brings up old wounds. Now go; and buy that woman some flowers on your way. Don't be a cheap ass."

"Yes, ma'am." He walks out the door.

As soon as he's gone, all the air sucks out of the room. I stare around and it just feels, soulless. All the life is gone. That's how all of Chicago feels to me, like I suffocate when I'm in this city.

Maybe some pizza from Giordano's can help fix it, a little anyway.

I'M on my second beer and I may need a shot soon if I keep reading these documents. The more I scan the pages, the more the hair on the back of my neck stands up. In a nutshell, Dad is a computer engineer. He worked for IBM for years at their regional headquarters in Chicago.

A lot of the tech stuff is way over my head, but Dad designed some kind of WiFi protocol that made things much more efficient for people to log in to the internet at home on their routers and modems, something with the way the devices talk to one another.

He made a couple million dollars when he sold it, then had a stream of revenue from maintaining and updating the code, all under his own business. A huge tech firm reverse engineered his work, filed for a patent, and then sued him and the big companies he sold it to. That's when the fun all started.

To make things better, the other companies bought the software from the tech firm, terminated their contracts with Dad, and sued him in return. He was pretty much a one-man operation. They've taken everything from him and there's not really anything I can do about it.

Bennett gave me two associates to help Dad out. I told him I would quit and work on my dad's case until it was finished and that was the compromise, to keep me working in New York City. It was just me, in my spare time, and them. I specialize in finance, not intellectual property.

I've had to sit and watch Dad lose everything he worked for, buried in legal filings and paperwork it'd take a team of high-powered specialist attorneys to fight. He developed this technology over years. Nobody will hire him now. He's basically a pariah in his field, which sucks even more, because it's what he loves more than anything. Well, ever since… yeah.

I look down at the document in front of me and my blood heats up even hotter. The firm who represented the big tech companies glares right back at me.

Collins and Associates, now The Hunter Group.

I should've quit my job in New York. I should've moved back here and worked on this full-time for Dad. He begged me not to, but it's what I should've done, and it's a regret I'll always have to live with.

Just when I think I can't get any more pissed off, I look up.

Donavan Collins walks through the door.

DONAVAN

YOU GOTTA BE FUCKING KIDDING me.

I'd know that stare anywhere. Paisley's sitting at the bar with a beer, empty plate, and papers scattered everywhere. She's right in the fucking middle too, taking up the whole thing.

I walk over, pretending to ignore her, and take a seat as far from her as I can get, which is two seats over. The bartender walks up.

"Call in for Collins."

"Want something to drink?"

"Maker's Mark, double, neat."

He walks away for a minute after pouring my drink, then comes back. "Got about fifteen minutes to go."

I nod and wish he'd go away. I wish everyone would go away. This is my spot and Paisley knows it. It was made very clear back at college when we talked about home. Giordano's is a ritual for me. I always come in twenty minutes early, get a Maker's Mark while I wait for my pie, then tip generously and leave.

Now, it's totally fucked, because of a woman sitting two barstools away.

An awkward silence stretches between us. I do anything I can to take my mind off her, sliding my index finger around the edge of the glass, staring at my reflection in the amber-colored bourbon.

I should get up and leave.

Fuck that. This is your place. Don't be a bitch.

Finally, Paisley says, "It's only going to get more awkward."

I whip around and snarl. "Why are you even here?"

"Uhh, they have good pizza."

I jab a finger into my chest. "This is *my* place and you know it."

"Oh really? They changed it to Collins' pizza?" She smirks. "Oh yeah, not many establishments with that name on them anymore."

Calm the fuck down. Change the subject.

I glance over at her papers all over the bar. "Thought you needed a job?"

She reaches around, like she's huddling them all together. "This is…personal."

"Oh yeah? Good luck with it." I do nothing to mask the contempt in my voice.

She shakes her head and looks back down, going through the papers. "Asshole."

"I always thought you liked that about me."

"We really doing this right now?"

"You came to my place looking for war. It is what it is."

"I was hungry. Jesus."

How does this woman get under my skin so damn bad? "You know I don't mean *this*. Don't be an idiot."

"Always quick to insult someone's intelligence."

"Call it like I see it."

"If I'm an idiot, what's that make you?"

I turn to face her. "What?"

"Well, I'm an idiot and I was number one in our class. What's that make you?"

My face heats up all over again. *Just fucking leave. It's not worth it.*

"Still holding on to old titles. Because you haven't accomplished shit since then."

She laughs. "Good one. God, you're so bitter, and insecure. Always were."

"For someone who wants a job at my firm, you're really doing yourself a lot of favors right now." I lean back, trying to appear slightly amused, but still fuming on the inside.

It doesn't help that she looks incredibly hot, even more so than at college. She's dressed casual in jeans and a Columbia Law t-shirt, hair pulled back in a high ponytail and my fingers twitch, wanting to yank her by the hair until she submits. There's no way I could do it. She'd call the cops. Can't really blame her for that.

"I'd have already gotten the rejection if it were up to you." She winks. "Just waiting on the phone call from the intelligent brother."

"So smug and condescending. Why the hell are you really here?"

"Told you I was hungry."

"Stop with the bullshit." I walk over.

She does her best not to look rattled, but I can see her pulse redlining in the side of her neck. Her legs go stiff under the barstool. She can act tough all she wants, but I still make her nervous as hell, all these years later. Good.

She swallows as I hover over her and she shuffles all her papers into the folder and slams it shut. "It's personal."

I eye her up and down, taking my time, just to make her sweat a little more. Just to watch her wipe her palms down her jeans and watch her lips part, ever so slightly.

"Yeah, so is you coming to my firm."

"Last I checked, Weston Hunter's name is on it."

"You know I'm a partner. It's mine."

She bats her eyelashes at me and speaks in the most condescending tone I've ever heard. "And I'll be a partner too, by the end of the week, so you really need to learn how to share, Donavan." She shakes her head. "God, that just eats you up inside, doesn't it? Poor little Donavan, not gonna get his way on this one. How many holes you punched in the wall at home, just thinking about what you know is about to happen?"

"Ohh, Pais. You flatter yourself with delusions that I think about you at all. It's comical really."

She stands up, doing her best to get eye to eye with me, but she's really about even with my throat. "Ohh, Donavan. What's comical is you think I'm not gonna spank your ass again, the same way I did in college." She pauses and grins. "Number two."

"Sir, I have your piz..." The bartender freezes when he sees the two of us, squared off at each other.

I tap the counter and toss my credit card out on it. He takes it and rings it up, then brings me back two pieces of receipt paper. I add a tip and sign one, pocketing the other.

I make a show of grabbing the pizza I ordered for Penn and me, then turn slowly back to Pais. She's breathing hard and her tits look incredible, even through a t-shirt. My cock hardens in my slacks and it takes a magnitude of willpower to keep my dick in check. Fuck, this woman drives me insane in so many ways it's impossible to keep track of them.

I lean down and scoff, then whisper, "I remember who did all the spanking back in college." I lean in even closer to her ear, so she can feel my warm breath on her neck. "And who begged for it...again and again and called herself Donavan's dirty little slut." I turn my back on her before she can say anything, but I feel her retinas burning a shotgun-sized hole in my back.

Fuck it. If she wants to make things personal, I'll make them personal.

This pizza is going to taste phenomenal.

PAISLEY

I walk into Dad's house and toss my to-go container in the refrigerator a little harder than needed.

Ugh! Fuck you, Donavan!

Don't let him get to you. It's what he does.

I pace around the guest room, where I'll be staying until I find my own place. I can't get his stare out of my head. And he went and made things personal, talking about him spanking me. The second I think about it, I can feel his big, strong hand on my ass and my blood heats up again. I can't believe after all these years he can still have this effect on me.

There's no way in hell a relationship, even a friendly one, would ever be possible with him. That's perfectly clear, but I haven't had sex in six months. I'm dying. And even if I had, nobody has ever compared. Not even close.

I stare at myself in the mirror.

"Look at yourself. You're a hot mess."

I need a release. There's an orgasm of epic proportions building between my legs, and the cause is one broody, self-centered, narcissistic asshole, and I absolutely hate myself for letting him turn me into this.

I stare at my suitcase, where I know my vibrator rests just inside it. Then I stare at myself in the mirror. Back and forth. Back and forth.

Do not do it, Paisley!

But I need to. This is not going away!

No, if you do it, he wins!

I walk out to the living room, still pacing, trying to get those dark blue eyes out of my head. That two-day scruff that could scratch up against my thighs. When I sit down on the couch, my leg practically shakes, bouncing up and down. I grit my teeth.

Damn it!

I damn near sprint back to my room, flinging my suitcase open with one giant tug. Clothes go everywhere as I rifle through my stuff, searching for the toy that can make all my problems go away. Finally, my fingers find purchase and I grip it in my palm and sling it onto the bed.

My fingers go crazy over my jeans, trying to get them unbuttoned and the whole time I curse Donavan repeatedly under my breath.

"Smug prick. Think you can talk to me that way? That's why I kicked your ass back then and I'll kick it again, every damn day if I have to."

My jeans get halfway down my thighs and I curse myself for not working out more. I've put on five pounds in the last six months, working nonstop on Dad's case and my own workload. It's not really noticeable at all, except when I'm trying to get a pair of skinny jeans off so I can rub one out to my arch nemesis.

After hobbling around for a moment, I finally just let myself fall to the bed. To hell with it, I don't need my jeans off to do what needs done. I click the vibrator on and it's between my legs.

My thighs are practically pushed together because of my jeans, and the tension at my ankles reminds me how Donavan used to pin me down or tie me up. All the memories flood back.

At least have some respect and think about someone else.

I wish my brain would turn off for two seconds so I could get this done. I can shame myself enough for it later, thank you very much.

Right now, all I can see are his eyes. Me bent over his lap, doing exactly what he said in Giordano's. When he whispered that in my ear, it was... I don't even know how to say it. It stoked a fire that had been dormant for seven years and kindled it right back to life.

How can you hate someone so much, have them drive you so crazy, and yet all you want to do is feel their touch one more time?

I tell myself it's all biological, but is it, really?

The moment my vibrator comes in contact with my clit I know my answer.

Totally biological. Those real feelings are long gone.

Don't say his name. Have some kind of dignity.

Before long, I'm lost, right on the edge. Sure enough, I say his name because the feeling is so intense if I don't get this frustration out of me, I might die.

He pins my arms over my head and thrusts into me, hard and slow, taking his time, knowing he's about to explode, but he wants me pushed right to the edge. He wants to shove into me at the last second while I come undone all over him. No matter what the foreplay was, no matter what we were doing, that's how it always finished.

"So close, Donavan. So close," I whisper the words.

Even now, in my mind, he has to say it before I can give in. Even in a ridiculous fantasy, I still have to please him for some reason. Have to obey and do as he says.

"That's it, Pais. Come..."

I'm about to unload the mother of all orgasms when the front door flies open.

"Fuck!" I cover my mouth and toss the vibrator between the bed and the wall.

"Pais, you here?" Dad calls out from the living room.

I flail around on the bed, doing my best to yank my jeans back up over my hips. If women can get blue balls, I'm going to have an epic case tomorrow. I may need medical attention.

"Be right there!" God, I hope I didn't sound out of breath.

I know I did.

"Everything okay?"

"Yeah." I squeak the word out. "Just a sec!"

Finally, by some will of the gods, I get my jeans back up and buttoned. I look in the mirror and my face is flushed. I take a few deep breaths, trying to compose myself.

"Okay, you want something to drink?"

"No, I'm good, thanks."

I straighten up my clothes and fly onto the bed, searching for the vibrator. It's going crazy up against the wall, reverberating through the sheetrock.

"What is that?"

"Just my phone!" I grab it and click it off, then bury it at the bottom of my suitcase.

After one last horrifying look in the mirror, I walk out of the bedroom, praying the shame isn't written across my face. Four years of high school, sneaking around with boys, and the one time he walks in the house is when I'm about to turn thirty.

Finally, I walk out. "Hey, how was the hot date?"

"Went great." He smiles and twists the cap off a beer. "Already made plans for another one."

"That's great, Dad. Really great. It's great that you're getting out there, ya know?" I do the punch the air thing, like he's giving it the old college try.

Dad's eyes roll up to mine. "You okay?"

"Yeah. Totally. Why?"

His brows narrow. "You said 'great' like three times, and then 'totally.'"

I shrug, trying to play it off. "Well, you know, I just feel like a kid again, back at home, I guess."

He nods toward the couch.

I huff out a sigh, but go sit down because now it's going to be about me and there's no way I'll get out of it. I plop down on the sofa.

"What's going on?"

I stare up at the ceiling. "Nothing... I mean, I don't know."

"It's about *him*."

I shake my head. "No, I'm just, a little stressed, I guess. With Grandma and Grandpa and your situation, but don't feel bad. I want to help."

"Well, kid, as embarrassing as it is, I'm in no position to turn down your help anyway. So you're off the hook. I just worry about you. Putting your career on hold, moving home."

"I'm not putting my career on hold. I'll be at a firm by the end of the week."

He shakes his head. "Yeah, but it's not the same. The place in New York is your life. I mean, I saw it in your eyes the first time you visited Columbia."

"Saw what?"

"That it was for you. That Chicago would always come second after that."

I go to say something, and he holds up his hand to stop me.

"That's not a bad thing. I'm not knocking you for it. You always were looking to something bigger and better, even as a girl. I knew you'd grow up and leave this city one day." He stares off at the wall, but he's looking beyond. "There was more to the world than what this place could offer. And as much as it broke mine and your mother's heart when you left, we understood. We always understood, Pais, and we were damn proud of you. We still are."

"Dad, you don't have to…"

"It's okay to talk about her. I'm okay with it."

He says that, but the look in his eyes says otherwise. He's doing it for me, and I don't want to put him through that again. "Dad, it's okay. I still think about her and remember her. You don't…"

His face hardens. "Yes, I do. She deserves it, deserves to be talked about, even if this isn't our old home."

"How did the date really go, Dad?"

"It was okay, but she doesn't compare."

"She never will. It's not fair to either of you to do that."

He nods and it looks like he might cry, but he won't. "I know." He looks at the ground. "I just… ahh, this is hard."

I walk over, bend down, and hook my arms around his neck. "It's okay to meet someone else, and when you meet the right one, she'll understand." I lean back and wave my hand at Dad. "All this. She'll get it, or she's not the right one."

"It just feels so wrong. Like I'm being unfaithful. The whole ride home, I just apologized to your mom over and over."

"It's been seven years. Mom would understand."

"I know she would. She would want me to do this. It makes it harder."

I need to change the subject. "My night wasn't much better."

"Didn't find that smoking gun you're always looking for?"

I shake my head. "No. I'm sorry."

"Don't apologize. You've gone above and beyond, and like you said, something else will come up. I'm good at what I do. Nobody will care about me being blackballed if I come up with another idea. It's how the tech field works. You're nothing until you have something they want."

"It was your life's work. We have to fight for it."

"Some fights you can't win, sweetie. I know I always told you to fight for everything, but sometimes you lose, and you have to know when to walk away so you can fight another day."

I've never seen him this down. He's barely holding it together. "*He* showed up, at Giordano's."

"Who?"

I stare at him like he just sprouted three heads.

"Oh. *Him.*" Dad's look morphs from sad to pissed off.

He refuses to say Donavan's name, like he's Lord Voldemort.

"Yep." I pop the p.

"Well, I guess you better get used to being around him, if you're going to go work there."

I sigh. "Yeah."

"Just forget about my thing, Pais. It's done. I want you to have a life. You're in your prime years right now. You shouldn't be worrying about me and Grandma and Grandpa."

"You're repeating yourself."

"Yeah, well, it's not right. Deserves being said twice."

"Don't worry about me, Dad. And don't worry about Grandma and Grandpa. Unlike some areas in my life, I have that one covered. They'll be fine. Okay?"

He nods. "Okay, kiddo."

"I just have to figure out a way to deal with you know who."

"I'm sure you will. You kicked his ass once. You'll do it again."

I give Dad another big hug and nuzzle into his shoulder. "Thanks, Dad. You always know the right things to say."

We both snicker and I walk back to the couch. The throb between my legs returns with a vengeance, and I know it's not going anywhere. It's what thoughts of Donavan do to me.

Yeah, I just need to figure out how to deal with this Donavan situation. No matter what happens, there's no way in hell I will let any of those assholes walk all over me at The Hunter Group. They might call me a bitch, but it's the same thing I had to do at Cooper and Associates.

No mercy, ever.

If Donavan gets in my way, I'll crush his nuts under my heel. Right after I rub one out after Dad goes to bed.

DONAVAN

IT'S BEEN a week and I haven't so much as heard a peep about the Paisley situation. Good, one less thing to worry about. Maybe Decker finally has a few brain cells firing.

I head up the elevator, *In My Time of Dying* by Led Zeppelin blaring in my headphones.

Finally, Paisley Williams is purged from my memory. She had a good run, stayed up there kicking around for a day or two or six. I may have jerked off thinking about the way I used to spank her little ass in my living room while staring out at the Manhattan skyline. It was a brief, fun trip down memory lane, but it's out of my system now.

Hell, I may even fuck one of these hot little interns walking around, just to piss Decker off for putting me through this. Or wait until one of them comes up from Dallas for training, then send her back home with tales of my dick for Weston to hear about.

As soon as I walk through the elevator onto our floor, I see a familiar pair of legs and I have to compose myself, so I don't throw my cup of coffee at the big granite THE HUNTER GROUP sign on the wall that's twice as big as the old COLLINS & ASSOCIATES.

Decker is showing Paisley around the office, laughing and smiling, like they've been friends for years. He didn't even tell me. Didn't even shoot a fucking email like *hey, we made our decision, prepare yourself when you walk in the office*. Not a goddamn word. No phone conference with Weston, so I could tell him my reservations.

Why do I still work here? Because it's family. It's what you do.

He finally glances my way and the color drains from his face, but he straightens his tie and then leads her over to Quinn. Quinn smiles and takes over the grand tour and Decker stomps in my direction.

I walk to my office and make him chase me all the way across the building because he fucking deserves it. At least I have a corner office in the criminal division with the best view of the city.

When I get to my desk, I glance back at Decker and he's marching his ass off through my department, people clearing out of the way. I haven't seen anyone that mad coming at my office since I sued Tate's client. Hah! What a fond memory. They deserved it. It was bad enough Decker merged the firm without discussing it with anyone. No partners. Nothing. He really needs to just retire because he's pussy-whipped, afraid of everyone, and doesn't communicate for shit. He's a fucking doormat.

As soon as I sit down, he flings the door open.

"My office, now."

"Not going anywhere." I hold my arms out like I just relaxed. "Haven't even had my coffee yet." I'm not going to his office. This is a pissing match and he doesn't have the nut sack to win it. He just wants me to walk all the way back across, so he can prove who's in control.

It's rookie shit and I'm not falling for his piss-poor attempt at psychological warfare.

Finally, he huffs out an exasperated sigh and says, "Fine, you want to fucking do it here. Let's do it here. Come on. Get it out of your system."

I shake my head. "Nothing to say. Clearly you made a decision."

He shakes a finger at me. "I knew you'd do this."

"Do what?"

"React like this."

"What way is 'this?'"

"Like a fucking passive-aggressive baby."

"What other way should I react? You don't listen to me. You knew I'd talk Weston out of it, and you couldn't let that happen. You always get your way. Might as well say 'bitch' on my door instead of 'managing partner.' So, I just grin and bear it, like always."

"There he goes. I knew the dramatic Donavan would come out to play. Maybe you should've gone to Tisch at NYU for a liberal arts degree instead of Columbia law."

Blood rushes into my face for reasons he has no idea about. I have to tamp down the anger building inside. It can't be healthy to be this pissed off nonstop, but Decker finds a way to get a rise out of me. Has since we were kids. I love my brothers. I really do, but our relationships are complicated. Most of the time, I want to choke the shit out of them, just until they pass out and shut up. Nothing life threatening.

I've had to learn how to pick my battles.

But you know what? Fuck them. I went to an Ivy League school and they didn't, and somehow, I'm a pussy because of that? What, because I did better than they did?

"You delivered the news. You can go now."

Decker stands there, a blank expression on his face. "Do you even want to know what's happening?"

"No. I got it. I'll stop by and say hello to my new coworker after a while. I'm a little busy at the moment."

He starts to say something, then turns to the door, then looks back.

I just can't help myself. I know better than to take the bait. I know I should just shut the fuck up and deal with it, but I can't. Under my breath, I say, "You just love pissing this place away, don't you?"

He shakes his head. "I fucking can't with you right now." He turns to walk away. "My wedding is in a month. I'm not dealing with this shit."

I stand up. "Yeah, and you need me to get along with you for that to happen. Or did you forget?" At Thanksgiving, Decker told us Tate wouldn't agree to marry him until he resolved a huge issue between us. Which is why he named me a managing partner, a title that has turned out to be worthless.

Decker's face goes hot as an iron and he spins around. "Are you trying to leverage my relationship to get your way? How pathetic can you be?" He stares at me like I'm beneath him. Like he's righteous and I'm a piece of shit.

My collar tightens around my neck and I bow up, jaw clenched. "Yeah, I'm the one always manipulating people. Justify your bullshit however you want. Just get out of my office."

"I came over here to discuss the situation and you can't even calm down for two minutes. Thinking everyone else is reckless and you're the only one who thinks through decisions. Fuck, you're the biggest narcissist I've ever met, and that's saying something around this building." He relaxes a little and sighs. "I have Rick investigating her. He's going to report directly to you. That's what I came to say."

All the air sucks out of my lungs and I can't do anything but stare. "What?"

"Yeah, have him do whatever you want to alleviate any concerns. If you're unsatisfied with what he finds, bring it to me, we'll talk it through. Is that an acceptable compromise?"

I want to tell him thank you, but I really shouldn't have to. This should've all been talked about before he walked in here and acted like an asshole, goading me. Just so he could then play the victim and act like this. It's ridiculous. At the same time, I take victories where I can get them. If there's an issue, Rick will most definitely find it.

Part of me wonders if he'll find anything. She might be telling the truth about why she's here, and then I'll look like an even bigger jackass, but hell. It's reckless to hire her. She worked directly for our biggest competition and she hates me.

"Fine, that'll work."

"She could be a major asset to our firm. You know that. But I want us to be careful."

I don't say anything.

Decker's shoulders fall, just slightly. "I don't like this tension between us, no matter how much you think I do. I want us to get along."

I blow out a breath and stare back at him. "I don't like being pissed at you either. I just…yeah. You know how I feel. At least I make it clear from the start."

"Yeah." Decker shuffles his feet, which tells me a compliment is coming, even though he sucks at giving them to me and doesn't like it. He can praise everyone else all day long, but everything is just expected from me. "I do appreciate the work you've taken off my plate with your new role. It's freed up a lot of time for the wedding, and with Jenny."

I am glad he's getting more time with Jenny. If he'd just ask for favors like a normal fucking human instead of doing everything backhanded, I'd be more than happy to help. I love working my ass off. It's what drives me. I'd take over everything if he'd let me, and I'd do a better job than he does.

Sometimes it's hard to even picture Jenny coming from him. They're so alike and so different at the same time. She's my niece and I love her more than just about anything else in the world. "Glad everything is working out. I really am."

He turns to walk off.

"Even if you are a pussy."

He whips back around and I'm grinning my ass off.

"You're still an asshole."

"Yeah, I am. At least I can admit it. Now say you're a pussy."

He's laughing now. "I'll kick your ass up and down this hall, and the other two at the same time. Don't tempt me. And be nice to Paisley, or stay away, I don't give a fuck which one it is. You're welcome for the Rick shit, by the way."

I lean back, grinning, and fold my arms over my chest.

Decker's brows knit together. "The fuck you look so smug for?"

"Tate made you do this, didn't she?"

His eyes widen, then narrow back on me. "What?"

"The Rick thing. She has reservations too and made you do it to appease me. That's why you did it. Don't lie, brother. I'll know if you are."

His jaw sets. "Just don't piss off Paisley."

"Hah! She did." I walk past him to go pay Rick a visit but shake my head at Decker as I pass by. "Trying to take credit for your woman's good deed. Your hypocrisy knows no bounds."

"Oh fuck off, Doc Holliday." Decker marches off in the other direction.

I head down toward Rick's office. Maybe he'll turn my day around after all. This dude is fucking awesome, and hilarious.

I rap twice on his door but don't bother waiting for an invitation. Rick's reading some Christian book that looks like it just came in from Amazon. *How to Know Your God Better* or something.

"You obeying the commandment that says you can't fuck until you're married?"

Rick laughs, and his eyes dart up from the book. "The only Collins brother who hasn't been neutered. What's up?"

"Decker give you all the details on Paisley Williams?"

Rick goes back to reading. "Yep. I'll get it done."

I lean down toward his desk. "Look, I want you to dig deep on this."

"How deep?"

"Map her fucking genome deep. Full cavity, double penetration, voyeur, dark web shit. I want to know everything down to when she sneezes and what kind of porn she jerks it to."

Rick leans back in his chair, clearly amused. He nods. "Okay."

This is the part where he's going to ask for a favor. That's how Rick operates, even though we pay him out the ass. You always have to barter something, just for him to do his job well. And we all give him whatever he wants, because he's the best at what he does.

"What do you want?"

"Tickets."

"To the Bears suite? Done."

He shakes his head. "No, man. I need tickets to *Jesus of Nazareth*, at the Chicago Center for Performing Arts."

I glance around, then down at his book. "Umm, okay. Shouldn't be a problem." I'll tell my secretary to get them. Should be easy.

He sighs and smiles. "Yeah, Mary's a fan."

"Magdalene? Someone told me you were chasing her around. I didn't believe them." I lean in close. "You hit that?"

He grins his ass off. "Oh no, not even close. Biding my time. Laying the groundwork."

What the fuck? I've never seen this guy chase a piece of ass longer than a day. He could easily fuck half the single women in the building. "Seriously?"

He shrugs. "When the heart knows, it knows. She's the one."

I have to get the hell out of this room. Didn't he just make fun of my brothers for being neutered? And at least they're getting laid. It feels like I'm in the *Twilight Zone*. "Whatever you say, man. I'll get the tickets, just email me the date and time."

"Will do, BC."

I grit my teeth. I fucking hate when he calls me that, but he's one man you want on your side at all times. Yes, it's short for Baby Collins.

As I'm walking toward the door he says, "Thinking about rekindling things?"

I stop in my tracks. "What?" I don't even turn around to look at him.

"With Ms. Williams?"

I just keep walking and hear his fucking laugh come from the office. How the hell does he do shit like that? He hasn't even started looking into her yet. The asshole knows everything about everyone.

I have to walk through finance, Dexter's department, as I make my way over to my office. I spot Paisley, messing around with her desk, adjusting her computer monitors. My morning did just improve and I'm in a better mood, so I should stop by and at least say something, so other people see it. Regardless of my personal feelings, I have to set an example for the associates.

I stand there, leaned up against her doorframe, while she's bent over fussing with some cables. Fuck, her ass looks incredible when her charcoal pencil skirt rides up her toned thighs.

When she sees me, it appears like she might shriek, but she cups a hand over her mouth.

I raise my eyebrows.

"How long have you been standing there?" She whisper-screams the words at me.

"Not long. Just stopped by because they made me. So welcome to the firm and don't let me know if you need anything."

I turn to walk away, but you can never get the last word with Paisley Williams.

Oh no, it never happens, and I should know better.

She rolls her eyes. I can't see it, but I feel it. "Always gonna be bitter that I beat you, aren't you, Collins?"

I spin around slowly, already grinning. I think part of me wanted this to happen. In fact, I know I wanted it to happen. "It's whatever. Water under the bridge."

She takes a few steps toward me and my heartbeat kicks up a notch. Fuck, she looks so damn hot with her button-down blouse, open just enough to get a peek at black lace underneath. I could easily turn her blinds down, lock the door, and bend her over the desk. Spank the shit out of her for talking to me the way she is. She'd keep it up. A woman like Paisley goads you. It's how she wins. She gets under your skin until you make a mistake, or conversely, dominate her in the bedroom. She gets off on that shit.

Her eyes, though. They're light blue and the contrast to her dirty-blonde hair is almost too much to bear. I remember the way she used to suck my dick and stare up at me, looking all innocent. She doesn't appear powerful, more like a girl next door, but that's her secret weapon. She's like that creature at the bottom of the ocean that pretends to look harmless, lures you in, and then the fangs come out and right before you die, you realize you were always the prey and never had the upper hand.

Her eyes land on me, and I can see the gears spinning. She's thinking. And when she thinks, it's dangerous. You're almost certainly going to lose, every damn time, even though I'd never tell her that.

"You're confident right now." She puts a hand on her hip and looks amused, standing about four feet away. "I wonder why."

Why does she have to look so damn sexy right now? Even if we got along, this can't happen. I need to stay on edge, keep my guard up around her, watch everything she does.

I shrug, because what else can I do. I *am* confident right now. Rick's going to find something, and this little problem will be wrapped up soon. Rick works fast.

"I know you didn't want to hire me. So, you were overridden. That's why you look constipated every time I see you. Like a big bucket of rage is sitting in your chest, waiting to explode, but you have to be professional. Oh, and Weston stole all your credit too. Yeah, you have a lot to be upset about, don't you?"

Fuck. My whole body tenses. I hate when she does this shit, works things out in front of me. Yet part of me loves the fuck out of it. She's not some chick you just fuck and send home. She's the real deal. The biggest challenge on the planet and she doesn't hold back, ever.

"You're a managing partner now, so seeing me here must really sting. Your concerns not being taken seriously." She walks over to the wall next to the door, and leans up against it, studying me. "We both know how you are. Always have to be right. Always have to be in control, of every situation. So what would they do? That's a good question. Decker would want to make you feel confident and relaxed, in control of something, like you are right now. You'd naturally use my last job as leverage. You'd tell them I worked for the competition, that we didn't get along at law school, anything you could come up with in that little brain of yours to torpedo my chances."

My face heats up another degree, and I shouldn't be angry right now, but she's going to get to me if I don't get out of here.

"You were always paranoid. One step short of a conspiracy theory documentary." She leans out to the side and peeks past me. "Which way did you just come from?"

"What?" I don't know where this is headed, and I nod back down the hallway.

My palms start to twitch, and I don't know how she consumes me with rage and makes me want to fuck her brains out at the same time. I want to kiss those tempting lips, just to shut her up. Judging by the smirk on her face, she can tell everything going through my mind.

Don't let her win, asshole.

She walks up to me.

What the hell?

Then she gets up on her tiptoes, right in my ear. It's so fucking hot. I glance down. Her pussy is just inches away from my dick, nothing but some air and a few layers of fabric between us. I could dig my fingers into her hips, and yank that skirt over her petite little ass. Put my handprint on it, just to remember what it looks like. Just to hear her beg me to do it again and again. Show her who runs shit, in the bedroom anyway.

My cock is hard as a rock and there's no way I can hide it.

Her lips are right next to my ear and she whispers, "I bet they agreed to investigate me, to alleviate your concerns. In fact, I'll bet the firm's PI has an office right down there, and that's where you just came from. That's why you have that smug, shit-eating grin across your stupid face. But when I walk back to my desk, it'll be gone. And you'll be nothing but angry again, like you always are." She pauses for a brief second, then whispers, "I'm not going anywhere, *asshole.*"

I try to bite back the rage the best I can, but it's no use. She'll see right through it. She always could. Instead, I just smirk right back at her. "I love how arrogant you are, Pais. You always thought you were the smartest one in the room."

She shakes her head, snickering. "Oh no, Donnie. That was *you*. I was smart enough to realize I wasn't always the smartest one in the room. And I know how to use that arrogance against you. Your guy won't find anything."

"You flatter yourself, thinking we'd spend resources looking into your uninteresting background."

"If you don't then you're definitely not the smartest guy in the room. I need this job for reasons your selfish ass would never understand, and it's personal. But do whatever you need to for your investigation. Know this, though." She leans back up to my ear and whispers, "If you fuck with me, I will eat you alive."

And just like that, she turns around and walks back over to her desk, swaying her hips, knowing I'm staring right at her ass.

I turn and walk away, hoping nobody notices my cock tenting my slacks. I shoot around the corner and duck into the bathroom. If I don't get a release, I'm going to go insane or do something I regret. The urge to hate-fuck Paisley Williams has never been stronger. One thing I do know, the second I get back to my desk, I'm going to send her a 'welcome to the firm' email for the ages. She won't get the last word.

PAISLEY

Decker pulls his SUV off I-290 onto Franklin Street. I stare way up in the sky at the top of the Willis Tower. It's the third tallest building in the United States. It would be impressive if I hadn't just moved back to the city from Manhattan.

An email pops up from Donavan, and I make the mistake of opening and reading it. My hackles rise, but I need to put it out of my mind. Then I see he sent it to the entire firm and copied all the partners on it. Asshole. I can't believe he even knew how to use a party popper emoji in the subject line.

Dexter is in the front passenger seat and I'm right behind him.

"Ready to give the good news?" Decker asks Dexter.

"Yeah," says Dexter.

They yanked me out of the office earlier, and I'm still not entirely sure what I'm doing here.

Dexter glances back as if he can read my thoughts. "Need you with us for a consult afterward."

I nod. Seems like usual business.

We park in the garage and head to the elevators. Decker punches in the fortieth floor and we rocket up. When the doors open, the office is gorgeous. A ton of beautiful women walk around in skirts and heels. I half expect Decker and Dexter to gawk at them but they don't. They soldier on toward the front desk, and I walk as fast as my shoes will allow, trying to keep pace.

A young woman reaches up and touches the headset on her ear, presumably to shut it off, then looks at both of them, then me. "Mr. Collins." She turns her head to Dexter. "And, uhh, Mr. Collins. Here for your meeting?"

"Yes please," says Decker. "We brought Paisley Williams with us."

"Nice to meet you." She pushes a button on her phone. "Mr. Miller, the Collins brothers and Paisley Williams are here to see you."

"Show them back." The voice booms out from the speaker on the phone.

She stands up and says, "Right this way please."

We pass a bullpen of cubicles, and offices line the perimeter. Split down the middle are conference rooms with floor-to-ceiling temporary walls made of glass. She leads us into one.

"Can I get you anything? Juice? Coffee?"

"No thank you," says Decker.

"No thank you," says Dexter.

She turns to me.

"No thank you, I'm fine."

"Mr. Miller will be right with you." She turns on her heel and exits before we can say anything else.

I set the folders they gave me on the table, and we sit and wait. A few minutes later a man walks in. He's the only person in the building not in business attire.

He has on tight, tattered jeans and a V-neck t-shirt that clings tight to his body. He's extremely good-looking, in the bad-boy, tough-guy sense. Tattoos cover both of his arms down to his wrists and he has dark brown hair and hazel eyes. His hair is disheveled, like he just looked in a mirror and messed it up then walked out the door. Dexter stands up first and they shake hands.

So, he's probably Dexter's friend and that's why he does business with the firm. Could be wrong, but the gut rarely is.

"Dexter, Decker, good to see you." He shakes hands with Decker then turns to me. "I don't think we've met. Cole Miller." He holds out a hand.

"Paisley Williams, I just started at the firm." I take his hand, and he has a hell of a grip.

Everyone has a seat.

Decker straightens up in his chair. "Got good news."

Cole Miller relaxes a little, like a huge burden just lifted off his shoulders.

Decker turns to me. "We've been battling a lawsuit for what?" He turns to Cole. "Eight months or more, going on nine?"

"Nine, for sure. My fucking hair's going gray."

Dexter laughs. "Hey, I hear silver fox is all the rage."

Cole laughs.

Decker cringes. "Jesus, with you two. Anyway, we reached a settlement." He turns back to me again. "Sorry, we didn't have a chance to brief Paisley. She just came to work for us, from New York. Cole owns a nationwide chain of gyms, Curve."

"Oh yeah, we had a few of those in Manhattan."

Cole grins. "Were you a member?"

I shake my head. "No, sorry. Always working and there wasn't one close to the office. I did go in and look around once."

He shrugs and grins. "No worries. I can get you hooked up, now that you're…"

Dexter cuts him off. "You gonna let us give you the news or do you want to pitch a fucking gym membership?"

Everyone but Decker laughs.

Decker sighs. "Always trying to sell some shit."

These guys *all* must go way back, the way they're talking to each other.

"They agreed to everything?" says Cole.

Decker nods. "Yeah, it was really just the courts and paperwork. I think they wanted it to stay in the news, she had a non-profit group behind her. I still can't believe this shit went on this long." He turns to me to explain. "The lady didn't want money, just a donation to an anti-online-bullying charity." His eyes move back to Cole. "She said multiple times she knows you didn't condone what your employee did and was happy with the way you handled it right from the start."

"What about the other part of the settlement?" says Cole.

"She was reluctant but accepted. Lifetime membership to Curve. She did ask for one more thing."

Cole cringes. "Yeah?"

"She wants you to start a program. The details we can discuss later, but she wants you to block off a time for certain classes or some shit, she used one of those pussy words everyone says now. Safe space or something. I don't really know what it means."

Dexter palms his forehead and shakes his head. Cole looks like he's about to die laughing.

"What?" says Decker.

"Nothing, you're just like an eighty-year-old conservative trapped in a forty-year-old attorney's body."

"I'm not forty yet, assholes. I have like two years to go."

"Coming up quick," says Dexter.

"Anyway, you were saying so eloquently, Decker. She wants a safe space in my gyms?"

"Yeah, a time block with some classes for insecure women."

Just looking at Decker I can see how uncomfortable he is talking about this stuff, and I have a feeling it's because I'm in the room and he might not want to offend me. It's hilarious.

"She wants, umm, curvier instructors. Basically, she wants you to do something so heavier, I guess, women feel more comfortable in the gym, when they're just getting started. Less intimidating. That's what she said."

Cole taps his chin. "Fuck, that's not a bad idea, actually."

Decker's eyebrows shoot up. "Really?"

Cole nods. "Yeah. A lot of women want to work out, they just don't always feel comfortable when they walk in and see abs and sports bras everywhere. They don't know how to use the equipment; they don't know what they're doing. They're afraid to hire a personal trainer, or they can't afford one. It's overwhelming for them, gives them anxiety which is something we're trying to combat here."

Decker shakes his head. "I'll never understand this generation of people. Afraid to do anything."

I swear I hear him mumble, "Pussies," but I can't be sure. I think it has more to do with personality types, and Decker looks as ambitious as they come. I can relate, somewhat, but everyone is different, and I think it's a great idea too.

Cole turns to Dexter. "Hey, when the smoke clears on this shit, is there anything in this lawsuit that would make it a bad idea to offer this lady a job?"

Dexter pops up in his seat a little. "Really?"

Cole nods. "Fuck yeah. I'll put her in my operations department. It makes sense anyway. She probably has a lot of insight into the minds of insecure women who want to work out. She knows what it's like to be body shamed on a national stage while trying to be healthy. I don't know what that's like. Do any of you?"

We all shake our heads.

"I try to put myself in the headspace of someone like her, so I can meet that demographic's demands, but it's not the same. She has first-hand knowledge of things we don't know about, other than through empathy. I should've done this shit a long time ago. Look at the name on the wall. It says Curve. The whole goal when I started was to make a place for all women, all shapes colors and sizes, to get healthier."

Decker sighs, as if he's tired of this conversation already. "Okay, so you're good with all the terms then?"

"Absolutely."

"Good." Decker stands up and shakes Cole's hand. "We'll make it final and I can get the fuck out of here before I get accused of microaggressions."

Everyone turns to him, eyes wide.

He shrugs. "I don't know what the fuck it means but one of the new associates told me I was doing it the other day. Tate thought it was hilarious. I told them to fuck off and get me the file I asked for before I showed them actual aggression."

Dexter shakes his head. "Sounds like you used actual aggression the whole time. I don't think there was anything micro about it."

Decker walks around and Cole stands up, so they're eye to eye. He smiles. "Glad we could take care of this for you."

"Seriously, Decker, thank you, for everything you and your firm did. It's incredible, and I'm glad everything is amicable. Just let me know where to write the check."

Decker says, "It's no problem, and I will. I want to do a press run and some social media stuff when you write it, and we'll do a formal press conference with the settlement. You'll get a ton of great PR value out of this. I think it may actually be a good thing overall."

"For sure. And we're good on the other thing too?"

"Yeah, I need to put you in touch with our HR manager and Dexter. I need to see if there are any additional tax or insurance benefits available, for providing gym memberships to all the employees."

Oh, that would be a nice job perk. I get excited for a moment, but I'm not sure how long I'll be in Chicago yet. Not to mention, I don't know when I'll have time to work out, if they work me anywhere near the same number of hours I put in at Cooper.

"Okay, I'm fucking off now. Have a great day." Decker turns to us. "You guys good to Uber back to the office? I didn't even think about that when we rode over together and I have a meeting."

"We're good," says Dexter.

Decker leaves and Cole sits back down at the table.

He laughs. "Your brother is very in tune with society today."

"Yeah, he's always been hardcore like that. Which is hilarious because he's liberal as hell. Just doesn't put up with laziness and feelings. He'll pay the shit out of some taxes though, for the good of the city."

"Hilarious." Cole leans back. "Now, the fun shit. Is Paisley up to speed?"

Dexter shakes his head. "No, I haven't had a chance to brief her." He turns to me. "Cole's looking to expand his business now that the lawsuit will be settled. His balance sheet is extremely healthy, just needs capital infusion. His tax structure is about as efficient as it can get, but I told him he needs to be very targeted, know exactly what he wants to try. Then, we go hunting for capital. I know this was your specialty in New York and I know you possibly have some connections to VCs and angel investors I don't."

I nod. "Absolutely, I can help. It'd be best to know what ideas you have first. I know VCs who specialize in certain sectors, so to put you in touch with the right people, I need to know your goals."

Cole's eyes light up like this is the conversation he's wanted to have. "I've narrowed it down to either health supplements or franchising."

I glance over at Dexter.

It almost seems like he's testing me right now. Wants to see how good I am. Well, Dexter, sit back and observe.

"Why franchising?"

He shrugs. "Well, I think it might be faster. I can bring in licensing fees with minimal oversight. Less work, more money. What's the downside?"

"Franchising can be good under certain circumstances. What's your managerial style?"

"Huh?"

"Are you laid back? Hands on? How much does your brand mean to you? When people see Curve, do their opinions and thoughts matter to you?"

"Of course, they do. I'm very involved. I can go to San Francisco and if I walk into one of my gyms, I want to get hands on, teach classes, show employees the way things should be done. Leadership."

I glance over at Dexter. He's doing his best to look indifferent.

Fuck it.

"I think franchising is a bad option. You can still expand, but you seem to like control. When you franchise, you can lay out terms and conditions, but it can be a pain in the ass to manage. I've seen it happen with entrepreneurs like you who see more than dollars and cents attached to their brand. You have to think like the investors who would be taking a chance, buying a Curve and managing it. They don't see your company the way you do. They see an investment. They want a return and that's it. Maybe you have one or two passionate ones, but it's not their calling like it is for you. They'll cut corners. They'll do anything they can to increase their bottom line. You can still expand, just get the capital and do it yourself. You have way more control and I can tell you like control. That's not a bad thing. It means you care about your company. You care what people think when they see Curve on the side of the wall. What they experience when they walk inside." I glance over at Dexter. "Just being honest."

"I like her." Cole grins. "You got all that, just by sitting in on one meeting?"

I shrug. "You pay for the best, you get the best advice. It's that simple."

"Okay, so what about products?"

"I'd draw up plans for both. Gym expansion and products. See which have the higher margins. Hell, why don't you do both? You already have an infrastructure built for selling products. I've been in your gyms and you're basically a store for other brands right now. And I would look and see how much cheaper you could have your own supplements made, versus what you already have. You sell them for a profit already, right?"

"Yeah. It's not much, but we make a few million each year from the sales."

"I think when you sit down and crunch the numbers, you'll find expansion the best option, financially. When you do that, you'll increase your product sales anyway. More gyms, more product going out the door."

"I think my reasoning for doing products is more brand related anyway. It gets me in front of more people. More people see Curve, maybe they think about coming to the gym."

"It's probably a good idea, but if you go to investors and say, hey, I want you to give me money to invest in these products, but it's to increase my margins in my other business you don't own a part of..." I hold out my hands and shrug.

"I see what you're saying. That makes sense." He mulls it over for a second. "Fuck, you're good. I see why they hired you."

"Thank you, sir."

Dexter glances at his watch. "Well, I think you have some stuff to think about. We can run the numbers. Oh, and here." He hands over a card. "Harlow wanted me to give you this. She just started a firm here in the city."

Cole's eyes light up, just a tiny bit, when he hears the name.

"I actually have a meeting with her when I get back to the office. She's going to do some work for us. Give her a call. She's young, smart as fuck, and she can help you with all the marketing and that type of shit while you're planning. She's a genius at all the new digital stuff. Get your proposition and everything together. Let me know if you want an associate of ours to help you draft it, but I think your people here can handle all the detail work. We'll start shopping for the right investors and set up meetings."

"Sounds awesome, man."

All of us stand up and we shake hands.

"Thank you, guys, so much. I'm really excited and it's a serious relief to know you have my back and can provide guidance on this. I mean that."

"No problem," says Dexter.

"Yeah, anything at all, just call." I smile.

We walk back, using the same route as before and head toward the bank of elevators.

Once we're inside, Dexter turns to me.

Before he can get a word out, I say, "Did I pass?"

He laughs. "Yeah, you passed."

"Good, I was a little nervous."

"Oh, like hell you were." He laughs again. "Great job. You said the exact same things I would've told him."

"It's no problem. That's why you hired me."

He eyes me for a moment, as if assessing everything about me, then nods. "Yeah, I think it's going to work well."

It should, if I can avoid your damn brother every day.

AFTER WE UBER BACK to the office, there's a younger woman, maybe mid-twenties, waiting for Dexter. She's gorgeous and intimidating. She's scowling and looks like she could kick any man's ass that even looked at her funny, but the second she sees Dexter her eyes light up.

She has on a super-cute, knee-length A-line cocktail dress. It's black and sleeveless. She has tattoos down both arms that are gorgeous. Her hair is jet black and she has icy blue eyes.

She looks like a female version of the Collins brothers and she must be the cousin Dexter has a meeting with. It's confirmed a moment later when she says, "Cousin!" and gives him a huge hug. Then she leans back and says, "Shit, sorry. Not very professional." She holds out a hand and keeps it there until he finally laughs and shakes it.

"This is Paisley." He turns to me and makes eye contact. "She's new at the firm. Just moved back from New York City."

"Oh man, I love Manhattan." Harlow shakes my hand.

Holy shit. She damn near crushes my fingers with her grip. She shakes hands like a damn man. I wonder if the Collins brothers made her this way, growing up around all boys. I don't think they had any sisters, but Donavan rarely talked about his family at law school.

"Yeah, it's great. I'm from the Chicago area originally, so it's nice to be home around family."

"Oh yeah, where'd you grow up?" She says it almost like it's a test.

What is it with the Collins family and their questions?

"Barrington."

"North side, right on. Okay, well..."

Dexter jolts a little, like he zoned out for a minute. "Yeah, right. The meeting, let's do it."

They start back toward the conference rooms, but I need to walk the same direction. I hang back, about ten feet behind them. I don't want them to think I'm tagging along for their meeting. I don't want to seem presumptuous or anything, make things uncomfortable.

Turns out, I don't have to do anything to make things awkward, because Donavan comes walking toward us and smirks right at me, like he won the pissing contest with his little email.

Shit. I really need to avoid him.

"Hey, Harlow." He gives her a hug and smiles. His eyes turn to ice the second they land on me, but he recovers quickly. "What's going on? You having lunch with Dexter and didn't invite me?"

She shakes her head. "No, I'm actually meeting with him to talk about maybe working with the finance department on some marketing."

Dexter looks away, like he's praying Donavan will leave it at that. I get the feeling it's not the reaction he expects, but the one he wants.

"Is that so?" Donavan's words are drawn out. He turns to Dexter. "Does Decker know about this?"

Dexter glares and looks like he wants to wail on Donavan but doesn't want to make Harlow uncomfortable.

Too late, Dexter. We're already there.

"What are you? In fifth grade? Does Decker know about this?" He gestures with his head toward the conference rooms. "Come on, Harlow. I know you're busy. Let's get to it."

Donavan's teeth are clenched. I know the look, seen it a million times. He's doing his best to stay calm, but his hands are fidgety. I can practically feel the tension radiating through his body. A tiny vein pops out on the side of his neck. "Just curious because nobody notified me. I figured you must have spoken with the other managing partner before you'd set a high-level marketing meeting regarding the use of firm resources." His eyes dart over to mine, then back to Dexter.

Harlow shrinks back a little, something I didn't expect from her. She looked so stoic and confident before. But she's young, and I get the feeling it's because it's family. Everything is always personal with family.

Dexter stares blankly, looks at Harlow, then right back at Donavan. "Okay, I apologize. It was clearly an oversight on my part. Can we discuss this later when a potential consultant is *not* present?"

Donavan grits his teeth, but says, "Fine."

Oh boy.

Harlow turns to Dexter. "Sorry, let's just do this another time, after you've talked to Donavan or whatever." She heads for the door.

Dexter holds his arm out and stops her, but his eyes never leave Donavan's.

"No. We're doing the meeting today. I gave you my word, at Thanksgiving. After you gave me the best damn pitch I've ever heard and convinced me you could help my department."

She freezes up, not knowing what to do. I can already tell what happened. Harlow just started a new firm and probably went to Dexter at Thanksgiving, when the family was together. Talked to him about consulting with the firm. I feel bad for her. It probably took a ton of courage to do that and now Donavan is shitting all over her. Why? I have no idea. Because he's always pissed off at the world, maybe? Because I'm standing here? Damn it! I should've walked away. I didn't even think maybe he saw me and that's why he's doing this.

Dexter hooks his arm around Harlow, like a big brother would do, then leads her over toward the conference room away from Donavan. Seriously, if she didn't look like she was made of steel, she probably would've broken down into tears.

Dexter squeezes Harlow a little more around the shoulders, and once she's inside the room with the door closed, he storms back over and gets in Donavan's face. "I'm not running shit by you and you better be gone when we're done." He sneers and looks Donavan up and down like he's disgusted. "Jesus." Then he walks back to Harlow.

I'm still standing there, because I don't know where the hell to go. I glance around and all the other employees have their heads popped up from their cubicles or out of their offices, but they're glancing around, pretending not to pay attention.

Donavan's eyes roll over and meet mine. I don't know exactly what he sees, but I'm pretty sure I'm scowling because inside I feel like I could tear his damn head off.

He scoffs, shakes his head, then storms away, down a hallway back toward Tate's office.

Like an idiot, I stand there for about two seconds, then chase after him.

He rounds a corner and I follow, getting madder with each step I take. Heels are such bullshit too. I'd pay good money to be able to walk around in flats like the men. It'd make running this asshole down ten times easier.

I get to the end of the hall and see the door to the stairs close.

Gotta be fucking kidding me.

I go up two flights of stairs and see an exit door. It's the only place he could've gone. I push it open and it's a rooftop. It's gorgeous too.

You can see all of Chicago from here, Lake Michigan to the east, the skyline all around.

Donavan's eyes meet mine and his face turns even more red. I don't give a shit. I stomp toward him and he looks like he's about to lay into me, but I don't give him the satisfaction.

"What the hell is wrong with you?"

He sneers. "Excuse me?"

"You heard me, dickhead."

He tries to walk past me, right back to the exit door, but I step right in his path. "Don't, Pais. Don't fucking do it."

"Why did you do that? Right in front of her like that?"

"It's a family matter and none of your goddamn business. Just like you have no business being at my firm."

"God, you're an asshole." I shake my head, then look down at the ground. "Tell me one thing and just be honest. Did you take your frustration out on her because I was standing there?"

He scoffs again, and it's so annoying and petty when he does it. "Don't flatter yourself."

I look up at him, trying to be civil and plead with him for just one second. "Could you not see your cousin's face? I don't even know her, and I could tell you destroyed her. And she looks mean, like she could take a punch."

He tries to say something, and I cut him off again.

I start to put my hand on his chest but stop myself when I realize what I'm doing. "Which means you must be really close with her, like a big brother. From what I could tell, this was a huge moment for her, and you steamrolled right over it. So, my previous question still stands. What the *hell* is wrong with you?"

He pauses for a second, and gulps. His face pales and becomes a little less red, like he's finally processing his actions. His voice calms. "I'll deal with Harlow. But I'm *not* discussing this with you." He turns to walk away.

"Do you still hate me that much?" My words hit him right in the back.

He freezes and exhales an audible breath. "I don't...hate you. I just don't understand why you're here. You know there's shit between us."

I walk around and get in front of him, forcing him to look at me. "You think I *want* to be here? I *have* to be here. For personal reasons."

"So you say." His eyebrows pinch together.

"You don't trust me, but I'm not the one who did anything to ruin the trust between us."

"No. That's not what I mean." He shakes his head. "Why here, at my firm? You could work at a thousand other places in Chicago."

My jaw clenches. "Why does it bother you so much? Because I beat you at school seven years ago?"

"Please, I'm over that."

"Sure you are. It's completely obvious. Why do you always have to be in control of *everything*? You were like that at Columbia and you're like that now. You can't stand anyone being better than you at anything. I was just doing my best at school and I beat you. I will never apologize for that."

"I said I'm over it."

"Then what's the *real* problem?"

His face screws up tight. Like seven years of resentment just bubbled to the surface. "I'm done discussing this."

"You owe me an explanation. What, you don't want me around your family?" Judging by his reaction I just nailed it.

He gets in my face. "You don't know shit about me and my family."

"Yeah, and that's my fault?"

He stands there, shaking his head like he wants to murder someone, completely silent.

"No, you never talked about them, remember?"

"You have no reason for being here."

I reach for his arm, trying my best to hold back tears that are forming. I told myself I'd never cry again, but I don't know how much longer I can take this. "Why did you do that to me at graduation? I told myself I didn't care, even years later, but I was lying to myself. Why did you do that to me?" My voice rises when I ask the last question.

Do not cry. Pull yourself together. Don't let him know he can still get to you.

He sighs and looks down at me. His face softens, just a hint, but he still doesn't say anything.

"Tell me, please. I deserve to know."

His jaw clenches. "I have to go."

"Donavan please."

He takes a step toward me. All the anger leaves his face and there's nothing but regret on it now, like he's warring with himself not to give in. "I didn't mean to…"

"Well, you did. Why?"

He stares out at the lake for a long few seconds, refusing to make eye contact. "I can't do this right now. I need to go. Just…meet me for a drink later. Maybe we can talk about some…"

I shake my head, cutting him off. "No. You don't get to set the terms." I turn to start for the exit door.

"I did love you, whether you believe me or not." His words hit me in the back. "Just have a fucking drink with me later, Jesus. Maybe we can be civil and get along while you're here."

I feel the tears still burning at the corners of my eyes and I won't give him the satisfaction. I shake my head. "You just had a chance to come clean and you didn't." I don't even look back as I say the words.

My feet fly down the stairs, hoping he won't catch up to me.

When I get back to the office I don't stop. I head straight for the elevator and ride it to the parking garage. My heels clack on the concrete as I walk to my car. I yank the door open, get in, and shut it behind me.

Everything slams into me at once and I gasp for air.

What the hell are you doing here, Paisley?

The tears start and I can't hold them back. I cover my face and cry straight into my palms. It wasn't supposed to be like this. I wasn't supposed to feel this way when I came to work here. Now, I can't breathe and it's worse than anything I've ever felt in my life. I want to curl into the fetal position and never show my face to the world again.

I glance at my face in the rearview mirror. So much for not crying a second time.

DONAVAN

I WALK into The Gage after work and Penn's waiting at the bar. He gives me a head nod when I walk in.

What a fucking day.

I can't believe I froze up like that on the roof. I just couldn't say the words, couldn't tell her. Can't believe I did that to Harlow either. Fuck, I crushed both of them. I'm on a damn roll.

What the hell is wrong with you?

I need a scotch, or four. I rub the back of my neck as I walk over. Could I do what Penn's doing? Just do nothing and travel for a while? Fuck some women and enjoy life on a beach or something? I have the money for it.

Don't be stupid. You'd go crazy.

I know my brain is right. I have to be competing, winning in the courtroom. It's the only thing that makes me happy. That and getting laid, until Paisley blew back into town like a fucking tornado.

I take a seat next to Penn and he already has a Glenlivet neat sitting in front of my stool. I knock it back with one gulp.

"Damn, hell of a day?"

I nod. "The worst."

"What happened?"

"Had it out with Pais. Shit all over my little cousin. Take your pick."

He turns and leans in, suddenly interested. "Damn, what happened with Pais?"

I sigh and tell him everything. Well, the important parts anyway.

"Fuck." He stares up at the ceiling, like he's reminiscing. "Man, she really did change after law school."

"What do you mean?"

"Don't you remember how nice she was at school? She'd do anything for

629

anyone. Always polite. I thought you two would get married and she wouldn't even use her law degree. Just start making little Donavans. I think that's all she wanted. You could tell."

"Yeah, she used to talk about it all the time."

Penn shakes his head. "Not anymore. She's a fucking stone-cold killer. You definitely changed her."

"You're not helping."

Penn laughs. "Well fuck, it's true. You did her a favor anyway. Look how successful she is. She made partner at Cooper. That's like being a Yankee right out of high school. Youngest person to ever do it."

"I don't think she'd see it as doing her a favor. Is she really *that* ruthless now?"

Penn eyes me for a long second, and apparently decides to go with honesty. He slow nods. "Yeah, man. She is. I'm surprised Cooper didn't open up an office for her here, just to have her still work for him. She was always at his side. Most valuable employee by a long shot."

I shake my head. "Fuck Cooper. I hate that prick."

"Oh, he's a prick for sure. A rich powerful one. You need to be careful going after him. Your brothers too."

"Who says we're going after him?"

He scoffs. "Please. He knows everything you do before you do it."

I start to say something, and my brothers walk in and their fiancées follow behind, all three of them.

Thanks for the invite, fam.

It looks like a triple date, but I'm all out of shitty things to say for one day. They all walk up, and I act civil and introduce Penn to everyone. He hits it off like he's part of the family. I'm not surprised, he's a likeable guy.

Tate glances over at me, a little gun shy. I don't blame her. She's my least favorite of all of them and there's a lot of bad blood there, but I really don't have the energy to spar with her.

My brothers, Quinn, and Abigail are busy chatting it up with Penn.

I look at Tate. "Buy you a drink?"

She raises her eyebrows. "Will it have arsenic in it?"

I snicker. "No."

She scoots in on a barstool as Jimmy, the bartender, walks over. "Hey, Jimmy. I'll have what he's having."

Jimmy eyes both of us. There's no telling what he's heard. Everyone from the firm hangs out here after work and he probably knows more of the office gossip than we do. "This a joke?"

I shake my head. "No, get it for her and hold the arsenic."

He glances back and forth like he doesn't understand but makes the drink anyway because we tip him like he's royalty.

"So, what happened?"

"What do you mean?"

"I mean you're talking to me. This is a huge step, Donavan. People might actually think we like each other."

I shrug. "Just a rough day."

"Does the problem start with a P?"

Fuck, she's smart. It's bad enough Tate came to the firm and I have to compete with her. She's a damn good attorney, maybe better than me. Now, Paisley is here, and she's definitely better than me. I just nod.

"Figured. She's a great attorney, but something doesn't sit right."

I nod again, finally glad someone else gets it. "Thank you. It was a terrible idea bringing her in."

"So, how long?"

"How long what?"

"Were you two together?"

I look away as soon as she says it and totally give myself away. Fuck.

"It's written all over you when she's in the room. The way you look at her. Your body language."

I stare down at the scotch in my glass. "During law school. Three years."

Decker walks over. "Wow. What's going on here?"

Tate grins. "Nothing. Just having a drink with my favorite colleague."

Decker's eyes widen and he looks like he doesn't know what the hell to do. It's hilarious, actually. Tate loves making him uncomfortable and it's maybe the one thing I like about her.

I glance up at him. "Yep, we might even go shopping together later."

Decker says, "Okay, spit it out."

"Spit what out?"

"The fucking punchline, asshole."

"It's not a joke."

Tate smiles.

"Seriously?" says Decker.

"Yeah, we just need to pick out some panties for you to wear under the wedding dress."

"I hate all of you." He walks off.

Tate laughs and slides her rocks glass over and bumps mine with it. "Nicely done."

Just as my mood turns around, Paisley walks through the door.

"Well...shit," says Tate.

Dexter waves her over to us.

I down my drink. "Gotta go."

"Donavan." Tate reaches for my arm, but I turn around and take a step before she can do it.

I scowl right at Paisley, then at everyone else. What the fuck? She can't have a drink with me, but she can with my family? I may not have told her what she wanted to hear right then, but I made a fucking attempt. It was better than nothing.

To hell with this.

I take off for the door. Paisley freezes in her tracks and watches me stomp past her. She looks like she's about to reach for my arm, but she doesn't do it.

Good, I don't want to hear her bullshit anyway.

It's always the same around this goddamn place, in this goddamn city. Me against everyone else.

I don't give a damn, though. I'm used to it. Fuck everyone.

PAISLEY

THE RIDE OUT to Barrington with Dad is slow and there's traffic everywhere. I haven't told him anything about Donavan and I don't really plan to. It's quiet most of the way.

When we pull into the retirement home, his eyes get big. "This place looks really nice."

He doesn't say it like *wow*. It's more like *how are we going to pay for this?*

To his credit, he doesn't mention it, though. There's a swimming pool and elderly people moving around with walkers. It looks brand new and it's nicely landscaped. The surrounding businesses are all new shopping centers that look like they were just built.

We walk up just as a van with BARRINGTON RETIREMENT COMMUNITY on the side pulls up.

"Perfect timing. I bet it's them." I rush over there to talk to the guy who gets out of the driver's side.

"Williams?" he says to Dad and me as he gets out.

"Yeah," says Dad.

"Got them in the back. No problems."

Dad wanted to go pick up Grandma and Grandpa, but the place said they had the transportation under control. I told Dad he was nuts anyway. There was no way we could drive them in either of our cars.

"We could've rented a van."

"Dad, they're not charging us for this."

"Yeah they are, it's built into the bill. Look at this place."

"Just stop, okay? It's taken care of."

Grandpa comes out first. They lower him down in his electric wheelchair with a ramp off to the side.

"Grandpa!" I run over and give him a hug, careful not to get tangled in his oxygen tubes that snake up and under his nose.

"Hey, baby girl!" He pats me on the back and squeezes me as hard as he can. "Okay, you're gonna have to let go of me so I can get out of the way."

"Right, sorry." I glance up to the driver.

He's all smiles, like he has all the time in the world.

This place really is perfect for my grandparents. Everyone is so nice and friendly and attentive. They'll get the care they need.

Grandpa's wheelchair buzzes as he drives it over out of the way.

Grandma is a little more complicated. The guy climbs into the back and undoes a few straps, then pushes her over on an elaborate stretcher, bigger than one they would use in an ambulance.

He gets her lined up, then slowly lowers both of them down, never letting go of it.

"Hi, Grandma!" I yell it before she's even to the ground.

An old, wrinkled hand pops up. "Hey, honey!"

I can't stop the excitement building in my chest, even though today is the worst day ever. My grandparents are the best. I practically grew up at their house.

Once they have her down and wheel her over, the four of us are led back to a big open area with chairs. Well, Grandma is pushed by the driver, but the rest of us follow. Once we're there, he gets Grandma down and into an electric wheelchair too.

A young, pretty woman, maybe mid-thirties, walks out and greets us. She looks at my grandparents. "Ready to move in? We're so excited you're here."

"Excited to cash the checks," Dad mumbles.

I elbow him in the ribs. "Knock it off," I whisper-scream the words at him. "I know it's a rough day, but c'mon." I use my best daughter stare to plead with him.

He holds up both hands in surrender. I can't be too upset with him. I know what this day does to both of us every year.

"I have good news," the woman says. "We had an apartment come available. I'll have to discuss price with you, but it's a suite and it has everything available so they could live together in it."

"Done, do it." I say the words without even looking at Dad because I know he'll object to the price.

Grandpa looks over. "It *would* be really nice, but we…"

I hold up a hand to stop him. "If it's possible for you two to live together, it's happening."

"I'll come back in a bit, so you guys can talk about things," the woman says apprehensively as she saunters away.

"Pais, we can't afford that. We can't even afford this place."

I shoot Dad a scowl. "What part of I'm taking care of all this do you not understand?"

Dad's always been a saver. A penny pincher, even when he had tons of money, but he's broke right now, and I know how he gets. He's always planning for worst-case scenario and it did save his ass when his company went under.

He shakes his head.

"He's right," says Grandma. "We shouldn't…"

"Look." I put my palms flat on my thighs. "Let's be honest. You guys need the care. I know, it's tough. You're independent. It's where him and me get it from. But it's time. Grandma just had hip surgery. She can't even walk. You had a good run, but this place is awesome and you're close to home. I saw both of your eyes when you saw it the first time. You'll love it here. You'll have a life, twenty-four seven care. And Dad and I will come visit all the time. You won't be able to get rid of us."

Dad stares. "I still don't know. How are you going to do this? Are you dipping into your retirement?"

I give him a glare. "Dad, listen to me and listen once, because I've about had it. I handle finances for the wealthiest hedge funds in the world and men with more money than you could make in a thousand lifetimes. I think I can handle my personal checkbook."

Grandpa's eyebrows rise. "Well, I guess that's settled then." He drives his wheelchair over to me and looks me in the eye. "Thank you."

Grandma reaches for me, smiling. I walk over and give her a big hug.

"Thank you, sweetie. And we would never get rid of you. You come visit anytime you damn well please."

"I will, Grandma. I promise."

Dad stands up and looks at me. He holds both hands up. "Okay, I won't say anything else." He pauses. "Thank you. I know how I can be, but I'm just… I'm really proud of you right now and it's tough…"

"I know, Dad." I rush into his arms and squeeze him tight. "I know."

His hand pats me on the back of my head and he smooths my hair down. Then he pulls back a little and puts both hands on my shoulders. I can already tell he wants to cry, but he doesn't do it. "You ready?"

I inhale a deep breath and nod. "Yeah, let's do it."

"Say hi for us, please," says Grandma.

Grandpa nods.

"Will do. Enjoy your new home."

DAD and I sit around Mom's grave, telling stories like she's there, drinking wine. Just like we always did in the kitchen when she was with us.

It's the anniversary of her death, seven years ago, and I always fly home and we do this. I don't know if I remember a night when Mom didn't have at least one glass of wine and tell stories. It was her favorite thing to do.

So, this is how we keep her memory alive.

Dad glances over at me. "It's about time."

I nod. "Yeah."

Neither one of us ever cry in front of Mom's grave. It's a rule we made. We have to smile and be happy because that's what she would've wanted. Cancer is a real asshole.

I bend down and drop a kiss on top of Mom's headstone. "I love you, Mom. And I miss you like crazy."

Dad plasters the fakest smile I've ever seen on his face, and I know he's barely holding it together, but he's a man of his word, always. He walks over and drops the same kiss on the headstone. "I love you, sweetheart. And I-I still miss you every day."

"Come on, Dad." I grab him gently by his forearm. "Let's let her rest." It's the only thing I can think to say because he looks like he's about to break down and then he'll feel even worse.

He nods. We get to the car and he sniffs loudly, but doesn't cry, after we climb in.

He turns to face me. "Thanks."

"For what?"

"Always being here, on this day. I couldn't do it alone. There's no way."

I lean over and give him a hug. "I'll always be here, no matter what." It was the one condition of my employment when I was at Cooper. Three days, every year, no matter what happened. I would *not* be there, I wouldn't answer my phone, I wouldn't look at anything client related. It drove Cooper mad, but he would always just grin and bear it.

"Let's go get some food," says Dad as he starts the car.

"Sure, sounds good."

He pulls around the end of the row, about to wind through the cemetery when I look back. I don't know why I do it, but I do.

I see a silhouette headed the direction of Mom's grave marker, but I don't think much of it at first. Could be anyone, a worker, someone going to visit another grave.

"Stop for a second, Dad."

He pulls over to the side. "What's going on?"

I stare and it looks like the man or woman stops right where Mom is.

I get out of the car.

"Pais, what are you…"

"Just stay here, I'll be right back."

I jog up the gravel road a little ways, then slow to a walk when I get near. *What. The. Fuck.*

It's Donavan, kneeling in front of my Mom's headstone. Blood rushes to my face. He's going to be lucky if he doesn't end up right next to her.

When I start to head that way, Dad pulls up next to me in the car. He glances over, and I see the recognition on his face. His hands grip the wheel and his face twists up. He reaches for the handle.

I hold a hand out. "No, I'll take care of this."

"Hell no, Pais."

I walk over and block him from opening his door. "I'll handle it, *Dad.*" I say through gritted teeth.

I'm sure he won't be happy about it, but he holds his hands up then shuts the door. "Hurry and get him the hell out of here." He practically rocks back and forth in his seat.

I nod and turn, storming right toward Donavan.

I still don't think he's seen me and he's saying something, but I can't make out the words.

When I get about thirty feet away, he looks up and goes white as a sheet. Then he looks over at the car, where Dad's sitting there, fuming.

He holds up both hands. "Shit, Pais, I'm sorry."

He backs up a few steps as I haul ass right toward him. "What the fuck are you doing here?" Every hair on the back of my neck is at attention and my skin prickles all over, like it's on fire.

Donavan shakes his head, quickly, like he's not going to say another word.

"I'm going to wait three seconds, and if you haven't explained yourself, I'm going to crack your fucking knee caps, Collins."

His eyes get big. "Jesus."

"You're gonna need Jesus when I'm done with you. I promise you that."

He turns to walk away and holds up a hand. "I'm leaving, okay. I'm sorry, I thought you'd gone already. I looked around and didn't see anyone."

"Yeah, well I'm here and you're here and that's the definition of a fucking problem."

He wheels around, finally tired of being polite it seems. "Oh, kinda like the one where I try to at least make things civil and you tell me to fuck off, then show up to have drinks with my brothers?"

"We're not talking about me right now and what I did the other day, we're talking about why you're at my mother's grave on the anniversary of her death after what you did to her, asshole!"

I glance down and his palms are trembling. I don't know if it's out of fear or anger or what, but I'm glad. He should be scared. If I had a gun this would be a very dangerous situation, with the kind of rage boiling in my veins.

He still stands there, saying nothing. His favorite go-to maneuver when he fucks up.

"Fuck this, I'm calling the police." I pull out my cell phone.

"Please. You're the one harassing me. I was here and you ran over and accosted me."

My eyebrows rise. Is he fucking serious right now? "Accosted you? You haven't seen accosted. The police will treat you way better than I do."

"Oh, I believe you. Just put the phone away. You're not calling anyone."

Dad gets halfway out of the car, and I turn and yell at him. "Stay in the damn car!"

He doesn't get back in, just stands there, watching. I don't think he can hear us unless I yell.

I turn back around and point a finger at Donavan's face. "What are you doing here?"

He just stands there, like he's not going to say anything, then finally lets out a huge, exasperated sigh. "I came to apologize, okay? I come every year." He looks up at the sky and exhales a long breath. "I talk to your mom for like five minutes and then I leave. I tell her I'm sorry I wasn't there for her, and that I'm sorry for hurting her daughter."

My heart pinches in my chest and I can't think. I don't even know how to process that. Before I can be reasonable and scream at him, I whisper, "You do?"

He nods. "Happy now?"

I move my eyes up to meet his. He looks remorseful and apologetic. I'm almost positive he's telling the truth. I've always been able to read him like a book, except when the shit went down at Columbia. Probably because he just disappeared after graduation and I never heard from him again.

I shake my head. "So, you can apologize to my mom, but you couldn't apologize to me all those years ago, or any year since? Why? Because she doesn't talk back? There's no accountability there?"

He stares up at the sky and huffs out a breath, then looks down at me. "I wanted to talk, remember? You said no."

"Two days ago, Donavan. And I didn't want to have drinks with you, I wanted an answer right then. It's been seven years. And if I hadn't shown back up to work at your firm, I'd still be waiting on an explanation that was never coming."

He shakes his head and turns and walks a few steps away. At the last second, he turns back. "Well, I still tried. You happy *now*? I offered on the rooftop." He sweeps his arm out. "You walked away. You don't have to forgive me, but I'm still trying. *Still*!" He turns and walks off.

I glance back at Dad and he looks like he wants to chase after Donavan and have words with him. I shake my head.

This whole situation is so damn complicated. It would be so much easier if I could just hate Donavan. I glance over at Mom's headstone. She wouldn't want me to hate him. She'd tell me to forgive him. She loved him. He was part of our family.

She had so much grace like that. You could treat her like shit, and she'd forgive you the next day, no matter what you did. I spy Dad in my peripheral vision.

Unfortunately, Dad and I hold grudges better than anyone in history.

I love being back home with my family, but I really need to get my grandparents settled in, stick around for a while to make sure everything is good with them, then get back to New York as soon as I can.

Donavan being like this is changing everything, and it's going to consume me from within.

DONAVAN

IT'S BEEN a long-ass week since the incident at the cemetery.

Can't believe I let that happen. I looked everywhere and didn't see a damn thing until Pais snuck up on me. At least I've been busy as hell. I was in court every day this week and didn't step a foot in the office.

The one thing eating at me is that Pais deserves an explanation, but I just don't know how I can tell her. It's been so damn long and it's so stupid, so petty and anticlimactic. I was young and an idiot and fucked up, and I just…

She's going to hate me even more than she already does when I say it, and I don't want that. I really don't. Something about when she's around, it brings back wounds, but it brings back a lot of good too. Things I haven't felt in years. Once I tell her, that will disappear, and I'll be right back to where I was before she showed up.

I'm supposed to meet up with Penn at The Gage, but I'm about ten minutes early. As soon as I walk in, I see Dexter and Abigail at the bar talking to Jimmy.

Perfect, I won't look like a loser drinking alone until he gets here.

Plus, Abigail is cool and I'm probably closer to Dex than any of my other brothers. I mean, we're all close. I love them, they just…yeah. Decker and I never see eye-to-eye on anything. I thought this whole managing partner role finally meant some respect, some recognition for my hard work. It was stupid. I shouldn't have fallen for it, but I did.

No matter what I do they always want more, and I realize now Decker did it just to resolve his own problems. It was the easy way out for him to get us back on good terms so he could marry Tate and get Dad off his ass. He still has all the authority and makes all the decisions. I'm never on any conference calls with Weston Hunter. Not that I'd be nice to him, but fuck. Managing partner. That means top level, overall. Yet, it's nothing more than a different title on my office

639

door. Nothing has changed, really, other than some extra administrative paperwork Decker didn't want to deal with.

I walk over to Dexter and Abigail. Abigail says, "Hi," and gives me a friendly wave.

"Hey, Abs."

Dexter looks like a deer in headlights.

"The fuck is wrong with you?"

He stands up. "You need to get the hell out of here."

Abigail turns to Dexter. "Why?"

"Shit, I didn't tell you what happened last week, did I?"

My eyes widen. "What the hell are you talking about?" I come here all the time. What's the damn problem?

"Too late." Dexter's eyes dart to the door.

I slowly turn, to see what he's looking at, and yeah, it's not good. I should've listened.

Harlow walks through the door, takes one look at me, and folds her arms over her chest. Her nostrils flare, and those frigid blue eyes of hers lock onto mine.

I look down and sigh. "Ahh fuck."

"Yeah, go take it like a man, asshole." Dexter looks away.

"What the hell did you do to Harlow?" asks Abigail.

I ignore her question because I'm sure she'll find out soon enough. I'm surprised she hasn't heard already, the way all the paralegals gossip around the office.

Harlow stands there, staring. It's like a scene from a spaghetti western film. The guy from out of town walks into the saloon and glares while the ominous music plays.

Dex appears behind me and claps a hand on my shoulder. "She's gonna kick your ass. You knew this day was coming. Might as well get it over with."

I saunter over there and it's the longest walk of my life. It's my own fault, not because of what I did, but the reason I'm about to have my ass beat. My brothers and I turned her into this. She probably would've grown up to be a really sweet girl if she hadn't had us around to corrupt her. But hey, no sane man would ever start shit with her, so there's a silver lining.

As soon as I'm about three feet away, she says the two words I knew were coming.

"Fuck. You."

I wince as she says the words right in my face. She doesn't flinch when she says them. Doesn't blink. Her jaw is set, and her hands are balled up into fists.

I hold both hands up, palms out. "Harlow, come on." I gesture over to the side where nobody is around. "Can we, you know?"

She doesn't respond, which I take as a yes. So, I walk gingerly over that way.

Reluctantly, I glance back, and she follows, keeping her distance. I can practically hear her breathing through her nose, forcing air in and out of her lungs.

Once she's in front of me again, I say, "Look, about the other day."

"When you were a fucking asshole and tried to sabotage my meeting?"

I nod, lightly. "Yes, that is the day to which I am referring."

"Do you have any idea how important that was to me?"

"I may have realized afterward, and my behavior had nothing…"

She finally just lets loose. "Why would you not want me to work with Dexter? What the fuck do you have against me? And measure your words carefully or I will put these pointy-toe shoes right through your fucking dick."

Jesus Christ.

I wince a little. "Can we refrain from the dick kicking please? He has a lot of good years left in him down there."

She points a finger in my face. "Don't make jokes right now. It's not fucking funny, asshole. You can't buy your way out of this shit with a cheap laugh, you little cocksucker."

I swear to God she could make a sailor blush. I start to say something else and she cuts me off.

"I looked up to you. You know that, right? You and your brothers were my heroes growing up. My best friends. You took me everywhere when you didn't have to, even though I was like a baby sister trying to tag along. All four of you protected me and glared at anyone who looked in my direction. So I just don't fucking get it. Why would you do that to me? If I was normal, I would've cried my eyes out."

I want to hug her so bad, but I don't, because she might kill me. She might break my neck or stomp on my balls.

I finally just give her the sincerest look I can muster and stare straight in her eyes. "It had nothing to do with you and I'm sorry, Harlow. I really am."

Her eyes widen and she looks like she's in a daze.

I keep going, unable to stop my train of thought. "It was a shitty thing to do and you didn't deserve it, I promise it had…"

She slams into me and wraps her arms around me so tight I can barely breathe. It almost knocks us to the ground, but I manage to keep us upright and her head presses up against my chest.

What the hell is happening right now? Is she tackling me or hugging me? No, if she were tackling me, I'd be on the ground for sure.

"You okay?" I pat her on the back a couple times.

She doesn't loosen her grip and doesn't say anything.

Finally, I say, "Jesus, what's your deal? I mean, I'll take it, but…"

She leans back, grinning. "I've never seen you apologize. Not once, for anything."

That can't be true. I tilt my head slightly to the side. "What? I apologize sometimes."

She laughs, shaking her head. "No, you really don't, ever. You're always right about everything."

I lean down and give her another hug, unable to process the weight of what she just told me. "Well, I really am sorry. It was wrong, what I did. I'm not just saying that. And I really am happy you're doing so well, like I knew you would. It makes me really proud."

"Thank you. I'm glad I didn't have to kick your ass."

I laugh. "Me too. I was seriously worried when you walked through the door." I glance over and Dexter and Abigail are both staring at us, wide-eyed.

"Good. Make them fear you, right? That's what you always told me."

"Indeed, but you take it to a whole new level."

She laughs. "Are you going to come over and have a drink with us?"

I shake my head. "No, I need to get back to work for a bit. This was enough excitement for one night."

I follow her over and Penn shows up. "Need to run to the office for something. I'll holler at you tomorrow. That cool?"

"Blowing me off already?" Penn laughs and glances toward the door. "No prob. Some pussy just walked in, so I'll be busy anyway."

I glance over, and strangely, I have no desire to even stick around and talk to the girls with him. "See you guys at the office tomorrow."

Penn wastes no time walking over to the three women. Dex, Abigail, and Harlow wave bye as I head out the door.

WHEN I GET to my floor, I head back to my office. I can't even remember what I came here for now, it was just so awkward I had to get the hell out of there. Surely, I apologize when I fuck up. Don't I?

No, you really don't.

Well, it's probably because I'm rarely wrong, but I did fuck up with Harlow. It was shitty. It's just... Anytime Paisley is around I lose my fucking mind. Her and Decker in the same building with me is a recipe for disaster. It's no excuse, but it is what it is.

Paisley.

Part of me wants her to just go back to New York and get the hell out of my life, and another part of me never wants her out of my sight. All these old feelings I thought I'd suppressed are bubbling back up, fast, and it's agony.

I need to get some air and think through a few cases, so I head up to the rooftop. It's the perfect place to ponder shit and form strategies when the city is all lit up. I love going up there at night when nobody else is around.

I take the stairs two at a time and push through the door... *Fuck.*

Really? Really universe?

What the hell is she doing here?

Paisley stands there, leaned over the guard rail, and she looks incredible. The pale moonlight highlights her high cheek bones and perfect bone structure. Her hair is down, flowing over her shoulders and she's still in her work dress. It's red with a zipper up the side, with matching red pumps.

Thoughts of yanking her dress up over her ass and bending her over the rail fill my mind, and I have to think about something else because the urge is so damn strong. Every memory of us crashes into my brain. The walks, the kissing, the holding hands through the streets of Manhattan and talking about how we'd run the world one day. Her talking about babies and how we'd get engaged and have a huge wedding. That was all she ever wanted, to have my kids and be my wife, when the time was right. She wanted to take care of our family. She wanted it more than being an attorney.

I turn around to leave.

At the same time, she looks back at me and mumbles, "Fuck."

Damn it.

I walk over there. I don't know why. Maybe it's because I'm hard-headed and this is my firm and I'll walk wherever I want. Maybe it's because I still love her and I don't want her out of my sight, even though I can barely stomach being around her.

The second I get over there, she starts right past me, like I don't even exist.

Before I know what I'm doing, I reach out and grab her arm.

She stares down at my hand then back up at me. "Let go." Her words come through her teeth.

"No." *Who the fuck am I right now?* It's like I have no control over my body or my words.

Her eyes widen. "I said let go of my fucking arm, Donavan."

I just stare at her, lost in those light blue eyes, even if they're glaring right at me. She yanks with her elbow, but I don't let go.

Her face heats up. She goes to say something, and I pull her into me and slam my mouth down on hers. She fights against it for a moment, but I shove my tongue against her mouth and her entire body relaxes in my arms. Her lips are reluctant for a split-second, but then they part and it's like we're back at Columbia all over again.

I put both palms on her face and her arms hook around my neck and our tongues roll and dance, there in the moonlight, with skyscrapers jutting up all around us. The kiss intensifies and my hands slide to her ass and I dig my fingers in. Fuck me, I've missed Paisley Williams so damn much. She was always the only woman for me.

I suck down her neck and my cock grows rock-hard up against her stomach. No matter how hard I kiss her, no matter how hard I feel her pressed against me, I want more. I want to be closer, fused together, until we're one person.

She grinds back against me, rolling her hips, trying to push into me as hard as I'm pushing into her.

I lean back and stare at her for a brief second, how innocent she looks, and I shake my head. "Fuck." Our lips meet again, and she mumbles something, but I can't make it out.

I pull her skirt up to her waist and knead her bare ass with my hands as I push her up against the railing. Her hands go to my belt and start unbuckling.

Suddenly, I hear the door shove open and a light comes on over on the side of the building.

"Shit!" I yank her dress back down and she shimmies it the rest of the way while I buckle my belt.

The regular security officer comes out, pulling a pack of cigarettes from his pocket. He looks up and it looks like he's just seen a ghost. "Oh, man, uhh, sorry, Mr. Collins."

Part of me wants to tear into him, but Paisley is standing right next to me and she'd lose her shit. I bite back everything I want to yell.

Before I can say anything else, Paisley is already on her way toward him. "It's okay." She doesn't turn back to look at me at all. "Perfect timing. You can walk me to my car."

"Umm, okay, Ms. Williams." He looks at me and shrugs like *I'm sorry*.

I stand there, out of breath from the kiss, face probably smeared with lipstick, watching Paisley walk away from me. She's the queen of mixed signals right now. I should be glad. I shouldn't have done that; kissed her. She just felt so fucking good, and now I feel like I'm lighter than air. Things are too complicated though. It'll never be how it was, especially after everything I've put her through.

She may still be attracted to me, but inside, I know she hates my guts, like most people.

I don't expect her to even turn around and look at me, but the security guard goes through the door first, and after he does, just before she goes through, she turns back and glances at me.

I flash her a smirk, because that's just who I am.

I don't see it, but I hear her huff out a loud, audible sigh before the door closes.

She may be pissed off and hurt, but I know that look on her face. I felt it in her body, the way she kissed me back, the way she grinded up against my cock.

She still wants me. She can't help herself. It was meant to be, and despite all the bullshit, no matter how big of an asshole I was, you can't fuck with fate when it has plans for you.

I shake my head. No, I'm not giving up on this.

I thought it was over, but it's not. Seven years later... Paisley Williams is still mine.

PAISLEY

Ugh! That smug bastard!

I shoot Dad a text that I'm going for a run and not to wait up for me. It's been at least ten years since I went for a jog along Lake Michigan, but it's spring, the weather is warm enough, and I have to burn off all this Donavan Collins frustration before it eats me alive.

I start off slow, finding my pace.

That kiss.

Double ugh!

How the hell does he do that? Make me forget everything for a moment so he can get what he wants? I should've decked him, grabbing me like that, with his big, strong hands, and rough fingers digging into my arm.

Why the hell does him doing that turn my legs to Jell-O?

The kiss was amazing. I wanted to float off into the clouds and it brought all the good times back to the forefront of my mind. How can I hate and love someone so much at the same time? He's so confusing.

I pass by a couple jogging the other way and stare out at the lake. It's so big and ominous with the moon sitting right above, it's light sparkling across the horizon.

He didn't come to my mother's funeral. Didn't say anything to my family after graduation and she died a week later. Just disappeared. Who does that? We were like the family he never had. We would come home and him and my mom would hang out. I wouldn't even have to be there. When the cancer diagnosis came in, I thought my dad was going to fall apart. Donavan was the glue that held my whole family together, through all of it, all the tough times, and then he just ghosted.

All I wanted was him, and he wasn't there.

How could I ever possibly forgive him for something like that?

Then he does things like he did at the cemetery. I had no idea he'd been going to see Mom.

Why didn't he do that for me? Why didn't he come back for *me*? Yeah, I would've made his life miserable for a while, but I would've taken him back.

Not now, though.

Fuck you, Donavan Collins. It's not happening. I don't give a shit how good he kisses me on a rooftop in the moonlight.

I need to get out of this city, but I can't. I have to take care of Grandma and Grandpa. I have to make sure Dad lands on his feet and finds some new creative spark for him to focus on, so he doesn't go stir crazy at home. If I'm being honest with myself, I'm going to be here for a while. It's not going to be a short stay.

One thing I definitely know is that I need to stay far away from Donavan. I thought I could do this; be at the firm and I wouldn't see him. Different departments and all that. Maybe I can talk to Dexter, volunteer for every single assignment that involves being out of the office. Maybe I can even talk him into letting me work from home some. Tell him I need to take care of my grandparents. He'd buy it and it's not untrue. The private investigator would see it and report back. I know he's been following me. I caught a glimpse of him on my street the other day, parked at the end of the road.

Everything was perfect last week when Donavan was at court and dealing with clients. I get the feeling he's not around all that often, probably because he micromanages every single case the firm gets. It'll be fine. It was just a fluke that he came up there on the rooftop the one night I stayed late.

It's settled. I'll just stay away from him and I'll be fine. Do my job, what I came here to do, for my family.

One thing is certain, though. I still have feelings for him. I can't make those go away, no matter how hard I try.

I don't trust myself not to end up in his bed, and it could make this whole ordeal a million times worse in the end.

PAISLEY

THE WIND BLOWS through my hair as Dexter and I head to Wells Covington's mansion. His car is a Chevelle, fully restored, and it's incredible. The vibration from the floorboard reverberates through my entire body as billboards whip past us on the way out of the city.

It's been a few days since the rooftop incident with Donavan and my stomach has been in a knot since. It felt so good and so wrong at the same time. I'm a mess, and I really should try to rid myself of the memory because I have bigger issues at hand.

I handled all of Covington's holdings when I was at my old firm, and Bennett Cooper is intensely aware of the relationship between Covington and Dexter. Right now, The Hunter Group is only handling a few of Covington's smaller, newer companies, but that could change any day. Cooper might act confident, but I can read him as well as anyone else. Where Covington goes, people follow. It's just the nature of Wall Street.

We pull up to the massive gate with a gold WC right in the middle.

Dexter shakes his head. "This fucking place."

I laugh. "Wells will be Wells."

"Truer words have never been spoken." Dexter leans out the window and barks at the butler on the other end to open up.

Both the gates swing inward, like we're heading into *Jurassic Park,* and the Chevelle rumbles through and snakes around a few turns. The place is huge and opulent, but my mind is still on Donavan and damn it... Why am I still thinking about him?

"What's on your mind?"

I turn my head to face Dexter with a blank look on my face. "Huh?" Shit, does he know I'm daydreaming about his brother?

"You just look indifferent. Most people have a different reaction when they see this place."

I exhale a sigh of relief. "Oh." I shrug. "You ever been to the Hamptons?"

He shakes his head. "No."

"Every mansion looks like this out there."

"Hmm. Makes sense."

He snakes us around a roundabout and parks right in front of the door, then turns to face me once the car comes to a stop. "So…"

Why's he being so weird? "What's up?" I hope a Donavan question isn't coming.

"I don't want to make things awkward or step on any toes."

Shit. It's about to get personal. "Look, Dexter, I…"

He cuts me off. "I've been avoiding the question, but business is business, you know?"

Wait, what? I must look like an idiot with a thousand-yard-stare, then it dawns on me what he really wants. "Oh. Yeah, I have a lot of contacts out there, in the Hamptons."

His eyes light up, and I can practically see the dollar signs in them. "I mean, you segued us perfectly to this topic, so I figured, now is the best time to take advantage."

"Look, I'll be blunt. Cooper isn't too worried about you. I mean, he is and he isn't. He knows you're going after Covington. He knows he already sent you some new businesses he acquired recently and we both concluded Covington was test-driving you and will possibly move all his holdings over to your firm."

"I don't buy it." Dex shakes his head. "The part about him not worrying. That guy latches on to anything that's his, and he doesn't give it up easy."

"Okay, here's the deal. Cooper sees things at a high level, as I'm sure you do as well. Sure, he stays close to the old money, and the material clients, but Wells isn't the wealthiest man on Wall Street. What Cooper doesn't know, and I do, because I'm on the ground, meeting with people, listening to the Street, is the way the winds are shifting. What people are thinking. What they do. And if you want Cooper's market share, you need Covington."

Dex nods, like we're on the same page.

"Everyone watches him like a hawk, because, well, he's the smartest man at what he does. They watch his holdings; they try to mimic his positions. They *listen* to him. Even if he doesn't tell them what to do."

"Absolutely agree. I went to school with Wells and I knew this is what he'd be one day. Everyone could see it. He has the brain and the drive and the work ethic. And the balls to take on enormous risks and trust his data."

"Definitely. He's your ticket to those high-priced clients, because no offense, but those people are loyal to the old ways. They like to deal in Manhattan. They like institutions that are a hundred years old, like Cooper and Associates. Not flashy firms in Chicago that have been around a decade."

Dex frowns.

648

"You pay me for the truth, not to blow smoke up your ass. I received an equity share when you hired me, I have skin in the game too."

"I like you."

I smile. The Chicago firm *is* growing on me, except for one of the brothers. I can't believe Donavan never told them about me, or introduced me to them. *Stop thinking about Donavan!* "So your ticket to those clients is through Wells. They listen to him. They won't listen to you. It's that simple. But he can get you in the room with them and give you an opportunity to pitch."

"Sounds like we have a game plan."

I nod.

"Okay, let's go in."

We both step out of the Chevelle and the butler opens the door just as we walk up the steps, like he was watching us from a camera on the other side. He leads us through the foyer, around a corner, and down a long corridor.

Dexter's head cranes around and his hands twitch slightly, like he's jittery.

I glance down at them and back up at him. "Haven't you been here before?"

"Not in this wing." He looks at me and shrugs, like he knows I notice he's nervous. "You never know what to expect with Wells."

"You think he has someone tied up right now?"

Dexter's head whips over to me, then his eyebrows waggle. "He hasn't shown me his dungeon yet, and I kinda want to see it."

I laugh. "I think he goes to clubs back in the city. He might keep it away from home." It's well-known in certain circles in Manhattan that Wells has peculiar sexual tastes and is very involved in BDSM. I think he may even own a secret club for that kind of thing. "He tried to take me to some underground place one time, but I was busy."

Dex nods. "Yeah, I'm not into that shit, but I'll admit, I'm kind of curious."

"It's natural to be curious about things." We walk a little farther and good God, does this hallway ever end?

"Like you and my brother?"

I damn near trip over a heel and stop abruptly on the tile. I don't mean to give Dex a dirty look, but it comes out that way. "What?"

He holds both hands up. "I don't know anything; it's just written all over both your faces. And judging by the way you just reacted, I was spot on."

Donavan never did tell them about me. I don't know why my heart pinches in my chest all these years later, but it does. "He never mentioned me back then. Did he?"

Dex looks like he doesn't want to upset me but doesn't want to lie either. He shakes his head. "No." He quickly holds out a hand as we continue following the butler. "I've never known him to date anyone. But, I mean, you know Donnie."

I nod. Yeah, better than I should.

"He's always been quiet. Kept to himself, unless he was yelling about something, or giving someone shit."

"Really? He was pretty social at Columbia. Always in a good mood, would talk to anybody."

"Hmm. Weird. Doesn't sound like him." He shrugs. "I don't know, maybe he just had to get away from home to open up. Having three brothers, you always had to fight for attention in our house."

"Yeah, I'm sure it was intimidating for him, with the rest of you. Trying to live up to that."

"I mean, yeah, we were hard on him sometimes." He gets this look of recognition on his face, then his lips mash into a thin line. "Picked on him more than we should've, probably. We were kids, though. I'm sure he understands."

It's not my place to say anything to Dexter, so I don't. I wish Donavan would just talk to his brothers. I can see they care about him more than he gives them credit for, and I know he cares about them too, even if he won't admit it. "I get it. We all do stuff when we're kids."

"Yeah."

The butler stops and ushers us into a massive library. We walk in and my eyes widen, and I crane my head around. It has a domed ceiling like something from Rome, with artwork scrolling across. There are floor-to-ceiling shelves lined with books, most likely all first editions. Wells is at the far end with a massive pile of them around him and he's rifling through spines.

"Collins!" He runs over and shakes Dexter's hand then turns to me. "And Ms. Williams, great to see you again, batting for the home team now."

I shrug. "It's good to be home."

"Come on, let's have a drink." He flies past both of us.

Dexter looks over at me and his eyebrows rise, then we both follow Wells.

A few minutes later, after walking the entire floor again, he leads us into his own sports bar inside his house. Wells goes behind the counter and pours three scotches neat in some rocks glasses then slides them over to us.

"What the hell were you doing back there?" says Dexter.

"Organizing my books."

"You don't have someone to do that for you?"

Wells snickers. "Not the way I can."

I glance up. "What's that mean?"

"It means I was organizing them all chronologically, as the events take place in the stories, by memory."

"Jesus." Dexter huffs out a breath. "You're fucking with us."

Wells shakes his head. "Nope. Just a little fun with my fiction. That's what I call it."

"Anyway," says Dexter. "Paisley is in a partnership role with finance, helping take some work off my plate, so I brought her along to make an introduction."

"We know each other. But you knew that already, so continue."

"No, really, that's it. Just a face to face. And a reason to drink your expensive scotch."

"Works for me," says Wells. "So, let's drink."

"Where's the bathroom in this monstrosity of a house?"

"Around the corner to the left."

Dexter gets up and walks out the door. Wells leans across the bar, eyeing me with that smirk of his. He's sizing me up, calculating things. I know exactly how he operates, and I hate it when he does this, because he usually figures out what's going on really quick.

Finally, I break the silence. "Just spit it out, asshole."

He dies laughing and shakes his head. "No, it's nothing. You're a shrewd one, though."

"What are you talking about now, Covington?"

"Oh, nothing. Just landing yourself a job at The Hunter Group." He holds both hands up. "To take care of your family, of course."

"You've been talking to Cooper. What'd he say?"

"Just that you moved home to care for your grandparents. Didn't seem happy about it. Can't believe you weaseled your way in at The Hunter Group, though. Most people couldn't pull that off."

"Yeah, well, I'm not most people. I'm good at what I do."

"That's a fact, Ms. Williams." He holds up a glass.

What does he know that he's not letting on?

"And yeah, it's true I'm not on great terms with Bennett right now."

"Understandable."

"Though I'm sure I could go back there if I wanted."

"Oh, I have no doubt about that either. Doesn't matter to me, either way I have access to your brain."

"Aww, thanks, Covington."

He grins, but his mind is miles away right now.

An awkward silence stretches between us and I've had enough. I want to get this shit moving and I need to score brownie points with Dexter to keep Donavan off my ass. "You moving the rest of your entities to Chicago or not?"

I say it right as he takes a sip and he damn near chokes when he laughs. "Fuck, you cut right to the chase when your boss is in the bathroom, don't you?"

I shrug. "No need to dance around the topic. You don't know until you ask."

His lips curl up into a smile, almost like the damn Grinch. "I like you. I've always liked you. Fuck it, why not?"

"Good, it's settled then." I know for a fact this isn't an impromptu decision and he's run the numbers a million different ways, done thousands of calculations, but I go with it anyway.

About that time, Dexter walks through the door. We both turn to stare at him.

He gets about five feet away and stops in his tracks. "What the fuck? I got something on my face?"

Wells walks over and stands in front of him. "Congratulations. You need to hire some new employees because I'm a demanding son of a bitch."

Dexter's entire face morphs into a devilish smile as the recognition sets in.

"Ms. Williams convinced me to bring the rest of my business under your purview while you were wicking your weed in my marble bathroom."

"You fucking with me?" Dexter's eyes roll over to mine, then back to Wells.

"I never joke about money. And you'd better make me more of it or I'll be gone."

I watch Dexter. He tries to play it cool, but inside I bet he's like a damn slot machine that just hit the jackpot. Bells and buzzers going off.

Wells walks us back to the front of the house and we both shake his hand at the door.

Dexter says, "I'll start getting contracts drawn up."

"Sounds great. Bring tequila next time."

"You have your own fucking bar."

"Don't be a cheap-ass on me, Collins."

We all laugh, and I follow Dexter back to the Chevelle. Once we're inside, and Wells has disappeared through the doors, Dexter turns to me. "Just earned yourself a nice fucking bonus."

Perfect. Mission accomplished. Things are looking great and Donavan can kiss my ass.

DONAVAN

As soon as she passes the door, my arm shoots out and I yank Pais into the breakroom. Craning my head around, I make sure nobody is watching, and pull her farther over to the corner.

Her eyes widen immediately, then one of the hardest glares I've ever seen follows as her brain processes what just happened. "What are you doing?" She yanks her arm away from me and smooths down her black skirt.

"Been busy the past few days." I lean in, closing the distance between us. "I'm not leaving things the way they were the other night."

Paisley sighs and looks away, maybe to see if anyone is watching us, or maybe because old feelings are coming up and it's tough to see my face. It doesn't matter. When I want something, I get it. It's that simple.

"Was a moment of weakness. Won't happen again."

"Bullshit."

Her head turns and our eyes meet. She shakes her head, just slightly. "Donavan, don't…"

"We're going to dinner tonight."

She lets out a light gasp that almost sounds like a laugh. "Not gonna happen. In what world do you think you'll get off that easy?"

I force her up against the wall with my chest, so that our faces are inches apart and she has nowhere to go, completely caged in. "Keep fighting this, but you're the one who'll get off easy." I grip her ass in my palm and give it a light squeeze. "Repeatedly."

She shakes her head again, but her eyes tell a different story. She's aroused and she knows it. Pais goes to say something, and I grip her ass even harder, digging my fingers in a little more. Finally, she mumbles, "I can't. It's not a good…"

I dig my fingers in even harder. "Keep telling me no, Pais. Watch what happens." I knead her ass in my hand, then slide it slowly up the back of her skirt.

"Donavan…" My name rolls off her tongue as a breathy whisper.

"Keep fighting this." I lean down next to her ear. "I want you to. It's not any fun if you don't."

Her hips roll toward my hand, despite all the reservations I know are coursing through her brain. It's an involuntary reaction, but I can sense she's holding back and it's taking everything she has to not give in.

My hand slides up a little higher, over her panties. "I'll drag you out there and kiss you in front of everyone. I dare you to give me a fucking reason. You're wet right now, just thinking about it."

"Shit," she says on a sigh.

That's right, Paisley. Submit, like you always do.

"You're not going to give up, are you?"

I lean next to her ear. "Not a single fucking chance of that happening."

I wait for her to do what she does best—negotiate—because I know it's coming next.

Her eyes harden and roll up to meet mine. "One drink. Happy hour."

My cock strains against my slacks when I see the fire in her eyes. How was I so stupid to let this one get away? We were always perfect for each other, no matter how much I tried to convince myself otherwise. It's always been *her* and nobody else.

I grin, amused at her feeble attempt, and shake my head. My fingers dig into her ass so hard it might leave bruises. "This isn't a negotiation. Dinner. I'll be at your Dad's house at six thirty."

Her eyes flutter closed, then roll up to meet mine and she nods, just barely.

I release her ass and walk off.

As I head toward the door, she exhales a light gasp, and I hear the heavy breaths leaving her slender, lithe body.

I smile where she can't see.

Fight it all you want, Pais. This isn't over between us. Not by a long shot.

PAISLEY

FUCK. Fuck. Fuck.

I can still feel his fingertips where he grabbed me. God, it feels so damn good too. I wanted to rip his suit off and climb him like a rock wall.

Even after everything he's done, I still want him so damn bad any time he steps in a room. I can already see it playing out now. I go to dinner. He tells me everything and I sit there and still fawn over him, like we're back in college, me practically worshipping the ground he walks on, forgiving him for everything.

There's just too much history there, and everything he's done... I don't trust myself with him. Why couldn't he have just done things differently? We could be happily married already with a family and he threw it all away like it was nothing.

I stare around the room, hyper-aware that I'm still breathing heavily.

I have to put a stop to this before it gets out of hand, and I know just what to do to keep him away from me.

I march through the door and straight to Decker's office. His assistant, Quinn, shoves the book she's studying under her desk when she sees me approach.

I smile and gesture toward his office. The door is closed. "Does he have a minute?"

Quinn reaches for the phone on her desk and holds up a hand, showing off her huge emerald engagement ring. She puts the phone to her ear. "Ms. Williams needs a word. Is it a good time?" She nods at no one in particular, then looks up at me. "Okay, I'll send her in."

That's all I need to hear, and I head toward his door and turn the knob. When I walk in, he's perched behind his desk and Tate sits in a chair off to the side of him, like I interrupted their conversation.

I stop in my tracks and glance back and forth at both of them. My eyes stop on Tate. "Sorry, I can come back."

Decker shakes his head. "No need."

I stare back and forth again, uneasy. "It's kind of a private thing. Would be better one on one…"

"Tate's a partner. It's fine. What is it?"

I hold up both hands. "I just… I don't want to upset anyone."

Both of them lean in toward me, suddenly taking much more of an interest.

I shake my head. "It's over already, I just…"

Tate's look is far more inquisitive and skeptical than Decker's.

"Why don't you just tell us what's on your mind," says Decker.

"It's not a…" I pause to try and gather my thoughts. It's not really necessary. This is all part of a performance. I need to look reluctant. "Look, I'm sure you have your PI looking into me."

Tate's eyebrows quirk up.

Decker stares, seemingly amused. "Why would you think that?"

I shrug. "It's what I would do."

Tate nods, just slightly. "I like her."

I glance to her then back at Decker. "Just please reserve judgment. I'm sure he hasn't brought you anything, *yet*."

"Just spit it out, Ms. Williams. Are you insinuating our PI will find something, if he *were* investigating you, which I'm not saying he is?"

I let out a sigh. I've built it up enough already, so I need to just get it out. "Your firm represented a company that sued my father. They ran him out of business."

Decker's eyes widen and his face turns a light shade of red. "And you're just telling us this now?"

I stare down at the ground. "I really needed the job. I'm sorry."

"Bullshit."

I glance up quickly. It wasn't the response I expected.

His jaw clenches. "This is about Donavan. Has his name written all over it. You could've found a job at any firm in the city, with your resume." He pauses and collects himself. "What else is Rick going to bring me?"

I shake my head. "Nothing, I swear."

His eyes are two dark slits and I can practically feel them burning a hole through my chest. It seems all the Collins men have that look down to an art form.

I swallow, hard. "I came to your firm because I wanted to work for the best, that was available to me anyway. It's the truth, I swear. Call me narcissistic or whatever you want. I can't not be the best at what I do. It's a personal thing."

"And this lawsuit with your father?"

"It's all wrapped up and settled now, I just knew you'd find it eventually if you dug hard enough and I wanted to tell you first. I couldn't stay in New York. I *had* to move back here for…" I take a deep breath, for dramatic effect. "My grandparents. They're elderly. And to help my dad land on his feet after the lawsuit. I swear."

I see Tate's eyes on me in my peripheral vision. She's studying, watching every little move I make, every facial tic, measuring my breaths. I've been in courtrooms with wolves and she's one of them, no doubt about it.

Decker exhales a long breath. "Why didn't you tell us about the lawsuit in the beginning?"

"You would've sent me right out the door. I would've never had a chance."

Tate still sits there, observing.

Decker mulls it over in his brain, making logical sense of this. I can see the wheels spinning in his head. Finally, he nods. "Okay. I get it." He steeples his fingers on his desk. "I understand why you didn't tell us up front. But..." He pauses. "If Rick comes to me with anything other than what you just told me, that's it. Your contract with the firm is terminated. Are we clear?"

I nod. "Absolutely, and you have nothing to worry about."

I can still feel Tate's eyes on me. She's skeptical, but she won't say anything until I leave the room. An ominous feeling takes over my body, knowing she's running a million calculations through her head and they all have to do with me. In a weird way, I can relate to her. I think I recognize a kindred spirit and she would worry me a little if I ever had to go up against her in court. She's formidable.

"Okay, well, I just came here to tell you that. Thank you for your time." I turn to walk out.

"Ms. Williams?"

I do a half turn, so I'm looking at him from the side. "Yes?"

"You'd better be on your damn A game."

Tate still sits there, quiet.

I nod and start to turn once more.

"Oh and stay away from Donavan for a while. He won't like this at all, and I have to tell him. Leave a little before five. I don't give a shit what you're working on. It can wait."

"Yes, sir." I walk out.

Once I'm past the threshold, I breathe out a sigh of relief.

At least Donavan will stop pursuing me and bringing up all these old feelings and desires.

I win. Again.

DONAVAN

It's the end of the day and I can't get out of this building fast enough. My heart races every time I think about Paisley. Squeezing her ass, the look in her eyes. Yeah, she thinks she's done with me, but this is a new beginning.

I still have it so bad for this woman I bump a meeting with a client to tomorrow. I never do that, ever. Fuck, what is she doing to me?

I wanted to kiss her so damn bad in the breakroom. She's completely submissive, like she always was, any time I touch her or so much as look in her direction even.

I glance down at my watch and the minutes tick by like each one is an hour. I can't remember the last time I left at five o'clock on the dot. It's probably never happened, but today it is.

I'm taking Paisley to dinner.

That familiar rush floods my veins, nerves, excitement. It's like I'm sixteen all over again with a crush on a girl.

At four fifty-eight on the dot, my desk phone rings.

I shake my head.

Don't answer it. It can wait.

I ignore it. It stops for a moment, then rings again.

Take the hint, motherfucker.

It stops then rings again, and I glance down. It's Decker's goddamn mobile number. I'll never get rid of him. He'll blow up my cell phone the rest of the night, and clearly he knows I'm in the office or he would've called it first.

"Shit." I pick up the phone and put it to my ear. "What do you want?"

"Need to see you in my office in five."

"I have somewhere…"

"Non-negotiable. Be there." He hangs up on me.

I cradle the phone and glare down at it, nostrils flaring. "Asshole."

This shit better not take long. I gather up all my stuff and shove it in my briefcase, then start toward his office. Quinn's still there, but I walk past her without acknowledging her because I don't have time for Decker and whatever anal-retentive shit he has to say. I have an hour and a half until I pick up Paisley, take her to dinner, then kiss the breath right out of her lungs. Maybe even eat her pussy, if I play my cards right.

I storm into his office and he's just sitting down, like he came in specifically for this.

"What is it? I'm running behind…"

"Just sit down for a minute."

I walk up to the chair in front of his desk and set my briefcase down but remain standing. "I'm serious, I don't have time…"

"Sit. Please. I'll make it as fast as I can."

Jesus Christ, he said please. That means it's bad news. Decker doesn't soften you up or utter that word unless shit is about to hit the fan.

I take a seat because I know his stubborn ass won't say anything until he's steered the conversation exactly where he needs to and everything in the room is just as he wants it.

He starts off slowly, flattering me, doing everything he can to lighten the tension in the room. My hands squeeze the arm rests on his chair until the whites of my knuckles show. Partially, because I know exactly what he's doing, and partially because I have a pretty good idea of where this is headed.

He finally drops the bomb, tells me all about Paisley coming into his office. Tells me exactly what time she came to the office, which uncoincidentally, was the second she left the breakroom.

Heat rushes into my face and I finally point right at him. "I told you. And I guarantee she's pissed about that lawsuit, but you believed her when she said she's just fine with it."

Decker sits there, shaking his head, like he knows what's coming and he's bracing for it. "Get it all out. Come on, just say it all instead of sitting back on your throne of judgment." He mocks me with his tone.

I stand up and pace back and forth. I can't believe he let this happen. "What is there to say? I told you—"

His eyes angle up to mine and he cuts me off. "You done yet?"

I stop mid-stride and my jaw ticks. What a fucking asshole. Just stay calm. I shrug. "You've made up your mind about whatever you're going to do, so why did you even call me in here?" Does he think he'll get my approval or something? Or that he can win me over? I'll never understand him.

"The lawsuit is settled. I already looked at it. We did what we had to for the client. Every law firm in the country would've done the same thing. She knows it's not personal, better than anyone."

"Okay."

"What do you mean okay? I know you have more to say than that."

I shrug again. "It doesn't matter. You'll do anything to prove you're right, instead of admit you made a mistake."

"Grow up."

"I'm the only one thinking like an adult in this office." I pause and inhale a huge breath, anything to keep from melting down. I take a step back and look away, so I don't want to punch Decker in his goddamn mouth.

"What's the deal with you two?"

"What?" I whip around.

"Tate said there's a history there. What's going on?"

I finally walk back over and take a seat, knowing the date tonight won't happen so I have all the time in the world. I give Decker the Cliffs notes version of our relationship, going all the way back to college. Why? I don't know. Maybe I did need to just get everything out, because it felt like an unnecessary burden just lifted off my shoulders.

"Why didn't you ever tell us about her if you were that serious?"

"Had my reasons."

Decker nods and thankfully doesn't press for more information I don't want to give.

As I sit there and talk to him, my mind clears, and all the dots start to connect. I swear to God dealing with Paisley Williams, how she is now, is a fucking game of three-dimensional chess. She did this to put distance between us. It was her trump card. She's using work to deal with personal shit, and it had nothing to do with her dad. I made her nervous in the breakroom. She's afraid of being hurt. She knew she'd have to wait a while to break this news to the firm. If she did it during her interview, even Decker wouldn't be dumb enough to hire her. I gave her the perfect opportunity to make this move.

"You okay?"

I glance up, and Decker's staring right at me. "Yeah, I'm fine. Just fuck... I wish you'd listen to me once in a while."

"I *do* listen to you. Your personal shit clouded your judgment. Dex says she's been killing it. A real asset to the firm."

I snicker in the most sarcastic manner possible, unable to tell Decker my professional concerns are gone, because if I do that, he wins. "Or she wants you to think that."

"Everything's a damn conspiracy with you. Sometimes people are just people and don't have hidden agendas. She seems like she really wants to be here, and her reasons are convincing."

"Keep telling yourself that." I stand up. "Maybe normal people, but not in our world. Everyone wants something and if we don't fight, they'll take everything."

"I protect what's ours."

I gather my briefcase and walk toward the door, then stop before I exit. "Right. Like you protected our name. Used to be right out there." I point to the entrance wall, beyond Quinn's desk, right where it says THE HUNTER GROUP. "Now, it isn't."

I walk out before he can say anything else.

By the time I take three steps, the conversation with Decker has already faded far away from my mind. The wheels are churning with nothing but Paisley Williams on a loop, over and over. What's my next move?

I need to do something, and I need to do what she least expects. She's not going to fucking beat me. It won't happen. Her motivation for going to Decker was to get out of our date, to put distance between us. I feel it in my bones.

So, she's going to get a goddamn date. Nice try, Pais, but I'm not losing this time.

You're mine. See you at six-thirty.

PAISLEY

I PULL down the street to Dad's house, practically bouncing in my seat. I found a perfect condo, right down the road from work with a gorgeous view of the lake. It just happened to be the last place I viewed after I left a little early, on Decker's orders.

I pull into Dad's driveway and can't even remember the drive home because I couldn't stop thinking about the condo. What's even better is they'll let me rent, month-to-month, until I make a decision about buying it. It's perfect. If my situation changes, I can bail at any time. If I need to stay longer, I can buy it and flip it for a profit when it's time to leave. If I ever need to leave.

I grab my phone and check it on the way to the front door.

Six forty-five.

I was supposed to meet with Donavan fifteen minutes ago, but that's not happening. Despite the fact I got what I wanted, my stomach still tightens. All I can think about is what could've been with us, and no matter how hard I try to suppress it, it's still there, in the deep recesses of my mind, in the corners of every cell in my body, refusing to let me flush it from my system.

You'll finally have your own place.

I do my best to focus on my happiness and good fortune, and rid myself of that strong, possessive hand gripping my ass in the breakroom.

"Dad, you'll never believe…" I turn the knob, open the door, and freeze in my tracks. My jaw has to be on the floor, but honestly, I have no idea what my face looks like right now. All I can do is stare at the scene in front of me.

Dad, in his recliner, glaring at the couch. On the couch sits Donavan fucking Collins, giving the glare right back to Dad. I don't know if I've ever been this uncomfortable in my life.

663

"What the...?" My brows knit together and the only other word that seems to make its way from my lips is just, "Huh?"

Donavan smiles the second he sees me, and I know he's furious on the inside and doing everything he can to hold back. It's so awkward he looks like one of those Stepford wives, faking their way through the day.

He stands up before I can embarrass myself any more and says, "You ready?"

What. The. Hell. Is. Happening. Here.

"Ready?"

"You forget about our date?"

"Our date?" I walk over and drop my keys on a side table.

"Yeah, I'm taking you to dinner." He walks over, fake-grinning, and talks through his teeth. "Grab your jacket. It might get chilly later."

Dad hasn't said a word. I glance over at him and he's still staring lasers at Donavan's back, then his eyes shift to me and I know I'll have to explain later, but I can't right now. Not with Donavan in the room.

Donavan walks out the front door and I follow without grabbing my jacket. As he's walking down the stoop, I reach for his forearm.

"Did Decker talk to you yet?"

His jaw clenches ever so slightly, telling me what I need to know, but I wait for him to respond anyway.

He nods, still smiling. "Yeah." He turns and heads to the passenger side of his car. I didn't even see it on the side of the road in front of the house when I pulled in. He reaches for the handle like he's going to open the door for me.

"You still want to do this?"

He freezes, then turns back around and storms toward me. He doesn't stop until he's all up in my personal space, just like in the breakroom. My heart thumps against my rib cage and I hear it beating in my ears. My throat goes dry, palms clam up.

His eyes narrow on me, and the smile disappears. "Nice try, Pais." He grits his teeth, even though he maintains a neutral expression. "Get your jacket and let's go."

Nothing good can come from this. I should tell him to fuck off, walk inside, and slam the door. It's what I should do. If I go with him, he wins. He gets his way.

God, that kiss the other night, and his hand on my ass.

How, how, how for the love of all things holy does he do this to me? I make stupid decisions constantly when he's in my vicinity. Why is the universe doing this to me? Why can't all our problems go away and we could just be together like a normal couple?

My brain screams "No!" the entire time, as I walk inside the door, grab my jacket, and tell Dad I'll be home later.

Donavan Collins has turned me into a damn zombie.

HE MAKES the turn onto N State Street and I already know where we're going, and he's an asshole for doing it.

I look over and damn it, the bridge of my nose tingles. I swear to God…

Do not fucking cry in front of him. Get your shit together.

"Donavan, don't." I can't even look at him while I say it.

His eyes dart over to mine, but he doesn't respond. Just keeps on down the road.

Maybe this is payback for what I did to him at the office, but this is way over the line, and he knows it. I shouldn't expect anything less from him. He's always done whatever he wanted, no matter who he hurt in the process, and part of me is actually glad he's still being himself. Maybe it'll make it easier to get this shit over with and suppress all the old feelings filtering back up to the surface.

The closer the neon sign gets as we approach, the more my stomach turns, until it's balled in a knot and I can barely breathe.

I reach for his arm and the fear and hurt has to be apparent in my eyes. I'd do anything to get him to end this right now, though. Anything else, I could handle. "Donavan, please…"

He glances over at me. "It'll be fine. I promise." He pulls in to the valet.

I just sit there as the valet opens my door, and I haven't even unbuckled my seat belt yet. I just stare at the huge neon sign that reads GIBSONS STEAK-FISH.

Donavan walks around to my side of the car and leans down. He holds out his hand. "Come on."

I shake my head. "Take me somewhere else or I'm going home."

"She wouldn't want…"

I point a finger at him and bare my teeth. "Don't tell me what she would or wouldn't have wanted."

Donavan takes a step back, and glances around. "Please, Pais? I need this, for us."

How the hell does he do that? Lighten the mood and look so vulnerable like that, in the blink of an eye. I think that's part of his allure. He always looks so pissed off, like he hates the world, that it just softens you when he shows you who he really is, even if it's for a split-second. It's a manipulation tactic. I'm sure of it, but I fall for it every damn time.

I glance around, and a car honks behind us. The valet taps his foot, but he's still trying to be polite, most likely because he wants a tip.

Reluctantly, I unbuckle the seat belt and climb out of the car.

We walk to the curb and I stand there, staring at the door. It's like my shoes are cinder blocks and I can't move.

"Why are you doing this to me?" I turn to him. "Is it because of what I did at the office? This some sort of sick retribution?"

He shakes his head and looks at me like I'm from outer space. "Of course not, Jesus, what do you think…" He stops himself. "Yeah, I'm not happy about that, but it has nothing to do with *this*."

I square up in front of him. "Then can we be honest with each other, for at least two minutes? What is this?" I hold up a hand in front of the famous Chicago steakhouse. "You know it was her favorite, where she always made us come, even when we told her it was overrated and nothing but a tourist hotspot where celebrities eat. You don't even like the food here."

"I'm not here for the food." His neck tenses and his eyes sear into mine.

"Why then?"

"I just…" He sighs and looks up at the sky before returning his gaze to mine.

Why is it so hard for him to just say what he's thinking? It's always a big dramatic event, trying to get the words out of him.

"I know you'll never go on another date with me again, and I… I just want a small piece of what I threw away. Just one more time, for an hour, I want to remember what it felt like, being with you."

Fuck me. Did he really just do that? Am I actually swooning on the inside? Who is this guy in front of me?

The Donavan you were with for three years, before he crushed you.

This whole thing feels so awkward and forced, but finally, I sigh. I think about what Mom would've wanted, because it's really not about me. She would've wanted Dad and me to still come here, talk about her, laugh. It's the one thing we haven't been able to do. Dad will kill me if he finds out I came here again, with Donavan of all people. I need to just go in. Maybe, a part of me, wants a small piece of what we had too. Just one more time.

I nod, and Donavan leads the way to the door.

He checks us in for our reservation and they lead us back to a two-top in the middle of everything, but there aren't many people around. It's kind of slow, actually.

We have a seat and order drinks, and surprisingly, it's not as bad as I thought it'd be. It's actually kind of nice, and it's so weird, but it's almost like I feel my mom smiling at us. Then again, she never knew what Donavan did, so of course she'd be smiling.

Dad thinks she still looks down on us, and I love going to her grave every year and remembering her, but when you're dead you're dead. I know she's not really with us, and yet this whole thing still feels very spiritual. I've never experienced anything like it. My brain tells me it's just chemicals firing in my body, years of evolution focused on survival, passed down from my great grandparents a thousand times over.

"What are you thinking about?"

"Huh?" My eyes fly up to meet Donavan's.

"You were smiling, and I'm positive it wasn't for me."

I can't stop the laugh that parts my lips, because he delivers the line so dry. "You're still as blunt as ever." I narrow my gaze on his. "And don't ask stupid questions you already know the answer to."

"Yeah, I…" He stops for a moment, gauging my reaction to what he's about to say, proceeding with caution. "I think about her a lot still."

I expect hurt, anger, sadness, all of them to overwhelm me, like back in the car, but it doesn't. My limbs relax, and I think it was just getting through the door that was the hard part. It seems so silly now.

We always came here for big occasions, celebrations. My brain tells me I should scream at him to stop talking about her, but I can't. Despite the absolute bullshit he pulled, I know in my heart he loved her. You can't fake something like that for three years. "I'm sure you do."

His eyebrows rise.

"I'm being serious, D. I know how you felt about her and how she felt about you, okay?"

"Thanks for that, Pais. I mean it."

I nod.

"So, your brother talked to you?" I can't look up at him, so I pretend to peruse the menu I know by heart and mumble, "How'd that go?"

"I imagine you know exactly how it went."

I can't help but smile at the way he says it, but I keep my eyes down. "The picture in my head is pretty clear."

The waiter stops by the table and drops off two rocks glasses full of Glenlivet, neat. I wait for him to leave and take a sip. It tastes amazing and the warm liquid heats up my chest on the way down.

"I probably could've pictured it even clearer if I'd known anything about them before I came to work there."

Donavan stares back at me like *we're really gonna go there?*

Yes, we are. You wanted this date, remember?

He grins. "Doesn't the mystery make the story better?"

I shake my head. "Not. One. Bit."

He takes a sip of his own scotch and sighs. "Yeah, I'm sure it doesn't."

"I just want to know why? Did you have another girlfriend or something back in Chicago? The one who got to actually meet your family?"

"God no, you were enough to put up with."

"Hey!" I reach over and flick his arm, harder than I intend to. My eyes widen. "Shit, sorry, it was just supposed…"

"Damn, woman." He mocks me, shaking his arm like I might've broken a bone.

I know he's using humor to deflect the conversation, which means I need to make him even more uncomfortable and press harder. I have no earthly clue why, but this is just how we've always operated. It comes natural to us.

"Well, maybe you should tell me why."

The vein on his neck bulges and he tugs at his tie, loosening it a little. "I just… I told you a lot of stuff about *me*, and it was all true, but there was a reason I never really talked about or took you to meet my family, okay?"

"Which is?"

"Fuck, this feels like a counseling session."

"You owe me the truth, Donavan. I deserve it, don't I?"

He stares for a long moment that feels like an eternity. "Yeah." He exhales a breath. "Yeah. You do."

I wave an arm forward like *continue.*

"My brothers and I, it's complicated. It's like I love them and hate them at the same time. And I don't like to complain about it, because I don't like to complain about shit I can't change."

"That's not an answer."

"Yeah it is. It just lacks the details you want."

"Then give me the details."

"Look, I didn't introduce you to them, because... Fuck... I didn't want to see you measuring me against them. I already got that shit my whole childhood, I didn't want the woman I love doing it too."

It's not lost on me that he just said "love" in the present tense. It's also not lost on me that my heart just redlined in my chest as he said it, and at the fact I know he's aware he said it and he didn't correct himself.

What the hell is happening right now?

"So, you just thought, I love this woman, she's the one I want to marry and have kids with one day, and maybe I can just keep her a secret from my family and they'll never have to interact?"

He shakes his head. "It was just the timing. I planned to do it all one day, I just... It was all supposed to happen different than what it did."

"Okay, so tell me the utopian version of how your life should've played out."

He shrugs. "That's easy. My plan was all mapped out in my head. I graduate number one in my class from Columbia, and stroll back home to Chicago the best, with the best girl in the world, and shove it in all their faces for picking on me, talking down to me, treating me like I was just an annoyance, like they were all better than me and I'd never live up to the Collins name."

My face heats up. "So that was your big master plan? Graduate number one from an Ivy League school and walk me into your parents' house with a shit-eating grin, and rub in their faces how much better you were? That you were the best?"

He traces the rim of his rocks glass with an index finger. "Look, I have regrets, a lot of them. I was twenty-four."

"So you can give yourself a pass at twenty-four, but you can't forgive your brothers for picking on you when you were actual children?"

He sighs. "Can we not..."

I shake my head. "You wanted a date with me. You got one." I pause for a quick moment, shaking my head. "I just, it still blows my mind. Is that why you left? Abandoned me and my family? Because I was number one in our class? Because your fucking plan didn't work out?" I lower my voice when I drop the f-bomb and glance around, but I feel like I might come out of my skin.

He looks at me and doesn't respond, just nods slightly.

I grind my teeth and bite back everything I want to unleash. I thought I'd be even madder than I am, but just the shock of something so petty seems to be taking center stage. "Couldn't you have come back home without being first in your class, without being the best and still had everything you wanted? Couldn't you have not broken my heart and shattered my life? You left me with nothing. I would've supported you through anything."

He can't even look at me and finally his eyes move to me. "I'm sorry, Pais. It was the biggest mistake of my life."

I clench my fingers around the fork on the table. I'm damn near shaking, but I know how hard it is for Donavan to apologize for anything. I really just need to let it all go. That doesn't mean I have to stick around and give in to whatever else he has planned with this little date of his. Finally, after the initial anger passes, I look down and mumble, "Okay."

"Okay? That's all you have to say?"

I start to get up and he reaches for my arm.

I yank it away from him. "Don't."

"Please, don't leave." His eyes drift up to mine.

"Why?" I talk to him through my teeth. "You did it to me. I got what I came here for."

"It's the biggest regret of my life and always will be. Just, please. I told you I'd tell you and I just did. I'm not proud of it. I just... I don't do well with this." He glances around, like someone might be listening. "Talking about things. But, I'm here and I'm doing it."

I sit down and lean back against my chair, shaking my head, putting as much distance as I can between us because I just don't understand him. Finally, I sigh, and manage to compose myself. "I mean this in the nicest way possible, Donavan, but maybe you should go see someone and get help with that."

His lips twitch, like he might lash out, a natural reaction, but then he stops himself and nods. "Maybe I should." He looks away when he says it, then his eyes fall back on mine. "I know I'm fucked up inside. I just see you and I... It hurts. Everything hurts all the time. I don't like who I am."

"You could've changed that. I would've done anything for you." I pause for a moment to collect my thoughts. As much as I want to pile it on him, he looks so sincere right now. At the same time, what does he expect me to do? Just forgive him? Like, hey, here's a get out of jail free card for turning your back on me and my family with no explanation whatsoever. "I'm just trying to picture the Donavan I knew. Yeah, you were driven, but I thought we knew everything about each other. I didn't realize you were fixated on fantasies in your head with such specific goals. You never told me number one in the class meant that much to you. I mean, yeah, I knew you wanted it. But I never thought if you didn't get it, you would seriously throw me and my family away like garbage. What was going through your head? I want to know. Did you picture us rolling down Michigan Avenue in a convertible, me on your side, but sitting just lower than you while you waved to the crowd with confetti blasting all around? Maybe a big banner that said 'Congratulations, Donavan. Number one in his Ivy League law class!', while your brothers stood on the side of the road, mouths agape, applauding you?"

"I don't know what else I can say at this point."

The waiter walks up, and I'm almost relieved because as much as I want answers, my blood is starting to boil again.

We both order bone-in ribeyes, medium rare. Same as we always did before.

After the waiter leaves, an awkward silence stretches between us. I turn my rocks glass in circles with my hand, over and over. It lasts until they bring out salad. Thank God my hands have something to do now.

"I told my mom about you."

He says it right as I take a bite and my eyes widen. I think maybe he did it to make me feel awkward. He knows I won't speak with food in my mouth. It's a huge pet peeve of mine. It feels like it takes me twenty minutes to chew and swallow, and it also feels like Donavan smirks right at me for the entire twenty minutes that's probably no more than five seconds.

I finally swallow. "Since I came back to work?"

He sets his fork down and shakes his head. "No. The first time I met you, and every time we spoke after that."

I stare right at him, eyes wide. "What?"

"When I first met you and the whole time we dated. I never told anyone in Chicago, except my mom. I'd talk to her about you on the phone."

"Why would you tell her and nobody else?"

He shrugs. "I never had to measure up to her, I guess. I don't know. She wasn't a great athlete or anything, didn't play favorites or compare me to my brothers. She was just my mom."

"So why was I never allowed to meet her?"

"I don't know. She was always with the family. It's not like I had many opportunities to get you alone around her. And we were always hanging out with your family."

"Because you never said a word about yours, ever."

"I know. It was my fault, all of it. Trust me, I know."

"Do you though?"

"Pais." He reaches out and grabs my hand.

I want to yank it back, but I can't because God, it feels so good when he touches me. There's no hurt there when his hand is on mine, and I want to just stop hurting. Seven years I've been this way and it never goes away unless Donavan Collins is touching me.

"If I could do things over..." He sighs. "I can't, though. It kills me, every damn day, twenty-four seven. I put that on anything."

I nod. "Well, I forgive you."

"You say that..."

I shake my head. "No, Donavan, I can't see there ever being anything more between us, but I do mean it. I'm being a hundred percent honest with you right now. I forgive you. I promise."

He swallows, hard, and nods. "O-okay. Thank you."

We finish the rest of our meal in awkward silence and I wonder if I really do mean what I said, not about forgiving him, but about there ever being more between us.

The waiter comes over and offers up a dessert menu. I feel like if I eat anything else, I might die. I didn't come close to finishing my steak, but I'll take the leftovers to Dad. Maybe he'll forgive me for Donavan coming over if I show up with part of a ribeye.

Damn it, no, he won't. I have to throw it out, because he'll see we went to Gibsons and lose his mind.

Donavan looks the menu over and smiles, then turns to the waiter and says, "Pecan pie, please."

My stomach lurches as the waiter walks away. "Why the hell did you order that?"

He stares at me like I must be insane. "What? You love it."

I shake my head. "Uhh, no, it's literally the worst."

"What? We ordered it on our first date, and you ate every bite and raved about it, more than once."

I burst out laughing. More of the tables have filled up around us and it's loud enough to elicit some glances.

Donavan snickers and stares at me like I've lost my mind. "What the hell?"

The laughing won't stop, and I stare at him. I wonder if I'm having a breakdown, or if this is just a natural response to all the other emotions that have run their course this evening. "I can't believe you remembered that."

"Our first date? How could I forget? We went to that little place over by campus. I could give you a play by play of the entire evening, down to the minute."

"Really?"

"Yeah, really." He leans back and smiles. "Hell, I was on top of the world that night."

I point at him, nodding. "And you did order pecan pie, I remember it all now. That was the one red mark on our date."

He pretends to be offended. "What? There were no red marks. I slayed. You said you loved it, repeatedly."

"Of course I did. It was our first date, and I'd wanted you to ask me out for so damn long. I had the biggest crush on you, and I wanted you to think you got every single thing right. So I pretended to like it because you liked it so much."

Donavan bursts into a laugh this time and now it's my turn to stare.

"What?" I can't help but start snickering now and attempt to deflect. "Someone take a picture. Holy shit. Donavan Collins is laughing in front of me. What's so funny?"

"I hate pecan pie too. It was terrible. I just thought you loved it so…"

We're both nearly in tears now and people stare at us like we're insane.

The waiter walks back over with it and sets it on the table. Donavan pays the check and we both get up and leave the whole giant wedge of pecan pie right in the middle of the table.

"Come on," he says. "There's somewhere else I want to take you."

He holds out his hand.

I stand there, staring at it, then look at him for a brief moment. I need to tell him to take me home. I kept my promise, came in, and had dinner with him. It's just when he smiles, when he's himself for a few minutes... What could it hurt?

To pretend things are fine for an hour and actually be happy. I deserve to be happy, for just a little bit. I want it more than anything.

Reluctantly, I reach out and take his hand.

DONAVAN PULLS us into the firm's parking garage.

"What the hell? You bringing me to work with you?"

"Oh zip it, woman." Donavan grins.

"I'm not logging any billable hours for your department."

He gets out of the car and walks around and opens my door for me. When I step out, I grab my jacket and put it on.

"We're not going to work. I just didn't want to walk a mile and a half."

"And..." I lift my eyebrows at him.

"Okay, I'm a cheap-ass and didn't want to pay to park or take a cab."

"There he is. Still in there, despite all the smiles and laughter." I can't help but notice I'm grinning more than I should be. Grinning more than I have in a very long time, actually.

He holds out a hand and this time I don't even think before I take it.

"Where are we going?"

"I'll show you in a minute." We head up the road and turn down Michigan Avenue.

"The Gage?"

He shakes his head then presses the button for us to cross the street at a stoplight. When it tells us we're free to walk, I freeze up.

"Donavan, I don't know..."

He squares his shoulders in front of me. "Come on, we used to always talk about coming here, and walking through the park, back when we were in New York. Then we always ended up staying in Manhattan and studying."

"Yeah, studying, that's exactly what we did in Manhattan." I shake my head at him, grinning.

The corners of his mouth turn up into a sly grin of his own. "I was trying to keep it PG out here."

His hand slides back down into mine, and our fingers intertwine. It's like we're twenty-three again, the second our fingers touch, and I can't stop that feeling that consumes me from within. The one that just wants to make Donavan happy and give him whatever he wants. We walk across the street, holding hands, and I shouldn't be doing this. I shouldn't be sending him mixed signals like this.

I already know what will happen the next time I put up any resistance. He'll say I'm playing games with his head, even though I told him at the restaurant he'll never have me again. That will conveniently slip his mind, but right now, the evening is kind of perfect. From dessert on, anyway.

I've been to Millennium Park dozens of times, as a child and a teen, but Donavan and I never made it here when we were in town at the same time.

We walk past the trees, and through the courtyards with the skyscrapers shooting up all around us on one edge, and the calm of the lake on the other side. It's a gorgeous spring night and the sun just set over the buildings, but it's still throwing up a light purple haze just over the top of the skyline. When I look out to the east, it's inky black with the stars surprisingly clear, even with all the light pollution from the city.

Both of us remain silent and take in the park as we stroll through. I keep glancing down at his hand, then back up, but he looks straight ahead. I can't help but wonder what he's thinking, what he's feeling. I'd pay good money to get inside that head of his just once. Just so I could know why he really did what he did to me and my family. Where did that all come from?

What, I had better grades than him? It seems so stupid to me, but clearly it isn't to him. Why is he the way he is? His family seems like a normal family to me.

I guess everyone's own experience in life is unique to just them. Our brains and programming are all wired from our own existence and perceptions. How can a man who seems to have it all—intelligence, looks, charm—be so tortured?

"This is nice, but I need to go home soon." I glance up at Donavan.

His eyes stay locked straight ahead. "I know, just one more thing first."

My chest tightens and my throat is dry, like it's filled with sand. This is so romantic, and his guard is down, and I know if I stick around much longer, I'll do exactly what he wants. I know myself and I'm playing with fire.

We come to a stop, right in front of Cloud Gate, the giant chrome bean. It's gorgeous like always, especially with the moonlight dancing off it. We stop in front of it, the stars bright overhead. I look around and take in everything.

It's beautiful. Perfect.

Not just the scene surrounding us, but Donavan too. I want to just forget everything that's happened and start fresh, a clean slate. But, I can't. The wounds are there, and they run too deep.

Both of his palms slide up to my cheeks and it's like he can read my thoughts, knows all my reservations. His eyes hold what they always held in them, the truth. Like he sees right through me, like it's all a façade and he knows all he has to do is say the right things and the walls will crumble.

I hate him for that, and at the same time I want him so damn bad, because I know there's not another man on the planet who can look at me the way he's looking at me right now.

Instinctively, I lean into his touch. I can't stop myself. It's just one night, anyway. Tomorrow, things will go back to exactly how they were.

"Pais, I'm sorry."

"Donavan, I…"

"I know, but this is the best I can do for a proper apology." He sighs, his eyes angling up to the sky, then back down to me. "It's all I've got. I know you said you forgive me, and that we'll never be together, and I understand. I just… You deserve *this* apology, the best I'm capable of."

I start to say something, but he leans down and our lips meet, gently. And just like that, I want to melt into him. His arms wrap around me, and I feel what I haven't felt in the seven years or so, since we were together for the last time— safe. My body comes alive, like an instant pain reliever. It all just washes away.

I don't want him to make me feel this way, but I can't help what I feel. I can't help the way he makes me want to give in. I want to hand my heart back to him, knowing he's going to drive a knife through it. In my mind, in this moment, it would all be worth it, just for a few seconds of—this.

My lips part and we stand there, in front of the bean, kissing while the rest of the world and the past fades away.

His hands slide down, and his fingers dig into my waist. It's so possessive, like he's afraid to let go, afraid to lose his grip on me. My heart comes alive, thudding in my chest. Every nerve ending in my body fires at once, all funneling down between my thighs, and I press into him even harder. His cock is hard in his slacks and presses up against my stomach.

You can't do this, Paisley. You can't.

Why can't my brain just shut up and give me one night of happiness? I haven't had that in so damn long it aches in every fiber of my being. Just one night without the anxiety, without missing what I lost so long ago.

Donavan's lips slide around to my neck and he yanks me to him, harder, pressing himself against me. I'm so wound up I might combust right here on the spot.

He kisses up my neck until his lips are next to my ear. "I need you."

My body is on fire for him, and I nod.

No!

"Donavan." My word comes out on a gasp as he nips at my ear.

"Don't tell me no."

"I can't do this."

"Yes." His teeth graze my neck as he pulls away and looks straight into my eyes. "You can. Come on."

He yanks on my hand, and I follow him.

I should tell him to piss off then sprint the opposite direction. "I can't go home with you."

"Yes you can. In fact, you are."

Despite me telling him no, I follow. "It's not a good idea."

He glances over at me and smirks. "Since when have we ever made good decisions together? Tonight is no different."

Shit.

One foot in front of the other, I walk behind him back toward his car. It's always been this way, and I should've known, coming back here, being in his presence, I'd make the same mistakes I already did. But I want him so damn bad.

I just want us both to smile, even if it's for a few hours.

This won't end well, but I do it.

I follow him, knowing one of us is bound to destroy the other.

DONAVAN

"Seriously, this is where you live? The Legacy building? Why'd you park at the firm's parking garage?"

"Didn't know if I was bringing you home or not."

She grins in the playful way that makes my dick even harder. "You didn't want me to know where you lived until you knew I was a sure thing tonight."

I pull her in close to me in the opulent lobby of my building and mash my lips against hers to do two things. One, shut her up, and two, keep her from thinking about shit until she's naked in my bed.

If there's one thing I know about Paisley Williams, it's that this moment is fleeting. If her brain gets churning, she'll be out the door—fast. I can't have that. I need her right now.

We're full-on making out in the middle of the lobby and I don't give one fuck. If a kiss could be rated R, this one is that. I grip her ass in both palms, and fuck, I don't even know how to describe what this woman does to me.

"I can't believe you don't like that song."

"That conversation is the furthest thing from my mind right now." I squeeze her ass harder in my palms. *Thinking Out Loud* came on the radio in the car, and Paisley went on and on about it.

Her eyes roll up for a second, then land back on mine. "But, it's Ed Sheeran. Everybody loves Ed Sheeran. And it's so romantic."

"All I said is it's not the most romantic song on the planet. I never said I don't like it." I lean down to her ear. "Though I'm liking it less every second we talk about it while I'm not inside you."

"Okay, I need to see your bedroom, immediately." She bites my lower lip.

I pick her up.

Her legs wrap around my waist and she digs her heels into my ass. I haul her straight toward the elevator, kissing a trail up her throat.

The elevator ride seems to take forever, way too long.

"You live in the penthouse or what, Collins?"

"I wish." We get off on the fortieth floor and I fumble for my keys in my pocket while simultaneously trying to kiss her and carry her to my door.

My cock is so fucking hard it aches, and she keeps grinding her pussy against me.

Finally, we get there, and I slam her back against my door, propping her up against the wall with my chest while I open the door with my key. I keep my eyes locked on hers the entire time.

It's been seven years, and holy hell have I missed her eyes, and just—this. No woman has ever been so in sync with me. I thought over the years, after Paisley, that I'd meet women with more experience, that surely law school sex with Paisley wasn't the best it was going to get. I was wrong. I'll never forget the first time she told me she liked it rough in the bedroom. That she liked to submit, but I had to earn it. That's what did it for her. It was exactly what I wanted too.

I finally get the key in the lock, but I can't take my eyes off her. She's so fierce and strong and smart, by far the most intelligent woman I've ever known. Looking in her eyes, I know what an idiot I was.

I was so caught up in my own little world and goals, with tunnel vision, not caring who I hurt or fucked over along the way, or how close they were to me. It was all about proving myself to everyone else, when I'd already done that with the one person who mattered.

Maybe this is only one night to revisit everything, all those old feelings and emotions, but I'm going to make every fucking second of it count with her.

I finally get the door open and we stumble through into the living room. Somehow, she peels my shirt off me before I even set her down on her feet. Once she's standing in front of me she moves for my pants, and I whip her around by the shoulders and have my hand around her throat, walking her toward the floor-to-ceiling windows that look out over Millennium Park and Lake Michigan behind it.

She gasps for air the second I do it, and I shove her up against the glass, my chest to her back. I pull her back far enough to palm both of her breasts and squeeze both nipples between my thumb and forefingers. Her head flies back, her eyes rolling up to her head. I can see every one of her reactions, barely, in her reflection on the window.

I lean next to her ear, so she can feel my breath play across her neck as I say, "I'm gonna strip you naked right here. So the whole goddamn world can see you're mine again."

"Holy shit." Her breaths grow ragged, and her neck tenses. "You haven't changed at all, have…"

I grip her by the hair and dig my knuckles against her scalp. With my other hand, I rip her blouse open. Buttons fly everywhere and rattle off the glass and the

678

hardwood floors. I slide one hand back around her throat, and one hand squeezes her breast over her black lace bra.

Fuck, I missed her tits, her ass, her mouth—everything. This back and forth between us has had me so wound up I can barely see straight. I slide my hand down her stomach and take my fingers just inside the hem of her skirt, teasing right above her pussy. "Do you know how much I've missed this fucking body, Pais?"

She shakes her head back and forth, staring at my eyes in the reflection of the window. I bypass her clit and cup her entire pussy in my hand, rough, digging my fingers in. "How much I've missed this pussy?"

She yelps, but I already know she enjoys this much more than she'll let on. I know how to push every button on her body and I damn sure haven't forgotten. Not a day has gone by I haven't thought about what I'd give to have this opportunity just one more time.

"Tell me what I want to hear. You know what it is." I dig my fingers in even harder. She'll be swollen tomorrow morning when she wakes up in my bed.

She shakes her head again, this time defiantly, but her lips are curled up slightly in a grin.

I squeeze my fist around her hair even tighter and yank her neck back, so her ear is right next to my mouth. "Say. It."

"It's not true anymore, Donavan." She gasps out the words, clearly goading me even more.

I smile right back at her reflection. "It's always been true. I'm not naïve enough to think you haven't fucked other men. They didn't compare though, did they? It's always been true. It was true then, just like it is now. Say it, and I'll give you everything you want."

She shakes her head again.

I slide two fingers through her slick folds, then shove them deep inside her. "Look how fucking wet you are, Pais." I apply even more pressure, and she squeezes around me. "Don't tell me it's not true." I pump my fingers a few times, and she gasps.

Just when she's starting to buck her hips against my hand, I pull them out and graze her clit.

She shudders against me.

"Say it, *Pais*." I grip the bottom of her skirt and slide it up, then run my hand over her ass. "I know what you want. Just say it."

She shakes her head once more, still defiant, but secretly loving every second of this. It's written all over her damn face. I dig my fingers into her firm ass, then massage the cheek, warming it up.

Finally, through several pants, she says, "Do what you have to do, Donavan."

I twist her head to the side, so this time I'm looking right into her eyes. "I will, trust me." I yank her panties down, pull my hand back, and smack her bare ass— hard. Hard enough to leave a bright red handprint right across it.

Her entire body jolts against the window. "Holy shit," she gasps, before a coo escapes her lips.

My hand immediately goes back to kneading her soft flesh where I just spanked her. Through gritted teeth I say, "Tell me what I want to hear, Pais." Before she can respond, I spank her again, a little harder this time. The sound of my hand colliding with her echoes through the empty condo, the walls and the glass amplifying the sound a thousand times over.

"Fuck," she gasps again.

Her chest rises and falls in huge waves, her eyes hungry, wanting more.

"I have all fucking night to spank you so hard you can't sit down in the morning." I swat her again, even harder this time, then release her hair and wrap my hand around her throat. My other hand slides around her ass and I take my fingers even deeper into her pussy this time, curling them up to hit the spot deep inside her that only I know about.

She glares into my eyes, then they close at the sudden intrusion. She slumps over a little, but I keep her held up by her throat.

When her eyes open again, I see it. What I've been waiting for. The submission.

The best fucking part about sex with Paisley Williams. She always put up a fight, but that moment of vulnerability is everything for me. It's like a precious gift she always made me work my ass off for, but then handed over like a present on Christmas morning.

I never thought I'd see it again, and my heart comes alive at the sight.

My lips curl up into a grin, and I know I have her.

My thumb circles her clit and my fingers relax around her throat.

I press my forehead against hers and stare right into her eyes. "Tell me," I whisper. "I need to hear it again, just one more time."

"It's yours, Donavan."

"What is?"

"My pussy. It belongs to you."

"Only me?"

"Only you."

I slip my fingers from her and pull her skirt down to the floor. She kicks it away after it puddles around her feet. I stand back up, taking my time, running my hands up the back of her legs, and I kiss my handprint on her ass, soothing the burn she has to be feeling. When I stand back up behind her, I slowly remove the tattered blouse from her shoulders and toss it aside with her skirt, then unclasp her bra and remove it from her arms. I slide her hair gently over her shoulders so her curls dangle down her back and run my fingertips slowly up her arms as I kiss around her neck.

"Fuck, I've dreamed about having you like this again. You in nothing but a pair of heels, pressed against my window, while you came repeatedly." I shove her forward, bending her over at the waist.

She gasps. "I'm so close, Donnie. You have no idea."

She's so helpless right now and it's hot as fuck. I can tell she needs this release just as bad as I do. If she's anything like me it's been coiling inside her nonstop. She needs me the same way I need her. It's always been that way. A yin and yang, push and pull. We've always been the other half of each other.

I take my time, working down her back, kissing her softly.

Her legs tremble every time I so much as exhale across her skin. She's so damn responsive it won't take long to make her come, but I'm going to tease it as long as I can, so it's that much better for her.

I can't help but admire her body. It hasn't changed much, but it's still different. More toned, stronger. She's hardened over the years, her interior as well as her exterior.

Once I'm on my knees behind her, I spread her ass and lick slowly from her clit all the way up her. Her entire body shakes and jolts, and she gasps out an audible exhale.

"Please, hurry."

I give her another smack on the ass, but not nearly as hard as earlier. Just enough to hold her orgasm off another minute or two. I want to take my time, worship her body from my knees. Also, if I'm being honest, I don't want this to end. I've never wanted it to end.

I let my pride and my ridiculous ego steal her away from me once, and I've told myself a million times I'd do anything for just one more night with her. This is a moment to be savored.

I slide my tongue back across her and flatten it on her pussy. The tip rests on her clit, and I slowly work circles around it.

Her thighs quake and her ass presses back against my face. "Don't stop. Please don't stop."

I spread her ass farther apart, giving me better access, and hum on her.

"So. Close." The words come out on a begging tone.

My cock is so fucking hard, I think I might pass out. I need to be inside her, buried deep as her pussy cinches around me.

The need is so bad it literally feels like the world will end, but I want to remind her how easily I can get her off.

I lean back and give her another swat, on the other ass cheek. "Not yet."

"Please." She draws out the word. "I need it. Please."

I growl, "When I say and not before."

I glance around and catch her nodding at her reflection. I have to hold her ass to keep her from shoving it back against me.

I move back in and exhale across her clit. Goosebumps break out up and down her thighs and ass.

"Stop. Teasing. Me." Her words come out on an exasperated sigh.

Energy radiates from her body, the release building in her ass and legs, and traveling up her spine. When she comes it's going to be fucking incredible.

I lift up onto my feet and stand next to her, bent down so my lips are next to her ear. "Fingers or mouth?"

"I don't care, just do it, please."

I grip under her chin and turn her head to face me, so our eyes are locked, then slide my thumb into my mouth and swirl my tongue around it, making sure it's properly lubricated.

Her eyes widen, but before she can say anything, I have two fingers inside her and my wet thumb pressed up against her tight, puckered asshole.

"Oh, fuck." Her eyes roll back in her head.

"Come for me, Pais."

Her hips begin to buck and shudder, and right when her orgasm crests, I slide my thumb in.

Her eyes vault open. "Holy. God. Donavan."

I watch in amusement as the orgasm rips up her spine and down through her legs, her whole body tensing and trembling in huge undulating waves.

Her pussy and ass squeeze tight around my fingers, so damn hard I wonder if I could even get them out of her now. I have them hooked into her from behind and I work them up and down as she gasps and smacks at the glass window, like she can't get any air.

Her eyes roll over to mine and she's lost right now. Caught in a whirlwind she's tried so hard to resist, but it still brought us back together years later as if fate determined it.

Fuck, this is the best part. When she looks like this, completely drained. I know it'll only last a minute or two, but it's just—perfect, taking care of her afterward. She's so soft and lithe—innocent.

I quickly scoop her up in my arms and hold her to my chest. She's completely limp as I carry her to the bedroom.

I lay her in my bed and slide down, so my face is between her legs, and just watch her. When her eyelashes finally flutter and stare down at me, my tongue is already on her clit.

"You're relentless," she says on a labored breath.

"You already knew this about me. It's why you came up here."

She shakes her head, but at the same time smiles and says, "Maybe."

It doesn't take long for me to have her on the edge of another orgasm. Despite all our problems, everything that has gone wrong, I've always been a master at knowing everything she wants and needs—in a physical sense. I know every possible way to touch her, which buttons to push.

With the tip of my tongue, I stroke across her clit slowly, left to right, right to left. Her thighs threaten to clench around my face, and I spread her wider with both hands.

She squirms against my touch, and I dig my fingers in to hold her in place.

She gasps for air. "Donavan, please…"

"Not yet." I growl the words against her inner thigh.

She groans like she's in the best kind of agony possible. I take her to the brink of an orgasm and then pull her back, over and over, until it feels like she might pass out with my face between her legs.

With one swift movement, I flip her over to her stomach and splay my fingers across her back, keeping her chest pinned down against the mattress. My tongue slides up the base of her spine, to the middle of her back, until my lips press up against her neck, just below her ear. Slowly, I pepper kisses along her ear, nipping at the shell.

"I've waited so goddamn long for this."

She gasps when she hears me unbuckling my belt. "Donavan, I…"

I slide my hand into her hair and make a fist while I free my cock from my slacks. It's hard as a rock and aches to be inside her.

Once my pants are off, I give her another smack on the ass, then yank her hips up so I'm lined up with her.

"I'm not on the pill."

Something about her admission causes my nostrils to flare even more. "Good."

Her whole body tightens, and I don't have to see her face to know there is shock written all over it.

The head of my dick parts her lips and she's so fucking hot and wet I can't stop the groan from low in my throat. I lean down next to her ear. "I'm going to blow deep inside you and whatever happens fucking happens."

"Donavan…" Her word sounds apprehensive, but at the same time she tries to push her ass back into me. She's so needy and wanting, like she's yearned for me and only me the last seven years.

"Tell me to stop if you don't want this." I growl the words into her ear.

She sucks in a deep breath but doesn't say anything.

I slide the tip against her clit and her back arches.

"Tell. Me. To. Stop."

She finally shakes her head. "Please don't stop."

That's what I fucking thought.

"This is mine, Paisley. It always has been, and it will *always* belong to me." I push inside her, and fuck, when her pussy squeezes around me a million memories come flooding back, a million feelings buried deep down. Feelings I've suppressed and tried to forget but couldn't. "Hide all you want, but you'll never escape me. No one else knows you the way I do."

My hips speed up as I fuck into her from behind, and holy hell, I don't know how long I'll be able to last.

Her hands reach out and my sheets ball up between her fingers. "Donavan…" She barely gets my name out.

My fist tightens in her hair, and I smack her on the ass. I look down at my fresh, red handprint, and then watch my cock go in and out of her, glistening in the moonlight as her wetness streams down the backs of her thighs.

My eyes roll up to the ceiling, then land on her slender, hourglass frame rocking back into me.

It was always meant to be. Why did I let her get away the last time?

Because you were an idiot.

I shake my head at my thoughts and dig my fingers into her hip, yanking her harder back into me as I thrust forward. "Okay, Pais." I nod. "Now, you can come."

Just as I say it, my hand slides around beneath her and I stroke her clit with my fingers.

Her back arches, and I pull her up to me from behind. Both of my hands cup her breasts and I hold her up as I fuck into her.

"Oh God, Donavan." My name comes from her throat on a squeak. Her entire body spasms as the orgasm rocks through her. Her hot pussy clamps down on me. She seizes up, shaking, like she would fall face-first on the bed if I let go of her.

Her walls squeeze so hard around my dick I don't know how much longer I can endure this. My balls tighten and lift, a huge load building pressure.

When she's finished, her chest heaves up and down with huge labored breaths. I'm about to blow everywhere, so I shove her down onto the mattress and flip her over.

When I see her eyes, they're wide, staring right back at me. In an instant, I'm on top of her and my cock is back inside her. Our foreheads press together, and I gaze into her eyes, seeing everything we've ever been through, every trial and tribulation playing out like a highlight reel.

"I want to look into your eyes when I come inside you."

"Holy shit, Don…" My name trails off as her eyes roll back, then land on me again.

I pump into her a few more times and I can't hold back any longer. My cock kicks and I let loose. My fingers grip the sheets on each side of her head, and I shove into her as hard and as deep as I possibly can.

A million primal instincts take over, mind separated from my body. This was what I was made to do, mark her as mine. Hot jets of come shoot into her, over and over, as she drains every last drop from my balls. Every muscle in my body tightens, and I groan repeatedly.

Her fingernails dig into my back and she finally breaks eye contact and looks over to the side, unable to stare at me.

I grip her by the chin and angle her gaze right back to my face. When our eyes lock again, no words need to be spoken. I just stare at her, telling her without words how sorry I am, how much I still want her, that I still love her and never stopped.

She finally breaks our silence and says, "Donavan…"

"It was always you, Pais."

She shakes her head. "Don't."

"Look at me. I'm not lying."

She pushes me off her and I roll to the side. Despite everything I want to tell her, I don't want her to be upset. Especially not after she just made me the happiest man in the world again, even if only for a brief time. I'd forgotten what that'd felt like, the tingling coursing through my body, the swell in my chest.

We lie next to each other, staring up at the ceiling, both of us still panting.

My eyes roll over to her and I can see her contemplating everything in her life in those few brief seconds, like she simultaneously hates me and loves me more than anything, all at the same time. How she should fight this. How she shouldn't have let it happen. I know her mind as well as I know mine.

Despite her expression, I slide my hand down into hers and her fingers wrap around it and squeeze. A tight squeeze that says, *I don't know what we're doing, but please don't ever let go.*

A smile forms on her lips and at the same time she tenses a little.

I won't let go. Not this time. She's mine and I'll fight to the death for her.

PAISLEY

When I wake up in Donavan's apartment, it's like I just started a new life. Everything feels different. It always did when I was with him. All the stress, all the worry has melted away and I feel like—me again.

This is always how it was meant to be. Then I think about everything he did and how, no matter how bad I want it to be, things will never be the same.

I sit up and wrap his thousand-thread-count sheets around me and look out at the balcony. Donavan's out there with a cup of coffee, staring at the sunrise off Lake Michigan.

It's beautiful.

He's beautiful.

He's wearing nothing but a pair of athletic shorts, lounging in a chair. No phone, no laptop, no suit. No distractions, just him and that ridiculous mind of his.

I want to join him, kiss him, tell him good morning, but I don't. Instead, I just sit there and watch for a few minutes, wondering what our lives would be if everything else hadn't happened, if he hadn't hurt me so bad, damaged me beyond repair. My stomach tightens again, and I feel like I might throw up.

Finally, I take a deep breath and walk out to the balcony.

His eyes light up the second he sees me. He rises from the chair, but I hold out a hand. "Good morning," he says softly.

I blush a little, because *hello*, Donavan Collins came inside me last night and basically said let the fates decide what happens. I mentally smack myself on the forehead. God, and I let him do it.

Of course you did. You always did.

"Morning." I have a seat.

He takes a sip of his coffee and he's still the boy I remember, but so different too. I can't put a finger on it exactly, but he's just—aged, more mature. At least he *looks* more mature. It's hot and I want to drag him back inside and put his manly body to more good use, but I can't. We *have* to talk, even if it might kill me. I have so many things to say to him, but I'm scared. So scared my fingers tremble and I grip the sheets tighter around me.

Finally, I inhale a deep breath. "Donavan…"

"I know, we need to talk."

I'm taken aback for a quick moment. Talking about feelings was not something I ever expected Donavan to be on board with, let alone bring up. He's always been quiet and always seemed like he was brooding, even when he was in a good mood. Finally, I just nod. "We can't do this and ignore everything else."

"I know."

My eyes widen a little more. *Who am I even talking to right now?* It's like I have an actual adult sitting next to me. "I really don't hold anything against you or your firm because of what happened with my dad."

He turns and looks at me. "I wish you would've called. I know it would've been difficult for you, but we wouldn't have represented them. I know you think I hated you or whatever, but the last thing I'd ever want to do is hurt your family more than I already did."

I nod. "I know, it's just…" I sigh, and grin to lighten the mood. "You know how the two of us are. Too proud. Don't want anyone else's help."

He grins and looks back out at the water. "Yeah, I get it. It's great for professional life, but not so much for personal stuff."

I shake my head, mainly at the fact I can't believe this conversation is flowing so easily between the two of us. It's not how I saw this going at all, and at the same time it makes things a million times worse. I think my life was actually easier when we hated each other. "That's the truth."

He glances back over, and his face is full of remorse. "I really am sorry about your mom. You know how much I loved her. And I'm sorry I never took you to meet mine."

We're entering shaky ground now, and all I want to do is run, sprint from this apartment, but I can't. No matter how bad I want to. I look down at the ground. "I thought you were ashamed of me. It hurt. I really wanted to meet your family. I thought we were it. We'd always be together, but that was always the thing that kept me on edge, worried we wouldn't make it."

"Pais."

When I look over at him, he looks like he's in genuine pain. I've never seen Donavan Collins look ashamed of anything he's ever done in his life, so it takes me by surprise, but it's there, written on his face.

"It had nothing to do with you and everything to do with how stupid I was. I just…couldn't let you see me like that."

"Like what?"

"Fourth best at everything."

I shake my head. "I don't even know what you're saying."

"In New York I was on top. Everyone looked up to me. I was best in the class, well, until you know…"

I nod. "Yeah, I know that part."

"But everything, socially. I was the king of that place and it felt like home to me. If I'd taken you to meet my family, you'd have seen me as the baby. That's all I am here. I'll always be the one who isn't good enough, doesn't do enough. Decker and Deacon were both at the top of their law class, after they were both going to be first round draft picks in the MLB and NFL. Hell, Dexter probably could've been too, if he'd even liked sports. But he's a finance wizard who could piss on something and turn it into gold. He wrote essays and did art stuff that was picked up for publication when he was in his teens. I sucked at sports. I sucked at art. I just… I didn't want you to see me like that."

I shake my head. "I wouldn't have cared, Donavan. I loved *you*." I lean back. "Like…bad. Like write Donavan Collins in my notebook over and over bad. You were it for me. Sometimes I'd wondered if you'd brainwashed me somehow. I didn't even plan on ever using my degree, I just got it as a backup plan. All I wanted to do was get married and support you, start a family. You were larger than life for me. I thought you'd end up being governor one day. Hell, maybe even president."

"Really?"

I nod. "Yes, really."

Donavan stares back out at the lake and the boats and the gorgeous sunrise but grits his teeth, just barely. "You have any relationships after me?"

I still can't believe how possessive he is all these years later, and how much I still love it, even though I shouldn't. I shake my head. "No. I…" I take a deep breath. "I changed, after us."

He glances back over, and the shame in his eyes socks me in the chest again.

"I'm not telling you this to get back at you, or to make you feel bad. It's just an exchange of information, and so you'll know I'm different now. I'm not the girl you knew. I put up walls and threw myself into work. Don't get me wrong, I had needs and had them taken care of."

His fingers tighten into fists when he hears that part, but his face doesn't show his frustration.

"It was just a release, though. Nothing more. I didn't feel anything. I haven't really *felt* anything since… You know. The only feeling I have is that my heart is encased in steel." I glance away and sigh. "Man, this conversation got heavy, sorry."

"Don't apologize." Donavan takes another sip of coffee. "It hurts to hear, but it's good to clear the air."

"So what about you?"

"Pretty much the same. I didn't want anything to do with women at all for about six months after. Then, I just went nuts, sleeping with any woman I could find." He pauses and glances over with wide eyes. "Always careful and a hundred percent safe."

I want to smile at how uncomfortable he just got. It's cute and obvious he still feels the same way about me as I do him. Why did he have to be such an idiot? We could've been so damn good together.

"Me and my brothers were all pretty wild for a while."

"I noticed they're all engaged."

Donavan sighs. "Yeah. They're all really happy. It's nice, I guess. Decker and I were on bad terms for a while, and that wasn't fun. I still can't stand Tate most of the time, but at least it's civil now."

"What happened?"

"It's a long story."

"We have time." I smile.

"She came from The Hunter Group, before we merged with them."

"Yeah, we heard about it in New York. Bennett paid some attention to it."

"That fucking guy." Donavan shakes his head. "Anyway, she came up to do all the due diligence shit, and just walked around like she owned the fucking place. Always mouthing off. Bossing people around. So, naturally, we didn't get along. She had a client in Texas, I had one here and saw an opportunity, and I filed a lawsuit against Tate's client."

I nod. "To create a conflict of interest." Of course, he would do that. He never goes down without a fight when it comes to everyone else.

Donavan grins a little, clearly still taking pride in his idea to tank a nine-figure merger. "Exactly. It didn't go over well."

"Oh, I can't imagine why not, Donavan. Jesus."

He laughs this time. A real, genuine laugh, and I love how he looks like a little boy again when he does it. "So yeah, Tate and I don't exactly get along all that well."

"She's been really nice to me. I kind of like her. She's smart. She does look at me like she doesn't trust me, though. Can't really blame her for that." I glance over, and he's still fidgety, his hands bouncing slightly against the side of his chair. "Why do you still seem on edge? About the merger and everything?"

His eyes dart over to mine. "You don't miss anything, do you?"

I shake my head. "Nope. What's so bad about merging with The Hunter Group? Don't you have an even bigger crim law department now? More cases? I'd think it'd make you happy."

"I don't know." He shakes his head. "Maybe because we didn't need them. We had everything we needed. Could've done it on our own and now it's like we have this asterisk next to our firm. No matter what we do people will say it's because we merged with them."

"Why did you guys merge?"

"Decker wanted to free up time. It was a valid reason. We were working crazy hours and he has a teenage daughter."

"I thought I saw a picture of an older girl in his office. He must've had her pretty young."

"Yeah, he was still in college. About to be drafted."

"I think it's kind of sweet he wanted to spend more time with her, work less. That's rare for people like us. Most people piss away their families and end up drowning in a bottle of scotch every day after work, wondering where it all went wrong. Good for him."

Donavan laughs. "Whose side are you on here, fuck?"

I can't help but smile. Giving him shit was always fun. "I see merits on both sides. But you're still dodging the question and you know it. What is it about the merger that ate at you so bad you'd divide your damn family over it?"

His eyes narrow, and I know I'm right on the edge of getting my answer. I think I already know what it is, but I want to hear him say it. It'll be good for him to get it out.

"I just... It was *ours*. We worked our asses off, blood, sweat, and tears. *We* built that fucking place, and even if Decker was managing partner and legally it was his right to do what he did, it was still bullshit. Our name was on the wall and he just sold it to the highest bidder, without telling us, without discussing it. It didn't say Decker on the building, it said Collins. We were the kings of this city." He leans back and shakes his head, clearly trying to rein in his temper.

Donavan is so intriguing and interesting. I think that's why I've always been so drawn to him. He rails on and on how he went away to New York to prove he was better than everyone else, prove he could do what they do. To get away and step out of the shadow of his family, when all he's ever really wanted is just to be seen and acknowledged. It's obvious he loves and cares about his family so much, takes pride in where he comes from, and then feels slighted, unappreciated, invisible.

Then, I came along, and I saw him. I saw his potential, and all the good in him.

I don't know why, but I think he just has to be the underdog. I think if he got the attention and praise he clearly craves, he wouldn't know what to do with himself.

Eventually, he looks over at me. "You're being quiet."

I nod. "I don't know how to work out what to say to all that. I've never been in that position, had my family's name on a wall or whatever, but at the end of the day, Donavan." I reach over and put a palm on his cheek. "It's just a fucking sign with letters on it. Our email signatures are just names with some letters attached to the end of them. An award for best criminal law department in the country is just words in a magazine. First in your law class is just something on the end of your name in an alumni mailer. Decker's daughter, your niece, those relationships are real. What we had was *real*. Those things matter more than any fucking title or achievement."

Donavan swallows, then stands up. He holds out a hand, and I take it as he gently lifts me up from my chair. We hug and he wraps his hand around the back of my head, pulling me to his chest. I want to nuzzle into it so damn bad. He makes me feel so safe, transported to some other place, some other life.

Finally, he kisses me on the forehead, and smiles. "I know. You're right."

"I'm always right." I grin.

"Oh, I know that too." He smiles. "How about we just take things slow? And try getting along first. Whatever happens after that, happens."

I nod, reluctantly. "O-okay. We can try." On the inside, my stomach twists and sours.

"I'm going to take a shower. I'm glad we did this, though. As hard as some of it was to hear."

I can't even look up at him. "Me too."

Donavan walks off, and I slowly follow him back inside from a safe distance. He heads toward his bedroom, and a few seconds later, I hear the shower come on. Once I hear the door close, anxiety slams into my chest.

What the hell am I doing?

I do whatever I can to shove all the hurt and anger back down, lock it away where it's resided the past seven years. All the resentment from being abandoned. This was so much easier when we were just enemies. When I wanted to punch him in the face, not stay in bed all day and kiss him.

This will *not* end well.

DONAVAN

"You gonna grin like an idiot or help me?"

I shake my head and kick the dolly under a stack of boxes in the back of the U-Haul. "Why didn't you pay someone to move all your shit for you? Hell, I would've paid for it. We could be at a restaurant, drinking booze while someone else did this."

"Would you look at the big, mighty Donavan Collins. Looks like he's never done a day of hard labor in his life."

She laughs, and damn that laugh again. If she's not careful I might fuck her in here.

"I know how to work hard, *princess*." I put a lot of extra emphasis on the word 'princess' as I shuffle all her shit down the ramp to the sidewalk.

She hops up on the truck and rifles through her boxes before I can grab her and drag her upstairs, away from all this—work. I pause for a second and look around. The place *is* nice, right down the road from the office. But it's not my place, where she belongs.

It's Saturday, and about two weeks have passed since I fucked Paisley at my apartment. We've been on a few dates and things have gone smoothly at the office. It all seems too good to be true. If I'm being honest with myself, I haven't been this happy in a long time.

Words can't describe what it's like to make Paisley smile again. I never thought I'd see the day.

I glance back, and she's bent over in a tight pair of jeans and the sight of her ass has my jaw clenching. God, she's so damn beautiful. I just want to bury myself inside her and never leave. I want to tell her fuck all this, she's moving into my place, no questions asked.

She'd never go for it. Not a chance in hell—yet.

In college, she would've done anything I said as soon as I said it. Not now, though. Paisley Williams is a different woman and I'm responsible for that transformation. It still eats at me every minute of every day. I took all her innocence, everything that was great about her, and turned her into, well—me.

The only thing I have left is hope that she's still in there. She brought out parts of me I never knew existed, and I want that back. I want it so damn bad, to let go of all the resentment, hate, insecurity, and just feel at home with her. Be who I was meant to be.

I don't know if it's even possible, but when she's around, there's at least a sliver of hope. So, if we need to take things slow, that's what we'll do, no matter how bad I want to pack up all this shit, tell her she's moving into my place, and tell her everything is going back to the way it was and that's final.

I groan at the sight of her, loud enough for her to hear. She smiles down at the boxes, knowing what her ass is doing to me.

I take off toward the building, hauling her shit.

"That's right. Keep it moving, Collins. This stuff isn't going to unload itself."

I grin the entire way to her apartment as I set the load of boxes down in her living room. On my way back out, she's practically bouncing as she carries one little box in her arms, her ponytail swaying from side to side with each step.

"I'm really enjoying this." She stops and gives me a peck on the cheek as she struts by.

"I hope so. You're going to pay for it later."

"We'll see." She sways her hips as she disappears into the building.

I haul the dolly up the ramp again, sweat beads forming across my forehead as I kick the dolly under another stack. I wipe my forehead with my shirt and stare at the never-ending boxes. "Worth it," I mutter.

I need brownie points, and this is the ultimate way to earn them. Everyone knows carrying heavy shit for women is the way to their heart. And I need the ultimate favor from her.

The Red Wedding (that's what I'm calling Tate and Decker's wedding, *Game-of-Thrones*-style) is coming up in two weeks and I need a date. I want Pais to go with me more than anything, and I know she'll be reluctant. For one, nobody really knows we're trying to rekindle our relationship. At the office, we keep things professional; even if I do want to drag her into a supply closet and have my way with her nonstop.

Every time I think about asking her, I tense up, afraid she'll say no. It'll be a huge event. The media will be everywhere. Every eye in Chicago is already anticipating it, probably outside of Chicago too. Definitely in Manhattan.

Chicago's power couple.

That's what all the headlines say.

I shake my head. I'm being stupid, worrying about it. Of course, she'll say yes. It's Paisley. I'll just give her a swat on the ass, over and over, until she agrees. I have nothing to worry about.

I'm about to lift another stack of boxes and haul it down the ramp when she comes out of nowhere behind me.

"Hey!"

I damn near piss myself and jolt upright. "What the hell, woman?" I start laughing.

Paisley tries to keep a straight face and taps her foot with both hands on her hips. "I don't see boxes moving. I have to get this truck back by four."

That's it. I can't take it anymore.

I head right at her and her eyes get big.

"Donavan, we don't—"

I slam my mouth into hers, and at the same time grip both her ass cheeks hard enough with my fingers it might leave marks. So be it. I yank her into me as I kiss the living shit out of her.

When she goes to say something, I press into her even harder, backing her up against the inside of the truck. The sound of us colliding with the wall echoes off the ceiling.

The kiss quickly grows needy, and I slide a hand up and grip one of her breasts through her t-shirt, pinching her nipple between my thumb and forefinger.

She gasps against my mouth.

"Keep talking that shit, Williams. Keep it up." I kiss down her neck and her throat.

Her greedy fingers dig into my ribs, like she doesn't ever want to let go of me. I smile against her ear at the effect I have on her. She tries to say something, but gasps when I cup her pussy in my hand over her jeans.

She's so wet the heat radiates through the denim. "You're only gonna make things worse for yourself when I get done."

"Maybe I won't mind," she says through labored breaths.

"I know you won't. So quit distracting me, so I can get this done then christen your new apartment with your toes curling into the mattress."

I pull back, breathing heavily, and just stare at her.

Fuck, she's gorgeous, looking at me the same way I'm looking at her, nothing but desire in her eyes. She wants me, and it's an amazing sight. I love this woman so damn much. She's never getting away from me again—ever. I don't care how far she tries to run or hide; I'll find her.

You can't escape fate, Pais.

Finally, she just nods. "Okay, uhh, yeah, let's get this done."

"What I thought." I snicker as I grab the dolly and take another load down the ramp.

At the door, I turn back, and she's biting her bottom lip, staring at me, one part hate, two parts love, the perfect ratio. She finally shakes her head and grins, then blushes and looks away, pretending to go back to work.

Yeah, I love her. More than anything.

TWO HOURS LATER, somehow, everything is at least inside her apartment. She moves toward the door, and I spin her around and pin her with my gaze.

"Not yet! We have to get the truck back."

"Fuck that. I'll pay for another day." I yank the keys from her hand and sling them across the kitchen tile. "I need you, now."

Her eyes get big. "Donavan…"

My mouth connects with her neck.

She nods. "Okay, you win."

I grin. "I need to ask you something first." I say the words as I trail my tongue down to her collar bone.

"Sure, yeah." She sighs playfully. "Ask me anything, just don't stop doing that."

I lean back, and she immediately looks disappointed I stopped. "It's a serious question."

Her lips mash into a thin line and she morphs back into serious Pais. Fuck.

"I want you to go to Decker's wedding with me." I shake my head. "I mean, fuck, will you go with me?"

"Asking and not demanding, you really have changed." She smiles for a split-second, probably at the thought of us getting all dressed up and going to a fairytale wedding together, but then her face hardens as the implications set in. "I don't know…"

"Yes you do." I smile, anything to try and lighten the mood. I just want her to say yes. I know if I can get her to go, it'll make things real. We'll zoom right past this taking-it-slow bullshit and get right into the heart of this. Right where I want us to be.

To my surprise, she smiles back and gets that playful look about her. "I'm serious, I really don't know. It's fast and people will talk."

I shrug like it's no biggie, even though I want to shake the shit out of her and make her see that I'm not that guy anymore, that I'll be whatever she wants me to be. "Okay, it was worth a shot. I guess I'll just have to ask—"

She grips my forearm. "Let's not be hasty."

I shake my head, knowing I have her right where I want her. "I know, I know, you want to take things slow, but I *have* to have a date, for appearances' sake. So I'm in a tough spot here, Pais. Surely you understand. I mean, I want it to be you, but if you're not ready…"

She cups my face in her palms and leans up to kiss me. "Such a jerk. Okay, I'll go with you."

I smile and say against her lips, "That's what I thought."

Her smile widens. "Asshole."

My hand goes to her ass, and I run my fingers across her pussy, needing her out of these jeans immediately. I don't give a shit how sweaty we are. My finger presses up against the crack of her ass. "Maybe, if you're lucky."

My mouth runs over her neck and I spin her around so that my chest is to her back. I sweep her hair out of the way and kiss her collar bone, my hands roaming what's mine, feeling every inch of it like I'm about to take it for a test drive.

"Such a filthy pervert."

"It's what you like about me, Pais." I reach around and unbutton her jeans, then slide them halfway down her thighs so she couldn't run if she tried.

She bends over the little breakfast bar and wiggles her ass at me, her panties still in my way. My cock gets even harder at the sight. I slide her panties down to her jeans, practically subduing her.

"Nowhere to go now."

"Fuck," she gasps when my mouth connects with her pussy.

"So helpless." I spread her ass in my hands and lick across her clit, running my tongue through her slick folds, the entire length of her slit. At the end, I tease my tongue all around the crack of her ass.

"I-I need to shower first."

I smack her on the ass, then rise up, my chest pressing down on her back, hard, smothering her against the breakfast bar. My hand grips her hair and she coos.

"Yeah, a shower. Then, I'm going to fuck this ass." I press a finger up against it.

She jolts. "If I say you can."

I laugh, like she must be out of her mind. "Oh, you will, Pais. Fight it all you want, but you know you will. I. Know. You."

"We'll see." She smiles with her face pressed against the counter.

"I still need you, though."

"Do something then and quit running your mouth. It's boring."

My jaw clenches. I love how bad she wants to get me worked up, so I'll fuck her even harder. It's always mind games with the two of us, and I get off on it. It's almost hotter than the actual sex.

Almost.

"Don't fucking move." I reach into my pocket and pull out a little black, round object.

Pais looks back and I show it to her. Her eyes get big. "What the hell is that?"

"A place holder." I reach in my other pocket and pull out a little bottle of lube. I always come prepared.

"I-I don't know…"

It's bullshit. She's on fire inside right now, wants it so damn bad. I can see it in her eyes.

I take my sweet time, squeezing out some of the lube onto the end of it, then smearing it all around to make sure it's evenly coated, until it's glistening in the light from her apartment.

She squirms a little as I hold it behind her.

"Hold still, Pais, or I won't be gentle. Last warning."

She nods. "O-okay."

I press it up against her and her legs tense.

"Relax."

She exhales a deep breath and nods her head.

"It doesn't come out until I say it does, understood?"

She nods again.

I take some more of the lube and squeeze it out on her ass, then smear it around her with my fingers. I press them up against her and a shudder rips through her body.

Good. It's how I like her best, squirming.

Slowly, I work one finger in and swirl it around, coating her up. I still remember the first time I took her ass, back in college. One look at her and I never thought she'd ever be up for it, but she was giddy with excitement.

Fuck, I can still remember how hard my cock was when she agreed to give it a go.

Her innocence only made it better, and I've never even thought about trying it with another woman after her. No woman has ever compared to her.

Before long, I have two fingers in, and Pais is cooing and gasping at the intrusion. Her eyes roll back and I know she's already close.

I take the plug and ever so gently, push it in, watching every reaction on her face. Once it's inside, I give it a little pat on the end for safekeeping.

"Fuck," she gasps.

I lean down to her ear. "It stays until I say."

"You said that already, asshole. Just hurry. I'm so close."

I grin and kiss her lightly on the cheek. "Not until I say."

I leave her bent over the counter, the plug in her ass, and walk around and pour myself a glass of water from the faucet. I stand there on the other side, watching her every single reaction with a smug, satisfied smile on my face.

The teasing makes this all a million times better.

Her eyes roll up to me, and I can see the frustration in them. "You get off on torturing me, don't you?"

I shrug. "Has its perks."

"Seriously, my legs are getting tired."

"Done running your mouth yet?" I smirk.

She shakes her head, then stops, grins at me and nods.

I know she's full of shit. She knows she's full of shit.

"Good, go take that shower. I'll wait."

Her eyes narrow. "What?"

"You heard me."

She doesn't even say the words, her eyes tell the whole story. *Please? I'm dying over here.*

"Go on. I'll wait." I gesture toward her bathroom. "I'll bring you a towel."

She pushes back from the counter, defiant as always. I knew this was what she'd do. She knows how to play the game as well as I do.

She does her best to not look irritated and nods. "Okay, Collins. I will take that shower."

She pulls her jeans up over her hips and takes her first few steps gingerly, because of the plug. When she sees me smirk at her, she straightens up and walks normally the rest of the way to the bathroom.

"Oh, and Pais?" I say, just as she's about to go through the door.

She lets out a frustrated sigh. "What?"

"It stays in, and no touching yourself."

Her jaw sets. "Fine."

I smile. "It'll be worth it, I promise."

I swear I hear her mutter, "It better be."

I HEAR Pais's ginger footsteps coming down the hall. I glance around and everything is ready. I hauled ass to get her bed put together and sheets on it. There's a nightstand on each side, and I have a few candles lit. It's as romantic as it can get.

I stand up at the edge of the bed, in nothing but a pair of boxer briefs, waiting to see her as she comes through the door.

She doesn't disappoint either.

She made sure to take her sweet-ass time in the shower, like I knew she would, just to spite me. She enters the room in a matching pair of black lace underwear, with black nylon garters halfway up each thigh.

I laid them out for her when I put the towel in the bathroom earlier.

The slow pace of her walk tells me the plug hasn't gone anywhere. She likes playing this little game as much as I do. She always did and always will.

Her eyes widen when she sees the bed and the candles, and a sly little smile threatens to show on her lips, despite the anticipation and frustration from all the teasing.

She starts to say something, but I cut her off.

"On the bed, *now*."

She doesn't hesitate, but she doesn't jump at my command either. She walks over and lays down on her stomach.

I walk slowly behind her around the bed, appraising every square inch of her perfect body. She belongs in a damn museum. Pais is just—beautiful. I don't know how to say it any other way than that. She's not fake, not plastic, just natural beauty. She's gorgeous in a gown or in sweatpants, makeup or no makeup.

I climb up behind her and lift her ass up to me while her chest stays pressed against the sheets. Slowly, I slide my hand down under her pussy, running my fingers the length of it, then lightly tap against her ass to make sure the plug is in place.

"It's still there," she whispers.

"That's not my concern." I lean down, and slowly pull the panties down her ass, and take my time running my tongue along her wet slit.

She shudders as my tongue glides across her.

"Did you touch yourself?"

"I wanted to."

"That's not what I asked, *Pais*."

Finally, she shakes her head. "No."

"That's a good girl." I run my hand along the back of her thigh, then take a finger under one of the garters. "I like this outfit."

"Oh, I'm sure you do." She pauses. "It was a pain in the ass to get it on, pun intended."

I smile but don't break character, then lean over, my chest against her back, and lick along the shell of her ear. My cock has been hard as a rock ever since she went to take a shower and it presses up against her pussy and ass. "Do you like it?"

"Like what?"

I thrust my cock up against the plug in her ass, jolting it forward. "This."

"Shit," she gasps. Then slowly, like she's being shy, nods her head. "Maybe."

I grip down on her collar bone. "Good, I'm going to fuck you while it's still in there."

"Holy..."

I slip my briefs down and line up my cock with her entrance. She's got her ass in the air, chest down on the mattress, and I tease my dick along her clit from underneath. "Good, you're wet." I part her lips and push inside before she can respond, and holy shit, it's euphoric.

She clenches down on me, and I feel the plug in her ass as I push in and out of her, and it's tighter, hotter, wetter, than I ever remember. I want nothing more than to fuck her as hard as I can until I blow deep inside her pussy, but I have to show restraint. It'll be over way too fast if I do that.

Reluctantly, I slide in and out of her in deep, hard strokes.

She's so damn wet it streams down her thighs onto the new sheets. I lean over her back and kiss along her neck as I fuck into her from behind. "You gonna come for me, Pais?"

She bites down on the sheets and nods her head.

"Do it then, come on my cock." I straighten up and pound into her harder.

Her entire body quivers and shakes.

I push my thumb up against the plug and apply pressure as the orgasm rips through her limbs. She shudders and everything tightens even more. Her pussy squeezes my dick so hard I might pass out, but I apply even more pressure and wiggle my thumb around.

"Holy. Shit. Donavan!" She's gasping for air, barely able to say the words.

I have no idea how I haven't blown already. I do whatever I can not to think about it, because I'm not done with her. I'm going to fuck her mouth and her ass too.

Once the orgasm courses through her limbs, I don't even give her a second to recover. I turn her over and suckle her clit. Goosebumps break out all over the insides of her thighs. I lick and suck, raking my teeth across the tender skin all around her.

Her hands fly down and her nails drag through my hair.

This is how she's meant to be. Writhing beneath me.

I glance up and her eyes are closed. Her arms press her tits together, and I slide up and take one of them in my mouth. When I bite down on her nipple, her chest arches up into me.

"Oh God."

I get up on my knees and straddle her. Her eyelashes flutter open just as I start fucking her tits, staring straight down at her eyes.

"Hold them there."

She nods and keeps them together with the insides of her arms as I thrust between them.

With one hand, I reach back and put two fingers inside her pussy and work her clit with my thumb. "I told you. I'm going to fuck everything on your goddamn body."

She goes to say something, and I take my fingers that were just inside her and push them into her mouth. My hips still thrusting my cock between her tits, I lean down, so we're eye to eye. "I'm going to fuck this mouth." I push my fingers in a little harder, to the point she gags a little.

Her eyes are two big, white orbs.

"Your tits. Your pussy. Your ass." I put my hand lightly around her throat, just so she knows it's there. "I want all of you, and I *will* have it."

I can practically feel her heart pounding inside her chest. I love how nervous I can still make her, and I love how her body comes alive when I touch her.

I lean over her and put one palm on the wall, so my cock is inches from her mouth. Her eyes roll up to mine, seemingly asking for permission, and I nod.

Then, and only then, her lips part and she takes me in her mouth. Fuck, fuck, fuck, I forgot how good it feels when Paisley sucks me.

I always tried to go down on her just as much as she went down on me, like it was a give and take, but damn, nobody else could ever compare to her. I have a feeling she's never done it for anyone else, either. I don't know why, and it wouldn't surprise me if I was the only one, but it's like I just know things with her.

It's the same way I've never been inside anyone else's ass. It just feels, I don't know—sacred, something for just us.

I'm already getting close. I can feel it in my balls, building and building, a huge pressure that needs relieved.

I pull myself out of her mouth and try not to grin. It doesn't fit the mood of the room, but all I want to do when I see her face is smile.

I work my way back down between her legs, and then place each hand on the back of her knees and shove them up to her shoulders. It angles her ass and pussy up at me, lifted off the bed, and I can see the end of the plug.

"Hold your legs."

She reaches around and grabs each one, holding them in place.

I grab the lube from the nightstand and toss it down on the bed next to me.

I take my time, slowly teasing around her ass and pussy with my tongue, licking and sucking, driving her crazy. Then I straighten up and look her right in the eye, as I slowly remove the plug.

Once it's out, I hold it up and look down at her. "Good girl."

Before she can respond, I dive back down, and lick all around her ass, just to tease her a little more.

"Please, Donavan, I'm almost there again."

"You will be, soon."

I take my tongue and work it in her ass. She writhes against the bed as I put some lube on my fingers, then suckle her clit while I work my fingers in and out of her, stretching her to accommodate me.

Once I'm satisfied, I lean back and cover my dick with it, from tip to base, until it's shiny and glistening.

I line it up with her and look down at her eyes.

She gives a slight, hesitant nod, and I sink down into her slowly. I don't want it to hurt her. I want to be gentle at first. I want her to like it just as much as I do.

She immediately tightens around me once I have an inch inside her, and holy fuck, I forgot how tight and wet it is. I pull back just slightly, then feed her more and more, slowly and surely, until she finally relaxes.

With my free hand I work lazy circles around her clit.

Her head flies back to the mattress, but she keeps her legs spread open for me with her ass angled up.

I watch myself go in and out, and it's the second best feeling in the world, next to blowing inside Paisley's sweet cunt.

"Tell me, Pais."

I look back up at her and she's in a daze, about to come again. It's like she didn't even hear me she's so caught up in the moment.

I thrust into her a little harder to get her attention and her eyes jolt open. "Pais, tell me."

"It's yours."

"What is?"

I fuck into her ass a little harder and her head flies to the side and she bites down on the sheets. "Everything. It's all yours, Donavan."

My hips speed up, pounding her harder and harder until Pais is writhing underneath me, the sound of our wet skin clapping together echoing around the room.

She's about to come again, and at the last second, I pull out of her ass and slam into her hot pussy.

"Oh my God."

Her fingers claw into my back, and I hook an arm around her leg and push it back toward her head, going even deeper.

"Come with me, Pais."

I press my sweaty forehead against hers and she nods against it.

"Okay."

I fuck her so hard she jolts back and forth, her tits shaking and pressing up against my chest. My balls tighten, and she clamps down on me right as I blow deep inside her.

It's reckless and stupid, but I don't give one fuck. I don't care. If she gets pregnant so be it. I hope she does. I want to take care of her. I want her to have my children. I always have.

Her back arches and her fingers claw against my ribs, like she's trying to shove me off her because the feeling is just too intense. After a few long strokes, her pussy milks everything from me, and I look down. I came so hard it streams out the sides of her and along my shaft.

I pull out of her and she tries to turn over, but I hold her in place.

I lift her legs again, so that her ass is back up in the air, and with my finger I slide it across, scooping up the part of my orgasm that streamed out of her and I push it back inside.

"What the hell are you doing?"

"Putting my baby inside you."

Her eyes widen. "Are you fucking nuts?"

"Yeah, I am, Pais. About you. I should've done this a long time ago. We should already have a family by now."

For the first time in forever, I can't read her face. I can't tell if she's raging mad, or elated, and it bothers me.

She leans up and folds her arms over her chest.

Fuck, I just want to know what she's thinking about right now.

"Take things slow, Donavan? Knocking me up isn't taking things slow."

Once I'm finished, I lower her legs and roll off to the side.

She stands up next to the bed to get dressed, then realizes her clothes aren't anywhere nearby.

"You mad at me?"

She glances back over, then crawls up on the bed and puts a palm on my cheek. "I'm not mad. I feel all the same things you do, like everything is going back to normal and it feels good, really fucking good."

"But?"

Her face hardens. "Things are never going to be the same, D. They're just not. And we don't *think* when we're together. Clearly." She looks down at herself, then back at me. "We're reckless idiots."

I shake my head. "I don't give a fuck. I like being out of control. I want *you*."

She leans over and kisses me on the mouth, and I can tell she's fighting the urge to straddle me and go for round two. "I want you too, I just…" She leans back. "I just want to be smart about it. I don't want what happened…"

"It won't."

She shakes her head. "You don't…" Her eyes close and then she opens them again. "You don't know that."

I wrap my arms around her slender waist and shrug. "I'll do whatever you want me to do. Just be with me, *please*."

She wraps her arms around me and presses my head to her chest. "I'm not going anywhere. I'm just scared."

PAISLEY

"You gonna hang out with us or look at your phone all day?"

I stare up at Grandpa and shake my head. "Sorry." It's probably impossible for me to hide my smile.

Donavan keeps sending me all kinds of sweet and dirty text messages, knowing I'm hanging out with my grandparents.

I sigh and pretend to look at my cards. Every time I start to think about what Donavan and I are doing, it makes my heart come alive, and then everything inside me threatens to crumble apart, knowing how this will all end. It's a vicious cycle, over and over. What did I get myself into?

I glance back up at Grandpa. "Go fish."

We've always played this game since I was a kid and I want nothing more than to just focus on having fun with him, seeing him and Grandma in their new surroundings, being taken care of by one of the top facilities in the world, but I can't. All I can think about is this pressure cooker situation with Donavan, and the fact I'm falling for him all over again. Scratch that, I never fell out of love with him, just buried it deep down inside and never let it escape, but the genie is out of the damn bottle now and I don't think it'll go back inside. We're like *Deepwater Horizon*, an emergency oil spill, and the well can't be capped.

"You have any threes?" Grandpa waggles his eyebrows, then frowns. "What's wrong, kiddo?"

I shake my head. "Nothing. Just a lot going on with work."

"And a guy?"

My eyes widen. "What?"

He shrugs. "You have that look about you I haven't seen in a long time. Like when you were at law school."

Shit. I really want to talk about anything but this right now.

I have no clue what to say, so I say the dumbest, lamest thing I can possibly come up with. "No I don't." I drag out the syllable at the end and everything.

Grandpa grins. "So, you two…"

"No, God…" I don't want to lie to him. "I don't know what we're doing right now, or where it's going."

"I always liked him, you know? Up until…"

"I know, Grandpa."

"People change, Pais. They get older, wiser. Sometimes not so much, but most people." He laughs.

I laugh right along with him, but inside my heart sinks. Now, it seems like I'm the one who changed for the worst. "Yeah."

"What's your dad think?"

I suck in a deep breath. "Well…"

"Don't worry, I'm sure I have a pretty good idea." He shuffles his cards around in his hands. Pretty well, actually, for his age. "What he did was wrong. And I wanted to fly to New York and kick his ass, just like your dad."

"I feel a but coming."

He grins. "But I've made mistakes. He's made mistakes. You make mistakes. It's what people do. It's not good to hold onto things the way your dad is." He holds up both hands. "I'm not judging him for it. You two have been through a lot of shit. The whole family has." I can't help but notice he glanced around before he said 'shit', making sure Grandma couldn't hear.

"I know, Grandpa. I don't think it's good for him either. It's not really up to us, though. We've never been in his shoes, losing everything he loves, twice. First Mom, then the company."

"That's right. You shouldn't criticize someone else." He looks around again. "*Shit* is never black and white. The world is gray and nuanced, things aren't simple."

"Truer words."

He nods.

My phone goes off and I see who the message is from. "Give me a minute, Grandpa."

"No problem. I need a drink anyway." He motors himself back inside their little suite.

I walk off toward a small courtyard with some chairs, away from everyone, to be alone for a minute. I don't open the message, though. Not yet.

Instead, I take a seat, staring around at the place, the smiling elderly people in their windows, getting the best healthcare and standard of living money can buy. I should be happy, but all I can think about is this situation between Donavan and me.

It seems so perfect right now, but I know it's going to end in disaster. How much longer can we keep all this up before it implodes? I should be staying away from him, not running into his arms.

You're not doing anything wrong.

The only thing is, it doesn't feel that way. No matter how many times I tell myself that.

DONAVAN

IT FEELS like Paisley is avoiding me at the office. I've looked everywhere for her and she's nowhere to be found. What the fuck? Maybe Dexter has her busy doing a bunch of shit.

As soon as I turn the corner I run into Quinn.

She has that look on her face. You know, one that suggests this greeting will be about anything but business, and everything to do with my relationship with Pais, even though we haven't told anyone.

"Quinn." I give her a head nod and try to keep walking. Doesn't work.

"Hey, how are you?" She drags out the 'you' like she's hoping to get some gossip. Fuck, there are nosy-ass people all over this office. Is this all they do?

Maybe this won't be a total waste, though. She might have some valuable intel on Paisley's whereabouts. "Great." I try to act casual. "Seen Paisley by any chance?"

I know it's a mistake as soon as I ask because Quinn's eyes light up like a Christmas tree. How can I be so good at reading asshole attorneys in a courtroom and so terrible at small-talk cues?

She shakes her head all slow but has that shit-eating smirk on her face like she knows exactly why I'm asking. "Nope. I could find out for you." She waggles her eyebrows.

Fuck. "It's fine. Just something to do with work."

"Oh yeah? She switch to criminal law?"

"Never mind." I start to walk off, but just as I'm about to make my escape, Tate walks up.

Motherfucker.

My eyes must tell the story because Tate holds up a hand at me.

"Oh relax. I just wanted to say great job. That girl is a keeper and a total badass."

"Is this what you two do all day?"

Tate ignores me and keeps going, jabbing her elbow at me playfully. "Bringing her to the wedding?"

"Yeah, we're all dying to know," says Quinn as she steps even closer into my personal space.

I stare right at Tate and sigh, ignoring Quinn. "Christ, you too? Thought you hated her."

Tate looks away. "Maybe I got some news that changed my mind about her."

"And I haven't been informed yet?"

"Shit, well, umm. You didn't hear anything from me."

"Hear what now?" says Quinn.

I just want this shit to be over. "Yes, I'm bringing her. Now, stop acting all girly, both of you." Someone kill me. I need to change the subject. "How's Decker holding up with all the wedding shit?"

Tate says, "Oh, he's great at this, working with the media. I think he's glad they're finally writing something he likes and not a hit piece."

I grin and glance back and forth at the two of them. "Well, I better go shit on his parade a little. Sounds like he's too happy."

"And, he's back," says Quinn as I walk away.

Without looking I say, "If either of you see Paisley, tell her I'm looking for her." I take two more steps and add, "And stop doing that swooning shit behind my back or I'll be an asshole to her just to make it stop."

This fucking morning. I don't know if I'm more irritated at the way they were looking at me or the fact I haven't seen Paisley's face and it's driving me up the wall. I don't know how to deal with all these goddamn—feelings. It's like I can't even make it through the workday if I don't at least see her, talk to her, or hear her laugh.

I make my way over to Decker's office and burst right in since Quinn isn't there to save his ass from unwanted visitors.

Decker's head pops up from behind his desk. "Nobody knocks in this fucking place, I swear."

I stroll over and take a seat, pretending to be much more comfortable than I am. "How's the wedding planning going, Martha Stewart?"

He eyes me for a minute, like he can't believe we're going to get along for once. "Pretty smooth, actually. I'm a little surprised at how easy it's all coming together."

I nod and smile. "That's great. I'm happy for you."

He stares back at me, smirking. "What's going on here?"

I shrug. "Nothing. Can't I be happy for you?"

"You're not happy for anyone. What the fuck?"

I hold up my hands like *what? I'm happy for you.*

"Things must be going well with Paisley." He steeples his fingers like he just got the upper hand.

About that time, Rick Lawrence walks in. He spots me, freezes for a second, doesn't say a word, then turns to walk out.

"Rick, it's fine," says Decker. "What do you got?"

Rick hesitates for a moment. I've never seen him look this nervous in his life. Fuck, does he have bad news?

"Actually, just the lawsuit. That was the only thing I found, and she was upfront about that. Well, kind of."

Decker's eyebrows shoot up "That's all there was?"

Rick nods. "Yeah."

"Give us details. How thorough were you?" I say.

"This is usually the part where I'd make some reference to anal sex and fisting, but since you two have been banging at your apartment, it's probably inappropriate."

I don't know why I want to laugh and punch him in the face at the same time. "I admire your restraint, Rick. Just tell us your methodology, please."

He glances around, then his eyes land back on us. "Hacked her bank accounts. They checked out. I social engineered a Cooper and Associates low-level employee over the phone to find out she does, in fact, no longer work there. She told me there was a falling out with Cooper because Ms. Williams had to leave the firm to take care of her grandparents. Cooper's still pissed off about it. Yes, the employee sent me unsolicited pictures of her tits. No, I didn't right click and save because Mary has my heart now."

Decker shakes his head. "Can anyone not fuck in this goddamn building? Jesus." He glances over at me. "I'll grant you a free pass since your relationship started way before you came to work here, but everyone else, Christ."

I snicker, but at the same time it feels like an enormous weight just lifted off my shoulders. I trust Paisley. That's what I tell myself. I trust her more every day, but I've been burned so many times in my life 'trust but verify' might be my personal mission statement. There's been this shadow over us, this nagging feeling something was being hidden, that she had some big secret. The verification just came in, though. Rick's the best there is. If there was something, he would've found it. Pais has been telling the truth this whole time.

Now, I want to see her and kiss her even more. I need her so damn bad, every minute of every day, and she's never getting rid of me, even if she wants to. Not gonna happen this time.

Like a true paranoid asshole, though, I just can't let it go. "Who's been paying for her grandparents' health care and place to stay? From what I could see in the file it's the best of the best and expensive as fuck."

Rick nods like he knew the question was coming. "Checked it out. It's a trust in her grandparents' name. The trail I followed looks like it came from cashing out her equity from her partnership at Cooper and Associates. That's my best assessment."

Wow, she's basically using her entire retirement and savings to care for her grandparents. It makes me love her even more. I should have never doubted her in the first place, but I just couldn't help myself. The shit I gave her when she came to work here was totally unwarranted. She was just trying to do what was best for her family and I was a total prick about it. I have to remind myself she's not me. She's never been me. I don't give a shit what Penn says, about how I turned her into a stone-cold killer after law school, you don't just change who you are. Paisley has always cared about other people more than herself. I can't say the same for me.

"Okay, great job, Rick, and that's awesome news," says Decker. "Now that that's out of the way, I need a favor, Donavan."

Hell, I'd probably agree to just about anything right now. I'm on top of the world. "What is it?"

"Mom and Dad won't be in town for the wedding until next week. Tate and I have some stuff we need to do tomorrow night. It's with the—"

"Will you just ask what you're asking? Stop skating around the issue like a pussy."

Decker laughs. "Can you watch Jenny tomorrow night?"

"Watch Jenny?" I chuckle. "She's about to turn sixteen for fuck's sake."

Decker's eyes narrow on mine. "Yeah, and I know for a fact that little boyfriend of hers is gonna show up." His jaw clenches. "I know that motherfucker will."

My entire demeanor changes. "Done. You want me to scare him if he does?"

Decker nods slowly, grinning. "Fuck yes."

Rick bursts into laughter and we both turn to him like we forgot he was still there.

He hooks a thumb over his shoulder. "Okay, I'll just fuck off now. Is there anything else?"

Decker looks at me, then back at Rick. "Nope, that's it."

Rick moves to leave.

"Oh, wait, Rick?" Decker stares at me even though he's talking to Rick.

"Yeah?"

Decker's eyes never leave mine. "Shred everything on Paisley, all your research, then have it destroyed."

Rick nods and walks out of the office.

I smile. Fuck, life is good.

PAISLEY

THE DOORBELL RINGS.

Damn. Donavan's early.

I'd been running around doing some things for the Wells Covington account at work, but it was mostly because I volunteered to do it for Dexter. I could've delegated it to an associate, but it's so hard to look at Donavan right now, knowing how serious we're getting.

He finally cornered me at the end of the day and told me we were going over to meet his sixteen-year-old niece. I should've said no and made up an excuse to get out of it, but it was impossible for two reasons.

One, I haven't seen Donavan look this happy, well, ever. Even in college I can't remember him like this, and it sucks, because he deserves to feel the way he does right now. Two, it's an opportunity to meet his niece.

I shake my head to snap out of my daydream down memory lane.

I make my way over to the door and open it. Donavan looks fantastic. Of course, he does.

He's dressed casual; some tattered designer jeans and a tight blue V-neck t-shirt. The shirt makes his eyes pop and his hair is slicked back. I can't remember the last time I saw him in something other than a suit, naked, or somewhere in between with the suit coming off.

I can't even get a word out because he marches through the door and announces his presence in true Donavan fashion, by planting a kiss right on my mouth, hard and firm.

The kiss quickly heats up and hands start to roam.

Part of me wants this to progress to more, because when he's kissing me or inside me, it takes me somewhere else, and all my anxiety about *us* disappears.

713

Against his lips, I say, "Your niece."

It's probably the only thing in the world that could get him to stop right now. We separate and he adjusts his shirt back down, then smiles. "Yeah, we should get going."

"Okay, I'm just gonna grab my clutch."

Donavan nods, and I walk off and retrieve it. I catch myself in the mirror and damn, I look like shit. My hair was twisted up in a bun all day and now it looks blah.

The way I catch Donavan smiling at me when I walk up tells me he doesn't care one bit about my hair or makeup.

We make our way to the elevator, through the lobby, and over to the parking garage. The drive to Decker's house takes about thirty minutes with traffic. It's nothing compared to driving through Manhattan, though.

I glance over at Donavan. It's so surreal. How did we end up here? A year ago, if you told me this would be my life right now, I might've fallen off a barstool and died laughing.

My throat feels like the Sahara, like words couldn't come out, even if I wanted them to. He's just so—happy. He's so happy it makes things awkward.

I glance back down at the floor, because looking at him is difficult.

"Just warning you, Jenny is going to ask a million questions."

My eyes widen. "Like an interrogation?"

"No, nothing like that." He glances over, smiling, and his hand slides onto my thigh. "She just gets really excited. I think she's glad to finally have more women around."

I nod. "Okay."

He gives me a side eye. "You all right?"

I nod again. "Yeah, I'm fine. Just a little nervous."

He pulls up the driveway to a giant house that sits right off Lake Michigan. I shouldn't expect anything less, considering Decker runs one of the largest law firms in the world. It looks tiny compared to Wells Covington's new mansion, but it's still beautiful.

Donavan leans over and kisses me after he puts the car in park. "Don't be nervous. She'll love you." He leans back and sighs. "I'm sorry I waited so long, you know? I-I'm…"

"It's okay." I cover his hand with mine, and I really don't want it to ever leave my leg.

He shakes his head. "No, it's not. I should've done this…"

"We can't fix the past, but we can make a new future." I say the words to make him feel better but simultaneously feel like the shittiest person in the world for them. I shouldn't have said that. I don't see how a future for us will ever be possible. There's just too much baggage.

I start to say something, but he opens his door and hops out. He hurries around the car and opens my door for me.

My stomach is in knots the whole way to the front entrance.

What if his niece hates me?

Donavan doesn't even get to knock, because the door flies open, and a beautiful teenage girl yanks him inside then does the same to me.

I barely spin around and she's already hugging me.

"You must be Paisley. Oh my God, I love your name. It's so beautiful." She stares back and forth between us. "Yep." She smiles wide. "I'm definitely shipping you two."

I glance to Donavan.

He shrugs and grins. "I don't know what it means, but I think it's good."

She launches into him, wrapping her arms around his waist. "Yes! It's a good thing! Come on." She yanks him by the hand and he almost trips and falls, and she leads us under a staircase and into the living room.

We all sit down on the couch and Jenny launches into full-blown question mode. I actually enjoy it because it takes my mind away from everything else. I forgot how much energy teenagers have.

We go through my entire biography, growing up in Barrington, where I went to high school and how I met Donavan. I leave out all the bad blood between Donavan and me, and he seems to silently thank me for it. I wouldn't do that to anyone, but especially now, the way Jenny looks at him. He's clearly a role model to her.

A million questions later, after Jenny finally seems satisfied and we've had a snack, she heads upstairs. "Okay, I'm going to bed."

"No phone."

Jenny shakes her head at Donavan. "Thought you were the coolest uncle."

He laughs. "Yeah, Dexter told me you tell him the same thing. Which means you use that shit on Deacon too."

She feigns innocence. "I would never." She fake-scowls. "You should know me better than that."

"Yeah right, asshole. Go to sleep. Love you!"

She grins. "Love you too, Uncle Donnie. And it was really nice to meet you, Paisley."

"Nice to meet you too." I smile once more as she disappears around the corner.

She was exactly how I pictured her in my head.

Donavan sits there, patiently waiting, until we finally hear her door close. He turns to me. "Thirty minutes."

I stare blankly. "What?"

"Thirty minutes."

"Until what?"

He leans over next to my ear. "In thirty minutes, I'm fucking you at the boss's house."

Holy. Shit.

IN TRUE DONAVAN FASHION, he sets everything up to make me incredibly nervous about what he's about to do. He gives me a tour of the place, showing me everything. The bedrooms, media room, garage, Decker's study, and then takes me over to a bar in the corner and pours me a drink.

I down it because I just want to get to whatever he has planned, but he takes his sweet-ass time, sipping a scotch and narrowing his eyes on me, like I'm next on the menu. He finally makes a show of savoring the last drop, then takes me by the hand and leads me out to a gorgeous deck that sits right on the lake.

We barely make it two steps out before Donavan turns me to face him and his hands go straight to my hips and pull me into him.

"Fuck, you're beautiful." He slowly takes his hand and pushes a few strands of hair behind my ear.

I don't even know how to accurately describe him, standing there in the pale moonlight with his razor-sharp jawline and eyes that are only for me. "Donavan, I—"

Before I can get my sentence out, he's flipped me around and pinned me up against the wall with his chest. "I wasn't joking, *Paisley*."

Hell, the way he says my name, growls it in my ear. I'm already wet for him. My heart runs a mile a minute, beating uncontrollably in my chest. How does he keep me on edge and at the same time make me feel so safe? It doesn't even make logical sense, but nothing is logical when it comes to Donavan and me.

"About what?"

He smiles against my neck. "That you're beautiful." His hand slides around my throat. "And that I'm going to fuck you."

"We can't. Your niece."

"She's asleep."

I try to turn to face him, but he pins me even harder and squeezes my ass in his palm over my jeans. "How do you know?" My words come out on heavy pants now, because damn, this is so hot.

"I just know." He pulls the collar of my blouse over and kisses down my neck. "And I walked by and peeked in her room."

Before I can respond he bites down on my collar bone, and I let out a soft yelp, coupled with a gasp. My thoughts go haywire on me as his fingers roam my body.

His hand goes to my pussy and he squeezes it in his palm.

My eyes roll back for a second, then I focus. "We shouldn't... Decker and Tate..."

Donavan unbuttons my jeans and shoves his hand down the front, then circles my clit with his middle finger. "You want to talk about my brother, or do you want me to fuck *this*?" He slides two fingers in deep and curls them at the end to hit my spot just right.

I damn near collapse at the waist but manage to hold myself up against the wall. I want him so damn bad I can't even see straight, words won't form, so I just nod.

"What I thought." He pulls his hand out of my jeans, and I immediately miss his fingers and clench around nothing but air.

With two strong hands, he doesn't even unbutton my pants the rest of the way, just shoves them down my ass. They're so tight it burns the sides of my thighs, but in the best way possible. Why the hell do I melt into a puddle when he manhandles me like this? It's always been this way. I used to think about it so much in college, like maybe there was something from my childhood or some psychology behind it. But I couldn't come up with anything. I just—like it, and Donavan knows.

The sound of him warring with his belt, like he can't be inside me fast enough only amps up how turned on I am. I push my ass back against him, and he stops what he's doing and spanks me, hard.

"Stay still, or it'll be worse."

I bump him again.

He yanks his jeans and briefs down and frees his cock, then in one fast motion he's up against me. He fists his cock with one hand and angles it up to me, and with the other he clamps it over my mouth.

He growls in my ear. "Did you think I was joking, Pais?"

I shake my head, needing him more than he'll ever know.

"That's right. You love being roughed up, don't you?" He tightens his grip on my mouth and teases the head of his cock underneath my clit, working it back and forth. "So. Fucking. Dirty. Aren't you?"

I nod again. "Yes, sir."

A low groan escapes his throat. "Fuck, Pais." He snaps back into character. "If you want to get off, you better do it before me. Because I only give a fuck about one thing right now. Blowing in this sweet cunt as fast as I can."

Before I can respond, he shoves into me from behind, and holy shit. He keeps his hand over my mouth, muffling my moans, as he fucks into me from behind. It's so intense. He doesn't hold back at all, doing exactly what he said he was going to do.

His free hand slides around my bare hip, and works down, until his index and middle finger circle my clit. I jerk my hips back, matching every one of his strokes.

"That's it, fuck me, Pais. Fuck me like a dirty little slut."

Oh. My. God.

I'm already on the edge, about to shatter into a thousand pieces then melt into the deck.

"You're close. I can feel it. You up against me, the way you're squeezing around me."

He still has my mouth covered with his palm, so I can't say anything, only nod and bite at his hand. He grips my face even harder and speeds his hips up.

"You better hurry. I'm almost there. Not to mention Decker and Tate will be here any second."

My eyes widen in shock, and his hand squeezes my face even harder. My moans get louder, until I can hear them through his hand, but he doesn't slow down.

His fingers speed up on my clit and before I know it fuzzy stars form in my vision and my whole body quakes and trembles.

Right in the middle of my orgasm, I hear a garage door motor start to turn.

I try to squirm and get away, but Donavan holds me still, and I can practically feel him grinning behind me. Fuck it.

I let the orgasm roll through me, and just as I finish, Donavan releases my mouth, grips my shoulder with one hand, and my hip with the other. He thrusts into me as hard and as deep as possible, maybe deeper than he's ever been. He grunts and his cock kicks. After a few more groans, I feel him stream out of me around the base of his shaft.

Lights come on in the house and I hear voices now, but Donavan stays buried inside me.

He holds me there another few seconds, until silhouettes dance through the windows, then he pulls out of me and we both haul ass to pull our pants back up.

I look up at him, half smiling with post-orgasm bliss, and half with murderous eyes that says he's a dead man. He just shrugs like *what can you do*?

Ugh, I want to kill him!

He still has that boyish smile on his face and pulls me over to him for a kiss.

Once we part ways, I stare at him. "We have to stop doing that."

"Stop fucking? Good one, Williams."

"No." I look away. "You coming inside me. Or I need to get on the pill."

His eyes narrow. "Like hell. You *will* have my kids."

How does the shit he says send me spiraling with worry and simultaneously make me the happiest woman on the planet? God, we're so... I don't even know what to call it. Volatile? Toxic? A disaster waiting to happen?

Only this time, it's my fault. I keep letting this go on.

You're here for your family.

I need some time away from him. Time to think.

Just as my thoughts are about to ruin me from the inside out, Decker and Tate walk out onto the deck.

"Hey, how'd it go?" says Tate.

"Great." Donavan looks over at me and grins.

"Anyone come by?" Decker says all nonchalant.

What the hell is he talking about? Who else would come by?

Donavan shakes his head. "Nope."

"Good."

Tate stares back and forth at both of them. "Is that why Donavan came over? Because you're afraid she'd sneak Nicholas in the house?"

"I'm not afraid. I know she'd do it," says Decker.

Tate's eyes narrow on Decker, and Donavan takes it as our cue to make an exit.

718

We say our goodbyes quickly, then Donavan leads me by the hand to his car.

My mind is spinning a million miles an hour.

What the hell am I going to do?

I really just need to put an end to this fling. I can see the head-on collision coming from miles away, but I keep speeding toward it anyway.

DONAVAN

THE WEDDING IS LESS than a week away and I don't know why I'm so goddamn nervous. Decker's the one getting married.

"How many times you gonna line that shit up, bitch?"

I glare back at Wells Covington. He nudges Penn, and Dexter laughs as I line up my putt for the third time on the eighteenth green of the golf course that sits right off his house.

"This is my one shot at a birdie today, cocksucker."

Fuck, I hate sports. It's embarrassing and I hate doing things I'm shitty at. The whole thing was unavoidable. Decker, Dad, Deacon, and Rick Lawrence already finished and they're at the clubhouse.

I finally putt and it rims out on the right side. "Fuck ass shit!" I want to beat the putter into the green *Happy-Gilmore*-style but manage to compose myself.

"So close." Wells grins as I walk off.

"Like you getting a blowjob in the red-light district."

He nods while Dexter and Penn can't stop laughing. "That hurts, Baby Collins. What a mean thing to say."

Him and Dex walk up to get in their cart, and I hop in one with Penn. He's driving.

"So what are you gonna do? Aren't you tired of being jobless?"

Penn takes a puff off one of Wells' cigars. "Not at all. Look at me. I'm living the same life as you without the work."

"Valid point."

He glances over as we pass by another hole that sits right on the edge of the lake. I watch the clubhouse and Wells' mansion grow larger in front of us.

Covington really is rich as fuck. This place is insane.

"I *am* getting a little restless, though."

I straighten up in my seat. "Oh yeah?"

He has a shit-eating grin on his face. "Yeah."

"Just let me know when."

He sighs. "Give me another few weeks of the good life, then I'll suit back up."

"I'll let Decker know. You can have your pick of what you want to do."

"And who."

I laugh. "Yeah, Decker's gonna love your ass working there."

"He likes money, doesn't he?"

"It's the only reason any of us still have jobs." I lean back and take a sip from a tallboy of Budweiser.

"So… Taking Pais to the wedding, huh?"

"Yeah." My heartrate spikes just thinking about her. I didn't want to leave her side to come out here on this guys' golf day or whatever the fuck they called it.

"It's like old times. It's nice." He stares ahead, like he's looking a hundred miles away.

"I don't know if it'll ever be like it was, but it feels like it might be."

"Yeah, haven't seen you this happy in a while."

About the time he says it, we pull up to Wells' clubhouse.

What in the fucking motherfuck?

Decker gets out and shakes hands with Weston Hunter and his other three main partners. One is his brother and two are his good friends from college, I think.

Decker glances back at me and glares, as if he's giving me some kind of non-verbal warning to play nice. To hell with that. That guy stole from me. Stole my respect, which is worse than stealing money.

I immediately think about Pais, just to calm myself down. In two hours, I'll be with her, and all will be well. We can talk about the wedding and everything we're going to do and wear and all that girly-ass shit that's a million times better than staring at Weston Hunter's face.

They're right in front of the clubhouse, and all my stuff is inside, so I have to walk right by them.

Penn smiles next to me, like he can already feel the tension in the air. Wells seems oblivious along with Dad, and Rick is probably looking for a piece of ass already because he's nowhere to be seen.

"Donavan." Weston holds his hand out as I walk up.

Goddamn it.

I shake it and resist the urge to crush his fingers. "Weston." I start to walk off, but he kind of sidesteps into my path to start up more conversation.

"Great job with the crim law department, you're killing it."

Before I can think, I say, "Great job with the photos. You're killing it at taking all the credit."

He smirks, and I want to punch him in his smug face, but at the same time he holds up his hands. "Whoa, sorry. Can't control what they print in magazines."

He's so full of shit.

"Goddamn it," mumbles Decker. At the same time his stare burns holes in the side of my head.

Just bite your tongue and let it go.

I shrug. "Sorry. Missed a birdie putt on eighteen and I'm still bitter. Good to see you guys." I walk off before I can say anything else.

But fuck that guy, fuck his brother, and those other two bitches. Fuck Decker for putting that asshole's name on our building. I could rip the walls of this place down right now.

"Holy shit." Penn bounces into the clubhouse behind me, then runs to catch up as I power walk toward the lockers.

"What?"

"That was some serious restraint. Thought for sure we were going to get a little show."

"Not worth it."

"Yeah, I mean, fuck, he'd never fire you. Even if you put his ass in the hospital. You're worth too much money to him."

I rifle through my locker for my wallet and shit and don't respond.

"It's one of the reasons I quit working at Cooper. Felt myself focusing on money so much I didn't realize how shitty I was treating people, just, the decisions you make when profit is the only variable that matters in the equation."

I straighten up and put a hand on his shoulder. "Won't be like that here. You'll make a difference, if that's what you're after. We have nonprofits and foundations you can work with. I have a specific group that works back and forth with the Innocence Project. It doesn't have to be about money, even if that cock maggot's name is on the building."

Decker walks in behind us, followed by Dex and Wells. Deacon and Dad must've run off somewhere. Thank God the assholes from Dallas didn't follow them in here.

"I swear to God, Donavan."

I hold up a hand. "Just don't. I'm having a decent day, despite all that shit, and I was nice."

"Well, they're coming to the wedding, and I swear if you get drunk and assault someone…"

"I'm not going to assault someone at your wedding, fuck."

"It might be fun," says Wells.

Decker shoots him a death glare.

"Stop treating me like a child, Decker. I know how to behave."

"I'm just saying, I don't want any problems. Tate's already…"

My head's about to explode. He's always been this way. Selectively picks out whatever facts he wants. Like we're not all brothers and basically the same. Like he doesn't have a fucking temper? Dexter headbutted some jackass in a bar a few months ago. Deacon is no stranger to blowing up and he's fucking huge. I heard him and Decker almost got into a fight at the office in front of employees.

But now, he wants to act all mature and like I'm irresponsible.

I shoulder past him. "I just want to leave. Is that okay with you?"

"You say you don't want to be treated like a baby, then you act like one."

I spin around, ready to unleash hell, but instead I keep my voice calm and collected. Just because I know he hates it even more when I don't blow up on him. "Did you even have my back out there? Or did you just get on your knees for Weston after I walked off?"

He steps up in my face, and Dexter moves to grab him by the arms.

"You did, didn't you?" I smirk. "You let him take all the credit from all of our hard work because you're too big of a pussy to put your foot down."

"Oh, now it's 'our' hard work, Donavan? You act like you're the only one who does shit at the firm. I gave you a managerial role."

"Yeah, a role that doesn't mean dick. It's just a title, that's it. Titles are worthless if the authority doesn't come with them. Your future wife has more of a say over firm business than I do."

He grits his teeth. "Leave her out of this."

I shake my head. I'm so tired of him doing this and I just want to go. I just want to be with Paisley right now and forget any of this ever happened. He doesn't have my back. He never did. None of them did. It's not worth all this anger and frustration sitting on my chest like a ten-ton elephant non-stop. I'm not living with it anymore. I have what I want.

I have Paisley.

"You know what? I'm sorry."

Everyone's eyes widen.

"You what?"

"This day, all this shit, Dad being in town. It's not about me. Sorry. Just, congrats man, I'm happy for you. Enjoy your wedding." I pat him on the arm and walk past.

It's not worth it, arguing with him. He'll never see me as anything but a nuisance, just like when we were kids and I'd follow him around wanting to be just like him. I'm done trying to impress these assholes.

PAISLEY

HOLY SHIT.

This is happening. The guilt has been slowly building and the crescendo is coming way before it's supposed to.

My fingers tap on the steering wheel as I turn down Dad's street. The rehearsal dinner is tonight, and I have a million things I need to talk to him about. Donavan is meeting me here in a bit and Dad has no idea. Why do I do these things to myself?

I know the answer to my question, yet I still ask myself over and over as I pull into the driveway.

I'm self-sabotaging. Punishing myself by forcing us all in a room together.

Plus, I just need my Dad. I want him to comfort me if I crack, because I feel it coming on, and I can't afford for it to happen at the wedding. I need to tell Dad everything I'm thinking, go with Donavan, have a great time, then reassess after the wedding. As soon as the wedding is over and Tate and Decker are a thousand miles away, I'll figure everything out. Surely, I can have fun at a big romantic wedding for a few days, before I have to act like an adult and do the mature thing.

I inhale a deep breath and head toward the door.

Dad opens it before I can knock. "Hey, kiddo."

"Hey." I can't even look up at him.

He eyes me up and down, then opens the door and nods at the couch. "I know that look. C'mon."

I walk slowly, like a prisoner on death row, all the way to the couch, biting back the shame in my chest. Once I'm seated, I say, "How's your work coming along?"

Dad sits in his recliner and stares. He's trying not to smile, which tells me he's onto something, but he wants to be polite and can see I'm conflicted. "No, let's talk about—"

"No, you first, Dad. Please. I need some good news before…" My words trail off.

"I think I'm onto something, Pais. I've been working non-stop the last week, all these ideas coming to me all at once." He looks like he wants to bounce out of his chair, but he's restraining his reaction remarkably well.

"That's… That's great, Dad." I nod.

"Pais, what's going on? Talk to me."

God, why is this so hard? I can deal with billionaires on Wall Street, but I can't even form words right now. I need to just tell him everything that's going on with me and Donavan and get it all out there.

"Dad, I…me and…" Just as I start to spill everything, I hear a car door in the driveway. I head toward the window and sure enough, it's him. "Shit. Donavan's early."

Dad turns to me. "*Donavan's* here, again?"

I nod and run over to Dad. "I'm sorry. I was about to tell you everything, but he showed up early. Please, I need something from you. Promise me."

Dad must notice the panic in my face. I'm practically trembling. He's caught right in the middle and I can see he's warring between going outside for a confrontation and consoling me.

"What is it you want me to do?"

I can't even look at him when I say it. "Please, just forgive him. Even if you don't want to, will you do it for me? Please?"

Dad's jaw sets and he glares at the door, then back at me. Finally, his face softens, just as I hear Donavan coming up the steps. "Okay." He nods. "Okay, I will."

I launch into him and wrap my arms around him. "Thank you. I'll tell you everything when I get a chance. I promise."

He smooths his hand down the back of my hair and kisses the top of my head. "Whatever you want, sweetie. I've got your back, a hundred percent."

"Thank you." I walk to the window, surprised Donavan hasn't knocked yet. I sneak a peek at him and he's a few feet away from the door.

He looks around, then takes a deep breath, like he's working up the courage to announce his presence.

My stomach is a pretzel right now, and yet somehow, him just being around sets me at ease at the same time. It's so frustrating. I can't even explain the emotions this man makes me feel.

He finally knocks. I answer.

His eyes light up the second he sees me.

"Hi."

His eyebrows shoot up. "Hi."

I open the door. "Come in."

He hesitates. "You sure?"

"Come on in, it's fine," Dad hollers from his recliner.

Donavan's eyes widen and he shrugs. "Umm, okay."

"Just have a seat," says Dad.

I can't thank Dad enough in my mind for taking charge right now because I'm a hot mess.

We walk over to the couch together and sit down. There's an awkward silence for a few seconds, though it feels like it's hours.

"Do you love my daughter?" Dad stares right at Donavan.

He damn near squirms on the couch. I never thought I'd see the day, Donavan Collins looking nervous, but it's happening.

"Yes, sir."

"Then the past is the past, isn't it?"

Donavan glances back and forth at both of us like *is this really happening right now?* Finally, he nods. "Yeah. I feel like I should say something, though."

Oh God, please don't let him go into humble mode right now, it might destroy me.

Donavan says, "I'm sorry. You'll never know how sorry I am. What I did to your daughter and your family…it was the biggest mistake of my life."

Shit. Shit. Feelings. Guilt.

Dad glances over at me, then back to Donavan. "We *all* make mistakes, son. I'm sure it won't be the last time someone in this family screws up."

My eyes start to burn when he refers to Donavan as family once again. I have to hold it together, but I don't know if I can.

Donavan nods, unable to say anything, but he exhales the loudest sigh of relief I've ever heard. He stands up and Dad does the same, and I have no idea what I'm even doing right now. I feel like I'm in quicksand. He wraps Donavan in a hug, but his eyes are fixed on mine the entire time.

Once they break free of their little moment, Donavan spins around to face me and he looks happier than I've ever seen him look. Despite wanting to run to my room and never come out, I put on my best game face and smile back at him.

"You ready to meet my family?"

Shit.

I've been so caught up in all this I totally forgot I'm about to meet his family for the first time too. Well, his parents anyway.

I nod.

Dad follows us to the door and shakes Donavan's hand again. "It's good to have you back. Take care of my little girl."

"I will, sir. I promise."

I need a drink, or ten.

PAISLEY

THE WEDDING IS at the Chicago Yacht Club and the drive over was mostly silent. I said a few words, but it was mostly me sitting there, stewing about this whole situation, while Donavan looked happier than I've ever seen him, like the weight of seven years lifted off his shoulders.

In a weird way, I resent him almost, for the way he feels right now. All I want is that. I want to enjoy this and be happy and meet his family, but I just can't. I wish I could just turn my brain off and enjoy this.

Donavan's hand slips into mine as we walk up, and I pray he can't feel how clammy my palms are. The wedding is going to be incredible. Spectacularly beautiful. They're already setting up a red carpet outside and people rush around, checking phones and tablets.

"You ready?"

My gaze angles up to Donavan. "For?"

"To meet them? Everything okay with you? You're really quiet."

Shit, his family. I keep forgetting. "Yeah, just really nervous."

"Don't be. Mom and Dad will love you. I promise."

We'll see.

We make it inside and there are three women with headsets talking to Tate. She looks like she wants to pull her hair out already. I can't blame her.

"Donnie!" A woman who must be Mrs. Collins damn near tackles Donavan, and as quickly as she has him wrapped up, she lets go and takes me by the hands. "You must be the infamous Paisley."

I nod, because I have no idea what to say. She's grinning from ear-to-ear and so not what I expected.

"You just…" She can't stop gushing, then wraps me up in a giant hug.

I hug her back because despite everything going on with me right now, it just

729

feels really good, and I immediately miss my mom. I haven't felt this type of comfort in forever, after walling myself off after Mom died.

"Gorgeous!" She turns to Donavan. "Isn't she gorgeous?"

"Yeah, Mom. She is. Try not to suffocate her, okay?"

She let's go. "Sorry. Sorry. Wow." She smiles so big at Donavan. "It was Thanksgiving, wasn't it?"

"Mom, we don't talk about Thanksgiving."

"What happened at Thanksgiving?" I say, grinning at Donavan.

"See what you did, Mother?"

"Oh, whatever." She waves him off with a hand. "Dex and Abigail made up and now they're together. It's water under the bridge. Anyway, Paisley, I gave Donavan a hard time about not keeping a woman happy."

"Jesus, here we go."

She turns and points a finger in his face. "What did I tell you about your language?"

I can't help but laugh. I love her already.

The other brothers see us and start in our direction.

"Can't believe Mom didn't tackle her to the ground," says Deacon as he walks up.

She wheels around on him. "Can't believe you haven't made me a grandbaby yet. Did you get your sperm tested like I told you?"

Deacon's face turns bright pink and he mouths, "Fuck," where she can't hear it.

Decker and Dexter are rolling. She begins to say something, and an older, stately man walks up. He has to be their father. He looks just how I picture Donavan when he's about sixty.

"Honey, will you ever let the girls breathe?" He holds out a hand. "David Collins."

I shake it. "Paisley Williams, nice to meet you, sir." I glance around. "The place is beautiful."

"Hell yeah it is, c'mon." Tate grabs me by the arm.

I don't even know where she came from, but I'm happy to have the attention off me. She pulls me over to a mimosa bar, thank God, and Quinn, Abigail, Tate's childhood friend Alexis, and Jenny follow us over there.

A bartender mixes the champagne and orange juice in flutes for us. The three women with headsets start toward us.

Tate immediately holds up a palm at them. "Five minutes, fuck."

I try my best not to laugh, but I can so relate to Tate right now. This would not be my thing either, especially with other people in charge bossing me around telling me what to do.

She turns to me, takes a deep breath, and says, "Glad you could make it. And you survived being accosted."

I glance around at all of them. "You guys all went through that too?"

They all nod.

"Grandma is awesome, she just gets excited," says Jenny, as she takes a drink of a flute with just orange juice in it.

Tate keeps eyeballing Quinn, but Quinn keeps looking away. "She's obsessed with having more grandkids."

"Would've never known." I laugh.

"You're lucky I pulled you out of there when I did. She was going to tell you what color eyes your and Donavan's babies would have."

"Hey, I wouldn't mind having some cousins." Jenny smiles.

Quinn keeps looking away.

Tate gets that sly smirk on her face. "Not thirsty, Quinn?" She eyes the full mimosa Quinn hasn't so much as had a sip of.

"N-naw, not really, I'm…"

"Feeling a little under the weather?" says Tate.

"What?" says Jenny, oblivious. "What's going on?"

Quinn yanks Tate aside, and leans in her ear and whispers something.

Tate rushes back over to us with Quinn on her heels.

Quinn says, "No, Tate, wait, please."

Tate turns back to her. "What? It's fantastic."

Quinn looks around at all of us, then smiles bigger than I've ever seen her smile, and she smiles all the time. "I'm pregnant."

"That's amazing!" I say.

"Congratulations!" says Abigail.

Quinn turns to Tate. "We were going to take you and Decker aside, before you fly out, and then announce it after you leave. We don't want to take anything away from your big day."

"Oh horseshit!" says Tate. "I would kill for some attention to be off me right now."

Tate walks toward all the family and friends and whistles so damn loud my ears actually ring. How the hell did she do that? Must be a Texas thing to call in the cattle or something.

Everyone freezes. Quinn is running after her. "No, Tate."

"Everybody! Quinn has an announcement to make."

"No, no I don't."

We all turn to Deacon and he looks like a deer in headlights. His eyes dart around then land on Quinn. She finally shrugs and then motions him over.

We all stand there, waiting, and Donavan walks up and puts his arm around me.

"What's this all about?"

"You'll see."

Decker sneaks in behind us and I hear him say, "There better not be any champagne in that."

"Dad, I don't drink."

"Mmhmm." He eyes her skeptically. "I'd complain about your boyfriend not being here, but I'm actually relieved."

"His band has a gig."

Decker damn near chokes and I'm not even sure he took a drink of anything. "A *gig*?"

"Yeah, you know where four guys bring instruments, play music and sing songs, for a crowd?"

"I know what a damn gig is. Wasn't aware he's in a band."

Jenny looks over at me and Abigail and grins. "It's pretty hot."

"Oh fu—" Decker stops himself. I glance back and his jaw is clenched shut.

Tate walks over to us, leaving Deacon and Quinn alone in front of everyone.

Before she even gets to us, Decker is marching toward her. "Did you know about a damn band gig?"

Tate smiles her ass off. "Not now. This is important."

"Not now? Are you—"

"Decker, I said not now."

Donavan's practically trembling he wants to laugh so bad.

"Umm, yeah, so everyone, I *guess* we have an announcement to make." Deacon glares over at Tate as he says 'guess', then turns back. "So... yeah, Quinn's pregnant."

"Oh! My! God! You had your sperm tested!" Mrs. Collins flies out toward them, arms extended at Quinn.

Quinn clutches her stomach, as if she's protecting the baby, and everyone else is doing the same because they can't stop laughing. Everyone except Mr. Collins, who palms his forehead, shaking his head as he walks out to congratulate them.

"Holy. Shit." I glance up at Donavan, after seeing his mom sprint toward Quinn like a linebacker.

"Yep." He grins at me, then leans down so we're eye level with each other. He whispers, "Get ready, you're next."

Before I can respond, his mouth is on mine and he's kissing me way harder than he should in front of his whole family, but my God, he knows how to kiss.

After a few minutes, everyone says their congratulations.

The women with the headsets are back and barking orders, wanting everyone to get ready to start rehearsing.

I give Donavan another quick peck on the lips. "I'll hang out over here while you're doing your thing."

"Okay, babe." He walks off.

Tate comes over and looks me up and down, from head to toe. "I have something to ask you, Paisley."

"Umm, okay. You need me to get you something? Or take care of some errands?"

Tate shakes her head and smiles. "No, no. Nothing like that. I want you to be a bridesmaid."

I must look like I've just seen an alien, because her request catches me off guard. "You umm, I'm sorry, what?"

"Yeah." She nods. "You can't say no to a bride. It's against the rules, you know?"

"Yeah, but I mean, why? You barely even know me."

Tate looks over at Donavan, then at Quinn, Abigail, Jenny, and Mrs. Collins. "You're in love with a Collins boy. You're one of us now."

My chest swells and I can't remember ever being so flattered, excited, happy. It's like she's asking me to be a part of their family, something I always wanted back in college, the same way he was with my family.

I shake my head. "But, a dress, I don't…"

"It's waiting for you. There's a tailor on standby to get it ready for tomorrow."

"Wait, wha-when did you order me a dress?"

Tate grins. "The first time I saw you and Donavan looking at each other in the office."

Finally, I nod. Because what else can you do when the bride asks you for something?

Just as I start to smile, the guilt floods back into my system, crashing into me twice as hard as before. How the hell am I going to do this without having a panic attack? I really don't know if I can go through with it.

DONAVAN

I USUALLY HATE weddings and big events, but this one isn't so bad. I watch Pais from across the room at the rehearsal dinner and everything just feels—right.

I take another flute of champagne from a server who walks by with a tray while watching her laugh and talk to my family like she's always been a part of it. How different would my life have been if I hadn't walked out on her? Would we have five kids by now? More? Married with a big townhouse in Manhattan, working for Cooper and Associates? Manhattan was always the plan.

She would've talked me into it. She was the only one with that ability. It would've been a nice middle finger to my brothers for always looking down their noses at me.

Mom walks up from behind and bumps me with her hip. "So, she's the one?"

I nod. "Yeah, always has been."

"Why didn't you ever bring her home to meet us? The way you talked about her when you told me all those years ago. I knew another girl would never have your heart."

"You know why." I look away from her, wishing I hadn't spent the last seven years alone.

"Your brothers love you, Donnie. Yeah, they might've picked on you some, and I probably should've intervened more than I did, but that's what older brothers do."

"If it weren't for you, I wouldn't have come back to Chicago."

She steps in front of me and squares up, so we're face to face. "Is it worth it?"

I smirk. "Is what worth it?"

She pokes a finger into my chest. "Hanging on to all that resentment, right there." She jabs me a little harder.

I stare right back in her eyes. "I would prefer there not to be a reason for any resentment."

She shakes her head. "I love all of you the same. So does your father."

I don't want to get into this shit right now. This should be reserved for a shrink's office, not Decker's rehearsal dinner. "I believe *you*. Dad, not so much."

"Donavan, I'm not going to sit here and pretend like your father couldn't have done better. Every parent in history could've done better at some point. Yeah, maybe he related to Decker and Deacon a little more with the sports, but he provided for all of us. He tried and it eats him up that you think he casted you aside and only cared about your brothers."

"Really?" I scoff. "You'd never know it from all the non-existent apologies. And I never complain to him. Collins men don't complain, we get things done, remember? So why would he think I feel that way? He has no idea."

"Is that what you need to make things better? An apology from him?"

I shake my head. "I don't know, Mom. I just...wanted to feel like a part of the family, and I didn't. It is what it is. I'm fine, okay? I have a great job, respect of my peers, an amazing girlfriend. I'm happy. I just want to leave the past where it is."

Her eyes narrow on me and she nods. "Okay. If you say so."

She goes in for a hug and I squeeze her back. Honestly, it feels kind of nice to get some of that off my chest. She's fooling herself if she thinks Dad ever showed even a remote interest in anything I wanted to do, but I can't change any of that.

I catch Pais staring at us out of the corner of her eye, and she politely dismisses herself and walks over. With her black clingy dress and pointy heels, she looks so damn beautiful it hurts.

Mom releases me and walks over to talk to Deacon and Dexter.

Pais strolls up next to me and it takes every ounce of restraint I have not to whisk her away into a broom closet and yank that dress off her.

"Is that Tate's family?" She nods off over to some men and women. There are three boys spread out a few years in age. The oldest one looks like he's maybe fifteen.

"I think so."

"They look nice."

"Yeah." I take another sip of champagne.

Just then, the oldest one walks over to Jenny. *What the fuck?*

Pais sees what I'm looking at. "Oh, the plot thickens. Doesn't she have a boyfriend?"

I nod. "Yep."

"And that's Tate's nephew, I'm assuming? The boyfriend isn't around?" She turns and hooks her arms around my neck. "This is like a YA taboo love triangle, playing out right before our eyes."

I laugh. "You look way too excited about this."

Tate's nephew reaches over and takes Jenny's hand as they speak, running his thumb over her knuckles, and fuck this shit. I pull away from Pais and start over there when Tate comes out of nowhere and grabs her nephew by the ear.

I laugh just as Pais sees what happens.

Tate's in the corner with her nephew shaking a finger at him, presumably telling him she's off limits and about to be family.

Paisley frowns. "And just like that, Tate takes an axe to the plot."

"So sad." I mock her.

She swats at my chest, but I snag her arm and pull her in for a kiss. It's really nice, but something seems off. I don't know what it is, but it's like there's this invisible barrier between us. On the outside, everything seems fine, but it's just like she's got one foot in, afraid to take the next step. She's distant. I can't really blame her after everything that's happened, but I'm not twenty-three anymore. Surely, she realizes that.

"What's going on with you?"

"Huh?" Her eyes dart up to mine.

"I don't know. Something just seems off."

Pais shakes her head and fakes a smile at me. "It's nothing, seriously. Just weddings and family, nerves, and it's all happening so fast."

It makes sense, I guess, she's a little overwhelmed. I have the remedy to that, though.

Leaving the rehearsal dinner, I hail us a cab and whisper our destination to the driver before opening the door for Pais.

"A cab, huh? Can't hold your booze?"

I slide in next to her. "Have a surprise."

"Oh really? Something tells me I'm not going to make it to my apartment tonight."

I nod slowly. "Your assumptions are correct." I block the view of the cab driver, putting my back to him, and my mouth collides with Pais. That wall is still up but I'm going to knock it down.

I keep it PG rated all the way to where we're going, even though it's the last thing I want to do. What I want to do is rip her clothes off and bury my cock inside her, right here in this cab.

It seems like it's only seconds later, but the cab comes to a halt, and I slide back over and open the door. I get out of the cab and hold my hand out. "C'mon."

She grips me and steps out, then looks up. "Ohh, the Waldorf."

"Let's go. I need you out of that dress."

She bites her lip and I pull her toward the front door. By the time we get to the entrance we're practically running and she's giggling, and fuck, there's nothing I love more than her laughing and happy.

Someone greets us at the door and hands me the packet with our keys. I take it like a hand off and keep going.

"Don't we need to check in?"

"Everything's taken care of."

She follows me into the elevator, and we head to the 26th floor, the presidential suite. It was the largest room they had.

I corner her in the elevator, backing her up against the wall and run my hands over her ass.

"You've been waiting all night for this, haven't you?"

I nod, not taking my eyes off her, then yank her into me. I kiss down her neck, then back up to her ear. "Just you and me, all night."

"We don't have clothes for tomorrow." She gasps when I nip at her ear.

"Won't need them. I plan on keeping you naked."

The elevator dings before I can make good on my promise right here. We step off and head to the room. I open the door and usher Pais inside.

"Holy… This place is amazing." She walks a few steps toward the bedroom. "Oh my…"

I wrap my arms around her waist from behind, then peek over her shoulder to make sure these fuckers got every detail right.

There are candles lit everywhere, and a trail of rose petals down the hall. I nudge her toward the door to the master bedroom, and the petals lead up to the bed. On a side table there are champagne and chocolate-covered strawberries. Right in the middle, is a single slice of pecan pie.

Paisley sees it then turns to me. "Are you trying to ruin the evening?"

I shrug. "It's like a tradition now. We don't have to eat it."

She laughs. "I do kind of like that we have a tradition, even if it's a disgusting one."

There's just something about the moment, staring into her eyes, the candles and rose petals. All night, I thought I'd get her up here, rip her clothes from her body, and fuck her so hard she'd have trouble walking at the wedding.

But, right now, after all the shit with my family, the talk with my mom, I just want to kiss her, hold her. I just don't want her to ever go anywhere or be anywhere else but right next to me. When she's away, I feel like I can't breathe. She's the only person who really knows me. Gets me.

I unzip the back of her dress until it falls and puddles around her feet. She has on a pair of matching black lace bra and panties. I take my time, reaching around and cupping her breasts in my palms as I kiss down her slender neck. At the same time, I unclasp her bra in the front and let it fall from her shoulders.

I don't know what comes over me, but I scoop her up in my arms, wedding-style and carry her to the bed. Her arms hook around my neck and she stares back at me.

I set her down gently on the bed.

She scoots back and props her head up on the pillows as I take off my shirt and pants until I'm in nothing but my boxer briefs.

I crawl up between her legs and kiss her, softly at first, until the kiss grows hungry. My hands roam her body, wanting to feel every square inch of her. My cock goes hard as a rock when she spreads her legs and grinds her pussy against me. She's so hot and wet I feel it through the fabric of her panties.

Slowly, I lean back and pull them down her thighs, then all the way off and toss them aside. For a brief moment, I sit there on my heels, staring at her spread out in front of me. Fuck, she's the most gorgeous thing I've ever seen, the perfect woman. She's so damn beautiful it physically hurts.

I slide my briefs off and crawl up between her legs, until we're face to face, and the head of my dick is pressed up against her. One small shift and I could easily glide into her she's so hot and wet, but I don't.

She stares back at me like she doesn't even know who I am right now, like she's expecting to be spanked or have her hair pulled. I kiss her again, even softer this time. I kiss down her neck, then exhale warm breath in her ear.

"I don't want to control you. I just want to be with you." I glide into her slowly as I say the words.

Our foreheads press together and our eyes lock as I slide in and out of her, in long, slow, deep strokes.

Her legs hook around my waist and her heels dig into my ass and it's fucking amazing, just being with her, here in the moment, joined together. It's cathartic, letting go, and for a moment I don't feel any pressures of the world. I haven't done anything wrong. I'm just here, present, sharing a connection between us. Something that's ours and nobody else's and nobody can ever take it away from us.

I push farther into her and a slight gasp parts her lips, and her eyes roll back for a second.

I glide into her, over and over in deep strokes. "I love you, Paisley. More than you'll ever know."

"I love you too." Her eyes are still closed when she says it, but my heart comes alive.

Every time she says those words to me, it's like a ray of sunlight in a dark cavern.

"I want you. Forever. There's nothing else I want in this world. You're it."

Pais nods, and I feel her body buzzing, and she's so close.

"Come for me, baby."

She nods again and her whole body tightens. Fuck, it's amazing. I can't hold back any longer either, and I come deep inside her. I can't remember ever making love to anyone like this before. Sex has always been an outlet, a way to release tension. Right now, it's like an entirely different experience, like we're one entity instead of two separate people. There's a spiritual connection, and fuck, I might feel alive for the first time in—hell, ever.

I'm still buried inside her when our eyes meet again, and I don't ever want to come out. I just want to stay here, locked in this moment, for eternity.

Her eyelashes flutter then a smile spreads across her face. "That was…"

"Incredible?"

"I was going to say, different." She covers her face. "Sorry, that sounded terrible."

I pull back her hands, and she still has her eyes squeezed close. "It's okay, Pais." I can't stop smiling at her.

"It was an awesome kind of different."

"I can still spank you if you want."

She smacks at my chest and I roll over, so we're both on our backs, lying next to each other staring up at the ceiling.

I glance over at her and she's looking at the wall.

"I meant what I said. I love you, more than anything."

"I love you too."

She says the words, but she still doesn't look over at me. I don't know what's going on with her. Maybe it just has to do with her dad and grandparents. I don't know, but I have the rest of our lives to get her to open up to me.

One thing I do know is she's not going anywhere. I'll never let her get away.

PAISLEY

TEARS ROLL DOWN my cheeks and land on the expensive hotel sheets. Donavan is passed out with his back to me.

I glance over at him and try not to sniff too hard and wake him up.

You'll never make it until after the wedding. You need to end this, now.

I want to rip this band-aid off so bad. I want to grab him by the shoulder and shake him awake, beg for him not to hate me and understand why we won't work. But, I just can't.

Part of me wonders if I'm doing this just to torture myself. Or because I'm selfish and want a few more days of seeing him smile.

Once it's done, it's done. He'll never talk to me again. He'll blow up and make a scene if I so much as suggest we shouldn't be together, that we have too many scars, that I have too much going on he wouldn't understand. I tell myself that's the reason I haven't broken this off yet, because he might ruin the wedding. If I break up with him now, he might not even show up, but I know that's not the actual reason I'm waiting.

It's really because I know once we have the conversation it will break him. He's so happy right now. Happier than I've ever seen him, and it will physically shatter him, and we'll never be the same.

I can't remember a time in my life where I've had anxiety so bad I could barely function. No amount of Xanax or any other pharmaceutical could take this pain out of my chest. I thought it would be easier with the wedding and staying busy, but it's not. It's a million times worse.

I reach over for his shoulder, like I've done about twenty times already, and at the last second, I pull my hand back again because I'm a chicken shit. I need to just tell him why I'm such a nervous wreck, but I can't.

Finally, I get up and make my way out to the balcony because lying next to him is too painful. I sit out there in a chair, hugging my knees to my chest, watching the city. It's nice out, beautiful. Nausea hits me all at once and I feel like I might puke everywhere. Maybe I'm coming down with the flu and it will get me out of all this. I can't remember the last time I got sick.

I sit out there for about an hour, constantly looking back in at Donavan, asleep by himself in the bed. His lips are curled into a grin. Every time I see it, I damn near break down again.

Eventually, I take a deep breath, walk inside, and crawl back into bed.

Twenty-four hours. I've thought about this a million times when I wasn't emotional. It's the right thing to do. Tate and Decker don't need the extra stress. If Donavan freaks out it could damage the firm with all the press that'll be at the wedding.

The next twenty-four hours will be hell, but after that, we can finally move on. Maybe tomorrow will be so damn busy, I won't be able to think about anything anyway, and time will fly by.

One can hope.

I take one last look at Donavan and nuzzle into him, knowing it might be the last time I ever get to do it.

DONAVAN

WE PULL up in a limousine outside the yacht club.

Paisley stares out the window with wide eyes at all the photographers waiting for us.

"You ready?" I hold out a hand to her.

I don't know what the deal is, maybe just nerves, but she's barely said a word all morning. I had to pry a conversation out of her at breakfast.

She takes my hand and we step out and walk toward the building.

Camera flashes go off from every angle. People holler questions at us.

An usher leads us over to the red carpet through the sea of paparazzi. The usher tells us where to stand and I look down at Pais and grip her hand tighter.

"Just smile and pose. It's almost over."

She smiles for the cameras and through her teeth says, "This is insane. Are the Chicago Bulls here?"

"Probably, we do some work for them. I'm sure MJ will be here. You watch basketball?"

"No, I just saw some really tall guys, so I took a guess."

"Well, just think of Decker as the Chicago version of Cooper. If Cooper got married, wouldn't it be like this?"

She stops posing and grins at me. "You have a point."

"Decker knows how to work PR. He's definitely capitalizing."

Finally, they lead us inside, away from the madness.

I think I might have a chance to talk to Paisley and catch a breather when three women with headsets rush up to us. Two of them grab each of us by the arm and march us toward rooms in the back.

This place is insane. It's nothing but people running around like crazy, holding flowers and candelabras. They lead us back to a large room with a huge buffet-style spread.

One of the ladies turns to us, scowls, and says, "Eat. You may not get to for a while. And don't get anything on your clothes."

Before I can say something shitty back to her, she turns on her heel, and marches from the room.

"Well, I guess we better eat." Pais walks over to the table.

I hang back and spot Deacon and Dexter, hanging out by themselves by a window.

"What's up, pussies?"

"Says the asshole with a leash on his dick." Dexter laughs. "She get you a ring yet?"

I stare back and forth at them. "You know that doesn't work when you're already engaged, right?"

"Fuck that," says Deacon. "It never gets old."

I nod. "Agreed. You assholes eat yet?"

They both look at each other, then shake their heads.

"Waiting on your women? Can't start without them?"

Two middle fingers fly up in my face, and I walk back over to join Pais. I fill my plate next to her when Decker and Tate both walk in.

My eyes widen. "Wait. What?" I wave a fork between them.

"Screw traditions," says Tate. She barrels past me and grabs a plate. "I'm fucking starving."

I glance over at Decker and he's pale as a ghost, like everything is just now setting in and he realizes what's about to happen tonight. "Better keep an eye on this." I point over at Tate. "The hips get wider. That's how it starts."

Tate doesn't even look up from the food. "I'd be insulted, but I'm so hungry I don't give a shit if I fit in my dress or not."

The rest of the family files in behind them, and damn, I didn't realize how many of us there are plus Tate's family.

Once her plate is full, her and Decker stand in front of everyone. She sets her food down and goes over all the plans. At the end she points at all the brothers. "You have one rule. Do *not* get drunk and embarrass me."

Just then, a cloud of smoke comes in from the entrance. It's Wells Covington puffing on a cigar with two scantily clad women on his arm. "Fuckers!"

"Jesus Christ." Tate palms her forehead and Decker rushes over to console her.

I laugh and Paisley smacks me in the chest.

"What the hell was that for?"

"It's *her* day. Not yours."

I nod, grinning. Thank God she seems to be coming out of her little funk. "Okay, I see how it is."

She smiles, then just as fast it disappears.

Shit.

We make our rounds and say hi to everyone, all the families. Mindless chit-chat and small talk.

Eventually, Pais ends up with the bridesmaids in another room, and it's Decker, Deacon, Dexter, and me in our own room.

Decker looks like a fucking ghost. A normal family might console him, but not ours.

"Jesus Christ, Casper, need some meds?" says Dexter.

"I'm fine. I'm fine," says Decker.

"Repeat that fourteen more times, maybe you'll believe it." I laugh.

"Fuck you guys," says Decker.

"You'll be okay." Deacon walks to the middle of the room like he's about to give a speech. "I mean, what could possibly go wrong, Decker?"

"Nothing is going wrong, assholes."

Dexter straightens up. "Well, now, let's do the math on this. How many people are attending the wedding?"

Decker turns his head, not liking where this is going. "Five hundred and change."

Dexter waves him off. "Oh, you got nothing to worry about. You know, I read the other day one in twenty-thousand people in the U.S. commit murder. That means there's a two point five percent chance there will be a murderer here. But, when you stop and think about lifestyles, the type of clients we represent... I'd maybe push it to ten percent. So, I mean, one in ten someone gets killed. I'd take those odds any day." He walks past Decker, grinning at Deacon and me.

Decker shakes his head. "Motherfuckers."

"That's just worst-case scenario, though," says Deacon. "Think about all the employees here, mingling, attachments to the firm. Healthy mix of male and female. All the pheromones in the air, champagne flowing, a gorgeous romance story unfolding in front of them. I mean, what are the odds of a giant inter-office orgy wrapping up as Decker and Tate board the plane for their honeymoon?"

I lose it at that point, damn near doubled over.

Decker stares like he doesn't even hear us. "I don't care." He looks down at us. "She's it, man."

The laughter disappears and the shit talk ceases.

"Happy for you." Dexter walks up and gives him a hug.

"Yeah, bullshit aside, it's gonna be great." Deacon hugs him too.

I walk up last. Decker looks at me and we have a brief moment, maybe three seconds, where we just stare.

There's so much between us, miles really. I don't know if I've totally forgiven him for all the shit with the firm. I want to say I have. I want it to be over, water under the bridge. Maybe I should just let it all go, because I don't know if they'll ever respect me the way I want them to, no matter what I do.

"I'm really happy for you. I mean that." I give him a hug.

"Thanks."

"Yep." I pat him on the shoulder and back away.

"Glad that shit's out of the way." Dexter sighs.

"Yep," Deacon and I say at the same time.

"It means a lot," says Decker. "Where the fuck is Dad? I thought he'd be back here with us."

About that time, one of the headset chicks rounds the corner. "Okay, thirty minutes for just the brothers is up. Come with me please."

"Guess that explains that." Decker walks toward her.

We all follow.

"Ain't even running your own shitshow of a wedding?" says Dexter.

"No man runs his fucking wedding." Decker stops in his tracks. "Wait, do you want to run yours?"

Dexter backpedals a little. "No, I was just…"

Decker laughs, eyes him up and down, then grins. "Sure, bitch. You pick out flower arrangements like a champion I bet, between the *Hallmark* movies."

Deacon and I are about to die.

On our way to the next room, Dexter mumbles, "I don't know shit about flowers."

Oh man, maybe this will be fun after all.

ALL THE BROTHERS except for Decker hang out around the front, mingling with people as they come in. It's our thirty-minute break before we have to go backstage or whatever and get ready to walk out to the music.

Dexter and Deacon walk off to chat with Wells and Cole Miller. Penn shows up with some woman I've never seen before. The bridesmaids aren't out here, and I miss Paisley like crazy. I hang out with Penn and his date to keep my mind off where she is and what she's doing.

Rick strolls in with a woman on his arm who looks vaguely familiar.

She's pretty hot, which is no surprise for Rick, but then I damn near choke on my drink when they get closer.

She has a rosary around her neck, and what the…

No. Fucking. Way.

Rick's smile widens when he sees the recognition on my face.

"Rick, good to see you." I shake his hand, then turn to the woman. "Mary?"

"Hello, Mr. Collins." We shake hands.

"Wow, you look…"

Rick shoots me a death stare.

I manage to recover. "Different. Not used to seeing you out like this."

She has on a black cocktail dress and her hair is down and wavy.

Rick gives me a sly wink and says, "Do you know what type of service this will be?"

What the fuck? "Huh?"

"Religious ceremony. It's not in a church, but who will be officiating?"

"Fuck if I know."

"Donavan." He tsks me.

I can barely keep from laughing, his ass is so transparent, and Mary isn't fucking stupid.

"Such language, young man."

"I'm going to go use the ladies' room." Mary excuses herself.

Once she's out of sight, Rick turns to me. "See her fucking tits in that dress? Mother of God!"

Four older ladies turn and glare at him when he says it.

He waves an arm at them. "Jealous old broads."

I shake my head. "You know she knows exactly what you're doing, right? Pretending to be religious or whatever? Can't believe you even got her to come."

"We're here as work colleagues, Collins. Nothing more. She made that part of the verbal contract very clear before accepting."

I shake my head at him again. "You could be fucking, well, not the bridesmaids, but look at all the ass around here. All the interns."

"Nah, I like the challenge. Besides, she's trying to 'save' me. I'm playing the long game." He winks and walks off, over to the bar.

I turn back to Penn and his date, who just watched everything, and we immediately shrug and burst into laughter. More small talk ensues.

I'm ready to just get this shit over with and take Pais back to the hotel already. It's exhausting. I remind myself to talk to Pais about eloping.

Right when it's about time for us to head to our positions, Weston Hunter and his little fuckboy partners cruise through the door.

Shit.

Deacon and Dexter walk their way, and I pretend not to see them and head up to where I'm supposed to be, five minutes early.

They need to get this shit show on the road.

IT'S TIME.

I can't stop staring over at Paisley in her bridesmaid dress. She's so damn beautiful it feels like my heart squeezes every time I look at her. I gaze around the room. It's covered in white linens and red roses, people from all over the world. The only thing going through my brain is what it would be like to do this with Pais. It doesn't scare me at all. It's like this is how it should've been all along if I hadn't fucked it up.

We would've had this moment.

You still can.

She smiles over at me and I return it. I should be focused on Decker right now, making sure he's okay, but all I can do is look at Paisley and have an entire conversation with only our stares.

Our moment is cut short when the music changes. I glance over at Decker and I don't think I've ever seen him look so neurotic in his life.

I mean, he's always neurotic, but this is different. It's like a nervous excited. He's practically trembling, and you can almost feel the energy coursing through his body. His face is pale and he gulps, but he's wearing the cheesiest fucking grin I've ever seen.

Jenny comes up the aisle, and wow, she looks beautiful. She's been dressing up more the last few years, wearing makeup, doing teenager shit, but right now, she looks like a woman. A strong, independent woman, and I feel the bridge of my nose start to tingle a little and I let out a little gasp.

She's still supposed to be our little niece, not—this.

Fuck.

This is more emotional than I thought it'd be.

I glance to the right and my brothers must be feeling the same shit, because they're trying to play it off but having a hard time as well. Dad is right in front of us and he's beaming at Jenny with pride. Mom is a fucking mess. She's already on her third tissue.

Decker is fucking done for. He's already trembling, just at the sight of Jenny smiling back at him. When Tate comes down the aisle, he's going to go down for the count. I can already see all of it playing out in my mind.

Just as the emotions are about to get to me, Dexter leans over in my ear and whispers, "Pussies."

I do my best not to laugh, but it was delivered with perfect timing. Just the thing I needed to break me out of this romance bullshit that was making me feel things.

"Yep." That's all I say in return, still looking forward.

Dex grins and we slyly fist bump down at our sides.

Deacon heard all of it and grins, then catches Quinn giving him the death stare. Her, Abigail, and Paisley must've witnessed the entire thing. All three of us straighten up.

The three women shake their heads.

"Women, always out to ruin a good time," whispers Dex.

Something about the moment. I don't know what it is, but I feel more relaxed and at ease with my brothers next to me than I have in a long time. My whole life I always felt like the odd one out, but this is different. It's like I belong here, with them. Maybe I need to just try a little harder on my end at this whole family social thing, and not so much on the work end.

Jenny finally makes it down the aisle, walks up to Decker, gives him a kiss on the cheek, whispers something in his ear, then stands next to him as his best man. Or best lady. Whatever it is, she's there and she deserves to be.

The music cuts off.

At the request of the pastor or priest or whatever, everyone stands up.

Here Comes the Bride comes on, and the doors at the back swing open.

There's a spotlight or something behind Tate as she walks in, because all I can see is a silhouette of her at first and then the light fades away and she comes into focus.

The crowd gasps, as crowds do at weddings, and her father walks her up the aisle.

Camera flashes go off all around the room.

Tate really does look amazing, and it's weird at the same time. I'm so used to her in her skirts, busting balls, talking shit, but right now she looks like she could be a princess in a Disney movie—with cowboy boots on.

She's beaming and her hair is done up. She doesn't look like a fierce attorney who says fuck every other word. She just looks—happy. As much shit as her and Decker give me, and how rocky our relationship has been since she arrived, one thing is true. She makes him happy.

I turn and look at Decker, and fuck me, I thought it would be bad, but it's really bad. He looks like he can't even breathe, but he's smiling through the whole thing. It'd be so easy to make fun of him right now, but I can't even process one-liners to give him shit because I get it. I know that feeling intimately.

That feeling of being so reliant on someone else to make you whole. That feeling when you think about what it'd be like if they left or were taken away and you can't even fathom it. Life would cease to exist without them. A feeling that's completely helpless, yet utterly addictive.

Decker does his best to wipe a tear away with his shoulder and beams right at Tate. She does the same right back at him, and fuck my ass, love is a pretty powerful thing if it can make these two cry in front of five hundred people.

The bridesmaids are already done for. Makeup ruined. They're clutching their bouquets to their chests and swooning.

I glance over at Dad. He's not crying, but it's as close as I've ever seen him come to it.

Tate's dad walks her up and let's go of her arm. He walks over and shakes Decker's hand, says something to him, and walks over to Tate's mom.

I had always thought at this part of the wedding the Dad always gave the daughter away, but at the rehearsal they'd asked Tate if they were doing that and she said, *"Fuck no. My Dad doesn't own me. He supports whatever decisions I make."*

Yeah, she's definitely Decker material.

Standing here, watching them together, promising their lives to each other while I steal glances at Paisley, it's all surreal. It's like some of the weight lifts off my shoulders. Strains with the family, shit at the firm, it all seems so meaningless right now. I can't believe it took a wedding of all things to make this shit clear.

The rest of the ceremony is as you'd expect. They do the things you're supposed to do and say the things they're supposed to say. Decker is choked up on his words at first, but eventually comes out of it. Flashes go off all around when they kiss.

Jenny let's out a, "Whooooop, Dad!"

Everyone laughs.

It really is pretty perfect.

They announce them as Mr. and Mrs. Collins, and I can't believe Tate didn't hyphenate her name. I thought for sure that would happen. I'm almost positive Paisley will insist on it. I really don't give a fuck. She can call herself whatever name she wants as long as she comes home to me every night.

I look over at her, ready to get her out of that dress and beneath me, wrapped in some sheets.

We follow Decker and Tate up the aisle, each of us waiting our turn and then walking with our women. Paisley and I bring up the rear as people cheer and clap.

Thank fuck, it's time for the fun part.

The reception.

DONAVAN

I'm over by the bar, three scotches in, feeling much better. Everything is perfect. I can't believe there hasn't been one hiccup. Nobody has made a scene. Champagne is flowing.

Mom and Dad are dancing, making fools of themselves. I literally can't believe that's my father out there, doing the chicken dance with Jenny and Mom. I have to blink a few times to make sure I'm not seeing things.

Jenny drags Paisley out to join them. I decline.

I could do it better than all of them, but I still have some dignity left. Fuck that.

Guests pass by, some I barely know, some I've known for years. I make the small talk, do the networking that keeps them sending business my way. Weston Hunter and his ilk stay across the room from me. At least they're smart. I might get boozed up enough to say more than I should. The night is still young, though. I might be turning over a new leaf with my family, but those assholes in Dallas can suck my dick, taking credit for everything I've built.

Paisley grins back at me, shaking and twisting her ass like it's Octoberfest.

I watch them all for another second or two, then head to the bathroom. It's time to break the seal. After I finish up at the urinal, I wash my hands and head out the door. There's a guy I've never seen before in a tux, standing there like he's waiting for me. He has this smug grin on his face.

I glance around, making sure there's nobody behind me.

"Can I help you with something?" What's this guy's fucking deal?

"I have something for you, Mr. Collins."

"Do I know you?"

"It's a wedding gift."

I snicker. "Wrong brother. There's a table somewhere in there." I start to walk past, and he shoves an envelope into my chest.

What the fuck?

I take it.

"Compliments of Bennett Cooper."

My jaw clenches. The guy just walks off, right out the front of the building. I stare down at the envelope that says Donavan Collins on it, clear as day.

What the fuck? Why is he stirring up shit at Decker's wedding?

I know I shouldn't open it. I should wait until later, but fuck. What if it's a subpoena? I don't know why he would subpoena me to court for something. I don't have anything to do with Cooper. His beef is really with Dexter and Decker over the Wells Covington shit. There's plenty of crime to go around the world, enough for both of our firms to not butt heads.

I head off to an empty table in the back away from everyone else.

When I pull the documents out, there's a note on top, handwritten.

For your enjoyment, BC

The second my brain processes the first page of information, my heart squeezes in my chest. Then, rage takes over. Everything around me turns red and I might kill someone. I don't know if I can contain it this time.

PAISLEY

WE'VE ALREADY DONE the chicken dance and moved on to the Electric Slide. I can't believe how much fun I'm having, but I really need to get back to Donavan. He walked off a few minutes ago toward the bathroom. Maybe I can go find him in the hallway and get a second or two alone with him, without a crowd of people asking us when we're getting married or his mom telling me how much my back will hurt carrying a baby.

I take two steps toward the tables, and he's marching right at me. His face is red, like a hot iron, and I don't know if I've ever seen him look like this before. His eyes zero in and he glares right at me and I feel about two feet tall.

He knows.

It's the only explanation for the way he's coming at me.

Not yet. God, please. Tomorrow. I was going to come clean and tell him everything *tomorrow*. This can't be happening right now.

I start to turn and walk off, let him follow me away from everyone else, so he doesn't blow up in front of the entire wedding party, but there's nowhere to go. I slam into a crowd of dresses and tuxedos and try to push my way through.

I manage to make it over to the edge of the room, by the wall with minimal people around when a firm hand grips my forearm from behind.

I don't want to turn around. I don't want to see him look at me the way I know he's looking at me, but I have to.

Before I can face him, his mouth is next to my ear.

"What the fuck did you do?" He growls the words in my ear.

Tears are already rolling down my cheeks and it's like my throat is closed off. I can't do anything but shake my head at him and start walking toward the front of the building, trying to make my way out of the room.

He's on my heels, visibly shaking, like he's doing everything he can to restrain himself from blowing up, but I know he won't be able to.

He speaks through gritted teeth, but still manages to halfway yell. "What the fuck did you do?"

We pass Dexter and Deacon. They see what's happening, and they run over and try to restrain him, but he breaks through them and comes after me even harder. Now, everyone around is staring.

I finally make it through the crowd and out the front door.

Donavan bursts through the door a second later, his brothers on his heels. "What the fuck did you do?" He screams the words this time.

I turn around and I just want to die. The way he's glaring at me, half rage, half agony, about five feet away.

I want to say so many things, but nothing will come out and I just cover my mouth and shake my head while tears stream down my face.

"You still fucking work for that asshole?" His voice carries down the street he yells it so loud, and Tate and Decker come up from behind and stand there behind him with Deacon and Dexter. "You pretend to be in love with me and fucking spy on our firm?"

"No." I barely get the word out, through the sobs. "It-it..." My throat is completely closed off and it's like there is no oxygen, like I have a plastic bag over my head.

Dexter and Deacon come up from behind and try to pull him back inside, but the entire Collins family glares at me while they do it.

I spot a cab in my peripheral vision and immediately take a step toward it, but Donavan yanks away from his brothers and comes after me. "Where the fuck do you think you're going?"

Just then, flashes go off and there are photographers taking pictures. They're probably from major publications in town, here to cover the wedding, like things couldn't get any worse.

I cover my mouth and run for the cab. I don't look back, I just sprint, even though it feels like I'm moving in slow motion. Donavan gets to me right as his brothers are on his heels.

Before I can get in the cab, he grabs me by the wrist and growls in my ear. "You make me sick. I loved you. Fuck you, Paisley." More flashes go off as the photographers run toward us.

His brothers yank him away, but the second he says those words my heart shatters into a million pieces. It wasn't supposed to happen this way.

As I get in the cab, he's standing there, his chest heaving up and down, with Deacon and Dexter in front of him, blocking his path.

He yells over their shoulders, "Never thought you'd be the type of person to fuck someone for a paycheck! You know that's prostitution, right? Bennett Cooper is your fucking pimp!"

I slam the door shut just as he says it, and as much as I don't want to look out the window at him, I do. Maybe because I'm punishing myself. Maybe because I just want to see his face one last time, even if he hates me now. I just want to grab him and hold onto him and not let him go until I can convince him it was real, and I didn't mean to hurt him like this. But, I can't.

I was supposed to be able to tell him everything after the wedding, and let him go off the deep end, but then he'd calm down and talk to me, and we'd see if we could salvage something out of this. That was how I saw it all playing out in my mind, away from everyone else, no spectators. Just him and me. Now, he hates me, and he'll never trust me again. Maybe there was a chance if I'd told him first.

How did this even happen? Why did I ever even give in and try to rekindle things with him? It was so shitty. I should've just stayed away from him as much as possible and did what I had to do.

I somehow manage to say my address to the cab driver, and I sink down in the seat. Bile creeps into my throat and I feel like I might puke everywhere.

One thing is certain, we are done. There's no coming back from this, and I can never show my face in their building again.

The worst part of this whole thing is…

I still love him. Even more than the first time.

PAISLEY

THE NEXT DAY, Dad comes over after I ignored five phone calls.

"Come in." I yell it from the couch.

I couldn't get up if I wanted to.

He walks in, takes one look at me, and sits down on a chair. "You okay? I've been worried."

I shake my head. "No." I try to keep it together. "No, I'm not okay at all."

"Well, what happened? Did Donavan do something?"

"No." I break down into tears. "I did something, Dad. Something terrible."

He rushes down to my side and halfway hugs me from a kneeling position. "Oh, Pais." He smooths down my hair.

I sniff and it's difficult to even get words out, but finally, I tell him everything that happened. Once he's consoled me to a point where I can have a conversation, he sits back down on the chair. "I guess I'm just confused. Why did you do it?"

I don't want to tell him, because he'll feel awful, but I know he won't let this go. "The reason most people do dumb shit. Money."

It takes him a second, and then the recognition appears on his face. "For me, and Grandma and Grandpa? That's how you've been paying for everything?"

I nod. "I had two salaries coming, one from Cooper one from Hunter, and Cooper has been paying for Grandma and Grandpa. It was all set up through a trust, so it'd look like it was my capital I cashed out, but it was him taking care of it. He let me keep all my equity in an off-shore account."

He lets out a long sigh. "Oh, Pais."

"I know I screwed up, okay? It was stupid. I just…"

"It's not stupid, sweetie. I get why you did it."

"Y-you do?"

He nods. "Of course."

757

I wipe my tears away with my shoulder. "I just wanted what was best for you guys. I never thought all these feelings would come back. I didn't think I still loved him, but I do."

"So that's why you had to go work *there*. I thought something was off about that." He nods for a second, like everything is clicking into place and making sense, then stares at me. "Pais, I'm proud that you wanted to take care of your family. I really am, but I could've told you this would happen. I wish you would've talked to me first and I'd have told you this would all blow up the way it did."

"How could you have known?"

"Because I know *you*. C'mon, sweetie. I knew the first time you brought him home from law school he was going to be my son-in-law one day. Love blinds us, but everyone else around can see it clear as day."

"I think part of me agreed to do this for Cooper because I hated what Donavan did to me. And part of me wanted him to feel just an ounce of that pain, but as soon as I started working there..." I can't even finish my sentence. I just stare at the ground and shake my head. "Am I a sociopath? How could I do that to him?"

"Pais?"

I glance up to him. "Yeah?"

"You're not a sociopath. Sociopaths don't feel remorse like this. And that makes me happy."

"What?"

He nods. "Yeah, I'm not happy because of what you did. It was wrong and you know that. But this reaction you're having, and the fact you wanted to take care of your family, it lets me know I raised a good human being. Yes, it hurts now, but you'll grow from it and learn from it." He pauses and sighs. "I held onto a lot of hate too when it came to Donavan. And I shouldn't have. He screwed up and you screwed up. It's what people do. You're a good person. Beat yourself up a little, but don't do it for too long. Okay, sweetheart?"

I shake my head. "I know I'll get through this, like I always do, but it doesn't feel like it'll ever end. Like I'm always going to have this void in my life. This hole in my chest."

Dad comes back over and sits down on the couch and hugs me for a while. "The pain will always be there, but it'll slowly fade and grow duller. I promise."

I know he's right, but it doesn't feel like it.

DONAVAN

IT'S BEEN about a week and a half since the blow up. I haven't seen or talked to Paisley and that's a good thing, because I didn't get to say everything I wanted to say to her. Thank fuck Tate and Decker have been on their honeymoon. I thought Tate was going to shove a foot up my ass for yelling at her outside the yacht club, but it took everything I had to remain as restrained as I was. It's not my fault all those photographers were taking a goddamn smoke break. I made sure to buy every copy of the paper I could find in a five-block radius of the firm and throw all of them away. Last thing I need is Decker framing a goddamn copy as a constant reminder.

If I'm being honest about my reaction to everything, truth be told, it happened so fast I don't even remember a lot of it, other than I said fuck you to her and told her she made me sick.

I'm just about back to normal, though. Back to my old self, not trusting anyone and kicking people's asses all over the courtroom. The highlight of my week was making a prosecutor cry. Good, they should fear me at the courthouse.

An added bonus is nobody tries to make small talk with me at work. I just come in, do my job, and everyone else can fuck off.

I'm in my office, eating some lunch before I have to get back to the courthouse for the afternoon rounds when Tate walks in.

Fuck me.

She already reamed me once at the reception. Enough is enough.

She doesn't look pissed off though. She's smiling and has a tan. They went to the Maldives or some shit and just got back.

She takes a seat and makes herself at home. Damn, this might take a while. I can't be mean to her and it's eating me up inside that she has the upper hand because of what I did.

"How are things, Donavan?"

I sigh. "Really?"

"Okay, maybe that was a shit question, but I really am worried about you."

"Why?" I shrug. "You don't even like me, and everything is easier now."

She glances at the wall, then back at me. "You can't bury this and forget it ever happened. Have you seen someone to talk about it?"

I snicker. "A shrink?"

She nods. "Uhh, yeah."

I shake my head. "Not really my style. And I'm kind of busy so…" I don't want to be rude to her, but I do not want to have this conversation either.

"Eating lunch?"

"Gotta be back to the courthouse—"

She cuts me off. "Have you talked to her?"

My eyes widen. "Uhh, no, she pretended to date me and tried to sabotage my family's business. Why the hell would I talk to her?"

"Because you love her."

"Not anymore I don't."

She sighs. "Don't be a stubborn asshole. Those feelings don't go away."

"Jesus Christ, Dr. Phil." I stop when her jaw clenches. "Look, sorry. But it's over. And I *am* sorry it went down that way. I actually mean that. I didn't mean to ruin your wedding."

Tate leans back in the chair. "Just part of the reception, the wedding was perfect."

My eyebrows shoot up. "So, you're not mad?"

"Oh, I'm still fucking furious. But…" She pauses and shakes her head. "Believe it or not, I don't hate you, and I'm worried about you. And, I want answers. Don't you want answers?"

"Not really."

"Donavan, there has to be a reason she did this other than just to be an asshole to you. You know her. Do you really believe she'd be that vindictive? And why now?"

I shrug. "I don't even know who she is anymore, so yeah, she's probably that vindictive. I abandoned her and her family when her mom died. Now, we're even. And I don't really care. It's over."

Tate stands up, tense. She walks to the door, then turns back. "I'm not going to tell you what to do, or make Decker force you to talk about shit you don't want to talk about, but you're my brother now, whether you like it or not, and I care about my family. That includes you. And as your sister, and not a coworker, you really should talk to someone. You can't keep this all bottled up. It'll kill you."

"Thanks, *sis*." I feel like an asshole, but what the fuck? Paisley did this. Not me. Tate needs to direct her line of inquiry elsewhere. I said I was sorry about making a scene at the wedding, the rest I'm wiping my hands of.

Tate huffs out a sigh. "Yeah, *bro*."

The second she walks out I exhale a long breath I'd been holding, and my palms twitch. Every feeling in the world creeps back into my chest again at the thought of Paisley. How close we were to fixing everything. Having everything. The walls start to close in on me and I can barely breathe.

It feels like I'm in a junk yard, where they smash the cars and that huge press is crushing me into a tiny block of metal. How did I get here? How did I put myself in this situation? Make myself vulnerable to this? I wanted to believe things had changed, that maybe I was better. But the fact is, I was weak. I let my guard down and got taken advantage of. It won't happen again.

I hate the world. I fucking hate everything.

PAISLEY

IT'S BEEN one month to the day, since the worst night of my life. I can still see Donavan's face. Every time I close my eyes, it's like he's right there in front of me, bright red, gripping me by the wrist, snarling at me. I can't even hear the words, all I see are his eyes, all the anger and hurt.

I haven't left my apartment. I walked out front once, and the sunlight hit my face, and I turned around and walked back in. I don't know what to do. Dad calls and I send him to voicemail. He stops by a few times a week, and I put on my game face enough for him to think I'm okay, then get him out as fast as I can, before I break down again.

This is what agony feels like. I thought it was bad back at the end of law school, but this is a whole other level.

My phone buzzes on the coffee table and I pick it up and stare at it.

Bennett Cooper.

I shouldn't answer. Why the hell is he even calling me? To gloat? I haven't talked to him since everything went down.

The anger building over the last month rushes into my face and I pick up the phone. "What?" I practically growl the word at him.

I swear he snickers on the other end, but I can't be sure. I'm sure he's doing that arrogant smirk of his.

"Look, Paisley…"

"You set it up, didn't you? Did you ever even care if I sent you information at all, or did you just want to destroy their family?"

Bennett sighs. "It wasn't personal. Just business."

"Just business?" My voice goes up about three notes. "You fucking hung me out to dry! You used me, asshole!"

He remains calm and collected. "Oh, look at the facts. Stop getting all emotional. It's not you."

"Did you basically just tell me to calm down?"

"Your grandparents are getting the best care money can buy. You're taking care of your family. Stepping up to the plate and doing what has to be done. It's why you're the best. You're a shark."

"What the hell are you even saying?"

"Come back to New York. Your desk is waiting for you."

"Fuck. You."

He snickers. "You'll come around." Then he hangs up before I can get another word out.

I toss my phone across the table and mumble, "Fucking asshole."

I sit there, stewing, steam coming out of my ears. Part of me wants to thank him for it. It's the first time in weeks I've been pissed off at someone other than myself. What the hell am I going to do?

There's no way in hell I'll go back to work for that piece of shit. I'll have to get a job at another firm. Maybe I'll go away, move somewhere new. But I can't. Grandma and Grandpa are here. I have to let Cooper keep paying for them until he realizes I'm not coming back, then have another plan ready.

What I want to do is just sit here and watch *Jerry McGuire* the rest of my life, eating ice cream and getting fat, never showing my face to the world. I'm already getting stir crazy, though. I need to be working. Doing something other than sitting here thinking about Donavan Collins and our roller coaster existence.

The worst part is, I still love him. I'll never stop loving him and my life would be so much easier if I could just turn that switch off. I watch these romance movies, thinking we'll have some big moment, where the two of us both admit how much we screwed up, both say that's what's so great about us, coming back together afterward and it making us even stronger.

Which is all a bunch of bullshit. I hurt him and he hurt me. It was like a heavyweight fight, and he knocked me out the first time, and I knocked him out the next one. We have the black eyes and bruises to prove it.

There's a knock at my door.

"Go away!" I yell, way harsher than intended. A second later, I take a deep breath. "Sorry, Dad, just now isn't a good time."

"It's not your dad." It's a woman's voice. It almost sounds like—Tate.

What the hell?

I walk over to the door and look through the peephole. Sure enough, it's her, the Chicago version of me, but with curly blonde hair.

"Tate, it's not…"

"You owe me." That's all she says, those three words.

She's right. Reluctantly, I sigh, and open the door.

The second I see her she doesn't look anywhere near as pissed off as I expect. She doesn't look angry at all. There's just one thing in her eyes—pity.

I offer her a weak smile and step out of the way.

She walks in. "Oh, uhh, wow."

"Sorry about the mess."

There are takeout boxes all over the table. I'm in sweat pants and a Columbia Law t-shirt.

"You've been hungry."

I do my best to hold it together, but it's so hard. Just seeing her reminds me of being in the office, Donavan in his suits, the wedding all over again.

"Look, Tate, I'm really—"

She holds up a hand and takes a seat on the couch. "Save it. I didn't come for an apology."

"Okay, umm, why are you here then? Because I have to be honest, I don't know how much more of this I can take right now."

Tate turns to the side and leans toward me. "I want to know why."

"Huh?"

"I want to know why. You had a reason for doing what you did. I've seen you look at Donavan. You're head over heels for him. Still are. Nobody is that good of an actress. Women like us don't get knocked down like this..." She cranes her head around the room. "Over a work setback. You're still in Chicago. I want to know what really happened."

"How did you know I was still here and not back in New York City?"

Tate leans back, and eyes me up and down. She's so much like me it's a little scary. "Can I trust you?"

I snicker. "You have no reason to. I wouldn't."

"Well, I'm going to, because you were just honest with me when you could've lied. Decker has people watching Bennett Cooper too. That's how I knew you haven't been back."

"Fair enough. He fucking deserves it."

Tate's eyes widen. "So, you're not going back?"

I shake my head. "I don't know what I'll do, but no."

Tate leans in. "Tell me what happened."

Just like that, the tears start up again and I bury my face in my hands and spill my guts.

I tell her everything, down to the last detail.

I don't even know how it happened, but Tate is next to me with her arms wrapped around my shoulders. It's utterly humiliating, and yet it feels so good to have someone comfort me. I just wish it was Donavan. He always made me feel so safe when I was with him, and right now I feel vulnerable from every angle possible. Like I'm completely naked without any protection and a speeding train is heading right for me.

I cry into Tate's shoulder, just trying to release everything inside me, all the anger, hurt, remorse.

"I-I didn't want to choose. I d-didn't want to do that to him. I was going to tell him as soon as you guys left, after the wedding. I swear on my life. It was killing me inside, every day."

Her hand smooths down my hair and I rock back and forth against her.

"I c-can't believe I did that to him."

"Well." Tate sighs. "The two of you are something else, that's for damn sure. I wouldn't give up on everything just yet, though."

I pull back and stare at her. "What?"

She nods. "You were taking care of your family. If Donavan doesn't realize that he has his head up his ass, and you'll just have to pull it out of there. And he may act hard, but I can see it written all over his face. There's no mistaking the fact he's still in love with you, and that means there's hope."

"I mean it. I was going to tell him, I was just, I didn't want to ruin your wedding and it got ruined anyway. I'm so sorry." The tears come back again, and I can't remember ever being so emotional in my life.

"Look, just cry it out, get it out of your system."

I shake my head and the tears won't stop coming. I bury my face in her shoulder again.

"Fuck, this is intense."

"You don't understand, Tate." I sniff again, because there's one more thing I have to tell her.

"Understand what?"

"I'm pregnant."

Tate leans back and puts her hands on my shoulders. "Really?" Her eyes light up, but then it's like the whole situation crashes back into her too. She shakes her head. "Fuck." She draws out the syllable.

I know the look on her face. She's concocting a plan, scheming.

I want to just die, and at the same time it feels like a little of the weight just lifted, giving me room to breathe. Not even Dad knows about the baby. Donavan's baby.

"Okay, look. Just cry it out a bit more, but then get your balls back. You're going to need them."

"What? Why?"

"To put up with all the assholes around the office."

I shake my head. "I can't go back there. It's not going to happen."

Tate puts her hands on my shoulders again, and she looks like she wants to shake me. "Trust me, he'll forgive you. And the other boys will too. They might act like hard asses, but they're soft as hell on the inside. And that baby is a Collins. It's part of the family. Nothing means more to all those boys than family, trust me."

"I appreciate it, Tate. I really do. But I just don't think I can. It's too much stress and I have someone else to think about now." My hands go down to my stomach. I still can't believe Donavan's child is in there, growing every day.

"Fuck it then. You're still a badass. Dust yourself off and find a new firm. You belong in the ocean with the sharks. There aren't enough of us around."

Tate gets up and I follow her to the door.

"Thank you for coming by. Seriously. Nobody else has even talked to me." I look away. "Not that I expected them to or anything, but it's very kind of you. You didn't have to do that, and it feels nice to know at least things are good between us."

She gives me a little nod and a smile.

I look off at the corner of the ceiling and sigh. "Bet you regret asking me to be a bridesmaid."

Tate smiles and shakes her head. "Not at all."

"Really?"

"Things happen that are supposed to happen." Her eyes narrow. "And don't worry about Decker. If you want to come back, he'll forgive you and make it work. I'll see to it."

DONAVAN

I'M AT MY DESK, still brooding, still pissed off at the world. Days go by and I do the same shit over and over. It's been a month and that ache in every bone in my body hasn't gone anywhere. If anything, it's amplified a little more each morning when I wake up. I don't know if it'll ever go away.

Tate is the only one who has even said anything. Everyone just goes on about their business, like we always do. Just ignore until it fades away, even though I know my brothers are secretly pissed about what I did at the wedding. Even though Decker's the one who hired Paisley, against my advice, without even consulting me.

But, hey, we've pretended nothing was wrong our entire lives, so we might as well keep the tradition going.

Thank God I'm up to my elbows in work. People keep committing crimes, and I keep getting paid to get them out of trouble.

Quinn's voice comes over my phone speaker. "Donavan, Decker needs to see you."

Fuck, I'll be glad when she passes the bar and I don't have to hear her bark those words at me. I'm sure he'll replace her with someone else who does it just as well.

"Tell him I'll be right there."

I lean back and look at all the papers strewn all over my desk and toss my highlighter down on top of them. I mumble, "What the fuck is it now?"

It better not be something petty, like how I bound together some paperwork wrong or took a file and didn't put it back the right way on the shelf. I might explode on his ass. Don't care if he just got married or not, the statute of limitations is up on the wedding fiasco and it's time for him to mellow the fuck out.

I walk through the office and people see me and just get out of the way. Good.

I walk past Quinn and into his office. He's sitting behind his desk and it's cleared. That's odd. It also tells me this is some kind of ambush, if he doesn't even have files out. What the hell is this?

I shake my head when I get halfway to the chair in front of his desk. "Not now." I turn on a dime and start to walk out.

About that time, Deacon and Dexter fill up the doorframe and cage me in.

Goddamn it.

They step inside the room and shut the doors.

I bow up in front of them. "Get out of the way."

They both glare at me. "We need to talk. You owe Decker an apology, it's been long enough."

I smirk. "Fuck off. I have work to do."

"We need to talk about this. I don't give a shit if you apologize, but we need to discuss things." I hear Decker's chair slide out from under him.

"That's good you don't care." I wheel around. "Because I'm not apologizing. Paisley did this." God, why does it hurt so bad to say her name? "I didn't do anything any of you wouldn't have. Yeah, I blew my top and maybe could've handled it better. But—" I spin around on the twin assholes. "You two did the exact same shit, did you not? And all of you hired her. Not me."

There's a light knock on the door.

Dexter cracks it open and mumbles, "Fuck."

What the hell?

The door opens and our father walks in.

I'm about to lose it now. What the hell is he doing here? The last thing I need is a lecture from him. Not now. I don't need his hard gaze and his tough love. My face heats to an alarming degree and my palms start to twitch.

I wheel around on Decker. "What the fuck is this?" I say through my teeth.

Just get out of the room. Just cool it and don't make a scene and get the hell out of here before permanent damage is done.

Decker holds up both hands. "We're just trying to help."

I can't take it anymore. It all boils up and I can't stop it. Thirty years of suppressing everything because I was taught to never show weakness, to suppress any type of emotion or feelings. Thirty fucking years of always being last, being unnoticed, an afterthought. Thirty years of trying to prove myself worthy of this family every goddamn day of my life just to be recognized, and now they all want to lecture me on behavior and how to treat someone. Fuck that and fuck them.

"I don't need your goddamn help, Decker!" I turn back to the others and I'm shaking I'm so damn mad.

Dad's doing his hard-stare bullshit right at me and I can't take it. "All I wanted was a fraction of what you gave them! And you gave me nothing!" My chest heaves and I don't know if I can fucking breathe right now. It doesn't feel like any oxygen is getting to my lungs. All I can see going through my mind are highlights of my childhood, being picked on, bullied by my brothers, me being tossed aside while my dad followed Decker to his baseball stuff, taught Dexter how to ride a bike, throwing a football with Deacon. I have none of those memories. Not one with just me and him. And all I can see is Paisley, the only person I ever really loved, and she betrayed me. I hurt her first, the biggest mistake of my life, but I thought she'd forgiven me, that it was real, and it wasn't. She was just setting me up the whole time, probably laughing behind my back on phone calls with Bennett Cooper. My entire life is humiliating.

I look down, sniff, and wipe a few tears from my eyes. "I liked to sing. I was in the choir." It's all I can say. I don't even really know where it comes from, the words just come out.

"What?" says Decker.

I turn to him. "It's what I loved when I was a kid. I loved music, and I liked to sing. And I joined the choir at school, in the fifth grade. You were in high school, and they were both in seventh grade."

Decker holds both his hands up. "Okay, I don't—"

"You laughed at me and called me a pussy. Said only girls sing in the choir." I turn to the twins.

They look like they have no idea what I'm talking about.

"You both laughed too. Thought it was hilarious. You pointed at me and you laughed." I turn to Dad.

He's still staring at me, hasn't said a word. His face is unreadable, he's just standing there with his jaw set.

"And you. You just shook your head and grinned at them, even with the shit they were saying to me, then went back to what you were doing. It crushed me. I ran off to my room and cried, not where anyone could hear, of course, because Collins men don't cry. I had to hide in my fucking house, ten years old, bawling, because I'd finally found something I was good at, that I loved to do, and I had to hide so I wouldn't get called a pussy and laughed at by my older brothers or my dad. The people I looked up to more than anyone."

"Donavan," says Decker. He moves to walk around his desk.

"Fucking don't. Just don't, okay? I've spent my entire life trying to fit in, to do what's right for this family, to be a part of it. I went to an Ivy League school. I tried to do everything better, just to get noticed. I have the number one criminal law department in the country. Still not good enough. You sold our fucking name off the wall, and nobody says shit to you about it." I turn to my dad and point a finger right at him. "So all this talk about family, family, family that you drilled into our heads nonstop, was a bunch of bullshit. It's nothing but lip service and empty words."

"Donnie…" Deacon and Dexter both start toward me, but Dad holds his hand up.

He still hasn't said a word. He walks toward me, hard eyes, narrowed in on mine.

My hands ball up into fists at my sides. Fuck it. I just said everything I've wanted to scream at them for twenty years. He gets closer and I back up a couple

771

steps, then sit down in a chair. I'm afraid of what he's going to say, what he's going to do. Even at thirty he can still strike fear in me. He's never hit me before, but he looks like he might and as bad as I want to stand up to him, fight him, whatever, I can't.

I drop my face in my hands. "You're going to protect them, take their side. It was always that way and nothing has changed." Everything finally hits me, everything I just said, in front of my brothers, in front of my dad. It feels like I might hyperventilate. Like there is no air in the room, all of it was just sucked out and I'm in a vacuum, alone. The same way I always end up.

He walks over and stops in front of me, and he bends down.

I finally look up, expecting him to be glaring, but his eyes look like he's in pain. They're soft, pleading even.

"I'm, I'm sorry you feel that way, son."

My chest is still heaving, but I don't even know what to do right now. My eyes just go wide.

I glance over, and my brothers all have the same shocked expressions on their faces, like they were waiting for him to take a swing at me.

I look back at Dad, and I can barely form words. "What?" The word comes out as a gasp.

His hand tightens on my shoulder. "I fucked up and I'm sorry. I've known it for years." He takes a deep breath. "I was just too big of a coward to do anything about it."

Tears roll down my cheeks and I still can't speak.

My brothers all look like their eyes might pop out of their heads. Our dad has never apologized for anything, not where we've heard anyway. He's always so quiet and stoic, no nonsense.

"When you fuck up, you apologize for it. I tried to do the best I could with you boys, but I..." His voice cracks a little. "You were the youngest and you got the short end of the stick when it came to my time and attention. It has eaten at me for years."

"It has?"

He nods. "I'm sorry I didn't make more time for you. It was... Things were tough financially, and I took the extra job, right when you were going from a boy to a man, and I should've been there for you more and I wasn't. You know what, just no." He stares around at my brothers then back at me. "I'm a hypocrite for not taking my own advice. Sometimes parents fuck up and I was too stubborn, too goddamn proud to put my ego aside, and for that I can't apologize enough, Donnie." His eyes soften again, and he leans down closer. "I could sit here and make excuses...working two jobs didn't have the time, blah blah, no. I had time. I was good at sports, I was good at coaching, I related to your brothers better. I was good at being what they needed, and you were different, and I didn't have any idea how to deal with that. It's no excuse though." He puts a palm on my cheek, and more tears roll down his face. He drops to his knees in front of me and chokes on his words. "I should've tried harder. You're my baby boy, and I failed you." He pulls me in close, so hard he almost crushes me to his chest, and his body trembles against me.

This is all I ever wanted from him, to know that I mattered too. That he gave a shit.

"I resorted to what I knew best, because it was easiest for me, and I'm so goddamn sorry. I know it's too late, but I want to do better from now on. I want to try. I love you."

I hug him back, even harder. "I love you too. I promise."

I pull my head back and wipe the tears from my eyes. Dad does the same. My brothers stare like *what the fuck just happened here*?

I look right at Dad. "That's all I ever wanted. To just know I existed, mattered. Like maybe I made you proud too."

We stand up and he pulls me into another hug, this time gives me a couple pats on the back. "You do, son. You always have."

I finally pull back and say, "Thank you."

"Don't thank me, it was my job to tell you that and I didn't. That's on me and something I have to live with the rest of my life. Can you forgive me?"

I nod. "Of course, I can. You're my dad."

He puts a hand on my shoulder and looks right in my eyes. "Thank you. I won't let you down again. I promise."

Then just like that, he returns to his usual self, standing there with his hard glare. I know what he wants me to do.

I turn, slowly, to face Decker. "I really am sorry, for blowing up like that at the wedding. I was so angry and hurt, I just... No excuses, I'm sorry." I turn to Deacon and Dexter and shrug, pleading. "I'm tired of holding grudges, burying all this shit inside. I just... I can't do it anymore."

They both nod then Deacon looks at Dexter and says, "Well, that's not how I saw this shit playing out."

I snicker and look at Dad. It's like my life just turned a one eighty, like everything just changed. I don't know what I thought about how he felt. I never imagined he was holding onto all that, and I can't believe it just spilled out of him.

Dad nods to the chair behind me, then to the other ones. All of us brothers have a seat, but Dad remains standing, pacing back and forth like he's thinking through a problem.

He finally grabs another chair, pulls it up, then sits down, and it's so surreal. Usually it seems like he's above us, on a different level, preaching down at us, but this time it's like he's actually here and not riding on the clouds like Zeus or a superhero.

Finally, he breaks the silence. "Look, I know I've always preached not to show weakness. All this shit about us being men." He shakes his head and sighs. "I have to tell you boys, the older you get, the more you think and the less you talk. You sit there, replaying your life over and over in your head, and you realize what an idiot you've been."

This all seems so unreal because it's like our family dogma is crashing and burning to the ground around us. Our whole identities. What makes us a Collins. It's like he's blowtorching it all to ashes, and there's something cathartic about it, and at the same time it's like my soul is being ripped from my body.

We all walked around worshipping this man twenty-four seven and now he's like, it's all bullshit.

He grimaces and points to his gut. "The more I've hung onto things, just tucked them all away, nice and compartmentalized—feelings. It's not good. It's not healthy to hold onto hate, regret, guilt." He holds up a hand. "I'm not saying to go out and start crying in front of the world like some pussy. That's not what I'm getting at here. You're still men." He turns to each of us and sighs. "It's okay, though, to be vulnerable to the woman you love. It's okay to be vulnerable to your family, tell them what needs to be said, emotionally. That's a blood bond that nobody can break. It's what makes us, us. You're still to provide. To step up and be the men you're supposed to be. When the tough situations come, and they never stop coming, you're the general, you know when to spring into action, and you better well be prepared to fight to the death to protect your family, and you take no fucking prisoners if anyone tries to harm them." He sighs again and looks right at me. "Tate called me after she went to see Paisley and filled me in."

Decker's eyebrows shoot up. "She did?"

"Wait, what? Tate went to talk to her?" My face heats up again.

Dad holds a hand up to both of us and gives us the death stare that can still rattle your bones. We both go quiet in an instant.

He turns to me. "Paisley did it for her family, not because of some vendetta between you two. I don't know your history because you never brought her around, even though Tate makes it sound like you were very serious in college. Tate explained other things to me too."

I sit there, shaking my head as he explains everything and all the details. My blood heats up, but I know I need to calm down and breathe. Some of it makes sense, and I want to believe him, I just... She completely betrayed me. She lied to me the entire time. I don't know what was real and what wasn't.

Finally, I shake my head again. "Why didn't she just tell me all of that?"

"Would you have listened?" Decker leans in with his elbows on his knees and stares at me. "Be honest with yourself. Would you have even come close to forgiving her if she'd told you?"

I look up at the ceiling and sigh. "No. I would've exploded no matter what."

He goes to say something, and I keep going.

"I deserved to know, though. I would've flipped out and caused a scene anywhere, but then I would've thought about it and calmed down some. Now, what the hell am I supposed to do?"

Everyone stares at me like I'm crazy.

"You don't know what we've been through, what I've done to her. I would've calmed down and went back. I would never hate her for taking care of her family. I would never hate her, period."

"So why haven't you done *that*? Calmed down and gone back?" says Dexter.

I give him a side eye. "Because I just found out."

"Because you didn't go after her. Give her a chance to explain," says Deacon. "Maybe it'd all be worked out already."

"Oh, okay, Saint Deacon and his disciples." I stop myself, before my blood pressure shoots through the roof again and take a deep breath. "Sorry, I just…"

Dad clears his throat and we all fall silent. He looks right at me and holds up a finger. "There's only one question that matters right now. The one thing that should determine your course of action."

I glance up at him. "What's that?"

"Do you love her?"

I can't even speak. I just nod lightly at him.

"You know what to do then."

I shake my head. "It's not that simple, Dad. There's no way she'll take me back after all that. After everything. Just, there's no way. The things I did, stuff I said… Just no."

Dexter stands up, cocks his head to each side, then makes a show of cracking his knuckles. He stares down at me. "You underestimate my skillset, brother. You just tell me what she loves, and I'll have you back together by tomorrow."

We all stand up. I have absolutely zero confidence in whatever he's thinking but fuck it. I have to try because these feelings aren't going away. They're just not. They didn't after I left her the first time, and they're not going to now.

At the last second, he turns back and pokes a finger in my chest, grinning his ass off. "Wait, you said you can sing, right?"

"Yeah. Pretty fucking good too, actually."

"Perfect," says Dexter, nodding, like he's in his own little world. "This shit will be legendary."

Dad pulls me in for another hug, then leans back. His eyes are dead serious. "It'll work, son. Trust me. Go after her, lay it all out there, and she'll take you back. Dads know shit too, even if we fuck up sometimes."

I nod. "Okay."

Even if she doesn't forgive me, at least I got my family back. At least I'll have tried and won't have that regret hanging over me.

PAISLEY

I'M AT MY GRANDPARENTS' retirement home with Dad, waiting for them to come back to the big living area to hang out with us. I can't keep my hands off my stomach, and every time I think about my baby, Donavan's face flashes in front of my eyes. At least I made it out of the house and I'm not ignoring my family.

I feel awful about the last month, but I just had to get that all out of my system. I just needed to get some distance, some time to think about my future.

Dad looks over like he can read my thoughts. "If he loves you, he'll come back. Just wait and see."

I roll my eyes so hard I'm surprised they don't fly out the back of my head. "That's such a cliché, Dad. That shit doesn't happen. *Especially* with guys like Donavan. You know him. He holds a grudge better than I do."

His eyes dart down to my hand on my stomach. "You should at least tell him. He deserves to know."

I shake my head. "No way, I can't. I can't see him right now."

He leans down and takes my hands. "Pais, that's what got you in this situation in the first place. He deserves to know."

He's right. I know he's right and yet, I just don't want to deal with it right now. I need to, so I nod at him. "Okay, I'll go tomorrow."

His eyebrows rise.

"I mean it. You can drive me if you want. I'll go tell him." I mean what I say. It's not fair to Donavan and if I wait much longer, he might accuse me of trying to hide it from him.

Grandma and Grandpa ride out to us on their electric wheelchairs, and there is a line of other people coming in too. Up front, there's a small stage and it looks like they're setting something up. I think they do games and stuff to promote social activities for all the people who live here.

Everyone scoots in, some of them with walkers, others with wheelchairs. One thing is certain, everyone in here looks so happy, and it kills me that I don't know how much longer I'll be able to afford to provide this for Grandma and Grandpa.

Financially, I should go back to work for Cooper, but I just can't.

Some teenage kid with shaggy hair, looking like a throwback to the punk era in a Ramone's t-shirt grabs a microphone and his voice blares through the loudspeaker.

Great. They're doing karaoke. Actually, this might be fun.

Grandma and Grandpa look totally into it, holding hands in their matching wheelchairs. Dad wraps an arm around me.

I glance back, and... what in the holy shit?

The entire Collins family is basically standing behind me. My mouth drops open. Even their mom and dad are here, and they're all smiling at me. My head whips back around. Dad's next to me, and his hand tightens around mine.

"In case you try to run."

"Dad, what the hell?" I start to get up, and he holds me by the forearm.

"Just sit." A smile forms on his face.

"What the hell is going on here?" I turn and say it right to his face, but he just grins.

"You'll see."

Shit. Shit. Shit.

I think back, trying to remember who I saw behind me. I didn't see Donavan, but can I be sure? It was a quick glance.

My heartbeat redlines and my pulse pounds in my ears. It's all happening so fast.

Donavan steps up on the stage, and what the hell? His eyes lock with mine, and he smiles, but I can see all the pain behind the smile.

The punk guy says, "They're all yours, sir." He hands Donavan the microphone.

Is he going to sing? No way. Donavan doesn't sing. There's absolutely no way.

The music starts, and oh my God, it's *Thinking Out Loud* by Ed Sheeran.

I squirm in my seat, because I'm already embarrassed and there's just no way. Can Donavan actually sing? He's going to humiliate himself in front of me. It's actually really sweet, but all the things he said to me, the way he blew up...

Donavan fakes his broody stare at me, and my heart comes alive even more, then at the last second, right before he puts the microphone to his mouth, he smiles. The boyish smile he only ever has when he looks at me.

He hits the first note, and what the ever-loving hell! Is this real right now?

The whole place gasps because he kills the note, and he walks toward me, singing the song flawlessly. He's a baritone, not a tenor like Ed Sheeran. God, it's so damn sexy.

I glance back and his whole family looks about the same way I do, eyes wide, mouths agape, completely shocked.

Donavan makes his way forward. He serenades a few of the older ladies in his path and they look like they might end up in serious medical condition if they clutch their hearts any harder.

He finally walks up to me and motions for me to stand up.

Even if I didn't want to, there's no way my body would have it. I'd do whatever the hell he told me at this point. Why has he never sung to me before?

Once I'm up, staring eye to eye with him, he hits the build up to the crescendo of the song and falls to his knees in front of me. He takes one of my hands and puts my palm to his cheek.

Tears stream down my face, and his voice cracks when he sees it, but he quickly recovers. Once he's finished, he clicks the microphone off but stays on his knees in front of me.

"I'm so sorry." He covers his mouth with his hand, and he's visibly shaking. Like he was holding it all in, just to make sure he got the song right for me, and it's all crashing into him at once.

I shake my head at him. "No, it was my fault. All of it." I glance over at Dad and he's just smiling, like he knew all of this was going to happen.

"It doesn't matter. You did what you had to do, and I didn't let you explain. I said things that…" He sighs and takes a deep breath. "You're everything to me and I will spend a lifetime trying to make up for the way I acted. I just love you. I can't live without you, Pais. Please, I'm begging you. I'm so alone without you. I don't want to be alone anymore. We can go away. We can go anywhere, be whatever, I just want you by my side."

I look around the room and every eye is on us, half of them holding tears. Quinn, Abigail, Tate, and Jenny all have their hands over their chests, doing the "aww" faces.

I hold my hand out to Donavan, telling him to stand up. He practically flies up to his feet and we're standing there. I motion for him to lean down. He does, until our foreheads press against each other.

"I'll forgive you if you forgive me."

Donavan sniffles. "Deal. I'll take that deal."

We both smile through the tears, then his fingers dig into my hips, and holy shit. My body comes alive all over again, just like it always does when he's around. He pulls me against him, then puts his hands on my face and kisses me. My arms go around his neck, and like always I'm floating on the clouds and could melt to the floor. I don't want to ever let go.

The walls of armor come up and I feel safe again.

"I'm so sorry, Donavan. Seriously. I never meant to hurt you, and I was going to—"

He shakes his head. "No. We're even, remember. Mine was even worse. And don't ever apologize for taking care of your family." He looks around behind him, then back at me. "There's nothing more important than family."

I glance around. "I can't believe you did this for me."

"I can." He pins me with his gaze. "You're worth it."

"*We're* worth it."

Donavan looks puzzled. "Yeah, that's what I meant. You and me."

"No, Donavan." I shake my head at him, then take his hand and put it on his baby. "*We.*"

He looks confused for a moment, then his face lights up. "What?" He falls to his knees right in front of me.

His hands go straight to my belly and he stares up. I don't know if he's ever going to let go of me now.

"Really?" His eyes are huge.

I nod and smile.

"Oh my God." He pulls me closer and plants his lips right on my stomach through my shirt.

Before I know what's happened, he turns to his family and he looks like a little boy on Christmas.

"Dad! Decker! Everyone, get over here!"

They all walk up. Decker and Mr. Collins are smiling like they already know. I'm assuming they do. I made Tate promise to let me tell Donavan, but I figured she wouldn't hide something from her husband. She must've told Mr. Collins too.

Donavan looks right at his father. "I'm gonna be a dad!"

Mr. Collins smiles right back at him.

Donavan kisses my stomach once more, then stands up and turns to his father. He cocks his head a little to the side and says, "You knew, didn't you? That day in the office."

"What day in the office?" I say.

Donavan shakes his head. "Nothing, I'll tell you later." He keeps staring at his father. "Thank you."

His dad puts a hand on Donavan's shoulder and says, "It's your job to be better than I was." He turns to me. "Congratulations, Paisley, and welcome to the family."

"Thank you, sir."

Everyone crowds around, saying congratulations, but Donavan is back on his knees, ignoring all of them. "I'm going to sing to you every night." He looks up at me and points to my stomach. "He's going to be the best damn attorney of all time."

"Oh, *he* will be?" I raise my eyebrows at him.

Donavan jumps back up and wraps me in his arms. "I don't care what he or she is, as long as I have the two of you."

I can't help but notice one of his hands is still on my stomach.

"Are you ever going to take your hand off our baby."

He looks down, shakes his head. "Nope." He raises his voice, like he's talking directly to our child. "Don't worry, you're the first, but you won't be the last."

I wrap my arms around his neck and gaze into his eyes. "That was always the plan. All I ever wanted with you."

"It was a long road, but we're here, Pais." He puts his palms on my face and kisses me, whispering against my lips, "We're here."

EPILOGUE

Four Months Later
Paisley

Bam! Bam!

My eyes vault open in Donavan's bed and I immediately clutch my stomach. There's a brief pause again then *bam bam!*

What in the hell?

A little bit of drywall crumbles from the ceiling and my hand shoots out for Donavan but he's not in the bed.

Slowly, I get up to see what's going on. It sounds like someone is ripping the condo down. The banging continues, growing louder as I walk down the hallway. Finally, when I'm a few feet away, it stops.

I take a deep breath once I'm fully awake because there's no telling what's going on in Donavan's freaking head right now, but I know it's him so I let out a sigh of relief. Before I can round the corner and yell at him for waking me up, his voice carries through the door, and I freeze in my tracks.

I clutch my chest and stand there, smiling like an idiot, because he starts singing *Baby of Mine* from the *Dumbo* movie. His voice is beautiful, and I still stand there gawking in disbelief every time I hear him sing. My hands go to my stomach and I whisper, "That's your daddy, singing to you. He can't wait for you to get here."

I peek around the corner and he's standing there, shirtless, with a tool belt strapped around his waist and headphones on.

Holy shit!

It looks like he's torn down half the wall between the nursery and the office next to it. I want to yell at him and ask what the hell he's doing, but he looks so damn sexy and he's singing, and I just can't.

I stand there and watch him, listening to him sing, smiling the entire time.

He finally turns and sees me and grins so wide his face might get permanently stuck that way. He stops singing and I immediately want to tell him not to, but he pulls out his phone and pauses the music then takes off the headphones.

I glance over to the wall, then at him. I do it a couple times for dramatic effect and raise my eyebrows at him.

He just stands there, trying to hold in a laugh, like he knows he's gone crazy, then he shrugs.

I tap my foot, trying my best to give him an irritated face, but I can't stop smiling.

"So, I was thinking…" He pauses, like he's testing the waters.

"You were thinking, all right." I glance to the wall again.

Finally, he rushes over and kisses me on the forehead, then falls to his knees like he always does. Part of me wonders if I'll ever get any attention once the baby gets here.

After he kisses my stomach and whispers, "I love you," his eyes roll up to meet mine. "I don't really need an office at home, and we could make the nursery so much bigger." He stands up gingerly, waiting for my reaction.

"It's pretty big already, you know?"

I watch his face go straight to attorney mode, like he's going to sell me an argument in the courtroom. He nods a few times. "It is. It is…" He grins like he knows I see right through this ploy. "But, think about it. My office is even closer to our room." He spins and points through the hole he just put in our wall. "We could put the crib on the far side, so the baby will be right up next to our wall. If a monitor malfunctions, we can still hear her or him crying." His eyebrows rise. "If there's an emergency, we can get there faster. There really are a plethora of advantages to this, Pais."

"A plethora?"

He grins and nods. "Indeed. And now, we'll have room for two cribs, hell, maybe even three." His eyes light up like he just thought of that.

Despite trying my best to look frustrated that he didn't even discuss this with me, my eyes keep roaming down his sweaty chest and ripped abs, and damn it, why does he have to be so hot? What is it about being pregnant that makes me want him even more? My hormones are off the charts.

He sees me glancing down and I see him processing everything immediately. Why does he have to be so damn smart?

A sly grin curls up on his lips, and he takes my hand from my belly and places it on his stomach. "Does that help? It's helping my cause, isn't it?" He waggles his eyebrows.

Despite the fact I know exactly what he's doing, my hand roams up his stomach to his chest. "This isn't fair, you know? Weaponizing sex to get out of the fact you did not discuss tearing down a freaking wall."

He pulls me into him and his hands go to my ass. I might combust. He has me and he knows it. His mouth is next to my ear. "It'll be best, you'll see."

I shake my head and try to wriggle out of his grip because I just want to win, no matter the cost. Plus, I'll get laid anyway if I want. I'm a woman after all and I know him. I take a few steps toward the wall, appraising his work.

I turn back and he smirks when I shake my head at him. "Do you even know what you're doing? Is the roof going to collapse on us?"

He scoffs. "Of course I know what I'm doing."

I nod. "Oh yeah, where'd you learn how to tear down walls in a high rise?"

He looks away and grins. "YouTube."

"Donavan Collins!"

He laughs. "What? They have tutorials and stuff. If I can graduate Columbia Law School, I think I can manage to knock out a wall." He takes a step toward me, his eyes lighting up even more. "You know what else I was thinking?"

"Oh Lord, what?"

"I was thinking why not just sell this place. We need a house like Decker's. A big place with a yard and I can hang a tire swing. Have rooms for all the kids."

On the inside I'm smiling so damn hard, but one of us has to keep us in reality when he gets this way. I love Donavan so much, but he's just going a million miles an hour right now and I feel like we need to pump the brakes, just a couple times at least.

"Sell this place after you just ripped a wall down?"

"It'll patch right up, no biggie."

I turn to the gigantic hole in the wall where I can see studs going up to the ceiling and I don't even know if he checked the wiring or anything else. He's lucky he didn't electrocute himself. Don't even know if it's a load-bearing wall or not. I turn back to him.

"They have YouTube videos for that too." He takes off running as soon as he says it, and I chase after him.

Finally, I corner him on the other side, and he pulls me in close. We both burst into laughter.

"We'll discuss this more later after the baby and I have had breakfast, which you're going to cook."

Donavan can cook breakfast like no other. He has magical powers in the kitchen, that only seem to work in the mornings.

"Deal."

I turn around and take a step.

"Pais?"

I don't know what it is, but there's something about the way he says it. The tone and the way it seemed to come up from the floor.

I turn around and all the breath leaves my body when I see him.

He's on one knee, in front of me, with a little black box held up with a huge diamond solitaire in the center. And I mean, it's huge.

I gasp for a second and start to say something, but it takes me by surprise and the words catch in my throat.

"I've thought of a million different ways I wanted to ask you this question— how, when, where... I thought of grand gestures in front of thousands of people, taking you on a trip across the world, at the top of the Eiffel tower... Literally, it's all I've thought about for months on end." He pauses and chokes up a bit. "But..." His voice cracks a little. "It's always been just you and me. It will always be just you and me, together, a two-person team. And I wanted this moment for us and no one else." He takes a deep breath. "I couldn't think of any place better, than in our home, where we'll raise our child, possibly more, if that's what we decide— together. I know I talk about tons of kids and houses and tearing down walls, and it seems like I run off and do my own thing sometimes because I get so excited, like this. But..." His eyes stay affixed on mine. "We are one. You're my best friend, the only other person on this earth who has ever gotten me, seen me, the real me. I am so damn grateful that I ever met you, that I know you, and that you want to be with me and feel the same way, even after we've been to the ends of hell and back more than once. I will walk through fire, take a thousand bullets for you, no matter how you answer what I'm about to ask you." He pauses and swallows. "Will you be my wife, Paisley Williams? Will you marry me?"

My hand is over my mouth and tears stream down my face. I try so hard to scream "YES!" at him, but the word won't come, and I just nod furiously.

He takes the ring out and his fingers are shaking so bad I don't even know if he can get it on my finger. He looks like I just made him the happiest man on the planet, and I must look the same way in return. He's practically bouncing as he slips the ring onto me and once it's on, he flies up from the floor.

His lips crash into mine and my fingers rake through his hair on the back of his head.

"Yes. God yes, nothing will make me happier."

After he provides me more than enough attention, he slides back down to his knees and grins at my stomach. His hands immediately go to my belly. "She said yes! You heard it, right?"

Just then, something happens. My hands fly down and cover Donavan's. "Oh my God! Did you feel that?"

I glance down at him, and I don't even know how to describe what I see. Donavan is staring right at my stomach, and there is nothing but just—pure love on his face. His eyes are wide, and he looks like a little boy discovering the world for the first time.

"I-I felt it." His eyes roam up to mine. "I felt our baby."

I can't do anything but smile at him, because he's looked so jealous the past month or so when I tell him I can feel the baby, but it's always been a flutter, like something bubbling inside me, but this time it was a definite kick.

Donavan's eyes immediately go back to my stomach and he says, "Well come on, kiddo, do it again! Tell us what you really think!"

I can't stop smiling.

Donavan stands back up and kisses me once more. He might be making jokes, but he almost looks like he's a different man now. Like his brain just realized he's actually a father, like the whole thing is real.

He takes out his phone and starts typing furiously into it and glancing at his watch.

"What are you doing?"

He holds up a hand, completely ignoring me. "Two seconds, not now."

I glare at him playfully, flabbergasted he just said that.

He shoves his phone back in his pocket and smiles at me. "Sorry."

"Yeah, you should be, what was that all about? Telling your family or something?"

His eyebrows rise, then he shakes his head. "Oh no, it was just..." His hand goes back to my stomach. "It's dumb."

"Tell me."

"I've been using the Notes app on my phone, and that was one of the most special moments of my life, and I just wrote down what happened, the time, where we are... I know, it's silly..." He shakes his head and looks away.

I fly into him and hug him even tighter. "It's not silly, babe. It might be the sweetest thing I've ever heard. You're forgiven for ignoring me."

"I love you." He rests his chin on my head and caresses my cheek. "I love our little three-man family, so damn much."

"I love us too, babe." My eyes roam over to the hole in the wall. "I even love our new hole in the wall."

Donavan laughs, then his hands roam down my back again. "Yeah, I need to make that up to you." He squeezes my ass. "Come with me, fiancée."

He takes me by the hand and leads me toward the door. I can't keep up fast enough.

Yeah, Donavan Collins was always right about one thing.

I'm definitely his.

We hope you enjoyed Arrogant Playboy as much as we did writing it.

Grab your BONUS Epilogue and more here! You don't want to miss this!

Order your copy of Inked Playboy - Book 5
Coming sooner than you think!

ABOUT ALEX WOLF

Alex hails from the Midwest and currently resides in Tampa, Florida with his girlfriend Chelle, his son and two cats. His daughter is currently serving in the U.S. Navy. He's a huge fan of THE Ohio State Buckeyes and the Cleveland Browns.

O-H…

He enjoys writing steamy romance but more importantly he enjoys the "research" required to produce the steamy scenes. If you like filthy-mouthed, possessive alpha heroes and steamy romance, then he's the author for you!

Join my facebook group!
Join Alex Wolf's Den

Where you can follow me

Printed in Great Britain
by Amazon